FORBIDDEN WINE

by

Fiona Harrowe

FAWCETT GOLD MEDAL • NEW YORK

FORBIDDEN WINE

Published by Fawcett Gold Medal Books, a unit of CBS Publications, the Consumer Publishing Division of CBS Inc.

ISBN: 0-449-14419-4

Printed in the United States of America

First Fawcett Gold Medal printing: August 1981

10 9 8 7 6 5 4 3 2 1

FORBIDDEN WINE

PART I

JOANNA

1356

"Fortunate men there have seen,
When she, fresh as a marguerite,
Down the bank came like a queen."

Pearl
Anonymous

Chapter I

Joanna Coke was six when she first learned that love had a secret, a pleasurable yet forbidden side, ten when she first met John Hawkwood. Both incidents left a profound mark, the former to haunt her intermittently through the years, the other to mold, to color and dominate all of her later life.

The lesson in love came about quite by chance.

On the morning of that fateful day she and her father, Ivo, having set out for Thexted Fair, had barely reached the forest which bounded the village when a wheel of their cart sprang loose. Assured by her father that it would take a little while to mend, Joanna decided to run back to their cot to fetch the packet of food Mariotta had prepared for their journey, a packet which Joanna, in her earlier haste and excitement, had forgotten.

No one appeared to be home when she reached it, and as she slipped the food packet into a withe basket she heard her mother giggle from behind the curtained alcove where the large bed stood. The tinkling laugh had a conspiratorial sound.

Tiptoeing across the room, Joanna quietly twitched the curtain aside and peeped in. On the bed a naked man was lying atop her mother; Clyde Bagley, she could tell by the dark springy hair. His white buttocks glimmered in the smoky gloom as they began to move up and down, up and down in a steady hypnotic rhythm. Mariotta moaned, a throaty, sensuous sound, and Joanna felt her face flame. Clyde was doing the same thing she had seen her father do with her mother in this very same bed. No one, not even Ernest, her oldest brother and source of odd bits of information, had explained adultery to her, but she knew instinctively that what she looked on now was forbidden. Clyde had usurped her father's place. Fascinated, ashamed, her heart tripping sickly, she stood watching, unable to turn away, held by the sound and movement on the big straw mattress.

As Joanna continued to gaze at the two figures, her mother's spread thighs moved farther apart and Joanna saw

Clyde's "thing," slippery and engorged, a long, thick, fleshy rod, moving in and out of Mariotta's private place.

"Clyde?" Mariotta whispered huskily. "Clyde? 'Tis not pleasuring me enough."

"I am trying," he muttered, his eyes screwed up, quickening his pace.

"Kiss me—nay—not my mouth—you know where."

Transfixed, Joanna watched as Clyde slid his naked body across Mariotta's belly and, grasping her thighs, brought his head down to the clutch of dark hair which grew there.

"Ah . . . !" Mariotta exclaimed. "Better—oh, so much better. Ah . . . ! Oh, oh, hurry . . . !"

Clyde lifted himself quickly and, straddling Mariotta, entered her once again. Suddenly she flung her arms about Clyde's neck and gasped, then she began to moan, "Oh—oh—oh—oh!" in time to Clyde's rising and falling hips. The sounds, the little cries and gasps, the moans were ones that frightened Joanna. She felt sure Clyde was hurting her mother, who, pinned under his heaving body, was helpless to throw him off.

"Mama! Mama!" Joanna called in terror.

But the pair on the bed did not hear her. Mariotta's gasps and moans increased, changing to a hoarse, rasping breathing intermingled with pleadings. "Oh—oh, please, please . . ."

Joanna, terrified that Clyde meant to kill Mariotta, dashed up to the bed and began to belabor Clyde's naked back with her fists. "Let her go! Let her go!" Joanna cried, tears of rage blinding her eyes.

Mariotta emitted a small shriek, which Clyde quickly covered with his hand as he collapsed limp and sweating upon her.

"Let her go!"

Clyde turned and winced as Joanna's small fist caught him in the eye. He grasped Joanna's wrist before she could deliver another blow.

"What's this?" he asked dazedly. "What's got into ye, lass?"

"Get away—get away from my mother!" she shouted. "If you don't leave her alone I shall fetch my father."

"Oh, God!" Mariotta groaned, and Clyde rolled quickly from her.

"Mama, Mama! Are you all right? Did he hurt you much?"

"I am not hurt at all. Don't take on so. 'Twas merely done . . y. Here—here now, don't cry." She took the sobbing girl . . r arms. "How is it you are not on your way to Thexted?"

"A wheel—b-broke," she blubbered, "and—and I came back for the packet."

"Ah."

In the meanwhile Clyde had slipped hastily into his smock. "You had best go," Mariotta said to him. "And Clyde," she called as he started through the door, "that will be five pence for the ale." Mariotta was one of three village alewives assized to brew and serve ale at a fixed stipend per ladle.

"Five pence!" he exclaimed.

"Five pence." She held out her hand. "Do not take time to argue, sweet. My husband should be along at any moment."

"All right. All right." Lifting his russet smock, he worked a small purse from his hip. He counted out the coins twice, moving his lips soundlessly, then dropped each into Mariotta's outstretched palm.

When he had gone, Mariotta pulled Joanna onto the bed and nestled her under her chin. "There now—good riddance, eh?"

"Mama..."

"Aye, we were only playing, a tumble done in fun."

"The baby game."

Joanna felt rather than saw her mother's smile. "Nay, 'twas done for pleasure."

"Pleasure? But Mama, you groaned so, as if you were in pain."

"Sometimes, dove, the delight is so great it hurts."

"Why?"

"One day—God willing—you will know."

"But Papa..."

She shifted Joanna from her. "I love Papa, make no mistake about that. I love him." She held Joanna by the shoulders, her violet eyes large, almost fierce in their intensity. "I love Papa, and it has nothing to do with the other. Do you hear me, child?"

Joanna stared at her.

Mariotta relaxed her hold. "I love Papa. He is kind and gentle and good. He is my husband. As for Clyde—well, I think 'twould be best not to mention him. 'Twould make Papa unhappy. So not a word. Promise?"

"I promise." There were so many questions that crowded her young mind. Why must she keep silent? Was the pleasure wicked, then, the pleasure that had made her mother so soft and loving? But Joanna remained silent. Somehow she sensed such questions were better left unasked.

11

The meeting with John Hawkwood came four years later.

It was 1347. Ivo Coke was then bailiff to Harold de Ander, Lord of Nareham, a fief in south-central England, as his father and father's father had been before him. A tall, raw-boned man with a shock of sun-bleached hair, Ivo prided himself on his free birth, on his inherited office and on the respect it commanded. He, together with Mariotta and their four children, of whom Joanna was the only girl, lived at the end of the village street in the bailiff's cot, a mile below the hilltop castle, their neatly thatched house somewhat larger than the daub-and-wattle huts occupied by the peasant farmers and castle serfs. In her childhood Joanna not only thought the bailiff's house superior to its neighbors, but felt that she herself was a cut above the village children. It was a conceit she acquired from her mother, rather than Ivo, for Mariotta was aloof and fiercely proud.

One late-October afternoon Joanna, returning from an errand on the far side of the village, was dawdling along the hedged lane when she heard the sound of approaching hoof-beats. As they drew closer, she stood to one side and watched as half a dozen hounds, tongues lolling, trotted past, followed by two horsemen, the young Thomas de Ander and one of the castle huntsmen, a hind slung over his saddle bow. Meat, Joanna thought enviously, her mouth watering; meat for the lord's table. The Cokes rarely ate meat, as the forest was the de Anders' private preserve and Ivo, unlike the villagers, would not poach nor permit the boys to do so.

Thomas, coming abreast of Joanna, drew rein. "Ho! Is it the bailiff's daughter?"

She gave a quick little bend to her knee, but did not lower her eyes. She remembered only too well how Thomas, a year earlier, had lobbed a stone at her in passing.

"Aye—I am Joanna Coke."

There were three de Ander sons, Robert the eldest, Thomas the next and Andrew the youngest. Joanna had never conversed with any of them, only seen them as they rode behind their father along the lane that led to the forest.

"You frown at me," Thomas said, poking her with his riding whip.

She had to restrain the impulse to snatch it from his hand.

"Cat got your tongue?" he asked, jabbing her again.

"You did me a hurt," she blurted.

"Me? How so?"

"You threw a stone at me."

"I don't remember," he said. "Did I hit you?"

"Aye. In the back of the neck."

"Ah." He paused. "I don't know why I did it."

It was not an apology, and Joanna did not expect one, yet he sounded rueful enough. She stared openly at him, a handsome lad, no doubt of that, and how well his beautiful hunting jerkin fit, a mouse-gray garment of finely tanned leather embossed with green velvet braid, the de Ander blazon stitched in green across the breast.

"Where are you going?" he asked.

Behind him the huntsman, the corners of his mouth turned down, sat waiting patiently for the lord's son to have done with the peasant child.

"To my home yonder," Joanna said, pointing.

"Would you like a ride?" he asked impulsively, patting the horse's rump. "Isn't it a beauty? My father's birthday gift to me."

Joanna looked at the horse, a smooth-coated chestnut gelding, a splendid animal.

"Come along." He smiled. "Give me your hands."

She held them out.

"Mayhap if I stood on yonder stone 'twould be easier," she suggested. She had not realized how tall the horse was, how far from the ground.

"No need for that," Thomas said and, turning to the huntsman, said, "Geoffrey, lift the girl."

Geoffrey's face turned a dusky red. Yeoman-bred, trained to ride and hunt as generations of Geoffreys had been before him, it was beneath his dignity to act the servant, especially when it came to a peasant.

"Pray, Geoffrey," Thomas said in a courteous voice. "'Twill be a boon to me."

Put that way, Geoffrey dismounted and, picking Joanna up by the armpits, deposited her behind Thomas as he would have done with a sack of grain.

"Have you ever been mounted on a horse before?" Thomas asked.

"Aye," Joanna answered scornfully.

They went at a leisurely trot down the lane. Joanna spoke the truth about riding a horse; she had ridden old Elfa, their cart nag, many times, but it was nothing like this, nothing. Elfa was skinny and small, hardly larger than a pony, and this long-legged creature elevated her to a new exalted height. How small the village looked, how mean and dirty the cots huddled about the commons at the foot of the hill, in contrast to the distant castle and its flying pennons. Suppose the castle was hers, she speculated, hers to go home to instead of the bailiff's house. Suppose she was riding now in a brocade gown and red leather shoes and a crimson silk scarf tied about her hair, riding in from the hunt. "Geoffrey," she would say, "go on ahead and see that supper is made ready. I shall have roast pheasant and a well-turned beeve and sugar-spun subtleties and good white bread. *White* bread, do you hear?" She had never tasted either, the sugary offerings she had heard so much about nor the white bread. "And plenty of red wine and..."

"Hold tight!" Thomas suddenly cried, kicking the gelding with his heels. The horse lunged forward, and Joanna, nearly knocked from her perch, grabbed Thomas's jerkin.

"Wait! Wait!"

The gelding flew down the lane, Thomas driving it on with his whip, laughing gleefully. "See what he can do—good old Rountour, good old Rountour! Faster, faster!"

The wind tore at Joanna's hair, whipping at her face, drawing the breath from her lungs, bringing stinging tears to her eyes. On they galloped, the village street spinning by to the thrum of pounding hooves. How mad, how exhilarating it was, how the heart pounded to ride this way. Mad, wild! It was as if the castle trumpets were sounding in her ear. Da—dadada! She was a great lady racing to hounds, not a lowly peasant, but exalted, a noble, the offspring of a lord, not the daughter of a bailiff, a girl with chilblained hands and a sniffling nose. And she did not want her glorious fantasy to end, not this wonderful thrilling sensation. She wanted to ride forever.

But end it did. They came to an abrupt halt at the edge of the moat. She could feel the horse's flanks heaving as he panted for breath. Thomas turned his head. "Do you not think he is wonderful?"

"Aye, aye! Oh, can we do it again?"

"Nay—I cannot risk winding him. You must get off."

"But—but I am a long way from home."

"'Tis not my concern. Get down!" And he gave her a shove with his elbow. But she clung to him, fearful she would harm herself if she fell from such a height.

"Get down, bitch!"

"You must help me." The huntsman had long since gone on to the castle.

"Why should I? You have had your ride." He twisted around, leaned back and cracked the whip across her face.

The searing pain set fire to her flesh, and she let go, slid sideways, grasping blindly for his clothing, her hands clutching desperately.

"I am your lord, do you hear?"

But she was sobbing now and could not answer.

"Get down!"

Tears streaked her grimy face. How could this kind boy turn so quickly to a monster?

"I shall teach you how to obey me," he shouted.

She cringed, eyes closed, clinging to Thomas as she waited for the fiery smart of the whip. But the expected lash did not come. She cocked one eye open.

A young man on horseback was holding Thomas's arm, restraining him. Why she had not heard his approach she could not fathom. But at the moment he seemed heaven-sent.

"Do you make a practice of beating children?" he wanted to know. A youth of about twenty-two with straight chestnut hair cut short below the ears, he had clear, direct, wide-set brown eyes, a high arched nose, thin lips and a firm jaw. Not handsome, but manly. Wearing the dress of a sergeant-at-arms, his broad shoulders straining at his tunic as if they would burst the cloth, he made Thomas beside him look weak and puny.

"She is a peasant. She stinks!" Thomas replied scornfully. "She will not dismount. And—besides—who the devil are you to be holding me thus?"

"I am called John Hawkwood," he said, taking a firmer grip on Thomas's arm.

"Hawkwood? I know you not. You are a common soldier."

"I am messenger to John de Vere," Hawkwood informed him coldly. "The Earl of Oxford."

"The earl?" Thomas ceased his squirming. "The same who fought at Crécy?"

"The same. My lord is journeying up to London, and he has sent me on ahead to beg hospitality for the night."

"The earl is my godfather, though I've not laid eyes on him since I was baptized. But I have heard of his exploits. And you, Hawkwood, were you at Crécy also?"

Everyone knew about Crécy. Minstrels were still singing the story of the famous victory in which English knights, with the aid of their skilled longbowmen, had soundly beaten the French.

"Aye, I was there."

"They say the English used a new weapon—the French call it *pot de fer.*"

"A cannon," John Hawkwood said. "It fires an iron bolt. Harmless in the main, except that it makes a loud noise."

Joanna had been following this conversation, mouth slightly ajar, her eyes fixed on John Hawkwood, who, to her, had already achieved the status of a warrior-saint, a savior who had rescued her from dire harm. He might be only a sergeant-at-arms, yet in her eyes he seemed as grand as a duke.

"And John de Vere is coming to Nareham?" Thomas asked, his face flushed with excitement. "How lucky I am to be home from Medway this week. I am training for squire there and must return Tuesday next. I shan't miss the earl, shall I?"

"I think not."

John Hawkwood's brown eyes rested on Joanna, who sat gazing at him in awe. He grinned suddenly, his face lighting up impishly.

"You won't see any angels on my shoulder, lass. Pretty little girl if she weren't so dirty, Master Thomas. But are you not a little green to be taking wenches to bed?"

"I was not taking her to bed," Thomas countered huffily. "I gave her a ride out of the kindness of my heart and now she refuses to get down."

"Is this true, lass?"

For a moment Joanna's tongue seemed to cleave to the roof of her mouth, but she managed a weak, whispery, "'Tis so far to the ground."

"A matter of no consequence," John said, dismounting.

Out of the saddle Joanna saw that he had a fine figure, not as tall as her father, but stout-chested and narrow-waisted. He lifted her down, and she felt the hard-muscled strength of his arms and had a whiff of leather and horseflesh before he set her on her feet.

"Run along now, lass. Well—go on, don't stand there and gawk. Go on!" He made a mock threatening gesture with his arm, and she picked up her heels and ran. Behind her she could hear them both laughing.

But he is not laughing at me, she told herself, as she raced across the meadow. 'Tis not a *mean* laugh like Thomas's, just a merry one.

Joanna slowly made her way down the muddy, dusk-shadowed village lane, deserted now, except for old man Dinwiddie, who with bucket and spade was gathering horse dung. It had been two weeks since her encounter with the earl's man, he of the impish smile and amused brown eyes, and she had been able to think of little else. She walked with laggard steps, wishing she did not have to go home, wishing she could keep on walking to—to where? Somewhere, a place, a castle where John Hawkwood would be waiting for her before a roaring fire, his face lighting up, his voice saying, "Good even, Joanna," giving her his arm, leading her to sit beside him at a table laden with roast venison and white loaves.

As she approached the Coke cot it suddenly seemed to look meaner and smaller. Even the spiral of gray smoke rising from the hole in the thatched roof and the glimmer of rush lights behind the shutters, always a comforting sight, did not cheer her. She hesitated a moment before the door, then opened it and stepped inside to a hearty burst of male laughter. Again she paused for a few moments, this time on the threshold of the outer room, which served as a storage place and roosting haven for hens. Joanna, peering past the chicken perches alive tonight with clucking and feathery rufflings to the curtained doorway beyond, heard the man laugh again.

Not Ivo, but one of Mariotta's ale customers. Popular with the men (the women disliked her), Mariotta sometimes had customers far into the evening, and Joanna wondered who she entertained now. Pray God no one who might bring a tight line to Ivo's mouth, shrill words from Mariotta, followed by a strong silence from her husband and to bed without supper for all.

As Joanna waited, a guttural voice exclaimed, "God's bones, but you do serve the best ale in Nareham!" and Joanna's heart shrank in her breast. It was Sir Theobold, the village priest, a cleric Ivo found not only distasteful but a disgrace to the church. "A glutton, a womanizer," Ivo called Theobold, whose title was a mere courtesy, since he came of peasant stock and had neither attended Cambridge nor received a knighthood. To make matters worse, Ivo could not summarily dismiss Theobold from his house as he could any other villager he disliked. Sir Theobold, disreputable and corrupt as he was, still had the power to act as God's go-between, a holy man who could excommunicate if he chose.

Joanna drew aside the curtain and stepped into the room

thick with smoke from the central hearth fire over which a blackened kettle of pottage sucked and burbled. Her mother and the priest sat on a rude bench at a trestle table in one corner, a wooden mug between them. On the floor close to the fire, Joanna's brothers, Arnulf, eight, and Jack, eleven, lay sprawled, playing with a litter of new pups. The third brother, Ernest, twelve, sat on a three-legged stool whittling away at a stick. No one looked up as Joanna entered, and it was some moments before her mother noticed her.

"So—'tis you, Joanna." Mariotta smiled crookedly, her speech a little slurred.

"Aye—and hungry," Joanna said truculently, resenting the priest.

"Hungry!" Sir Theobold exclaimed. "Isn't that the way with fledglings? Mouths always agape, wanting to be fed. Hungry, hungry, hungry. Well, my fine maid, aren't you going to give your *père* a respectful greeting?"

Joanna bent her knee and mumbled, "Good even."

Mariotta laughed heartily, throwing back her head and showing white teeth. "There, does that suit you, Sir Theobold?"

Mariotta, despite a life of toil and the birth of five children (one, a girl, coming after Joanna, had died), was still a beauty. She had white skin, much criticized and secretly envied by the village women, who looked upon her efforts to protect it through the use of wide-brimmed hats and cucumber cream as a sign of vanity and sloth. Her black lustrous hair she wore braided into thick ropes, coiled and pinned over her ears, hair which she washed and brushed regularly—another vanity. But why not? She did not want to become an old hag before her time. Let the biddies cluck. She had large, almond-shaped eyes, high cheekbones, a slightly aquiline longish nose and full sensual lips. Joanna thought her mother the loveliest creature she had ever seen. No one, least of all Mariotta, told Joanna that she resembled her, and Joanna herself had no idea, for she had never seen her own face except reflected in the dark depths of the village well.

"Come here, little pigeon," Sir Theobold coaxed. "Sit down beside me and have a sip of my ale." He edged his bulk a little closer to Mariotta. A fat man, gross, his chin larded, his pink cheeks glossy with good living, a notorious libertine, the known father of several illegitimate children, he nevertheless was well liked in the village. The Narehamers felt him a kindred spirit, for he had sprung from the same peasant stock

18

as they, the son of their own village carpenter, John Biggings. Though he could scarce read and write, garbled his Latin and often rearranged or forgot parts of the Mass, he did have a generous heart, and was tolerant to sinners and sympathetic to the unfortunate who fell upon hard or sorrowful times. Mariotta liked him. She found his company genial, his wit amusing, his manner charming and flattering. No one loved a pretty compliment and flowery words more than Mariotta, and God knew she received few of these from sober-faced Ivo.

"You are embarrassing the child," Mariotta chided.

"So I am, but you are a child yourself," he teased, tweaking one of her breasts.

She laughed again, her hearty, infectious laugh, and was still laughing when Ivo came into the room.

Joanna took one look at her father's stony face and her throat went dry.

"Ah—Father Theobold!" Ivo said bitingly. "Enjoying your ale?" The bailiff could never bring himself to address the priest as Sir Theobold, an oversight Theobold generously chose to ignore.

"Aye. Your wife here was kind enough to bid me stay for another draft."

"So I see." Ivo shot Mariotta a penetrating look, but she merely tossed her head. "It grows late, wife. Have you supped yet?"

"Aye, and the bread blessed by Sir Theobold himself," she answered.

"I hope our humble stew was to your liking," Ivo said, his sarcasm not lost on Theobold, who thought him a surly, strait-laced fellow hardly worthy of the beautiful Mariotta.

"Not stew but a pottage, Ivo," he corrected, smacking his lips. "And very good."

"Well, then, Father, since 'tis late and you've had your fill, I bid you a good night."

"Ivo...!" Mariotta exclaimed, shocked at her husband's discourtesy.

"Do not distress yourself, Mariotta." The priest patted her hand with his own plump, beringed one. "The bailiff is right. It has been a long day, and I know he is eager to find his bed." He winked lewdly, first at Ivo, then at Mariotta, as he rose clumsily from his seat, his protruding stomach shaking the unsteady trestle. "God bless you—this house," he added with an airy movement of his hand.

As he lumbered out, Mariotta called after him, "I shall be at church early for confession."

Ivo waited until the priest had gone before he spoke. "I daresay you have plenty to confess."

Mariotta fixed him with a cold stare. "And what does that mean?"

He did not answer but, turning his back, lifted a pair of iron tongs and began to poke at the lighted charcoal under the kettle.

"What does that mean?" Mariotta repeated, her voice rising.

Ivo, ignoring her, went on scraping at the embers on the hearth.

"Sir Theobold came in for a sip o' ale like any other and paid me good money. You do not like him, no fault of mine—or his. Why must you act the churl? Why?" A pause as she got to her feet. "Why? Are you listening? Churl! Insulting the priest, a holy man."

Ivo set the tongs down and, lifting a large wooden ladle from a hook on the wall, began to stir the mess cooking away in the caldron.

"Do you hear me? Why don't you answer? Answer!" Mariotta was shouting now. *"Answer!"*

Ivo went on stirring.

"Damn you—may your jealous soul rot in hell!" Mariotta scooped the wooden mug up from the table and hurled it at her husband. It hit him with a loud thwack between the shoulder blades. He did not flinch, did not turn.

Joanna licked her lips. The boys, all three of them, looked up; the two playing with the pups gathered up the litter and retreated out of harm's way.

"Answer me!" She clenched her fists and swallowed. "Nay—you will not because you are stubborn—a mule, an ass. An ass without feeling. Aye. Aye. You do not like my having guests, but you find the extra pence welcome enough."

Ivo had been saving two years now for the purchase of a plow ox, hoarding every penny and groat, and Mariotta's earnings were indeed welcome, but at the same time a sore point.

"Oaf! A pox on you to hold me in such low esteem. Oh—I know what you are thinking. Aye, aye, I know. You think I have bedded every man in the village. Including the priest. You don't say, but I know. Well—speak! *Speak!*"

She looked about wildly, then dashed to the wall, snatched

a wooden bowl from a peg and lobbed it at him. The bowl missed its mark and went crashing against the far wall, falling atop two of the puppies. They began to squeal and yelp, trying to run from the sudden engulfing darkness, making the bowl hop and wobble in erratic starts and fits.

Mariotta stared at it for a brief moment, mouth open, then suddenly burst into peals of laughter. "Oh—oh, oh! Look!" She pointed. "Look!" Then, running to Ivo, she flung her arms about his waist. "Look, husband, look!"

Ivo's gaze went up from the kettle.

It *was* funny, the blackened vessel dancing about seemingly on its own. "Ivo!" Mariotta cried. "Have you ever seen such a comical sight?"

Ivo did not laugh, though the tautness slipped from his shoulders. But the boys broke into loud guffaws, and Joanna, a load lifted from her heart, gave a nervous, high-pitched giggle.

Mariotta stood on tiptoe and kissed her husband's obdurate cheek. "You will stir a hole in that pot. Let me." She gave him a hurried squeeze and took the peeled wooden stick from his hand. "Fetch the bread, Joanna," she called, "and the beechen bowls."

It was over. Another storm weathered. In a trice a steaming hot supper of thick pottage and bread stood on the table, a bowl for Ivo and one for each of the children. Mariotta brought out a new cheese and cut a wedge for her husband, a sliver for the boys and Joanna, humming a lively tune as she worked. The firelight played on her face, the full moving lips and rounded cheeks. No one could go from one mood to another as quickly, no one could get as violently angry or as ecstatically happy as Mariotta. Joanna loved the intensity with which Mariotta lived, from brewing ale or plucking a hen to intoning prayers in the church nave. She was keenly aware of her father's disapproval, of Mariotta's friendliness to other men, of her scant attention to housewifely duty, of her fitful maternal feelings, now smothering her children with kisses, now cuffing them, now ignoring them altogether. She also knew that the village goodwives considered Mariotta wicked—they had made it plain enough, even calling her the "whore of Nareham," a phrase that was flippantly and graphically explained to Joanna by her oldest brother. The revelation had mystified, shocked and pained Joanna. She had heard the priest, Sir Theobold himself, in one of his rare sermons, exhort his congregation to beware of whores, calling them the handmaidens of the devil. In no way could Joanna picture Mariotta as in league with Satan. Her father, despite his periods of stoical anger, loved Mariotta, of this Joanna felt sure, and if such a good, honest man as Ivo could love a woman surely she could not be bad?

"How did the business go at Thexted?" Mariotta asked, pouring herself a mug of ale. Ivo had been sent by the steward, Sir Gregory, to pay for and collect a horse purchased by the Lord of Nareham.

"Well, very well," Ivo answered. "Except the steward has accused me of holding back four marks."

"Did you?"

He gave her a hard look.

She laughed. "I meant it in jest, husband. Of course you did not. You—of all people. What an idea! Sir Gregory was serious?"

"Never more."

"Accusing you?" She slammed her mug down on the table. "Why, the whoreson! Son of a bitch! May his tongue rot, may his—"

"Mariotta—pray, hush!"

"Why? Because 'tis not meet to revile a noble? They do not frighten me, not the steward nor any of them. Nobles!" She spat. "Sir Gregory hates all honest men. He would steal the eyes from his own mother's head if he thought 'twould profit him."

Ivo made no comment. He chewed thoughtfully on a mouthful of bread.

"Whatever he says or thinks," Mariotta went on, "I doubt the steward will go to the lord with this trumped-up tale. Sir Harold will never believe him."

"He's already told de Ander, and whether he believes him remains to be seen."

"Pshaw! I should not worry about it."

But early next morning a house carl arrived at their door summoning Ivo to the castle.

"The steward says you are to make no delay," he ordered sternly, a pasty-faced youth who sniffled when he spoke.

"Take care!" Mariotta warned. "You are speaking to the bailiff. You—you stripling, to command my husband in that tone. Has the de Ander livery gone to your head? Underneath your fine clothes and badge you are still a louse-infested villein."

Joanna, listening from the outer room where she was root-

22

ing for eggs, felt a bubble of pride rise in her throat. Whatever the village might say, however wayward they might name Mariotta, they could never criticize her when it came to standing up for her family.

"We shall see about that," the house carl sneered.

"Get out!" Mariotta shouted, raising her fist. And as the youth fled through the outer room, Joanna flung an egg, hitting him in the small of the back, splattering yolk over his tunic. A waste of an egg, her father would say, but what satisfaction, what joy to have struck an agent of the despised steward and the lords in the castle. It almost made up for the whip lash Joanna had received from Thomas.

Ivo returned just as the supper pot was beginning to boil, his face wearing a grim expression.

"They have discharged me as bailiff," he said without preamble, sitting heavily down at the table.

"What?" Mariotta cried. "What are you saying? *Discharged?* Surely you jest, husband."

"I wish to God 'twere a jest. But 'tis true enough. Sir Gregory says I'm no longer bailiff."

"Sir Gregory!" she said disdainfully. "And what of Harold de Ander? He has known you since childhood, and your father too who was bailiff before you."

"De Ander says I'm to go."

"He said that to your face?"

"He said, 'I leave it to my steward. I trust his judgment.' And then he walked from the room."

"Like that. But why—why?"

"It's the four marks the steward says I withheld."

"But 'tis a lie! A lie! God's blood, I could kill that little Sussex cock with my bare hands. Did you tell Harold de Ander 'twas a lie?"

"Mariotta, of what use would it be? You know very well a peasant's word cannot stand up to a knight's."

"But you are freeborn."

"As if that mattered." He bowed his head, and sat for a long while staring down at his strong, brown, work-scarred hands folded before him on the table.

A sick knot formed in the pit of Joanna's stomach. She had never, never seen her father less than strong, iron-spined, jaw outthrust and head held proudly.

"Papa...!"

He started up, and seeing Joanna's frightened face, gave

her a twisted, wry smile. "'Tis all right, sweet, do not be afraid. 'Twas the shock, the first shock. But 'tis over now. We shall manage—be sure of that. We shall manage. And it could have been worse, much worse. They are not going to hang me, at least. And that is something to thank God for."

"Oh—Papa!"

Mariotta, hands planted on hips, said, "There's more, husband. You haven't told me all. They're not going to hang you—I should hope not—what then? Throw you in gaol?"

"Nay. We shall have to move from the bailiff's house."

"And...?"

"I must pay the four marks and two more as a fine."

"Six marks! Six!" Mariotta exploded. "And where, pray, are we to get six marks? The steward might as well have asked for the moon."

"We'll have to sell the cart—the horse and the plow." He looked around. "And our good iron pot, the new scythe, the horn cups..."

"Sell! Sell—sell! Sell *everything!* Sell me, if you will. How are we to live?"

"Others far poorer than we manage."

"Manage," she echoed mockingly. "Like animals, they manage. Never enough to eat, scrounging for a crust, dressed in tatters, and if the harvest falls short, starving. Manage! Pshaw!" She spat. "You are a knave, a fool!"

"Mariotta...!" Ivo warned.

"Knave, fool! Fool!"

"Curb your tongue, shrew!" he commanded angrily, lifting his hand as if to strike.

"Who then should I give the edge of my tongue to? God?" she retorted, nevertheless gauging the raised fist. Ivo was not a wife or child beater, but when provoked could deliver a telling blow.

"Your friend the priest can tell you the answer to that," Ivo said bitterly.

"Oh ho! So mayhap 'twas his fault, his fault that we are losing everything, the very roof over our heads."

Ivo flashed her a look of contempt, then, turning to Joanna, said, "Draw me a cup of ale, child."

Joanna ran to obey, glad for the interruption, hoping her mother, in another moment or two, would make one of her abrupt changes from anger to sweet-tempered amity.

But an outraged Mariotta went on in the same vein. "If you were not such a pietist, not such—such a *saint*—if you

24

had only taken a bribe here, stolen a sack of grain there, collected an extra fine, killed a hare in the forest, the steward would have looked on you with a less jaundiced eye. He would have *respected* you."

"Respect from one thief to another? God's bones, woman, but you have a poor idea of me. I'd sooner be respected by the devil."

"For *our* sakes, lackwit. For *our* sakes! You might have thought of us, you might have known that sooner or later Sir Gregory would resent your piddling God Almighty honesty, your..."

Joanna delivered the ale, and Ivo, snatching the cup, drained it, then rose, his face hard as stone, and made for the door. But Mariotta would not let him go. Spluttering with rage, she flew at him, tearing at his hair, beating on his back with her fists.

Ivo wheeled, holding her at bay with extended arms, while she still flailed at him, muttering curses, every foul, demeaning word she could think of, until at last, tears spilling from her eyes, she ceased to struggle, and Ivo, his hard face suddenly softening, drew her to his breast, where she lay for a long time sobbing broken-heartedly.

Nothing could be done. Harold de Ander, even if Ivo had been bold enough to approach him again, had gone to his estate at Horlick. The boys, too, had left, though separately, Robert as squire to Connington, Thomas to Medway and Andrew as page to Bolingbroke. Sir Gregory, now in sole charge, was adamant. The new bailiff had been hired already, he said, a more pliant, cooperative overseer than Ivo, coming from Marlow and due to arrive within a week's time.

"I expect you to vacate the house before the new man arrives," the steward said, sitting his horse easily, looking down his nose at Ivo standing behind the hedge.

The house where he had been born, where he had brought his bride, where his own children had been born. Leaving it would be like leaving part of himself.

"There's an empty cot down the lane. John Hyman's," the steward went on. "He's long gone to his rest, and his children have cots of their own."

"Aye." Ivo had already examined it, a mean miserable hut, but the only one unoccupied in the village.

"The rent will be cheap enough," Sir Gregory said. Freemen, unlike serfs at Nareham, paid a small rent each year, though the bailiff's house had cost nothing. "Four shillings—due each Christmas."

"Four..." Ivo clamped his mouth shut. Four. Of course. Two for the steward and two for his master. Four shillings for a tumbledown one-room cot.

"You committed a grave wrong," the steward said, frowning down at Ivo. "At the least Harold de Ander could have confiscated your land. So be grateful." He wheeled his horse about, holding it in check. "I want you out by nightfall Friday."

Ivo sold the horse and cart, his plow, the new scythe, and the extra iron spade to John Biggings and his sons, getting much less for them (and that in promise) than he had hoped. The harrow went to the miller. The pig, the cow, a half-dozen chickens and a rooster he kept. The goodwife Hester Doakes gave a shilling for a sack of feathers Mariotta had been saving toward a feather bed (and where did Hester get the money?); three wooden bowls and two mugs were bought by the cook in the castle. The Cokes would have to share utensils at mealtimes, as most of the villagers did.

For a while Mariotta feared she would be banned from brewing ale, but the steward merely raised the assizes—the extra fee he, of course, would pocket himself.

They moved into their new home on a gray blustering day, hauling the last of their few meager possessions down the muddy lane, Mariotta carrying a bundle of pots and blankets balanced on her head, Joanna driving the chickens before her with a stick, Ernest leading the pig. The bulkier items, like the trestle table and benches, the spade and rakes, had been installed earlier. Now as they progressed, the wind slapping at them with a bone-keening sharpness, Joanna became conscious of watching eyes from the gaping windows as they passed. Once she heard a jeering laugh and saw her mother turn toward it, teeth bared. But for the most part their short journey from bailiff's house to serf's cot was accomplished in silence without comment.

It was scarcely a place to cheer one even on a bright day, a wretched dwelling huddling behind a ragged hedge, the close mired in mud, the one window shutterless. Rats apparently had been at the thatch, eating portions of it away, in some places down to the rotting crucks, while the walls, pockmarked by heavy rain, showed the skeleton beneath, the twigs, debris and wattle. A lone apple tree grew to the side, a stunted thing, leafless and spindly, leaning away from the wind.

The hennery, a prickly-hedged enclosure, was situated behind the cot at the top of a slope, and there Joanna shooed the chickens and the one remaining lordly cock. She lingered a bit, throwing the silly, fluttering females a handful of pulled weed, watching them peck eagerly away, not knowing why she felt reluctant to turn and go up to the house.

"Joanna!" her mother called. "Joanna! Where are you?"

"Here!" Joanna answered, and leaving the chickens, trudged around to the open doorway.

"I need you. Where have you been?"

"Feeding the chickens."

There was one room. One room. Smoke-blackened, dim, an earthen floor bare of rushes. The hearth placed in the center had no iron grill, only a few stones, the sooty walls only two hooks. They would sleep on straw pallets, all of them; they would have their trestle table and the benches, true, but in winter they would share that one small chamber with whatever domestic animals they possessed. And their eyes would water, their chests constrict with a hacking cough from the smoke of the hearth, which could not escape except through the narrow window and a small clay hole in the roof.

Joanna, her throat tight, took it all in with a child's eyes, feeling resentment against her father, against the fate which had snatched her from her comfortable home, thrusting her into this miserable cot. As she gazed dumbly about the dark, malodorous room, she suddenly thought again of John Hawkwood, of his impish smile, the way he had stayed Thomas's whip, the feel of his strong protective arms as he lifted her down from the horse. He had come to her rescue once, why not now? But she knew it was a foolish question, knew that she had suddenly become too old for such childish hopes and fantasies.

Chapter II

Spring came late that year, trumpeting across the manor lands in gusting, squally fits as if to mock the Cokes further in their downfall. An anxious Ivo at the first break in the weather took to the fields to prepare the ground for planting, working his own strips as well as John Crykes's in return for the use of Crykes's plow and ox. Once the soil had been sufficiently turned and harrowed the entire family was called upon to help with the sowing.

Except to shoo crows and pigeons from newly planted seed, more of a lark than labor, Joanna had never worked in the fields. Nor since her marriage had Mariotta—another source of universal envy, for all peasant women toiled alongside their men. Heretofore the bailiff had been able to pay the extra help he needed for his own farming, but now he could ill afford to part with as much as a penny, and all six of them must lend a hand. It made Joanna feel important to be included among her elders, to be doing her share. The warm sun, the fragrance of wind and earth, the birds chirping and twittering and the faraway sound of peasants singing as they sowed all combined to give her prospective task the nature of a genial outing. As she stood watching a sparrow fluttering over the upturned earth her mother called.

"Joanna! Why are you standing there like a lackwit? Get to work!"

Joanna picked up her stick. "Where must I begin, Mama?"

As the day wore on Joanna's cheerful eagerness vanished. The stick with which she was dibbling—planting beans—grew heavy, and her right hand developed a blister between thumb and forefinger where the skin took the pressure of each downward thrust. Her back ached, and the seed in her pockets seemed like weights. It was hot work even on a cool day. Perspiration rolled down her face like tears, dampened her back and formed in sticky blobs under her armpits and behind her knees. The breeze soon died, and the friendly sun so welcome in the chill morning now became an enemy, its brassy rays beating down on her bare head. The strip seemed endless, marching ahead of her into a heat-hazed distance. On she went, on and on. Another twist of the stick, a seed dropped in—ah, it missed again—stop to retrieve it, brush the dirt over with grimed fingers, another step, another twist, two seeds by mistake in this hole, but it didn't matter, no one would see, cover it quickly, straighten up, another step, another twist, another seed, stoop, cover, straighten up. Would they never finish?

At long last Mariotta called a noon halt. The family, flinging themselves down in the sparse shade of a twisted, half-dead oak, ate their scant meal in silence. Joanna, wolfing her share down, finished quickly, then, leaning her back against the tree trunk, she let her eyes wander. All over the field peasant families were breaking their fast, some sitting in the blazing sun, others improvising shade with shirts hoisted and stretched on spades or harrows. The oak was on Ivo's land, the only tree within comfortable distance, but no one joined them. Joanna could feel their isolation, but it did not bother her. Her father as bailiff had never been popular; he had driven some too hard, had meted out too many fines, the memories of which still rankled, and, of course, her mother had never taken the trouble to endear herself to the women of the village.

"Look!" Mariotta exclaimed. "We are going to have a visitor."

Stepping daintily and carefully across the planted rows, Katrine Flemyng, the miller's daughter, approached them, a pudding-faced girl of fifteen, her tucked-up kirtle revealing dusty, bulging calves.

"Good day," Ivo greeted her pleasantly.

She colored, flushing a deep red. "Good morrow, Ivo." She darted a vague, nervous smile at the others.

"Morning," the children replied, a chorus from four throats while four pair of eyes gazed at her with curiosity.

There was a short silence as Katrine stood tongue-tied, twisting her apron between pudgy hands.

"Did you come to pass the time of day?" Mariotta asked sarcastically. "Or did you want something?"

Katrine shot a quick frightened look at Mariotta. "I—I . . ." she began and fell silent.

"Speak up, lass," Ivo coaxed gently.

"My father," she stumbled, her eyes fixed on her dirt-encrusted toes, "my father—asks if ye would help with his sowing. He—his legs give him trouble." She swallowed and darted a rapt look at Ivo. "He—he says if he does not get a hand his fields will have to go by this year."

The miller too was a freeman, getting so much for each

sack of flour ground, pence and shillings he must divide with the lord of the manor, who owned the mill. His crops helped to feed a large and ever growing family.

"I'll be glad to help," Ivo said.

Mariotta spoke up. "For pay, Katrine. Ivo will want a wage."

"Now, Mariotta..."

"You cannot do it for naught. Not now. Well, Katrine?"

"I know not for certain," the girl stammered, avoiding Mariotta's eyes. "Mayhap..."

"We shall settle the business later," Ivo said, frowning at his wife. "Go along."

"Thank 'ee," she whispered, throwing him a look of gratitude.

Mariotta laughed. "That simpleton is gone on you, Ivo. Madly in love."

"Don't talk gibberish."

Mariotta gave him a wide grin, her violet eyes dancing. "I can't say I blame her. You are a handsome beast." She flung her arms about his neck, kissing him soundly on the mouth.

"Mariotta!" he exclaimed. "Enough—enough! You forget yourself. Come now, enough I say. We've dawdled too long. To work—all of you. Up—up!"

Ivo's gruff tone covered embarrassment, but underneath he was pleased to be the recipient of Mariotta's affection, and Joanna, sensing his pleasure, was glad. It meant an abeyance of her parents' quarreling, which lately had grown more bitter and acrimonious.

"To work!" Ivo repeated, urging the boys on. "You, Joanna, on your feet!"

They had been working only a short while when Joanna heard the sound of horses' hooves and, looking up, saw the steward galloping toward the wood in a cloud of dust. Behind him rode a man and a woman, and Joanna, her heart suddenly thumping, stared at the man, the wide shoulders, the sun-caught brown-reddish hair. Could it be—was it John Hawkwood? Would he slow his horse, smile down at her? She wanted, hoped for nothing more than a smile, a look of recognition. It would make up for her blistered hands, the ache in the small of her back, sustain her for the endless hours to come.

She shaded her eyes against the sun. No. No. She had been mistaken, bitterly so. It was not him, not John Hawkwood, but a knight and his lady, strangers she had never seen before.

Across the fields they came, heedless of the peasants' sowing in the harrowed rows, trampling the new plantings, churning the earth which had been so carefully prepared in their wake. But not a single voice was raised in protest. The nobility had the right of passage, and if they chose to cross plowed or planted land, the villeins must bear with them, accepting their selfish unconcern without argument. The peasants muttered, but under their breath as they touched forelocks respectfully to the steward and his company sweeping past.

Only Mariotta raised her fist, and Joanna had a moment of heart-palpitating fear, for the steward was known to punish those who showed disrespect. But Sir Gregory did not see Mariotta, and as the small cavalcade went by Joanna stared at the lady riding behind the knight, a young woman with golden hair caught in two glittering cauls, smooth of brow, carrying a gray falcon on her wrist. She wore a tawny-colored tunic and the long white scarf twisted about her throat floated out behind her as she rode. It seemed to Joanna that an angel had passed, a creature so removed from her everyday life as to be not of this world.

"A murrain on them!" her mother growled. "May they rot in hell. They think we are no more than beasts, that we have no feelings. Oh God, if only I could *do* something. That bitch, did you see her with her nose stuck up in the air, and the jaw like a nag's?"

Joanna, feeling her angel somewhat tarnished, said, "Aye, Mama."

Mariotta still bedded with Clyde Bagley, though it was harder now to find the time and place to do so. It never occurred to her to give him up. Not that she loved Clyde—far from it. She found him stupid, his speech gross, his grin irritating and his presence a trial. It was Ivo she loved, Ivo she had given her heart to, the gentle, kind man who had saved her from a life of abject poverty and clawing hunger, the husband who had released her from serfdom. But Ivo's lovemaking was as stolid as his manner, and her body craved hot passion, it thirsted for strong, ruthless hands, for frantic caresses, for a hungry mouth kissing and probing into forbidden places. Though Clyde Bagley did not quite fit her notion of an ideal lover, he was better than most. Further, his vanity did not suffer, as so many masculine vanities did, when she told him what to do in order to bring her to climax.

Only once had she met a man who required no instruction,

who took her wordlessly, in erotic, barely controlled savagery, in a sexual assault that drove her wild with excitement.

Tom Fixe was his name, an itinerant peddler who had come through Nareham on his way to Thexted. Tall, powerfully built, with a thick head of fair hair and narrow, amber eyes, he had caught Mariotta's attention the moment he stopped his one-wheeled barrow laden with its hodgepodge of kettles, iron pokers, needles, thread and pretties outside the bailiff's house. She had run out and bartered with him, settling on a ribbon in exchange for a mug of ale. She recalled how he had followed her into the house, so close behind she could feel the heat of his body through his dirty jerkin. Seated at the trestle table where two of her customers, Isaac and Charles Crykes, were just finishing a stoup, he seemed even larger than he had in the lane. The shirt under his jerkin was torn and she could see his darkly matted chest, broad and muscled like a blacksmith's. Mariotta served him ale, and his hand touching hers made her skin jump. It was a sun-browned hand with bleached hairs on the back, a strong, callused hand, and as she watched it curve around the mug she pictured it curving about her breast, the thought of those warm fingers setting her on fire. Suddenly she wanted him, she wanted him with a desire that throbbed and pounded in her blood. Her body ached with a hot, unbearable craving. She wanted him as a thirsty man wants water, as a parched drunkard a cup of ale. She *had* to have him; she could not let him get away. And when at last she lifted her gaze from those mesmerizing hands and looked into his eyes she saw that he already understood.

But there were Isaac and Charles still lingering.

When Tom Fixe rose to go, she said, "Oh, peddler, I have changed my mind about the ribbon. Might I have the red instead?"

"'Tis one and the same to me," he answered with a small smile. "Come outside."

Over the lip of the barrow she murmured, "Tonight—the stack at the bottom of the garden," and grasping the red ribbon hurried back to the two men inside, who had been watching her through the window, and now, to cover their rude curiosity, had decided to have another stoup.

That evening Mariotta did not leave the house until everyone had long been asleep. Slipping through the door, she went around the back, shushing the dogs, careful of her footing in the blackness. He was waiting for her as she groped her way toward the haystack, catching hold of her shoulders, pulling her into his arms, bringing his mouth down in a hungry kiss, moaning low in his throat as he worked his lips back and forth. She pressed her body into his, rubbing her stomach against his rising hardness, exulting in the taste and odor of him. He had a feral smell, a lusty animal odor that fed the fire which had begun to race through her veins. His hands, those splendid, light-haired hands, went down her back, stroking, caressing, squeezing her buttocks, up again, down. He lifted the edge of her bodice, and when it would not give, he reached in front and tore it apart, releasing her full breasts for the pleasure of his seeking mouth and tongue.

Not a word was spoken. She could not see him in the darkness, but it mattered little. When he brought her to the ground and shoved her skirts above her waist, her loins were already pulsating. She sensed rather than saw his dark hulk above her and in her urgency reached out, intending to guide his entry. But he grabbed her wrists, crossing them, holding them tightly over her belly. Then she felt the tip of his rigid member just inside, going no farther but rubbing against the little button that grew there. Soon, very soon, she began to feel waves of quivering heat race through her body, wave after wave, building, building until she heard herself crying, "Oh—oh! Ah—oh!" while her hands clawed his back as if she were trying to escape her exquisite torment, a torment that carried her mind and body to new, almost frightening limits. Finally when she thought she could endure it no longer, he jammed himself inside, going deep, deep, driving savagely, thrusting again and again. The final paroxysm when it came, a moment before his own orgasm, was an explosion, a disintegration into a thousand wonderful glittering fragments.

They lay side by side panting, wet with perspiration, spent with passion. But even then they remained silent. It was only after he had taken her the second time that he spoke.

"I've never met a woman like ye. Never."

"Nor I a man," she said.

"Come with me then. I'd be a meaching fool to let ye go."

She laughed. "And I'd be a peddler's whore if I said aye."

She knew instinctively that she would not meet or have another lover to equal this one, a physical counterpart in passion and untamed ardor. He had given her a lusty, erotic, savage, loving night and could give her many more of the same if she went with him. But Mariotta knew that this would not be enough. She had always been able to separate

33

herself, to put her extramarital affairs in one compartment and feelings for her husband in another. As long as she held Ivo in her heart, she reasoned, she was faithful to him. Living with him, for all his irritable piety, gave her more than a sense of comfort; it gave her a feeling of being loved, of love returned, for she *did* love Ivo. He was father, mother, brother, dear husband and cherished friend—all these things—and she could never turn her back on him. And though Tom Fixe's urgings tempted her, she bade him goodbye with a lingering kiss and only a faint regret.

Gentle rain showers in the middle of May turned the fields into a striped green velvet carpet that soon tufted and gradually grew thicker and taller. Smiles appeared on the village street, faces became less stern. A special Mass of thanks was conducted by Sir Theobold to which the whole village, including Ivo, came. The bailiff (and Ivo still thought of himself, and was thought of, as bailiff, never mind the new one) had not shed his dislike nor his poor opinion of the priest, even though Sir Theobold remained one of the few drinking customers who still patronized Mariotta. The men of the village did not enjoy imbibing their ale in the crowded Coke cot, not as much as they had in the bigger house, and some complained the ale was not as good. Sir Theobold saw no difference, in fact thought it a better brew than last year's. As ever, he bore no malice toward Ivo, nor did he taunt him with his reduced circumstances. Yet Ivo could not warm to the man. However, since he could no longer attend the castle chapel he had no choice but to go to Theobold's. Not to be present at such a Mass of thanksgiving was unthinkable.

Nevertheless, some of Sir Theobold's flock, those hardened and sun-blackened peasants who had lived through many seasons, felt thanks were a little premature. One could never be certain of God's bounty until the grain and corn were cut, stacked, dried or threshed. Too many improbables could intervene. An ill wind, a blight, a bug, a capricious storm and all would be lost. Best save the thanks for later.

And they were right, for after the fourth week of May, it stopped raining. Those who waited anxiously, scanning the heavens for a single dark promising cloud, did so in vain. As day passed into day, the sun shone even brighter, shone with a kind of intense defiance, a fiery implacable ball in the hard blue sky. Prayers were said, candles lit, the Virgin, the Mother of all, invoked. And still no rain fell. None. Not a drop. The green blades of wheat, rye and barley (barley so necessary to Mariotta's ale) withered, the curling tendrils of peas, the shoots of beans turning yellow as one week went into the next without moisture. Everything, the entire landscape, slowly baked to straw, the lifegiving growth shriveling before the villagers' helpless eyes. The house gardens could be watered with buckets dragged up from the stream (now sunk to a muddy trickle between sere banks), the fruit trees, too, might be nurtured, but the fields themselves waited, cracked and thirsty, panting in the heat.

To Mariotta the drought seemed unjust, God's spiteful malediction, a cruel, twisted joke aimed solely at them. Hadn't they paid for their sins already? Hadn't they given up the comfort of their large cozy house for a miserable cot? Hadn't they worked and toiled in the fields, breaking their backs?

"Why has He done this to us?" Mariotta railed. "What kind of a merciful God is He?"

"Hush," Ivo warned. "You blaspheme."

"Would you want me to thank Him? 'Thank you, God, for blessing us with misfortune,'" she mocked.

"Hush! 'Tis well a priest does not hear you."

But she said the same to Sir Theobold, and he only laughed. "You are a lusty wench with a sharp tongue. But I know that in your heart you still revere and fear Him."

"And how do *you* know what is in my heart?"

July came, and except for brief thundershowers which did little more than wet the ground and raise hopes, the weather continued dry. Dust added to their torment, dust swirling down the main village street, covering what was left of the garden with a dull powdery gray, seeping into windows, blowing down the smoke holes, settling over food, ale and water, creeping into hair, eyes and nostrils. A gritty taste clung to their mouths, a dryness to their throats.

It wasn't long before the cow ceased to give milk. The loss affected Mariotta more than the others. Partial to cheese and butter, she saw no way of obtaining either now, nor did they have the extra coins to purchase such delicacies from the castle, where they still managed to feed and water their dairy animals. She grew morose, her eyes smoldered.

"I cannot bear it!" Mariotta cried, throwing down the spindle, so that the hempen yarn unraveled on the dirt floor.

Joanna, sitting at her feet, looked up from the flax fibers she was carding. It was August. Ivo and the boys had hired themselves out to help with the lord's harvest, not a bountiful

35

one, in fact quite scanty, but a harvest nevertheless, since his fields had been planted earlier than the villagers' and consequently had escaped the brunt of the drought.

"I cannot bear it!" Mariotta repeated, rocking her head between her hands. "Why? And we can do nothing but sit by and let it all—all—slip from us. I don't want to be hungry. Do you hear, Joanna? I don't *want* to be hungry."

"Aye, Mama." Joanna watched her mother anxiously.

"Aye—aye. You say that and know nothing. But *I* know. Because I have been hungry. Oh, I don't mean hungry from one meal to the next, but hungry day in and day out. No food in the cot, not a crumb and no hope of a crumb. We had to go to the abbey and beg for bread. They gave—they gave crusts, all right, not the good bread they sat down to at supper, but their moldy wormy leavings. Damn them!" She paused, biting her lip.

"Mama," Joanna ventured timidly, "was that before you came to Nareham?"

"Aye. Before. My mother and father and two brothers died. They starved to death. But *I* didn't. I took good care not to. I *stole* whatever food I could lay hands on, a bit here, a bit there. If your father ever knew I had been a thief—ah—your father..." Her voice trailed off.

"Papa says we'll manage."

"Papa," Mariotta echoed, gazing past Joanna.

Joanna resumed her carding, but her mother sat with folded hands, still looking into some unknown distance, the spindle lying on the floor forgotten. A hen hopped over the sill, clucking and fluttering its wings. The straw thatch rustled overhead, and Joanna heard the gnawing, chewing sound that was the bane of Ivo's existence. A rat at the roof again.

"Come!" Mariotta spoke so suddenly Joanna jumped. "Come, daughter, we are going to see someone who will help us."

She rose and went to the rush basket where she kept her kitchen tools and, selecting a sharp knife, tucked it into her bodice. "You must tell no one," she warned, "least of all your father. Do you promise?"

"Aye, Mama. But what...?"

"Ask no questions. Make the cross and promise."

Joanna did as she was told.

Mariotta scooped up the chicken as it pecked at the floor and tucked it, squawking and fluttering, under her arm. Then, with Joanna close at her heels, she went from the cot down to the riverbank. "We can cross here, 'tis shallow enough," Mariotta said. They splashed through the muddy water in their bare feet and scrambled up the farther bank.

"Are we going into the forest?" Joanna asked fearfully.

"Aye, but not far."

The fallen pine needles crackled and pricked their horny soles as they trudged along. Mariotta led the way. They took a narrow animal track through the undergrowth, tinder-dry and less lush than usual because of the paucity of rain. Patches of withered mushrooms lay beneath the oaks, scabrous excrescences of yellow and brown. Twigs snapped with a popping noise that made Joanna's heart race. Not a single living creature could be seen or heard, not a hare, not a squirrel, not even a bird. The forest was ominously silent, the heat under the trees stifling. Soon they came to a glen, the parched grass dotted with a circle of gray stones which, to Joanna's frightened eyes, resembled shrouded human bodies. A ring of stones— where had she heard of them? Aye, she remembered now. Ernest had told her that the stones had been placed in a circle by Azazil, a place where he could be worshiped in the form of a black goat, the devil's favorite disguise.

Joanna clutched her mother's arm. "Mama, let us go home. I don't like it here."

"Be quiet."

The struggling chicken screeched, and Mariotta squeezed it more firmly under her arm.

"Now sit there," she instructed Joanna, pointing to one of the stones.

"Mama..."

"Sit!"

"It should be done by the light of the moon," Mariotta muttered. "But 'twill have to do now. I cannot wait for the moon."

"What are you going to do, Mama?"

"You shall see. When you hear me call, 'Melusine!' you are to say, 'Amen!' Do you understand? Otherwise, you are to be silent."

Mariotta went to the center of the clearing and, facing the largest stone, stood for a long time without speaking. Crows zigzagged lazily over the treetops, their distant cawing echoing eerily in the stillness. Mariotta got down on her knees and began a strange chant, words Joanna had not heard before, words she could not understand, except for the occasional loud enunciation of "Melusine!" which she dutifully echoed with an "Amen." She had not the vaguest notion of why Mariotta was acting in such a weird and terrifying manner, kneeling and calling upon a strange god. Was her mother a— a wi...Nay. She could not even say the awful word in her mind. Not her mother, *never* her mother.

Mariotta would have been surprised to learn that Joanna suspected her of being a witch. Far from it. She was as Godfearing as any Christian. But it certainly did no harm to call on a spirit for help when it seemed apparent that God's attention had been drawn elsewhere. What she chanted was pure gibberish, as meaningless to her (except for the invocation of Melusine) as to Joanna. Once as a child, she, together with a Cornish tinker's daughter, had secretly witnessed a strange rite performed by the latter's mother. The circle of stones, the chanting, the calling on Melusine, the witness echoing "Amen," she remembered vividly, as well as the part played by the chicken. The tinker's daughter had told Mariotta that her mother did not resort too frequently to Melusine lest the fairy queen become bored with a mere mortal's entreaties, but if one pleaded only in dire circumstances for help it was usually granted. Mariotta had forgotten the tinker's daughter, her mother, the rite, until her mind going around and around in desperation suddenly recalled them. Why not? she thought. She had reached the point where she was willing to try anything.

When she felt she had reached the ear of Melusine, she took the hen from under her arm and held it up on high with one hand while in the other the knife glittered. But the chicken with a sudden twist wriggled free and started to hop, flutter and fly across the clearing.

"Catch it!" Mariotta shouted. "Catch it!"

Joanna darted forward and grabbed the hen by the legs.

"Hold it for me," her mother ordered. "On the stone."

Joanna, frightened yet fascinated, anchored the struggling fowl, holding onto it. The knife flashed and the shrill scream of protest died as the chicken's blood spouted, spattering the stone and Joanna's arms.

Mariotta got down on her knees again. "Melusine—give us rain and harvest and plenty," she intoned. "Give us back our house and Ivo his place of importance."

Joanna shivered and instinctively crossed herself.

"There!" Mariotta said. "You may think it a waste of a hen. But wait and see."

Mariotta's wishes *were* granted, but in a way she never foresaw.

Chapter III

The Cokes did not prosper. As the next winter drew itself out, Ivo was forced to sell two sacks of his precious grain in order to pay the rent and the first installment of his fine. Opportunities for income were few. Had he been able to keep his horse and cart he might have earned a few shillings by hauling produce to market. Nor was he able to obtain work as a paid laborer mending roads and dikes. For each of these jobs there were twenty applicants, and the new bailiff who did the hiring passed Ivo over for men who slipped him a bribe. Ivo could not do this any more than he could whine and beg. Not once did he complain or bemoan his fate or bend his head as he had done in a moment of weakness when he had first been dismissed. He was like a rock, strong, obdurate, a granite wall that faced wind and storm squarely without flinching. "We shall manage," he maintained in the face of each fresh setback. His attitude exasperated Mariotta. But her anger could alter neither her husband's optimism nor the stark reality of their situation. She cooked their one meal a day now with a much less lavish hand, and each time she reached into the shrinking flour sack she had to suppress a little spurt of fear.

One morning after Ivo had taken the boys to the field to begin the winter plowing, Mariotta set Joanna to weeding the garden. It was a cold day, the wind coming off the gray brimming river in chilled gusts. Joanna on her knees felt every blast as it struck the back of her neck and worked its way down her spine. Her numb fingers tore at the nettles and tares, despised plants yesterday, saved today, the tenderer shoots going into one pile for a meatless stew, the tougher ones into another to be thrown later to the chickens. She hated weeding. She would much rather have been inside, thick with smoke as it was from the central fire, than out in the wind grubbing in the dirt with chilblained hands. She had been at her task for perhaps an hour when her mother called to her.

"Joanna! Go down to Freyda's and ask to borrow her latten bowl. I'll need it for brewing."

Joanna sprang to her feet, grateful for the interruption, though she had no liking for Freyda, the village midwife, a tart, grumpy harridan.

"And what if she refuses, Mama?" Joanna asked.

"I'll break her jaw. Tell her that!" and Mariotta laughed.

Joanna was glad to see her mother in such good humor again. Thank God they had been able to salvage some of the barley. Brewing always made Mariotta happy. It was the one chore she enjoyed above others.

Joanna found Freyda spinning, her gray head bent, her thin mouth pursed. Nareham distaffs and spindles were seldom idle. Homespun supplied all needs: cloth, sheets, shirts, smocks, girths and ropes; some woven from "carle" hemp, the finer kind from "fimble" hemp.

"The Coke child," Freyda said, looking up, squinting at Joanna. "What pray, brings you here?"

"My mother wishes to borrow your latten," Joanna said, pointing to the outsized yellow clay bowl hanging on the opposite wall.

"Does she now?" Freyda asked crossly, hands on hips. "I must say she has gall, since she still owes me for a packet of herbs I gave her last summer. Bitch!"

Joanna ignored the jibe. A pot was simmering on the hob, and her stomach rumbled.

"Mama must have forgot." She looked longingly at the pot—stew. Her nose twitched. Rabbit? Chicken?

"Forgot? Mariotta? Not likely. She doesn't want to pay."

"Oh, she will, she will." If Freyda would only invite her to have a spoonful, just a small little dribble on a wedge of coarse bread, she would be eternally grateful. She licked her lips.

"I should hope so."

Freyda saw the girl eyeing the pot and noted how thin she was—bones like a bird's. But she steeled herself against pity. She had three men and two half-grown boys to feed, and the stew would make scant enough fare. She could not start providing food for the neighbors' children; one exception and they would all be down on her like a pack of wolves.

Joanna said, "My mother will be so grateful."

"Ye have good manners, girl. More than ye deserve." She got up and, unhooking the bowl from its wooden peg, gave it to Joanna. "See that yer mother returns it—and soon."

Clutching the utensil to her breast, Joanna left Freyda's cot, gritting her teeth as she faced into the wind. The muddy lane was deserted except for a bony, humpbacked, skeletal dog foraging in the running ditch and two small ragged barefoot children chasing a sow with a stick, their cries growing fainter as they disappeared behind a wall.

41

Joanna reached home to find her mother's cheerful mood had vanished.

"What took you so long?" Mariotta demanded irritably.

"I came as quick as I could."

"Well, never mind, never mind. I don't feel up to brewing." Her face looked flushed, and her hands shook as she hung the bowl on a peg.

By the time Ivo returned in the evening Mariotta had a raging fever. Between bouts of violent retching, she coughed, spasmodic, breath-catching coughs which she could not seem to control.

A worried Ivo sent Joanna back to fetch Freyda.

She arrived huddled in her shawl, muttering and cursing, her black gimlet eyes brimming with hostility. The sound of Mariotta's ragged breathing seemed to fill the room now.

Ivo sat at her side, his face a stony mask. "You brought a poultice?" he asked Freyda.

"I brought the makings, no thanks from ye. Rousing an old woman out of bed and not even a cup of ale offered to warm her. Well—where's the hot water? How can I make a poultice if there ain't hot water?"

"The water's heating in the kettle, you old fool," Ivo said.

He had stuck a lighted brand upright in the floor next to Mariotta's pallet, and now he leaned over and blew it out. Except for a flickering circle of light at the hearth, the room lay in darkness.

"How can I see, ye knave?" Freyda complained.

"You can see well enough," Ivo answered. "Wood is dear and brands dearer. Go about your business."

Grumbling and calling upon God to witness her goodness of heart and the ingratitude of churls, she steeped the herbs she had brought in the kettle over the fire, stirring, narrowing her eyes against the steam which rose in aromatic vapors. Mariotta, who had been thrashing about on her pallet, became suddenly quiet. Then a moment later she began to speak.

"Ivo," she said clearly. "Ivo, where is the red ribbon you promised me for my hair? Where is it? Where? Oh, Ivo..." And she laughed, a laugh so full of joy Joanna's heart turned over.

"Hush," Ivo soothed. "Hush."

"Ivo—oh, my sweet Ivo."

He held her hand, bending over her, his eyes glittering with tears.

"God will punish me," Mariotta went on. "But I fear it not. If I burn in hell, then so be it."

"Hush," Ivo begged. "Oh, hush."

The poultice made up and cooled, Freyda carried it to Mariotta. Leaning over, she hesitated, staring through the gloom at the invalid's face, then she placed it on her forehead.

"Somethin's awry here," she muttered. She got to her feet, waddled to the fire and, reaching for a stick of wood, lighted it.

"What are you about?" Ivo demanded, striding across the room with the intent of snatching it from her. But she thrust it out at him, her arm quivering with anger.

"I shall scorch the skin from yer loutish face if ye don't stand aside," she threatened.

"You—you vile old woman." He lunged at her.

The brand moved and Ivo cried out as the flame singed his hair and brushed with fiery heat past his nose.

"I mean what I say, bailiff."

He kept his distance as Freyda cautiously edged her way past him, holding the outstretched torch between them. She lifted the brand high over Mariotta to get a better look and gasped in shock. The white skin of the sick woman's bare outflung arms was mottled in livid spots; her face had a strange purplish tinge, and there was a swelling on the side of her neck large as a hen's egg.

"God preserve us!" Freyda gasped. "Oh merciful Jesus. God keep us and help us all. God! God! The plague!"

She dropped the brand and without bothering to collect her shawl stumbled past the startled boys.

"The plague!" she shouted as she ran through the door.

Icy fear squeezed Joanna's heart. She had been two, hardly out of swaddling clothes, when the first great wave of the dread disease (known as the Black Death in later years) swept the countryside. Though she herself could not remember the dim, gloomy house, the closed shutters and clouds of stinking sulfuric smoke burned to ward off the disease, she knew the plague well enough through hearsay. Tales were still repeated of how entire villages had been devastated, how in the towns men piled bodies in the streets, afraid even to bury their own dead, how the fatal illness indiscriminately took the rich and the poor, a horrible affliction which brought pus-laden buboes to armpit, neck and groin, a sickness that strangled some and produced fatal hemorrhaging in others.

Ivo himself had survived it, and by wisely isolating himself from his family when the first symptoms appeared, had managed to keep them from contamination. In any case, the plague, for various reasons, had not struck Nareham with the same force and intensity with which it had stunned other villages.

Suddenly Mariotta's voice queried, "Ivo? I want the priest, Ivo. I want Sir Theobold. I—I haven't long—Ivo?"

Ivo was at her side. "Do not fret, sweetheart." He had not called her sweetheart for many years. "Theobold will be here shortly."

He turned to Joanna. "Run, get the priest," he whispered. "Tell him to hurry; she is calling for him."

But Joanna could not move. The thought of venturing out in the haunted night again and to the priest's house, so close to the graveyard, terrified her. "Papa..."

"Never mind, I'll go, 'twill be quicker," Ivo, torn with anxiety and worry, said impatiently. "Do not stay too close to your mother. Keep your distance. If she calls, say Father Theobold is on his way."

The boys curled up and were soon sound asleep. But Joanna sat by the fire and waited. It was a long time before Ivo returned with Sir Theobold. The priest, wearing a greasy stole, his breath smelling strongly of ale, came gingerly into the room. He carried the consecrated wine and bread of the Eucharist in a small basket.

"Papa, she has been very quiet," Joanna said.

Theobold tiptoed over to the pallet and peeked down at Mariotta, touching one limp hand. He withdrew his own quickly and genuflected.

"She is dead," he said, his pendulous lower lip quivering.

"Oh, my God!" Ivo fell to his knees. "It can't be! So soon? Surely not—?" He looked appealingly at Theobold.

"Dead. And I failed her—she is unshriven."

Theobold closed her eyes.

"May God in heaven succor and absolve her," Ivo said. "I should have gone sooner to fetch you—but I thought—such a bad sign, a priest—she might take fright—and I hoped she would get better. And now—God forgive me." Tears began to trickle down his grooved, weathered face.

Joanna seeing her father cry was too terrified to do anything but stand twisting her skirt, her eyes going from Ivo to the priest and back again. She could not fully comprehend that Mariotta was dead, gone, a lifeless corpse to be put into the ground, the volatile voice stilled, the beautiful face smothered with black, wormy earth. How could such a warm being, a mother so alive only a few hours earlier, be inert now, unhearing and mute?

Ivo, his shoulders shaking, lowered his head. Joanna burst into tears, and the boys, awakened, sat up, rubbing their eyes.

Theobold, a look of compassion on his heavy-fleshed face, put a hand on Ivo's shoulder. "All is not lost. Come, we shall say the prayers for the dead. She was a good woman with a generous heart. God will take pity on her."

He knelt beside Ivo and began to murmur. After a long while Ivo joined him, moving his lips soundlessly to an *Ave*.

"You will have to bury her," Sir Theobold said. "The sooner the better."

Daylight was seeping in through the shutters.

"Now?"

"Now. If the villagers should find out, even a single one ..."

"Freyda has been here."

"Then you can be sure she will lose no time spreading the word."

Ivo got stiffly to his feet. He felt drained, exhausted, but he would manage. The tears of remorse and grief he had shed, the long hours of prayer, had purged him—not of the pain, for that would take time, but of his feeling of helplessness, the feeling that God had deserted him, that Mariotta's death had been the last straw. During the night he had wanted to lie down beside her and die too, but it was morning now and life went on. He had the children to think of.

"Father, I thank you for what you have done here this night," Ivo said. "But I ask one more boon. Take my boys and girl with you. They've not had the plague, and if they could get away ..."

"What are you saying?" the priest broke in, shocked. "That is impossible."

"If they stay in this cot they will sicken."

"I cannot take the children. A priest's house is—is sanctified. A priest ..." He paused, because Ivo was looking at him. It was common gossip that what went on in the priest's house was not all prayer and sanctity.

"Every man comes to the same reckoning in the end," Ivo said. "Sinners as well as saints. You have your own soul to think of, Father. It is never too late. If you save four children, God's grace will serve you well."

Theobold's jowls shook as he looked at the silent children, who stared back at him with frightened eyes.

He was not a bad man, or selfish, but he too was afraid. And yet he knew as well as any that the plague was God's punishment for man's sins. He had sinned, there was no denying that, he had sinned mightily both in thought and fact. "It is never too late," Ivo had said. *Never too late.* Should he? Should he not?

"I will take them," he said, coming to a quick decision, a decision made out of a wish to receive God's pardon as well as a sincere pity for the children.

"Bless, bless you."

Theobold waved his hand. "About Mariotta's burial. You will have to prepare her yourself, since I'm certain Freyda will not. We will bury her after sundown. Now then, come, children—come as you are—nay, no food, none from this cot. I will have to burn your clothes before you enter my house. Come along—be quick!" He herded them toward the outer door. Beyond it came a murmur of voices. The priest looked at Ivo questioningly.

Ivo shrugged. "Mayhap 'tis a few who have come for a cup of morning ale."

But when Sir Theobold drew the door open they saw not a few but a large crowd of angry villagers, some with sticks in their hands, others armed with scythes and hooks. Freyda had already spread the word.

"The Cokes are to stay inside!" John Crykes shouted, brandishing a rake. "The bailiff, his wife—that plague-ridden witch!—and the brats. We shall kill the first that puts his foot into the lane!"

The children shrank back. Ivo brushed past. "Go on about your business," he commanded. "You, John—and you, Clyde—Roger—Tom—Avice—all of you. Off with you! Whether I come or go is my own concern."

"Take heed, bailiff! We mean what we say." A loud chorus of ayes agreed with John Crykes.

Ivo was neither afraid nor angry—annoyed, mayhap, for he understood the terror which drove them to menace him with shouts and bludgeons.

"Go home—all of you!" he repeated.

A stone struck the door lintel, and Ivo would have stepped forward had not Sir Theobold grasped his arm. "Stand back," he urged. "They mean harm."

The crowd had begun to shout obscenities and to wave

their sticks. Sir Theobold held up his hand, and the tumult subsided to an irate muttering. "What of me? Would you strike your priest too?"

"Nay, Father," John Crykes said. "You are a man of God—protected from the pestilence." Where he had received this bit of misinformation Sir Theobold did not ask. He knew that during the last epidemic priests died along with laymen, many doomed at the start because they were called upon to administer the last rites to the ill.

"Then let me bring the children through."

"You cannot," John Crykes argued. "They are fouled with the disease. We will not risk it."

"Would you prevent me?"

"You are a holy man. None would dare strike you, Sir Theobold. But as God is my witness I cannot answer for the safety of the brats. Nor can any of us." A murmur of assent went around the sullen crowd.

Sir Theobold knew his parishioners too well to doubt their intent. They hated Ivo, now more than ever, hated him, his wife, his offspring. They would kill his sons and his daughter, just as they would kill the vermin in the fields.

Ivo too saw where further debate was useless. "Go, Father," Ivo said. "Nothing is to be gained by nattering with these foolish folk. Go—pray for us. That is all you can do."

"I shall pray. I shall light a candle to St. Roch, the patron saint of the plague-afflicted, but more, I shall return. You will need healing herbs, bread and fresh water."

"'Tis kind of you, Father." But Ivo was too much of a realist to expect Sir Theobold to keep his promise.

When Ivo turned to reenter his cot, he saw that a great red cross had been painted on his door. The rays of the rising sun suddenly struck it in a shaft of scarlet light, and the cross seemed to pulse and shimmer like a symbol of the cursed and the doomed. Ivo stared at it for a long moment, then motioned the children inside and, following them, slammed the door behind.

After Mariotta had been laid to rest in the churchyard, Ivo burned her pallet, the clothes she had worn in her illness, even the wooden ladle she had drunk from, though it was their only one. He had Joanna sweep up the rushes and throw them into the fire too. Next he sprinkled the floor with vinegar and made the children wash their hands, mouth and nostrils with the same. He had heard that rosewater and a pomander ball stuck with precious cloves also proved good antidotes, but such luxuries were beyond his reach. Only the manor-born could afford them. Vinegar and prayer would have to do.

However, neither proved enough. Two days later Ernest awoke from a restless sleep complaining of a terrible thirst. His throat, his back and his legs hurt. Given ale, he vomited and then lay back on his pallet flushed and trembling. Soon he began to thrash about in a high fever, calling upon his dead mother, imploring her to keep the demon who was sitting on his chest from impaling him with a red-hot pitchfork.

On the second day after Ernest had taken ill, Sir Theobold returned, much to Ivo's surprise, bringing three loaves and a cheese.

"So the boy ails, does he? Don't lose heart, Ivo," he said cheerfully. "The young fare much better with this sickness than the old. Many recover."

"I hope to God you are right, Father," Ivo said, a new respect in his voice. He had never thought to see Father Theobold while the danger of plague still hung over them. "But are you not taking a risk?"

"There's no risk to doing the Lord's work."

"Ah, but you came." He gave Theobold a wan smile.

"Humpphh! Well—well!" Sir Theobold cleared his throat, embarrassed, but pleased. "Mayhap. Now—as for the villagers harming you, you may rest easy. I have put the fear of the Devil into them, and leastwise they cannot blame you now for spreading the plague."

"There are others who have it?"

"Three: Tom Flemyng and William and Agnes Chickley. I have heard the steward, Sir Gregory, is feeling poorly too. Fortunately, Harold de Ander has not returned from Horlick, and I doubt he and his lady will until the pestilence has run its course."

That evening while Joanna prepared supper—the last chicken killed for the pot—she felt a little giddy. At first she thought it was the thick smoke rising from the damp sticks sputtering on the hearth and stepped away to clear her head. But then the smell of the boiling fowl, one moment delicious and appetizing, became suddenly sickening, and bile rose to her throat. She tried to swallow it, could not, and, dropping the stirring stick, ran to the door. Her father, hearing her retching, came to hold her heaving shoulders.

"'Twill be all right, daughter. Your brow is cool, thanks to God," Ivo said, pressing it with a hand.

But she saw the flicker of apprehension in his eyes and her stomach knotted anew.

"Sit, Joanna. You will feel better in a moment."

She sat on a stool and watched Ivo take up the stick to stir the steaming pottage. His figure swam before her eyes. She tried to focus, but could not; the broth was making her sick again, and when she got up her legs doubled under her like broken straws. She heard her father gasp and then remembered no more.

From the bottom of the red-hot pit where she lay, Joanna heard the murmur of voices.

"Jesus, Lord of Mercy—have mercy—have mercy..."

The prayers for the dead. She tried to pull herself up, but glowing pincers grasped her by the head and she could not move. She was thirsty, her throat was parched, her tongue so dry it seemed to rattle in her mouth. "Water...!" a voice croaked. Her own? "Papa—water..." A cool horn cup touched her lips and her throat ached as she lapped at it, sipped and drank, the water running down her chin. She opened her eyes.

A haggard man with red-streaked eyes and a coarse beard sprouting on his chin bent over her, a stranger, someone who meant her harm, and she flailed out, knocking the cup from his hand.

"Papa!" she screamed. "Oh, Papa, where are you? Papa!" And the engulfing darkness swept over her again.

A long while passed, an age in which horrendous dreams and monstrous fantasies tormented her. John Hawkwood would appear in those dreams, a John Hawkwood astride a black, black horse, riding along a forest path. She would be separated from him by a screen of mist-shrouded trees, a barrier she tried desperately to breach, stumbling over roots and clawed branches, running and sobbing, calling his name, begging him to stop, to look, to smile, to speak, to save her. Then the dream would fade into distorted nightmares again.

After what seemed an eternity, a timeless time, during which she grew hot and cold by turns, her body sometimes shrinking to a droplet, sometimes swelling, swelling like a blown pig's bladder, she found her own shape; the pain and bad dreams receded, finally vanishing altogether.

She opened her eyes. The man again, the face more gaunt, the beard thicker, streaked with gray. A stranger. She blinked her eyes.

"God—oh God! I thank Thee for Thy mercy," the stranger whispered.

"I am hungry," Joanna muttered, and the man smiled, a smile she knew. Not a stranger, but her father. "Papa...? Oh, Papa."

His fingers brushed her forehead. "Hungry, you say? Bread soaked in milk for the invalid. Wait but a few moments and I shall fetch it."

"Papa!" She grasped his sleeve. "Was I ill?"

"Very, my daughter, but you have come through it, and you will get well now."

"And Ernest—is he better too?"

Ivo crossed himself. "Your brother—God absolve his soul— died."

A tear caught in her lashes and then slowly coursed down her cheek, but she was too weak to shed more. Ernest dead— and—aye, aye, she suddenly remembered, her mother too.

Ivo went to the hearthstone and poured some milk from a pitcher. Milk, she wondered in her dazed mind. Where did Papa get milk? And so dear. He came back with a bowl and offered her a bit of sopping bread from his fingers.

"Don't wolf it, eat slowly—that's it, slowly."

Ah, but it tasted good, like nothing else she had ever tasted before. She ate three mouthfuls and would have gone on, but Ivo took the bowl away. "Your belly's shrunk—and you will only lose it."

She lay back on the pallet, light-headed but lucid. She understood now—she had somehow survived the illness which had taken her mother and brother. She saw the shadow of her father dancing on the walls as he stirred the fire. It was strangely quiet, so quiet; no hens clucked (but the last had gone into the pot, she recalled), no voices, no murmurings from the other pallets.

"Is it night?" she asked.

"'Tis day," Ivo answered.

The bell from the village church began to toll, cutting the silence with clanging, brassy peals. "Someone has died," Joanna said, counting the gonging sounds.

"Many, daughter, many."

She looked about the room. "Arnulf—and Jack...?"

"Dead too." He had wanted to break the news gently, but he was too weary to think. "Dead too."

Chapter IV

Not one household in the village escaped the plague. Death had knocked at every cot door, sometimes taking entire families, fathers, mothers, children, old and young, male and female. The new graves overflowed the parish cemetery, crowding into the field beyond, makeshift burials hastily performed at dusk or in the predawn dark. Crykeses, Flemyngs, Bagleys, Chickleys, Trypes, Biggingses, Cokes, all had suffered losses, all had seen their line diminished, some dying knowing they were the last. The survivors, those who had recovered and the very few who had not fallen ill, either sat about in a helpless, mumbling daze or made merry, carousing and drinking, sure that their hours were numbered whatever they did. The unplowed fields shimmered under gray skies, fallow, lonely, unpeopled, a vast demesne awash with mud and winter rain. Not a single strip had been visited, let alone touched.

Dikes had fallen into ruin, ditches overflowed, walls crumbled, thatch rotted, and gardens struggled against overgrown nettles and vines. The animals, those that had not sickened and perished, ran wild. Chickens, pigs, geese, sheep, even the precious oxen and a few stray horses grazed on the verges along the hedgerows, wandering and drifting into the forest itself. The cows, milked only intermittently, lowed piteously, and few seemed to mind, for who needed milk? The healthy drank ale and the sick would soon die in any case.

At the manor house, Sir Gregory, the despised steward, had died, as had his lady, a son and three daughters. At the first sign of illness the new bailiff, taking his family, had run off, no one knew where. Cold comfort, Ivo thought when he heard the news.

Sir Theobold, miraculously untouched by the plague, was among the survivors, a changed man even in physical appearance, for he had shed pounds of flesh. Skin hung from his chin in loose, quivering dewlaps, and his gown fitted him now like a shapeless tent. But the merry smile was still there. He had redeemed himself a thousand times over. Courageously tending the ill as best he could, he had shriven the dying, sped their souls on to a Christian heaven and murmured his rote-learned prayers for the dead at their grave-sides. For the first time in his life he truly believed in a benevolent God—for had he, Theobold, a repentant sinner, not been spared?

When Ivo had finally emerged from the cot and saw the devastated village, the gaping doors and banging shutters, the lane clogged with debris and dead animals, the fields gone to the wild, his heart said, *I don't care.* He had been through a harrowing ordeal, had lost a wife and three sons, a loss that had stunned and shattered him. He could not understand why he, Ivo Coke, had been spared. For what? To suffer, to grieve, to mourn? He would have gladly exchanged places with Mariotta, Ernest, Arnulf or Jack, any or all of them, gladly have fitted himself into one of the graves next to the village church, gladly given his life for theirs. But he could not, and the self-pity he felt now was a weakness he could ill afford. He must grapple with his fate, put the pieces back together, not weep for what he could not alter. For some mysterious reason God had allowed him to live—and Joanna, too; he must not forget Joanna. For her he was grateful. Thanks to the Almighty's mercy he was not entirely alone.

So he stood there, eyes narrowed, resolutely putting aside his pain, his mind taking stock of the situation. If he and his neighbors were to eat they must get to work at once and salvage what they could. They would have to work hard and together—and there for a moment his heart balked again, the bitterness flooding in. He recalled only too plainly the menacing crowd gathered outside his cot, John Crykes (gone to his reward too) waving a scythe, the curses, the shouts, not a hand raised to help him, but all lifted to beat him down. But this moment like the earlier one passed, and the bailiff in him took over again.

He stepped into the mud-rutted street beyond his close and with a firm tread began to move from cot to cot. At each place still inhabited by a man or boy of working age, he explained what had to be done, sternly advising against letting things go on as they were. Most of the surviving villagers, drained now of old enmities, exhausted by sorrow and fear, rallied surprisingly under Ivo's prodding. Glad to have someone with purpose in command, they went to work willingly, forgetting their former hatred of the bailiff, even welcoming his brusque orders, for only in the long hours of toil did life seem bearable again. And it was hard labor. Ivo drove them mercilessly from morning until night, men, women and children; anyone able to milk a cow or pull a weed was dragooned, threatened, coerced into doing his or her share. There was so much to be done and so few to do it.

Rumors from the castle itself were disquieting. The manor varlets, who had run off to the forest in panic, were now slinking back and, finding those in authority either dead or gone, had taken over. Ivo flinched when he heard of varlets tumbling the kitchen maids in the lord's beds, eating off gold plate and making merry with the Anders' wine. His ties to Nareham's master were too strong, duties passed from father to son too ingrained, for him to remain indifferent. After he had organized the villagers, serf and freeman alike, to their various tasks, he hurried up the hill to the castle. The gates had been left ajar, and when Ivo entered the courtyard he was shocked at the sight. Animals lay where they had fallen, their rotting corpses stinking to high heaven, ordure piled ankle deep, refuse, broken implements and furniture thrown helter-skelter into the manor yard. The well had been fouled, and it was plain to see by the discarded empty wine kegs what the servants had been drinking in place of water. Inside the house the same chaos, the same filth reigned. Ivo rounded up the varlets and by knocking heads together, cracking jaws, kicking the drunk into sobriety and threatening them all with a hanging he soon had them scurrying about under his orders.

While Ivo was occupied setting the castle to rights, Joanna, still weak and trembling, sat on a stool peeling onions for the noonday meal and talking to Sarah Biggings. Sarah, a young girl of fourteen, had come by to borrow an awl and had tarried a bit to exchange a few words with Joanna. She too had lost most of her family and like Joanna had taken dangerously ill with the plague and survived. They were comparing their present state of health, their exhaustion and lassitude, when suddenly a shadow loomed in the doorway. The next moment three men entered the room, three strangers, dressed in tattered jerkins and drawers, their legs wrapped in rags. They were an ugly-looking trio, one with a horribly pockmarked face, another with a broken nose, all with unkempt beards.

"We are hungry, lass," the pockmarked man said, looking around. "Have ye anythin' to spare for a couple o' pilgrims?"

"Pilgrims!" Sarah retorted scornfully. "From the looks of ye, ye be brigands or I miss my guess. Be off with ye!"

The pockmarked man lunged forward and gave her a resounding slap which knocked her from the stool.

Joanna, terrified, sprang up and made for the door. But one of the "pilgrims" was ahead of her. "Not yet, brat!" He flung her back into the room.

She wanted to scream, even though she knew it was useless—all her neighbors, everyone in the village strong enough to wield a hoe, had gone to work in the fields—but she was afraid of being slapped as Sarah had been.

"Where's the food?"

Joanna tried to swallow her fright before she stuttered, "Th—there's onions here, cheese and bread in yon coffer."

The pockmarked man flipped open the coffer and grasped a loaf. "Is this all ye've got?"

"Ah—ah—all," she managed, hoping they would take what they found and be on their way.

Sarah had regained her seat on the stool and sat silently, eyes glowering, her hand nursing her bruised jaw.

It took no more than a minute or two for the men to gobble the cheese and bread down.

"I heard chickens in the back," one of them suggested.

"Aye—chickens—but wait," the pockmarked man said, his gaze lighting on Sarah. "There's somethin' else I been hungry for." He leered at her.

"If you touch me," she threatened, "my brother will tear you limb from limb."

"Yer brother'll do aught. There's no one about. Harry," he directed the broken-nosed man, "ye stand guard at the door."

"Me? Why should I? I could use a bit o' tit and ass myself."

"Don't whine. Ye'll get yer turn, never fear. Go on, go on!"

Sarah rose up, grabbed a fire tong and faced the men defiantly, while Joanna, her eyes wide, her throat dry, began to sidle toward the window. But Harry, on the way to the door, reached out and shoved Joanna against the wall with such force she slithered to the floor.

Through a daze she heard Sarah scream, saw the pockmarked man relieve her of the poker, saw him ripping her kirtle from her body, revealing her thin, naked form with its small applelike breasts.

"Hold her hands," he instructed the third man. "Christ—she's got nails."

Pinned to the floor, Sarah moved her head from side to

side, arching her body, her bared white breasts heaving convulsively as she tried to free herself.

The pockmarked man was on her, his swollen member free. "Keep her still, damn you!" When he entered Sarah, she screamed, her legs flailing. "Ah—haha!" the man exclaimed, his nude buttocks rising and falling. "Tight as a drum."

"Ye son of a whore!" his companion cried. "Hurry, damn ye. I'm fit to burst." He wiggled out of his drawers, letting go of Sarah, who had ceased to struggle.

Harry now turned away from the door, his mouth slack, his forehead beaded with sweat, and stood watching. "Let's have her between us," he suggested. "Ye in front, me—"

"Shut up!" the third man spat. "If ye're so damn horny, take the brat."

Joanna made herself small, shrinking back, wishing she could disappear into the floor.

Harry moved toward the copulating pockmarked man, anger glinting in his small eyes, his fists balled. "Ye want to do me out o' a turn—foisting me off. I know ye, turd, hogging that bit there..."

Joanna, seeing that no one was looking, quietly crawled to the open doorway and noiselessly scuttled through. Once outside she began to run, sheer terror giving her weak legs speed, her heart pounding, her chest constricted with rasping sobs as she fled.

Blinded by tears, she did not see the horse and its rider until she was almost upon them. She stopped short as the mounted man drew rein.

"What's this, little miss, do you wish to be run down?"

Joanna, wiping her nose and eyes, looked up into a sun-bronzed face. She drew her sleeve across her eyes again. Was it the same dream? Was she still ill? And the nightmare behind her...

"'Tis really you? John Hawkwood?"

He smiled, his brown eyes crinkling at the corners. "Aye, 'tis me. How do you know my name?"

Choked up, unable to answer, she burst into tears. Laughing, he leaned down and lifted her into the saddle. "Such a pretty little lass to be crying. A beating, a scolding?"

Between sobs she tried to tell him, pointing at the cot, from which the men were just emerging. Hawkwood, finally catching the drift of her story, spurred his horse into a gallop, but the men, seeing him, had picked up their heels, fleeing from sight around the corner of the cot.

Sarah was dead. Her heart, weakened by illness, had not been able to bear the further shock of fear and revulsion and so had simply stopped. To Joanna the whole incident, the manner of Sarah's death, was so horrifying she managed to blot it from her mind, and years later when she recalled Sarah, it was to think of her as dying in the plague. The only memory of that day she carried with her was her meeting with Hawkwood and the feeling that he had rescued her from some dark disaster, the details of which she was never able to recall.

But she remembered Hawkwood himself, the way he looked, the short bristle-lashed lids hooding brown eyes, the white flashing grin, the smell of leather and horse, the feel of his strong arms holding her, the way the top of her head fitted in under his chin as they trotted toward the castle to meet her father. She remembered every word he said (except those which pertained to Sarah), the sound of his deep voice, every gesture, even his laugh.

He had come looking for Harold de Ander, he told Ivo, to collect a debt owed to the Earl of Oxford, now fighting in France. The plague there had decimated the earl's ranks, and he needed money to hire new recruits.

"The lord and his family are at Horlick," Ivo explained. "They have been there since before the sickness came to Nareham, and likely to stay for several months, according to what I hear."

"Horlick—a long ride," Hawkwood observed.

Joanna stood by listening to this conversation, her eyes never leaving John Hawkwood's face. She loved him. She loved him with all the fervor and passion of a child who has found an idol to adore. She did not want him to go to Horlick; she did not want him to go anywhere. She wanted him to stay. She loved him as much as if not more than (God forgive her) her father.

She said, her voice piping, a little high, "I never told you how I knew your name."

"That's so. But I suppose we have met before. How could I forget?"

"My name is Joanna."

"Aye. Well, Joanna, may God be with you—and you, Ivo. As I said, a long ride, so I'd best be off."

As Joanna stood gazing raptly at him, he threw her a kiss, then wheeled his horse and galloped from the yard.

Joanna reverently touched the cheek where she imagined Hawkwood's airy kiss had fallen. A kiss—even at a distance—so much more than she had ever expected.

The de Anders returned to Nareham in April. They came clattering across the causeway and down the road toward the castle at the tail end of a sunny spring day, Harold and his squires leading an entourage of vassal knights and huntsmen carrying their falcons, their dogs loping beside them. Following behind, the ladies rode in a painted wagon blazoned with the de Ander coat of arms while four baggage carts piled high with household and personal belongings brought up the rear.

Sir Theobold, catching sight of the calvacade, hurriedly mounted his gray cob and trotted toward the drawbridge to intercept them.

"God's greetings, sire," he called to Lord Harold as he drew near.

Harold, reining in his blooded mount, narrowed his eyes against the setting sun and saw a shabby cleric in a greasy, mud-stained habit, a gaunt monkish figure with a beaked nose. A mendicant friar, he decided, one of those begging frauds that cluttered the countryside these days, importuning alms in the name of the Holy Trinity. He nodded to his squire, and the man rode forward. "Give the shaveling a shilling."

"Nay—nay," Sir Theobold protested. "'Tis me, my lord, not a beggar. Do you not recognize your village priest? 'Tis Sir Theobold."

"Theobold...? Theobold. By God's belly, I did not know you. Have you been stricken too?"

"Nay, thanks to God. But the village..." He waved his hand toward the clustered cots. "Nearly half gone, may God rest their souls, and the castle folk too. Sir Gregory was among the first to die."

"Sir Gregory—aye—so I have been told. The plague was bad in these parts, eh? Well, God works in mysterious ways, does He not?" He smiled, showing yellow teeth, a big-boned man with brown curling hair, close-set eyes and a skin tanned by wind and sun.

"The village looks better than I had supposed," Harold said. "Much better than some I passed on the way. And the fields plowed and planted, mine also."

"Thanks there goes to the bailiff—not that Roger Peyte who scurried off like a weasel at the first sign of trouble, but Nareham's old bailiff, Ivo Coke. If it had not been for him, everything here would still be rack and ruin. 'Twas he who got the men together, those in the castle too. Put them to work, toiled right along with them, punished the shirkers, had them at their tasks even on the Sabbath."

"The bailiff? Ivo Coke? Wasn't there something...? Ah, yes. He kept back money on the purchase of a horse."

"A mistake, my lord. Sir Gregory was mistaken. He confessed as much on his deathbed."

"Ah?"

A small lie. Sir Gregory had confessed nothing. May he burn in hell. But Ivo was worth ten of him. "'Tis so. You know—as we all do—Ivo Coke's reputation. Straight and honest as the day is long. I would swear on the Holy Cross itself, on the Virgin Mary, on the grave of my dead mother, that Ivo Coke never cheated or lied, never was a party to a crooked dealing in his entire life."

"Hmmmm. Mayhap you are right, at that."

Two days later Ivo was summoned to the castle and shown into the great hall by the lord's own squire. Walking across the rushes toward the dais he had a few moments of trepidation. He had borrowed a heavy yoke for the oxen from his old home, the bailiff's house, now empty, and suspected that some serf, seeking to curry favor, had reported it as a theft. He would deny it, of course. But then Harold de Ander had not believed his earlier denial over the purchase of the horse. A thief once, a thief always, he would say.

So, suspecting the worst, Ivo approached and bent his knee.

"Ah—Coke." De Ander smiled with his yellow teeth. "I hear that order was restored by you—that because of you Nareham will have a crop."

"I did what I could, my lord."

"A humble man, not boastful. I like that. I have decided to bestow a great favor upon you." Again the broad, yellow-toothed smile. "An honor, in point of fact. Can you guess? Ah, I see by your face you cannot. Well, I shan't keep you on a short line. It's this: I want to make you my steward, a steward who will oversee the whole of Nareham."

Ivo's face went blank. Was the lord jesting? Was he making mock of him before he let the ax fall?

"Well, what do you think of it? Speak up, Coke."

"A steward, sire. I—we have always been bailiffs. I know not..."

"I need a steward more than a bailiff. Come now, Coke, is it so hard to say aye? You come with the best recommendation—years of service to the lords of Nareham, and Sir Theobold has put in a good word for you also. Well?"

"I—I shall be eternally grateful. I never dreamed..."

"Of course you did not. But it's done. Tomorrow early, you may move into the upper apartment of the keep. I am given to understand that the rooms are comfortable. In festive times it has been used to house an overflow of guests. And there is only you and a daughter, I believe?"

"Aye. Just the two of us. I do not know how to thank you. It is most unexpected and I pledge—"

"Good," the Lord of Nareham interrupted with a wave of dismissal.

Alys de Ander had objected when her husband first proposed elevating a peasant to stewardship, even if he had once been their bailiff. It was a position filled more often than not by the minor nobility, a place of honor and respect. But Harold had pointed out that they must be realistic. Who else could they ask? The plague had killed off a host of men, nobles as well as yeomen, leaving a dearth of available candidates to choose from. He knew of no one who could fill the post, not one that he could trust. Ivo, he explained, was loyal, clever, hard-working, honest. The business with Sir Gregory had been unfortunate, but he now suspected Gregory of having made "mistakes" on other matters. Ivo, being a peasant, would certainly be more careful.

"Very well," Alys had finally capitulated. "But I hope you are not thinking of having him under our roof?"

"Do you take me for a fool?"

And hence the old keep. A flattered, pleased Ivo did not give his intended quarters a thought, did not for a single instant compare his place in the castle yard to that of Sir Gregory, who, of course, had lived and eaten with the de Anders as an equal.

Nor did it pass through Joanna's mind that they had been relegated to inferior accommodations. She was delighted, ecstatic with the tower, a world apart from their cramped, smoke-filled cot. True, it was dark—the deeply embrasured slit windows let in only a trickle of light—but their new home had three good-sized alcoves, rooms separated with hangings, more space than even the bailiff's house. And such elegant furnishings! Sturdy stools, two coffers carved with cabbage roses and kitchen utensils of every kind, of every description, even a tapestry, much faded and moth-eaten, but a tapestry nevertheless.

Not until Joanna visited the manor house itself did she realize that the keep was not the ultimate in comfort or magnificence she first believed it to be. Her father, expected to dine in the great hall at his lord's pleasure, had taken her with him a week after their arrival, and when they stepped into the long, high-arched room, Joanna, standing behind Ivo, gave an involuntary gasp. She had never seen such a chamber, and the stories about this beautiful room gave it scant justice. Strewn with sweet-smelling rushes, flanked at each end by enormous fireplaces, the walls hung with rich tapestries of glowing colors and lighted by gilded flambeaux, it seemed like a fairy-tale hall, vastly superior to the musty, bare keep.

Stumbling behind her father, she followed him down the hall through the crowd of trestle tables where the lesser folk customarily dined. At the far end of the room on a raised dais sat the Lord and Lady of Nareham and their noble guests. Ivo paused at the trestle table beneath them. At the head of it a place for him and his daughter had been reserved, below the salt, a position, a term, Joanna was one day to find demeaning. But for now her proximity to the master and mistress of Nareham awed if not overwhelmed her. Ivo kept prodding her to eat, not to gape.

They had been living at the keep for three years. Joanna was fifteen now, a beautiful girl, full-lipped, violet-eyed, tall with a narrow waist and firm, rounded breasts. Her raven hair, braided into two thick ropes, reached well below her waist and swung provocatively against her rump as she walked. Even the gray peasant kirtle and hempen bodice she wore could not hide the ripe litheness of her figure, nor the hint of sensuality in the movement of her hips. Of this, of her good looks, of her female charm, Joanna was unaware. Boys and men ogled, winked and cat-called after her, true, but then it was more or less expected of men to do so at anything in skirts. Even old Bess with her tattered shawl and wrinkled cheeks sweeping the flags with her straw besom received her share of lewd invitations.

One morning as Joanna was drawing water from the well, she heard the gates creak open and, glancing up, saw John Hawkwood ride through, carrying the de Vere pennon fluttering at the end of a pike. She gazed transfixed, oblivious to the water spilling from her bucket, staring at the tawny-haired Hawkwood sitting his large gray stallion with the easy grace of skilled self-assurance.

John Hawkwood! Not in a dream but in the flesh. John Hawkwood! Her hero, her chivalrous hero, the idol who had scooped her up into his saddle, dried her tears, thrown her a kiss.

He was already riding past when she called his name.

Drawing rein, he turned his head, and she smiled, the smile freezing on her face as their eyes met and an inexplicable emotion jolted through her. It was the same man, John Hawkwood, giving her not the same amused look she remembered as a child, but one that pierced her to the marrow. In the brief silence that followed his arrogant eyes examined her with surprise, admiration and curiosity while she struggled for words.

"I—we—we have met before."

"Indeed?" He lifted one brow, his face reflecting a man's pleased response to a desirable woman.

And it flustered Joanna, flustered, frightened, yet excited her. "Aye—we have met—twice, some years ago."

Again his eyes flicked over her. "Could I have disremembered such a meeting?"

He had, he had. Had she changed so then? And what must he think of her? Accosting him like a wanton, like a dairy maid eager for a tumble. "My name is Joanna Coke—you..."

But before she could finish a groom came running. "This way, sergeant, my lord awaits you."

Hawkwood leaned down from the saddle. "We shall see one another again, lass. We shall." And he gave her a knowing wink.

She looked after him as he trotted across the courtyard, a feeling of mortification rising in her breast. He *had* thought her bold, shameless. How could she fault him for that? How could she have expected him to remember their two brief chance encounters? And those years ago. It was natural for him to think of her as the usual peasant girl, forward and compliant as so many were. He had no way of knowing that she was Ivo Coke's, the steward's, daughter, that she had been brought up to prize her virginity, that she believed with all her heart that it was a sin to come to her marriage bed other than pure.

And until the moment John Hawkwood had looked at her, her beliefs had never wavered. To be good, decent, to be well thought of, to think well of herself, formed the basis of her pride. In the past she had never had occasion to doubt herself. She had never felt desire for a man, never the rising heat to the face, the fluttery heart, the longing to touch, kiss or copulate under the hedges as the kitchen wenches often did. No man had captured her fancy, none had ever moved her to ecstasy or tears. Toward the few would-be suitors who had dared approach her she had felt only a cold contempt. But now...it was as if she were a ship that had suddenly come loose from its mooring. Was she in love? Nay, nay. How could that be? Hawkwood was a face, only a face, that belonged to a childish memory. Then why this confusion? She did not know. She had no powers of introspection, she only sensed a vague uneasiness, a formless, perplexing discomfort as if her skin no longer fit.

And the feeling did not go away. In the early evening, still restless, she went down to the courtyard to chat awhile with the carpenter's daughter, Elthreda. But Elthreda was at chapel and Joanna, having no desire to join her, began to stroll aimlessly across the courtyard past the manor house. At the gate of the pleasaunce, Alys de Ander's private pleasure garden, she paused. Enclosed by a tall hawthorn hedge, it was forbidden to all but the de Anders and their guests, though Joanna, out of curiosity, had secretly inspected it shortly after she had moved to the keep. She had not been able to understand why the pleasaunce should be so special when it contained nothing more than a plot of grass, a small stagnant pond scummed with dirty ice (she had seen it in winter), a few trees and several moribund flower beds.

No one was in sight, so she unlatched the wooden gate, closed it behind her and commenced walking slowly along the graveled path. Finding a stone bench, she sank down and leaned back with a sigh, looking up at the sky. Tattered mauve streamers tinged with gold lingered in the afterglow of the setting sun. The evening star glittered high above, a pinpoint of diamond light, a jewel set in pale lavender velvet. Joanna was seldom moved by displays of the physical universe. Growing up, she and nature had been adversaries. The sky was scanned for possible rain, not for its glorious sunsets. The greening of the earth was noted anxiously, hopefully, not with detached wonder or poetic enjoyment; those yellow flowering blooms could turn to weeds, casting their seed pods on the tilled soil to compete with life-giving grain; the silvered trees harbored birds that pecked, tore and ate the new growth.

A bank of delicate snowdrops, wild roses or bluebells, the forest's colorful autumnal finery, were traps to lull the unwary into thinking nature was beautiful and benign. The elements had to be watched carefully and cautiously and when necessary fought tooth and nail.

But on this evening, Joanna felt strangely affected by the summer twilight, her heart heavy with a bittersweet nostalgia. Nostalgia for what? She did not know. She sighed again. A bird began to trill in the hawthorn bush, rustling the branches, showering little pink petals upon the turf, and their perfume made her throat ache. The bird sang on, the notes swelling and caroling in piercing sweetness.

"Oh hush!" she cried angrily. She hated the bird, the flowering hawthorn, the sweet-scented dusk, the heavy feeling under her ribs. She had the terrible urge to put her head down in her hands and weep and weep. "Hush!"

She heard the crunch of footsteps and, looking up, saw John Hawkwood peering at her over the hedge.

"I thought I heard a voice."

Lips parted, she stared at him.

"A maid. A maid meeting a lover," he taunted, his voice lightly mocking.

"N-nay..."

His head disappeared, and a few moments later she saw him coming toward her. She experienced a flash of panic, not so much because she had been discovered trespassing but because she felt trapped, forced by chance and her own foolishness to face John Hawkwood alone. Rising, she found her knees had gone weak.

"Ah—the pretty maid at the well."

Her lips trembled as she tried to offer some excuse for her presence in the lady's garden, "I—I came hence—to—to pluck a bouquet for..."

But he did not seem interested. Again he was looking at her with the sort of look she resented or ignored in others. But now, no resentment, no indifference, only a disquieting apprehension, and that same curious excitement as if a hand had lightly caressed her bare skin.

"You said we had met before?" he asked politely in a tone at odds with the liquid warmth of his eyes.

"Aye," she answered unsteadily. "Aye—some years ago."

"I cannot recall."

"I was still a child, not quite eleven, riding pillion with

Thomas de Ander, and he—he was using his whip—you stopped him."

He creased his brow. "I cannot recall," he repeated. "I should, but I cannot."

She had thought that when she reminded him, he might, just possibly might, remember. But now the thought struck her that all these years when John Hawkwood had been so clear in her dreams and fantasies, *she* had never once been in his. He had forgotten, most likely dismissing her from his mind, the moment she had gone from his presence. She tried not to feel disappointment, asking herself what grown man (and an earl's sergeant-at-arms at that) would recall a chance encounter with a child. But still...

"And you are what age now?" he was asking.

"I lack two months to sixteen." And for one moment she wished she was not nearly sixteen; she wished that she was eleven again, that she could feel the same awe and delight in his presence, not this disconcerting agitation.

"And so comely. You are called Joanna, I believe you said?"

"Joanna Coke, the steward's daughter."

"The steward." He nodded his head, his brown eyes sweeping over her again.

"I—I must leave..."

"You are going to run off? When we have hardly become acquainted," he chided.

"I must..."

"Come sit awhile. There's no harm in that." He laughed as he flung himself on the bench, drawing her down beside him.

His touch, his nearness, came like a shock, unnerving her even more.

"You say your father is steward?"

She could feel his thigh through the stuff of her gown, hard-muscled and warm. Never had she been so acutely aware of a man's physical presence.

"These past three years. He was bailiff before."

"Ah—tell me about it."

He leaned back while she narrated in a hesitant voice the toll the plague had taken, her mother's and brothers' deaths, Harold de Ander's summons to the keep, while her mind flitted uneasily here and there, until she realized that her story was boring him.

"I talk overmuch." She lifted her eyes. "What of yourself?"

The sky had darkened to night, and a sickle moon rising

slowly over the hedge seemed to poise there, a luminous blade of pale light.

"Why, there is hardly anything remarkable about my life," he said wryly, taking both her hands in his. "I have seen strange countries, fought, met many people, among them ladies of high and low rank. But Joanna," and his eyes smiled into hers, "never have I met such as you."

It was a banal compliment. She had received several much like it and guessed it to be a prelude to seduction. Yet...

She ran her tongue over her lips. "Thank you."

He lifted her hand and kissed it, a kiss that seemed to sear her flesh. Further she did not know how to respond. Only the nobility indulged in such gallantries. Was he mocking her?

"Joanna." He smiled into her eyes again. He had a thin, brutal mouth, and she had a great longing to feel it, to press it with her own.

"I must go," she heard herself repeat, but she could not find the strength to rise. "My—my father will be wondering." Anything, any excuse. To remain would be fatal. She should not tarry with this man. She must leave, she must—now, now.

Suddenly a loud voice close at hand exclaimed, "But someone's here!"

Out of the darkness, two staggering figures appeared, a man with his arm about a woman's waist. By the dim light of the moon Joanna recognized Sir Robert Langley and Margaret, Countess of Callendar, two visiting nobles pointed out earlier by her father and both obviously drunk.

From habit she rose to her feet.

"What's this?" the countess slurred in a wine-sotted voice. "Who's here?"

"A thousand pardons, my lady," Joanna murmured and, picking up her skirts, fled.

John Hawkwood caught her outside the hedge. "Joanna, you cannot go now."

"I must," she said, freeing herself, hurrying on, gripped with another, different, frightening sensation that this had all happened before. Where? The pursuit, the cold fear of doom. Where had it happened? In a dream? No. For in her dreams *she* had been the pursuer, he unattainable, seen from a romantic distance, not like the Hawkwood of the garden, bold, masculine—dangerous. Yet there he was, the same man who had melted her heart so long ago. But no, she must not think of it. She must get away. Quickly. *Run, run, run!*

But he was too quick for her. He caught her and, whirling her around, crushed her to his chest, bringing that hard, thin mouth down on hers, his savage kiss shocking her so that her body stiffened. His lips moved back and forth on her reluctant ones, back and forth, and the voice that had cried "Run!" faded. An insidious sensuous warmth crept through her veins, sapping the will from her, leaving her weak and yielding. She clung to him, her lips parting to receive his tongue, the sweet melting languor drowning memory, thought, reason, until it seemed that nothing existed but the man and herself.

When he finally let her go she felt shattered, boneless.

"You're a virgin," he said. "It hardly seems possible, a ripe plum like you, but I'll stake my sword on it."

She waited before she spoke, clenching her fists, trying to stiffen her shaking voice, her trembling knees. "I—I am still a maid." Already her innate peasant common sense was returning, bringing a measure of calm. "I see no reason for *that* to be your concern."

"You are wrong. 'Tis my concern. For you see, I am herewith making a bid for your maidenhead."

"You mock me." Astonish was more like it. She thought only the village men made abrupt, coarse proposals.

"Never was I more serious." His fingers brushed her face, and for a moment she thought he would kiss her again. But he made no move to take her into his arms. "I want you as much as any man could want a woman. And if I am any judge, you desire me also."

"You are wrong. Wrong! I—I am promised." She threw the lie at him out of desperation.

"To whom? To some village lout, who smells, who will beat you, who will go at you like a hog humping a sow. Nay, sweet one, let me teach you the ways of love. I will be gentle. I will bring you nothing but great pleasure."

"I cannot. I know that virtue is lightly held these days. But *I* cannot. My father..."

"No one need know. Your father least of all."

"God will know."

He laughed. "God will forgive. Confess, do a small penance. 'Tis worth a night of love, do you not think? I see that you do not. But that is because you have never had such a night. Come, lovely," he coaxed, taking her hand, "let me teach you."

"I cannot!" she cried, snatching her hand away.

"Think on it a bit. You will change your mind, lovely," he

said with confidence. "Later, tonight—after Matins. I shall be waiting here. And you'll come. You will." He leaned over to kiss her, but she backed away. "Tonight, sweet."

"Never!" And she turned and walked quickly away. He did not pursue her, but she could hear his soft, mocking laughter.

Still angry, she went to bed early, determined to forget John Hawkwood. Meet her in the garden? What did he take her for? A pox on him, she thought, pulling the cover up to her chin, settling herself more comfortably.

But for all her determination, she slept little that night, tossing and turning, her thoughts going around and around like a mill wheel. I must not think of him, she told herself over and over. I must clear my mind, think of other things, a hare to be dressed, a pot to be mended, a shift to be sewn. But whenever she closed her eyes she saw him, the thick mane of chestnut hair, the masculine jaw, the sensual mouth. Ah—that mouth! Her bruised lips still ached. Never had she been kissed in that way, never had a man fired her blood so, making her forget time and place. Yet it would be folly to give herself to him, an experienced lover, years older than herself, a man of war, a sergeant-at-arms. Fighting men, she had heard, were great wenchers, coupling with women wherever, whenever they could. Whores, virgins, matrons, tavern wenches were all the same; two breasts, a pair of spread legs and a receptacle for their hard, swollen members. And after they finished with their pumping and grunting off they would go. John was no different. A night of pleasure indeed! He would bed her, take her maidenhead and disappear before cockcrow without a backward glance. And then her belly would grow.

She thought of her father and how he prized virtue. He wanted her to be happy, to marry well, and when he spoke of it his stern face would break into a gentle smile. She was Ivo's daughter; she wanted to please him, she could not throw his good name away by giving her virginity to a man, no matter how compelling his kisses.

When she finally fell asleep it was to dream not of her father or John Hawkwood but strangely enough of her mother, the black hair fanning out from a face lit with ecstasy as she lay under a moving Clyde Bagley. The dream disturbed her, and she woke from it feeling perplexed and guilty. Her mother—God have mercy on her soul—had spoken of pleasure too. But her mother had sinned, she realized that now. Poor,

poor Mariotta. Was she still in purgatory? Joanna crossed herself. She must pray for Mariotta, for herself. And shun John Hawkwood.

But by morning he was gone. From idle talk at the well she heard that he and Harold de Ander had left at dawn, and the sudden wayward twinge of disappointment which pinched at her heart she put down with a firm muttered "Good riddance!"

It was not that easy to banish Hawkwood from her mind, however, and she went on thinking of him, dreaming the old romantic dreams, feeling safe to do so now that he was no longer near.

But one evening her father gave her a jolt which cut through her preoccupation and crowded everything else from her thoughts.

They were in their quarters, sitting at their evening meal, she and Ivo, dining on a mutton pie with a crimped crust (the crust having been noted, admired and copied by Joanna from the manor cook), when Ivo suddenly said, "What would you think, daughter, if I were to marry again?"

"What? You, marry? Why, you are jesting."

He was not.

"It has been over four years since your mother died—God absolve her—four years since the boys went." He paused. It still saddened him to talk of Mariotta and his sons, a sadness tinged with regret and not a little guilt. If only he had been able to provide decently for them, able to give them what he had now, plenty of food, a relief from hard toil, warm clothing, a solid roof over their heads, perhaps they would have been able to weather the plague, perhaps...

"Papa, why should you marry? Are my meals not to your liking? The pie, mayhap..." The mutton churned disagreeably in her stomach. "Mayhap, less fat?"

"The pie is the best a father could wish," he assured her. "I can find no fault with your cooking, dove, nor with the way you keep the house. But a man needs a wife. I am not old and doddering yet, and I can still have sons, an heir to carry on my name."

"An heir," she echoed numbly.

"Wouldn't you like a mother?"

"I had one."

"But you must be lonely here without another woman. A

girl growing up needs, well—ah, needs advice a man cannot give."

"I don't want another woman," she said sullenly.

"You will change your mind once I bring a wife home."

"Who?" she asked sharply. "Who? Have you picked her out?"

"I was thinking of Katrine Flemyng."

"Katrine!" she wailed. "Oh, I knew it! I knew it! Papa—she's been making eyes at you ever since I can remember."

After the plague and Mariotta's death Katrine, the same miller's daughter who had blushed so profusely in Ivo's presence, had paid more than one visit to their cot, bringing a loaf, a clutch of eggs, a wedge of cheese to the bereaved widower, blushing even more, stammering, fluttering her lashes at Ivo.

"She is sly, Papa."

"Hush!" he warned, suddenly irritated. "Katrine is freeborn, she is young, she is healthy and strong. She could have a younger man, but she wants me."

"Oh, if Mama only knew. She *hated* Katrine!"

"Hold your tongue or I'll give you a clout you won't forget!" he threatened, disturbed at Joanna's reference to Mariotta. He had the strange feeling that his departed wife was glaring at him from some shadowy limbo. She had always been jealous, though he had never given her cause then, or now. He did not feel for Katrine what he had once long ago felt for Mariotta, a passion and a desire that made him overlook her bad temper, lack of family, dower and perhaps even her virginity. Mariotta had been a fire in his blood, his brief wild moment of youth. Even after they had settled into fitful, sometimes rasping domesticity, his pulses had quickened at her touch. But she was gone, and he was not foolish enough to think that he, a man approaching forty, would find a woman to rouse him in the same way. He was not in love with Katrine, barely fond mayhap, but it hardly mattered; she would make a good wife and, he hoped, a good breeder. Joanna's objections irritated him, but in no way swayed his decision. He had cosseted his daughter for too long. She would have to accustom herself to his new wife and that was the end to that.

"'Tis all settled. The banns will be read this Sunday. And"—leaning forward, shaking a finger at her to forestall further protests—"you'd best behave or so help me I'll give you that clout and more besides."

They were married at the end of the harvest, the couple joined by a beaming, wine-flown Sir Theobold, Ivo secretly wishing that the good father could have remained sober for the occasion. But he would not have had another perform the rite. He had not forgotten how Theobold had been his only friend during the plague and knew it would hurt the village priest deeply if he had chosen to be wed in the castle chapel.

After the ceremony, at the invitation of Harold de Ander, the entire village trooped to the outer bailey for the marriage feast. The master, grateful for a good harvest and for his steward's diligence, had provided bountifully. Long trestle tables groaned under loaves and round cheeses, platters of sausage, meat pies, savories and eel jellies. Four pigs and two ewes turned slowly on the spit, and three large casks of ale stood ready.

Joanna sat at the newlyweds' table, resenting Katrine, the look of joy on her sweating peasant's face, a plump face resembling a well-fed sow's. Ivo, decorous, minding his manners, offered his new wife the first sip of ale from his cup, as was customary, then drank himself. Toasts went around, ribald jests were made, the meat was served, cut and gobbled amid laughter and shouting. Someone brought out a tambourine, and Ab Bagley tottled his pipe while a quartet of inebriates sang in disharmony. The guests banged their cups, clapped hands, stamped their feet in time to the music, and presently the noise became deafening. All, even those who disliked Ivo, were there—none stayed away. "Be a fool to," Joanna heard Sim Crykes say with a loud belch. "Ale for the asking, not the swill they serve on boon days, but ale that's been aged in the cask."

The lord and his lady put in a brief appearance, drank to the health of the bride and groom and said a few words, while all stood on their feet, hanging their heads, shuffling, fidgeting, shushing the drunkards. Once they had gone, the clamor, the clatter of wooden mugs, the strident, high-pitched, tipsy voices and brassy music redoubled. Joanna hated them all. She hated them for their two-faced hypocrisy, for their grimy, black-rimmed nails, for their coarse jests and greasy, spotted clothes. She looked at her father, dressed in a clean blue tunic, his fair hair combed and brushed back from his high brow, and for the tenth time thought him the handsomest man present. Only John Hawkwood could equal Ivo in comeliness and bearing. John Hawkwood. Suppose he were here now. Suppose it was he sitting in Ivo's place and she in Katrine's. Bride and groom. Married. She sighed heavily.

But how foolish even to fancy it. He might be of noble blood for all she knew and would never, even remotely, consider a peasant as wife. Besides, a man with honorable intentions does not pursue a girl with unabashed, blatant seduction in mind.

When the dancing began, Joanna was drawn willy-nilly into the circle. Everyone except the stupefied, the sleeping drunks and babes in arms danced; the bridal couple, girls and boys, men, women and children snaking in and out, clapping their hands. Her earlier ill humor smoothed away by two cups of ale, Joanna, who after all was young, vibrant and alive, found herself caught up in the excitement and she let herself go, stepping lightly, heel-and-toe, skip, heel-and-toe, skip, clapping in time to the beat of the tambourine and jingle of bells. She did not even notice when Katrine and Ivo broke away, disappearing toward the keep in the gathering dusk, nor hear the catcalls that followed them. Around she went, around and around, in and out, singing, "Tra-la-lala," laughing at a misstep, enjoying herself for the first time that evening. Suddenly, a hot, heavy hand grasped her shoulder.

"Joanna!" It was Jack, the bride's older, widowed brother. "What a pretty thing ye've grown into. Let me dance with ye." His arm went around her waist, and he leered at her with protruding pale-blue eyes set in the same pudding face as his sister's.

"Go away!" Joanna ordered.

But he broke into the circle, taking her hand with his grubby, sweating one, treading on her feet, spoiling the fun. Sobered now, Joanna wrenched herself from his grasp and began to walk away from the smoking fires and sounds of revelry toward the inner courtyard. She had just reached the well when she heard running footsteps.

"Joanna!"

It was Jack again, hurrying after her. She was not afraid, for she did not yet fully realize what he wanted. Her father's position as steward had more or less protected her from the village lechers. What she felt now was annoyance. But before she could elude Jack, he sprang at her, his arms clutching her, his wet mouth coming down on hers. She struggled to free herself, but he held her fast while his hot, rough tongue tried to pry her lips open. She raised her fist and struck him on the side of the head, a bone-crunching blow, but he only grunted, forcing her back until she lost her balance and fell to the ground.

He was upon her in an instant, tearing at her bodice, his dirt-encrusted, calloused hands pinching and kneading her exposed breasts. She beat his face as he brought his slobbering, ale-fouled mouth down again, gnashing her teeth in outrage, too angry to scream or call for help.

"Lie still, bitch, lie still!" He pinioned her arms with one hand while the other scrabbled at her skirts. She lifted her knee, catching him in the groin.

"Damn you, witch's spawn!" he cried, slapping her with his calloused hand, a slap that rattled her teeth and made her head ring.

He kneed her legs apart, his freed, swollen member poking at her thighs. Frightened now as well as angry, she opened her mouth, shouting, "Papa! Papa!"

Suddenly a torch flared and a looming shadow asked, "What is happening here?"

"This—this churl," Joanna sputtered, "this churl—would force me."

"Get up, you knave. Up!" the shadow commanded in accents that were plainly not a peasant's.

Jack hobbled to his feet.

"Who are you and why are you attacking this girl?"

Jack cringed when he saw it was young Thomas de Ander, and began to babble about how the girl had lured him on and being drunk he had not had the sense to resist her.

Joanna, indignant, sprang up, crying, "He lies, he lies! The whoreson lies!"

"I did her no harm," Jack said petulantly. "She's still got her maidenhead."

"Is this true?" Thomas asked.

"Aye—but for you, Master Thomas, I would have lost it. The devil take him!"

"You are the bailiff's daughter?"

"Steward," Joanna corrected, drawing her bodice together, her fingers trembling as she did up the laces.

"Ah, yes. Steward now. Joanna, I believe you are called?" He smiled at her with white teeth. Twenty, the handsome boy had grown into a handsome man.

"Do you wish to bring this knave to manor court?"

She glared at Jack. She wished—what did she wish? To put a knife through his rotten heart. To have him broken on the wheel, to have him flayed. To have him at least disgraced in front of the entire village. But she had enough sense to realize even in the heat of anger what a scandal it would cause—her father's new brother-in-law accused of attempted rape, and all the Narehamers siding with Jack against Ivo.

"Make him swear to hold his tongue on pain of having it torn out," Joanna said. "I don't want to spoil my father's wedding day."

"Do you swear?" Thomas asked Jack.

Jack swore, on the cross, on the Holy Virgin, on his dead mother's grave. Then, dismissed, he scurried off.

Joanna, watching him go, brushed the dirt from her skirt. Thomas leaned against the well. "So your father has married," he said.

"Aye."

"You do not sound very happy about it. Don't you like your stepmother?"

Joanna flung back her hair. "Not very much."

The torch sputtered and hissed. In the distance they could hear raucous laughter and a drunken baritone singing a refrain.

"You have not been at Nareham for a long while," Joanna said, breaking a silence.

"I am squire at Medway, now," he said. "Next spring, God willing, I shall be dubbed knight."

"If I were a man I should like to be a knight too."

"*You?* Why, you are just a peasant."

She had no reply for that. It was true; it was as true as the sun coming up in the morning and going down in the evening; she was a peasant. But something stirred within her, a sense of shame, a vague resentment, a feeling that somehow she had to redeem herself.

"I am going to be a nun," she lied, drawing herself up, looking him square in the eye.

He laughed. "My sister said the same. And now she is married to Edgar du Trolaine and has three children and another on the way. So much for girls who want to be nuns."

"But *I* shan't change my mind."

"A pretty girl like yourself?" He reached out and lightly caressed her cheek with the back of his hand.

She drew away.

"So pretty, and such beautiful eyes."

She tried to remember what gossips had said about Thomas de Ander, Harold's second son. Was he a womanizer, a skirt chaser, a seducer of kitchen and dairy maids? He had been away for most of his growing-up years, and she did recall old Bess once saying that Alys de Ander frowned upon the men in her family bedding the castle retainers. Still, the look in his eyes was unmistakable, and she was too embarrassed to look down and see if she had laced her bodice properly.

"Thank you, Master Thomas," she said sweetly, moving back a little more. "For the compliment *and* for saving me from Jack. I would like to stay, but I must be going."

And before he could argue, she turned and hurried away.

Katrine went into her marriage with an honest attempt to win Joanna, not because she liked her, but to please Ivo. However, it was not easy to befriend Joanna, a girl whose barely concealed resentment cut like a whip lash.

When they were alone, Joanna would be openly antagonistic, speaking in a manner she would never have dared use in Ivo's presence, defying at every turn Katrine's position as mistress of the house. In front of her father, however, Joanna curbed her tongue, using a clever subtleness to undermine her stepmother.

For his part, Ivo, his head full of estate matters, remained ignorant of the strained undercurrents in his household, while Katrine, enduring Joanna's insolence in silence, consoled herself with the knowledge that Joanna would one day marry and leave. In the meanwhile, she bided her time, hoping that she could gain ascendancy by producing the son and heir Ivo longed for.

And she did. A year almost to the day of her wedding, she bore a male child, a son whom a delighted Ivo named Charles. Katrine, feeling more secure now, began to defend herself, throwing back Joanna's taunts with a tongue all the shriller for the silence it had so long endured. They had bitter quarrels, fighting over trivia, the consistency of a sauce, the turn of a spitted fowl, the length of a flaxen thread.

Ivo, finally becoming aware of domestic dissension, pretended at first to ignore it. But one evening when open warfare broke out between Joanna and Katrine, he realized something had to be done. He loved Joanna, his daughter, the living reminder of Mariotta, but he could not condone her behavior.

"Show some respect for your stepmother," he warned sternly. "She is my wife, the mother of my child. Remember that."

"Papa, I do all the hard, dirty work, while she—"

"Liar! Before God, she lies!" Katrine shrilled.

Ivo brought his fist down on the table. "Hush! Both of you!"

He sat silent for a few moments, crumbling a piece of bread in his fingers, contemplating Joanna, the full mouth, the black brows and fringed lashes.

"It's time you were married," he said, speaking at last.

"Marry! You want to be rid of me. Oh, Papa."

"I want a peaceful house."

"Who would you have me marry? Who? A peasant farmer, a drover?" A vision of John Hawkwood rose in her mind, Hawkwood, ruggedly handsome, astride his gray charger, the straight spine, the thick neck, the tawny hair. "I don't want a villager for husband. I shan't have him!"

"Hold your tongue! I'll decide, not you." He leaned toward her, his keen eyes scanning her face. "You are not thinking you are grand enough to marry into the nobility?"

"Of course not." What was John Hawkwood? Suppose he was not of noble descent after all. "Whatever gave you such a notion?"

"Well, see to it that you do not become the plaything of some feckless knight who'll put his bastard in your belly."

"I have no such intent, Papa," she replied indignantly. "You ought to know me better than that."

"Hmmm. Still, I would be happier to have you wed. Let me think on it awhile."

Ivo was still mulling over the possible candidates for husband to Joanna (he wished his only daughter to marry well, a burgher's son if it could be arranged) when he was summoned to the manor house by Harold de Ander. The master of Nareham had just returned from a long, circuitous visit to his various scattered fiefdoms, a tiresome journey during which he had suffered from a nervous stomach and a painful swelling in his left foot. In addition, he had received distressing news. His eldest son, Robert, fighting in France with the Black Prince, had been wounded at Poitiers.

"Thanks be to God he was not killed," Harold said. "Though many were. The English did well, I am told, and King John of France himself, together with a dozen of his high-placed nobles, have been made our captives. Still, that does not make my son whole, does it?"

"Nay, my lord. Was it a bad wound?"

"Bad enough. An arm gone. Amputated."

"I am sorry to hear that, my lord."

"No sorrier than I." He looked down at the accounts Ivo

had brought him, not a word or figure of which he could read. "You have done well, Ivo."

"Thank you, my lord."

Harold rustled the parchment, stroked his chin. "Oh—by the way, before I forget, I wonder if you could find a lass to assist my wife's seamstress. She has two helpers but is needing a third."

A place in the lord's household that wanted a lass. Ivo thought quickly. The quarreling under his own roof—Joanna not yet married. Should he? Joanna might object. What of it? It was time she learned how to knuckle under.

"A seamstress, you say. I believe I have just the right girl without having to look further. My daughter. Most handy with a needle, and an angel when it comes to embroidery."

"Your daughter?"

"She is young, but skilled, a hard worker, not one to shirk or lie idle."

"Hmmmm. Sounds suitable. Very well. Send her to see her ladyship."

And that, Ivo thought, relieved, takes care of my difficulties, at least for now.

Chapter V

Offended at having been forced out of her home by Katrine (who else? A small triumph for the bitch, may she rot in hell), still smarting, Joanna nevertheless could not help but feel a small thrill of nervous anticipation as she followed the haughty house carl up a staircase and down a short corridor to the solar where Alys de Ander would receive her.

After all, Joanna reasoned, it was not every lass who can come into the manor house as a seamstress's assistant rather than as a lowly kitchen maid or pot scrubber. Katrine could never aspire to such a position. Never. A seamstress's assistant! She hoped that she would make the desired impression upon her ladyship, for she had taken great pains with her appearance, wearing her best kirtle, her hair newly washed, brushed and plaited into two dark gleaming ropes. As she walked she tried to remember Ivo's last-minute instructions: Bend your knee, speak only when spoken to and then shortly, keep your eyes modestly on the floor.

The carl stopped at a heavy oaken door, opened it and announced in a loud voice, "Joanna Coke, the steward's daughter, my lady."

Joanna, her eyes lowered, heard a murmuring, the rustle of silk, then silence.

"Come forward, girl," a voice commanded. "I cannot see you if you skulk behind like that."

Joanna stepped out, red flaming her cheeks, steeling herself to ignore the stares of perhaps a half-dozen pairs of eyes. Waiting women to her mistress.

Alys de Ander herself was seated at an embroidery frame, thread and needle poised in midair. "So you have come to help my seamstress."

"Aye, lady," Joanna answered, giving a small, inexpert curtsy. Up close Alys did not seem as young as she did from afar. The forehead under a gilded headdress had fine lines running across it and two deep grooves between the brows, as though the lady were perpetually displeased with the world. The eyes were searching, a little cold, superior, the mouth turned down at the corners.

"Can you sew a fine seam?" Alys de Ander asked and,

without waiting for an answer, turned to an older woman seated on a stool next to her. "Dame Elizabeth, lend her a piece of cloth and a needle."

The cloth and needle in her hands, Joanna bit her lip to keep her fingers steady. She was conscious of the other women watching her, some at embroidery like Alys, others seated in deep-embrasured, cushioned windows. A fragrance seemed to emanate from them, the perfume of spring violets. She forced herself to concentrate on her sewing, not to think of the ladies, of their sweet smell, of their enviable lives. With slow deliberation she took tiny, tiny straight stitches down the length of the cloth.

"Good—good enough," Alys de Ander said, examining her work. "You may go with Dame Elizabeth. She will show you what to do."

Dame Elizabeth gave her lady a deep curtsy and, nodding for Joanna to follow, left the room. A short, dumpy woman, she walked in silence ahead of Joanna with quick little steps, her skirts rustling at her ankles. Up a dark, narrow staircase that creaked and trembled, they went up and around and still up until they came to a small room with a sloping ceiling. Sparsely furnished, it held a table, a chest, several straw pallets, a long bench and a trestle table on which lay scraps of cloth and a large pair of shears. Dame Elizabeth went to the window and threw the shutters open. No paned glass here. And no fireplace. The room was very cold.

"Our workplace," Dame Elizabeth said. "You will sleep there"—pointing to the pallets—"with Bella and Marta. They are on an errand now but should be back soon." She had a harsh, rather hoarse voice. "I, of course, am bedded elsewhere. You will receive board and a shilling a month. Can you cut to measurement without wasting cloth?"

"Aye."

"Aye, *madam!*" she corrected sternly.

Dame Elizabeth had a tendency to bully. A poor relation of Alys de Ander's, a cousin twice removed who had been married off to a wool merchant, long since drowned at sea, she had been left penniless. Taken in by Alys on the recommendation of the chapel chaplain, Elizabeth had lived and worked in the de Ander household for ten years, eating at their table, but at the far end among the children and lesser folk. Treated only slightly better than a servant, mostly ignored, she had worked diligently through the years, earning her keep many times over. It was hard for her not to feel

78

resentment, for she craved some recognition, some praise, some warmth from her relatives, none of which she ever received. To compensate, to assuage her bitter rejection, she had taken to drinking—the good wine, not the ale. Even drunk she could sew better than the best seamstresses in London (so she assured herself), though of late her hands had developed a slight morning tremor and her stitches slipped a little. Joanna, from the small cloth sample she had seen in the solar, would do well, making up for the dame's deficiencies, much better than the two idiotic girl assistants they had given her at Horlick.

"Her ladyship wishes a new gown for her grandaughter's christening," Dame Elizabeth said. "Have you ever cut velvet?"

Joanna debated for a fraction before deciding to answer truthfully. "Nay, madam."

"Then let me show you."

Quick and skillful, Joanna soon learned everything Dame Elizabeth had to teach her and began to take on more and more of the sewing. As time passed, Dame Elizabeth drank openly and often. Too tipsy and unsteady to attend to her mistress's measurements and fittings, she would send Joanna in her stead. Joanna did not mind. She enjoyed taking her ribbon measure and her little basket of pins and needles and going down to the lady's bedchamber or the solar, loved the sweet fragrances that scented the air, the soft carpets to kneel upon and the tiring women's chatter interspersed with French (still the favored language of the Norman nobility in England) as they gossiped of castle intrigue. She learned that most of the ladies painted their faces, daubed cheeks and lips with red paste and used a dark pigment to outline their eyes. Some even dyed their hair with saffron, for yellow hair was considered more fashionable. Joanna noted how they walked, how they sat, how they carried their heads, observing their posture and movements carefully, mimicking them whenever she could snatch a few moments of privacy. Why she copied the ladies she could not say. She knew she would never rise above her humble station, that such airs were foolish. Still she went on watching closely, at mealtime too, the way they sipped from a cup and wielded their knives, how they dipped their soiled fingers in the water bowl, daintily wiping them on the edge of the cloth. And they never picked their teeth.

Dame Elizabeth, catching her out at her mimicry once,

laughed. "Idiot! Peasant! Do you think you can change? A sow's ear never made a purse."

But Joanna could see no harm in imitating the ladies and went on with it.

Early in May, Thomas de Ander arrived at Nareham for his knighting, the ceremony and attendant festivities having been set for the twenty-fifth of the month. Thomas's godfather, John de Vere, the Earl of Oxford, would publicly dub him in the courtyard before an assembly of Nareham's villagers, the castle folk and a host of visiting nobility. The bishop himself, escorted by a retinue of distinguished clergymen, was said to be on the way, having accepted the invitation to say the special Mass.

And now Alys de Ander, suddenly realizing that she must begin to prepare for the great event if she were to be ready in time, instructed Joanna to make her a new cape and two gowns, "as soon as possible." In addition, she wanted three shifts of finest linen to give to the earl's lady as a gift, and no one to stitch them up but Joanna. Since Dame Elizabeth, deteriorating into sodden uselessness, had been packed off to a convent (Joanna in the meanwhile seizing the opportunity to appropriate her room and soft feather bed), Alys herself offered to help with the embroidery.

On hearing that the de Veres were expected, Joanna had a few moments of wild excitement—John Hawkwood would surely accompany his lord—before she reminded herself (again) that Hawkwood was not the man of her childish fantasies, but one who must be avoided at all costs. He was a libertine, an accomplished seducer, and this time he might very well succeed where he had failed before. What if she succumbed, gave in, disgraced herself? But no, no, she was not that weak, not that susceptible. These last few months had given her a new poise, a new maturity; she would never allow herself to be tricked, to be shamed. She had only to think of the numerous women Hawkwood must have tumbled—he had implied as much—to put him in a bad light, making him easier to resist.

In any case, it would be weeks before he arrived, and in the meanwhile she had much to do. Working long into the night by candlelight, Joanna kept at her stitching, sleeping and eating in her room, having food sent up, meals brought by a dirty, cheerful lad invariably half spilled and cold. As she plied her needle, Joanna thought obliquely of Thomas, wondering if the fuss and bustle all in his honor had turned his head. A second son was rarely given such an extravagant knighting, and she suspected it had more to do with Harold's penchant for lordly show, an excuse to play the rich bountiful host, than any desire to please Thomas. Nevertheless, Joanna had the feeling that Thomas's vanity would rise to the occasion. Milking every drop of glory from the ceremony, he would make sure he was not pushed aside by anyone, especially his father. She could imagine him busy, officious, greeting the guests, offering them wine, seeing to their comfort.

So she was somewhat surprised to find him at her door one late afternoon.

"I made inquiries," he said, with a flashing smile. "And wonder of wonders found you were under our very roof. May I enter?"

"Of course. I did not think you would wish to leave your guests."

"Why not? They are all very dull." He sat down on a stool. "And I wanted to see you."

"Your mother..."

"She has already warned me. 'No scandal.'" He mimicked Alys, giving a good imitation of her. "'Remember she is the steward's daughter.'"

Joanna smiled but said nothing. Seating herself at the table where she had been sewing small seed pearls at the neckline of a gown, she resumed her work.

After a short silence Thomas asked, "Do you think I am capable of seducing you?"

The question, half expected in some form, did not alarm her. "Capable, Master Thomas, but I am afraid you cannot count on my willingness." How odd, she thought, this man does not tempt me in the least, not at all. His visit does not even flatter me.

"That is most unkind," Thomas said, reaching across to take her hand. She slipped it away, a slight easy movement as she took up a ball of thread.

"I have thought of you often," he went on.

"Have you?"

"All these months since the night I rescued you from that lout, remember?"

She looked up from her sewing. "Aye—'tis a wonder to me that you have not forgotten. Surely there must have been a maid or two who caught your fancy in the meanwhile."

"Trollops." He had indeed slept with a few women, but

only whores or lowborn serving wenches, for he had been taught at Medway that a man of good blood does not corrupt a noblewoman. But this one, this dazzling beauty, Joanna, fell somewhere in between, and he did not quite know how to deal with her.

"But I have never been in love until this moment." It suddenly occurred to him that it might be true. For why else would he be taking the time to woo her? Again he tried to reach for her hand and again she moved it away.

"You are not very friendly," he accused.

"I believe my manners are correct," she said. "You are my lady's son, and I have shown you deference as is seemly."

"I do not want your 'deference,'" he said, abruptly lunging forward and this time catching hold of her wrist. "I want your friendship, sweet Joanna. I want at least a kiss."

"That would not do," she answered coolly. "If I were a kinswoman, aye, but I am not related to you."

He smiled. "You would deny me then?" Was she a virgin? he wondered. But no, how could she be with those breasts? His eyes lingered on them, noting how they pressed against her bodice, the nipples delectably outlined, nipples surely teased by a man's fingers. And that slender waist. He lowered his eyes, visualizing her naked; the belly, hips, thighs and the place between. Someone had been there before him, but no matter. It would be easier for him to enter her. And thinking of it sent the blood rushing to his face. His fingers tightened on her wrist.

"Let me go, sir. You are hurting me."

For one wild moment he thought to throw her upon the floor, fall upon her and have his will. But she might fight and scream, an embarrassment if someone came or if his mother should hear of it. Besides—he clenched a fist, trying to control his burgeoning passion—it would be that much more pleasurable if she gave herself to him willingly.

He dropped his hand, though it cost him a great effort. "I would not want to hurt you, my sweet Joanna."

She said nothing, but continued to sew, making neat and precise stitches, knotting each pearl in place.

"You might at least speak to me," he said after a long silence. "Did you not think of me, miss me too?"

"That is not a fair question, Master Thomas. We were hardly close friends before you went away." She was wondering how to get rid of him. She did not want anyone, servant or otherwise, to find Thomas in her room. They would think the worst. A woman, regardless of birth, was always looked upon as loose, a seductress, in such a situation.

"The question is fair enough. Why don't you look at me?"

She lifted limpid violet eyes and fixed him with a level gaze, wide eyes which promised nothing, yet in some obscure way challenged. A pulse began to beat in his throat again. She smelled of lavender. Did she wear a sachet, a little bag of the fragrant dried blossoms between her breasts, as some women did? White breasts, each to fit a hand. He dove at her, catching her around the waist, and brought his mouth down on hers, prying her lips open, drinking of the sweet softness within.

She struggled free, and when he tried to take her in his arms again, she grasped the shears and pressed the sharp tip to his breast.

Astonished, he looked down at them, then at her. "You would not..."

"I would."

"They would hang you."

"Aye. But you would not be here to see."

The scissors glinted under his chin. Suddenly he threw his head back and laughed. "You have spirit, Joanna. Are you paying me back?"

"Paying you—for what?"

"I recall hitting you with a whip. I had given you a ride."

"I shan't ever forget it."

"Then I am forgiven?"

"If you promise to behave."

"I shall try. But I do want you. I do love you. And how can you be unkind to a man so in love?"

"I mean no unkindness. I am honored by your declaration, believe me. But—you see—I am betrothed." The convenient lie again. But a tumble with the young fool de Ander might cost her dear, the loss of her position, not to speak of a possible by-blow pregnancy.

"You are so young to marry," he protested.

"I am sixteen."

"Ahh..."

She put the shears back on the table and took up her sewing.

"I must say this," Thomas went on. "You have certainly learned how to turn a phrase. And you have lost your country accent too. You do not sound like a villager."

The oblique reference to her peasant origin was not lost on Joanna. It only strengthened her desire to be free of him.

"Thank you. And now, if I have your permission to go on with my work?"

That night a wide-eyed Joanna lay on her bed gazing up into the dark, thinking of Thomas de Ander. Was he truly smitten, really in love, or was he wanting her out of pure animal lust? He had sworn that he loved her, begged her to be his. Harold's son. And yet she had felt nothing. True, he was handsome, clean of breath, courteous too, for he might have forced her. Nobles often thought it their right to take peasant women at their will, but he had not. He wanted her, but only if she consented. Why then did he leave her cold? She had not felt the faintest rise in her pulses when he kissed her, no change of heartbeat, not the least flutter, nothing like the frightening, shivery thrill when Hawkwood had done the same. She had not even been afraid of Thomas. Why?

Restless, she rose from the feather bed and went to the window, opened the shutter and looked out. The castle yard lay silently sleeping, bathed in white moonlight, the shadowed corners beckoning mysteriously. The same courtyard she had looked upon a good part of her life; why did it seem so different tonight? She could not answer. None of the questions she had asked herself had an answer. As she stood there, her eyes suddenly stung with tears.

The guests began to arrive two weeks before Thomas's knighting. They came by horse, carriage, cart and mule, a stream of nobles; Harold de Ander's comrades at arms, men he had fought with in France, the barons and knights he had met in London, his vassals, neighbors, kinsmen; the de Ander daughters with their husbands and children, the eldest son, Robert, with his wife (childless but still hoping), each bringing their own household servants. John de Vere, the Earl of Oxford, announced by a fanfare of trumpets, rode through Nareham's gates followed by a retinue that stretched clear across the bridged moat and outer field. This crowd of well-wishers and their menials had to be put up somehow, but Alys, efficient, skilled as a chatelaine, managed adroitly, without fuss and with a fine eye to rank and importance. Quietly she assigned chambers, and bedding-down places, the more prominent to be housed at the manor, the less distinguished at the castle keep, the common folk to sleep in the tower, barricades and barns. Joanna, pressed into sharing her room with two of the Countess of Oxford's maids, gave up her feather bed and slept on the floor.

The hall at mealtimes, however, especially in the late afternoons, got beyond Alys's control. Here the trestle tables crammed from wall to wall held the visiting servants as well as the castle's men-at-arms, sergeants, scriveners, clerks and friars, seated by rank also (for a falconer or huntsman would consider it an insult to be placed next to a potboy or house carl), and squabbles often broke out when some forward or drunken retainer forgot his rightful place. The nobility crowded upon the dais, busy with toasts, chatter and laughter, paid little heed to those below, while the clumsy servitors recruited for this occasion from the village dashed from kitchen to hall sweating and swearing (and sworn at) with huge platters of roasts and savories.

On the eve of Thomas's dubbing his knightly dress was displayed on the banquet table; the spotless white shirt, the costly robe of ermine and the spurs of gold. If the hall had been noisy beforehand, it now rang with a din that threatened to blast the ears. All who had been invited (and some who had not) were there. Joanna, sitting next to her father and Katrine, took it all in, enjoying the stir and excitement and the entertainers especially hired for the week-long celebration. She sang along with the gleemen, humming when she did not know the words, and laughed at the mirth-mongers and tumblers. Her eyes roaming the hall, keenly aware, noted everything, missed nothing. She watched with interest how Lady Oxford, reputed to be an arbiter of fashion at King Edward's court and a confidante of Queen Philippa's, was dressed. On this evening the lady had her forehead banded with a gilded fillet to which were attached two circular cases of gold fretwork ornamented with precious stones, cauls into which her hair (a modish dyed yellow) had been tucked. A gorget covered her throat, a cloth climbing from neckline to chin and attached to the coiffed hair with beaded pins. It was her dress, however, which intrigued the seamstress in Joanna, the cloth-of-gold surcoat covered with an intricate, delicate pattern of blue and green embroidered beasts, birds and foliage, a piece of stitchery that must have cost someone strained eyes and numb fingers.

As she continued to gaze at the dais she saw a knight of medium height with broad shoulders step up and thread his way past the waiting squires and pages. When he stopped behind John de Vere, leaning over to speak into the earl's ear, Joanna had a full view of him, and her heart turned over. The hooked nose, the assertive jaw. John Hawkwood! Oh, God! God! So he came, he is here!

Joanna waited a few moments until her heart had ceased to hammer so loudly, then turned to Ivo. "Papa, the knight yonder." She indicated him with a nod of her head. "Did we not once meet him as a sergeant-at-arms?"

Ivo, who took it upon himself to know everyone of rank that came to the castle, drew his brows together. "Aye. 'Tis Sir John Hawkwood, lately knighted, I believe. Where or when I know not, but so many are knighted on the field now. The earl has a few such in his retinue. Why do you ask?"

"No reason, Papa."

Ivo turned to speak to the priest on his left, and Joanna looked up at the dais once more. How had she missed noticing Hawkwood before this? Mayhap he had just arrived or taken his meals elsewhere. But there he was, his face more weatherbeaten than she remembered, and now scarred with a red slash across his right cheek. A private duel? Or had a Frenchman's sword caught him a glancing blow at Poitiers? He was dressed in a smooth-fitting white cotehardie devoid of embroidery, its very plainness bringing out the deep bronze of his skin. She was still gazing intently at him when he lifted his head and their eyes met, and his, flashing with recognition, smiled into hers. Then, as he had done before, he gave her an eloquent, arrogant look, a look that undressed, admired and desired all in one sweeping glance.

"Your face is on fire," she heard Katrine say spitefully. "Too much wine."

Joanna did not reply. Her father nudged her. "You've barely touched your food."

"I'm eating, Papa."

She took a bite of capon, chewed, swallowed, then glanced up at the dais from under her lashes. He was standing in profile a little back from the seated diners, talking in earnest to one of John de Vere's squires. Not handsome, she thought, not in the least; in fact, he resembled a beaked bird of prey. She remembered how awed she had been when he rescued her from Thomas's whip, when she had run to him in the lane, how godlike he had seemed. But that had happened an age ago, in the hoary past of her childhood. She was grown now, and it was idiotic to go all hot over a look from a man who thought of her only as a maid he could seduce.

But her appetite had vanished. The noise, the smoke from

the hearth fires and sconced torches, the smell of roasted meat and sweating bodies suddenly seemed to press down on her, forming a tight hot band across her forehead. The performers no longer amused her. She had seen the Morris dancers and their Maypole antics, had seen the mummers in a parody of a comically botched hunt. The music clanged loudly, twisting the invisible band around her head a notch tighter. Everything that had excited her earlier now seemed drab and irritating. She got to her feet.

"Joanna?" Ivo turned an inquiring face to her.

"I'm all right, Papa. A little tired. I shall see you tomorrow."

Katrine leaned up. "But the savories are yet to come."

"Then I shall have to miss them," Joanna said, and began to push through the crowd. Stumbling over a dairy maid lying under a bench the worse for what Katrine called "rich wine," dodging a pair of rough, dirty hands that would pull her down and a leering sergeant-at-arms that would block her way, she finally reached the hall's threshold, where a shabbily gowned friar beseeched her to show him the way to the privy. Instead of going down the stone passage to the small staircase which led to her room, Joanna opened the large outer doors and stepped onto the porch and there drew a long, grateful breath. Vesper bells were ringing, a tinny clang-clang-clang, filling the stillness with brassy sound. It had been a long day. The feast inside, begun shortly after noon, would go on for hours yet, far into the night mayhap, though Thomas would leave early for the chapel to commence his ten-hour vigil in preparation for his knighting on the morrow.

A loud burst of laughter from the hall moved her to descend the two steps to the courtyard, and turning to the left she walked beyond the manor house, pausing at the entrance of Alys's private little garden.

No one was in sight, so she unlatched the wooden gate and entered. The deserted pleasaunce lay slumbering in the soft evening light. The tranquil air smelled of day lilies and jonquils blossoming palely yellow and white in beds beyond the graveled path. She stooped to pluck a lily, pressing the cool moist little bells to her nose, inhaling the sweet scent. Filled with the by now familiar yet still obscure yearning, she went on, walking slowly past a pear tree in late bloom, a small tree haloed with a froth of white, the petals scattered like snow at its feet. Every blossom in the dew-drenched garden seemed to be opening its heart to receive the languorous dusk.

Hot, unaccountable tears filled her eyes, and she crushed the lily bells between her fingers, the ruined flower falling from her hands.

Suddenly she heard the sound of a light, firm tread. Footsteps crunching the gravel behind her. She stood still without turning, her heart thumping wildly in her breast.

"Joanna!"

Her name. Had he followed her? Was she surprised? Glad? No, no, she had promised herself *not* to be glad; she had sworn to be calm, strong.

"Joanna!"

She took a deep breath, and though her knees felt like straw, she gave him a curtsy. "Good—good even, Sir John." She curtsied again.

"There's no need for that," he said.

"But you are a knight now."

"Dubbed by the Black Prince himself, but still a tanner's son, a yeoman. So from a pretty maid as yourself, a smile will do."

A yeoman, not a noble. Her lips trembled at the corners.

"We were to meet in the garden, if I recall, when I was last here at Nareham. But you did not come, Joanna."

So he remembered. And she could see by the look that was undressing her once more that he meant to take up where he had left off.

"I told you I would not come," she said, forcing her voice to steadiness. "I have nothing to apologize for. And now, if you will let me pass, Sir John?"

To her surprise he stepped aside and with a gallant flourish indicated that her way was free.

She swept past him, her fists clenched to her sides, for he was grinning, a grin that in no way detracted from the aura of masculinity which seemed to reach out as if to hold her. She ignored it, ignored him, ignored her own leaping pulses. She had nearly reached the gate when he suddenly called again.

"Joanna—wait!"

She hesitated, her back rigid.

He was behind her, and before she could move again she felt his hand resting on her shoulder. "Joanna..."

"I cannot..."

He repeated her name, his voice low, his fingers tightening, digging into her flesh.

"I..."

He turned her about, and seeing his face, the hint of the

88

old impish smile in his eyes, her defenses crumbled. She went into his arms, silently, trembling as if she had prepared for it, as if she had always known this would happen, giving her mouth to him with a low, sobbing moan. His kiss, soft at first, grew hard, passionate, demanding, hungry. The shawl fell from her shoulders. She felt the bones in her body melting, her muscles, every fiber dissolving, flowing along a dark river, flowing away from the safe, lighted shore. His mouth moved to her cheek, to her brow, her ear, her throat, resting there for a moment, then to her breast, his hands moving up and down her back, pressing her buttocks closer to his lean, strong thighs. She felt the bulge of his rising passion, and a responding stab fired her loins.

With one hand he began to unlace the ribbon at her collar, still silent, his face now lost in shadow. She herself had not the strength to utter a word, not even his name. She wanted to remain pressed to his body, feel his kisses, she wanted the tumult and sweet forgetting, the flowing river, to go on and on. He bared her shoulders, sinking his teeth gently into the smooth satiny flesh; pushed her bodice down, found her breast, covering it with quick little kisses, his mouth resting on a taut nipple. He licked it and little shivers ran down her back. When he took it between his teeth, she gasped, "Nay...!" to stem a drowning, a breathless immersion in dark, dark waters.

He was lifting her as if she were weightless, and again she heard herself utter a protest in a weak, choked voice. What was he doing? Where was he taking her, why did she not stop him? She could cry out, call for help. Crushed against his chest, feeling herself moving through the night, these thoughts flared, flickered and went out.

He lowered her on the damp grass. "Joanna." Her eyes were luminous in the faint light.

He hesitated, looking down into those wide violet eyes. She was young, untried and innocent. Innocent. Should he? There were other wenches to be had, girls who had lain with men, young too, ripe, not wholly spoiled yet, lasses who knew what it was all about. Why this one? Her hand fluttered up, brushing his bared chest. Damn my soul, he thought savagely, am I getting soft? And he fell on her, kissing her passionately, tasting of her breast again, pushing her gown up, freeing her legs.

"You are hurting me," she whispered.

"Lie still." He forced himself to go more slowly, though the blood throbbed in his head, using his hands to fondle and caress her, wondering why, in the back of his mind, he took so much trouble with her, more trouble than he had ever taken with another woman. He stroked the inside of her thighs, his fingers finding the place between. She began to writhe and moan under him, and he, no longer able to contain himself, entered her with more force than he intended. She gave a sharp cry, raised her fist and struck him, called him a varlet, a dastard, but he could not stop now, not if the earth yawned beneath them and swallowed them whole.

Spent, he sprawled over her, his hand tangled in her hair. She was very quiet, no tears, no sobs, no curses. He lifted himself on his elbows and looked down into her face. She gave him a soft, knowing smile, the pink mouth so honey-sweet and sensuous parting over her white teeth. Desire stirred in him anew. He bent and kissed her forehead.

"My sweet," he murmured. "'Twill be better for you in the future."

"John, dear heart, are we to be together, then? Are we to be betrothed?"

Betrothed. The word acted like a bucket of cold water dashed in his face. Desire fled. He rolled away. "God's belly, nay!"

"But I thought—and you told me you are not nobly born—"

"You thought wrong. I am not a marrying man. I am a soldier."

In the darkness Joanna's lips curved into a smile. He did not mean it; no man who had behaved so passionately toward a woman could possibly not love and want her. He had said, "in the future," and that to her meant marriage. She would not give herself to him again unless he spoke to her father and slipped a betrothal ring upon her finger.

Chapter VI

John Hawkwood had been born in Sible Hedingham, a small village in Essex. Clever, inordinately vain, he possessed the arrogant, driving ambition characteristic of many second sons, lads who saw the bulk of their father's legacy going to the eldest male of the line. In his case John had lost out to his older brother, also named John, their father, Gilbert Hawkwood, a prosperous tanner and yeoman, having left his principal heir the farmland, livestock, tannery and a half-timbered house, a prize in itself boasting adze-hewn beams and set-in windows. But John the younger had not been entirely forgotten. To him had been bequeathed ten pounds and a hundred solidi, five quarters each of wheat and oats, and bed and maintenance for one year under his father's, now his brother's, roof. That Nicholas, the third son, destined for the church, received even less, that his four sisters were hardly mentioned in Gilbert's will, did not diminish John's resentment against the fates which had made him second instead of first.

However, John was not one to go on and on wasting his time in fruitless umbrage. Assessing his situation (one which in all honesty was to be expected), he saw where perhaps his inheritance might have worked to his advantage. To be Gilbert's successor meant carrying on with the tannery, an odorous trade, and working the farm with backbreaking labor. And while both vocations would earn him a decent living, there was no real money or advancement in either. The wealth and glory lay in soldiering. He knew that because his uncle, Bernard, had repeatedly told him so.

Uncle Bernard, a crossbowman in the service of the Earl of Oxford, had accumulated through years of intermittent foreign wars a tidy trove to see him into his old age, which he had barely started to enjoy before misfortune overcame him. Returning home one foggy night from the Hedingham pothouse he had lost his footing on the narrow bridge crossing the Colne, a river customarily shallow nine months of the year but then, as luck would have it, in full flood, and tumbling in, he had drowned. Dead but not forgotten, Bernard's words came back to John now:

"My boy, war is the only decent occupation for a *real* man, the only way to better yourself. And why? Booty! That's the reward, not the two pence a day they give you, but booty! Horses, saddles, swords, and if you are lucky, gold. Aye—for the taking, lad. Even after the nobles have grabbed their share there's plenty left over. More—if you're brave, if you fight well and catch the eye of a lord, you can be dubbed knight right there on the field. S'truth, I've seen men rise from serfdom to knight at the tap of a grateful duke's sword."

Even given that Bernard had what John's father called "a blown bladder for a head" there must have been some truth in Bernard's tales of plunder. For how else could he have come by a fine Spanish gelding, leather-saddled and harnessed with crimson balls and little silver bells, a fur-lined cape, a topaz signet ring and the wherewithal to buy a small cob house? If Bernard, hardly known for his quick-wittedness, had done well, he, John, could do better.

Not one, even then, to jump into a venture haphazardly, he planned with forethought. He sought his uncle's old friend Tillbury, a one-legged veteran of the Scottish wars, and asked how best to enter the business of soldiering. "Not as a pikeman," John cautioned. He had no intention of starting at the bottom if he could possibly help it.

"Archery, lad," Tillbury advised. "Get yourself a bow."

But which? There were two in current use, the longbow and the crossbow. Which?

Tillbury could not say. But young John decided it would be to his advantage to become skilled at both. One never knew what opportunities might arise.

Practice was made easy, since King Edward, needing expert archers for his armies in the English and French wars, encouraged archery as a sport, and in fact for a time put a ban on any other. Hedingham had its own butts, and there John went each day, at first under the tutelage of Tillbury, later on his own. John was a quick learner, and the muscles he had developed in arms, shoulders and back on the farm with plow and scythe stood him in good stead. Of the right height and build, not too short so that the six-foot bow towered over him, nor so tall that he lacked balance, and with a natural eye for distance, he soon mastered both weapons. By the end of three months he could hit a bull's-eye at a hundred yards, at the end of six could do the same at two hundred yards.

When John heard that the Earl of Oxford, liege lord of the

Hawkwoods, had been called upon by King Edward to provide a fighting force to assist in the repulsion of a projected French invasion of England's south coast, he thought it an auspicious time to offer his services. This rumored coastal attack was just one more ploy, one more counterplot, in the long and bitter struggle between England and France. It was a dispute that dated back in part to friction over the Duchy of Aquitaine, a huge chunk of France acquired by the English crown when Henry II married the beautiful but infamous Eleanor of Aquitaine, two hundred years earlier. The French monarch, King John, now claimed the English king to be his vassal, a position Edward III, Henry's descendant, took exception to. More, King John was not only making trouble between the English wool merchants and the weavers of Flanders (a French fiefdom) but also supported an anti-English claimant to the Scottish throne.

On the day John Hawkwood left the tannery and set out to enlist with the earl, the fight had already been in progress for two years, a war that was to span a century and go down in history as the Hundred Years War.

John Hawkwood, of course, had no way of knowing this, nor would it have impressed him if he had. Wars were a part of life; he could not imagine the world long without one. So he whistled as he walked on this beautiful May morning, the kind of blue-skied, sun-bright morning that always seems happily prophetic to those about to launch on a new venture. Wearing new hose and a woolsey cape, bow in hand, his quivered arrows slung across one shoulder, he stood at the gate tower of Hedingham Castle and boldly called upon the warden, "Ho, there! Ho!" in a commanding tone which, like his archery, he had practiced beforehand. Queried, he stated his business. "I wish to see the captain on matters of urgency."

It was easy, easier than he had thought. The captain, impressed with his air of self-assurance, his display of marksmanship, took him on. "Two pence a day and your keep."

Housed in the barracks with some twenty-five other archers, John had enough sense to bridle his tongue and assume a more modest demeanor. He did not want to antagonize, to cause trouble, to rub his comrades the wrong way—especially the old veterans. He wanted merely to get ahead and knew he could best do this by looking and listening and continuing to practice with bow and arrow.

Not long after entering service for the earl, John became involved with a young girl, Roscilla, an interval in his life he never spoke of until years afterward. Roscilla was one of Lady Oxford's tiring women, the bastard offspring of a noble cousin and a serving girl. Twenty, pretty, high-bosomed, with flaxen hair and blue eyes, she could be seen in the courtyard every now and again playing with one of those silly, fluffy lap dogs. One day toward dusk as John was crossing from the well to the stables she ran up to him in tears, saying she had lost her little Flora in the garden and would he help her find her?

The garden, situated beyond the far courtyard, laid out with trees and flower beds, graveled walks, little copses and quaint wooden bridges over fish ponds, was a new sight to John. There had been no reason for him to visit it before, a place reserved exclusively for ladies, one that had never piqued his curiosity. Now, looking upon it, his yeoman's eye was rather shocked by so much good soil given over to what he considered frippery. But he did have to admit that the smells were lovely, if not a trifle heady, for it was mid-June and Lady Oxford's roses, languishing in full, blowsy bloom, perfumed the summer air.

"Here, Flora!" Roscilla called. "She must be in there," she said to John, pointing to a flowering hydrangea. "I see the bushes move."

Parting the heavy blossom-laden branches, their shoulders touched, and John, feeling the soft silky skin of Roscilla's arm, the warm closeness of her body, experienced a shock, a surge of longing, of desire, which shot up from his loins like a leaping stab of fire. He grasped her hand and they went in under the trees. Once in the shadowy recess of the thicket, he pulled Roscilla into his arms and kissed her. Far from resisting in outrage as he expected, she flung her arms about his neck, returning kiss for kiss like a starveling presented with a heaped platter of sweets.

He took her there on the mossy sod with the night mists closing in about them, took her wordlessly, in silence, not once but twice, she wrapping white limbs around his back, clinging to him as he drove into her with his feverish need. Afterward he could not say whether she had been a virgin or not; his experience with women had been too limited. Besides, as he later told himself, the entire episode had happened so fast such minor considerations as an intact maidenhead seemed irrelevant. The dog too. What happened to it he never knew.

Nor did he see Roscilla again until two months later when

94

he was summoned to the earl's private parlor. Following behind the house carl, torn between fear—what have I done?—and expectation—mayhap he has seen me at the butts and is going to reward my skill with a purse—he entered the large room hung with silken tapestries and carpeted with colorful wool rugs. To his surprise the earl sat on the dais flanked by two women, the countess and Roscilla.

De Vere did not mince words. Roscilla was pregnant by John. No query, "Is this true?" No opportunity for him to say yea, nay, or mayhap.

"Under ordinary circumstances," the earl said, frowning, "I would run you through with my own sword or have you strung up like a varlet. But these are not ordinary circumstances. I understand you are a good archer—and we need you. So I am giving you the honor of becoming Roscilla's husband."

Giving, not asking.

"You will have quarters in the west tower, something less than this slut—" He caught himself. "—than Roscilla is accustomed to, but then she has no choice—do you, my dear? And let's not make a big thing of the wedding, eh, lady?"

Lady Oxford said, "I think this marriage is a shame and a disgrace. Roscilla has noble blood. If you were not in such a hurry I could provide her with a squire, at the least, someone of good family."

"And fob off another man's child?" the earl asked.

"It is done all the time."

Was it? John wondered.

The earl had turned red at the jowls. "Would you have me wait until her belly shows? She will have to take the best I can find. John here comes of decent stock. He will make a satisfactory husband. She can expect no more."

They were married quietly in the castle's private chapel. But if John thought it could be kept a secret, he was wrong. The men in the barracks had somehow got wind of the forced wedding and teased him unmercifully. "Caught you, did she?" "The wench snared you proper, eh?" "Couldn't keep your drawers up, lad—ha, ha!"

For all her noble blood, Roscilla proved a poor wife. Slovenly, lazy, she spent most of her days playing with a replacement for Flora (curse the yapping beastie!) or combing her long yellow hair. She neither swept, spun nor cooked, nor did she know how to instruct the little serf girl, Lady Oxford's wedding present, in these matters. Even her sexual appeal

95

had dissipated, and John soon found the sight of her thickening waist and rounding belly repellent. One morning, coming to their quarters unexpectedly, he interrupted his wife and Sir Rupert, the earl's server and carver, an old man with a drooping lip and thin, stringy hair, humping noisily on the bed. Furious, John had no choice but to keep his anger in check. A yeoman does not challenge a knight, no matter how provoked, but what ran through his head as Rupert, hastily and with much fumbling, got into his clothes, was Lady Oxford's, "It is done all the time."

Now he doubted the baby was his; he told Roscilla so. She swore Rupert was merely trying to console her for being so lonely; she had given up so much to marry John, all her old friends, and this was the first time they had bedded. He did not believe a word of it.

She gave birth in the autumn to twins, two boys, and they were Hawkwoods. No mistake. He could see it even in the red wrinkled faces, in the shape of the heads, in the birthmarks that would one day be covered by tawny hair at the base of the skulls. He was rather stunned. He knew he ought to feel proud—that was standard for fathers of boys—but he disliked Roscilla and their miserable marriage so he found it hard to summon the necessary pride.

Roscilla herself did not seem to care. She was too grateful to have the entire horror of labor over and done with. She gave her babies suck with a look of annoyance on her face, and when she proved dry handed them to the midwife with a sigh of relief. "Find a wet nurse. Anyone, it doesn't matter."

Lady Oxford came the following morning to visit with Roscilla privately, so the midwife said, and while Roscilla seemed to be recovering splendidly, she took a bad turn in the afternoon and died that evening just after Vespers. The midwife hinted at dark doings, saying, wasn't it lucky the boys were with Bess Wheelspinner at the time? John was not without his own suspicions—poison was always handy in a large castle, and Roscilla had disgraced the de Veres—but he kept his thoughts to himself.

After a hushed-up and hasty funeral, John scraped together a little money to pay Bess to keep the boys, but in truth he wanted to forget them and the marriage, so he put it from his mind as if it had never happened. And when he moved back to the barracks and took up his old routine, it seemed that it never had.

* * *

By the time John Hawkwood fought at Crécy in 1346 he was a seasoned soldier, and because he displayed great courage and boldness (where it did the most good) the earl promoted him to sergeant-at-arms. It was a promotion that pleased but did not overwhelm him. He had loftier ambitions. He observed that the choicest booty went to those high on the heap, and he meant to get there, though he realized now that his Uncle Bernard had greatly exaggerated the opportunities for doing so. Never mind Uncle Bernard. He had great faith in his own abilities, his own excellence, and if the goal was elusive, so much more appealing the challenge to reach it. The political aspects of warfare, the kingly moves and ducal parlays, held little interest for him. His energies, his will, his enthusiasm focused on fighting—and winning. A loser never earned praise, prizes or advancement.

He liked soldiering. Never having suffered the slightest repugnance at killing, the way some of his fellow novice archers had, he took to warfare like a duck to water. He did not mind sleeping on the hard ground and eating salted meat and worm-infested bread, did not mind the forced marches, the rain, the blistering heat or the freezing cold. He minded only idleness, the times between battles when he and his company were at loose ends and half pay.

He had weathered the Black Death with a grim determination mixed with prayer and quantities of ale while scores fell around him. Tough, imbued with a healthy body, he managed to be one of the few in his company who survived to fight at Poitiers. There, with the Earl of Oxford under the supreme command of the Black Prince, John, after expending his last arrow, distinguished himself by picking up mace and ax from a decapitated footman and hacking his way through the disintegrating French lines. The prince himself had dubbed him on the field, "Sir John Hawkwood."

John, a knight now, with the coveted gold spurs but without land and still in the pay of his lord, felt he had come to another crossroads in his life. Except for the title his situation seemed little better than it had been before. As he saw it, he could go one of two ways: either continue with the Earl of Oxford at peacetime half pay (the capture of King John and the Treaty of Brétigny ensured the cessation of Franco-English hostilities for a time at least) or quit his service and join the Tard Venus.

These Tards were troops of disbanded soldiers, English, Flemings, Gascons, Bretons and Germans, men who chose not to return to their native lands but to stay on and ravage the French countryside. In their ranks could be found landless knights like John, disgruntled squires, avaricious clerics, lords who became too fond of a life by the sword, and French barons themselves who had lost holdings to the English. Nobles, yeomen and peasants joined with the lawless riffraff of city and farm under a leader, a loose-jointed though cohesive whole, to plunder what was left in the wake of war, to hire themselves out as mercenaries, or to blackmail isolated chatelains for "protection."

Influenced in part by King Edward's attitude, which was that whatever weakened the French strengthened the English, Hawkwood had elected to throw in his lot with this movement, the "latecomers," the *routiers*, seeing in them his opportunity to obtain the riches and power he could never hope to acquire under the earl. He had come back to England and to Nareham to collect his back pay and to sever his connection with the Earl of Oxford, John de Vere, as amicably as possible, assuring his seigneur he would never take arms against England. The two parted friends (the earl had long since forgotten the Roscilla incident), de Vere wishing him God's blessing.

John, his business completed, would have gone on but for Joanna. She intrigued him. Never before had he considered a woman important enough to effect his slightest change of plan. His forced marriage had made him wary of entanglements. He had consorted mostly with whores and willing peasant women, taking from them what he needed, a tumble, a hasty coupling in a hayfield, behind a barn, against a stone wall, an easement of flaring lust, forgetting these faceless creatures the moment after his last orgiastic gasp. If asked he could not rightly say why Joanna should stay him. He knew nothing of love, in fact scorned it as a pastime indulged in by pasty-faced fopdoodles. Perhaps it was the way other men looked at her, Sir Thomas for instance. What others wanted always posed a dare for him. Or it could have been Joanna's beauty itself, her youth, those alarmingly blue-violet eyes, the voluptuous mouth, the sensuality which he seemed to rouse in her. To make her limp, to hear her sigh, acted as an aphrodisiac, a new experience he found exciting.

As for Joanna—she was in love. No question of why or wherefore; she gave herself over completely to John Hawkwood. The heavy heart, the inexplicable sorrow, the longing had vanished. She exhibited all the lovelorn signs, dreaming over her needle, humming, smiling secretly to herself, misty-eyed, pink-cheeked, softened. She met him every night now. Because they feared discovery in Alys's garden, John had found a secluded nook high in one of the wall towers, a stone-floored room with two slitted windows. He had dragged a straw pallet there, and on it they lay through the darkened hours, entwined, making love, sometimes savage, sometimes tender, kissing, fondling, embracing, exploring one another's bodies anew. It had not taken long for Joanna to discover ecstasy, to learn how to give and receive pleasure. The girl who had once thought herself cold and unfeeling had become alive, a warm, passionate creature. She had only to see John's strong brown hand grasp the door handle and shut the world out and her blood was roused. Her own nakedness gave her joy. She loved the feel of her satiny skin next to John's mus-cled chest, loved to feel his hard knee separating her bare thighs, the way her nipples rose between his lips. And always, always in the back of her mind she told herself it was not a sin to love thus, that John, whatever foolish denial he made, would wed her in the end.

He tarried a month, much longer than he intended. He was loath to leave, though he knew he must go. But Joanna had captivated him, opened up strange vistas, vistas he ex-amined with wonder, tentatively, gingerly.

One night she was late for their rendezvous, and he, like any headlong, impatient lover, went rushing up to her room, something he had not done before, bolting the stairs two at a time, his mind rehearsing the words with which he would scold her. He paused at the door, his hand raised to open it, when he heard a man's voice.

"Let me kiss you, sweet, just once, before I leave."

"'Tis late, Sir Thomas...pray..." Joanna replied.

Hawkwood did not wait to hear more but shrank back in the shadows, his mind in turmoil. Sir Thomas, the fledgling knight—in there with *her!* Thomas, the vain cockerel, a raw lad hardly out of swaddling clothes, the lord's son. Had they bedded, made love? Of course, you fool, you fool! "It is done all the time"—Lady Oxford's words came back to him. This girl, this chit who had sworn to love him eternally, copulating with Thomas, white breasts and limbs bared, gasping, sigh-ing, clinging—the picture rose sharp and vivid before him. Had she made the same little cries, the same little moans, whispered the same little endearments? What an ass, what a bumpkin to have allowed himself to be taken in by the wench!

He resisted the impulse to hurl himself through the door and tear them both limb from limb. Cool reason, which had served him in more than one crisis, overrode his rage. To confront Thomas, to strike him, would surely lead to a duel, a fight over a woman, when he had always felt only a jackanapes would waste himself in such futile combat. And what if he injured this de Ander, or worse, killed him? The attendant scandal would sully his name, and he wished to leave England with the honor he had won at Poitiers intact, not dragged in the dirt.

He moved farther into the shadows as he heard the door open and saw Thomas, dressed only in hose and shirt, depart. After his footsteps died on the staircase, Hawkwood thought to go in and confront Joanna, but again decided against it. There would be a scene, an unpleasant exchange of shrill demeaning words, and his pride would not allow him to fall into the role of a petty, wronged lover. Let her indulge in bed sport with as many as she liked, open her legs to whoever caught her fancy, he thought bitterly as he stood there. Women were all alike; not one to be trusted. He had given more of himself to this girl than he had to any. His heart, if truth be told. And it hurt, it hurt. He would not do it again.

Instead of going in to berate Joanna he decided to return to the tower room and wait for her there, pretending nothing had happened. They would have their night of love and in the morning he would leave.

When she came into his arms a half hour later, dewy-eyed, black hair falling across her white shoulders and bared breasts, he felt a stab of anger—had she come thus to Thomas? The whore! Female Judas! But then their mouths met and he gave himself up to her voluptuous passion and his own driving desire. He made love to her that night with a savagery that bewildered, frightened, yet excited her, and she clung to him, muttering, moaning, whispering his name over and over.

He was the first to wake in the predawn light to the crowing of cocks in the outer bailey. Looking down at her, the hair fanning across her sleeping face, the black, crescent eyelashes on flushed, smooth cheeks, he felt a sudden surge of regret, an emotion he rarely if ever experienced. He bent down and, brushing the hair aside, kissed her earlobe.

Her eyes fluttered open and she gave him a smile, the sort

of intimate smile only a woman deeply in love can give. But Hawkwood, gazing at her, found somehow Thomas's face suddenly coming between the smile and himself.

"Joanna," he said abruptly, drawing back. "I must quit Nareham. The longer I stay, the more I lose. I shan't get ahead in France by lingering here."

"Of course, you must go, sweet. You must improve your situation, now more than ever."

"Now?" he asked suspiciously, surprised because she was making no fuss.

She gave him a tender smile. "Can you not guess? Oh, sweeting, I am carrying your child."

She had suspected it a week earlier, not sure until she awakened one morning sick, her breasts swollen and painful. Jubilant because she had conceived her lover's child, certain Hawkwood would share her feelings, she had imagined all that would happen: John speaking to her father, Ivo's hearty handshake sealing pleased consent, the hasty banns, the wedding on the church porch, and lastly herself, Lady Joanna (Lady Joanna!), riding pillion behind her husband as they went through the gates of Nareham toward a new life in France.

But the prospective father was anything but delighted. His brows came together. "You are in pup? My God! Are you sure?"

It was a question that at the moment seemed more dismaying than redundant. "I am sure, sweet. I thought..." Her voice trembled a little because he went on looking at her in a chilling way, not taking her in his arms, kissing her, saying he hoped it would be a boy. "I thought the news would gladden you."

"Gladden me? God's bones! The last thing... I suppose you got it into your goose head I would marry you."

She could hardly believe her ears. How could he change so quickly? One moment the tender, passionate lover, the next, cold, cold as ice. "Aye. I thought..." she began tremulously.

"...that it is done all the time," he provided with a biting sarcasm.

"Nay," she whispered, the sudden lump in her throat strangling her voice.

"Have I led you to believe so?"

"Nay." He had not said he loved her—true—not in so many

words. But surely a man who bided because of a maid, a lover who took such pains to caress, to stroke, to bring the loved one to burning flame, would want to keep her as wife?

"You are a tasty bit, my sweet. But I am not a sentimental fool like some. I have told you that, have I not?"

When? Where? She could not remember, but it must be if he said so, and she nodded dumbly.

"Should I ever marry," he went on, twisting the knife, "I shall do so with a lady born, an heiress, some noblewoman, old and ugly, who will not only be faithful but will consider herself fortunate to have even a tanner's son as husband."

The knot swelled in her throat, threatening tears. She clenched her fists. "My father would give me a good dowry."

He threw his head back and laughed. "I don't want a 'good dowry,' goose. I want land, a fief, *money,* money to throw away if I choose. I want to be the *lord* of a manor."

"And a steward's daughter..." Oh, how it hurt to talk. "A steward's..."

"Now, sweet, don't take on so. We have had good sport, you and I, have we not?" He cupped her chin with his hand, but she pushed it away. "Besides, I am not too sure the child is mine."

She gazed at him with brimming eyes. "The child? But there's been no one else."

"So all women caught with a brat in their gut claim."

She sprang up and lashed out at him in a fury, striking his face with her fists. He caught her arms.

"How—how can you say, even *think* there was someone else?" she spluttered. "You know very well you were the first."

"Aye. I'll not deny that." He gazed down at her, a sardonic look on his face. "But I saw Sir Thomas leave your chamber last night."

"Ah, so *that* is it. Sir Thomas. Nothing happened, I swear. Nothing, *nothing.* Why do you look at me like that? I tell you nothing happened. He came to me, he wanted to bed me, I'll not deny that, but I sent him away. As I have done before. I would not have him, now or then, or ever."

"And you expect me to believe it?"

"You have only to ask."

"I shall do nothing of the sort. Make a fool of myself?"

"I swear, John, I swear by all that is holy, I swear on my dead mother's grave, I swear..."

"Save yourself from perdition. You do not love me, you never have."

"How cruel you are, how cruel! You are only using Thomas as an excuse because you have grown tired of me, because you do not want to acknowledge your child."

"My child? Spare me, Joanna. You expect me to swallow that lie when I hear a man asking for another kiss and then see him coming from your chamber half undressed?"

"It was *not* what you thought," she repeated, anger rising.

"Wasn't it?" he asked mockingly. "But why upset yourself? All is not lost, sweet. You are tough. Mayhap you can find a villager who will marry you. If you do it straight off he will never know the babe is not his."

"A pox on you! Turd! Pisspot!"

He grinned and then suddenly, swiftly, brought his mouth down on hers in a hard, bruising kiss. She kicked and pummeled, trying to get free, but he continued to hold and kiss her, and gradually the fight drained from her and the familiar warm tide of pleasant helplessness washed over her. He couldn't mean to leave her, not when he kissed her like this. He couldn't. She clung to him, trying to hold him, but he unwound her arms from his neck and pushed her away.

"Goodbye, sweet. I shan't be back," and stepping away, he opened the door and went through.

She heard his dying footsteps on the stone stairs and sank slowly down on the pallet. For a long space she did nothing but sit, listening to the heavy beat of her heart. A cold little chill crept through the slitted windows, teasing a fringe of hair on her forehead. She looked up at the mortared walls, at the thin ray of morning sun touching the stone brick, without seeing, blind. The courtyard below came gradually to life; voices, the cluck of hens, the scrape and whine of the well winch, a whistled tune, the bark of a dog. Presently through her frozen numbness Joanna heard the clatter of hooves. John? By straining her ears she could just make out the sound of the creaking gates as they opened. The hoofbeats receded, faded away.

Gone. He had not believed her sworn denial, had not *wanted* to believe she had turned Thomas away, had used the incident as an excuse to leave her behind. He was gone. He would not come back—he had said so. She would never see him again. He did not love her. He had bedded her as he would any loose woman, any weak-willed, foolish maid who had given herself to him. Their nights of rapture, his kisses, the "sweetings" and "doves" had meant nothing. He would make his way to France, taking his women where he found them, saying the same things, kissing and fondling them the way he had done with her, coupling with them, leaving them and moving on. He would marry a lady born, rich, her coffers filled with gold and jewels, a lady who would make him the lord of a manor. Not a steward's daughter who could bring him only a simple dowry; not a peasant.

Humiliation burned her cheeks. Tears stung her eyes and began to course down her face, hot, blinding, bitter tears. She put her head down on the cold stone floor and wept, sobbing wildly, her body racked, pouring out all the pain and chagrin, her unhappiness, her disappointment. Finally when she had finished, when there was not another sob or tear left, she dried her eyes on her discarded gown, then slowly got to her feet. She pulled the gown over her nakedness, adjusting the bodice. She stood for a few moments looking down at the straw pallet where she and John had lain. Her mouth twisted wryly. She had been duped like the country goose she was, seduced and abandoned by a man she trusted and thought she loved. What a fool, what an idiot! Loved? How could she ever have imagined it? She hated him, hated him with an anger growing by the moment, an anger that drowned out hurt and shame. She wanted revenge, she wanted to inflict pain, to make him suffer. She wanted to kill him. But she could do none of those things. "I shan't be back," he'd said. She hoped an arrow would pierce his heart. No, not an arrow—that would be too easy. Better if he were run through with an ugly barbed spear so that it would take him a long, lingering, agonizing time to die.

It was broad daylight when she emerged from the tower, and the sunny courtyard was bustling with humanity. She hesitated a moment, shrinking into the shadows, not wanting to be seen. She hated to be the butt of gossip. This past month she had made sure to leave the trysting place long before dawn, crossing the yard in the darkness and stealing into her room without once meeting anyone on the way. But now— well, it could not be helped. She stiffened her spine, and squaring her shoulders stepped out from the doorway. Simon, the swineherd, and Ethbert, a stableboy, gawked at her, but she ignored them, sweeping past, head held high. Tess, the washwoman, drawing water at the well, called to her, "Joanna! You are out early."

"I had an errand," Joanna replied shortly, not stopping to chat as she might have done in times past.

She had nearly reached the little side door which led

through to a passage to the staircase when she saw Sir Thomas coming toward her. Too late to avoid him. "Good morrow, Joanna." He smiled, showing all his white teeth, his eyes going over her, resting on her bodice.

"Good morrow." She did not bend her knee; she knew that she should, but she could not, seeing him suddenly as the cause of her grief. She did not let herself think that Hawkwood would have left her in any case, churl that he was, but only that Thomas's appearance in her room had turned her lover against her.

And now he was here, smiling at her as if nothing had happened, his superior air making mock of her misfortune, of her pride. She was freeborn, but to him, to Hawkwood, to others of their ilk, she was still a peasant, a breed to be held in contempt. Oh, she had heard them, the ladies in the solar, gossiping while she measured them for gowns, speaking one to another as though she, Joanna, were invisible or an inanimate object like the cushioned benches and embroidery frames.

To the nobility the villagers were dirty, sly, unwashed and foul-smelling. They made no distinction between freeborn and serf, deeming them all little better than beasts. How Joanna hated them, the painted lollipops, the aristocrats, the entire lordly class! She recalled her years of poverty, the mean hut, the unceasing toil, the hunger, all caused by a cheating nobleman whose word had been taken over her father's. She could understand her mother's clenched fist now, her passionate, bold outcries against privilege, against her overlords.

"How lovely you look this morning, Joanna." Moving closer, Thomas took her hand and began to gently knead her fingers.

She resisted the impulse to snatch them away. "Thank you, Sir Thomas. And though I am a bit tardy, I believe I have never congratulated you on your knighthood. May you have a long and illustrious course."

"Your good wishes are most kind, and our meeting so opportune. I was on my way to bid you goodbye. I have just learned of my appointment to King Edward's personal guard."

"Oh? An honor, I am sure."

"My godfather, the earl, managed it. He is privy to the king's ear, you know, a man of great importance, and I should have been overjoyed at the result of his efforts were it not for leaving you."

A pretty speech, Joanna thought, anticipating what would come next. She was not disappointed.

"Since I must go on the morrow I was hoping we could spend the evening together." He gave her a meaningful look.

She forced herself to smile. "I should like nothing better, but unfortunately your lady mother has requested I finish a cape."

"I could speak to her," he suggested.

"I do not think she would be pleased."

He seemed to mull that over for a few moments. "Mayhap another time *would* be best, when we can enjoy each other's company at leisure. I plan to return at Christmas. Mayhap then."

"Aye, Sir Thomas, mayhap," she murmured, and freeing her hand dropped one knee quickly, then turned and walked away.

Upstairs, alone in her room, Joanna's first thought was to rid herself of the child. Murder, a sin against God, the priest would say, but she did not care. She would rather suffer in some future hell than face the shame of the here and now. A purge was what she needed, a strong, noxious purge. Recalling her mother, she was sure now that Mariotta had used some brew of her own making to flush more than one unwanted baby from her belly, but her mother was dead and she must look elsewhere. She had heard that Edith, who had taken Freyda's place as midwife in the village, could be persuaded with a coin or two to dispense a powerful herbal concoction that would do the trick, but Edith was also a notorious gossip. Approach her and the whole village would know. Still, she might make her request in a roundabout way. A potion for a friend, mayhap? Would Edith see through the subterfuge? Probably.

Gradually she began to turn over a new idea. Suppose she had the baby. Suppose, just suppose. Further, suppose it was a boy. John Hawkwood's son. She closed her eyes and saw not a child but a man, a younger version of her lover, the same brown eyes and auburn hair, the same eagle profile and thickset torso. John Hawkwood's son, a son who had grown up to hate the father who refused him a name. Ah, yes, she would tell him, her child, her bastard son, tell him everything, she would teach him to hate—and *he* would be her instrument of revenge. Just how this would be accomplished was vague in her mind, but the notion appealed to her. Her son would exact retribution; a debt would be paid.

For a short while her fear of shame—she could never have the baby in secret—struggled with her desire for revenge, but only for a short while. In the end she decided to have it.

Once she had made up her mind, she never considered that her plan might go awry, that it was presumptuous, farfetched, unchristian (the least of her considerations, had she had them), or even that she might have a girl. The child would be male, it would be hale and hearty, it would look like its father, it would someday right the wrong John Hawkwood had done her. Only the first name was uncertain, a choice between John and Edward.

By the fifth month, fast approaching the stage where concealment would be impossible, she decided to tell her father, an ordeal she dreaded. Ivo's good opinion mattered, far more than anyone's, and, in fact, her fear of gossip and shame was mostly motivated by what he would think. She had given herself to a man out of wedlock, making a mock of the high moral principle Ivo had tried to instill in her. That half of the village girls came to marriage with the seed already planted made it all the worse. She, Joanna, was the steward's daughter, freeborn, a cut above those who conceived under a hedge. How could she demean herself, demean *him*, so? And too, there were those who, remembering Mariotta's capricious, wanton ways, would point and say—like mother, like daughter. And that would hurt him too.

Joanna climbed the keep's winding stair one evening, her knees trembling and fear in her heart. When she entered her father's chambers he was still at his meal, and the smile he gave her, the way he pushed out a stool, beckoning her to join him, made her wish she were dead.

"I have already eaten, Papa." She sat down. "But thank you just the same."

Katrine did not greet her. The youngest child (there were three now), sitting on his father's knee, gurgled at her and waved pudgy arms. The other two mumbled a perfunctory "Even, Aunt Joanna," and went back to their game of straws.

"We do not see much of you these days," her father said.

"Her ladyship keeps me busy, Papa," she replied, using the time-worn excuse.

"The work must suit you, then. You look well, rosy cheeks, and you've put on flesh."

Joanna's face burned red.

Katrine cleared her throat, bristling in silence as she always did whenever Ivo paid Joanna the least compliment.

Joanna wished she did not have to speak in front of her stepmother, but there was no way to avoid it, unless she caught Ivo by chance in the stables or in the little room he shared with the clerk where the accounts were kept.

"Papa..." she commenced, looking down at her folded hands, "Papa, I have committed a grave sin."

Ivo bounced the child from one knee to the other, a sturdy boy with flaxen hair. "A grave sin? I cannot imagine what. Have you confessed?"

"Aye—to Father Imbard."

"The new pastor, ah." He nodded approvingly.

For some reason she could not quite understand (perhaps it had something to do with Sir Theobold's old association with her mother) Joanna had not gone to the village priest but to Father Imbard, recently brought to Nareham to take over some of Brother Robert's duties, chiefly those of hearing confession of the castle servants and giving them communion. A pale cleric with cold blue eyes and a pinched, snuffling nose, he had already heard the whole category of sins, from adultery to sodomy, from lying to stealing, petty and grand, many times over. Peasants had little imagination. Joanna's tale was by now old. He listened, ordered her to say fifty *Aves* and to give five groats to the first passing pilgrim. Joanna had not expected more, she had not looked for relief, for a lightening of the heart, for true forgiveness, but had only gone that morning so that when her father asked her she did not have to lie.

"And you have done penance?"

"I am doing it, Papa, but..." He looked at her, eyebrows raised, waiting, and her heart quailed.

"Papa—I am with child."

A stunned silence filled the room. Even the fire seemed to have paused in its crackling, and the little one too, sensing something amiss, looked blankly up into his father's shocked eyes.

"Are you sure?" Ivo asked.

"I am in my fifth month."

Katrine made a sound in the back of her throat, folded her hands on her ample lap, a smug curve to her lips.

Ivo set the child from him, and Joanna braced herself for a storm of words, for an angry torrent; recrimination, curses, a threatened whipping. But nothing came. Ivo stared at her, his face blanched. He suddenly appeared older, old, the blond hair graying, the brow furrowing it seemed before her eyes.

Nothing he could have done could have been worse than this silent shock, this crumpling. She needed his wrath, a scourge, to help her bear the guilt she had managed to put away earlier in her desire for revenge.

"Papa—please, say something."

He stared at her for a few moments longer, and when he spoke it was in a flat, dull voice. "Whose? Who is the father?"

"Sir John Hawkwood."

"Did he force you?"

She hesitated—a small lie, he would never know—but she could not. "Nay, Papa," in a low, barely audible voice.

Ivo got up, mug in hand, and went to the ale cask in the corner, where he refilled it.

Katrine said, "Ivo, if I were you—"

"Hush!"

He came back to his seat, his face set, only the eyes betraying his deep hurt. Still Joanna waited, hoping that his anger might yet come.

"So—so you will present your old father with a bastard," he said in the same cold voice.

"Papa—I am sorry, truly sorry."

He made a helpless gesture with his hand. "Sorry will not help now, will it? Aside from me and Katrine, who knows?"

"No one. I have told no one but Father Imbard."

"And he can be trusted to hold his tongue. Father Imbard—a good priest."

He toyed with his mug. She wanted to speak, to tell him she did not care what others would say, she would take her shame as punishment gladly if only she could spare him.

"Heed me, Joanna," he said, breaking a long silence. "Your mother has kin, cousins, in Harnun. You could go there. I would explain your absence by saying there's been a death in the family, a widow left with five small children, and you are needed. You could have the baby without anyone here being the wiser. Then afterward—afterward..." He drummed on the table with stained, callused fingers. "The sisters at Waltham sometimes take orphans in."

"Papa! Give my child up? I cannot."

"But you must. 'Tis the only way, Joanna."

"Abandon my child? 'Twill be a sin, Papa, a sin against God." That particular sin had no terror for her, but she could not tell him the true reason for her wanting to keep the child. "Whether a babe is born in wedlock or not, it has a God-given right to mother love. To shunt it off to someone who might not care, someone who would neglect, starve it—Papa—for Mother Mary's sake..."

She went on and on in this vein, her argument larded heavily with Mother Marys and maternal love, finally winning Ivo over.

He agreed to let her have the child, in the end accepting his daughter's disgrace, resolved to bear it with the same stoicism that had pulled him through so many disappointments and tragedies. She could come home to the keep if she liked—now; she needn't wait. But Joanna felt that Alys de Ander would not dismiss her because of her pregnancy. She was too good a seamstress. The lady might deplore Joanna's stupidity, her loose behavior, asking, "What can one expect from a peasant?" but she would keep her on.

In point of fact, Joanna's condition, the stomach swelling and bulging under her apron, caused less comment than she had supposed. The ladies were too busy chattering over the most recent news from London. King John of France, held captive in London since the Battle of Poitiers, was to be released in exchange for lesser, but still illustrious, hostages. A large band of French nobles, headed by the four "fleurs-delys," the king's own two sons, Louis and Jean, in addition to the Duc d'Orléans and the Duc de Bourbon, were arriving in England to replace their monarch as prisoners. Naturally, their ladies and household would accompany them, the royal entourage to be put up in suitable quarters, though they must stand their own expenses. Speculation as to the latest fashion in hairstyles, gowns, jewels and shoes of this prospective feminine invasion dominated the talk in the solar so much so that a servant big with child—or even rumors of the plague reappearing in London—hardly caused a stir.

Joanna, growing larger in advanced pregnancy, moved through the talk, impervious, unheeding, like a leisurely swimmer moving through water. She found her unaccustomed languor, the slowness of her pace, strange, but not wholly unpleasant. The weight she carried seemed to enfold her, isolating her in a floating cocoon. She listened with a calm, attentive inner ear to the life stirring inside, the little kicks, throbs and pulsations, wondering but never astonished.

More and more as her time drew near she nested like the plump wrens in the hawthorn hedge, rarely leaving her chamber, sending little Cecily to measure and to deliver the finished capes and gowns in her stead. She could not explain it, she did not try; she thought of her vowed revenge every now and again, but as some distant, faraway goal. For the present, this moment and the next, her entire being, her will, every part of her body, the very beat of her heart was bent to one purpose—birth.

Her time came before she expected it, a single cramp that took her breath away, disappearing only to return some minutes later, vanishing again, coming back, advancing with less and less pause in between until there was nothing but a continuous grinding and twisting. She thought of Ivo, how she had promised to come home, but Alys de Ander's midwife, summoned by the frightened Cecily, advised her not to move. Remembering other women's cries, screams and hoarse moans, she had believed she was prepared for the agony of birth, but she found the reality far worse. Her determination to suffer stoically, grimly and silently vanished with the first monstrous pain, and she heard herself shrieking like a mindless idiot, a raging animal. She endured, screamed, called upon God to kill her, through the hours, an eternity, hating the thing that had caused her such unbearable torture. If she had been flayed, quartered or hung by the thumbs she could not have suffered more.

It was born at dawn, a boy, a red scrap of humanity taken from her, cleansed and swaddled. Exhausted, she lay on her bed while Cecily mopped her damp brow.

"Such a beautiful boy," the midwife said, placing the child in her arms. She looked down at the sleeping infant, the blondish poll, the snub nose, the blue-veined lids, the little pink-nailed fist clenched at the tiny, puckered mouth. She gazed at it, her baby, her son, and saw that it did not resemble in the least John Hawkwood. It was Ivo, her father as he might have been at birth, the shape of the face, the forehead, the promise of a nose, Ivo not John. But she saw more. She saw her child, her first, and something she had not planned, never imagined or supposed, happened. She fell in love with the mite, the infant that had caused her shame, anger and a burning desire for revenge. She loved him from that first moment as she was to love him for the rest of her life.

Chapter VII

The child was named Edmund. He was given the breast whenever he mewed, sucking eagerly five, six times a day; his
cheeks soon rounded out like rosy apples, the chin and neck
dimpled. His eyes changed to a light brown color (John's eyes),
his fair hair grew into wispy little curls. Ivo in his own un-
demonstrative manner loved it and would have been proud
of his little grandson if Katrine had not constantly reminded
him that it was illegitimate. She called it a bastard, a by-
blow, but only when Joanna was out of earshot.

However, one day Joanna, overhearing her, attacked Katrine with a besom, fully intending to knock out her teeth.
Only the intervention of Ivo prevented bloodshed, and Joanna
vowed that she would never set foot in the keep again.
Fiercely protective, Joanna also scotched the snide remarks
and bawdy jokes the manor servants aimed at her offspring,
giving them the benefit of her lashing tongue and black scowl.
They kept their distance, agreeing among themselves that
illegitimate motherhood, far from humbling Joanna, had
made her even more haughty. As for Alys, she simply remarked, "So you are back. About time. Here—take this gown
and see what you can do. Such a mess! That little girl, your
helper—what is her name?—Cecily—made a botch of it."

But then Alys had other things on her mind.

Her youngest son, Andrew, was to be married to the Damosel Cecilia de Braybroke in two weeks. A hasty betrothal,
a hasty wedding. For the noble class this could mean only
one thing: Andrew had gotten the girl in the family way. No
question as to why or what to do, as in Joanna's case; no
queries, no options, simply a single solution—marriage. Alys,
mortified at the scandal, trying to ignore the clacking
tongues, had to console herself with the fact that her new
daughter-in-law came from a good family and brought with
her a respectable dowry.

Joanna was immediately put to work making the wedding
clothes, a new gown and a half-dozen shifts for Alys. Her old
energy restored, Joanna managed without difficulty to stitch
and embroider while at the same time tending to the baby's
needs. He slept by her bedside, the child's chance stirrings

and mumblings bringing Joanna out of sleep to lean over and soothe it. She fed it herself, although she could have had a wet nurse if she wished, a returned favor from one of the dairy maids. But Joanna had plenty of milk, she said; why hand it over to a stranger?

However, she had not relinquished the idea of getting back at Hawkwood. But now her thoughts of redress had taken a subtler twist. Edmund, too dear and far too worthy to be forged into a cold and calculating tool of vengeance, would grow to splendid manhood and on his own, out of love and respect for his mother, call his errant father to account. She pictured the scene in her mind time and again; Edmund, tall and handsome, a youth of noble bearing, confronting his father, the latter surprised, dismayed, impressed and finally moved, falling on his son's neck, weeping, asking for forgiveness. Edmund might forgive him, but Joanna never would. Never. If John Hawkwood crawled on his knees and implored her in the name of God, the Holy Ghost, Jesus and Mother Mary, she would never, *never* pardon him.

Where John Hawkwood was now she had no idea. She only knew that he had sailed for France some seven months earlier with ten newly recruited bowmen, five footmen and four horses. The hayward's nephew who enlisted with Hawkwood as a foot soldier had sent news of their departure back to the village, and the hayward boastfully passed the information on to Ivo, unaware that Hawkwood had sired Joanna's child. As far as Ivo could learn, no one associated the departed Hawkwood with Joanna, though Edmund's paternity was a source of much speculation.

As time went on, however, Ivo began to feel that the boy should be publicly acknowledged by his natural father. "It would relieve much of the stigma," he told his daughter. "As a knight and a man of honor, I am sure Sir John, once he knows he has a son, will proclaim Edmund as his and provide for him too."

Joanna, though she might daydream about impossible confrontations, was too much a realist to believe that John Hawkwood would do any such thing. "He is selfish. He is concerned for no one but himself. His knightly vows only serve to put a sword in his hand; otherwise they mean nothing. He never had any wish to protect the weak, give to the poor or love God," she said bitterly. "He is a dastard, and I don't want to say or hear another word about him."

Yet whenever conversation among the ladies in the solar turned to France, Joanna's ears picked up.

"I understand the Tard Venus are overrunning the French countryside," Harold de Ander said to his lady one cold blustery March morning. He had come up to the solar, a room warmer and less drafty than the great hall, and now sat red-nosed, his eyes watering, hunched over the hearth fire toasting his hands.

Alys shifted her feet as Joanna knelt before her, marking the hem of her gown. "I was given to understand the king gave orders for all stragglers to return to England."

"The peace treaty did make a point of calling the men home, and King Edward gave the proviso lip service. But I doubt if very many of the brigands plaguing France now will heed such injunctions."

Lady Thérèse, one of Alys's cousins and a frequent visitor to Nareham, spoke up. "What can you expect of common rogues?"

"I wish to God they were only common rogues," Harold replied. "But I am told many knights have joined them. I believe Sir John Hawkwood is now in their ranks. He was here at Thomas's knighting, if you recall."

"Oh," said Lady Thérèse faintly.

Joanna, looking up at her quickly and seeing pink tinge the lady's cheek, thought, So she knew my John. I wonder how well. Did he sleep with her too, make love, bite her ear, say she was beautiful? If she had not already been married would he have tried to make her his wife? Marry her, pregnant or not?

Thomas de Ander did not come home to Nareham at Christmas but at Easter, almost a year after his knighting. He wore a short, bristly beard, obviously a new one which he kept fingering and stroking, and his curly hair was cut short just below the ears. A life away from the castle had given him a wider perspective, and he found it difficult not to look down at manor-house folk, even his father and mother, as countrified and somewhat beneath him. Only his good looks and natural charm excused him from what in others would be criticized as snobbery.

He had not forgotten Joanna, however, nor did he snub her, for he had been at Nareham only a few hours when he sought her out in her workroom.

"I have a tear here on the collar of my tunic," he said. "Could you mend it for me?"

"Certainly, Sir Thomas," Joanna replied coolly, not at all flustered, the way Cecily and her two Scottish assistants were, blushing and curtsying, bobbing up and down, casting looks at Thomas from under fluttering eyelids. "Will you remove it?"

He took it off, a particolored garment of cherry red and lemon yellow, revealing a muscled chest as smooth and white as a girl's. The Scottish maids began to giggle but were stopped by a stern look from Joanna.

"I failed to parry a dagger thrust," Thomas said, "hence the tear."

"A fight?" Joanna asked, threading her needle.

"Aye, over some trifle, I cannot remember. I near killed the man—would have, had not my squire come between."

"Ah," said Joanna, feeling that his tale was invented to impress her. Coxcomb, she thought.

"You are as lovely as ever," he said.

One of the little maids, choking on a giggle, began to cough. The other clapped her on the back. Ignoring them, Thomas went on.

"And you have a son."

"Aye—Edmund," she answered proudly, pointing to him as he slept wrapped in his withe cradle.

"So you are not the sweet virgin any longer."

"I never was—sweet, that is, sir knight."

He laughed. "Ah—Joanna."

Cecily tittered.

"Are you never alone?" he asked.

"Never."

He made a wry face, then, turning to Joanna's three little assistants, said, "Here—you make too much noise, out with you. Out, I say!" He raised his hand. "Well—what are you waiting for?"

Terrified, they scrambled for the door.

Joanna, concentrating on her sewing in the silence that followed, felt Thomas's eyes resting on her. There was only one reason he wanted to be alone with her. Wary, she braced herself for an attack.

But he made no move to touch her. "You are still the loveliest woman I have ever seen," he said finally. "The beautiful steward's daughter."

The allusion to her status rankled. "The steward's daugh-

115

ter"—exactly the phrase John Hawkwood had thrown at her. They were all the same. Thomas had not thought her beautiful when she was a half-starved child. Suddenly she recalled their meeting in the mud-puddled lane, the ride on the chestnut gelding, the malicious look on Thomas's face as he raised his whip and ordered her to dismount. The entire scene came back in a rush of bitter resentment, and with it an anger she could barely control. Her needle shook, she did not meet his eyes.

"I want you," Thomas said in a low urgent voice. "I love you. I have thought of no one else all these months away."

The needle flashed in and out. "Not one of the court ladies looked upon you with favor? Oh, Sir Thomas..." She managed a wan smile. "That is hard to believe."

"They may have looked upon me, but I looked at no one. Compared to you they were all dross."

"You flatter me."

"Not at all." He leaned forward and kissed her lightly on the top of her head. "I love you," he repeated.

Was he sincere? She shot him a quick look. Sweat beaded his brow, his earnest eyes gazed at her like a hound dog's. He wanted her, there was no mistaking it, wanted her badly. But love?

"Joanna!" He got down on one knee, grasped her hand and kissed it. The passionate suitor. "Joanna, I will be your slave."

Real or not, the sight of him at her feet dissipated her anger, and she had a sudden strange feeling of elation, of power. He was actually begging her.

"I love you," he continued earnestly, "and if you were to give me your fair body I would be the happiest man on God's earth."

She considered for a moment before she spoke. "As you know, Sir Thomas, I am in your mother's employ. Freeborn, but still her servant. You can have your will of me if you so choose and no one will gainsay you."

He brushed her hand with his lips. "You must come to me because *you* wish it. A man never forces the woman he loves."

God's bones, Joanna thought, mayhap he really means it. How I would like to have him, to make his desire so great as to crowd out his overweaning vanity, to destroy him if I could. And if she destroyed him, might she in some oblique way get back at the other, the knight who had betrayed her?

"I must confess, Sir Thomas..."

"Thomas."

"Thomas"—was she being elevated from peasant?—"that I have held a high regard for you for many years." She could lie prettily too. She had learned a great deal from John Hawkwood.

His eyes glowed, resting hungrily on her breasts. "Come to bed with me, Joanna. Isn't that how a man and woman show love for one another?"

Of course. She knew that, had known since John Hawkwood had taken her in a May garden.

"'Tis a sin," she parried, feeling very sure of herself now. "One that I have already committed, God knows. I shan't do it a second time."

"'Tis no sin if two people love one another."

Did they all borrow the same words from each other's mouths? If two people loved one another. How he presumed! The smug peacock in his red-and-yellow particolors taking it as a matter of course that she loved him.

"Joanna—have pity on me."

So hot, so eager. Well—why not? Hawkwood had already convinced himself she was unfaithful, so what did it matter? Besides, Thomas might help to restore some of her self-esteem.

"I cannot—not tonight," she said, frowning, pretending to give the matter thought. Let him wait, let him stew a little.

"When, then? You have only to say when."

"We must be discreet. If your lady mother should hear of it..." She did not mind Alys knowing—she felt secure enough to face her anger, even a threat of dismissal—but she shrank at the thought of her father finding out.

"I will tread lightly, breathe not a word, I promise. When can I come to your chamber?"

"I—I should think—let me see—Saturday, next Saturday night." It would not do to put the panting lordling off for too long. He might lose interest, find someone else for all his avowal of love.

"I shall die before Saturday."

She smiled.

"You will not change your mind? Ah, then, let me kiss you."

He clutched her, his mouth coming down on hers, moving back and forth, kissing her hungrily. She bore his assault passively, but when she felt his hands fumbling, pushing the neck of her gown apart, she resisted and, using her elbows, managed to struggle free.

117

"Sir Thomas! You promised. You said..."

"I cannot help myself."

She got hastily to her feet, shoving the stool between them. Then, reaching down, she picked up the tunic where it had fallen to the floor. "I believe you will find this mended now."

"Joanna..."

She went to the door and opened it. "Next Saturday night, Sir Thomas. It will be all the sweeter."

"If I must." And when he made another move toward her she adroitly propelled him across the threshold with the closing edge of the door.

Saturday night came quickly enough. Joanna had taken a bath earlier in tepid water the Scottish girls had brought up in a vat from the kitchen. Now she perfumed the hollow of her neck and the cleft between her breasts with a few drops of gillyflower water from a half-vial Alys had inadvertently thrown away. She put on a clean linen shift and braided her hair so that it hung down her back in a single, thick, glossy rope (not for Thomas the unbound, flowing hair). When darkness came she lighted the stub of a taper and sprinkled the sheets on the bed with rosemary and bane's tooth, a remedy said to protect a woman from pregnancy. She'd not be caught again; she loved Edmund, but she did not want another. She gave the coverlet one last pat, then sat down to wait. Hands folded, she listened to the distant murmur of diners from the great hall, the muted laughter, the tinkle of a gittern. Her girls had been instructed not to disturb her—what they thought she could guess, but she was not going to let it worry her. Edmund, given over to the dairy maid, would spend the night with her. She missed the child's presence. He had begun to coo and gurgle, making little mewing sounds, and to smile and dimple when she leaned over him. A sweet baby, he looked more and more like Ivo each day. Except for the eyes, those brown eyes so like John's.

A step outside startled her from her thoughts, and a moment later Thomas entered the room.

"Have I been overlong?" His teeth gleamed in the flickering light.

"Nay," she replied calmly. Except for a slight dampness of her palms she felt no apprehension, no uneasiness.

"I have brought a small cask of wine," he said, putting it down. "Do you own a mug?"

"Aye." She got up and took it down from the shelf, a wooden

mug, fancifully carved, a present from her father when she had left home.

"Good. Wine always helps love along, does it not?"

He was nervous. The noble's spawn nervous of a peasant's daughter! Oh, how it pleased her, how she wished it were John Hawkwood who stood there in Thomas's place, so that she could show him she did not care.

He sipped at the mug and offered it to her. She tasted, observing him over the rim.

"I have never seen such beautiful eyes—blue—blue like cornflowers." He took the mug from her and pulled her into his arms, kissing her, his mouth spreading over hers, his tongue forcing her lips open with a greedy passion. She suffered his tongue, his mouth, as she had done before, in unperturbable silence, wishing he would cease his slobbering and get down to the business at hand. She wanted it to be over—and quickly.

He began to fumble with the laces at the neck of her gown, his inept fingers knotting the strings so badly Joanna at last reached up and undid them herself. As she did so she could not help but think how skillfully John Hawkwood had managed even this simple task. How he had caressed her, kissed her, bringing the hot blood to her face. John's hands, his mouth... A pang twisted her heart. God knew she had loved him, going to him in innocence, wanting only his love in return. But he had laughed, betrayed her.

Thomas, breathing hard into her hair, was working the gown from her shoulders. He paused to kiss each breast through her shift, then finished easing the dress past her hips. It fell about her ankles with a soft, slithering sound. The shift came next. She had embroidered it in blue knots and cross-stitches herself. He pulled it over her face, catching the ribbon which banded her forehead, yanking the shift and bringing the ribbon with it too. Had he never undressed a woman? she wondered impatiently.

"Turn—turn—just so, Joanna, so that I may look at you in the light. God's bones but you are lovely. A waist the span of my hands—the breasts—no one would guess you have had a child."

He gazed at her for another few moments, then suddenly scooped her up in his arms and carried her to the bed. She lay there, unmoving, unmoved, while he hastily got out of his clothes, muttering an oath at an obstinate lace, a stubborn hook. She saw his shadow looming against the wall as he

119

bent to blow out the taper, and the next moment felt the mattress shift slightly with his weight. She expected nothing, not even revulsion. The feeling, the passion, the insurmountable tension would all be his. She would not try to pretend, as she had heard some women did. *He* would never notice.

He kissed her wetly on the lips, on the cheeks, on the lips again. She lay detached, resigned. He mounted her, nuzzling her throat, his jaw grating her breastbone. She could feel his hardness pressed against her knee. He gripped her shoulders, moving his head, and took a nipple between his teeth.

The sharp searing flame shot through her before she had a chance to think. "Thomas—do not...!" But he had the nipple firmly between his lips, and his tongue ran around it as he sucked and drew. This was not what she had expected, certainly not from his kisses.

"Thomas!" To be touched *there*, in this way, always undid her, made her blood run hot, and her body arched into his, thirsty, longing for his hard member to enter and assuage the ache in her loins. She tried feebly to push him away, but he was inside now, moving, moving with a pleasurable slowness that robbed her completely of her earlier resolve. She felt herself responding, her hips rising to meet his every downward thrust, and somewhere in the back of her mind she heard a faint voice utter, *Fool! Fool!* But caught up in the mindless, ecstatic ascent, the voice was drowned, lost, lost until the ultimate blinding thrill shuddered through her.

It was over. The whole episode had not lasted more than half a minute, but her body had betrayed her. She had not imagined it could happen, but it had, and she hated herself. She thought of her mother, who had loved her father but given herself to others, a woman who could never get enough of male love play. Mariotta, the whore of Nareham. Was she, Joanna, the same?

After a long while Thomas said, "I have never been so pleasured. And you, my sweet?"

Joanna was too chagrined to reply.

"Speechless, are you?" he said, his voice smiling. "But we shall have more, many more hours like this." He burrowed his head in her breasts, his lips caressing the delicious cleft between, his hand roaming her thighs. In the darkness Joanna scowled at him.

"Thomas..."

"Aye?" came a rumble in his throat.

She felt him rising, knew that in a moment it would all

begin again. She grasped him by the hair, not too gently. "Thomas, we must leave off. The nurse I hired will be back with Edmund shortly." The lie came quickly to her lips.

"But I thought—you said—"

"He has an earache, and Maria cannot seem to quiet him the way I can when he cries."

"The child be damned!" he exclaimed and tried to pull her toward him again. But she eased herself away, rolled over and got to her feet.

"Joanna, where are you going?"

"I shall only be a moment."

Feeling her way in the dark, she found the doused taper and, slipping out into the passage, lighted it from a flaming torch on the wall. When she returned, Thomas was still abed.

She picked up his discarded drawers and linen shirt. "You must dress, Sir Thomas. I beg of you."

He groaned again, sat up and scratched his head. She dropped his clothes into his lap. He picked up his drawers and slowly began to pull them on. "'Tis not right to send a man from a warm, loving bed out into the cold night. Joanna . . ." A pause. "Joanna, I have been thinking we should find a better place. There is a room in the north court tower—"

"Nay!" There was only one empty chamber in the north court, the room she and John had made love in. She couldn't. "Listen, sweet, I shall see to it that no one disturbs us next time. We shall have the entire night here—I promise."

"When? Tomorrow? My stay at Nareham is only for two weeks, and I want to make up for lost time."

"Tomorrow—but . . ." She bit her lip. "I will have to bribe the girls." She had thought of it suddenly; why not make him pay a little? A boon bought with hard cash was often valued above one acquired freely.

"Bribe three serfs?"

"They are not serfs, Thomas. And if I wish them to hold their tongues, I must give them something. A shilling each."

Had she asked too much, too little? "And one for the nurse." She would keep the shillings for herself, of course.

"Ah—well," he said, reaching for his purse, "'tis money well spent." He took out a handful of coins and put them on the table. She saw the four shillings and a gold solidus, a coin worth considerably more.

"I only wanted four shillings," she said quickly.

"The solidus is for you. Buy yourself a pretty the next time the pack peddler comes by. A gift from me in gratitude."

She looked at the winking bit of gold, more than she could possibly earn in six months, and thought, What does it matter? If I was willing to accept four shillings, the solidus will make me no more a whore.

"Thank you, Sir Thomas."

"Thomas," he corrected, taking her in his arms and kissing her on the mouth, not so wetly this time.

The next evening after the last brassy clang of Compline echoed over the courtyard, Thomas hurried into Joanna's chamber, breathless, eager, sweeping her into his arms with a laugh. Whether she had warmed to him because of the coins he had given her, or whether he had somehow become a more experienced lover in the last twenty-four hours, his kisses pleased her in a way they had not the night before, pleased her so much she hardly had to pretend. Nevertheless, once he had her on the bed she reminded herself sternly, even while making false little sighs and gasps, that she would not let him sweep her away. Not again. A promise, alas, she was incapable of keeping. Though she tried to stem the mounting tide and nearly succeeded, a sudden picture of John Hawkwood's naked body flashed before her and she found herself letting go, carried, swept along. It was John holding her, John's thrusts she responded to, rising and falling with a twist of her hips to grasp the full, sensuous hardness inside her. *John, John!* Higher and higher she rose, borne upward on a towering wave, flung and hurled into that brief but all-consuming moment of ecstasy.

Beached and sobered now, brought back to reality with Thomas still panting over her, she felt betrayed by herself once more. I must be a doxy after all, she thought ruefully. And in the shadows John Hawkwood seemed to mock her.

The next day when Joanna took up her sewing basket and descended the stairs to consult with Alys de Ander in the solar as she did every morning, she fully expected the worst, certain that by this time Alys would have learned of Thomas's visit to her room. Bedding with Thomas was a far different affair from bedding with John Hawkwood. Sir John had been one visitor among scores, his comings and goings of no special interest, while Thomas, a member of the lord's family, was under the scrutiny of at least a dozen servants, who observed, noted and gossiped about his every move. The giggling Scottish girls most likely had not kept silent either, and Joanna braced herself for a sound scolding.

The lady, however, had not yet made her appearance, and Joanna entered the solar amid gossip of another kind. The women were discussing Thomas and his possible betrothal.

"My parents are trying to make an alliance between the du Pynne girl and my brother," Aelenor du Trolaine, Thomas's older sister, was saying.

"Hulda du Pynne? Why, she is only eight years old and a lackwit to boot," Damosel Maude of Saffron Walden remarked. Maude was a frequent visitor to Nareham, one, Joanna guessed (and rightly), that Alys did not welcome warmly.

"She will grow into marriageable age. And as for being a lackwit, what matters?" Aelenor countered. "She is an heiress. She is very rich."

"Rich—but will she give Sir Thomas an heir?" asked the damosel.

Maude had her eye on Thomas. She was passionately in love with him, had been for two years, wanted desperately to marry him and felt she had every chance of succeeding. No one could fault Maude's background and her illustrious lineage or her auburn-haired, creamy-skinned beauty. Unfortunately, however, Maude's estates did not match the du Pynne heiress's, and Harold de Ander, under his wife's strict instructions, had politely turned away the girl's proposal made through her guardian, a doting old uncle.

Maude, however, was not discouraged. Thomas she wanted and Thomas she would have. And Alys, aware of her son's weakness for comely women and Maude's determination, had vowed to prevent any such alliance. This duel for the young curly-headed knight went on between Maude and Alys under a cloak of false smiles and stiffly polite small talk. Meanwhile, the other ladies were equally divided in their opinion as to who would wed Thomas—Maude or du Pynne.

Joanna, listening to them debate, wondered what the women would say if she brashly broke into the conversation and told them that du Pynne and Maude were furthest from Thomas de Ander's mind, that he had declared his love for *her,* and had begged to be allowed to come to her bed every night as long as he remained at Nareham. Watching them in their silken gowns, their hair bound in gilded nets, the white hands aglitter with jeweled rings, hands that never had done anything more arduous than holding an embroidery needle or strum a lute, she had to admit they would think nothing. A brow might be raised, a shoulder shrugged. What of it? Nobles were always taking serving girls to bed, and if a knight said a few silly words to entice one of them, it was no more important than offering a child a sweet. Only Alys would care.

"Thomas deserves a wife who can give him a lusty son," Maude went on. "Someone like me, someone—" She stopped short as Alys swept into the room.

Alys shot Maude a sharp look, a moment before her lips parted in a sugary smile. "Ah—dear Maude! How good to see you. I am sorry I was still abed when you and Sir Roger arrived, else I would have given you the welcome you deserve."

"Thank you, lady. Your hospitality is always most generous." Maude bent her knee in deference to age and marital status, returning Alys's smile with a flash of white even teeth. Those teeth were her special pride. Few women could boast such a smile, and Maude knew it. Alys's teeth were slightly crooked, and a lower one in front was missing, a fact which did not make her fonder of Maude.

"Now then, ladies and damosels," Alys said briskly. "Shall we get to work on the altar cloth?" The altar cloth, done to Alys's own design, St. George rescuing a pale, virginal maiden, was destined for the castle chapel.

Joanna waited on her feet, the basket held in two slightly damp hands, until Alys finished with the women.

At last she turned to her. "I have nothing for you today," she said in the same brisk voice. "You may go."

Joanna stared for a moment into her mistress's face. Was it possible she did not know about her and Thomas?

"Well—why do you gawk? I said, go!"

Someone snickered as Joanna went through the door. Lady Sybil, one of the most malicious of the gossips, said, "Have a care with servants who take liberties. I do not like to say, but they tell me Thomas, your son, has..."

Joanna climbed the stairs to her room with flaming cheeks. Oh, why should she fret over their silly gabbling, why should she give it a second thought? Why should she even listen? Her life had nothing to do with theirs; it went on in a different world. She must learn to close her eyes, her mind, to their cruel, sly remarks. Even if it hurt. Oh—damn the lot of them!

By late afternoon everyone from the spit boy to the chamberlain knew she had slept with Thomas de Ander. Fortunately Ivo had gone to Gore, a town some twenty miles distant, to settle a suit on Harold's behalf and would be absent for at least a month. And Katrine had little to do with the manor. Joanna hoped by the time her father returned to Nareham Thomas would be long gone and interest in her affairs would have died.

Hardly anyone condemned her. A few sly gibes and a clucking of tongues by the older servants, but for the most part, especially among the younger women, she was the object of envy. Thomas de Ander's good looks had caused many a soulful sigh in the kitchen and dairy rooms, and because Joanna had snared him, not for one night but for more to come (how they knew *that* remained a mystery), she acquired a special luster. The cook's wife had taken it upon herself to give Joanna advice. "If ye do not wish to have his bastards, my friend, the best remedy is a rowan branch."

"And what am I to do with it?"

"Have one cut, either in flower or in berry, and wave it over the bed."

The boy Joanna sent to fetch the branch was hard put to find a rowan tree, and Joanna, waiting, was beginning to despair when he arrived toward dusk, breathless, red in the face, triumphantly presenting her with the branch. Not only did Joanna use the rowan branch but she sprinkled the sheets again, this time with tansy and hensbane, also known for their efficacious properties in preventing conception. The apprentices watched this procedure with round eyes.

"Well, be off with you now," Joanna ordered. "Take Edmund. And if anything befalls him I shall boil you in oil for certain."

Because she wanted to keep Thomas enraptured she resolved to be less cool in his embrace, less passive, though God knew she had been anything but passive in the final throes the night before. There too, however, she would exert more control. Kiss him ardently, she forewarned herself, because his kisses do not arouse, and later when he took her while his passion was at its height she would think of something else and only feign the ecstasy. She must, above all, retain a sense of balance, never lose mastery of the situation, not melt into lovesickness as she had with John Hawkwood, for she had decided to make gain from this encounter. She was tired of her servitude, tired of being snubbed and scorned or treated as if she did not exist. Her efforts were taken for granted, her wages, that one shilling paid not as money earned, but as a grand charitable gesture, a reminder that she was and would always be a peasant minion.

Joanna did not aspire to the nobility—one does not aspire to the unimaginable, the preposterously out of reach, not in this life—but she did want to better herself. She wanted more than what she had now both for herself and for Edmund.

Ever since Thomas had left the golden solidus she had been thinking. There was a life away from the manor in the towns, where the freeborn were rising in importance, some even gaining wealth. She remembered the grain merchant, Pickard, a man of no better class than her own who had started out with very little. Through diligence and luck and with the aid of a little capital he had amassed enough money to build a fine house, make honorable marriages for his children, become a man, Ivo had told her, who was respected and admired. His wife wore miniver, in spite of the royal decrees banning fur for all but the nobility, displayed jewels on her fingers, in her hair and ears, and owned a splinter of the True Cross, which she carried in a gold-embossed reliquary around her neck.

Joanna reasoned that if she saved enough gold coins to set herself up in a tailoring or seamstress's shop in Thexted, she could sew for the rich burghers' wives and little by little accumulate a sizable purse. When Edmund came of age she would apprentice him to a wine seller, a wool merchant or a goldsmith so that he could learn a respectable trade. He might, if so inclined, go to school and read for the law. Oh, she had dreams and visions for her son; Edmund splendidly dressed, riding a fine-bred horse, looked up to, a man to be reckoned with in the town. "Good morrow, Master Coke." "If you will allow me to say, Master Coke." Asked for advice, listened to, bowed to. And the ultimate, the finishing stroke, his meeting with John Hawkwood, the wayward father made humble.

By the time Thomas left Nareham with promises that he would return soon, very soon, Joanna had managed to squirrel away several pounds. Since she had never paid for her keep or engaged in a transaction which had involved more than a shilling or two, she knew little about the cost of things outside Nareham. To her the small hoard she had saved seemed sufficient for her purpose, and she decided to leave the manor as soon as she could arrange it.

When Ivo got back from Gore, she revealed her plan to

him. Listening, he did not know whether to laugh or scold. "My dear child, you cannot be serious?"

"Oh, Papa, I am. Just think—a little shop of my own."

"Joanna, are you daft? Firstly—did you honestly think I would let you go, a young girl alone with a child? Why, you would be branded whore for sure before you set foot inside Thexted's gates."

"Then I shall take someone with me, some old hag from the village, to make it respectable."

"You will take—who? And what of her ladyship? Do you think she will let you go?"

"She cannot prevent me. I am freeborn, I can go where I like."

"You are freeborn, my girl, but you cannot go where you like. Alys de Ander *can* prevent you, and if she does not, I will. You have no husband, and I, as your father, still have the say-so."

She pleaded with him, using the argument that here at Nareham Edmund would forever be maligned as bastard, while if she left and went to Thexted she could pose as a widow whose husband had been killed soldiering in France. Further, she would let it be known that because her husband had died saving a knight's life she had been granted a small pension. To augment it she would sew for the more fortunate matrons of the town.

Ivo said no. He wanted her to marry; he had not given up on that score. She was young and attractive, and if he could find her a suitable husband, an older man to be sure, one who would accept the child, Joanna would fare much better than by going off alone on some idiotic venture.

Joanna countered by saying she would not marry, that she wanted to spend the rest of her life looking after her son, that was enough for her. She did not want an older man, she did not want *any* man.

Finally, out of desperation, she resorted to tears. Ivo, not one to be melted by a woman's weeping, nevertheless felt compassion for Joanna. She was still his little girl, and she had suffered so much in the past, the death of her mother, that terrible illness and lastly the seduction from which she had learned a bitter lesson.

"There, there," he soothed. "Dry your eyes. I'll think on it. But, dove, five pounds will not do much for you at Thexted."

"I can ask her ladyship for a raise in my wages."

"And get a few pence more if you are lucky? She is not too

generous, and if she thought you planned to leave her, I doubt she would give you anything."

"Then, Papa, will you lend me the money?"

"I don't know . . ."

"My dowry money," she pleaded with tear-lashed eyes.

"We shall see."

She knew he would give it to her, it was only a matter of an outright aye, and so she began to make ready. From an old gown, musty and riddled with moths, that a waiting woman had discarded she managed to piece together a particolored cape. She begged leather for shoes from the tanner, and pilfered enough linen to make two new shifts, which she embroidered prettily with violets and daffodils entwined. She added to her store of coins by offering to sew for the cook's wife and the chamberlain's daughter and niece, often staying up past Matins, stitching by rush light until her red-rimmed eyes closed with fatigue. From Ivo, from the beadle, a passing tinker, from anyone who had ever been to Thexted whether for a day or a year, she gleaned information, how many mercers, tailors, how many houses for rent. What was the cost of a loaf, of a round of cheese? Could one get fresh eggs daily? Her long-ago visits to Thexted made in the company of her father had been to the market square, not the town proper, and in any case the situation might have changed in the interim. She wanted to know everything, to be prepared for any contingency. She wanted to succeed in Thexted, not come back like a dog with her tail between her legs.

Ivo, seeing her determination, finally agreed to let her go, with the stipulation, however, that she stay in the house of an elderly couple he knew, a goldsmith and his wife. "They will charge you little for rent, and keep an eye out for you and the babe."

It was not exactly what she had in mind; she would have preferred living by herself. But she was too delighted to quibble. Preparing at last to tell Alys, she awoke one morning with a queasy nausea roiling her stomach, and as she hung over the slop jar retching and gasping, she suddenly realized that her breasts ached too. Swollen breasts with distended nipples.

She was pregnant again.

Chapter VIII

She tried every known method short of killing herself to get rid of it. She drank foul-tasting potions, took scalding baths and slept with her feet propped above her head. She rode a bucking mule with a burr under its saddle around the courtyard, wore a cloth of scarlet tightly banded across her stomach and a bracelet of owl's feathers on her ankle. Nothing worked. The alien seed which was destined to grow and grow shamelessly remained stubbornly inside her. She hated it. She did not want another child. She did not want Thomas's bastard.

But it seemed she was powerless to do anything about it. Consumed by a feeling of helplessness and rage, she tossed through a week of nights, her mind darting this way and that in an attempt to resolve her terrible dilemma. What, oh what was she to do? How could she possibly manage now with two children pulling at her skirts? How was she to have her shop? What of Edmund's future? Worst of all—oh, far, far the worst—how was she to tell Ivo?

Finally, after much painful deliberation, she decided to go on with her original plan. It would be best to leave Nareham at once before she began to show. She simply could not face Ivo with this second disaster. Later, mayhap, but not now. She would think of something. For the present, however, she had to get away. Her place in Thexted had already been arranged, her clothes packed, the cart spoken for; she had only to tell Alys de Ander.

On a morning two weeks after her fateful discovery, Joanna went to the solar, her little speech prepared. Alys, busy with instructing a trio of new arrivals (young kinswomen who had been sent to Nareham to learn the amenities of noble housewifery) in tapestry work, did not see her enter. Joanna hovered near the doorway waiting for recognition. She felt a little giddy and longed to sit down. But a servant remained on her feet unless invited otherwise, an invitation which rarely if ever came. Even Ivo in his high position as steward always stood cap in hand in the presence of nobility.

The room was stifling. Though May and warm outside, all the shutters were closed and two braziers burned in the center of the floor, the scented coals sending up a thin stream of white smoke.

"My dear Bernadine," Alys was saying to a bucktoothed maiden, "your stitches are like bird tracks. You will have to do better than that." She moved on to the next damosel, leaning over her work, her brow wrinkled. "Aye, that is a little better, but let me show you..."

Joanna wiped her perspiring hands against the sides of her skirt. The heat became more and more oppressive; she could hardly breathe.

"...and your knots must not show. They must be tiny, very tiny, almost invisible. See..."

Her heart began to flutter in a disconcerting way. If she could only sit down, fan her heated face...

"...Mabelle, you have done well, except for the loops. They are a little crooked."

Her stomach rumbled and a sour taste rose to her throat. Sweat broke out on her forehead, a cold clammy sweat, and little black dots began to dance before her eyes.

"I can see where each of you has much to learn," Alys's voice rasped on, "but before you leave Nareham I expect you to be accomplished not only at embroidery and tapestry work, but at the lute, in dance and song and good manners. And now—oh, Joanna, there you are."

Joanna saw her lady's face through a darkening mist; she had one horrible moment during which she grappled with the enclosing blackness, and then she remembered no more.

When Joanna came to she was lying where she had fallen and someone was slapping her with a rag soaked in vinegar. She sneezed, lifting her head.

"Can you get up?" Alys asked. "Or shall I call one of the serving maids?"

"I—I can get up, my lady." No one offered her a hand, but with the aid of the doorpost she managed to bring herself falteringly to her feet. Her knees trembled so she feared she might fall again, and so she stood clutching the post.

Alys did not ask her to sit down, not because she was particularly cruel but because it simply did not occur to her. Nor did she think to take the girl aside before she bluntly asked, "Are you with child?"

Joanna, shaken, unprepared for this direct question, murmured, "Aye," without thinking.

"I am not surprised."

Joanna wet her lips. Her throat ached, and she would have given anything for a sip of water.

"Who is the father? Well—speak up!"

"I cannot say, my lady."

"Was it Sir Thomas?"

Joanna worked her painful throat, trying to swallow.

"Oh, you need not try to hide it. I asked only for form's sake. I have long been aware of my son's lust for you. And truthfully, I expected this to happen. So I set a spy on you to see if there were others who came to your bed." She paused, observing Joanna, her head tilted slightly, her thin mouth pursed.

"There were no others," Joanna managed in a hoarse, whispery voice. A spy? Who? One of the Scottish girls? Hardly, they seemed so stupid. Cecily, perhaps.

"How far gone are you?"

They were all staring at her now: Lady Thérèse, Aelenor du Trolaine, Maude, the new damosels. One of them, Bernadine, the bucktoothed girl, tittered behind her hand.

Joanna lifted her head. "Two, lady, two months, I believe."

Alys's cold, dispassionate probing went on. "Does your father know of this?"

"Oh, nay, nay! God forbid!" Her heart began to beat violently again and she was afraid she would faint a second time. "I do not want him to know."

"And how are you to prevent it, pray?"

"I was hoping to leave Nareham, lady."

There followed a long silence. Maude kept staring at Joanna, but the other ladies and damosels soon lost interest—servant girls were forever getting pregnant—and went back to their embroidery and idle chit-chat.

"Leave Nareham?" Alys's pale brows lifted. "Without my permission?"

"I planned to ask for it this morning, lady."

"I see."

Maude spoke. "If you will forgive me, my lady, it seems your son would do well to marry—a young wife, of course, who will keep him out of mischief."

Alys was too affronted by this impertinent interruption to even attempt a false smile. "Thank you for your kind advice," she said bitingly, "but I daresay I can do without it. This matter is of no concern to you."

Maude colored and turned away, but Joanna could tell by the rigid set of her shoulders that she was still listening.

"Before I make any decision," Alys said, "I think it is only just to inform your father."

"Oh—my lady, pray not! 'Twill go hard for him." Oh, why had she fainted? And having done so, why had she confessed the truth so meekly afterward? "My lady, it would serve no purpose except to distress him."

"Too late to think of that now, is it not?" she said dryly.

"If I leave..."

"Did you think I would allow you to leave with my son's child?" Each syllable was pronounced with icy precision. "A bastard he might be, but he will have de Ander blood."

"I am born free. You cannot—"

"Do you dare? You whore, do you dare?" she demanded, her face turning a mottled red. "Do you dare tell me what I cannot do?"

Joanna lowered her eyes and held her tongue. I shall run away, she thought. She cannot keep me. I shall run away, and no law in the land can force me back. I am freeborn, not a serf, free.

"You are not to speak to me of leaving again. Do you understand? Very well." She walked to a peg on the wall and took down a blue gown. "If you will sew new braid on this, Joanna. I fear the old is rather frayed. The silver braid, there is some left?"

"Aye, my lady."

The minute Joanna reached the workroom she threw the gown down on the bench in disgust and, going to the water bucket, lifted the brimming dipper. She drank thirstily, wiping the moisture from her lips with the back of her hand. The two Scottish girls and Cecily, who had been waiting for her return, stared at her.

"Well, what are you gawking at, you fools?" Joanna demanded. "Go on, get out. Go on, go on! I can't stand the sight of your stupid faces."

They fled, crashing the door behind them. Joanna moved to the window and looked down at the courtyard. She must leave as soon as possible, tomorrow morning, early, at first light, before word got to Ivo. She could not take her coffers now, just her money, a bundle with a change of clothes and Edmund. She could get through the gate with the child wrapped in her cloak, pretending to be one of the dairy maids. Perhaps once on the road she could get a ride in a passing cart. Beyond that she would not think.

Hours later, still wakeful, she began to feel queasy again,

her hasty supper of bread and green cheese sitting like a hard sour rock under her heart. She tossed and turned restlessly, waking Edmund, who began to fret. Held in her arms, he soon dozed off, but Joanna, far from sleepy, felt the hard lump in her stomach moving up to her throat with the taste of bile. She rose quickly and ran to the slop jar, leaning over it, vomiting. The baby murmured, an overhead beam creaked loudly. Joanna drank some water and lost that too.

She felt miserable; her back ached and her head hurt. She crept into bed and lay there, her mind going around and around in its now familiar groove. Oh, why, why did she have to get pregnant? The rowan branch and the tansy and hensbane—what a fraud, what an old wives' tale! It hadn't worked. And damn Thomas, damn him! Just when she thought she had her life arranged.

Toward dawn she fell asleep and knew nothing until she felt a hand shaking her awake. It was Cecily.

"Peter, the stableboy, is at the door with a message."

"What is it?" Joanna asked in a drugged voice.

The boy, peering around the door, said, "Yer father wishes to see ye at once."

Joanna sat up. Sunlight shafting in through the open shutter fell on her bed. God's bones! She had overslept! Too late to leave. Too late.

"He said to come at once," the boy repeated.

"Very well." Ivo knew. He would not have sent for her otherwise, and for one wild moment she thought of picking up the baby, dashing down the stairs and out the gate. But she knew, even close to panic, how futile such an attempt would be. "I shall be along presently."

He was waiting for her, sitting upright on a stool, his back ramrod-stiff, his face expressionless except for an occasional twitch at the corner of his white, hard mouth. The two older boys had been sent down to the courtyard to play, but Katrine was there, her baby on her lap, a gleam of satisfaction lurking in her boiled fish eyes.

"Good morrow, Papa." Joanna gave him a tentative smile.

He said nothing, did not return her greeting, did not smile, did not nod, just stared at her.

"Peter said you wanted to see me. What is it, Papa?"

He continued to stare at her in silence, the twitch of his mouth becoming more and more pronounced. A little tremor ran down Joanna's spine. The story she had concocted on the way over repeated itself in her mind. She had been attacked, she would tell him, raped, a story she would not have dared tell Alys, but one she hoped Ivo would believe. Sir Thomas, she would say, forced his way into her room one night and had taken her. Why had she not raised a hue and cry? Two reasons, she would explain—one does not cry out against a ravisher who is the lord's son, and her own shame.

But Ivo did not question her; he said nothing. The silence grew. The baby laughed; Katrine hushed it, clucking her tongue. Somewhere under them in the keep a man began to whistle "God send thee good ale," a woman laughed, the man went on whistling.

"Papa . . ."

Ivo's throat worked. "Come here," he ordered in a harsh voice. "Closer—*closer!*"

When she reached him, he lifted his hand and struck her full across the face so hard she staggered back. Stunned, her fingers went to the painful welt rising on her cheek. "Papa . . . !"

"Whore! Trollop!" he roared.

"Papa . . ."

"I could kill you—kill you with my bare hands!" He half rose from the stool, and she shrank back in fright. The veins on his forehead stood out like purple ropes, and his eyes were black with rage. Never, never in all her life, not even with Mariotta, had Joanna seen him in such a state. It was as if all the suppressed anger of a lifetime had exploded.

"Why?" he shouted. "Answer me, why?"

"Papa—he . . ."

"Why have you done this to me? Shamed me in front of the whole castle, noble and varlet alike? Why? Do you think I ought to allow you to live after this? Do you? Answer me!"

"Papa . . . he . . ."

"When this happened the first time . . ." He swallowed, making a visible effort to control himself, for the baby had started to scream in fright. "The first time I forgave you—but—but to sin again in such a way—would you have me grandfather to a string of bastards? Well—answer me!"

She tried. "Papa—he . . ."

"Do not lie, trollop, do not try to fob me off with that old, hoary tale—'He forced me!'"

"But, Papa—he did!"

He rose up like a shot, and even as she took a step back he slammed her full across the mouth. "That is for lying! I warned you!"

She felt the blood oozing from her lip, but she made no

move to wipe it away. She knew Katrine was watching, was enjoying every minute of this nightmarish scene, and hate twisted her heart. It was unfair, unfair, unfair, *unfair!* If her father had not married, if he had gone on living just with her, he would have been more lenient, understood, and if she found herself pregnant, Ivo would have forgiven her as he had done earlier. But Katrine had poisoned his mind against her, turned him into this sudden, frightening stranger she did not recognize. Katrine, nattering and nagging, Katrine who hated her.

"The first time—the first time," Ivo repeated, his voice choking, "I took into account your youth, your innocence— but to have you wantonly bed with a man again! Nay, God forgive me for siring such a trollop. You are your mother all over again, and He is punishing me for having turned a blind eye to her wickedness. Aye—I knew—God help me, I knew she cuckolded me. I knew. But I could not—she was—she had such a wretched life when she was a child—abused—starved and so unhappy. Better for her soul had I beaten and up-braided her. And now God is taking His revenge. *You.* I will not make the same mistake twice. I give you no forgiveness. May God damn you! May God..."

"Papa!" she cried in terror.

He stared at her out of bloodshot eyes. "Let the church curse you then, I shan't. I do not know you. I have never known you. You are not my daughter. I never want to see you again. Leave Nareham, just as you planned, but not to Thexted. If you dare show your face there I shall have you whipped through the streets as a whore. Go—I care not where—anywhere as long as people do not know me and cannot point to you as my shame."

"Oh, Papa—please..." she begged. But he rose and, turning his back on her, went to the window, where he stood staring blindly out at the chapel tower across the yard.

She had a frightening moment of vertigo, as if she had suddenly been cast headlong into an abyss. Clinging to the brink, conscious of Katrine's smirk, she recovered enough to make one more attempt.

"Papa! Please..." But it was useless. She flung a last appealing look at the obdurate back and, resisting the impulse to shout "Damn you!" to Katrine, left the room.

Once on the stair outside, her knees buckled again, and it took her a few moments before she could gather the strength to descend to the courtyard. As she made her way back to the manor house she felt the tears burning her eyes, but she did not weep. The hurt had gone too deep for weeping. She had anticipated Ivo's displeasure, but never had she imagined he would disown her, cutting her off from the one human tie she always felt could never be severed. He had denied her as his flesh and blood; she was no longer his daughter, and she knew that he would not change his mind. He was inflexible, righteous, a pietist, and yet she loved him. That was why her heart ached with such a terrible pain. If she had been indifferent toward him, his repudiation might have disturbed her, but she would not have been as devastated as she was now. She loved him, adored him; he had been her guiding star from childhood on. To have fallen out with him in such a final way was like death itself.

Curiously she felt no remorse for having gone to bed with Thomas. Her regret was that she had been caught at it; she had conceived. And she hated the child inside her more than ever, hated it as an excrescence, an abomination which had mysteriously taken hold and would not let go. She was trapped with it, trapped here at Nareham. Her father had meant what he said about having her whipped through the streets of Thexted. But he could not banish her from Nareham, as he threatened, if Alys chose for her to stay.

In the weeks that followed, Alys made no reference to Joanna's condition. Her youngest son, Andrew, had come home to Nareham for his dubbing, and she was too preoccupied with arranging the festivities which would mark the ceremony to think of much else.

Then one morning, Andrew stumbled in dismounting from his horse and fell on a rusty hoe. He received only a bloody scratch and paid no further heed to it, until he woke the following day to find his leg painfully swollen and streaked with red. By evening he was in a raging fever. A leech hurriedly fetched from Thexted bled him, and when that did not relieve his condition amputation was advised. Andrew's wife, Cecilia, screamed, "Nay!" His mother forbade it, and a distraught Harold de Ander, easily persuaded by the women, ordered the leech from the castle. Two days later young Andrew died, leaving a weeping wife and an unborn, fatherless child.

Thomas was summoned home for the funeral. Joanna witnessed his arrival from her window, drawn to it by a commotion and clatter of hooves in the courtyard. She saw her erstwhile lover riding past the well head, his squire and two men-at-arms behind him. He was dressed for the road, but elegantly, in a thigh-length fawn-colored cotehardie of Sicilian silk figured with a pattern of branched leaves, the fitted sleeves buttoned from wrist to elbow. Around his hips rode a jeweled belt. His tights were particolored, horizontally striped in red and green, as were his hose, while his feet were shod in red-and-white-checkered leather. Bareheaded, his brimless hat in his lap, he seemed to be riding to a wedding rather than a funeral.

When he dismounted he glanced up at Joanna's window. She hesitated before she waved and smiled, but he had already turned away. She wondered if he would deny the child, as John Hawkwood had done. Strange that it had not occurred to her before. Suppose, too, that Alys had changed her mind? She had accepted the child as Thomas's the day Joanna fainted in the solar, but she had not said a single word about it since.

Joanna sat down on the bench and folded her hands, a sic dreariness seeping into her blood. She was not carrying this baby well. The nausea, which should have left her after the first few weeks, persisted; she could scarcely keep more than hard, stale bread dipped in wine on her stomach. She had grown thin, pale. There was not a morning she did not wake wishing she would have a miscarriage before nightfall. But she did not miscarry; the baby was still there. And now if Thomas denied paternity, Alys, upset by Andrew's death, might pack her off to God knew where.

Joanna gazed disconsolately at a spot on the floor. Never had she felt so exhausted, so torpid, so heavy-hearted. It seemed that her longings when she had walked in the garden that May evening long ago to encounter John Hawkwood had been light compared to the burden she carried now. Her father had not spoken to her since that frightening scene in the keep. He had tried to avoid a chance meeting, and when he could not, looked through her as if she did not exist. He hated her. And here at the manor house she was surrounded by hostility too, by people of ill will. The moment Alys withdrew her protection they would goad, taunt, spit on her, openly call Edmund a bastard. She realized now that the castle servants had always disliked her, secretly hoarding their petty jealousies, their enmity, waiting for a sign of weakness or a fall from favor to spill their hatred out.

She thought of the house carls who could snub or fawn, the servitors, the silly kitchen maids, the grooms, the hall porter, the horde of pale-faced menials lined up against her and Edmund. Lickspittles! All of them. And as she pictured them a sudden anger kindled in her breast. Why should she care what *they* thought, what *they* said? Petty bow-wows, mincing varlets. Her back stiffened; she lifted her head. The strong fiber that was her heritage, the muscle, sinew, nerves, the core of her soul which had been tempered by hunger, hardship and pain, refused to grovel or to admit defeat. Let them say or do what they would, let them try to insult, to mock, she would meet them with the ultimate weapon—indifference. As for her present predicament, there was a way out, there must be, and she would find it, for Edmund's sake as well as her own. She had money, not much, but if she could not go to Thexted then she would go somewhere else, a larger town, London perhaps, a place where two bastards more or less would hardly be noticed. She would turn her hand to anything—sewing, baking pies, cleaning poultry, washing clothes, anything that would earn a shilling or two. Hard work had never dismayed her.

Nones—three o'clock. Summoned by Alys, Joanna stood at the solar door, hesitated, then knocked. She went in, as always, without waiting to be asked and found Alys alone.

She bent her knee in a deep curtsy.

"I wanted to talk to you in private," Alys said. The black mourning gown she wore gave a sallow cast to her skin, made her look unwell, but in no way diminished her air of cold haughtiness. She was not one to mourn openly; only her puffy eyelids indicated her personal grief. Andrew, the youngest, her baby, had been her favorite.

"I have been discussing you at some length with Sir Thomas," Alys said. "Have you seen him since his arrival?"

"Nay, lady." Joanna squelched a dart of fear, clenching her fists at her sides, bringing her chin up unconsciously as if about to receive a mortal blow.

"It seems Sir Thomas is still infatuated with you." Alys surveyed her, the cool eyes passing over her body as though she were a cow set out at Thexted Fair. "He acknowledges the child you are carrying is his."

Joanna tried not to smile. "He is a man of honor, my lady."

"I do not need you to tell me what a fine and noble man my son is. What I want to know is—do you love him?"

The question startled Joanna. Love him? What difference did it make? A knight to be loved by a seamstress? But she said, with the proper amount of feeling, "I do. I love Sir Thomas with all my heart."

"And the father of your first child? You have never told me who he was."

"A passing knight, one who came to the banquet when Sir Thomas was dubbed. He did not tell me his name. But I feel nothing for him—nothing."

"And if he should return?"

"I would spit in his face, lady."

Alys drew back. This was a little too vehement, a servant spitting at a nobleman! The effrontery of the wench! But she decided to gloss it over. "I want to make sure of your loyalty to Sir Thomas. I would not want you to be carrying on with another."

"I care for no man, lady, but Sir Thomas. I would not look at anyone else."

"I should hope not. He is a lusty youth, as you mayhap know, and he needs a mistress. His betrothed, Hulda du Pynne, is still too young for marriage."

So the du Pynne female had won.

"He must have a woman," Alys continued. "Not a depraved trollop who will give him a disease. Do you understand? And since he seems to desire your body, I feel that you can best satisfy his needs."

"Thank you, my lady."

"I have a dower manor, Thorsby. It has been neglected somewhat. The plague killed off most of the village, and the remaining peasants have managed through the years to buy their freedom and have gone elsewhere. The manor's fields lie fallow, but you will be comfortable there. It is closer to London, and Sir Thomas can come and visit you more frequently."

At one time Joanna might have been somewhat dismayed by this offer, but in her present situation she could hardly believe her good fortune. What luck, what incredible luck! To be the acknowledged paramour of a knight was a position no one among her equals could scorn. She would be leaving Nareham without shame, after all, and established in a manor house, not as a servant, but as its mistress. She would have nothing to do there but please Thomas. A manor house! How generous of Alys, who was rarely generous! My God, Joanna thought, why is she doing this? To get Thomas away from Damosel Maude, who still lurked about? Perhaps his mother was afraid that despite the du Pynne betrothal her second son might get involved with Maude the way Andrew had become with Cecilia. Alys did not want him at Nareham; she had given him a plaything to amuse himself with at Thorsby. And Joanna was not in the least disturbed to be Thomas's diversion.

"You are to gather your belongings at once, since you will be leaving before Prime in the morning."

"I shall be ready."

"The child, the other one..."

And for a moment Joanna's heart stopped.

"I suppose it will be all right. Thomas does not seem to mind as long as it is kept out of his way."

"He's little trouble, a good child. He—"

"Remember. You are to be loyal and true to Sir Thomas. If I should hear of anything, the merest whisper, 'twill go bad for you."

"I promise by the cross. I shall be faithful and loyal, lady. And, again, my thanks."

She had much to be thankful for. She would not have to go to London, to struggle there in God knew what poverty. She was going to be nurtured, protected. And Edmund too. That was the important thing. Edmund.

The one and only thing Joanna regretted as she rode through the gates with Edmund in her arms was not being able to say goodbye to her father. After her interview with Alys de Ander she had gone to the village, pleading with Sir Theobold to intercede on her behalf. The priest had aged considerably in the last six months. Some secret malady was eating his flesh away so that his jowls hung down in quivering dewlaps just as they had done during the plague. His head as well as his hands shook, but he had the same cheerful smile, the same willingness to be of help. He had agreed to talk to Ivo, a conversation which he later reported had been short and fruitless. "I had three sons," Ivo was reported to have said. "All died. I never had a daughter."

Joanna tried not to think of it. Shifting Edmund in her arms, she waved to the grumpy gateward. She was glad to be leaving, glad that she had Thorsby to look forward to. Thomas had come to her bed last night, ardent, eager, tender, and she had let herself go, allowed her body to respond to his with keen enjoyment. What if she did not love him? What did it matter? She could not remember what love was, why she had ever thought she loved John Hawkwood. She had given

140

him all the fiery passion of her young girlhood; it had been spent, squandered on a man who had thrust her away with a laugh. Love, her love, centered now on Edmund; for the rest she cared not a whit.

Ahead of her rode her future, Sir Thomas in his silken cotehardie. *He* swore he loved her. That she doubted, but again, what did it matter? Behind on a pair of mules rode her servants—*hers*—a crone, Ursula, and two kitchen maids, Beth and Agnes. Ursula, thin as a stick, with snapping black eyes and a yellow, gap-toothed smile, had experience as a midwife and looked capable enough, but the maids, frightened and tearful, seemed rather simpleminded. Nevertheless, Joanna was glad to have them; even a lackwit could be taught something.

They stopped at an inn for the night, a half-timbered hostel that seemed to Joanna rather grand, for it boasted two stories and a tall breastwork chimney. They ate a good supper in the common room, roast mutton washed down with ale, and were later shown to an upper chamber, which they shared with a merchant and his two assistants. The servants and Thomas's squire and men-at-arms slept in the stable.

They traveled all the next day under a hazy September sky. Every now and again a flock of migrating birds passed overhead, cawing and flapping as they winged southward over forests tinged with the first hint of gold, yellow and flame. Thomas fell back to ride beside her, pointing out the sights, a castle, a bridge, an old Roman wall, touching her hand, smiling at her. She was hardly conscious of the unfolding scenery, however, of the people they met on the road, wayfarers plodding along on foot, clerics astride mules, knights with their meinies at a gallop, raising clouds of dust. She had always been a poor traveler, and now, burdened by the child in her arms and the uneasy life beginning to kick and make itself known inside, she found the long hours in the saddle a torture. Only the prospect of journey's end at Thorsby kept her spirits from lagging.

Toward evening of the fourth day, just as the crimson sun began to descend the western horizon, they crossed a meadow and a shallow grassy ditch which Joanna realized must once have been a moat. Climbing a slope, the little train paused before a pair of iron gates set in a crumbling stone wall. A small gatehouse, also in half ruin, perched above it, deserted, its slitted windows leering down at them.

Thorsby? Joanna wondered. Oh, no, it couldn't be. Not

Thorsby, not yet. They were stopping here for the night, seeking shelter at some poor manor house that belonged to a friend of the de Anders.

"Ho! Gateward!" Thomas's squire, Will, shouted. "Ho!"

Thomas leaned down and clapped Will on the shoulder. "There's no one there, you fool, can't you see? Open the gates yourself."

The squire dismounted, and by heaving his shoulders against the scaling gates, broke the rusted chain which held them together, and they crashed open with a dull clang. The company rode through. Just inside, against the ruined wall, stood a forlorn cottage, its thatched roof sagging, its broken door agape, its garden choked with tall weeds. No smoke rose from its clay-hole chimney, no face appeared at the small unshuttered window. It reminded Joanna of the deserted cots at Nareham just after the plague, and she shivered. Ahead of them on either side an impregnable thicket overgrown with thistles and creeping vines barred the way.

Will said, "I see no road, sir."

"Idiot! Use your sword and clear one."

Slashing through the thorny undergrowth, Will rode ahead. Joanna's horse balked, refusing to pass through the torn hedge. She dug her heels into its flanks, beat at it with her free hand, but it remained stubbornly unmoving, shaking its head with little shuddering snorts. Behind her, Ursula clucked, hawked and spat, "Give it the back o' yer hand." Joanna kicked it again, but she might as well have kicked a stone wall. Finally Thomas dropped back, took the bridle angrily and yanked the reluctant beast forward.

A wall of bilious green closed around them, the jagged thorns tearing at their clothes, monstrous shrubs and plants, brake, dock and giant thistle slapping at their faces. Rising above the dense, tangled vegetation stood a tall, solitary, leafless beech, and in its skeletal forked branches a hunched, beady-eyed black rook perched, peering down at them. It croaked loudly and ruffled its wings as Joanna passed beneath, and a shiver of uneasiness ran up her spine. Edmund stirred, awoke, gazing up at her with large, trusting eyes. "'Tis all right," she whispered, holding him closer.

Presently a path of sorts appeared and though still rank with weeds, the going became easier. They were riding now beneath an avenue of lofty wych elms, and through their high branches gleamed the red sunset sky streaked with livid purple. In the fading light Joanna discerned several tumbledown cots with caved-in roofs and broken shutters, ghostly and deserted, like the lonely gate lodge, and a moment later they were lost to view behind a towering row of hedges. On they rode, in single file, Will at the head, then the two men-at-arms, followed by Thomas and Joanna, with the servants and baggage bringing up the rear.

Suddenly a strong wind arose from out of the west, a cold gusting wind whipping at the slender trees, bending and swaying them in wildly creaking torment. Joanna reached around and brought her hood up over her head only to have it blown back to her shoulders again. Clutching the reins tightly with one hand, she replaced the hood with the other and held onto it. The gusts grew stronger, shrieking, whistling, howling, lowering to an eerie moan, then suddenly letting out a hoot that made Joanna's heart jump and her skin crawl. The sky grew a deeper purple, then slowly began to darken into slate gray, and yet they rode on with no manor house, not another cot, not a single habitation of any sort in sight. The men had long since fallen into grim-faced silence. The birds seemed to have vanished. Even the rooks who had been wheeling high above the trees suddenly disappeared. The sound of the raging wind filled the dusky, eerie world, the lost, lost wind, abandoned, angry like the spirits of the unshriven dead who come back to haunt the living.

"Thomas..." Joanna ventured during a brief lull. "Thomas, where are we going?"

But he did not answer, did not even turn to look at her.

She clutched Edmund closer. The leather rein bit into her flesh, and when she let go of the hood to adjust the rein, her mount, feeling the slackness, pranced sideways, and would have gone off under the trees had she not jerked it back. The wind again snatched the hood from her head, teasing and tangling her hair. She felt cold, frozen and anxious, an anxiety slowly turning to fear.

Where were they? To what destination were they riding? None, Joanna decided. They were traveling nowhere. They had left the world of real people, familiar objects and known landmarks far behind and had stumbled into a strange country, a place beyond the pale. They were lost, irretrievably lost. Else why should Thomas remain so strangely quiet? Lost and night falling fast. The elms thrashed, the wind galloped, even the clip-clop sound of the horses' hooves were drowned out by the rush of the ghostly tempest.

Suddenly a dog began to bark and the file halted. Joanna,

rising slightly in the stirrups, saw the edge of a mortared wall and a black roof. Will, still at the head, started once more, the others following, passing another gate, this one opened wide. Beyond an ancient gnarled oak rose the manor house, a huddle of gray stone beneath an ugly square tower. An old man with bleary eyes stood before the ponderous oaken door restraining a mastiff that growled and showed yellow teeth.

"'Tis ye?" He peered up at Thomas. "'Tis ye, Harold de Ander, Lord of Nareham?"

"Nay, his son, Sir Thomas."

"Ah—Sir Thomas." The oldster nodded his gray head. "Welcome then, sir knight, welcome to Thorsby."

High above through the trees a wisp of ragged cloud revealed the last red reflection of the dying sun in a narrow, bloodshot, malevolent leer.

Chapter IX

The interior of Thorsby proved no more inviting than the outside. As Joanna entered the great hall with Edmund clinging to her neck, she was struck by the dank chill and the sour odor of mildew, the effluvium of a house long closed up and fouled with its own air. The chamber, lit only by a feeble fire on the central hearth, seemed vast, receding into smoke-stained shadowy stone walls and a ceiling vaulted with rotting, cobwebbed timbers. The packed-earth floor, where the keeper's mastiff crouched eyeing them warily, was devoid of rushes and littered with debris, old gnawed bones, discarded cheese rinds and broken bits and pieces of God knew what. At the farthest end the lord's dais sat on a raised platform over which hung a blackened shield bearing Alys's family arms. The trestle tables and benches were stacked against one sweating wall, a wall decorated with a single dingy tapestry. Dead leaves had drifted in through the shuttered windows and lay along the deep ledges and in crumpled little husks on the floor.

Ursula dragged forward a bench, and Joanna, stiff with cold, exhaustion and disappointment, sank down upon it. She had not expected this, not this blight, this ruin. Her imagination had painted a house, smaller than Nareham, a little less elegant perhaps, but still weathertight, the floor rush-strewn, a corner hearth, furniture, an arras-covered wall. Why—why, Thorsby was little better than the bailiff's cot in the village! Only larger and uglier. And how she had prided herself, fool that she had been, mistress of a manor house, Joanna of Thorsby. Ha!

Thomas was saying to his squire, "Ride to the village, rouse someone. We need food, a small keg of ale. Wait—you will have to pay for it; they are not serfs." He took a few coins from his pouch.

Dull-eyed, numb, Joanna stared at the smoking fire. She might have known that Alys would give grudgingly, that this manor house would be of little worth, a poor residence, a gray fungus on the desolate landscape. "You will be comfortable there," Alys had said. Comfortable. Joanna shivered again.

Thomas went to the door and ordered the men-at-arms to

stable the horses. "See what hay you can find," he called. Then, turning to the two maids who stood huddled over the hearth, he said, "Why do you stand there like dolts? Fetch wood. Go on, go on! Get on with you now!"

"Where are we to get it, Sir Thomas?" Beth asked in a small frightened voice.

"How should I know? Outside, you imbeciles, find some outside."

"But 'tis dark, sire," Beth whined, her fear of the night greater than her fear of Thomas.

"I know 'tis dark, rabbits. Go!" He raised his hand, and the two girls fled.

"And you, you old crone, get busy. The kitchen is behind, there must be a pot somewhere."

"And what am I to put in it, my good knight?" Ursula demanded, unruffled by Thomas's scowl and threats. She had received too many blows in her long life to fret about taking another now.

"Find something. Water, if nothing else."

When she had gone he turned to Joanna. "Tired, sweet?"

"Aye."

"I did not realize Thorsby would be in quite such a state of disrepair. Why—why it has been years—not since I was a small boy..." His voice trailed off as he looked around, trying not to show his own dismay. The truth was he had no recollection of Thorsby at all, having been brought there when a babe in arms. Though his mother had spoken of it— her dower castle—he had no idea a noble household could be so shockingly plain, so poverty-stricken, even if neglected.

"Ah well," he sighed, "we shall soon put it to rights, eh, love? Give us a kiss." She lifted her head, but as he pressed her lips, Edmund began to whimper.

"I won't want him in our bed," Thomas reminded her.

She said nothing. She was too tired to speak. Her ankles had swollen to throbbing painfulness, her head to a pulsating ache. The gloomy hall, the chill little eddies playing on the back of her neck, Thomas's rejection of Edmund—no matter how oblique—combined to weigh her already drooping spirits. She felt lonely and depressed. And she was hungry. They had not eaten since morning, a hasty meal of bread and ale which she had lost on the way.

Thomas went to the fire, crouching on his heels before it, holding his hands to the flame. Watching him, she suddenly thought of her father, and a sick longing for Nareham twisted her heart. Not for the manor house or the keep chambers, but for the cot, the bailiff's cot she still remembered well. In her mind's eye she saw the close, the yellow blooming asphodel that came up every spring at the doorsill, the apple trees feathered in pale pink, the hens clucking and pecking at her as she rooted for eggs, her mother, vibrant, alive, warm Mariotta, sitting with a customer over a cup of ale. She could feel her father's hand on her head. "Joanna"—and his blue eyes smiling affectionately at her. "Joanna."

Suddenly Edmund began to cry. She shifted him, held his small body closer.

She could not go back; nothing, not even God, could bring the past alive again. She must do what she could; no self-pity, no hankering, no tears. She had set herself a course, unwittingly, mayhap, but it was a course she must follow to the end.

"Hush." She rocked the child in her arms.

Ursula shuffled back into the hall, balancing a tripod over one shoulder, her other sagging with the weight of a large iron pot.

Thomas rose to his feet, but he made no move to help her. Not only was it beneath a man (any man) to assist with womanly tasks, but for a noble to extend a hand to a servant was unthinkable, unheard of. Ursula could have fallen into the fire and he would not have made the slightest move to drag her out. Nor would the crone expect anything from her master. He would have demeaned himself in her eyes if he had suddenly said, "Here—let me."

Ursula set the tripod up and, looking over at Joanna, said, "What ails the boy?"

"He is tired and hungry," Joanna answered, bouncing him lightly in her arms.

Thomas went up to the lord's dais and sat down in the great carved chair, the place of honor. "Aye," he pronounced, "we shall be quite cozy here."

The two maids returned, their arms laden with twigs and branches. Throwing them on the fire, piece by piece, they built it up into a roaring tower of flames.

"Not all of it," Joanna warned. "We must have some to cook with."

Cook what? their eyes asked.

"Go out to the kitchen and help Ursula."

In a little while the men-at-arms returned, one carrying a cask, a portion of which he and the other must have sampled, for they both were unsteady on their feet. "We found this in the stable, Sir Thomas," the beefy one said. The other lurched up and set Thomas's saddlebags on the dais table.

"Aye, and drank most," Thomas said. "Well, let's have it, then."

Thomas rummaged in his bag and brought out a horn cup. He filled it, drank, made a wry face and spat. "'Tis not worth swill for pigs. I wondered why you bothered to bring it to me rather than drink it all yourselves. God curse you." The curse, however, was delivered perfunctorily. They were his father's retainers, men he must provide for, as he must for even the old crone, the two imbecilic maids, and his Joanna. His Joanna. He had made a grave error in not bringing sufficient supplies to tide them over. But he had assumed the village would provide him with whatever he needed; he had assumed the old goat of a keeper would have something set by in the larder. But the old goat had conveniently disappeared, and according to Ursula the cupboard was bare.

Restive, the men retired to the shadows. Edmund, at last, slept in his mother's arms. The maids returned and sat down on the floor and stared into the fire. At least the room had become warmer—not much, but some. No one spoke. The wind outside, quiescent one moment, the next whooping past, rattled the shutters. The fire spit and crackled. They sat, each sunk in his own silence, while time ebbed and flowed.

Ursula finally managed to find a parcel of stale oaten cakes, a stinking chunk of cheese and some dried beans, and by foraging around at the kitchen door a few hen's eggs. All these she put into the pot, mixing them with water and ale, and before long had a meal, sparse, scant, but providing a mouthful or two for each of the company.

When they had finished, Will arrived with a mordant goose he had found outside the courtyard wall. "'Tis the best I could do, sire," he apologized. "There is no village closer than Shurbridge across the fen. I shall have to go in the morning, though I am told the folk there are not a friendly lot."

"Who has said so?"

"The old gatekeeper. The Shurbridge peasants claim Thorsby is bewitched."

The maids gasped and looked around with white-rimmed eyes; the two men-at-arms crossed themselves.

"Ha! Ghosties we have, do we?" Thomas said, annoyed. "A murrain on them! Lazy improvident churls. God's bones, they'll make up any story to keep themselves amused."

"Thorsby is very old," Thomas explained as he lighted the way up the outside stone staircase to the bedchamber above. "Some say it goes back to Saxon times."

Joanna's teeth were chattering. She had given Edmund over to Ursula, and she missed the warmth of his little body.

"My mother comes from a proud family," Thomas went on, pushing open a heavy door. They entered a shadowy room as cold and as bare as the hall below. "One William de Grenon held this castle for three months against King John in—what?—1215, I believe 'twas."

He fixed the lighted rush in a sconce on the wall. Joanna saw a huge box-shaped bed covered with several moldy fur skins and a lidless coffer at its foot. There was nothing else; not even a crude stool or a bench on which to sit.

"Thorsby was also said to have sheltered one of Thomas à Becket's assassins," Thomas continued, removing his cloak, hanging it on a rusty peg. "But no one can really vouch for that. However, my mother has a parchment which states that Eleanor of Aquitaine tarried here for a fortnight. Mayhap slept in this very room."

Joanna managed through blue lips, "Oh?"

"Come, sweet, give me your cloak." He stretched out his hands.

"I—I cannot. I am so cold, Thomas."

"I shall warm you." He took her into his arms and kissed her, and she clung to him, not so much from affection as from a need to shut out the cold.

He finally got her to shed her clothes, done hurriedly with no time for kisses in between, and he gallantly carried her to bed. Despite her exhaustion it was a sleepless night. For one, Thomas, denied her body for these past few nights, made love to her not once but several times, and for another, the odorous, stained mattress beneath, prickly with quilled goosefeathers, was infested with fleas, flitting, hopping monsters who, finding her white limbs more tasty than Thomas's tougher flesh, attacked her with hungry malice. She scratched, she yawned, she twisted and turned, and in between tried not to think of Edmund, how he was faring with Ursula, tried not to dwell on Thorsby, damply rotting and decrepit, Thorsby, her new home.

She finally fell asleep toward morning, and when she woke she found Thomas had been up before her. Hastily getting into her clothes, she came down to the hall. It was deserted, but she heard sounds coming from beyond the dais, and following them she entered the kitchen, a large chamber which at one time had been part of the hall. Ursula was plucking the goose. Close by on the floor sat Edmund, smiling and waving his arms at his mother. Such a good child, she thought, even-tempered, happy, complaining only when hungry.

Joanna lifted him and held him against her cheek, and his lips brushed her cheek in an inadvertent kiss. Joanna laughed. "My darling," she muttered.

Edmund said, "Mama..." very distinctly.

"How bright he is, Ursula, how quick to learn."

Ursula took a knife and hacked the goose down the middle. "'Twill be a wonder he won't grow up crooked," she said sourly. She believed any child removed from swaddling clothes before two years of age, as Edmund had been, was doomed to the life of a cripple. Joanna, however, could not bear to see her son bound and trussed like a fowl, his face red with heat, and so had freed him before setting out for Thorsby.

Edmund's fat little fingers tugged at her hair and earrings, and Joanna laughed again, delighted. What a love, what an angel! How could she be anything but happy with such a son? Supposing the manor was not what she had expected. She could make it into a pleasanter place, more habitable, more attractive. She would wheedle money from Thomas, hire a carpenter to fashion decent stools and chairs. She, Ursula and the maids would whitewash the walls, and when they were through they could start on a tapestry. She had canvas and thread in her coffer. The shield over the dais could be burnished, a cloth put on the table, the lord's chair padded in crimson, rushes strewn on the floor—oh, so many improvements made. It would be a house for Edmund to love, to be happy in. And Thomas's bastard too. Would not Thomas want his child, a son with noble blood in his veins, to have a proper home? Surely he could see that no matter how many illustrious people had slept at Thorsby the house lacked comfort. And for the first time she began to look upon the coming child with something less than distaste. She had to admit now that perhaps her pregnancy had been fortunate. Thomas, in acknowledging the baby, would provide for it and go on doing so even if he should tire of her (not likely, at least for years), a provision that would benefit both her and Edmund. She must try to be kinder, more affectionate, to her lover, let him believe that bearing his child meant a great deal to her.

Reminded of him, she said, "Have you seen Sir Thomas this morning?"

"The master and his squire's gone out to get meat for the table," Ursula replied, separating the yellow-clawed feet from the goose's legs with a well-aimed blow.

"Oh? There can't be very good hunting in the thicket."

"There's supposed to be deer beyond old Thorsby village."

"The empty cots we saw?"

"Aye. The village has long been shut of its people." She hacked off the goose's head and tossed it in the pot. "So Geralt, the gatekeeper, says. A talky person when he has the inclination. He told me a good many things."

Joanna nudged the child's playful hand from her lips. "What things?"

Ursula looked up and hastily crossed herself with a bloody hand. "Geralt says there's a curse on this place—'tis haunted by a creature half man, half beast. They call it the Centaur."

"Pshaw! You heard what Sir Thomas said last night. There *are* no haunts. Yet you believe Geralt, swallowing an old wives' tale." But even as she said it, she remembered the wind shrieking in the dark tossing elms and made a surreptitious sign of the cross with her thumbs.

"That's what I told Geralt—an old wives' tale. But he said why did I think the peasants cleared out of Thorsby, those that were left after the sickness—and not a single one ever came back. No one who knows Thorsby at all will set foot inside the gate."

"Then why did the old fool of a gatekeeper stay?"

"That's what I asked, and he got an answer for that too. Says he's too old to leave, got no kin to offer him a roof anyway. He's made himself comfortable here, so he can put up with the haunt. Whenever the Centaur goes galloping past he just says an *Ave* fast as he can and it disappears."

"I shouldn't say anything to Sir Thomas," Joanna warned. "He doesn't take kindly to such talk. By the by, where are Beth and Agnes?"

"Gathering firewood. They don't have sense to do much else."

They came in shortly, both white-faced, breathless, spilling sticks of wood from their trembling arms.

"Ursula—oh, Ursula," Agnes began, "what are we to do?"

"What is it?" Joanna asked. "One would think you had seen a ghost."

They squealed, dropping the remainder of the wood.

"Has Geralt been talking to you?" Ursula asked. "Aha, I might have known."

"He says..."

"You silly goosehead. Never mind what he says. Get busy with the fire. If we're to have food on the table before Judgment Day we ought to make a start with it."

Four days later, on a morning sparkling with cold dew, Joanna bade Thomas goodbye, kissing him as he bent from the saddle. He was returning to London, and he did not know how long he would be gone. He gave her a purse to buy provisions from the village and left the two men-at-arms to serve as guards.

"The old fool at the gate is worthless," he said. "But you will be safe with the others, my pretty. Remember, you are mistress here now, Dame Joanna."

He had been good to her, and she could not help but feel a little flash of tenderness as she kissed him again. But then she had never actually *disliked* him, she assured herself (forgetting the times past when she had). How could one dislike a young, handsome man who made love so ardently? It was just that he could not compare to Hawkwood (to give the devil his due), and except for the moments in bed when he brought her to ecstasy, he aroused no real feelings of passion, no longing, no desire. The notion of love she dismissed with scorn. She was neither sorry nor glad to see him leave, and a half hour after he had disappeared through the gate she found herself humming a tune as she sat down to begin the tapestry she had in mind to grace one of the bare walls.

He returned two months later as the autumn waned and the naked elms along the ride stood in drifts of brown, fallen leaves. She had grown in girth and was out of sorts. This baby was more troublesome to carry than Edmund had ever been. Her ankles remained swollen, her breath came in ragged gasps whenever she climbed the stairs, and a terrible lethargy gripped her, not like the former one when she seemed to be floating, but one that dragged at her spirits, weighed on her heart. She felt clumsy, ungainly, trapped in a body that was not her own. She had long since given up the tapestry. The makeshift frame sat in a corner of the hall, pushed aside, forgotten. She had left the cooking and the ordering of food from the village all to Ursula. Even Edmund, vaguely loved, receded into the background. While Thomas was there she tried to make herself pretty, combing her hair, bathing, putting on fresh clothes, returning his kisses, all the while wishing she were alone, wishing she could sink into some kind of blissful oblivion.

Wrapped in her own discomfort, depressed by her burden which grew heavier each day, she nevertheless sensed a change in Thomas—not in his love, for he was still as ardent as ever, but in his mannerisms, in his demeanor. He had always been rather cocky, often assuming a boy's I-dare-you stance, but his cockiness had become subdued, transformed into a self-possession, a mature vanity, sure of itself. Court life, again, had done it. He moved among dukes, princes and barons, the king's and the Black Prince's meinies, men he admired, whose manners and dress he aped. Always fashionable, his clothes now glittered with peacock hues and sparkled with semiprecious gems and gold thread. He wore shirts and drawers of sheerest linen and gold-stamped leather shoes which came to an exaggerated point. His nails, cleaned with the tip of his dagger, never showed the least speck of grime, and his beard, clipped short, neatly barbered, rode his chin with authority. He ordered the servants about with a quiet but firm voice of command and insisted they all address Joanna as dame. Thorsby, which he had accepted earlier, did not measure up now. He spoke of new furnishings, a cushioned settle for the great hall, a new table for the dais, a new feather bed. All to come later, of course, in the future, when he could get his hands on some money, for at present he was embarrassingly short.

After five days he instructed his squire to pack his gear once more. "I hate having to part with you so soon," he told Joanna. "But I have been commissioned by Queen Philippa to carry letters to her kin in Hainault." A duchy in the Low Countries, Hainault was the queen's birthplace, and she often sent couriers there to exchange news and greetings with Flemish relatives. "The ship sails in a fortnight. God willing, I shall be back soon, sweet."

He would have to dismiss the men-at-arms and send them back to Nareham. Their wages and keep were a little more than his strained finances could support at the moment. He did leave a purse, however, for provisions, not as generous as the last, but as he explained while Joanna helped him into

153

his glittering surcoat, "I am in debt to the moneylenders. I receive very little from my royal patron and still less from my illustrious parents. The bulk of my father's largess goes to my older brother, Robert, which I suppose is right, but it does make for hardship."

In November they had their first big storm, a rain that lashed at Thorsby for two solid days and nights. The rotting roof sprang a dozen leaks, and water plunked dismally onto the earthen floor in the great hall or ran in little rivulets down the stone walls. A fairly large trickle falling on Joanna's bed forced her to have it moved to a drier corner, a task which took the maids the better part of a day. The manor house, never warm or dry in any weather, became still damper, the chill wintry mizzle setting green mold upon food and clothes alike. Firewood gathered in the wet burned feebly on the hearth, giving out thick clouds of smoke, smarting and stinging their eyes, sending them into spasms of coughing if they hovered too close.

After the rain abated, the clouds hung on, a low ceiling of shifting gray that seemed to meld with the sodden landscape. Chilled and disheartened, Joanna, sitting as near to the kitchen fire as she dared, would numbly watch Ursula at her work while the maids spoke to one another in hushed voices. Neither Beth nor Agnes had reconciled herself to Thorsby. They lived in constant, agitated fear, a fear which they fed by telling each other remembered stories of past hauntings and evil enchantments. Aside from fetching water and wood and emptying slops there was little for them to do, and the idle hours gave them the leisure to whisper, to speculate and to shiver.

"We must be careful with our stores," Ursula said one morning. She and Geralt had traveled to Shurbridge the preceding day in a mule-drawn cart; the mule, left from their journey to Thorsby, was their sole beast of transport, and the cart had been resurrected from the stable yard, a creaking, complaining contrivance whose wheels threatened to spin loose at every turn. In that rig they had jolted to the village, a distance of some three leagues, for the purpose of buying provisions. They had hoped to bring back a load of foodstuffs but had found most of the peasants away at a fair in Wodd Sapney. From those who remained they bought some chickens, a sack of apples and flour, an old sow and a cask of new ale, paying twice their worth.

"There's not much left in the purse, mistress."

Joanna roused herself. "We can surely make do with what's there until Sir Thomas returns."

"And when will that be?"

"He said not long."

Ursula pursed her lips and kept her counsel.

One morning, Joanna, after a restless night transfused with frightening dreams in which she saw the ghostly Centaur gallop past her window on thundering hooves, came down to the kitchen to find Ursula and Geralt sitting on a bench by the fire sharing a mug of ale. Edmund, on Ursula's lap, gumming a crust of bread, grinned happily at her.

Geralt rose to his feet, removing his high-crowned hat respectfully. "Good morrow, dame."

He stood head bowed, his gnarled hands clutching his hat, a menial in the presence of his mistress. But his subservient manner was a sham. He had lived too many years on his own, and his betters did not awe him. When he could get away with it, he did as he pleased. In Thomas's absence he forsook the gatetower and slept in a small loft above the storeroom at the west end of the great hall, a nook warmer and more weathertight than the drafty tower. Joanna, even if she had noticed his defection from guard duty, did not have the energy or will to remonstrate. Besides, as Geralt himself put it, who in his right mind would want to attack Thorsby?

Ursula, whose respect lapsed as Geralt's attention to duty did when Thomas was away, did not get to her feet (*she* knew Joanna's origins, knew Joanna had no more claim to the title "dame" than she had), but she did notice her mistress's white, blanched face.

"Are you feeling poorly this morning?" she asked anxiously.

"I slept badly." She looked around. "Where are Beth and Agnes?"

"They went out to feed the chickens. Come to think on it, that's been hours ago. Geralt, go find 'em. Tell them to get their lazy hides inside."

He came back shortly, saying he had searched everywhere but neither Agnes nor Beth was to be found. "The chickens ain't been fed either," he complained. "They near et me alive."

"Could they have decided to walk to the village?" Joanna asked.

"What, them? They'd as soon walk to London."

Nevertheless, he was sent to the village to inquire. He

came back at dusk without either Beth or Agnes. No one, he said, had seen them, though he had gone from house to house.

Joanna, listening to him, felt a thrill of fear run down her spine. Ursula said, "They've run off, the fools."

"Did they?" Geralt asked. "Mayhap the Centaur came last night and got 'em."

"Shut up, you lackwit!" Ursula ordered. "They'll be back, you'll see."

But they did not return, not that day or the next or the next. They had simply vanished. No one saw them again. Where they had gone, what had happened, was to remain a mystery, one that continued to haunt them, especially on cold, gusty nights when the wind howled and tore at the shutters.

The world beyond Thorsby soon receded into a distant dream. It seemed to Joanna that she had lived forever in this ancient crumbling manor house with the rain beating against the leaking roof, closed in by damp and mold-pitted walls, hampered by the kicking burden in her belly. She would sit for hours, a piece of unfinished sewing in her hand, staring into the fire. Every now and again she would give a soulful sigh. She wished—she wished what? No sense in wishing for Nareham—that was impossible. And Hawkwood? If he had been a different sort of person, an honorable man, she would be his wife now, carrying his second child. If... But it was futile to follow *that* dream again. She was here—at Thorsby. Still—and her thoughts would take flight again—still, if Thorsby could only have been the place she had imagined, warm, wood-paneled, with carpets strewn over the floor and a comfortable feather bed, if Thomas could come more frequently, stay longer, if—and the "ifs" rolled themselves out in an endless fancy of what might have been.

There were just the three of them now, just the three. Joanna no longer went up to the large chamber, not since the night the girls had disappeared. She had Geralt bring the mattress down and slept on the hall floor, like a serf, Ursula said disapprovingly. But Joanna did not care. To go out in the cold and the wet and climb the stone steps with a wavering torch, to enter that large, inky room where the wind whistled and moaned, not knowing what lay in the shadows, what the night might bring, was more than her faltering courage could face.

One morning she was awakened by a sharp, stabbing

cramp in her loins, the familiar, twisting pain which announced her time had come. She welcomed it, for now, soon, she would be relieved of her burden. A few hard, wrenching pains and it would be over. They said the second child always came much easier than the first.

But they—whoever—were wrong, at least in Joanna's case. She moaned, cursed and suffered hour after hour while Ursula sponged the sweat from her brow, coaxing her to be patient. However, patience was not one of Joanna's strong points, and even a Griselda would have been provoked into shrieking complaint, for it took Joanna two days of agonizing, wrenching labor before the child was born.

It was a boy. But Joanna, worn out by her trial, did not even ask to see it. Turning on her side, she fell into an exhausted sleep.

Chapter X

The child had to be baptized.

His brother had been blessed at the font in Nareham by Sir Theobold, and though Joanna felt little fondness for this second infant she could not condemn it to a life outside the pale. He was of her flesh, after all. But what to name him? Since Thomas was not there to express his wish in the matter, Joanna chose Aleyn. It seemed to her lofty enough for a babe half de Ander.

The priest at Shurbridge, informed by Geralt of Joanna's intent, was less than enthusiastic. A stooped man with failing eyesight, he suggested she go to Wodd Sapney instead. But Geralt, for once roused out of his self-interest, remonstrated—why he himself did not exactly know. Perhaps it was the priest's lordly attitude, perhaps it was the sticking memory of the pastor who long ago had forbidden consecrated burial of his poor mother, who had cut her own throat in a fit of despondency. He reared up and said, "Would ye denȳ saving a soul for Christ?"

Father Simon, taken aback, not expecting this challenge from such a sorry-looking peasant, said, "Certainly I should never deny anyone."

"Then you must baptize this infant." Geralt, of course, neglected to say that said infant was a bastard.

But apparently Father Simon knew. "I find it hard to sanction the fruit of an illegal union."

"What has the child got to do with it?" Geralt asked crossly. The priest, he reasoned, must have learned of the child's bastardy through village gossip, spread by the two men-at-arms, who had wandered over to a Shurbridge alehouse during their stay at Thorsby. The loose-tongued pisspots!

"If the father and mother agree to be married," the priest said, "then I could see my way..."

"Marry? That's their affair, parson. But what of the child?"

Geralt and the priest continued to argue until finally Father Simon reluctantly agreed to the baptism.

Joanna was still weak and ailing when she rode in the mule-drawn cart to Shurbridge, holding Aleyn bundled under her cape against the winter's cold. Ursula with Edmund, capped and wrapped warmly too, jounced alongside her, while Geralt drove the cart, cursing at the mule, spitting every so often over the wheel with truculent vehemence. His argument with the priest having been won, he thought his duty accomplished, and he felt put upon to be called from the warm kitchen fire to whip the mule across the fen on such a bitter day.

The lowering gray sky and the chill little wind nipping at their noses promised snow. A thin scum of ice lay on the muddy road, crunching beneath the wheels, breaking under the mule's step as they lurched through iced-over puddles and jolted across stiff, frozen ridges. They passed a few bare hickory and thorn trees, their black, weblike branches hung with old nests and parasitic mistletoe or bending with the weight of rows of silent sparrows. As they wound their way across the marsh the road became rougher. Here tall coarse grass grew in jigsaw islands surrounded by glassy water reflecting the slate-colored clouds. A white-bellied duck flapped its wings as it skidded across a patch of ice and took off into the wintery air.

When they finally crossed the arched wooden bridge which gave Shurbridge its name, they could look down the hill to the village proper. Two dozen or so daub-and-wattle cots and a forge ringed a green covered with yellowed grass on which grazed a few dirty sheep. The mill and the bakehouse stood apart from the houses across the green facing the church, a spired, whitewashed building with a latticed round window in the steeple. As they rode toward it a child carrying a bucket paused to gawk at them. A woman's voice from behind the hedged close of the nearest cot called, "Jack! Jack!"

A stone suddenly went zinging past Joanna's ear. She turned, and another stone, deflected by her hood, grazed the edge of her forehead. The first stone might have been mischance, but not the second. An upsurge of anger roused her from her lethargy. Her eyes raked the cots. Where? Who? A third stone hit the side of the wagon, and a shrill voice called, "Whore! Whore of Thorsby!"

But Joanna saw nobody; the houses had their backs to her, blank walls and no windows. She scanned the hedges.

A handful of pebbles spattered the backboard. "Best pull yer heads in," Geralt advised, snaking his whip over the mule's back, trying to hurry it along. A small rock narrowly missed his nose. "Imbeciles!"

A stone caught the mule in the rump, and its ears twitched.

Another plunked against its gray hide, and the mule stopped short, kicking its heels in an effort to break free from the cart. Geralt climbed painfully down, cursing and shaking his fist, and began to tug the anxious beast along by the bridle. As they rumbled past the cots the stones commenced to fly fast, stones and offal and rotten eggs. One splattered Joanna's head. The infant began to howl. Edmund sat with round eyes, too terrified to utter a sound. Joanna put her arm around the child, drawing him from Ursula's lap to her own. They crouched low, but still the pellets flew. Did the varlets mean to stone them to death? Joanna could hear the old woman, so rarely ruffled, praying in a frightened voice.

The cottagers, seeing they had nothing to fear in the way of reprisal, began to emerge from the shelter of the hedges, and soon a mob was closing in on them from all sides, waving fists, shouting, "Whore! Trollop!" with a ferocity that chilled the blood. A woman, her head bound in a red rag, her teeth bared, screamed, "Throw the harlot in the river!" A mingy-faced man in a peaked woolen hat thrust a stick between the wheels, halting the cart with a lurching jolt. They swarmed about the wagon, ugly, menacing, their features twisted in mindless, animal rage. An idiot, a pasty-faced lout with a drooling, slack mouth, stuck his chin over the cart's side and grimaced at Joanna. Geralt, who would have fled had he the chance, tried to use his whip, but it was wrested from him.

Terror dried Joanna's mouth, and her heart thumped sickeningly under her ribs. She clutched Edmund and the baby, trying to shield them, cowering, waiting for the first blow.

Suddenly a loud voice ringing with command rose above the tumult. "Stop! Stop! Or by all that is holy I'll see you fry in hell!"

There was a startled pause, hands held in midair, indrawn breaths, an exclamation, "'Tis himself!" and the tide of savagery ebbed, the madness seeping away from the mob's eyes. They parted, and a black-robed figure with a crucifix dangling from his roped belt moved through to the cart.

"God bless ye, Father," Geralt said. "In another moment they'd have had us."

Joanna, a little dizzy, the lump on her forehead throbbing, said, "I, too, thank you, good Father."

"I could not have you stoned in the street by people who have foolishly lost their heads."

Geralt screwed up his eyes, staring at the priest, a tall

man with copper red hair and rugged features. "But you are not Father Simon!"

"Nay," replied the cleric. "I am Father Mark, abbot of Kenham Abbey."

"My lord abbot," Joanna said, bowing her head and kissing his extended hand. Ursula, crossing herself, did the same.

"Father Simon is a pious man," the abbot explained, "and would have intervened in my stead, but he is a little fearful of mobs. One should not blame him overmuch. Fortunately, I had business in Shurbridge and was at the church when I heard the shouting."

The crowd had slowly melted away. Only the little boy with the bucket lingered, but when his mother shrieked, "Jack, come at once!" he fled.

"What is it that you have done to bring these good villagers out for your blood?" the abbot asked Joanna.

"My lord, I have done nothing. They wish to harm me because—because..."

"Because you are Thomas de Ander's concubine?"

"Aye," she answered, more surprised than shamed.

"'Tis true you have been living in sin as Father Simon has told me, then. And you have had this bastard by him. Still— I would rather God judged you than *they*."

"Mayhap He will not judge me too harshly, my lord abbot," Joanna murmured, lowering her eyes. "We love one another truly."

He said nothing, and Joanna, looking up, met a pair of steely blue eyes. He had guessed her lie. There was something about the set of his proud head and the directness of his gaze which made Joanna instinctively feel that this man was different from the clerics she had dealt with in the past, Sir Theobold, Brother Robert, Father Imbard—different and superior.

And she was right. Father Mark came of aristocratic lineage. A second son without a prospective legacy, he had gone into the church because the ecclesiastic hierarchy offered the only honorable opportunity for a nobleman who did not choose a martial career. To his surprise he found he had a calling. He took to theology, to Latin and Greek, to prayer, to fasting, with sincere faith and genuine devotion. Serving God gave him a joy that renewed itself each time he entered a church, each time he went through the ritual of Mass. And he liked people. He loved the good and the bad, the pious and the sinners; the sinners sometimes a little more, for they were most in need of God's pity.

"So you love him," Father Mark said.

Joanna looked away, unable to meet those knowledgeable eyes. "There—there are times when I do."

"Times." He nodded.

Geralt shuffled his feet. Were they going to stand in the middle of the lane all day? He was thirsty, and he needed to answer a call of nature. Did he dare leave them and go over to the side of the ditch? Did one walk away from an abbot without his permission? If he could only sit down. The mule nudged him, nipped at his cheek, and Geralt gave it an angry blow across the muzzle. The mule bared large yellow teeth and brayed.

Edmund laughed delightedly. And the abbot, looking down at the child, smiled. "This is your firstborn?"

"Aye," Joanna replied, adding quickly, "He is baptized Edmund."

"Edmund, ah. And his father?"

"Sir John Hawkwood." It was like making confession, only this was in the open with Geralt and Ursula staring at her.

"Were you his lawful wife?"

"Nay, my lord abbot, he would not marry me." Sin compounded. "But I did love him. I loved him with all my heart," she added, willing tears to her eyes to underscore her sincerity. "I was very young, very foolish. I—I was seduced."

"Seduced the first time—and the second?"

"Sir Thomas was after me—I—I . . ." Her voice faltered as the blue eyes searched her face.

"Did he force you?" The same question her father had asked. But again she found it hard to dissemble.

"Nay, but—but he followed me about, he begged, he implored, he even threatened." A small lie, a little one, a mere stretching of the truth? "And I was a servant in his father's house. I could not refuse him."

"I can see where a man might be persuasive with someone as comely as you, Joanna. They call you Joanna, I am given to understand. Still—to go on living with him . . ."

"'Twas his mother's wish. The babe is his. They, the de Anders, acknowledge him."

Father Mark had put his hand on the edge of the cart as he stood there, and Edmund, drawn by the flash of his ruby ring, had crawled from his mother's lap. Half rising, he grasped hold of the abbot's finger.

Father Mark's face broke into a smile. "He is a handsome lad, bastard or no. Here, Edmund, would you like my ring?" The child, looking up into his eyes, gave a joyous laugh. The abbot leaned down and picked him up, and the child's arms went about his neck as naturally as if he had known this stranger all his brief life.

Joanna had conflicting emotions. She was proud of Edmund's sturdy good looks, his rosy cheeks, his thick fair hair, proud that he had been noticed, had been praised as handsome by no less than an abbot. But she also felt a pang of jealousy, of resentment, that Edmund should show affection for this cleric who had called her sinner and who, in a few minutes, she was sure, would try to wring contrition from her.

The abbot set Edmund back in the cart. "We shall take this matter up, my daughter, after the business at hand. I am sure Father Simon is wondering why we dally here."

Geralt remained outside with the mule and the cart, while the abbot, Ursula, Joanna and her two children entered the church.

Father Simon stood by the font, frowning, stroking his crucifix. The stone bowl which held the holy water was covered by a wooden lid, crisscrossed with a heavy padlocked chain.

Ursula and Joanna gazed at the odd-looking contraption suspiciously.

"Is this the babe?" Father Simon asked the obvious crossly.

"Aye, this is he. I..." Joanna paused uncertainly. "I—I want him to have a proper baptism, Father."

"And why should it not be proper?" he bristled.

"The font..."

The abbot broke in, "Do you not have the same in your parish church?"

"Nay," Joanna denied. Ursula shook her head.

"Why, 'tis simple enough. The good people of Shurbridge and their pastor fear the holy water will be stolen for purposes of sorcery or witchcraft, and so they lock it up."

"You have witches?" Joanna asked, crossing herself hastily.

The abbot smiled. "God forbid. But one cannot be too sure," he added with a faint hint of mockery in his voice.

Father Simon threw him a reproving look. "The devil lurks in the most unsuspected guises," he said with asperity. "In places where one would never think to look. And devil worshipers *will* steal the water for their unholy rites, for their Black Masses. I feel it my duty to keep the blessed water safe and untainted."

"And quite rightly," the abbot assured him, smoothing his face to soberness. "I hope you do not consider me a meddler, nor wonder why I don't stay in my abbey as any decent lord abbot would do. But unfortunately business calls me away from time to time. Now—if you wish me to step aside...?"

"Not at all, not at all," Father Simon said, rather testily, shaking out the full sleeves of his robe, wanting to get on with it. "Who is to stand godfather to the child?"

"I had hoped you would call Sir Thomas his godfather," Joanna said.

"The real father—and without his consent?"

"I know not when he will return to Thorsby."

"Then I cannot see—wait...there is your servant."

Geralt had just sidled in through the door.

"Not my servant," Joanna protested. "The de Anders would never forgive me."

"Without a godfather..."

Father Mark stepped forward. "Let me. I shall be proud to stand for the child."

Father Simon shot him a look from beneath his white bushy brows as if to say, "What is Mother Church coming to?"

"As you will, my lord abbot."

The abbot took the child in his arms and Father Simon intoned, *"Patris et Filii et Spiritus Sancti..."* hurrying through the baptismal recitation as if the hounds of hell were barking at the church door. He finished by dipping the child so precipitately into the water it sputtered and coughed, its face turning purple, unable to cry until the abbot gave it a whack between its shoulder blades.

Holding the howling infant, the abbot asked, "Dame Joanna, do you wish to confess now?"

She did not want to confess, she certainly did not want to repent. But she could not refuse the abbot's polite offer, so close to a command. However skeptical she might be of priests, her upbringing had been too full of the threat of hellfire and brimstone to make it easy to decline. And the painting above the font did not help. Done in vivid colors, it depicted a horned black devil taunting Sloth and Greed with a red-hot pitchfork and his demon helpers roasting an adulteress, a patricide and a thief, each on a spit over a raging

164

fire. She had seen a similar painting in the new castle chapel at Nareham, each figure pointed out and explained by Brother Robert. The one of the adulteress she thought particularly grim.

"Aye, my lord abbot, if you will," Joanna answered.

She followed him down through the nave to the side, where a confessional box stood. When the shutter over the grille slid back she took a deep breath and began, her recitation starting with John Hawkwood. Her speech was mechanical, hurried, garbled, as if she herself did not want to hear it.

But when she came to the part where her father disowned her, she faltered and genuine tears rose to her eyes. "He—he said I disgraced him, that he had no daughter, that he had never had one."

"And you love your father?" the abbot asked kindly.

"Aye, aye. He was good to me all my life—when I was ill." She bit her lip as the tears brimmed and spilled down her cheeks. "I tried to be like him, God-fearing, honest, virtuous, but—but I don't know—things happened, things I somehow could not help. And then he—he said he never had a daughter."

The abbot waited a minute or two while she struggled with her tears. "You have suffered much over this, my child?"

"Aye," she answered in a low voice.

"The Almighty is your heavenly father as well as your earthly one. If you make reparation you will know His forgiveness. Repent, abjure your sinful life, give up your lover."

She leaned her head against the cold grille. "But, my lord abbot, where am I to go if I leave Thorsby? Who will take me and the children?"

"If you truly repent there is always a way. A nunnery, mayhap, where you can earn your keep. There you might find peace and contentment. But the children, the children, you must relinquish as part of your penance."

Startled, she lifted her head. "Give them up?" Aleyn mayhap, but not Edmund. Never Edmund. Yield him—to who? Someone who would mistreat him, beat him, call him bastard. It would destroy her.

"You wish me to surrender my children," she said. "I would be a poor mother if I did so."

"Would you renounce your chance for salvation?"

"Nay, but surely I can find another way to do penance?"

"I shan't press you now," he said after a moment.

He sympathized with Joanna's dilemma, her vague wish

on the one hand to find grace, to be "good," and on the other to keep her children. He did wonder, however, if her reluctance to seek shelter in a nunnery did not also stem from an unwillingness to forgo the comforts of concubinage. Still, for now, he would give her the benefit of the doubt.

"Go in peace," he said. "When you are ready to come to terms with God, I shall be waiting. The abbey is not that far from Thorsby."

"I promise I shall think on it," she said. "And I thank you, my lord abbot."

By the time she reached Thorsby, however, Joanna's practical self began to look at the abbot's demands as sheer folly. To give up Edmund—as repentance? Fiddlefaddle. God in His heaven did not decree a mother should abandon her son, for anyone, anything. Jesus may have been the exception, but then He had not been abandoned; besides, hadn't He died for the world's sinners? She could not relinquish Edmund just to save her own soul. It didn't make sense. The abbot, a holy man, sanctified, knew little of everyday living, knew less of a woman's struggle to survive. Isolated, surrounded by luxuries (she knew how such abbots lived—like dukes), they could not possibly appreciate the hardships of common folk. "Earn your keep," he had said. In a nunnery. She could see herself on her knees, scrubbing stone-flagged floors, despised by the sisters, thin-lipped, whey-faced females, eating hard bread, sleeping on thin sacking, just as Sir Theobold had once described it. A nunnery—without Edmund. She would find another way to atone. Perhaps later she could go on a pilgrimage to Walsingham or Glastonbury. She would take to the road like so many penitents she had seen stopping at the gates of Nareham for a meal and a place in the barns to bed down. Some of these pilgrims had committed sins far worse than she—murder and robbery—and had been redeemed. Why should *she* be expected to surrender her whole life when others gave only the few weeks it took to travel to a religious shrine?

Thomas did not return to Thorsby until the last of January. By then, the small household was running dangerously low on food, since Geralt refused to set foot in Shurbridge again. "What, and get my head knocked silly?" he grumbled. Neither would he go beyond Shurbridge to the next village for supplies; the weather was too uncertain, the mule would never make the journey—he had a dozen and one excuses, all reasonable. So they had to make do with snared rabbits and bread Ursula baked, mixing chaff with flour.

When Thomas finally came riding through the broken tower gate they welcomed him with an enthusiasm that bordered on hysteria. Joanna wept real tears. Thomas was touched. Did she think he had forgotten her? He would never do that, never. She had been in his mind constantly since he left. He still loved her passionately. He had brought a new feather bed to prove it. A feather bed, a beef pie, two hams and a young deer his squire had speared in the thicket. Fresh meat. After weeks of sawdust bread and gamy rabbit. Joanna covered his face with kisses. Impatient, he did not wait for the new bed to be installed but carried Joanna up the stairs and, spreading his fur-lined cape on the hard floor, brought her down into his arms.

"How I have missed you," he muttered, nuzzling her neck, fumbling with the laces of her gown, his fingers as always tangling them to a knot. She began to undo them herself while his mouth worked her lips open and his tongue darted inside.

"God's bones, hurry!" he urged.

As she pulled the gown over her head he quickly rolled down his hose, his drawers. Grabbing her, he mounted and entered her, climaxing almost at once.

Afterward he continued to hold her, breathing heavily into her ear. She tried not to feel cheated or resentful, telling herself she ought to praise heaven at having a man in her bed again. But—couldn't he have taken more time, made some attempt to please her?

Lying there in Thomas's arms, she began to think of Hawkwood. No comparison. None. Churl that he was, John had never made love to her in such a hurried, unthinking manner. John. She closed her eyes and let herself sink into a drowsy reverie, picturing her former lover, his face, his eyes and how they would narrow with admiration and desire whenever they scanned her bare breasts. She could almost feel his thin, demanding mouth pressing hers, trailing fire along her cheek, her throat, her shoulders, the silky, soft clefts and hollows of her sweetly aching body. Her nipples burned when she thought how he would thrust a leg over her hip, rolling her over on her back; hard, rigid, barely holding himself in check, he would take the time to fondle, to kiss, to caress, before he entered her. Joanna was so lost in her fantasy she moaned aloud. A roused Thomas asked:

"What is it, sweet?"

"Take me," she whispered.

He embraced her and held her for a long moment before shifting his weight, rising slightly to hover above her for a moment. Then he was over her, kissing her, his hands sliding down under her hips, lifting her buttocks as he entered her. And now, once more, it was the John Hawkwood of her erotic fantasy she responded to, John she rose to meet again and again, John who sent her pulses pounding, her heart racing, the hot flush to her cheeks. John who made her cry out as they reached the final, shuddering ecstasy.

But it was Thomas who spoke into the dark and said, "Sweet, you are a mistress any man would envy."

Joanna now began to realize that Thomas, despite his first few bursts of generosity, was miserly. Only for himself, his clothing, his accouterments, his comfort did he spend freely. He would have gone off again, making inadequate provision for Joanna despite her description of their plight. She had already recounted her harrowing experience with the villagers at Shurbridge and how prior to that they had only sold foodstuffs to them at exorbitant prices. Thomas promised to speak to the peasants, to see that they were properly punished, but so far had done nothing.

Meanwhile he was leaving, God knew for how long, and they must have food set by.

"What is it you want?" Thomas asked.

"You must send your squire to Shurbridge," Joanna replied. "Farther away if need be. Have him fetch several sacks of fine milled flour, one of corn, one of oats, another of peas, and a keg of dried herring. Also—a cow, a good milker. And a sturdy boy. We could do with another servant, bright and willing. Oh—and I should like to have cloth for a gown."

"But, sweet," he said, a little stunned at the long list, yet trying to sound reasonable, "why a new gown? Who is there to see you at Thorsby?"

Joanna bit back the hot retort which flew to her tongue. It was true, no one would see her except the children, her ancient, creaking retainers, the crows and the chickens, because Alys had planned it so. Let her son keep his toy, his lowborn trollop, hidden in a ruined manor house that shook and shuddered each time the wind blew. Out of sight, far from gossip and scandal.

"One would think..."

"I am the mother of your son, whatever you think," Joanna said with asperity. "And for that alone I should have a new gown."

The odd thing was that Thomas had taken to his son, Aleyn, at once, a fondness which should have made him willing to loosen his purse strings. But somehow it did not. He had learned that one could be fond without throwing one's money about, money so hard to come by and always so short in supply.

"But, Joanna sweet, if you could do with less..."

"I *cannot* do with less," she interrupted stubbornly. "Would you have us go hungry, in rags?"

In the end he grudgingly conceded, sending out his squire and two men-at-arms. They scoured the countryside and by sharp bargaining, cajoling and threatening managed to bring back most of what Joanna had ordered, including a length of cloth for a new gown and a boy servant. However, the lad was not the sturdy one Joanna had requested, but rather a sorry-looking creature, thin to the point of emaciation, with large, frightened eyes and a cringing air. He called himself Timkin, and was the youngest of thirteen. His father, a poor free farmer, the owner of a small holding on the other side of Shurbridge, had been happy enough to be rid of him. The lad, he averred, was a wee simpleminded, but he could work well enough if given the whip. When Timkin came to Thorsby his back and arms carried old scars as well as recent ones festering with pus. Ursula, seeing them, clicked her tongue and got busy. Using dock leaves and boiled mustard seed, she made up a poultice and applied it to the boy's sores. It was the first time anyone had been kind to him, had cared whether he suffered or not, and the moment Ursula laid the steaming bag to his skin he became her slave for life.

Aside from the boy, Joanna had no complaint, and she sent Thomas off with a warm embrace, many kisses and a few tears. But his departure, like the last one, was not a wrenching one, and he had hardly passed from view when she ceased to mourn. Now she could spend more time with Edmund. Understandably her lover did not relish another man's child underfoot, and while Thomas was at Thorsby Joanna kept Edmund out of sight. But with Thomas gone she made up for her neglect, playing with Edmund by the hour, talking to him, teaching him to sing a few simple airs. He was a bright little urchin, walking now, getting into innocent mischief, and had to be cautioned lest he fall into the fire. Aleyn she left to Ursula. Since she could not hire a wet nurse she nursed him herself, a task which she disliked, and before long she had Ursula wean him on a false teat soaked in cow's milk. His wails, his cries of protest on being taken from his mother's warm breast and given a substitute, she shrugged off as bad temper, a tantrum that would soon pass.

Winter now descended on them in earnest. A howling wind brought a snowstorm that raged for days, leaving high drifts level with the windows and wedging the door closed. Geralt and Timkin had to dig a path to the barn in order to feed the chickens, pig, mule and cow. The boy, under good treatment, proved much more intelligent than his father had thought. With two satisfying meals a day his sticklike arms and legs filled out, grew strong and muscular. It was he who gathered their firewood, chopping down the dead trees, hauling them sometimes for a mile to be split into smaller pieces in the courtyard. Thanks to Timkin they had fires to warm them against the inclement weather and rush tapers to light the darkening days. Joanna sewed on her new gown, singing under her breath, casting a look of love every now and again at Edmund, who played at her feet.

One morning when the snow still lay thick a loud commanding voice hallooed from the yard. Because of the snow no one had heard the sound of an approaching horse, and when the first shout of "Gateward—open up!" reached them they thought that some pilgrim on foot had inadvertently strayed into their yard.

Geralt inched open the door cautiously. He hated pilgrims—beggars, he called them—living off decent people with their tales of sin and woe.

"What is it?" Joanna could hear his peevish query.

"For God's sake!" a male voice boomed. "You give a traveler cold welcome. I am looking for Joanna of Nareham, Ivo Coke's daughter."

Joanna's heart turned over. Before she could order Geralt to shut the door their unexpected visitor came striding into the great hall—John Hawkwood, as flamboyant and as self-assured as ever.

Chapter XI

"Joanna, my sweet, there you are—at last!"

Dressed in a tight-fitting, buff-colored cotehardie and a fur-lined, swirling cape thrown back rakishly from his heavy shoulders, he came toward her, his ruddy cheeks glowing with the January wind. "My lovely, beautiful Joanna." He removed his pearl-encrusted leather gloves with a flourish and gave her a mock bow.

"How did you find me?" she managed coldly, her heart still knocking against her ribs. "More to the point—why?"

He made a deprecatory sound in the back of his throat. "What a sorry greeting for one who has been riding over the countryside this past week searching for you."

"I thought never to see you again," she said, ignoring his little speech, the memory of his rejection rising sharply, knifing anger, honing her will. This was not the man of her dreams, of her idle amorous fantasies these past months, but the real flesh-and-blood dastard who had shamed her. "I do not know how you have the effrontery to face me."

"Come now, that was what—two years, give or take, ago? Surely you can find it in your heart to let the past be."

"What a pity you were not killed," she said.

"The French—and not a few Italians—unfortunately feel the same, but here I am, whole and sound." He grinned. "My lovely, I have been through hell's fire fighting for king and glory; can you not give me a kind word?"

His hand reached out and grasped hers, and before she could withdraw it, he lifted it to his lips. His breath, the pressure of his cool mouth upon her skin, sent the blood rushing to her face. That Hawkwood could still make her blush unnerved her. She had thought bitterness sufficient to make her immune, rancor strong enough to put a cold, angry distance between them.

"There—that is better," he said, releasing her hand. "The frown's gone. And now, if you try, mayhap you can give me a smile." His eyes danced with a merry gleam.

Quickly, her brows drew together again. She must not allow him to think for a moment that he was welcome. "You—

you have no warrant to come here. Thorsby is Thomas de Ander's manor."

"And you are his mistress—as you were at Nareham."

She tossed her head. If he wished to go on believing his own falsehood, let him. "Aye. He loves me."

"And—there is talk of marriage. I suppose."

"'Tis none of your concern."

"Oh—I disremember. He is nobly born, so you would not presume—would you?"

"You have a spiteful tongue, sir knight."

"My Joanna." He grinned at her again. "You are right, forgive me. And it was I, after all, who asked that we let the past be."

His gaze passed to the servitors, Geralt, Ursula and Timkin, who had been standing in the background. They bobbed, Geralt's old knees creaking audibly.

"These are your household?" Hawkwood asked Joanna.

"There are more," she lied, "busy with tasks in the barn and kitchen."

"Ah!" He looked around speculatively. "'Tis not much, Castle Thorsby, is it?"

"More than you can call home," she retorted spitefully.

"Mayhap for the present," he replied, unperturbed. "But I will soon have enough to build three of these and tear them down on a whim if I choose."

The braggart, Joanna thought. Braggart. "Have you come to see your son, Sir John?"

"What son? I recall no son." He leaned forward but did not touch her, his eyes caressing her face. "I came to see you."

She laughed, an unsteady laugh quickly cut off. "You flatter yourself, my knight. I have no intention of giving myself to you. What passed between us is over, done with, the folly of a young, ignorant girl."

"You expect me to believe that? You liked it well enough. You were crazy for it, starved."

"I am not starved now. I have Thomas—a man who does very well by me in bed."

"Does he, now? If I remember him rightly, he has the looks of a girl."

"He is handsome, manly."

"That bespangled fop?"

"You are jealous!" she threw at him. "Green with envy. You do not have his birth or breeding. You do not have me!"

172

"Jealous, am I?" he said between his teeth, reaching out and pulling her into his arms.

Crushed against his chest, rebellious, she fought to push him away, but his embrace was like steel. One hand gripped the back of her skull as he brought his thin mouth down on hers, kissing her savagely, and she felt his desire racing through her pinioned body in waves of shock. Abruptly her struggles ceased; dizzy, her nerve ends quivering, she went limp.

"There," he said with an air of satisfaction, releasing her finally. "I'll wager our good Sir Thomas has never kissed you like that."

She put her trembling fingers to her bruised mouth. "You cannot..." she began, trying to control the sound of her ragged breathing, "you cannot—come back and expect—expect everything to be as it was. You cannot."

"I can and I did. Why do you quibble with me, sweet? Why the coyness? Did you not say you would love me always?"

"The girl who said that no longer exists. Pray—go."

"You want me to leave? Truly?"

"Aye." She rubbed her moist hands along the sides of her skirt.

"You would send me out into the cold with night falling? A beggar knocking on your gate would receive more courteous treatment. You have a hard, cruel heart."

"'Tis you who have the hard heart."

"Was the kiss I gave you that of a hard, unfeeling man? Oh, Joanna, be considerate. Show me the hospitality you would extend to the least stranger."

She stepped back, away from him. "Very well. You and your squire may spend the night. But here in the hall. You may break bread with us—but no more."

They ate on the dais, Ursula bringing roast fowl, a cabbage stew and bread in from the kitchen, serving Joanna. The squire, a long-jawed youth with a blond cowlick, waited on Sir John. Hawkwood had brought with him a small keg of wine, Gascony wine, he explained to Joanna, not as good as the Burgundy, but passable. Joanna thought it excellent but forbore to compliment it. The meal for the most part passed in silence, a strained silence which Joanna felt more than John. He ate with gusto, throwing her little side glances, little smiles, which she pretended to ignore.

"Are you not going to ask me where I have been, what I have been doing?" he said, wiping his mouth with a cloth his squire had presented. "We can, at least, be civil. They tell me you have another child. A boy."

"Aye. Sir Thomas's. And *he,* like the fine nobleman he is, has acknowledged his son."

John Hawkwood let the barb pass. "You look none the worse for your ordeal," he said, smiling, flashing white teeth in a sun-bronzed face. "Living well while I have been at war."

"War—you prate on war. I thought there was peace between the English and the French."

"Aye, but there is always fighting somewhere. Since I last saw you I have joined forces with a German knight of great courage and enterprise, Albrecht Sturz. He leads a large band of Tard Venus, stalwarts, brave warriors to the last man, the pick of the lion-hearted. 'Tis called the White Company. Mayhap you have heard of us."

"I think not."

"If you ask why *White* Company," he went on, ignoring her indifference, "the answer is simple. We keep our arms and our mail polished mirror-bright. Albrecht and I both insist on daily scourings of pikes, shields, visors and armor with cooking fat and sand. Now, that ought to tickle your housewifely fancy. Cooking fat and sand. The men grumble and complain—women's work, they say—but you should see us formed in tight ranks, pikes and lances upright, steel glinting and sparkling in the sun."

"Hmmm, a pretty picture, I daresay," Joanna murmured, selecting a chicken leg and bringing it to her mouth.

"More than pretty. We are the new breed of fighting men, Joanna, with a new way of battle the English taught us at Poitiers. We are not like the haughty French knights who scorn their common soldiers, elite snobs encased in outmoded steel caskets clumsily mounted on heavily accoutered horses. Nay, we travel lightly, swiftly, and our footmen are skilled with bow or lance or sword. *Sword,* Joanna—can you imagine a knight of old allowing a yeoman or peasant to lift a sword?"

His eyes glowed. Nothing, no subject, could make him as voluble as war, fighting, battles, horses, armor, anything that had to do with martial matters. He felt comfortable with these topics, on familiar ground, more so than when trying to make fine speeches and speak love words to a woman.

"There are many of these free companies forming now, in Burgundy, Picardy, Brittany and the valley of the Rhone, all in search of booty. But we happen to be superior; victory comes easily to us. Why? Because we are disciplined, we fight *together,* as one. Everything falling in our path, villages, fields, cots, castles...."

Joanna turned to him and in his eyes saw the gleaming reflection of fired ramparts, the leaping flames, licking, crackling, towering skyward, saw the mirrored images of shadowy figures fleeing in panic against a background of fiery timbers, smoking walls and blackened ruins.

"So you pillage and rape and burn!" she said scornfully. "You are nothing more than brigands. How vile!"

"Is it?" He grinned. "Do you believe the nobly born are less base? You deceive yourself. Chivalry is but a mask for bloody violence, for grasping greed and unbridled lust. Lords are not saints. A knight murders, sacks and pillages with the same zeal as a peasant—more, mayhap, since God has blessed his sword and he has the church on his side."

"The nobly born are instilled with honor from childhood up, they set an example..."

"Pshaw! You know you do not mean that. You have no more love for the aristocracy than I have. Your father may toady to them..."

"You dare!" She drew in her breath, her eyes flashing. "You dare speak of my father thus?"

"Dare?" His eyebrows went up. "From the gist of the gossip at Nareham I deduced Ivo had disowned you. Under the circumstances I should think you would view him more dispassionately. He does bow and scrape, you know, butters Harold up..."

"Be quiet!" She gripped her eating knife in a white-knuckled fist. "You are not to speak of my father, do you hear?"

"Not at all?"

"Nay. You degrade him. I won't have it!"

His eyes opened in mock fear. "My, but aren't you the wildcat? And so beautiful too when you are angry."

She rose from the table, her indignation somewhat spoiled by the need to steady herself from a sudden giddiness brought on by the Gascony wine.

"Sweet," he said in a conciliatory tone, pulling her down beside him, "there's no need to be angry. I swear I shan't mention the good steward, Ivo, again." He lifted his horn mug in a gallant gesture and drank, then offered it to her. "Nay—not a sip? Very well, I shall not press you. Now where were we—ah yes, chivalry and pillage and the nobility."

He took another sip of wine and continued. "The Black Prince, aye, even King Edward, fought at Crécy and Poitiers—

175

why? So they could cling to their French possessions. And how did they weaken their enemies? By burning and sacking. I've fired village after village myself under the Earl of Oxford's orders, riding down among the houses, a torch in one hand and a spear in the other, touching the brand to thatch, watching the flames spurt and crackle like dry tinder and seeing the poor peasants running out like ants. Always behind me came the earl's house guard on horse, like vultures, to drive away sheep, chickens and geese, gathering up the peasants' little hordes of coins. For whom? For the noble earl, and very little for me, who had too often risked my life for him. Can you blame me—and those of like mind—for wanting to reward ourselves in a more generous fashion?"

"But 'tis different with the king and the earl."

"Different? Can you tell me how?"

She could not. She knew he was right. At Nareham, listening to the ladies recounting their husbands' stories in the solar, catching snatches of Harold de Ander's braggadocio, she had secretly come to the same conclusion. The nobility were a pack of ruffians disguised as knights of honor. Defending them as she was doing now went against the grain, but she had no intention of agreeing with Hawkwood, even if she should find herself arguing in the devil's favor.

"They are nobles fighting bravely for England," she said rather primly.

"They are nobles fighting because they simply like fighting or they like fighting for gain, or both. What if I were to tell you that among our so-called bands of outlaws and brigands several wellborn men, knights of good name, if you will, ride with us?"

"I would not believe you."

He threw back his head and laughed. "Just like a woman. When the argument is not going her way she either says 'I don't want to talk about it' or 'I don't believe you.'"

"How can I, when I must take your word for it? Your word is hardly trustworthy."

"Why do you say that? I cannot remember that I ever went back on it in our dealings."

She gave him a haughty look.

"Well, did I? Be just, Joanna, I never declared myself, never promised undying love, never promised or even asked to marry you."

It was true, all too true, and she hated him the more for it. "You led me to believe..."

"I led you nowhere. You came to me because you wanted to."

"Well, more the fool I," she said, glaring at him.

"But you have done better with Sir Thomas, have you not? A chivalrous noble, whose generosity"—he looked pointedly around the dismal hall, its bleak furnishings, its damp, chill walls—"knows no bounds."

"If you find such fault with the hospitality at Thorsby," she said acidly, "then you are free to leave."

"And forgo your charming company? Hardly."

"Then you will forgive me if I find your company less than charming. Pray, excuse me." She got to her feet again, making certain this time not to stagger by holding onto the edge of the table.

"Joanna, the evening is young." He put his hand over hers.

"I am tired. I bid you a good night."

She walked across the hall, teeth set, head held rigidly, conscious of his eyes upon her. Slipping a lighted brand from a wall sconce, she went out into the dark night, swirling now with a light, frosty snow. She would have preferred bedding down in the kitchen or in the hall—as she did when Thomas was absent—rather than having to climb the stairs to the cold chamber, but she wished to put as much distance between herself and John Hawkwood as possible. Pray God he would take himself off in the morning. She did not flatter herself for a moment into believing he had come to Thorsby for the sole purpose of seeing her. He had stopped because he needed shelter. On his way from Nareham to somewhere, London mayhap, he had found himself miles from an inn and so, having heard of Thorsby, perhaps from the de Anders themselves, had presumed on her hospitality.

The chamber was freezing, and she regretted having left the hall in such haste without her cloak, but there was no returning. She secured the light in a rusty wall holder, then turned back to the door. It had an old, worn wooden bolt which she tried to shoot, a bolt she had never used before even in fear of the ghostly Centaur. After several attempts to budge it with her bare hands, she looked about for something to knock it free, and her eye lit upon a pair of flaking fire tongs. One mighty whack and the bolt came loose. She slid it across the door, tested its efficiency, then, satisfied, began to undress hurriedly.

Sinking down into the feather mattress, safe now, she let her mind dwell on Hawkwood. There was no denying his

177

masculine appeal. When he entered a room his raw vitality seemed to charge the air, rebounding from the walls like a magnetic echo. He had brought into the gloomy hall below a feeling of hearty cheer, a lusty love of living, such as Thomas, for all his good looks and splendid clothes, had never been able to do. Even the hearth fire seemed to burn brighter. Aye, John Hawkwood had an irresistible draw, the assessing eyes that seemed to challenge and charm simultaneously, the mocking half-smile, the strong, suntanned hands that could send the blood leaping with the merest touch. She knew and feared his power to excite her, his power to make her lose her head. Like the Gascony wine. Now thinking calmly, she was more determined than ever not to become embroiled with him. She would not give in, not let him shame her as he had done once before. Even yielding to the kiss had been a mistake. It would not happen again.

The wind tugged at the shutters, made a plaintive little cry, so human Joanna shuddered. She thought briefly of the two maids who had disappeared, of the Centaur and its thundering hooves, and snuggled deeper into the featherbed. She was just dropping down into a confused, frightening dream of the creature, half man, half horse, when the rattling of the door brought her wide awake with a heart-thudding jolt. Lifting herself on her elbows, her nightmare-clouded brain pictured the monster breathing hard, its nostrils exuding puffs of sulfurous brimstone as it panted outside the door. "It" had come after her! She was certain the Centaur had mounted the stairs on silent hooves and was now attempting to open the door. The door shook again. Holy Mother of God! Perspiration broke out on her brow. Why had she not slept downstairs with Ursula and the children? Why had she come up to the chamber? To escape John Hawkwood. Now she was trapped.

A shattering rat-a-tat knock on the door sent her heart leaping anew. "Go away!" she called hoarsely. "Oh, please, go away." Mother Mary protect me, I beseech Thee...

Something heavy hurled itself against the wood paneling. "Go *away!*"—her voice louder, strangled, close to hysteria. Another crashing thud; the door buckled on its hinges, and she heard the bolt snap. The door flew open, slamming against the wall.

A lamp flickered on the threshold, outlining a dark, hulking figure. She cowered on the bed, the covers drawn up to her chin, too frightened to scream.

"Damn!" a voice cursed.

Disbelief mingled with relief brought her upright.

"I nigh broke my shoulder on your stinking door." Hawkwood strode into the room carrying an oil lantern. "Bolted, too. 'Tis the first time I've had a door bolted 'gainst me."

"Get out! Get out at once!" Joanna ordered, finding her voice, the fear of a few moments ago now funneled into outrage. "You are drunk! You must be, for I did not invite you here."

"Not in so many words." He winked at her, shutting the door with a jerk of his elbow.

"I want you gone. Leave, do you hear? *Leave!*"

"Must you shout? You know very well you do not want me to leave." He held the lantern high so he could look at her. His eyes gleamed in the flickering light, and it seemed to her they could see through the covers to her naked body.

"You assume too much," Joanna said tartly. "I am not one of your camp harlots."

"Nay—never. You are too beautiful, my Joanna of Thorsby. No woman who sells her favors, none that I have met, leastwise, can compare with you."

"I am not flattered, not with such a comparison. Pray—go."

"Give me a kiss then, a goodnight kiss."

"I shall give you the back of my hand if you dare touch me."

He stared at her, and for a moment his eyes narrowed unpleasantly. Then he was smiling again, smiling with a faint hint of mockery twisting his lips.

"So you would. Well, then, I shall not torment you with my presence. Gentle dreams to you, my Joanna."

He turned to leave, and she felt an inexplicable twinge of disappointment, one that urged her to call his name. She ignored the urge. He reopened the door; the wind came whistling and romping through, lifting his cape, belling it about his ankles. He hesitated on the threshold, and she saw the blackness beyond his head, the solitary night with the snowflakes lit by the lamp's rays fluttering about like swarms of flying moths.

John! she wanted to call.

Still he stood on the threshold, muttering something she could not hear. Suddenly he slammed the door and whirled about. Setting the lamp down, he kicked it across the floor so that it slid upright to the foot of the bed. He strode toward her, divesting himself of his cape as he moved, and tossed it, a swirl of fur-lined wool, into a corner.

Joanna cried, "Don't!" as he flung himself upon the bed, grasping her shoulders.

"Scream," he dared. "Go on—go on, scream."

"You...! You dog—you...!"

Half-lifting her, he crushed her to his chest, his mouth closing hers with a hungry, devouring kiss. She tried to fight him, she tried, she tried, but the poison of surrender was already creeping through her veins, flooding her with an exquisite weakness. Her flailing arms fell, her breasts, stomach, thighs, her very bones seemed to melt and flow into his hard, masculine body. Oh, curse him for coming back into her life, yet even as she cursed her blood sang, her loins throbbed. These past two years she had been asleep, dozing, passing her days in dull apathy, but now she was rekindled, reborn—*alive!*

He undressed quickly while she lay and watched as if in a trance. And now he was kissing her mouth, her face, her throat, his lips lingering on her shoulders, the cleft between her breasts. He did not speak, he was silent, unlike Thomas, who kept up a constant stream of murmuring. But she did not mind. His touch and his kisses were far more exciting than Thomas's ever could be. He paused and looked down at her in the wavering light, his eyes large with desire.

"Let me see your hair, sweet."

She sat up and nimbly undid the thick braids until the hair flowed in a dark torrent about her white shoulders. He buried his head in that black wealth, buried his head in her throat, biting it, biting the flesh above her breast, kissing her hair, her cheeks, biting her breast again.

"Don't," she pleaded. Even the pain he inflicted sent shivers of delight through her body.

He mounted her, his hands running down her thighs, nudging her legs apart. He bent his tawny head and kissed the soft sensitive skin in the inner thigh, his lips pressing, sucking, biting.

"Don't." The word was a moan.

He gathered her close and entered her, his manhood huge, filling her with indescribable pleasure. They began to move in unison, hip to hip, slowly at first, then faster and faster. Her mind fled. Had she felt anger, resentment for this man? She did not remember. Only the moment counted, was real. Each thrust brought her closer to the edge of panic, the edge of the ultimate, and she clung to him, moaning, sobbing, her hands clutched to his thick hair—until the world erupted in a blaze of light. She loved him, she had never stopped loving him. God—God! The heart-shattering wonder of it!

They lay entwined, without speaking. He brought his head up, found her cheek, kissed it tenderly. Tears sprang to her eyes. She wanted to hold him thus forever. She did not want their moment to end. She wanted the lovely glow to go on and on, wanted to feel that he too shared a wish to prolong their joy. She wanted him to love her as she loved him.

After a long while he shifted, drawing over them the covers, which had been pushed to the foot of the bed in their frantic lovemaking.

"You see, Joanna, I said you would enjoy it, didn't I? Confess—you have been missing me more than you realized."

They were not exactly the words she wanted to hear, not now, not when the enchantment still lingered. "And did you miss *me*, John?"

"Aye, I have already told you so. But then I knew Sir Thomas was taking good care of you."

She turned to him. He smiled, but she saw a shadow—of jealousy? regret?—lurking in his eyes. "Why must you speak of him?" she wanted to know.

"Because we are here, in his bed, where he must have taken you many times. Do you love him?"

"Nay, I have never loved him."

"But of course he does not know that," he said wryly.

"John—pray—don't. Even though you have treated me badly, it is you I love."

"So you have always led me to believe."

"How can you be so—so mulish? I love you, and you, *you* love *me*. I know it. I am sure."

He looked at her, an enigmatic look that softened as his eyes roamed her face. "Joanna..."

She waited. "*Say* it," she demanded impatiently. "Say you love me."

But he could not. There was something about the word that made him cautious, wary. And yet his feeling for this woman reached deep into his soul. Why could he not trust her, then, why not reveal the tenderness he brought with his passion, a tenderness only she could evoke? Was it because of Thomas, Thomas the lordling who had fathered the son she had tried to foist on him? When he thought of the night he heard Thomas behind Joanna's door—"Give me a kiss, sweet." When he thought of them here together...

"Women!" he said mockingly. "I sought you out again, isn't that enough?"

"You tell me I am beautiful, flatter me, but you won't say the one thing that makes it true."

He brushed back the mane of hair from his forehead with a quick, impatient movement. "I know nothing of 'love.' I hear the minstrels sing of it—but to me 'tis a feminine conceit. Like hair ribbons and silken tippets."

"You do not think bedding with me a feminine conceit." The glow had vanished, and the bitterness of regret was already whispering, *Fool! Fool!*

"Bedding you? My lovely Joanna, next to fighting 'tis the most enjoyable pastime I can think of."

"Then mayhap you'd best go back to your fighting."

"Sweet," he said gently, turning toward her, gathering her in his arms, "do not pout. We have such little time, you and I. There is not one who has or who can give me happier memories."

Did she have to settle for that? Was wanting more a cry for the moon she could not have? But perhaps he said the same to his other women, perhaps... But soon it did not matter, for he was kissing her again, his hands and mouth doing things to her body, sending the hot blood coursing through her veins, making her nerve ends jump and twitch pleasurably, blotting out doubt, speculation, argument, regret. It was the moment she grasped now, the moment which made her cry out at the end, "God, how I love you!" and answering his murmured, "Always?" she whispered, "Always."

The next morning as John was breaking his fast with the last of the Gascony wine and half a loaf, Joanna brought Edmund into the hall. The child, walking well now, held to his mother's hand.

"Sir John," Joanna said, "may I present your son to you."

John paused in his eating, a chunk of bread speared on his knife. "Mine? I have no son in these parts that I remember. Who is this little fellow?"

"He is Edmund, and by God, by Jesus, by all the saints in heaven, I swear he is yours."

"Swearing does not make it so," he said amiably. "I will not have a strange child fobbed off as mine."

"How can you say that?" she questioned heatedly. "*Look* at him. See the likeness."

He surveyed the child with a furrowed brow. "Hmmm. A likeness to Ivo Coke, mayhap, not to me. The only likeness is that he has a face, two eyes, a mouth and nose. But otherwise I see nothing that reminds me of myself."

"He has your eyes."

"They are brown—true. But were I to acknowledge every brown-eyed brat as mine I'd have thousands." He grinned. "And I am not *that* virile."

"Oh! You—you beast! You are impossible! Scurvy varlet...!"

"I must remind you I was knighted Sir John Hawkwood. Neither scurvy nor varlet, sweet."

The boy, who had been watching the stranger, taking a cue from his merry eyes, broke into a laugh.

"He finds me amusing," John said. "A winning child as children go, but *not* mine."

A rush of scathing words flew to her tongue, but she forced them back. Her rage would only incite him to mocking laughter, and she had had enough of that. Giving Edmund over to Ursula, she retired to her tapestry frame, where she took up the long-neglected wall hanging. She worked swiftly, her brows drawn together, plying her needle with a set face, trying to hide her disappointment and mortification. She heard him speak to his squire, ordering him to saddle his horse and make ready to leave.

"Joanna." He was standing over her, but she did not look up. "Joanna, my sweet, let us not part in discord."

She shrugged indifferently, her eyes on the needle stitching away at the outline of a leaf.

"Sweet, will you not look at me?"

"For what purpose? Goodbye. I wish you Godspeed, and good journey"—all said without feeling, her eyes averted.

She felt his hand on her shoulder; it burned like a brand through the cloth of her gown. "That is not a proper farewell, Joanna, and you know it."

"You have had your will of me. What else could you want?"

"Your blessing. A goodbye kiss." And when she did not answer, "At least come into the courtyard and see me off. 'Twould be discourteous not to."

She got to her feet and followed him as he picked up his cape and went through the door.

The snow had stopped some time during the night and lay like a dazzling blanket under a blinding morning sun. White had covered the old shambled stables, the broken flags, the crumbling wall, the drifts hiding piles of refuse, cow dung and rusting wheels, transforming Thorsby into a sugary castle, a fanciful tower-frosted sweet.

John's horse, a dark gray stallion with a brass-studded harness, stood by, shaking his head, his breath rising in steam from his nostrils. The squire mounted on a brown gelding held his bridle.

"Farewell, my sweet," John said, taking Joanna into his arms, kissing her on her turned-away cheek. "Come now, is that a way to send me off? Let us part friends."

An ache rose in her throat as she gave him her lips. She could already feel the terrible loneliness closing in around her, the empty days, the black nights. On sudden impulse she said, "Don't leave me behind. Take me with you, John. Let me go with you."

"What? What are you saying?" He searched her face. "You would come with me now, now as you are, go from Thomas's protection without a backward glance?"

"Aye. Myself and our son."

The look of expectancy in his eyes vanished and his face froze. "*Our* son. You will persist. I cannot take you. I cannot load myself down with baggage."

Crushed with mortification, her cheeks stinging, she retorted, "When you call me baggage, you call me whore! Damn you! Damn your soul to eternal hell!"

"Hush! Hush!" He covered her mouth with his gloved hand. "Is that the way to speak to a soldier?"

She pulled away. "If the French do not kill you, I shall. By God—I swear, someday..."

He laughed merrily. "And last night in my arms you swore you would love me always."

February dragged slowly into March. The piled and dirty drifted snow melted, disappearing into slushy puddles under pelting rain. In an abandoned orchard a few stunted apple trees sprouted pink-and-white blossoms, and beneath their branches lupine pushed green spikes up from the sodden black soil. An early Easter came and went. Thomas sent provisions, money and a message by way of a dispatcher leading a pack pony. He still loved her. But he himself stayed away. Joanna finished the tapestry and hung it on the wall, hiding an ugly damp spot which had long annoyed her. She began another, her needle twinkling in the firelight, her head bowed over the frame, while Edmund played and the swaddled Aleyn fretted in a makeshift basket at her feet.

When she was not at her tapestry she found other things to do. She polished the dais table, gathered eggs, baked bread, carried water, tasks she had not performed since she had lived with her father, but if she kept busy she had little time to think. Even so her mind would often probe and question, going over and over the old arguments, the old debates. Had she bettered herself that much? Had Thomas, had Thorsby, really improved her situation? Would Edmund when he came of age have the advantages she hoped for him? She wanted Edmund to be apprenticed to a cloth or wine merchant or some respectable tradesman. That would cost money, a good sum, for no master accepted a lad unless he was well paid for his trouble. Would Thomas pay the fee of indenture, if asked? Perhaps she should have wrung that promise from her lover at the very beginning, when his ardor was at its peak. Had his interest waned? (She had warned Ursula, Timkin and Geralt on pain of a horrible, lingering death not to say one word about John Hawkwood's visit—an unnecessary warning, since they had all aligned themselves with Joanna rather than Thomas from the start.) What would she do if she were exiled at Thorsby for the rest of her life? Nay, nay, she would not think of that. There was time, plenty of time to worry over something that might never come to pass.

As the days lengthened, Joanna took to sitting in the window embrasure of the tower bedchamber in the afternoons. There she had a view beyond the gatehouse down the elm-lined ride which led to the high road. She told herself she was looking for Thomas, but in her heart it was John Hawkwood she waited for. Though she knew he would not return, her eyes, staring past the rubble and twisted vines, hoped for the sight of a dark gray stallion carrying a broad-shouldered man in a fur-lined cape. She hated him; he had treated her shabbily again, taken her at will, shamed her. And yet her thoughts were full of him, the feel of his thick tawny hair under her hands, the knotted muscles of his strong arms, the pressure of his hungry mouth, so eloquent, so sure, so quick to bring her joy. She did not love Thomas; she would never love Thomas. Did she love John Hawkwood? How could she love and hate a man at the same time? Was it possible? She did not know.

One afternoon she saw two horsemen approaching, and she held her breath, her heart thumping wildly, until she recognized the horseman in the lead as the abbot, Father Mark, riding a sleek bay. Behind him rode a monk dressed in the black-and-white habit of a Dominican. Disappointed, she withdrew from the window before he should see her. She could guess the reason for the abbot's visit. He was determined to save her soul. She had hoped he had forgotten, that the salvation of an ordinary woman such as herself could hardly matter to a man of high clerical office. But apparently it did.

She waited until Ursula came puffing up the stairs. "'Tis his grace," the old woman wheezed, awed, flustered, trying to catch her breath. "His grace himself."

"Well—don't take on so. It's not the pope."

Ursula crossed herself. "He wants to see ye."

"Tell him I shall be down in a moment."

Joanna smoothed her hair, tucking a strand into her headband, inspected her gown to see that it was clean. What difference does it make how I look? she asked herself. But feminine vanity would not allow her to appear before the abbot looking less than her best. She could face him with more assurance as Dame Joanna of Thorsby than as Joanna, a slatternly concubine.

She came down the stairs and entered the hall, spine straight, chin high, walking with the same proud grace that had surprised Father Mark the first time he had seen her moving down the nave at Shurbridge church.

"My lord abbot," Joanna murmured, kneeling quickly to kiss the outstretched ring, "to what do I owe this honor?"

"I was in the neighborhood on abbey business, and I thought I would stop by to see if you have reflected on our last discussion."

She rose. "I have been thinking..."

"I had also hoped," he said, sweeping past her, looking around, "that you would no longer be here. That you would have given up this sort of life."

"I cannot leave Thorsby. I must stay for the sake of my babies. I have already told you I have nowhere to go, and I will not sacrifice them—their right to have a mother—for my own deliverance."

The abbot lifted his brows. "I must say you argue well. Suppose you tell me what you plan to do to earn God's forgiveness?"

"Why, I shall—I shall make a pilgrimage to Canterbury, to the tomb of Thomas à Becket, this summer."

He smiled. "If I can hazard a guess, Dame Joanna? You have no intention of doing so. 'Tis said solely for my benefit. I would ask you not to further imperil your immortal soul by a falsehood."

Her cheeks reddened, but she did not lower her eyes. "'Tis a possibility."

He waved the possibility aside. "I should give you the benefit of the doubt, as, I might add, I have done before, but I cannot see you trudging to Canterbury. Well—it seems you are going to be my hardest, most recalcitrant sinner yet."

"I am not hardened, my lord abbot," she said defensively.

"Pardon—'hardest' was a little excessive—but you will be, unless you take care. If you wish, I can hear your confession now."

Confession! She would have to tell him about John Hawkwood. God in heaven, she could not.

"But," he went on, "mayhap you can do that at Shurbridge. I have so little time. My cellarer and I are making the rounds to see that the plowing is done on the Kenham glebes beyond Thorsby."

Relieved, let off the hook, Joanna became the generous hostess of the manor house. "Will you not have a cup of wine, at least? I have some Burgundy I have been keeping for just such an esteemed guest as yourself."

"Thank you, but only a cup."

She called to Ursula, who, lately going deaf, did not hear her. Geralt and Timkin were out, so she went into the kitchen and fetched the wine herself. When she returned, the cellarer, a short, thin man, fidgeted nervously in the background while the abbot, seated on a stool, conversed with Edmund. The child spoke now, not in isolated words but in full sentences, rather fluently for all the little childish twists and mispronunciations.

"And you are not lonesome without playmates?" the abbot was asking.

"I have my bruvver."

"But your brother is too small to play yet."

"I talk to him," Edmund averred seriously.

The abbot looked up. "You have a very quick child here, Dame Joanna. I have never known one to be so intelligent at such an early age."

Joanna smiled, her heart suddenly warming toward the abbot. To compliment Edmund—without danger of the child's

187

affections straying—was to compliment her. "How kind of you. I thank you, my lord abbot."

"'Tis a pity to waste such a mind," he went on, taking the proffered wine. Joanna was sorry she had not brought the silver cup for him. The plain horn one would have done for the cellarer.

"Have you thought about his future?"

Her heart skipped a beat. "Often, my lord. From the very first, if truth be told, I have known him to be out of the ordinary. 'Tis not a mother's affection speaking, believe me; you yourself have seen how it is. God has smiled on him by making him handsome and clever, and I will try my best to see that he goes forward in life."

"And how would you want him to go forward?" He sipped at the wine, his eyes smiling kindly.

"Why, I should like him to be a wine merchant, or a dealer in wool. Respectable trades, yet ones where his birth will not be questioned and thrown at him."

"Aye—his birth. A pity, that. I myself think he has the makings of an excellent churchman."

The church! Holy Christ! She wanted her son to be rich, respected, but she did not want to lose him. She wanted to be a part of his life, to have him marry, beget sons, to have a household in which she would share. But the church! The church would take and devour him if it did not make a hypocrite of him first. She could see him like Father Theobold placed in some poor village, going about his duties with a rusty soutane, cadging a chicken here, a goose there, ale from the alewife, or if he was lucky acting as scrivener to some pinchpenny bishop who kept him on crusts and rotten fish.

"I had not thought of the church," she murmured.

"Of course he could not be ordained; his bastardy would prevent that—unless I could manage a dispensation. I have heard of it done—rare, but feasible."

He was serious. He was actually going over the possibilities, practical possibilities. Joanna instinctively took Edmund's hand in hers. "'Tis kind of you to be concerned. And I thank you for it. But do you not think it early to make plans? Mayhap he will not have the inclination, the vocation."

"I can usually tell if a child has the vocation. And I think your Edmund does. However, we shall see."

We shan't see, she thought determinedly. You shall never have my Edmund. And she had to resist the impulse to order the abbot from the house.

Chapter XII

Thomas came in August, impatient, somewhat testy. He stayed five days. He had no money, he told Joanna, though he was dressed as resplendently as ever. Five marks was all he could spare. When she brought up the question of apprenticing Edmund, he brushed it aside.

"I have Aleyn to think of."

"My lord . . ."

"Do not badger me," he snapped.

They quarreled, not a bitter quarrel nor an especially heated one, but their first, a short, vituperative exchange. They made it up, of course, Joanna apologizing for losing her temper, Thomas saying the blame was his. Certainly he would take care of Edmund, but later, when the time was ripe. They parted on good terms, after a night of frantic yet passionless love.

"God go with you," Joanna said. "And oh, Thomas, I shall miss you so." She meant it, not Thomas so much as human company, someone from the outside world to breach the loneliness. Aside from Hawkwood and the abbot, who each in his own way had left her perturbed, no one had come to Thorsby.

"I shall try to return by Michaelmas."

September slowly passed, the apples dropping onto the sere orchard grass, the nights growing cooler, the air hazed with woodsmoke. Before they knew it, Michaelmas slid by and it was October. Ducks gathered for flight in the swampland, the last of the leaves fell from the elms. Frost began to appear in the mornings.

Geralt had resumed his dealings with the Shurbridgers, both he and they approaching each other warily with barely concealed hostility. The peasants, though they hated Geralt and tried to cheat him, accepted his money, good coin of the realm. Besides, Father Simon, at the instigation of the abbot, had warned them against any show of nastiness. As for Geralt, though he detested his enemies, he did not detest them enough to bypass Shurbridge and make the longer trip to Wodd Sapney or Kenham for supplies.

At the end of October a messenger came riding to Thorsby bringing word from Thomas. His older brother, Robert, had died, and Thomas was now heir to Nareham. Joanna received this bit of news with only passing interest. Robert had been a stranger to her, and Thomas's inheritance had to wait on his father's death, an event which might be many years away. In any case, her lover's elevation to a lordship would make little difference to her status.

What did dismay Joanna, however, was the further message that Thomas was being sent to Aquitaine and might be gone for two years. Two years! Two years for one who had watched and waited from day to day anticipating his imminent return seemed like an eternity. Soon the dreary winter, her second, would close down on Thorsby, a lonely echoing time, the months stretching away in endless monotony, cold, gray, damp as a tomb. It did not bear thinking. And when she shook out the purse he had sent and saw only a handful of gold coins, her heart shrank even more. Two years—and this. How were they to live?

For the first time since she had arrived at Thorsby she sat down and with a clear head took stock of her situation. In the past she had leaned on Thomas, feeling that he loved her, that he would provide one way or another, but there was no evading it; Thomas's ardor, his interest, had cooled. She might have expected it—a sensible mistress would—but even if she had, how could she have foreseen that Thomas would tire of their affair so soon?

Her lover, vain, handsome, charming, must have met many beautiful women in London, women, even highborn ones, willing, if not eager, to bed him. He might have another mistress, even another child. The thought made her wince, but had to be faced. Tightfisted as he was, he could hardly be expected to feed Joanna and her children when a more recent bedmate had claims, however tenuous, on his limited generosity. To go on depending upon Thomas entirely would be unwise. Perhaps the purses brought or sent would get leaner and leaner. And if Thomas forgot them altogether, what then? No, she would not think of that yet—later, but not now. In the meanwhile the long winter ahead would have to be gotten through somehow, their supplies eked out, their money hoarded. She remembered only too well her early days at Nareham when hunger pangs probed her ribcage and rumbled her stomach. She did not want Edmund to know what it meant to go to bed each night and dream of food, to wake with the same gnawing inside, assuaged by a slice of dry, stale bread, if one was lucky, or a mess of boiled grasses, never filling one up except with bilious gas. No, she did not want that for her son. She would manage somehow; she had to.

The cow and calf, a few pigs and a dozen chickens would not suffice, of course. It would be folly to imagine they could subsist on that alone. They would have to somehow acquire more pigs and grow a garden, and mayhap they could plow a small strip and plant corn. Not too late for it; she remembered how her father and the villagers had sown winter corn in October for June harvest. Why hadn't she thought of putting in a garden months ago? They could have had cabbages and beans, leeks and garlic to gather and put down in a cool place for winter use. Beans and garlic made a satisfying stew. And... But no sense to cry about it now. They must do what they could. She herself was not afraid of hard work. She did not like it, but it held no fear for her.

Geralt, after living a life of comparative ease for many years, was less than eager to take up the chore of farming. He invented all sorts of excuses. They had no plow, and should they have one, the mule would die in its tracks pulling it. The soil was poor, he had no way of clearing it without a strong man's help, his rheumatism bothered him; he was too old, old, *old*. He even sobbed a little. But Joanna was not a bailiff's daughter in vain.

"We work or we starve," she said. "He that sits idle will go hungry. As for a plow, look in the stables; there must be something we can use."

They found a plow, rusted and a little dull, but not past repair, and several spades and hoes, an ax, and best of all, a honing stone. The next morning, carrying their sharpened implements, they went out beyond the orchard to a spot that seemed to offer the likeliest growing field. The weeds and a tangle of vines and bushes would have to be removed before they could plow, so they set to work under Joanna's instructions and began to hack away with spades and the ax.

Geralt soon began to complain bitterly; his back hurt, his side had a stitch in it, his legs pained him. Cursing at each root torn from the soil, he swore that he would not last the day out. At their noon pause, he flung himself down and sobbed, begging Joanna to send for the priest; he was dying, couldn't she see? Disgusted, Joanna gave up prodding him and decided he was more trouble than he was worth. Early the next morning she sent him to Shurbridge. Putting two marks in his hand, she directed him to buy seed corn as well as seed for cabbages and leeks, and, if he could, a piglet they could fatten for Christmas.

"Dame Joanna," Geralt said, looking at the few coins in his gnarled, callused hand, "ye've not been to the village lately, I can see. I couldn't buy an old broken-down one-legged goose with what ye've given me."

"I cannot spare more. Do what you can."

Geralt had hardly gone when Timkin, whose job it was to do the morning milking, came into the hall and announced that the cow was acting strangely.

"She was all right last night," Joanna said. "What ails her?"

"Come see, dame."

Joanna, with Ursula hobbling behind, hurried to the barn. The cow was lying on its side breathing heavily, its eyes bloodshot, too weak to bawl. Joanna, reaching back in her memory to girlhood, tried to remember the afflictions cows fell heir to. Sheep had murrain, often, if not almost always, fatal, and there was cowpox, but this creature had no pustules on her udders. What had sickened her she could only guess. Probably standing in water for a week she had caught the animal version of the sweating flux.

"Ursula, we must make up one of your remedies, and quickly." To lose the cow was to lose a precious source of food.

"Which? I've all sorts of remedies, mistress."

"I don't know which—something, anything, but hurry!"

A brew was mixed, mashed with some ale and dribbled down the cow's throat. The beast seemed to rally for a brief spell, giving Joanna a glazed look and emitting a low moan which seemed to both women a heartening sign. However, an hour later it jerked convulsively, rolled over and died.

It was a terrible blow, but Joanna did not give herself time to mourn. "We must fletch it and salt down as much of the meat as we can."

They worked all that night on the dead cow; a botched-up job, bloodier and messier than even Joanna had imagined. But by morning they had the carcass dismembered and skinned, great chunks of it ready to be put down in brine, the salt fortunately brought home by Geralt on his last foray. Two of the haunches Joanna decided to smoke. The rest they would eat until the meat turned rancid and maggoty, which then would be thrown to the pigs.

Geralt had been gone two days when Joanna began to worry. "If he could not get the seed in Shurbridge he might have gone farther afield," Joanna, airing her concern, said to Ursula. "Still, he should have been back by now."

"He's a scoundrel," Ursula snapped. "Ye was wrong to trust him."

"I had no reason to *mistrust* him. He's always returned before."

"Returned when he knowed he got a place that's warm to come to, a place where he can be sure of fillin' his belly. Lazy varlet. Now that he has to work on short rations he's took off."

"I cannot believe he would do such a thing. An old man, where would he go?"

Ursula shrugged. "Where? Lots of places. Don't forget he got him a cart, a mule and a couple of marks in his fist."

"Still, unless something has befallen him, he will be back."

But the week passed into another, and Geralt did not return. Joanna felt he had come upon some misadventure, that the wagon somehow had tipped over crossing the fen and it and he had disappeared into the bog. But she soon learned differently when a passing pair of pilgrims who had lost their way stopped at the gate. Given a meal, they were asked if they had seen an old peasant, Joanna describing the bushy eyebrows, the limping gait, the cart and the mule.

"Indeed," said one, a short man with a humped shoulder. "We saw him at the Cat and Mouse in Kettering. Said he was on his way to Leicester, where a burgher had promised him a job as gateward in—in—I have forgotten the manor. Do you remember, Harry?"

"I cannot recall the name of the manor," Harry replied, "but the old peasant sticks in my mind. A bit of a braggart, wasn't he?"

Joanna needed no further proof to convince her that Geralt had indeed deserted them. The rapscallion! She did not mind his desertion (and in some ways was glad to be rid of him) as much as she minded the loss of the cart and mule. And the money. They could make the oats Thomas had provided stretch through the winter, but after that—what?

If I could only get the seed, Joanna thought, then I would drag the plow myself or break up the soil spade by spade. The seed. The villagers, peasants who had their own bellies to look to, would give her nothing, certainly not without payment. She thought of leaving Thorsby and trying to return to Nareham, but she could not take to the road on foot with two small children.

It was then that she remembered the abbot. He was the only friend, if he could be called that, in the entire countryside. She felt sure he would give her the seed, loan her another mule or ox, mayhap even send a man to help her plow. Or would he? Would he again advise her to leave Thorsby, renounce her concubinage, although the reason for her concubinage seemed to have quite forgotten her?

As the days wore on, growing shorter and colder, she became more and more concerned and finally decided she had no alternative but to test the abbot's goodwill. Since she did not want to leave Ursula alone with the children, she informed Timkin that he would have to go.

The prospect frightened him. He knew how to reach the village, but he had never been farther west than his old home, a league beyond it. He was terrified of getting lost, of wandering into a forest or bog from which he might not emerge. Geralt had told him the story of the two maids, and he felt sure they had either gone down in the sucking muck or been set upon by wolves.

"Nonsense," Joanna chided. "You will be in no more danger than you were in the cart with Geralt. And as for getting lost, you have only to ask directions at the church in Shurbridge. Once you are well on the road behind it you can't miss the abbey—anyone can direct you. And I am certain the abbot will send you home with the seed I asked for in a cart. You will not have to return on foot."

He left armed with a kitchen knife and a stout club, a thin lad, squaring his shoulders as he went through the gate, much like a jouster going forth to do battle against heavy odds. Watching him, Joanna felt a slight twinge, one that quickly passed, however, since she had much to do; there was the puddled garden to be drained, firewood to be gathered, chicken and calf manure to be spread, all the heavy work which now fell on her shoulders.

Timkin returned five days later, trudging wearily through the gate on foot and alone, dirty, his underlip swollen, his clothes torn and muddied, dragging a hempen sack behind him.

"Is this all the abbot could spare?" Joanna asked, looking inside. "Onion and cabbage seed?"

"The abbot weren't there, mistress. And pray, can I have a sip o' water and a bite of bread?"

"Later—tell me what happened."

By prodding she finally got the disjointed story from him. After having taken a wrong turn in the road and blundering about for half a day he had finally been set in the right direction by a kindly traveling friar. Once at the abbey he discovered that Father Mark had gone up to London. No one there had heard of a Dame Joanna, but the porter, taking pity on him, had given him seed for the garden.

"Dear God, could you not have used your head?" Joanna asked. "You might have left a message."

"I did not think on it, mistress."

"God preserve me from such an idiot!"

"Mistress," he said, "they stoned me."

"Who? Who stoned you?"

"The villagers at Shurbridge as I passed back through."

"Damn them!" she muttered. "Well—all right, all right, I shan't harm you, though God knows you deserve a whipping for your stupidity. Ursula will give you your supper."

November.

They found a patch of wild rye and another of barley. Reaping the grasses, they ground them up in a hand mill to augment their oaten flour. One barrel of meat turned bad and had to be thrown away. Timkin redeemed himself somewhat by setting snares and catching small birds and a few hares, once a fox.

December.

They had grown weary of salted meat and at Christmas (what they guessed was Christmas) slaughtered a pig. It was delicious, all tender and juicy and the outside crisp and crackling. Ursula made a sparrow and onion pie and a custard of eggs and honey, and brought out one of their precious cheeses. They drank cider and sang Christmas hymns, "Sweet Jesus, King of bliss, my heart's life, my heart's joy," the great hall echoing with their voices and the laughter of the children. Edmund's eyes shone as he watched his mother leading the singing, his piping notes following hers, catching both tune and words quickly. They could not feast the entire Twelve Days as the castle folk did at Nareham, and the next morning Joanna put them on short rations again, but they did not grumble. Full-stomached, Ursula and Timkin did not look ahead, and Joanna tried not to. But sometimes in the dark of the night, listening to the rising wind, a stab of fear would go through her like a knife. Five mouths to feed; the children ate little, true, but they did eat, and no matter how sparingly they were all fed, their provisions could not last indefinitely.

January.

The snow came with a howling northwest wind, and they brought the animals into the great hall. The wood, burning wetly, sent huge billows of smoke into the rafters but gave little heat. The air turned foul, a mixture of ordure, smoke, rot and damp. Ursula coughed almost constantly and one morning could not rise out of bed. It frightened Joanna. She had leaned on the old woman more than she realized. Her sour tongue, her insolence, had, on occasion, goaded Joanna into anger. But for all the old woman's disrespect and tartness, she had proved to be loyal, a staunch servitor, one who would never desert her mistress. She would cleave to Joanna until they both went down together, starving, frozen by the cold, or devoured by the rapacious crows sitting on the bleak walls and naked limbs of the orchard outside. To Joanna, Ursula's knowledge of simples and potions was a hedge against illness; to have the herbalist, the healer herself, sicken seemed the direst of omens.

Instructed by Ursula in a gasping, choking voice, Joanna brewed a pinch of rosemary with the last of their hoard of honey and the dried toad's foot and offered it to the ailing woman. She drank it, trying hard not to cough in the meanwhile, her bulging eyes running with tears. But by evening she breathed easier, and the next day she was able to get up and toddle about the kitchen.

The weather turned bitter, the cold seeping in through the cracked and broken shutters, a bone-aching cold, chilling them all to the marrow. They slept by the fire, huddled together under all the covers they could find, the two children fitted like spoons between Ursula and Joanna. Mornings they had to break the ice in the bucket so they could heat up a thin gruel to warm their stomachs. The chickens molted, laying few if any eggs and those hard to find, as they would sometimes fly to a ledge under the arched rafters and there nest. One night the door flew open, unknown to them, and the calf wandered out. The next morning when Timkin was sent to look for it he returned empty-handed. He had walked for miles, calling, searching without success, and feared it had wandered into the bog.

Joanna gave him a halfhearted clout. "It seems you cannot do anything right, idiot." And she went out herself, struggling against the wind that whipped at the skirt of her cloak. Snow lay everywhere. Great drifts had blown up against the walls of the stable, shutting the doors tightly so that the heifer could not have strayed back to its old home. There were no tracks. The wind had obliterated all signs of bird or animal life, leaving only faint shifting ripples of whiteness. The sky, pregnant with dark, swollen clouds, frowned down on her as she plowed forward, sometimes sinking knee deep, struggling on through the gate into the orchard and thence to the fields where the fierce wind had laid bare several patches of frozen black earth. She had thought the calf might be grazing there, or trying to graze, but there was no sign of it. Her eyes scanned the icy blue vastness that stretched to the bog. Nothing. She turned and tried to make her way down the ride between the clacking, wildly thrashing elms, but the funneled wind clawed at her, pushing her back. Her cheeks and nose had stiffened with cold; her slippers had soaked through, and her feet had lost all feeling. She gave up. The calf was gone— another bitter loss. God, why? Why? What had gone wrong? She who had sworn to rise out of poverty, who had made something of herself at Nareham—why this now?

Damn Thomas! He was to blame. He and her own foolishness. She should have never given herself to him, never trusted him to care for her as he promised. What a goose she had been! Damn Thomas, the vain, conceited ass in his bejeweled tunics and particolored hose. A gust of wind staggered her as she turned to go back. Was God punishing her for producing two bastards? Was the abbot right when he said that to be shriven of sin she must give up her babies? Aleyn she did not mind, Aleyn somehow had never been hers; but Edmund ... God, God, what a coil! If I could only get through the winter, only, dear God, she prayed as she sank and floundered and fought her way through the snow, I shall go on pilgrimage if I have to carry both children all the way in my arms.

February.

Winter stuck fast in a gray, cold timelessness went on and on and on. Mewed up behind Thorsby's walls, Joanna lost track of the days. Was it Sunday, Tuesday—Saturday, mayhap? Sometimes when the wind let up and the air cleared for a brief spell, they could hear the faint tolling of the village church bells. Tierce, Nones? Was it morning or noon? She could not tell. Night she knew, night with its blackness when the roused wind spoke in hoarse, crying voices. She would wait tense and listening on those nights for the sound of ghostly hooves. But the Centaur never came. Instead very often above the whine and whistle of the wind she could hear the howling of wolves. She knew they were wolves because they had lurked in the forest on the edge of Nareham. During the cold season when Harold de Ander was not in residence and there were no nobles to organize a hunt the wolves grew bolder, sometimes crossing the river to raid the hen runs and the cowsheds. She had seen a pack of them once, lean, hungry, bloody-snouted beasts, tearing the entrails from a fallen ox before they had been driven off with sticks and stones.

One morning for the first time in a long while they awoke to bright sunshine. Did it mean the long siege was over? Did it mean the snow would soon melt? Ursula said yes. She knew, she felt it in her bones. Still cold, but the sting had gone out of the air, and the wind had ceased. The old woman looked unwell, gaunter than ever, ancient, her pasty face so furrowed now the eyes were mere slits lost in a web of wrinkles. None of them was eating enough, and Joanna had taken her gown in twice. They were hungry, but not starving, not yet. Not yet.

Joanna sent Timkin out to the woodpile. "Try to get some sticks that are dry. If you lift the top ones you might find a few."

He had been gone only a few minutes when they heard a loud thud, then a rattle and rumble, as if logs were tumbling and rolling over and over. Joanna said, "The stupid idiot, he's probably upset the whole pile."

"I'll go," Ursula volunteered. The cold swept in as she opened the door.

Joanna raked the embered ashes, throwing on a few twigs, coaxing a small flame from them. Suddenly through the thick walls she heard an eerie scream. God, what now? "Keep away from the fire," she shouted at the children as she rushed out into the courtyard without cloak or shawl.

Ursula was kneeling in the melting trampled snow amid a helter-skelter of sticks and logs. Joanna had a queer view of Timkin's shod feet and baggy-hosed legs. The rest of him was hidden by Ursula.

"What is it? What happened? Did the idiot...?"

She saw the gray slab of stone, a small rubble of mortar, before she saw Timkin's head.

"Mistress—don't come."

But Joanna did, biting her lip, her fists clenched. It was a horrible sight. Timkin lay in a pool of blood, the top of his head smashed in, his face gone, brains, flesh and bone splattered about. Apparently a stone from the edge of the crumbling rooftop had come loose and fallen, hitting him squarely on the top of the skull as he rummaged in the woodpile.

They threw a blanket over him where he lay, and the next morning with the sun climbing the yellow sky, Joanna dug a shallow grave for him at the bottom of the garden. The ground had already begun to thaw, but not enough to make spading the flintlike earth less than a grinding task.

"He's not shriven, poor soul," Ursula said, tears oozing down her seamy face. Despite her scolding and verbal scorn, she had been very fond of Timkin. "Poor innocent, never did a fly harm. And now—not even a priest."

"We shall say *Aves* for him," Joanna said. "And later we shall buy him a Mass."

The question "When?" hung in the air.

Joanna shoveled the black earth as gently as she could upon the shrouded corpse. She found it hard to believe he was dead, the little mite, not bright, sometimes stupid, but always cheerful and eager to please. He had worked side by side with her, not complaining, whistling between his teeth, willing to do whatever she asked (even going to the abbey) and dying at the last task she had given him. The injustice of it all choked her; she wanted to weep as Ursula did, but life at Thorsby seemed to have hardened her against tears.

She could not weep, but kneeling at the graveside, head bowed, she again felt a sudden stab of fear. This was not the end, there was more. God the Almighty, the Avenging Father, would not let her go. He would break her yet, break her for her pride, for flaunting His holy laws. The scales were weighed in His favor, for He in His angry righteousness had the power to unleash famine, disease, death, and she, she was only a weak helpless mortal. Why go on? she thought, a great weariness washing over her. If she could only lie down, close her eyes and sleep, the dreamless sleep of exhaustion; admit defeat, give up, let it all go.

But even as despair gripped her she seemed to see her father's face looking out at the falling rain, Ivo lifting his head, squaring his shoulders, after his dismissal as bailiff, Ivo, a wife and three sons buried in the cemetery, standing in the doorway of their cot, squinting against the light, assessing what had to be done. Ivo refusing to be crushed. And what of Mariotta? Her mother, Mariotta, shaking an angry fist at the world, crying, *God damn them all!*

No. She could not submit, yield, surrender. Only those who allowed themselves to be broken were ground under His heel. Not her. She was Ivo and Mariotta's daughter; their blood ran in her veins. She could not give up. She could not bow down, submit, not while she had Edmund to fight for, not while she had a breath in her body. They would survive. They must. Hadn't they come through the winter? True, Timkin was dead and the food slowly giving out, but they were not finished, they were still there, she, Ursula and the two children.

When the last of the patchy snow thawed and melted away they put the chickens, pigs and geese out. Ursula swept the hall, throwing wide the windows and door to let the fresh air in. Joanna went to the garden and began spading the earth, careful to avoid Timkin's grave, turning over and breaking each clod with a silent prayer. Once the soil was prepared, she spread the seed that had come from the abbey.

Was it March, April? Ursula thought only March. Spring. It would be planting time at Nareham. Ivo would be riding the fields on a bay, giving orders to the reeve, the hayward, seeing that Harold de Ander's strips were planted to corn, oats and barley. He would overlook the calving and the lambing himself, count the chickens and the geese. Winter stores would be assessed, the manor court held, fines levied. And the soft, sweet-scented breezes would be sighing in Alys's garden, the lilies, the rose bushes.... But she mustn't, she mustn't. She would die of homesickness if she let her mind dwell on the pleasant memories. Better to recall the unpleasant ones, the hunger, the cold, the dirty smoke-filled cot, the awful plague, the servility, the bowing and scraping in the manor house and her father's thunderous brow, his cold voice disowning her, a wound that had not, would never, heal.

The days continued warm and sunny as if to make up for the terrible winter past. The sprouts in Joanna's garden lifted green heads and spread into leafy shoots. She liked to think that Timkin's presence under the sod had something to do with their steady growth. She became fairly proficient at snaring; it not only put rabbits in their kettle, but kept the voracious pests from devouring the young plants. The chickens began to lay again. She, Ursula and the children were eating, not their fill but at least they did not go to bed hungry. Edmund could be trusted to do simple tasks now, gathering twigs, chasing the hens from the garden and throwing stones at the crows. He was a tractable child, mild-tempered, happy, nothing like Aleyn, who pouted and wept, sometimes rolling on the floor in a fit when he did not have his way.

One morning Ursula came in from the orchard to announce that rain was brewing. "I don't think 'twill be a bad storm," she said. But when Joanna went out to look a little later the sky was livid with massed clouds. Streaks of white lightning silently throbbed and shimmered. The wind was cold, icy cold. She had a premonition, one she could not place, but somewhere in the past she had seen the same sky, felt and smelled the same wind.

She ran back into the house. "Get blankets, sheets, cloths," she ordered Ursula as she moved quickly from pallet to pallet snatching at the coverings.

They hurried out into a whirling chaos carrying their bundles, Ursula following Joanna as fast as her old crippled legs could carry her.

"We must cover the plants," Joanna shouted against the wind. Together, each holding an edge, they laid down the billowing cloths, anchoring them with rocks. They had just finished when it began to rain, a cold, steely rain, and by the time they had reached the front door the rain had turned to hail.

It lasted less time than it took to boil a pot of water, but the clattering hailstones, the size of large marbles, had flattened the grass, torn the blossoms from the apple and cherry trees and sent the chickens and geese scurrying into the barn. A damaging hail, the kind that Joanna had seen before.

When it was over and a weak sun emerged, Joanna went out and down to the garden. Lifting blankets and sheets, she saw that only a portion of the new growth had been destroyed.

"What is left is as good as harvested," Joanna said happily, adding confidently, "The worst is over."

"Pray God ye be right," Ursula replied, crossing herself twice.

Chapter XIII

Two days after the hailstorm, Joanna, hoeing her garden, heard a distant shout and a few minutes later the sound of approaching voices. Thinking she had visitors—who she could not imagine—she ran to a breach in the wall and, clambering up the heap of rubbled stone, looked over. Coming toward her from the direction of Shurbridge was a crowd of people, men, women and a scattering of children, many of them carrying flails, scythes and hooks. Every so often someone would raise an implement and wave it in a menacing manner. Joanna watched, a cold hand squeezing her heart. As they neared she heard the murmur and babble of angry voices, and then a shrill female cry rang out:

"Kill the witch of Thorsby! Death to the whore!"

Sliding down, she ran to the house, fear pounding in her lungs. Once through the door she slammed it shut.

"What is it?" Ursula asked, startled by the white face, the distended eyes.

"I—I don't rightly know," Joanna gasped. "But I believe the villagers have come."

"Here? What fer?"

"Oh—listen! Listen!" The shouting had come closer. "For God's sake, help me bar the door!" Joanna shot the worm-eaten wooden bolt and then together with Ursula dragged a bench across to fit under it. "The trestles, too!" They brought four trestles to the door, piling one upon the other.

"What do they want?" Ursula asked, her chin quivering.

"I know not. But they sound—oh, God, the windows! And the kitchen door! Mother Mary, I almost forgot."

They shuttered the narrow windows—there were only two in the hall—then ran to the kitchen. This door also had a heavy wooden bolt, a little sturdier than the one in the hall, and they banged it down, securing it tightly. Then they hastily shoved the heavy cutting block against it.

Edmund stood in the center of the hall holding his younger brother's hand. Both children, catching the women's panicked urgency, stared at them with round frightened eyes as they dashed hither and thither. Aleyn stuck his fist in his mouth and began to cry.

"Oh, hush!" Joanna ordered impatiently, while her eyes scanned the room. She ran down to the west end and, picking up her skirts, clambered up the rickety ladder to the loft Geralt had used as a sleeping place. Stumbling over a straw pallet, she reached the small window and began to tug at the smoke-grimed shutters. Unused for years, they refused to give until Joanna by pounding and pulling savagely managed to yank them back.

She looked down on the courtyard just as the howling mob came boiling out from under the gate tower. Thorsby gained, their cries redoubled, the stragglers catching up, screaming, too, at the top of their lungs as they rushed toward the door, a human pack in full cry. Joanna recognized some of them, the woman with the dirty scarlet rag bound about her head, waving a billy hook now instead of a stone, the mingy-faced man in the peaked woolen hat armed with a scythe, the drooling idiot, his mouth open, showing blackened teeth.

"Kill the witch!"

They were a miserable ragged lot, thinned by a lean winter, the men stubble-bearded, the women sallow-faced, the children hollow-eyed, a pathetic bunch, but feral and vicious. Those in the lead began to pound on the door, the sound echoing hollowly in the hall.

Bang! Bang! Bang!

Joanna, shrinking back, called down to Ursula, "Get the fire going. Melt what lard we have until it bubbles."

"Mistress, there is barely enough lard to fill a pipkin."

"God's bones, boil water then—hot, hot, lots of it in the big kettle."

The pounding continued. "Come out!" a voice cried. "Come out and get yer just rewards! Witch! Witch!"

Should she attempt to talk, to reason with them? But they were mad, insane. They would never listen. Could she try? The window was too high for any of them to do her harm, the wall too steep and slippery for even the nimblest to climb. Thorsby manor had, after all, been built as a castle-fortress, for which she was now grateful. Should she address them sternly, threaten them for trespassing?

Bang-bang-bang! "Come out or we'll come in and drag yer out!" This from the mingy-faced man in the peaked woolen hat.

"We want to duck yer in the river to see if ye can swim," a woman yelled stridently.

Mad. And yet she remembered her father telling her of a

mob at Thexted Fair he had once seen converging on a peddler, a stranger, who had been accused by two peasants of cheating them. The man, his wits about him, had nimbly jumped to a mounting block and, holding up his hands, had quelled them, according to Ivo, simply by seeming unafraid. He talked to them, outshouting the loudest, then, addressing them in a calm and reasonable voice, explained that he had made an honest error and was willing to rectify it.

"Witch! Witch of Thorsby! Witch! Witch!" the crowd chanted.

She pulled herself up on the sill of the window and called down.

"Folk of Shurbridge!"

At first the milling mob did not hear her, so intent were they on breaking the door down. Someone had brought up a heavy log and they were ramming away with it. "Witch! Witch! Witch!"

"Folk of Shurbridge!"

A man with sun-bleached yellow hair and a squint looked up. "There she be! Look! Look! The witch herself ready to fly!"

The crowd, almost as one, raised their heads, mouths gapping. "The witch...shhh...!"

"Folk of Shurbridge..." Joanna swallowed, wiping her clammy hands against her skirt. "What would you want of me? Why do you come to my house in such rage? I am no more witch than you—or you." She pointed down at them, the two women singled out shrinking back in horror. "I live here without troubling you. I live in peace with my neighbors. I have never harmed you, not one—"

"That's a lie!" the mingy-faced man cried. "Since ye've come to Thorsby we've had naught but trouble. Aye, and this last is too much. The hail—*ye* brought it on!"

"The hail killed my garden, too," Joanna said.

"'Taint true!" a lad on the fringe of the assembly shouted. "I been down to the garden and the cabbages is growing—aye—growing!"

"That's because I put down covers, I—" Joanna began, but the voices below had swelled into an uproar, drowning out speech.

Someone found an old cow turd and flung it at Joanna, and it plopped against the ledge. Others began scrabbling around for turds, stones, sticks, anything to hurl.

Joanna withdrew, leaving the shutters slightly ajar.

"Fly away, witch, fly away if you can!" someone sang out mockingly.

Joanna, leaning over the loft railing, looked down on a white-faced Ursula and the two children staring up at her in mute fright.

"Is the water hot?" Joanna asked.

"Not yet. Almost."

She thought quickly. She must find a way to get the heavy kettle up without scalding herself. Descending, she hurried into the kitchen and took down a length of rope hanging from a peg on the wall. When the water began to boil, she and Ursula, using cloths, lifted it from the fire and carried it to a spot just below the balcony. Joanna quickly looped the rope through the arched wooden handle. Then she climbed the ladder with one end of the rope in her hand. Ursula followed, more slowly, carefully, her old knees quivering. "Hurry!" Joanna urged.

Together they hauled the kettle up without losing too much of the steaming water. Joanna opened the shutters quietly, and she and Ursula hoisted the pot onto the sill.

Down below they were still hammering at the door, a stout oaken one, thank God, a door that had weathered many another rougher siege. "She be hard to get," a man said. "The witch has put a spell on the door."

"Someone got a cross?" the woolen-hatted man shouted. "Make one, then, and hold it up. Everyone knows witches have no power against the cross. Now the rest of ye—put a little muscle behind this log."

Joanna tipped the kettle, and the scalding water spilled in a small torrent on the invaders' heads. Piercing shrieks rang out as those closest to the door received the full impact of the boiling water. "Yah! Yah!" They leaped and danced, knocking down a brown-shawled woman and a child as they hastened to back out of the way.

"There's more!" Joanna cried. "My servants"—and she tried to make it sound like a small army—"have been busy. Next time 'twill be boiled oil and pitch. So clear out!"

The crowd withdrew across the courtyard to confer. Joanna, watching, heard them arguing in low tones, and though she could not catch what they said except for an occasional curse and the word "witch" repeated many times, she guessed that some had had a bellyful and were ready to go home. But the mingy-faced man shook his fist, exhorting them, railing, and once shouting, "Do ye want more o' the same? I tell ye she's cast her evil eye on Shurbridge."

They were not going to leave. The lumpish varlets, the craven vultures! God's curse on them! For the first time since they had arrived she forgot fear and caution as a raging, fist-shaking anger took hold. Stay, would they? Call her witch! Stone her, drown her? Burn her at the stake? She would show the blathering knaves.

"Come, Ursula." Closing the shutters, she hurried down with the kettle. "More water." She ran into the kitchen and placed the pot on the fire and emptied the water bucket into it. If they only had pitch. If they only had weapons, arrows, lances, anything to make those mad peasant dogs think there were a few men inside, soldiers under her orders. But arms, if any, would have been kept in the gate tower. The only weapon to hand was a rusty pike standing in one corner of the great hall. One pike against that frenzied horde. But—but, she thought, if she could pick off the man who seemed to be their leader, the one with the woolen hat, perhaps the others would lose heart and retreat.

She found the lance, surprised at its weight, disappointed at its blunt tip. She sharpened it on a small whetstone in the kitchen, keeping an eye cocked for the water to boil.

Presently she heard the crowd banging at the door again. Evidently they had been persuaded to continue their assault. "Witch! Witch!" the muted shout rose above the pounding.

Joanna, grasping the pike, hurried up to the loft window and opened the shutters. Pulling herself up to the ledge, she knelt there, aiming for the wool-hatted man. Just as she launched the pike, its heft nearly pulling her from the sill, a woman on the outer edge of the throng shouted, "Watch out!" There was a scrambling and the crowd parted as the pike clattered harmlessly to the court's broken flags.

Joanna called, "There's more! I swear we shall skewer you all. My men are fitting their arrows now."

"Ha! Why ain't they been at us afore?" the mingy-faced man cried.

Joanna retreated. With Ursula's help she dragged up the second pot of water. But now, the leader, a little wiser, had placed a lookout across the court from the window, and the moment the shutter opened, the door rammers scattered, and they stayed out of reach, watching Joanna, trying to lob stones at her. After a while, knowing the water had cooled, the group who formed the vanguard went back to their work at the door. Joanna emptied her pot on them nonetheless, but despite a drenching they went on with their grim work.

"Mistress!" Ursula called. "They's some at the back!"

They were attempting to get in through the kitchen, and there were more at the two wooden-shuttered windows in the hall, for they heard a cracking sound as one of the slats broke through. Joanna slithered down the ladder and, picking up an iron poker, stationed herself by the window.

"Find yourself a weapon," Joanna ordered, "and stand guard at the other window."

Ursula hobbled out and returned with a meat hook.

They waited. Another slat cracked open and a head poked through. Joanna raised the iron poker and hit with every ounce of her furious strength. There was a bloodcurdling shriek and the head was withdrawn quickly, pulled back by those on the outside. She did not know whether she had injured or killed the man. Killed, she hoped.

"The next one who tries to come in will get more of the same!" she shouted.

She heard the murmur of voices, vehement curses, but they seemed to think better of the window and left it alone.

The light through the chinked shutters faded. The hall darkened into dense shadow. The children, silent until now, paralyzed with fear, had sat huddled together near the hearth. Now Aleyn began to cry again. He was hungry. Joanna, afraid to leave her post, afraid to allow Ursula to move either, instructed Edmund to bring his brother some bread. "There's an oat cake on a ledge next to the spit. Mind the fire."

He was thirsty, too, Aleyn said. There was not much water left, but they had a keg of cider.

Suddenly, it became quiet outside, ominously so. Joanna put her eye to a missing slat in the shutter. Evening had come with a blood-red afterglow staining the milky pale sky. She saw the crowd conferring at the gatehouse again. Would they leave, go home? It did not seem likely. The villagers were afraid of the dark and would never walk across the fen after nightfall. She guessed they were trying to decide how to fill their bellies—for by this time they were surely hungry—and where to bed down. She was right, for presently they dispersed. The mingy-faced man returned in a few minutes and kneeled on the courtyard flags. He had his back to Joanna and she could not see what he was doing. She clambered up the ladder and, opening the shutter, leaned out. He had a handful of dry straw and a small whetstone. He was starting a fire. One of the lads appeared with an armful of sticks. Joanna hoped they were too damp to take the feeble flicker that licked at the straw. But the mingy-faced man, like all peasants, could start a fire in the midst of a marsh if need be, and before long flames were leaping skyward. The woman with the red headcloth emerged from the gloom, laughing, holding three flapping chickens in each hand. Joanna clenched her fists as the hot, angry blood rushed to her face. Her chickens, *her* chickens, the ones she had coddled and nurtured through the long winter, saved from the pot because they were such good layers. *Her* chickens!

"You kill those," she shouted, "and I'll put a curse on them."

Pale, firelit faces looked up at her.

"Any one of you who tastes of those chickens will sicken and die. I call on Melusine, the Lady of Darkness, on the devil and all his demons..."

There was a horrified shriek, and the woman dropped the cackling chickens, which promptly hopped and fluttered away.

"Ye fools!" their leader shouted. "She can't harm us as long as we have the cross. Where's the cross, who's got the cross?"

"The cross," Joanna said loudly, "will do you no good. 'Tis not blest."

"Ye are wrong," the woolen-capped man retorted. "Rowena here wears a brass cross blessed by the priest. That and my hedgehog foot will protect us." He held it up.

If it is such good protection, Joanna wanted to ask, why are you here? Why? Because, she answered her own question, they think me a witch. A witch, that is why. Suddenly her mind raced back to childhood, a clearing, a rock, Mariotta mouthing gibberish, a fluttering hen with its head severed—blood spattering. Had her mother harbored some taint and passed it on to her? Were those frothing, angry Shurbridgers right? Was she, Joanna, a minion of Satan? Oh, no. Nay. Not her. She could not, would not ever believe that. The villagers were at Thorsby because they needed a scapegoat, someone outside, a stranger they could blame for their misfortunes, the bad crops, the hail. Stupid, idiotic varlets!

"Go on," the woolen-capped man commanded. "Fetch the chickens, ye boobies. Do ye want to go hungry? Say an *Ave* over them, that'll chase the she-witch's curse away."

They killed the chickens, all six of them. Someone had rounded up the pigs, too, and there followed a debate as to whether to slaughter them now or take them back to the village. Those arguing in favor of saving them for future use won, and the pigs were hastily trussed.

Watching them, Joanna felt as though she would choke with rage. *Her* pigs, reared, fattened on scraps carefully hoarded. "Damn you!" she shouted, shaking her fist.

Ignoring her, the villagers set up a tripod, spitted the hastily plucked chickens and hung them over the fire. Presently the smell of roast fowl wafted up to Joanna.

She banged the shutters to and went back down the ladder. Ursula and the children looked at her trustingly. She loathed that look, hated their trust, wanted to shout, "I don't know what to do!" She was tired, hungry, her nerves were frayed. She wished she could shift the burden of her fear to someone else's shoulders, someone strong and capable who would reassure her, who would say, "Do not worry, I will take care of everything." But there was no one. Thomas had gone, leaving her without protection. John Hawkwood, thinking only of his pleasure, had deserted her twice. And her father had disowned her. She did not have anyone who could stand up to that mad throng outside, disperse them and send them packing, a man who would guard her against terror. There was no one but herself.

"Mama, are they going to hurt us?" Edmund asked anxiously.

"Nay." She went to him and, stooping, kissed him quickly, holding him for a brief moment. And because Aleyn had begun to sniffle again she held him, too.

"Nay, sweets, no one will harm you while I am here."

Somehow she must live through the nightmare, somehow she must outwit those fools camped in the courtyard, those ignorant, superstitious peasants, but hate alone would not rid her of them.

As she could see it now her only salvation lay in time. The longer she could hold out the more chance she had of remaining alive. Again she reminded herself that Thorsby was a fortress, one that must have successfully withstood attacks in the past. True, she had no men-at-arms or weapons to back her up, and the castle walls presented a far less formidable barrier than they had years earlier, but if she could delay the mob, keep them at bay outside until their tempers cooled, she hoped they would grow weary of milling about and go home.

"What have we in the kitchen, Ursula?" she asked.

"There's several loaves, a cheese and a few pieces of meat in brine. Some root, the onion root, I call it, and cider. A rabbit I stewed this morning. A few eggs."

"Good." More than she expected. If the door held they would not suffer from hunger. "Is there anything else we can put to the doors?"

"The table on the dais?" Ursula suggested.

It was a stout table, hewn from oak and nailed to the floor. They could not budge it. They heaved the last bench on top of the pile already under the latch, then sat down on the floor to cold rabbit pie and cider.

Joanna said, "Do you smell smoke?"

"Nay. Only the fire on the hearth."

"I hear something, the..." Rising quickly, she ran up the ladder and climbed up.

"What is it?" Ursula asked.

"They've set fire to the door!"

Someone shouted, "Smoke them out!"

Ursula put her hand over her mouth.

Joanna scooted down the ladder. "Come—quickly!" She grabbed Edmund's hand. "Take Aleyn. We shall try to slip out the back."

But as they came through the kitchen they heard the ominous crackling sound, smelled the wood burning. That too!

Joanna wheeled and ran back into the hall. God, oh God! The shutters were on fire, too!

A ring of fire. They would be in, the whole screaming mob, as soon as the first shutter or door gave. "The windows!" she yelled at Ursula. "Hit the first head that comes through!"

But she could do nothing about the door. And there was no place to hide, none. The kitchen and the hall. Not a nook or cranny where they might conceal themselves. A simple manor castle, it had been built years and years ago, when the walls were stout, and the gate tower and the tower chamber were all that was needed to repulse an enemy. She stood by the hearth, her heart pounding, her knees trembling, stood there, facing the door, her children clinging to her skirts, waiting for the worst. She saw the flames beginning to lick through the wood, heard the mob, revived by a good meal, shouting jubilantly at the prospect of success.

"God in heaven, kind, merciful Mother Mary, Jesus, my Lord, I have sinned, forgive me," Ursula prayed.

Joanna stooped and lighted a stick of wood, then held it above her head. She would fight fire with fire. The first one who tried to touch her would get the flame in his face.

The door fell open with a smothered crash, scattering trestles and benches, the timbered panels alight with dancing fire. Beyond, in the dark, torches flared. The smell of smoke and unwashed bodies rushed in on the chill night air. Joanna, standing stiffly, saw their bloodshot eyes, the mingy-faced man waving a cudgel, the woman with the red-bound head, her lips drawn back from fanglike eyeteeth.

"Burn her! Burn the witch!"

Joanna's stomach churned sickly, and she felt darkness closing in. She fought it, she fought against the loud banging under ribs, straining through a dizzy mist, fought to remain on her feet, when suddenly, as if in a dream, the advancing rabble halted, froze. From a long way off she heard a clear loud voice command, "Stop! On pain of God's wrath—and my own—I order you to stop!"

The abbot!

"Would you dare me to excommunicate each and every one of you? I will, I will!"

Joanna felt Ursula's hand on her arm. "Mistress..." and still the darkness came in great billowing waves.

"Mistress, come sit, we are saved."

"Nay," she said weakly but resolute. "I shall stand."

The mob fell away as the abbot, followed by his cellarer and two monks, strode over the smoldering door.

"Are you harmed, Dame Joanna?" he asked.

"Nay—nay, my lord abbot."

He took the still-burning torch from Joanna's hand and gave it to his cellarer. Then, turning to the villagers, he coldly ordered them to stamp out the last of the fire. "And be sure you get every ember, you loutish knaves!"

They fell over one another rushing to obey, and soon the air was filled with the stench of singed wool and leather as they slapped their jerkins and shirts against the shutters and doors.

"Lift the torch, Barnaby," the abbot commanded his cellarer. "I want to look at these good Christians. I want to see everyone plainly."

The torch flared and sputtered, casting a garish light over the motley crowd, no longer savage, but cowed, crestfallen.

They stared at their feet and shuffled, averting their eyes from the angry ones of the abbot. No one spoke, no one uttered a sound. The torch crackled and spat.

"Heathens!" The abbot spoke at last, hurling the word at them, his anger so monumental he had difficulty controlling the impulse to reach out and strangle the nearest man with his bare hands. "Heathens!"

There was a little murmur in the back, and a voice said, "My lord abbot—'twas John who—"

"Hush! I do not want to know who your leader is. I do not want to hear you tell me someone else was to blame. You are *all* to blame. All! Sheep! Pagan sheep!"

It was true. For all their obsequious mouthings of God, Jesus, Mary and the Holy Cross, they were still pagans, Saxon pagans more at home with idols, Beltane and Melusine. Peasants. It was at times like these he felt doubt, the uselessness of his calling, the futility of the struggle against ingrained idolatry and turgid minds. "Shame! Shame to you! This woman has done you no harm. She has only set foot in Shurbridge once—and then was stoned. Shame for shame. Why do you call her witch? What proof?"

Silence.

"Did you imagine that by firing Lady de Ander's castle you would get off scot-free? Did you? Let me tell you I have seen men hang for less."

There was an answering mutter, the shaking of bowed heads.

"Go home, then. Go home, and if I should hear of one of you coming within a league of Thorsby I'll have you thrown in the stocks. Is that plain?"

A slight stir, a few whispers, a cough, and the voice in the back said, "Sire, pray—could we not remain the night in the barn here? We shall be quiet as mice, but if we..."

"Afraid of the dark, are you? Why don't you call on your pagan gods to protect you, then? Nay, you cannot stay. Go home. Light your way with the damnable fire you used trying to burn Thorsby down."

They left, not as they had come, but crestfallen, woebegone, stepping on one another's heels, in an effort not to be either too far ahead or too far behind.

When they had disappeared, the abbot turned to Joanna, pale but recovered.

She curtsied. "My lord abbot, I cannot begin to tell you my thanks."

He waved his hand. "I only regret I did not come sooner."

"But for you..." Joanna bit her lip. She looked unwell, thin, almost gaunt, her eyes enormous in her heart-shaped face. "How—how came you here, my lord?"

"By God's design. We, my esteemed cellarer and my brothers, were riding through Shurbridge on our way to Luton when I happened to notice how empty the village was, how very quiet. I inquired of the miller, a laconical fellow, and he told me they had all gone to 'burn the witch.' It did not take much to reckon who they meant."

"I shall be forever grateful."

She might be a peasant and a whore, he thought, but she had the dignity and poise of a lady born. And intelligent, too. Ah—*that* was the difference he had sought to explain to himself earlier, the difference between her and the other concubines he had not bothered to redeem. Joanna was not only beautiful and proud, but intelligent as well. Perhaps that was why she had such a clever child. But what a pity God had wasted so fine a mentality on a woman.

"I would offer a glass of wine and supper," she said, "but I am afraid we have no wine and our supper is poor."

"The wine I have with me, and as for supper, we have fasted before."

The monks brought him a bench, and he sat down. "Fetch the keg," he instructed. Then, turning to Joanna, "Your paramour has not returned?"

"He has not been here for some time now."

"How have you lived, then?"

"As best we could."

"How, Dame Joanna?"

She gave a brief, almost dry recitation of their troubles, telling him she had sent Timkin to Kenham to get help and how the lad had later died.

"Poor simpleton. Timkin had only to leave word and I should have been here long ere this. And you have had such a hard time of it. But..." The abbot gave her a rueful smile. "You don't want my pity, you don't want me to tell you that your travail was God's punishment, a penance. You want my assistance. Am I right?"

"If you could—a loan?"

"A loan to a sinner." It was petty of him to make such a remark. He knew it, but the words had slipped out despite himself.

"Not for me, my lord abbot," she said, flushing, "but for my children and my old servant here."

"Of course, I will do everything I can."

"I—I must be honest. I do not know how or when I can repay you."

He smiled again. "I would be a poor giver if I expected anything in return. Besides," and he patted Edmund on the head, "I would hate to see my future scrivener starve for lack of Christian charity."

The abbot left the next morning after saying a Mass over poor Timkin's grave. But he did not forget his promise to Joanna, and two days later an ox-drawn cart laden with provisions rumbled into the courtyard. The abbot had sent flour, chickens, a keg of ale, a sack of onions, two piglets (male and female), corn, a basket of garden seeds, a huge round of cheese and a fierce dog of mixed breed to act as guard replacing Geralt's mastiff. And as if that were not enough he had instructed the driver, a lay brother, to unhitch the ox and use it to plow Joanna's strips, "and whatever else it would take a man's hand to do."

By the time the lay brother left three days later, Joanna not only had her field plowed and planted and a garden dug but the doors and shutters repaired as well.

One April afternoon two men mounted atop a sorry nag came trotting up the elm-lined ride. A mean-looking, bedraggled pair, one with an eye missing, the other with a heavily scarred face, they carried a roll of cloth for Joanna, a gift, they said, from a knight whose name they had forgotten. Joanna at once thought of Thomas. The cloth had been entrusted to them at Dover by a ship's captain for delivery at Thorsby. Claiming to be discharged soldiers from Aquitaine, they recounted a sad tale of hard luck, wounds, dismissal without pay and hunger.

"Good dame," the one-eyed man said, "we came a long road out o' our way to give ye this. Near got our throats cut twice, ain't it so, Jack?"

Jack nodded in agreement. "Weren't for the goodness o' God we wouldna be here. We was promised two nobles for our trouble."

"Two nobles!" Joanna exclaimed, aghast, fingering the coarse woolsey cloth of faded blue. Wasn't it like pinchpenny Thomas to send her such a poor offering and expect her to pay for its transport? With what? "I haven't any money.

Here—you'd best take it back." She shoved the roll into the one-eyed man's arms. "Mayhap you can sell it for a few pence."

"We couldn't. We doan want it. Not even one noble?"

"Not even one."

"Nothin'? I tell ye what, dame—we'll settle for a good meal and a flagon o' wine each."

"Ale I have, and cider. You are welcome to it. My—my serving men are out in the field and will be in presently," she added as an afterthought. She did not like the way they were looking around, assessing the hall. She could read their minds as if their skulls were clear glass. Not worth putting up a fuss, nothing here to take, except the wench herself. And menservants, no telling how many or how soon they'll return.

The wench, armed with a poker, sat watching them warily as they stuffed themselves with bread and cheese, washing bulging mouthfuls down with swigs of cider.

After they had gone, Ursula started to unroll the cloth. "We might be able to make some warm shifts for the children," she said to Joanna.

"I can't see how. Even those thieves didn't want it—full of moth holes, mildewed."

"Hmm." Ursula flipped over another fold. "Mistress! Look ye! Look! There's a purse here—here, sewn on the inside!"

She ripped out the stitches with her teeth. It was a purse of the same faded material as the cloth. Undoing the strings, she turned it upside down. A shower of gold coins dropped upon the table, some falling to the floor and rolling away. Ursula scrambled on her knees, her old bones creaking painfully, to gather them.

"They're foreign, mistress." She bit one, then another. "But good, good. Golden coins. And so many! God bless Sir Thomas!"

Joanna pressed her hands to her flushed face. So he *had* remembered, he *had* thought of her. Thomas had not forgotten. He still loved her.

PART II

JOHN HAWKWOOD

A hundred lords had he in his rout,
Armed full well with hearts stern and stout.

"The Knight's Tale"
Chaucer

Chapter XIV

Joanna and Ursula had made an understandable error in thinking the blue purse had been sent by Thomas. The coins were foreign, Thomas was in Aquitaine, and he was the only one who had ever sent them money. But in point of fact, it was John Hawkwood who had dispatched the roll of cloth with its golden bounty.

Hawkwood had suddenly thought of Joanna one evening in Italy shortly after his latest victory while dining with his captive, a Pisan, the Count of Perlonti. He could not exactly say what had prompted his memory, the exotic girl with the long black hair moving her hips so seductively as she danced for them, the sweet, savory, heady wine, or the smell of new earth mingled with lime blossoms wafting in from the garden, but think of Joanna he did. Remembering her drab surroundings, it amused him to imagine how surprised she would be when she received his gift. He had also inserted a small piece of parchment into the purse, a fragment large enough to hold his name, which he had himself laboriously signed—John Hawkwood—though he had no way of knowing that when Ursula had up-ended the purse, the parchment had stuck to the bottom. In any case both she and Joanna would have made little of it, since they, like Hawkwood, were unlettered and could not read. Again it was something Hawkwood had not foreseen, for he was certain Joanna, receiving his largesse, would compare it to Sir Thomas's stinginess and would be impressed.

A hundred florins. A tidy sum he would have felt in the old days, but his recent successes had made him a rich man in so little time, swiftly if one looked back, far quicker than he had imagined. How long had it been since they had decided to leave France, he and Albrecht Sturz and their White Company? Five, six months, aye, nearly six months. Champagne, Burgundy and the Languedoc had been swarming with mercenaries. Sir Robert Knolly's arm of three thousand had already skimmed the cream, taking the richest villages, towns and manors, leaving the dross for others to squabble over. Now even the dross had been reduced to worthless rubble, and so the White Company and others of their ilk had marched down the valley of the Rhone and on their way bullied Pope Urban VI at Avignon out of 200,000 florins. With their pockets jingling with gold, Hawkwood and Sturz rode through the Cenis Pass of the Maritime Alps to Italy, joined on the way by other companies coming in under their white banner, all seeking new fields for booty. A formidable army now, 3,500 horses and 2,000 foot, each pike, helm and belt buckle polished to a dazzling gleam, each mounted man in a white surcoat, they advanced under the fluttering white ensigns. Marching from the Piedmont into Lombardy, they had halted within six miles of Milan and set up camp.

Hawkwood recalled it all, every detail stamped on his memory.

He remembered how quickly a messenger had arrived from the lords of Milan offering to make peace, how the company had pretended to accept the offer and then a few days later, on New Year's Eve, had attacked and overpowered the unsuspecting Milanese in the midst of their holiday. By a stroke of luck the Count of Perlonti and a host of other wealthy nobles were captured, tied one to another on a long rope, each man representing a large ransom.

It turned out to be a rewarding night's work, for 100,000 gold florins were collected, and John, as one of the leaders, sharing generously in this booty, hardly missed the hundred florins he had sent to Joanna. Indeed, Hawkwood, dining with the count, had reason to be pleased with himself. He could see where Albrecht Sturz had given wise advice; Italy was a veritable golden cornucopia. He would stay—there was no going back. For him France was no better than a corpse picked clean. England held nothing for him either. Though, as he had said many times over, he would never fight against the English, he did not see profit in fighting *for* them. Let King Edward continue his quarrel with the French King John, God speed him, but Edward's fight held no interest for him. Someday when he was established in a villa of his own, he might send for his sons. Should he do the same with Joanna? Have her come to Italy?

He leaned back and let his mind dwell on Joanna, remembering Thorsby, the bleak tower room, the wind howling outside the window. He recalled how she looked as he leaned over her, those beautiful eyes filled with love, the rich black hair fanned out from her face, one thick lock falling over a white breast. She had wanted to come with him, had begged....

He frowned at the memory. Aye, she had offered to go away with him, taking "our son." "*Our* son." Why did she insist on this blackmail? Did she think if she kept prodding him he would buckle under, give in, agree? Never. He was not some puling, weak-kneed milksop like her Thomas. (And stingy to boot. The hundred florins would show her how generous a *real* man could be.) Let her stay with her paramour, the bitch! In the meanwhile, he thought, eyeing the black-haired dancer, there were a plentitude of comely women who would gladly share his bed.

He liked the count, his captive, and for the first time in his life was sorry he could speak no language but English. He tried to have the count repeat his own name—John Hawkwood—even drew a hawk and a tree on the table cover. But apparently the Italian tongue could not work its way around the Anglo-Saxon syllables, and the closest the count came was Giovina Acuto, a name with several variations that John was eventually to be known by throughout the Italian peninsula.

Within two years John Hawkwood replaced Albrecht Sturz as sole leader of the White Company and as such put himself and his men under the jurisdiction of Pisa, now waging war against Florence. After months of interminable battle, of seesaw victories and defeat, John was beginning to feel bored with the entire campaign when he had an amusing if not pleasurable interlude.

His men had captured a Florentine merchant on his way home from a transaction in Sienna, and John Hawkwood decided to hold him for ransom. Words were shouted to the ramparts of Florence announcing the merchant's detention, his name, Nicola Torenzetti, and the amount wanted, fifteen thousand florins. Nicola pleaded that he was a poor man, that his family could not possibly raise such a sum, that he was neutral in this war, an innocent bystander. He argued in vain. Fifteen thousand it was and would remain.

That evening a lone cloaked horseman carrying a white flag of truce emerged from the city gates and rode toward the camp. "A member of the Torenzetti family, Sir John," Hawkwood's squire announced to his captain as he sat in his tent.

"Can you not take care of it yourself?" It was a petty matter, and Hawkwood had already lost interest in his prisoner and his numerous complaints.

"Nay, he insists on seeing you alone."

"Well, if he thinks I shall settle for less he is much mistaken. Who is it—a son?"

"I know not, captain. He will not say."

"Very well, have him come in."

A moment later a tall figure muffled in a dark-blue woolen cloak entered the room.

"Have you brought the money?" John asked as his page poured him a goblet of wine.

"I wish to speak to you alone," the figure said in hoarse broken English.

"So? And how do I know you will not draw a knife the moment my page and squire are gone?"

The figure crossed itself. "I swear on the tomb of our beloved Lord, Jesus, I shall do nothing to harm you."

Hawkwood's squire advised against leaving, but John laughed. "I'd be a sorry soldier if I could not take care of one Florentine—and a civilian at that."

When they were alone, Hawkwood lifted the goblet to his lips. "Well then, say your piece and be quick. And for God's sake, take that cloak from your face. I don't like talking to a mask."

"Aye, sir knight." The cloak was thrown open.

Hawkwood gaped. It was a woman, a young girl, a beautiful young girl with gray almond-shaped eyes, a short, perfect nose and lovely white skin.

"God's bones!" He set the goblet down and leaned forward.

"I am Torenzetti's daughter, Angelica." Removing the cloak, she let it fall to the floor. Her yellow clinging gown revealed a superb figure, high round breasts, a slender waist and smoothly curved hips. She shook out her dark chestnut hair, and it rippled over her shoulders in thick waves.

"I never dreamed that prattling old man..."

"He is my father," she reminded him coldly.

"And you, *you* want to bargain with me?"

"Aye."

"I see." He lifted his goblet and drank, watching her over the rim. "Pray—have a seat?" He motioned to a camp stool.

"I will stand."

"Wine? Nay, then. The price is fifteen thousand, and you want to ransom him for less."

"We have little money," she said. "My father's business has not done well because of this war. It has come close to impoverishing us."

"You don't look impoverished."

She gave him a faint smile. "I speak the truth. We have been forced to sell our villa and other properties. We are barely able to get along. Fifteen thousand florins is out of the question."

"What can you offer?"

She looked him squarely in the eyes. "I offer myself."

Hawkwood leaned back. "You are serious?" Girls of good family were as closely guarded as gold.

"Never more. I offer myself for a night."

"Does your father...?"

"He must never know. That is one of the conditions."

Hawkwood's eyes went slowly over her. He was not a wencher and had long given up the camp whores, dirty, odorous trollops whom his men found so satisfying. His tastes were more discriminate, but women of a higher order were not easy to come by, so he had done without. "Are you a virgin?" he asked.

She blushed.

"And you put one night's worth at fifteen thousand florins?"

She lifted her chin. "I do."

"Well then, I should like to see what I am getting." He rose and unhooked the tent's flap, letting it fall into place. The interior, lit by a single oil lamp, danced with shadows.

"You will have to show me," John said when she made no move. "Surely you as a merchant's daughter must know that a customer will not buy unless he can first examine the wares offered."

She bit her lip. Her slim-fingered, trembling hand tugged at the neck ribbon of her gown. Slowly she began to unlace the bodice. John smiled his encouragement. She shrugged, and her round creamy shoulders emerged from the silk; the breasts, suddenly released, sprang out, white, pink-nippled mounds.

"Does that suit you?" she asked haughtily, a spot of red burning on either cheek.

"Let us see the rest."

He was tormenting her, he knew, but in some obscure way she had made him angry. If this had been his daughter (and God knew he was old enough) he would have killed her. A woman of good name did not offer her body under any circumstances. Her virginity stood as her honor. Yet—he asked himself—why did he suddenly think of honor, why now when

223

he had always scoffed at it? Was it because *she* was the seducer, not he?

She worked the gown over her hips, and it slid with a soft whispery sound to the floor, lying in a yellow heap at her feet. Her satiny skin gleamed in the lamplight. He felt an ache in his loins as he stared at the firm breasts, the white stomach and the patch of dark hair between her legs. A man would have to be of stone to resist. He forgot his anger, his reluctance. He got to his feet, and when he started to take her in his arms, she drew back.

"You may look," she said, "but not touch unless you are willing to buy."

"I am willing, damn you," he growled, pulling her roughly against his chest.

Her lips tasted of wine, and it passed through his mind that she must have drunk a flagon or two for courage before she set out on her mission, but the knowledge did not soften him or cool his desire. He kissed her hard and long, his tongue probing her velvety mouth, his fingers digging into her back. When he released her, her eyes were veiled, but fear glimmered in their depths. He picked her up and carried her to his cot.

It took only a matter of moments for him to get out of his clothes, and then he fell upon her, grasping her shoulders, kissing her mouth, cheeks and throat, his mouth playing over her breasts and finally grasping a nipple. She gasped, her hips rose, and he kneed her thighs apart. He was aware that she was struggling—last-minute regret, no doubt—but he was too far gone to heed anything but his own animal need. His member swollen to a sweet intolerable ache, he entered her—ah! ah!—God, how he had missed a woman—how he had needed one. The moist warmth engulfed his senses, sent him thrusting again and again, and again, the tension building up until the one blazing explosion.

He collapsed, shuddering, holding her, the blaze slowly dying. She had not been a virgin, but every florin of the fifteen thousand had been worth it.

Several months later, John Hawkwood, still loyal to the Pisans in principle, became embroiled in their internal affairs. An ambitious, very wealthy merchant by the name of Giovanni Agnello—John the Lamb—had long been plotting to seize power and oust the commune of Pisa. He offered Hawkwood thirty thousand florins to aid him in his bid for stewardship, and Hawkwood, by now dissatisfied with his former Pisan employers, agreed. One hot summer night when the city slept, Hawkwood's soldiers stole into the campanile of the palazzo Santas Maria de Firoe and took over peacefully from the napping guards. The following morning at cockcrow, Giovanni had his followers assemble the people and from a balcony announced that the Virgin Mary had appeared to him in a dream, ordering him to assume temporary command of the troubled city. He, with Her blessed approval, was to be their doge.

Hawkwood, of course, was not fooled either by the dream or by Agnello's promise of a "temporary" lordship. He knew the beak-nosed, smiling, glitter-eyed merchant meant to be a tyrant, a rigid autocratic ruler, for as long as he possibly could. Still, he did not refuse Agnello's offer to be his "captain," though he never formed a liking for the man, and at times secretly loathed him. But he looked upon his position from the eyes of a professional soldier, a contract to be honored, a job to be done, a man to be served with cool integrity, regardless of his personal opinion.

His grasp of the Italian language had reached the point where he could converse, although still overlaying his words with a thick English accent, but people understood him, and he them.

Established in comfortable headquarters, he decided to send for Joanna after all. Time and distance had quelled his anger, and he missed her. Not even the lovely Florentine, Angelica, had satisfied him as Joanna had. His current mistress, a sleek Pisan courtesan with silky olive skin and high pointed breasts, had amused him for a while, but she was too demanding and had begun to bore him. He wanted Joanna. For some reason which he was chary of probing he felt he needed her. She was the only woman who could give him something other than a beautiful body, but what that "something" was he could no more explain than his need. So he had his clerk write a letter, telling her to come (without the brats), and enclosed five hundred florins in a packet, instructing the courier to put it on a ship bound for England.

Then he turned back to the business of advancing John Hawkwood's—or Giovinni Acuto's—affairs.

Chapter XV

Joanna received neither packet nor letter. The ship on which Hawkwood's golden summons had been placed went down off the coast of Portugal in a storm. All hands, all cargo. Nothing remained of what had once been the *Santa Sofia* but two floating kegs of wine; and the clinking coins wrapped in the parchment of words dictated with such a peremptory flourish vanished beneath the waves.

At Thorsby, Joanna, sparing with the last of her provisions, tended her garden, harvested her corn, still waiting for Thomas to appear. It had been over three years now, three years and seven months since she had last seen him. In that time she had woven a fantasy in which she convinced herself that she loved him, a fantasy born of loneliness rather than any genuine feeling. Occasionally she would think of John Hawkwood, remembering his kisses, the passion of his caresses, but the memory would be overlaid quickly with the recollection of his demeaning farewell. Baggage, he had called her. The hateful viper! To give him a single thought was to betray her own self. No, it was Thomas who, at last, had won her heart.

Then one windy, rain-lashed night, as she and Ursula sat over the central hearth, the dog the abbot had given them began to bark in the courtyard.

"Someone's here," Ursula said, her head cocked, listening to the clip-clop of horses' hooves distinguishable above the hoarse, frantic barking. She looked at Joanna questioningly

"It must be a stranger," Joanna said.

A loud, banging knock echoed through the hall. "Open up. Open up!" a male voice commanded. "In the name of Thomas de Ander, open up!"

Joanna blanched. She and Ursula exchanged a startled glance. "But 'tis not his squire's voice," Ursula whispered.

"Open up!"

"He may have a different squire," Joanna answered. Had he come back? Had her Thomas really returned?

"It may be a trick," Ursula cautioned.

"Open up! In the name of de Ander!"

Suppose it *was* him, oh, just suppose. Her impulse was to rush to the door and fling it open, but instead she motioned to Ursula. "See to it."

A suspicious Ursula cautiously inched the door open, clutching at the frame with white-knuckled, gnarled hands.

"Sir Thomas de Ander and company wish a night's lodging," the voice said.

Ursula, peering out into the pouring rain, seeing the looming shapes, the dark-cloaked horsemen, took fright and began to close the door, but the man stuck his foot in the crack. "Where is your master, you old bag of bones? Be quick, I say, and fetch him!"

Joanna, listening, thought; it couldn't be Thomas, his squire would surely know that he had rightful entry to Thorsby.

"We have no master," Ursula replied. "There's only Dame Joanna and a few servants." The servants she added to make herself, Joanna and the children, sleeping peaceably in the kitchen, seem less defenseless.

"Then fetch Dame Joanna," the intruder demanded.

Ursula tried to shut the door again, but the foot remained squarely wedged against the jamb. She scurried out of earshot to Joanna. "What shall we do? There's a whole pack of 'em. Couldn't see, but they might be thieves, robbers or worse."

"Did the man sound like a thief, a ruffian?"

Ursula shrugged. "One never knows."

"What did he look like?"

"A young man with a scowl."

"And his clothes?"

"Rain-soaked. Ah—but he was wearing a badge. I could not make it out, but 'twas a badge."

The knock again, the banging of an impatient fist.

"Let them in—and Ursula, do it graciously."

Ursula went back to the door. "My mistress says welcome. She has scanty provender, but what is hers is yours."

Joanna did not rise from her stool by the fire until she saw Thomas enter on the heels of his squire. Though she had been prepared by the exchange at the door, she could hardly believe her eyes, hardly believe her dream of his return had come true. But it had, it had. He was *here*, standing before her in the flesh just as she had imagined a thousand times before. Thomas. He loved her, he had come back.

"Thomas...!" Oh, she had been angry, but now, now all

was forgiven, the long bitter years, the waiting, wiped away. "Thomas!"

The look on his face warned her, and she caught herself. Behind Thomas appeared the cloaked figure of a woman, the hood thrown back from a beautiful face glowing with youth.

The mind, even in shock, even in dismay, works quickly. Her body stiffened, the smile fled from her face.

She heard herself saying, "You are welcome, Sir Thomas," in a voice she scarcely recognized as her own. But she could not curtsy, her knees refused.

"Thank—thank you, Dame Joanna," Thomas said, his voice slightly hesitant as if unsure of his welcome. He had changed little; his dress was still elegant, and except for the slight initial pause, his air snobbish and vain. Time had not aged him; he seemed as young and comely as ever. "But for the weather I should not have disturbed you."

So he had not told the woman, whoever she was, about her or Thorsby. He was going to make it seem as though the manor had cropped up on this stormy night, an opportune stopping place.

"You did not disturb me, Sir Thomas," Joanna said, standing very straight, conscious suddenly of her poor, coarse dress, the poverty of Thorsby's great hall.

"This," said Thomas, taking the woman by the hand and drawing her forward, "is Lady Rosamonde of Tribourne, my betrothed."

Betrothed! But what had happened to the witless du Pynne girl? Joanna forced her obstinate knee to bend. "Welcome, lady."

Rosamonde. A noblewoman, of course. His betrothed. An incomparable white skin, a rosebud mouth, blue, blue eyes and hair the color of an autumn leaf. Beautiful, and younger than she. "Welcome to Thorsby," Joanna repeated, and the words seemed to stick in her throat.

"Thank you, dame. It is kind of you to receive us." And a sweet, sweet feminine voice. Docile, not one to demand, to order a sack of flour and a bolt of cloth, not one to argue. Joanna had known all along that Thomas would marry, had known from the start, but while it had been an event of the future, some nebulous, vague happening, a marriage contract with an ugly lackwit, she had not minded. But—Lady Rosamonde. She could tell by the way Thomas had introduced her that this lady was special, even adored.

God damn him! she thought bitterly. So this is why he had

not come. Lady Rosamonde. Rich, too, she had no doubt. Thomas's mother, Alys (never mind his ineffectual father), would never have consented to a marriage unless it brought land and wealth.

"Whatever I have is yours," Joanna said.

"We have brought our own food," Thomas said curtly.

Joanna felt heat sting her cheeks. Damn the gilt-spurred cockerel. It was because of him she could not set a decent table. Except for the purse of gold coins, he had sent her nothing in the last three and a half years, and now no gracious greeting, no smile, not even the least indication that he had ever known her.

"Ah—there!" Wind and rain lashed through the open door as two men-at-arms entered, one carrying two sacks slung over a shoulder, the other with a sack and a small keg cradled under one arm. Joanna led them to the kitchen. Hams and meat pies, salted herring and brawn were laid out on the butcher's block.

Ursula clucked her tongue. "My lord still eats well, I see. Feeds his belly while others—whom I won't name—go hungry."

Joanna, ignoring her servant's remarks, tied a coarse apron about her waist and began to help with the preparation of the meal.

The two men-at-arms lounged against the wall, one picking his teeth with a splinter of wood, both eyeing Joanna covetously. The shorter, thick-muscled one spoke.

"I say, mistress, what a waste to have such a morsel as yourself condemned to this godforsaken shambles. What did you do? Help cuckold your husband with those fair breasts?"

The other tittered, "Got the wrong man between her legs, no doubt."

Joanna turned on them, a cutting knife in her hands. "Get out!" she ordered. "Get out of this kitchen before your lord has your gizzards for his supper. Get!" She advanced menacingly.

"What a shrew!" the short one said. Nevertheless, he and the other left, but not before the short one had turned his head and given Joanna a lewd wink.

As they cut up the ham, Ursula began to mutter again. "Seems—he could have sent a message—some word. Not right—not right—leave ye to rot—the mother of his..."

"Oh, hush!" Joanna hissed.

In the great hall Thomas had seated himself in the place

of honor on the dais with his lady-to-be beside him. Joanna served them; it was her duty, the peasant serving the master, a chore she had performed through the years and for Thomas most gladly, but Rosamonde's presence shamed her. Did the lady know, was she aware, that Joanna had been (was?) Thomas's mistress? And if she did, did she resent it? Mayhap not. Having mistresses, taking women, especially those of low birth, was a noble's privilege. Their wives and affianced ladies simply ignored it, assuming that a man could do no less if he was to be counted as virile.

Yet it hurt. She was just as human as the beautiful lady to whom she offered a platter of meat, human, a woman who could feel jealousy, anger, rage, love, hate and degradation. That was the worst, the dishonor, the ignominy, the scorn. She did not love Thomas; what fantasies she had woven in his absence had been dispelled at the first cold glance he had given her. Nor did he love her any longer, but he could have treated her with a modicum of courtesy. She had borne his son. She deserved better.

Rosamonde was given the tower chamber. The men-at-arms had bedded down in the stable, the squire in Geralt's loft, and Thomas before the hearth in the hall. Joanna and Ursula retired to the kitchen, where the two children lay sleeping on their pallets, oblivious to Thorsby's guests.

Joanna, however, found it impossible to sleep. She wondered now that Rosamonde was safely ensconced in the upper room why Thomas did not come to her, at least to give her some explanation for his long absence, or to see their son. She fretted, tossing and turning, torn between rage, indecision and her self-imposed calm, a false tranquillity which was as unnatural to her in time of crisis as fire to water. Finally she rose and, taking a brand from the hearth, went into the hall.

Thomas slept, lying on his back, one arm flung out, the other cradling his head. Joanna stood over him gazing down into his face, smooth except for a slight frown between his brows. How Aleyn resembled him, she thought dispassionately, without warmth or pride. She could not say why she felt such a lack of affection for her son. Perhaps it was because she had never really loved his father. Perhaps she was an unnatural mother, perhaps all the maternal feelings she was capable of were expended on Edmund.

Thomas stirred. Of what was he dreaming? she wondered. Lady Rosamonde? Of glory, of honor, of right against wrong, of victory over defeat, of valor over the coward's retreat? Of her? She leaned closer, and a spark fell on his sleeve. His eyes flew open, for a moment dazed, then clearing. His frown grew deeper.

"Joanna."

"Sir Thomas," she said acidly, "it has been a long time."

He pushed himself up on his elbows. "You are not going to start a quarrel? I meant to send a message, but I have been away—across the sea."

"Italy?" The abbot, stopping in to see how they fared and shown the coins, had told Joanna they were Italian florins. "But along with the purse you might have added a word or two."

"Purse? What purse?" He seemed genuinely surprised.

"A purse of florins. One hundred of them."

"Florins? They were not mine. I wish to God they were, but I had no florins to give."

There was no reason why Thomas should lie. On the contrary, if he had sent the money he would boast of it. But he seemed genuinely puzzled. Strangely, the thought that it might have been John Hawkwood never entered her mind.

"Did the messenger who brought them say from whom they came?" Thomas asked.

"Only that it was from a knight."

"Mayhap he had you confused with another Joanna and delivered the purse in error. I am sorry, but I had nothing to spare."

Nothing to spare. The same old tale. Close-fisted, mean, he had sent her nothing. She might have known. One hundred florins was more than Thomas would have given her even at his most eager. How could she have possibly thought otherwise? What a fool to believe such largesse, such a generous gift, had been his.

"How," she asked bitterly, "did you expect me to live?"

"Why, I thought you would petition your father. He makes a good wage, a very good wage."

"You know as well as I," she retorted, spacing out her words deliberately to keep from shouting, "that he has disowned me. Because of *you*—God damn you...!"

"Hush! Do you want to wake the others? All right, mayhap I was wrong in thinking Ivo would help. But *I* could not."

"Because of *her?*"

"I would warn you, Joanna, to be more respectful. Lady Rosamonde comes of noble lineage."

"Not like mine. Peasant that I am."

"Why are you behaving in this ridiculous manner? You have no claim on me."

"I bore your son."

"Aye—*he* may have the claim. But never you. Consider yourself lucky to have conceived a child with noble blood. I recognize him, and I always shall. Not you."

"So you would discard me."

"Aye, 'discard,' if you wish to call it that. Remember, Joanna, that I have already done far more for you than the father of your first child. I am in no way bound to you."

He was right. He was not bound to her. Why then had she permitted herself to engage in this futile, if not demeaning, argument? Because he had promised her comfort and she had had nothing but cold, drafty Thorsby, near starvation and hard toil. What, then, had he really "done" for her? Very little. She met his gaze squarely, pride and anger flashing from her eyes. If he expected her to cringe or to break into copious tears, then he would have to wait until snow fell in hell. No self-pity, not a single word about her years of privation, her brush with the savage mob of Shurbridge. Though she longed to fling accusations in his face, to shout and let go of the anger and recrimination she had carried for so long locked in her breast, she held back. She would not give him the satisfaction of calling her a hell-hag.

Swallowing the sour lump in her throat, she said, "Sir Thomas, I had thought you loved me—'passionately,' I believe, was the word—but it seems I was mistaken. No matter. Since I never loved you either the break will cause little pain."

He twisted his mouth in a wry grimace. "Unlike you, I expected as much. After all, a strumpet who willingly comes to a man's bed knows nothing of love."

"Damn you!" Joanna uttered in a low voice choked with emotion. "Damn your rotten soul!" She raised a clenched fist.

"My sweet Joanna, contain yourself. Ah, that is better. Let us part without a fuss, eh?"

He reached up, cupping her breast with his hand. She knocked it away, but not before it had sent a shocking thrill through her body.

"If you think..." she began.

"For old time's sake, Joanna?"

"Nay, never." The brand had gone out, and as she turned

to go he leaned forward and grabbed her skirt. "Let me go! You will tear it, the last gown..."

But he was on his knees, his arms about her legs. He pulled, jerking her toward him, and she fell, the spent torch tumbling from her hand. Still clutching her tightly, he brought her full length on top of him. She hated him. She meant to fight, she meant to, but when she felt the hard ridged pressure of his swollen member against her thighs a surge of hot blood rushed to her face and her raised fists unclenched, her hands falling weakly to his shoulders. His arms tightened about her waist, pressing her closer, and she ceased to think of Thomas. It was as if he had suddenly been replaced by John Hawkwood—as he had been so many times before—and she could only think how good it was to be held thus, that it had been so long, an age, since she had been bedded, since she had felt John inside her, and her loins ached with an intolerable need. His hand slid up between her legs, and they parted as if they had a will of their own.

"You could not say nay, you know you could not," Thomas murmured.

She did not speak but buried her head in his chest. He pulled her skirts above her waist and began to stroke the tender, silky skin of her inner thighs. Each caress sent a shiver up her spine, each brush of his fingers made her pulses leap and jerk. He rolled her over on her back, and she closed her eyes as her arms went up, twining about his neck. Her breasts flattened against his hard chest, she felt him enter her, and on her closed lids John's face darkened with passion seemed to hover, his hooded eyes, his mouth, touching, kissing, devouring hers. She had forgotten the dizzy wonder of it, the sweet, sweet agony, the delicious sensation of moving up and up. Her nails dug into his back—oh, hurry! hurry!—now, now, hurry!—there, there, oh there! She came into a sweeping climax, a shuddering gasping climax that left every nerve tingling.

Thomas lay back and sighed. "Well—are you sorry?"

She said nothing. The vision of John Hawkwood fled, and she steeled herself against guilt, against shame. But she had nothing to be ashamed of, she thought. If a man could relieve himself sexually, why could not a woman? Yet she knew in her case, at least, it was not true. She had betrayed not John Hawkwood, for whom she felt both love and hate, but Joanna Coke. She had given herself to a man she had never *really* loved. More, Thomas had made her position all too clear; she could never be his equal even in bed. She was a strumpet, wasn't that what he had called her? A strumpet. He hadn't even bothered to undress her.

She sat up, pulled down her skirt and got to her feet.

"Wait," he said, putting his hand on her arm. "There is something I should tell you. I had meant to come to Thorsby at some future date and settle this matter, but now that I am here, I might as well finish it. My mother has sold Thorsby, and you must vacate—the sooner the better. The new owners are anxious to take possession."

Taken aback, she could only stare at him. How quickly a man could go from sexual excitement to chill practicality.

"What? What are you saying?"

"You must leave Thorsby. It has been sold."

Sold! Of all the difficulties, the calamities, she had anticipated, she had least expected this one. Though she had no fondness for Thorsby, she had grown accustomed to it and had begun to look upon it as her home. She had plowed, planted and harvested the earth here, buried Timkin in the garden, worked, worried, been afraid, had borne a child within its walls. It was hers, hers by the sweat of her brow. And now she must vacate.

"Lord Hazelton has bought it for his daughter as part of her dowry."

"And I..."

"You can always go back to Nareham."

"I—I cannot. I cannot. My father—I cannot live at the castle when he has disowned me."

"I have been told that your father is quite ill."

"Ill?" She brushed a strand of hair from her forehead. "'Tis not a serious disability, is it? What ails him?"

"I know not, but the messenger I spoke to in London thought he was dying."

Her hand flew to her throat. She felt as though the abyss which had started to open beneath her feet when Thomas first introduced her to Lady Rosamonde and had continued to widen since now made its final lurch. For a few moments she struggled to breathe, to keep her knees from giving way.

"God, oh, my God! Are you sure?"

"So they say."

"Why did you not tell me sooner?"

"I had forgotten."

"Forgotten? How could you?"

Dying. Ivo—Ivo dying. Somehow, deep down, her heart

had always harbored the faint hope that one day when her father's anger had cooled he would send word that he had forgiven her. She had never imagined him dying. Never. It *couldn't* be. Yet he was mortal like any other. No longer a young man, old by the reckoning of his fellows, he had to die sometime, did he not? But nay, not now, she thought wildly. Not now before he has forgiven me, before he has blessed my sons, blessed Edmund.

"I am certain," Thomas said, "that the good steward, facing the Almighty, will welcome his daughter back."

"I must go to him at once," she said, not listening, her mind grappling with this new worry, this new despair. What if Ivo had already departed this life and was even at this moment lying in his grave? Nay, nay, she must not think of it. He still lived, and if God was good—Jesus, my Lord, make it so—he would recover. But she must not delay, not for a moment.

"How am I to make the journey, Thomas? Mayhap I can join your party." In her anxiety, her need for haste, she had forgotten her enmity toward Thomas, his insults, his dismissal. She thought only of the road ahead, the road that led to Nareham. "I shan't need to take much, the children and..."

"You cannot come with us," Thomas broke in. "We are going to Tribourne, Lady Rosamonde's home. Her mother too is ill, mayhap dying. Aside from that, it would not do to have you along. A past mistress—how would it look? Lady Rosamonde does not yet know, but she would guess."

Joanna's lip curled. "Aye—'twould look bad, I vow. Especially if she should see Aleyn. But I will get to Nareham if I have to ask the lady herself."

"You dare not."

"You would have to chain me to prevent it," she retorted, her face flushed.

He bit his lip in exasperation. "All right then, I shall give you a horse and a man to ride with you."

"One horse? For the four of us?"

"One horse for you and the two children. The old bag of bones can stay behind."

"Indeed not. That old bag of bones, as you call her, stood by me through flood and fire, and I have no intention of abandoning her. Two horses—and a purse. Do not look so horrified. I need money to buy us a bed at an inn. I refuse to sleep in the ditch along the way."

"Very well, a purse."

"Now," she said, holding out her hand.

He opened his pouch and, bringing out a handful of coins, slowly counted fifteen shillings into Joanna's outstretched palm. "This will do you well enough," he said truculently, adding, "To think I would allow myself to be cadged by a trollop."

"You are getting off cheaply as it is," she said acidly. "One of your London whores would cost you dearer."

She knew little of professional whores, nothing of the ones who plied their trade in London, but apparently Thomas, he of the proud name and conceited posturing, did. He flushed before he said, "I daresay I might have received more for my money with less trouble."

"I daresay," she replied coolly.

"One more thing, Joanna. I shall want Aleyn."

"Want him?"

"He is mine; he has noble blood. It would be a disgrace for me to have him brought up by a peasant's daughter. So leave him at Nareham. My mother will see to his care."

"But I am his mother," she asserted, though in truth she had rarely felt so, even now when faced with relinquishing the child. Nor was she especially shocked or taken aback by Thomas's request. She knew nobility sometimes cherished their bastards, knew that the father had a right to them and the mother no rights at all. Still, she disliked giving in to him without some show of protest. "I carried him, I gave birth."

"Joanna," he chided, "let us not dissemble. From what little I have observed, Aleyn might as well have been spawned by a stranger. You favor the other bastard. Admit it."

"One always favors the firstborn."

"You have an answer for everything. Waxy, I give you that."

It was not a compliment, nor did Joanna construe it as such. Men with quick tongues were considered amusing and sagacious, while women with the same gift of glibness were counted shrews.

"I have no doubt you could argue well with the very devil," Thomas added.

Joanna turned away, suddenly weary. She had no wish to go on bandying words with Thomas; it gave her no pleasure. She wanted only to go home, to see her father; she wanted to feel his hand on her brow, wanted to see him smile, hear him say that he regretted his bitter words, that he had missed her, that she was his daughter, his dove, his child.

"Joanna," Thomas called to her back. "Look at me." She turned. "I want you to promise to do as I say."

"And what is that?" she asked dejectedly.

"We shall take to the road on the morrow. I would like you to keep Aleyn out of sight until after we have gone."

She raised her brows. "So that Lady Rosamonde will not see him? But she will have to know if she is to be your wife."

"Once we are married it will not matter."

Joanna wanted to laugh. What a craven specimen he was, this knightly gallant. His lady must be powerful as well as beautiful and rich. Pious too, no doubt. And here was Thomas shivering in his painted yellow shoes lest his betrothed find his bastard. I should like nothing better than to cause trouble between them, she thought spitefully. It would make up a little for Thomas's neglect and the insulting manner in which he cast me aside.

Later that night she lay on her pallet still thinking of revenge, imagining all sort of scenes in which she confronted Thomas in Lady Rosamonde's presence. She might confess they had spent a lusty interlude together and that Thomas had hinted more of the same in the future. A lie, but what of it? Or she might bring Aleyn into the lady's chamber, Aleyn, who looked so much like his father, or send the child in to call, "Father, Father!" She hated Rosamonde, envied her with a passion, not for Thomas's love—fie on that!—but because Rosamonde was a woman who obviously had never known a day of hunger, an hour of fear, never had to wear the same gown month in and month out, never had to plow or hoe or carry a load heavier than a ball of embroidery thread, never had to butcher, to swill pigs, to coarsen her hands with rough work. Living in comfort, she had been cosseted, petted, perfumed, loved. Simply by being born she had all the good things of life fall into her lap.

When Joanna finally fell asleep, she dreamed not of revenge but of her father at Nareham. They were living in the bailiff's house again, and Ivo was peering at her through the smoke of the hearth fire. "Where are you, daughter?" he asked in an old man's querulous voice. "Where are you, dove?"

"Here, Papa. I am here, can you not see?"

But he did not seem to hear, for he kept calling, "Joanna, where are you? Why are you hiding from me?"

"I am not hiding. Oh, Papa, reach across, give me your hand, help me, help me, Papa."

She awoke to find that she had been weeping and the pallet cover beneath her face was wet with tears.

Chapter XVI

Joanna, the two children and Ursula, riding behind Thomas's man, approached Nareham on a late afternoon in early April. Tattered clouds scudding before the chill wind cast swiftly moving shadows across fields sprouting with delicate green. She rode through sunlight and shadow down the village street past the thatch-roofed cots toward the ramparts of the castle. The de Ander pennant snapping in the breeze, the stagnant moat, the wooden bridge, the gate tower and the throaty challenge that came from it were exactly the same as she remembered. Nothing seemed to have changed. Passing through the outer bailey into the inner courtyard, she saw the manor house, the porch, the well, the two gnarled trees shading it, the house servants drawing water, the old woman sweeping the flags with a straw besom, the Nareham she had carried in memory.

She felt a tightness in her chest, and tears pressed her eyes as she was helped to dismount. She had not imagined she had missed it so. She had been glad enough to leave— God alone knew—but now the past unhappiness was forgotten in a rush of warmth as she looked upon the familiar, the known.

Ursula and she parted with a tearful embrace, Ursula going off in the direction of the mews where her grandson lived in a small cot with his family. Then, holding Edmund's hand and with Aleyn clinging to her neck, Joanna climbed the worn stone stairs of the keep. Long before she reached the heavy oaken door she smelled the boiled cabbage and onions, heard a child's piping voice, the scrape of a chair. Her heart began to beat faster, to thump against her ribs. Perhaps she should have sent a servant on ahead to announce her arrival, to cushion the shock. What if her father should order her out, what if he should refuse to see her? What if he should look right through her, pretend she was a stranger he did not know, and instruct Katrine to close the door in her face? She paused, leaning against the stone wall to catch her breath, to collect herself, to postpone the moment she had hurried so anxiously toward, the moment now looming over her in all its frightening uncertainty.

Edmund tugged at her hand. "Shall we stay here, Mother? Or go to the top?"

"Go to the top," she breathed. "Let us pray your grandfather is well enough to receive us."

She started up again, finally reaching the passage. Setting Aleyn on his feet, she pushed open the slightly ajar door and went in.

Katrine sat on a stool, plucking a dead chicken lodged between her knees. When Joanna entered she did not look up but frowned, saying, "Well—what is it?"

"Good day," Joanna said.

Katrine lifted her head, astonishment spreading over her round lumpish features.

A little girl Joanna had not seen before ran to her mother's side and gazed at Joanna with startled eyes, one grimy fist clutching Katrine's skirt, the other jammed into her mouth.

"What do you do here?" Katrine asked, putting the chicken aside.

Joanna saw then that she was wearing a black apron over her gray kirtle, and her heart seemed to stop. An icy fear ran through her veins, and she could scarce find her voice. She could only stare at the black cloth speckled with brown feathers, unable to take her eyes from it. Black, black, black, it seemed to grow before her, getting larger and larger, until she thought that the awful blackness would swallow her whole.

"Why are you here?" Katrine's voice grated sharply.

"My father..." Joanna wet her lips. "Papa..." She looked beyond to the bed in the corner, its covers smooth, no invalid, no body there. "Father..."

"He died a fortnight ago," Katrine said coldly.

"But—but he couldn't—he..."

"We buried him in the churchyard," Katrine went on. "He died a man united with Christ, we, his wife and children, at his bedside."

"But—he could not—I—I wanted his forgiveness. I wanted him to bless my sons."

"He would never have forgiven you. Not once did he speak of you in this household. He had forgotten you entirely."

It was a cruel lie, for Ivo had died with the names of Mariotta and Joanna on his lips. But Katrine would not give her that, not the bitch, the black-haired bitch who had been a constant reminder to Ivo of his first wife, the trollop who had made her early days of marriage so unbearable.

240

"But if I had come in time," Joanna said, the pain in her throat strangling her voice, "if I had come in time, if he would have seen them..."

Edmund piped up, "Is Grandfather dead?"

Katrine ignored the child. "You would have been a stranger to him, someone he would not have wanted to see. So why make over it?"

Joanna did not answer. She was too overcome with disappointment, with grief, to think of anything but that she had been too late.

"The sorrow you caused him with your wanton behavior hastened his death," Katrine went on, unable to leave well enough alone. "If you had been a good, decent daughter, if you had married as he wished you to do, he would be alive today. Alive and well. But no, you had to bed with everything that wore hose, you had to have not one but *two* bastards. The last broke his heart. He was never the same man again."

"Don't—don't. I cannot listen, pray..."

"A broken man, hardly able to do his work. Harold de Ander would have replaced him."

Joanna sank to her knees, Aleyn and Edmund watching her with frightened eyes. Had she killed him, the one man, the one person, she loved so dearly? An image of Ivo rose in her mind, Ivo, his brow clouded, his voice cold, without feeling, and she had come too late to erase that picture, to replace it with one that she could live with, a gentle, forgiving face. Too late.

"And because of you I am left a widow with five little ones. What am I to do?"

(But later, Joanna discovered that Ivo had left Katrine well provided for, even after a death tax had been paid. To his wife he had given his strips of land and the benefits of the harvest to keep until his oldest son became of age, his oxen, his plow, the farm implements and fifty pounds. Fifty pounds, a fortune.)

"What am I to do?" Katrine complained. "They are taking the roof over my head away. The next steward will want it. And where am I to go?"

Joanna covered her face with her hands. Too late. Oh, why could she not have come sooner? Why couldn't Ivo have sent for her when he first took ill? Why?

"I cared for him as a good wife should, I saw to his needs, and I was *faithful*, not like some I know."

"Oh, God, I wanted so..." Joanna bit her lip, her eyes

going to the bed where he must have taken his final breath. "Who—who gave him the last rites?"

"Sir Theobold, the old scapegrace."

A sudden hope rose to Joanna's breast. Perhaps Ivo in his final confession had forgiven her, perhaps he had said something.

"Ivo was already too far gone and could not respond," Katrine added spitefully.

It was the truth. Katrine, fearing that Ivo with death staring him in the face might relent and not only forgive his daughter but leave her part of his property, had waited until the last possible moment before fetching the priest.

"I shall speak to Sir Theobold, in any case." Joanna rose to her feet. "You have had Masses said?"

"Surely. What do you take me for?"

"I will light a candle. Katrine, may I have something, a small token, a glove, a medal, to remember him by?"

"Certainly not! He would turn over in his shroud if I were to give you as much as a splinter from his table."

"You have a hard heart. I doubt you grieved overmuch when Papa died. But then you have always been a selfish bitch."

"Slut!" Katrine spat at her, her pasty face flushing. "You are one to call me bitch! This is still my house, you trollop, and I demand that you leave."

"Gladly. Come, children," taking each by a hand, "let us not tarry in the witch's presence. She might give us the evil eye."

"May your tongue rot, may your..."

But the rest was drowned out in the noise of the slamming door.

Joanna did see Sir Theobold, who confirmed what Katrine had said. "Aye, he did not even know me. He was barely breathing. I scolded Katrine for waiting so long, but she said he seemed on the mend, then got suddenly worse. Well, these things happen, you know. I myself had to prize his mouth open to place the wafer there."

"Poor Papa," she mourned, clasping her hands, wringing them.

They were standing in the priest's kitchen, where Joanna had found him earlier reckoning sums on a tally stick.

"Ivo was a good man," Sir Theobold said. "I have never known a finer. And I am sure, could he have confessed on his death bed, as was proper, he would have begged your pardon."

242

"It is I who should have begged him." Choked with tears, unable to hold them back any longer, she began to weep. Sir Theobold patted her awkwardly on the shoulder and murmured a few sympathetic phrases. "There, there, 'tis a shame. Can't be helped." But Joanna, sinking down on the bench and resting her head on the trestle table, went on sobbing, everything inside cracking, snapping, disintegrating in wild sorrow, an agony of grief. Sir Theobold's housekeeper, a fat peasant woman in her middle thirties, came waddling in, and seeing Joanna she put her arm about her waist in an effort to comfort her.

After a long while, Joanna raised her tear-stained face. "Do you think the dead have the power to look down and forgive?"

"I do not know, child." Theobold's grizzled jowls shook. "God forgives. Remember that. Here now—nay, nay, do not start again."

It was too much, too much. She blamed herself again for not coming sooner, for not trying to see him. God, God! Alive he had been in her thoughts, the hope that someday...but not now, not ever. "Dead, he is dead," she sobbed.

Theobold, deeply upset, sent Mary to fetch some of the sacramental wine. He poured a cup and urged Joanna to drink. The wine was sweet and warming. She emptied the horn cup and sat holding it between her hands, staring at the red-stained interior.

Theobold cleared his throat. "Do not be too hard on yourself, daughter. Had Ivo been aware when shriven, I feel certain he would have forgiven you. I have never known a man or woman who did not pardon even his worst enemy before departing this life. You must rest easy on that score. More wine?"

She shook her head.

Motherhood had made her even more beautiful, so much like Mariotta—may God rest her soul—with the fringed eyes of so strange a blue color, almost violet in the shadow. Theobold sighed. What a pity he was no longer young.

"What will you do now?" he asked, breaking a long silence. "Return to Thorsby?"

"I have been evicted," she said, crooking her lips in a painful smile. "Thomas no longer wants me, and his mother has sold the manor."

"Will you stay at Nareham then?"

"I know not. Katrine has made it plain I have no place in

243

her house. Mayhap—mayhap Alys de Ander will take me back as her seamstress."

"The lady has been ailing of late. You know that her eldest died. Aye, it's been several years now, but she cannot seem to get over it."

"I did not realize she was so fond of him."

"Fond enough. And remember, she is getting old too—as we all are."

"Is she still haughty?"

"Aye. That she will always be."

Aleyn tugged at her knees and tried to climb into her lap, but she set him down. "Sir Theobold, may I spend the night here? I and my two children?"

"Stay as long as you like, child," Sir Theobold said warmly.

In the morning, Joanna, taking Aleyn, presented herself at the manor house and requested an audience with Alys. She was informed that the lady would be unable to see her. "Tell her I have Sir Thomas's child."

The house carl, the same snobbish cockadore, grown a little bent but managing to sneer all the same, said, "I shall convey your message."

He returned shortly. "My lady says leave the boy. But she cannot see you."

"She must!" Joanna protested. "I have come all the way from Thorsby. She must!"

"How dare you! You—you peasant bitch! My lady *must* indeed. She will not see you, she cannot. She does not want to see you, now or ever. So begone!" He made a threatening gesture.

Joanna stooped and kissed Aleyn, who, sensing some kind of unknown and therefore horrific change in his life, began to cry.

"Be brave," she commanded. "Don't whimper. Your grandmama will take care of you and love you."

He clung to her skirts, and she pried his hands loose, not thinking of the child, hardly able to sympathize with his fright and bewilderment, only angry with Alys's snub and the servant's superior air. "Go on," she said, urging him forward, giving him another quick kiss. "Your father will see that no harm comes to you."

Joanna visited Ivo's grave and remained kneeling by the side of the freshly mounded sod for a long time. The small walled cemetery was flooded with spring sunshine. New grass

244

lay like a velvet carpet between the stones, and from a drooping willow tree a cuckoo called. She did not cry. The weeping, the sobbing, the breast-beating were behind her. Now she must think of tomorrow in earnest, what she would do, where she would go. She could not stay at Nareham. Already there was talk, there were whispers, sidelong knowing looks, snide remarks about her spending the night at Sir Theobold's. "The old lecher," she heard one woman at early Mass whisper, "he still has an itch for girls. And Joanna—well—ye know who her mother was—ha!"

No, she could not stay at Nareham. Thorsby was lost to her. She might, she thought, go to Thexted and see if she could find employment there. Mayhap the goldsmith and his wife, Ivo's old friends, would take her and Edmund in. She could still sew, she had not lost her skill, and she could earn her keep.

But suppose they were dead? Suppose they, like Alys, refused to take her in?

She sighed, trying to ease the ache that had settled on her heart. She was back where she had started. She was not one whit better off than she had been four years ago; she had not advanced herself, had not made any progress toward her dream for Edmund. Had it been foolish of her to have such ambitions? Had God, as the priests lectured, ordained each to his place on this earth where he or she must stay from birth to death? Was it presumptuous to want more? Both Sir Theobold and the abbot would have said aye. But even now, still grieving, still smarting with hurt and disappointment, she refused to meekly accept such a fate. She would not, could not abandon hope.

The next morning she gave a shilling to an old drover to take her and Edmund to Thexted in his cart. Only five shillings remained in her purse, and she had no idea how and when she could replenish her funds. She counted on the goldsmith, but not heavily, bracing herself against the worst.

It was well that she did, for the goldsmith's wife, summoned by a servant, confronted Joanna in the narrow entryway without inviting her into the hall. "So 'tis you, steward Coke's daughter. And you wish employment? Shelter?"

"Mistress, I must find a means to earn my bread."

"I have nothing for you. Another bastard, I am told." She threw Edmund a look. "Nevertheless, I daresay you will do well." Her eyes raked Joanna from head to toe. "Your kind always does."

Joanna, her face flaming, swallowed her anger and left the house.

For a while she stood in the street with Edmund, not knowing where to go. But passersby began to stare at her curiously, and when one man approached her with a lewd suggestion, she grasped the child's hand and fled. She put up at a poor inn that night, one of her shillings buying her a place in a corner of the common room. She had no friends, no one to turn to in her need, not a single soul, until she thought of the abbot of Kenham, as she had once before. Father Mark had helped her on three separate occasions, the last time rescuing her from the brink of starvation with a generous loan of food and seed, a loan whose repayment he had graciously waived. Kenham was a long way from Thexted, but she still had four shillings. If she used them judiciously, if she got a free ride, found cheap hostels, ate little, she could manage the journey. She must; she could think of no other alternative.

The abbot received her in the parlor, a bare room awash with rainbow-prismed light from a single high-arched stained-glass window depicting Christ on the Cross. The window, donated by a rich widow, was one of his treasures.

"And so you have come to me," the abbot said, but not unkindly. He had heard Joanna's story through without interruption, his head bent a little, for he found that his hearing was prematurely beginning to fail.

"I had no one else, your grace."

He wanted to say, "Except God," but knew that to her such a reminder would be fatuous.

"And so circumstances have made you give up your paramour, or more correctly, he has given you up. I need not tell you how easy it would be for you to find another."

"I do not want another." Her gaze turned briefly to Christ bleeding on the blue-and-purple window before she spoke again. "What has my life with Sir Thomas profited me? Naught but humiliation. I cannot, I will not, sink back into whoredom. I wish to earn my bread honestly."

He studied her beautiful face, now thin and a little sad. "I believe you. And I take it you still are reluctant to enter a nunnery?"

"Only as a last resort."

"I see. You are a seamstress, I think you once told me?"

"A good one, if you will forgive my lack of modesty. I can

246

also bake, weave, spin. I can do anything, even clean horse troughs, if need be."

"I see." He stroked his chin. "There is no employment hereabouts. So I would suggest London. I am told some of the mercers hire women to sew for their customers. Your wages will be meager, if you receive any at all. Your bed and board most likely are the only compensation you can expect."

"That will be enough. I ask nothing more for Edmund and myself."

"You are not planning to take Edmund?"

She took a firmer grip on the child's hand. "He goes wherever I go."

"My daughter, be sensible. It will be difficult enough, but with a child, impossible. No employer will consider you, no master will want to feed another mouth, one that is useless to him. You must think of Edmund and what is best for him."

"I *am* thinking of Edmund. I think of him all the time."

"Then leave the boy with me. He will have a good home here. He will not be fed on hard crusts, I promise, nor worked like a slavey. Nor will his bastardy be thrown in his face. I shall have him taught. He will learn to read and write so that you can be proud of him."

Proud! She did not want Edmund to become a scrivener or monk. She wanted him to be a rich merchant. She wanted him to rise above poverty, to be more than a servant within cloistered walls. She wanted them to be together.

"I see you still have doubts. But if Edmund went with you, you both might very well be reduced to begging in the streets. Can you see that for the son you profess to love?"

"But surely some kindhearted person would..."

"Did you find such a person at Nareham? At Thexted?" he interrupted.

"Nay." She remembered only too well Alys's refusal to see her, the goldsmith's wife's insulting remarks.

"What makes you think shopkeepers will be more generous in London? The city itself can be hostile if you are without kin or means. Its maze of streets is infested with criminals of the worst kind waiting to pounce on the innocent. London is not a place for the homeless to wander about in with safety. And supposing by some evil mischance you and Edmund are separated there? How would you find him again?"

The abbot was right, of course. He knew more of the world than she, and even her limited experience had taught her that people cared little for a lone woman with a bastard child. Ah, but it was hard, hard to give him up. If there was only some other way.

"I promise," the abbot was saying, "that I will not force him to stay if he wishes to leave when the time comes. And if you do well, 'twill only be a little while."

Only a little while.

She thought: I will earn money, find a place, send for him, and we will be together again. He will be fed here and be warm, and the abbot is a kindly man. Only a little while. "Your grace," Joanna began, speaking with difficulty, for the decision was not coming easily, "forgive me for showing so little gratitude. Another in my place might have been full of thanks, but I know you understand how painful this parting will be. I..."

"I understand. And I think it will help if we do not draw it out. Believe me, painful farewells only make matters worse. Pray, do not worry about your child. We shall take very good care of him, I promise. Kiss your mother goodbye, Edmund."

Joanna knelt and clasped the boy to her heart, hugging, kissing him, trying not to cry, though the tears crowded and stung her lashes. "Goodbye," she whispered. "Do not forget the mother who loves you."

She clung to him, and he, childlike, growing impatient, tried to struggle free. At last she released him. "Goodbye, Edmund."

The abbot had taken his hand, and he seemed already to have forgotten her, but when they reached the door Edmund turned and gave her a smile of such sweet purity and love she wanted to rush forward and snatch him back, to shout, "Nay! I have changed my mind!"

But the porter had come forward and was touching her elbow. "Come, daughter, I will show you to the hostel."

Chapter XVII

Joanna, armed with a purse containing fifteen shillings generously advanced by the abbot, started out for London the following day. She had obtained transport in an abbey cart carrying several bales of greasy wool shorn from abbey sheep, fleeces to be sold at Chepe, where the abbot expected to get a better price for them than he could locally. She paid a penny for her ride, a penny donated to charity, as the abbot explained, and was expected to stand her own expenses for food and lodging in the various monastery hostels along the way.

The ox-drawn cart was not the pleasantest manner to make a journey of any duration. It was a square-shaped timbrel made of heavy planks borne on two springless nail-studded wheels, and it jolted and bounced mercilessly as it creaked and rumbled along the rutted road. The pile of wool stank and at every jounce threatened to topple over and smother Joanna. She could not see out unless she stood on tiptoe clinging to the sides, a stance hardly more comfortable than sitting. The cart caused such a racket conversation was impossible, even if the monk and lay driver perched on the board bench above her had been so inclined.

They stopped at Boldnor Abbey the first night, not at the abbey proper, which was reserved only for sojourners of high rank, but at the guest house, a building standing by itself outside the walls of the monastery. Simply designed, it consisted of a hall with an open hearth on which meals could be cooked and sleeping rooms opening up on either side. The house was already crowded by the time Joanna arrived, filled with pilgrims, wandering friars, laborers in search of work, musicians, tumblers, herbalists and wayfarers of every description, folk who eschewed the inns because they were too dear, or as in the case of a few merchants who could afford them, because they were infested with rats, lice and cutthroats.

Most of the travelers were men. Each must share his bed with two or three fellows, and Joanna looked about for an old graybeard or devout-appearing cleric, someone who was not apt to commence fumbling her in the darkness of night. Heretofore she had traveled with the children or with Sir Thomas, who protected her against covert lechers, but now alone (the monk and lay brother, afraid of theft, had bedded down in the cart), without a husband or man to fend off unpleasant advances, she felt for the first time her vulnerable position. She was accustomed to being alone—she had been that at Thorsby—but being alone and out in the world was a different matter.

She bought bread from a lay brother who came in with a sheaf of loaves under his arm, hawking them for a ha'penny each to those who had the means (very few did, or said they did), and had him fill her cup with ale. Her eyes were roaming the benches for a space where she might sit down and have her supper when a female voice exclaimed, "Why, here is another woman!"

Turning, Joanna saw a rosy-cheeked matron, her hair hidden by a wimple.

"Good morrow, young miss," the woman said in a hearty voice. "Where are you bound for?"

"London, mistress," Joanna said, responding with a smile to the other's friendliness, her merry blue eyes.

"Indeed. So are my husband and myself. We live in that benighted city, though I must admit I have missed it sorely. We are just come from a visit with our daughter—her first baby, a girl, a pity, but such a sweet thing. And you and your husband...?" She gave the man sitting on the bench nearest to Joanna a sliding glance, a burly brute clad in cast-offs, tearing at his loaf with jagged teeth.

"I have no husband," Joanna said. "He—God absolve his soul—died a month ago of the sweating sickness." She dabbed at her eyes with the edge of her sleeve. The lie had not been made up on the spur of the moment, for she had decided to pose as a childless widow before she left the abbey. Widowhood, she reasoned, would make her more respectable.

"Tsk, tsk! I am sorry to hear that," the matron commiserated, relief flickering for a moment in her eyes as she cast another look at the burly man. "And are you traveling alone?"

"Nay. I am in the company of a monk and lay brother from Kenham Abbey. The abbot was a good friend of my late husband's."

"Ah. Here, Bertrand," she said, pushing at her husband with stout hips, "let the little mistress sit between us, so's we can talk."

Invited, Joanna wedged herself in between the woman and Bertrand, a thin baldheaded man with a pendulous lip.

"My name is Elizabeth Wheelwright," the matron introduced herself, then added proudly, "and my husband, Bertrand here, is an armorer in the pay of the Duke of Lancaster."

Joanna was duly impressed. Later she was to discover that Bertrand was not actually an armorer but a spurrier, a smithy whose duties were confined to fashioning spurs for Savoy horsemen. Still, to be in the service of the great duke—the king's third son—was no mean honor.

"And you, young mistress, how are you called?" Elizabeth asked.

"Joanna, Joanna of Thorsby. My husband was steward there."

"Ah—I knew it. I knew from the moment I spied you that you were a cut above the average yeoman's daughter." She leaned forward and asked in a confidential, intimate tone, "Have you noble blood?"

"I know not," Joanna said, resisting the impulse to say yes. "There are rumors that my great-grandfather was sired by a Norman, but of that I am not sure."

Elizabeth nodded knowingly. "You have the look, a certain air which says good blood. Well, my dear, and have you kin in London?"

"None. My husband, God forgive him, left me penniless."

"A steward—penniless?"

Joanna, her story prepared, twisted her mouth wryly. "Aye. Since I was childless his goods and chattels went to his brother, the next in line."

"What a pity. And no provision for you?"

"So my brother-in-law claims."

"He's cheated you!" the good wife cried. "No one is without a portion. You must get a man of the law to bring suit."

"The abbot says I have no cause." She sighed. "I accept my lot. 'Tis God's will. And I am young and strong. I can find some way to earn my bread. I sew a fine hand. I can work for a tailor."

"Tailors, my child, are guildsmen. They accept only men."

"Mayhap some fine lady will want her private seamstress, then."

"Mayhap. Bertrand..." She turned to her husband, who was sitting slumped forward, his chin resting on his chest. "Is there a lady in the duke's household who could use a seamstress?"

Apparently he had dozed off. She gave him a sharp jab

with her elbow, and his startled eyes popped open. She repeated her question.

"What—what? A seamstress? I know not. But I shall be happy to inquire."

Elizabeth turned a beaming face to Joanna. "You see, God must have smiled on you, my child. It will be arranged. And in the meanwhile—why do we not finish our journey together?"

"Why, I thank you, Mistress Elizabeth."

"Elizabeth. Let us not be formal. And you must stay with us. Now that our last daughter has married we are alone, and I would consider it a pleasure if not an honor to have you."

Joanna could barely conceal her delight. To think she had fallen in with these two, when only an hour earlier she had been faced with a bleak, uncertain future.

"I shall be happy to accept your invitation," she said with dignity, "but only until I can fend for myself."

"Nonsense!" Elizabeth patted her hand. "We want you to stay for a long, long time, do we not, Bertrand?" A jab and Bertrand muttered, "Of course, of course."

Joanna's first sight of London was of a cluster of roofs and the spire of St. Paul's rising grandly above the outer walls. Though the abbot had described the metropolis in unflattering, if not fearsome, terms, she still thought of London as a fabled city. And as they clattered through Aldergate she gawked at the people, men, women and children, hurrying alongside, more people than she had ever seen on the Thexted byways even on a fair day.

"We are taking the long way around," Elizabeth explained to Joanna. "I wish to stop at Chepe and make some purchases, cloth and a few loaves of bread for our supper. There's a Stratford baker there who sells his leftovers at the end of the day at half price. Good bread, too, much better than what we can bake at the duke's palace."

Approaching Chepe, the streets became more and more crowded. Their squeaking cart jostled other conveyances, carts and painted wagons alike, wheels hitting wheels, sending sparks flying as they slowly progressed through the throng. And what a motley mob! Bare-armed men pushing barrows, ruddy-faced peasants dragging sacks, wimpled old women toting baskets, imperious horsemen restraining mounts, friars on muleback, street vendors on foot and beggars extending skinny, clawed hands in supplication, whining shrilly, "For the love of God! A penny! A penny!"

The market itself was a sea of activity, a market held every day, Joanna was told, not twice a week as in Thexted. Every day! The smell of roast meat, of hot bread, of simmering pasties filled Joanna's twitching nostrils. She did not know where to look first. The stalls lining the street, one after another, were heaped with vegetables, fish, poultry, bales of cloth, iron pots, baskets; and behind them the shops of the furriers, the mercers, the glove sellers, tailors and goldsmiths, each with a man outside hawking his wares. The noise was deafening, the shouts of the merchants, the shrill, bargaining housewives, the rumble of wheels, the whinnying of horses, the cries of servants, "Make way, make way!" as they herded their masters' litters through. Bells and gongs and horses' hooves, the bang of a drum and pipe of a flute as the bearward put his charge through its lumbering paces.

Joanna, her mouth agape, could scarce take it all in, her head turning this way and that. She felt like a child again. Thexted was so small in comparison to this, so dull, so provincial. She loved London. She loved the way it stirred her blood, set her heart to dancing. Oh, how could she have endured the loneliness, the boredom, of Thorsby for so long? Why had she not fled that gray moldering heap of stones ere this? There was life here, busy, energetic life, joyful and thrilling!

They stopped before a bread stall, and the baker, flaunting a brimless, towering hat stuck with a cock's orange-red feather, recognized his old customers and grinned widely. "So ye're back, are ye, Mistress Elizabeth? Didn't find bread like this on yer travels, I'll warrant."

They bickered over the price, and finally the baker, with a muttered curse but the same good-natured grin, threw four loaves into the cart, while Bertrand leaned down to pay him.

"Got you a nice lass from the country?" he asked, inclining his head toward Joanna. "Needs plumping up a bit, but she'll do."

Joanna had a bad moment. The abbot had warned her of city procurers who scoured the countryside looking for young girls to sell to brothels. Were the Wheelwrights panders? She stole a glance at Elizabeth, who was still bandying with the baker, her eyes brimming with amusement. How could she be? So kind, and her husband such a sober man. Ah, but a voice told her, it was decent-appearing people such as these who could entice silly girls. She thought of jumping from the wagon, of running through the crowded streets and losing herself among the throng, but then she heard Mistress Elizabeth say, "Shush, you clattermouth. Enough! Why, this is Joanna of Thorsby; she is a respectable widow, I'll have you know. Shame to speak so in front of honest folk."

No, Joanna thought with relief, brothels wanted green virgins, not respectable widows. She had done the virtuous Wheelwrights a wrong by associating them with whoremongers if even in thought.

They made one more stop at a cloth merchant's stall, where Elizabeth bought a length of scarlet, some thread and some braid. Joanna, overcome with gratitude (mixed with a little guilt), offered to make up the gown for her benefactress.

"Why, how generous!" Elizabeth exclaimed.

They left the market and drove past St. Paul's Cathedral, and Joanna, looking up at it, thought she had never seen a church so imposing. Out through Ludgate they crossed the Fleet River and jolted down past the Temple Bar, coming to the wide gray Thames and driving beside it until the crenellated walls of the duke's residence came into view. If Joanna had felt awed earlier she was now rendered speechless. So vast she could hardly take it in. This, all of *this*, one nobleman's residence? Nareham by comparison seemed a poor country castle.

"We call it the Savoy," Elizabeth told her, smiling in a proprietary manner. "It covers three acres. Aye, three acres. And it doesn't sprawl like some. 'Twas all planned in a series of—of what is it called, Bertrand?"

"Quadrangles," he replied laconically.

"Quadrangles," Elizabeth repeated. "There are smithies and a great treasure chamber. There are mews for the duke's falcons and stables and pleasure gardens and docks for the pleasure barges. And see—see the huge clock? 'Tis Flemish. The hours are struck by dwarves who come out from the little door at the bottom of the clock's face. Clever, is it not? Ah—there—there is Beaufort Tower." She pointed to a whitewashed tower rising above the walls. "The state chambers have buff and cream tile on the floors and great silken tapestries, some woven with thread of gold. See the windows? Most are glazed, you know, hundreds of them."

As Joanna looked, the reflection of the setting sun glinted like struck fire from a row of panes, and she wondered who stood behind those windows, what royal personage was there, shading his or her eyes, gazing down at them.

"There are mantels carved in stone and a grand staircase and rugs brought all the way from Turkey. The duke has a gilded chair cushioned in black velvet..."

Elizabeth went on and on, gushing over the splendors of the Savoy, so much so that Joanna began to believe they would be housed there and could scarcely conceal her disappointment when they stopped before one of the armorers' shops and Mistress Elizabeth said, "Here we are—home at last!"

Joanna, clutching her bundle, was helped from the cart and followed Elizabeth as she climbed a wooden ladder at the side. They entered a large, loftlike room, the sloping ceiling disappearing into wooden rafters chinked with rubble and thatch. A curtained bed stood in one corner, a chimneyless fireplace in the center. The stools and trestle table shoved against one wall could have been the same they had used in her father's house at Nareham.

"We shall get a pallet for you straightaway," Elizabeth said, throwing the bread on the table.

A pallet. Where were the down beds all canopied in brocade Elizabeth had spoken of so glowingly?

"My—and the dust. Be a sweet, Joanna, there's a besom there on a peg—would you get the cobwebs?"

Elizabeth banged two pots together, turning them upside down to dislodge the accumulated debris. "These will have to be scoured—ah, what a mess!" She went to the window and, throwing open the shutter, shouted, "Bring a brand for the fire, Bertrand! Bertrand?" She turned back to Joanna. "He did not hear me—deaf when it comes to doing something for me, deaf. Be an angel, Joanna, would you go down to the shop and fetch a light?"

When Joanna returned she found Mistress Elizabeth seated on a stool eating an apple. "Good girl. You'll find wood in a corner, somewhere—behind that keg." She pointed with the apple.

After Joanna had built the fire, she was sent to fetch a bucket of water from the well. It was Joanna who got their supper, Joanna who scraped the platters and scoured the dirty pots, each request prefaced by a "Be an angel." The pallet not forthcoming the first night, Joanna had to lie on the dirty floor in her cloak and listen to the scampering of the rats in the rafters before she finally fell asleep.

And so it went the next day and the next. On the third day, Joanna, struggling up the ladder with yet another bucket of water, wanted to weep with chagrin. It seemed she could do no more than travel in circles. Just when she thought she had advanced herself, that her luck had changed for the better, fate or the devil (certainly not God, or was it?) gave her a shove back to the old place. Mistress Elizabeth was not planning to sell her to a brothel—after all, she was a good Christian and could hardly traffic in harlotry—but instead had made a servant of Joanna, a grateful servant who would work without pay.

I shan't let her, Joanna thought grimly. I shan't.

One afternoon when Elizabeth lay sprawled on the curtained bed, taking her midday nap, Joanna put on her good gown, the one she had done up so long ago from a roll of cloth Thomas had brought her in their early days together. Plaiting her hair, she fixed the black, glossy braids at the nape of her neck in two coils. She smoothed her eyebrows and pinched her cheeks to make them rosy, wishing she had a mirror to see how she looked. She regretted her lack of headdress or cauls. Her ring and earrings had been sold long ago, one winter at Thorsby, and her only ornaments were a plain silver brooch pinned to her collar and an enameled crucifix and a disc-shaped wooden charm against illness suspended on a short brass chain which she kept tucked inside the neck of her bodice.

In the courtyard she stopped a pimply-faced page and asked him the way to the wardrobe. "'Tis through yon gate," he said, pointing, "next to the kitchens."

Joanna lost her way three times before she found the right door. A man with a scar on his cheek and stiff, crimped hair opened it. "Good morrow, sir," she said cheerfully into his scowl. "I wish to offer my services." His assessing look made her stumble. "As—as a seamstress."

"A seamstress. Is that what you are calling yourselves now?"

"How dare you!" She drew herself up, her face flaming. "I have come in all honesty, asking for work. I sew a fine hand with the needle and wish to be employed in the making of the duchess's gowns."

"*You*? I have never seen nor heard of you. Aside from which, we employ only men here, all master tailors. I advise you take your—ah, what did you call it?—'services' elsewhere." And he slammed the door.

She faced the busy courtyard, biting her lip, trying to

control her anger. The insufferable varlet! The petty jack-anapes! How dare he insult her! He dared, a voice told her, because she was less than nothing to him; she had no name or face. In his mind she was either a menial or a whore. Joanna stood for a few moments watching the stream of servants pass on their separate errands, the water carrier balancing two buckets on a pole across his shoulder, laundresses bearing baskets of linen on their heads, the shoemaker with half a score of felt slippers slung around his scrawny neck by their laces, the woodman with his cart piled high. The driver, a young, broad-shouldered youth showing white teeth in a grin, shouted, "Will ye lie with me, fair miss?"

She turned and walked rapidly away. It took several inquiries, a wrong turn and a short backtracking before she found herself at an ornate door which she guessed led to the duchess's privy suite. Drawing a deep breath, she knocked loudly, her balled fist rat-a-tatting with authority.

A wizened little man in crimson, gold-embroidered livery opened the door.

"I wish to see one of the duchess's ladies-in-waiting," she stated loudly, still smarting from her last insult. "Any one of them will do. 'Tis a private matter," she added imperiously.

"Wait here," he said in a dubious tone, but at least he did not shut the door.

A few minutes later, just as Joanna's nerve was beginning to desert her, a pretty young woman came to the door. She was exquisitely dressed. Her peach-colored bliaut, embroidered in an intricate pattern of griffins and peacocks, covered a green silk gown trimmed in martin. Across her forehead she wore a band of pendant pearls, and her saffron-colored hair was bound up in a silk fillet, the fillet's long ends hanging down her back. Her eyebrows had been shaved, and the painted ones above them gave her a look of unblinking surprise. Joanna, staring at her, felt countrified, dowdy.

"Well?" the young damsel asked, her eyes making the same humiliating assessment as the scar-faced servant's. "What is your 'private' business?"

"I am seeking employment as a seamstress," Joanna said, omitting the requisite curtsy and instead lifting her chin. "I have sewn for Alys de Ander at Nareham. I was head seamstress there for some years. The lady herself thought highly of me."

"Alys de Ander?" She wrinkled her nose. "I am afraid I am unacquainted with her. But it matters not. The duchess

257

has all the seamstresses she can use. Besides, she is in residence at Bolingbroke now."

"Oh," said Joanna.

"You might find employment at an alestake," the young woman suggested.

Joanna colored. The maids at alestakes were notoriously free with their favors.

"I am not a whore," she said heatedly. "Whatever you and your ilk may think. I am no more trollop than you. Simply because I do not wear a fine gown, nor dye my hair, nor paint false eyebrows..."

The door, again, was slammed in her face.

As she trudged back to the loft the sun went in and a sudden chill wind swooped down, belling the skirts at her ankles. Dust and whirling debris scampered over the cobbles, blowing in gusts, slapping her face, and she tasted grit with her bitter, unshed tears. She felt tired, dispirited; she thought of walking on, going past the loft, out the gate and into the city. Anywhere to get away, to leave, so that she did not have to face Mistress Elizabeth again. She hated her. Hatred burned in her heart for everyone, for Thomas, for Katrine, for Alys, for the varlet at the wardrobe, for the damsel with the saffron-dyed hair. Contemptible fools! Oh, if she could get back at them, if she could revenge herself on them all!

And she missed Edmund. There had not been a night since she had left him at the abbey that she did not weep a little, did not wonder what he was doing, wonder if he missed her too, and worry over how she was to get him back.

She came to the armorer's shop and looked up at the apartment above. The shutters were open, and she heard Mistress Elizabeth's carefree laugh. The air smelled of rain, cold rain, and the wind blew harder, beating at her, molding her dress to her body. She had no money. The shillings the abbot had given her had been "loaned" to Elizabeth. She knew no one in London. How could she leave? How far could she get? She thought of St. Helen's, the convent where her girlhood friend Elthreda had spent a year. But she did not know where it was or how to find it. And without the abbot's intercession, she doubted they would take her, a stranger, in. The sisters might even give her the same insulting suggestion she had received here at the Savoy.

Slowly, she climbed the ladder.

When she came into the loft chamber she saw the Wheelwrights had a visitor, a young man dressed in a knee-length blue cotehardie, a simple garment, unadorned but of good cloth, and blue hose and felt shoes that buckled across the instep. He had a broad forehead, a finely molded, clean-shaven chin and thick blond hair cut squarely at the neck. His blue eyes met Joanna's with a look of surprise.

"Ah!" Mistress Elizabeth exclaimed. "Here is my adopted daughter, Joanna of Thorsby, an unfortunate widow we have taken in."

He got to his feet, the look of surprise still stamped on his face.

"Our honored guest, Sir Richard Smithborne," Elizabeth said and beamed.

Sir—a knight—*here?* Joanna bent her knee, wondering if her hair had come awry in the wind but glad she was wearing her good gown.

"Sir Richard," she murmured.

"Sir Richard is an old friend," Elizabeth explained. "The blacksmith's son. He was knighted in the field at Auray in France. Oh, I know the whole story, Richard, you needn't be so modest. Your father has told it ten times at least, how your liege lord, Sir Granfort, was unhorsed, his squire killed, and how you plucked up his sword and stood by Sir Granfort, fighting off the savage Bretons until horsemen could come to his rescue. Brave, brave lad."

Sir Richard blushed.

"Well, there and then dubbed, you, only a pikeman, made a knight on the field by no less than the most eminent warrior in England—the Black Prince's own constable, Sir John Chandos!"

Sir Richard's color deepened.

"You are too modest," she repeated, shaking a finger at him. "A knight! You are one of the nobility now. You must not blush, you must be proud. A handsome young man like you. Throw your chest out, strut. Cockadoodle-do!" she crowed, her face turning red, her chin shaking. "I wager the ladies are all over you. Eh? You'll make a fine match—some heiress will grab you up or my name is not Elizabeth Wheelwright. Ha ha!"

Bertrand rose and shuffled his feet. "I—I should be getting back to the shop," he said, embarrassed, obviously uncertain as to whether he ought to bow or shake his guest's hand, a guest whom he had known as just another boy in the courtyard. "The duke's steward will want his spurs ready for the jousting tomorrow."

"Oh, get along then," Elizabeth said impatiently, and Bertrand, finally deciding on a nod, slipped out of the room as his wife continued, "Richard—pardon, *Sir* Richard—you are to be in the tourney tomorrow?"

"Aye, that is why I am here in London." He had a pleasant deep voice with a pronounced Saxon accent. "I am to duel against a knight from Wales."

"My husband and I shall be watching from the barricades," Elizabeth said.

Richard turned to Joanna. "And you, mistress, will you be there also?"

Elizabeth quickly broke in. "Not likely. Tomorrow is laundry day—our turn at the wash well. Joanna cannot possibly go."

"Oh?" said Richard, disappointed.

Joanna smiled at him, her prettiest smile, showing the dimple at the side of her mouth. "I should love to watch you."

"Why—Joanna," Elizabeth chided.

Richard said, "Then she must. It would pleasure me, Mistress Elizabeth, if your adopted daughter could be there."

"Well!" Elizabeth exclaimed in a put-upon tone.

"You see," he went on, "I meant to ask if—if Mistress Joanna would allow me to wear her favor."

Shock rendered Elizabeth momentarily speechless. A knight going into tourney always wore a lady's favor, a sleeve, a ribbon, a flower or tippet. But a *lady's* favor.

"Does—does that meet with your approval, Mistress Joanna?" Richard said, looking at her, coloring to the roots of his hair. "I do crave a token to bring me luck."

Joanna, her heart beating fast, sought wildly in her mind for something to give him. She did not want to tear the sleeve from her gown as was sometimes customary. It would spoil it. "I have a ribbon—will that do?"

"Most certainly."

She rummaged in her little pack of belongings and brought out a bright-red ribbon, one that she had bought from a peddler on the way from the abbey.

"Thank you," he said as she gave it to him. Their hands brushed, and Joanna felt him start. "I—I shall wear this proudly and hope to do your token of esteem credit. Good even. Good even, Mistress Elizabeth."

When he had gone, Elizabeth let out her breath. "Well! Well, I never. I must say. The effrontery! Is this the thanks I get for taking you in, a poor widow without kith or kin?"

"I am sorry about the laundry," Joanna said.

"You could have refused him."

"I did not want to," Joanna said.

"Did not want to? After we have fed and housed you these many weeks? Brought you to London? Where would you be without us, eh? Selling your body in some lice-infested brothel."

"I've not only earned my keep but paid shillings for it into the bargain," Joanna said stolidly. "I've swept, cooked, fetched, washed, done every patch of work that had to be done, and without wages, mind you."

"We fed you—and well," Elizabeth repeated, her eyes popping with anger. "We *fed* you."

"So you did. But you forget I am not a serf who must work simply to fill her belly. I am *freeborn.*"

"Pshaw!" Elizabeth spat. "Freeborn! You are no more so than the next country girl who comes to the city. Freeborn. And will that buy you bread, a fine gown?"

"Nay, but I am going to the tourney, like you, like *them,*"— she inclined her head toward the window—"whatever you say."

"Aha! You think because Richard is taken with you—oh, I could see it, the looks, the little blushes, the stuttering—he will be your protector? Or is it marriage, my good, eager widow, that is in the back of your mind? Well, let me tell you, his father went into debt to equip him; to buy the great destrier he rides at tournament, the armor, the very spurs for his boots. His father, Master Smithborne, is a practical man. He looks for repayment, he looks for his son to marry a girl with a dowry, mayhap not from the nobility, but many a merchant father would be happy to give a well-dowered daughter as wife to a knight. So if you have hopes in that direction, I advise you to put them away."

"Sir Richard only asked to wear my favor, mistress, not to marry me."

"Aye, and pray remember that," Elizabeth said maliciously.

How, thought Joanna, did I ever think this woman to be a friend of mine? She is jealous, green with envy. She resents Sir Richard's attentions, his request for a favor. She finds the idea of a servant, *her* servant, attracting a man of distinction insulting. Ha! Let her stew, the old biddy.

The next morning a young page came to the loft. He had a message for Mistress Elizabeth, he said. He was to conduct her, her husband and Mistress Joanna to the lists, where Sir Richard had reserved a space for them. When Elizabeth heard this she was considerably mollified, although she maintained that Richard had procured this more prestigious seating arrangement on the basis of their old friendship. Joanna knew better, but for the sake of peace kept her counsel.

She dressed with care, donning her good gown, brushing her hair until it shone, plaiting it with a broad yellow ribbon. Over her glossy head she threw a wispy veil she had found in her belongings. At the last moment Bertrand decided he would rather go with his cronies, smiths and armorers who could watch from the stables on the field. There they could do a little betting, could shout or curse and drink as much as their exuberance dictated without having to worry about scoldings from their wives. So it was Mistress Elizabeth and Joanna who followed the page to the waiting cart below. Several other women, wives of lesser knights and squires, were also to be transported, and Joanna, noting how well they were dressed as opposed to herself, lifted her chin a little higher. Not one of them spoke to her or to Mistress Elizabeth on the long ride to Smithfield, where the tourney was to be held, but chattered and giggled and laughed among themselves, occasionally casting a cutting glance in her direction.

As they rode on Joanna gradually lost her resentment. She was not going to let a group of foolish women spoil her day. Who were *they*? She had been invited by Sir Richard and had every right to be in the wagon, every right. She would not be peeking through the barriers like ordinary folk, but would be sitting in a loge. *And* a knight would be wearing her favor.

Their loge was not the canopied, velvet-cushioned one she had imagined, however, but a line of benches set up next to the luxurious ones, uncovered, open to the glaring sun. No matter—Joanna, the country girl from Nareham, who had never been to a tournament outside the ones held on the weed-choked turf at home, was enchanted. Dimly aware of blaring trumpets, the herald's loud voice shouting the names of contenders, the thunder of hooves, she, like Mistress Elizabeth, was too busy scrutinizing the spectators to take much heed of the goings-on in the field.

There—over there, could it be . . . ? She asked her neighbor, a plump girl wearing a horned headdress, "Who is that?" She pointed in the direction of a gilded loge.

The girl looked at her in surprise. "Why—that is the king. King Edward himself."

She might have known. How ignorant. The loge, a striped canopy covering it and the banners down in front, the lily and leopard banners of the king.

"The king loves tournaments," the girl added.

King Edward. And was that his queen? It must be. Oh, how wonderful, how exciting! It was all she could do to sit still. She forgot her plain dress, her lack of a remarkable head-dress and jewels. She stretched her neck to take in the sights, the women in their dazzling gowns, the men in their richly embroidered surcoats. "And who is that?" nudging the plump girl again. "And that?" She wanted to know everybody, their names, their rank. She never had been so close to royalty, never shared an entertainment with them, and she reveled in it. Her presence at any function at Nareham had always been as servitor, one of a horde, but now she felt, despite the hard bench, that she had suddenly come up in the world.

"Sir Richard Smithborne!"

The shouted name caught her with a jolt of surprise. She turned her eyes to the field, shielding them against the glare. At a short distance to her left a visored man sat a large heavy-footed destrier, a glinting lance couched in the crook of his elbow. She would not have known him except for the red ribbon tied about his steel-encased arm. Sir Richard! Gazing at him she saw not the bashful young man she had met in the Wheelwright loft, but a gallant, a romantic warrior, a heroic knight. Her pulses leaped, her heart began to beat faster. Until now she had never been much interested in jousting, but this was different. The manly figure astride his horse on the field for all to see was to fight for her, *her!* She felt giddy, drunk with the thought. He was not a cowardly suitor to keep her in secret or one to sneak out after dark for a rendezvous, but a knight who had asked her courteously, openly, for a favor, one who would do battle to honor her.

Another blare of trumpets echoed across the field.

The marshal cried, "In the name of God and St. George, come forth to do battle!"

And then Richard was thundering down the field, the sod flying in spurts under the horse's hooves, galloping, charging toward his opponent. Shields and visors lowered, the two met with an explosion of wood and metal that rang out over the noise of the crowd. Both men held their seats; separating, wheeling, they galloped back to their starting places. Again the hollow drumming of hooves, the lance and shield streaking across the arena, the shouts—"Go to it! Unseat him! Kill him!" Thunder, lightning, a crash like God's hammer. The crowd roared, and Joanna found herself screaming and shouting with the others, not really knowing why, but intoxicated with excitement. Once more a loud roar arose, then a collective groan, and Richard's opponent tumbled to the ground. Joanna shouted and cheered until she was hoarse.

Richard rode up to the king's loge. A cup was presented, a few words spoken, words Joanna could not hear. Then Richard cantered down to the benches, the visor under his crested helm lifted. His smile and his eyes were directed at Joanna. He raised his gloved hand and threw her a kiss. Conscious of the stares of the women around her, she flushed prettily and fluttered her lashes. A few minutes later a page approached and whispered in her ear, "Sir Richard wishes for you and Mistress Elizabeth to wait for him outside the barracks."

They were walking now along the dusk-purpled banks of the Thames, having left a complaining Mistress Elizabeth, who could not keep up with them, far, far behind.

"Yesterday when I saw you," Richard said, "I thought I had never laid eyes on a more beautiful creature."

"Why, thank you, sir knight," Joanna said demurely.

"The truth is..." He paused and turned, gazing down at her with softened eyes. "I—I fell in love."

She laughed lightly. "But you hardly know me. We have not spoken three words together."

"I feel as though I have known you all my life," he said fervently, the tried and true avowal of all newly smitten.

"Come now," she chided.

"'Tis true, I swear it. And you, Mistress Joanna, do you think—oh, I know this is hasty and all wrong, yet I—I cannot help but ask—if you felt in your heart you could be—could be the least fond of me?"

"Sir Richard, I must remind you again, we are still strangers, and that is not a proper question," she said primly, suddenly regretting having gone on without Mistress Elizabeth. As much as Joanna disliked the woman, a chaperon would have come in handy now, a safeguard to respectability. It was time she stopped being so impulsive. Only a loose woman or a green country girl would go walking alone with a man, and she was neither. She had no intention of giving herself to this one. None. If he wanted her, he must marry her. Farfetched? Mistress Elizabeth believed so. But, Joanna thought, stealing a glance at Richard, not so completely out of reason, not with that spaniel look in his eyes. He wanted her, that was plain, but how much?

"You must think me a wanton," she continued, looking down at the tips of her shoes, wishing she could force a blush. "Alone with you like this. But—I had no—no idea. I—I am not accustomed to being out in the world. You see, I was given in marriage early, very young...." She felt his intent gaze, and now she did blush.

"I have upset you, my dear Mistress Joanna," he said, touching her hand briefly as if to take it. "I pressed my suit too quickly. I could cut out my tongue. I hold you in the greatest esteem, and I swear I meant no disrespect in speaking of love. You must believe me. I do not for a moment think you a wanton. Pray, Mistress Joanna, say you forgive me."

"I do not know what to say. I should never have left Mistress Elizabeth's side." She raised blue eyes large and moist with a distress that was not wholly feigned. "I—I do not like to speak against her, but she—she does not like me as it is. She was most unhappy about the favor—she..." At the thought of Elizabeth and the unfairness of her treatment, the brutal unfairness of life in general, it was not difficult for Joanna to suddenly burst into genuine tears.

He hovered helplessly over her, embarrassed, discomfited, not knowing whether to take her in his arms or not. Would she resent the intimacy, accuse him of further insult?

She solved his dilemma by leaning toward him, reaching blindly out for support, and without quite knowing how it happened he found her head on his shoulder as she sobbed, mumbling something about being treated like a servant, beaten, not having enough to eat, sleeping on the hard, wooden floor, an orphan, without kin.

"There, there," he said, patting her back. He had little experience with tearful females, his mother having died when he was quite young. His three sisters, many years older than he, had left the home with their husbands by the time he was ten. Soldiering, he had had a whore or two, not from lust, but merely because it was the thing to do, and whores had never wept in his company. As for other women, he had never really been taken with a particular one, or even more than mildly interested, until he had seen Joanna come in the door of the spurrier's loft, her gown outlining her slim figure with its high, rounded breasts. The eyes, the windblown rosy cheeks, the sensuous mouth, all had enchanted him. And now she was in his arms weeping, the scent of hair in his nostrils, her warm body pressed to his. He felt a surge of desire. But he felt protective too. Manly.

"What am I to do?" she wept. "Now, my reputation..."

"Oh, my sweet Joanna, nay, nay. I can't tell you often enough how much I respect you. Why—you are like an angel. The sweetest, most virtuous woman I know. I have thought of no one but you since yesterday. I—I want you to be my wife."

She swallowed, paused in her weeping. Oh, God, so soon? Wife. Perhaps he did not mean it. Perhaps it was said on impulse.

"Sir Richard, you must not try to placate me with a jest," she murmured against his chest.

"A jest—never. Never!" He lifted her head so that he could look into her eyes, blue-black eyes with tears clinging to their lashes. "Joanna, I swear on my mother's grave I spoke from the heart. I want you to be my wife."

"Do you?"

He leaned down and kissed her lips chastely. "With all my heart."

"But—but your father..." Experience had taught her to think of contingencies, not to spring to hasty conclusions. "Your father—what will he say? I have no dowry, no family. I am just a poor widow. A freeman's daughter."

"He would be pleased. He would rather have me marry a woman who will accept him as he is than the richest lady in the land, one who would stick up her nose at his lowly origins, his humble speech and the dirt under his fingernails." He grasped her hand. "But none of that matters. I do love you, Joanna. Say aye, say you will marry me!"

She lowered her eyes. He meant it, he *meant* it! Wife! She would be lady, Lady Smithborne. Wife! He wanted to marry her. Should she accept at once? Would that be another sign of her forwardness, another blunder? On the other hand, if she let him go home without an answer, he might think his proposition over and have doubts, or he might be persuaded by his father to change his mind.

"You are silent, Joanna. Is it because I have been too forward, because I have asked you directly and not gone about the matter as custom demands? But who could I ask, if you have no father, no guardian? Perhaps Mistress Elizabeth..."

"Oh, nay, nay. She hates me, she wants to keep me with her because if I go she will have to hire and pay a servant. Do not ask her, promise." She laid a slim finger on his lips, and holding her wrist he softly kissed it.

"Tell me you love me, my sweet Joanna. Tell me you will be my wife."

"I love you," she whispered. "And, aye, I will be your wife."

On the way back to the Savoy, riding pillion behind Richard (Mistress Elizabeth having found her own ride), Joanna, leaning against his back, began to cry again. When he asked her why she told him that she dreaded facing Elizabeth, repeating how the woman had mistreated her and embellishing her story of woe.

"The base woman! And to think all these years I regarded her as a friend. Nay, sweet, you need not ever see her again. You will stay in my father's house until the banns are read and we are married."

The elder Smithborne also had living quarters above his shop, more spacious and better furnished than the Wheelwrights', but housing more people: Richard's older brother, Hugh, Hugh's wife, Ellen, and their child, a boy of three, Richard's uncle, Herbert, and his wife, Bess. When Richard brought Joanna home and introduced her, giving a brief explanation of who she was and his intention to marry her, there were varying reactions, none of them favorable.

Tom Smithborne, contrary to his son's enthusiastic avowal of how delighted he would be, took the news with a sour grunt, eyeing Joanna sideways. A widow, not the young virgin maid he had in mind for his handsome, knighted son, but used goods and no dowry. Not a farthing.

When he had the opportunity to take Richard aside, he pointed this out. "Ye'll not get any money from me, son," he said. "I've too many mouths to feed here. Ye'll have to make yer own way."

"I intend to, Father. I have means of earning a good livelihood."

Richard Smithborne was a knight errant, a professional jouster who went from tourney to tourney competing for prize money and ransoms. Fortunately, thanks mainly to King Edward's enthusiastic interest, jousting had become the premier sport of the land. One could always find a tournament in progress somewhere—Dover, Reading, Colchester, Salisbury, Bury St. Edmunds, Windsor, any number of cities or castles drew contestants and spectators from far and wide.

Despite Richard's assurance to his father, it was a precarious way to earn a living. Prizes for the lesser knights were meager, a silver cup, an engraved medallion and infrequently a modest purse of gold. The ransoms, however, sometimes made up for the skimpy rewards. A knight unhorsed in mock battle or a duel, or bested in hand-to-hand fighting and taken "prisoner" by his opponent, sued him for release by promising to pay a ransom. The loser was also required to give up his horse and arms, but that custom was dying out. Richard did well enough, an excellent horseman, competent with lance and sword; he enjoyed his mode of living and felt himself fortunate for not having been Tom Smithborne's oldest son and so condemned to the forge for the rest of his life. He liked jousting, liked the pageantry, the crowd's acclaim, the nervous feeling in the pit of his stomach when his name was called out to the throng, the sound of the wind whistling past his helmeted head as he thundered down the field. Asked once why he had not remained in France after the wars and tried to make his fortune in booty as so many of his compatriots had done, he answered that he had no stomach for brigandage. It was one thing to fight a man fairly, sword to sword or pike to pike, but to rob and loot and murder the defenseless peasant went against the grain. "Too soft," his older brother chided.

Richard's and Joanna's banns were read in a small chapel at the Savoy, the wedding date set for the second week after Easter, when Richard should return from a tournament at Windsor. It seemed like a long time away to Joanna, and she tried not to show her impatience, an impatience to leave and set up her own household, rather than any eagerness to be Richard's wife. The Smithbornes all shared Tom's disappointment at the young knight's choice of a dowerless widow, and their chilly disapproval was not lost on Joanna. She looked forward to leaving them. She liked Richard, was even fond of him, though his mild, often hesitant and blushing manner sometimes annoyed her. She wished he had more fire, more resolution. It seemed he saved all that for the tourney field—how else could he be a success at such a bold warlike sport?—and she wondered why he could not carry some of that zest away with him. Nevertheless, she promised herself that once she became Lady Smithborne she would make a good wife; he would never have cause to be sorry, never regret having married her.

One afternoon, a few days after Richard had left the Savoy riding his great warhorse with his squire following behind bearing his armor and shield, a boy climbed the ladder to the Smithborne chambers asking for Joanna.

"There's a man with a message from Nareham," he said.

"Nareham," Joanna echoed, the blood draining from her face. She had mentioned her birthplace to Richard, but had kept silent about her illicit affairs and the fruit thereof, Edmund and Aleyn. She was afraid to reveal their existence, afraid Richard would be reluctant to marry her if he knew. And his family! God, it was bad enough for their Sir Richard to wed a penniless widow without her bringing two children, and bastards at that, to him. Such news would send her prospective in-laws into hysteria, and Tom, the father, would openly forbid Richard to take her as wife.

"Where is he?" Joanna asked. If the messenger was from Nareham it must be concerning Aleyn, although she could not imagine how he had found her. Still, he was here at the Savoy. Perhaps Alys had changed her mind and did not want Aleyn. And for one moment she felt the old resentment against the child she had never been able to love.

"He is waiting near the stables," the boy replied.

Richard's sister-in-law, Ellen, said, "Why does he not come to her here?"

Nay! Joanna wanted to shout, not here and reveal all!

But the boy answered, "I do not know, mistress."

"I'll come. 'Twill be no trouble, I'll come now," Joanna said hastily.

She clambered down the ladder and hurried toward the stables, passing the well, the gardens, the mews at a half-run. She rounded the last corner and was beginning to cross the flagged court when she saw him standing in the shadows. But she recognized him. She would have known him anywhere.

Chapter XVIII

As John Hawkwood stood out of the wind, waiting for Joanna, a faint, ironic smile formed on his lips. He had missed England more than he imagined, especially during the long days and interminable nights just past, the endless months he had spent in an Italian prison. A year of disagreeable confinement. Although he had always known that capture and incarceration were hazards of his profession, that most if not all *condottieri* suffered this fate sooner or later, it had still made him bitter. He had had a year in which to cool his heels, a year in which to consider his mistakes.

Long gone from Pisa, he and his White Company had hired out to Bernabò Visconti, Lord of Milan, and at his employer's behest had gone to the aid of Perugia, a city-state at war with the city of Arezzo and its ally, the pope. Overconfidence coupled with exhaustion had made Hawkwood vulnerable. He should have rested his men, not made that hazardous journey through Bologna and Romagna at such reckless speed. And he had underestimated the mustered strength of Arezzo, the cunning and fierceness of their German mercenaries. Outnumbered, the White Company, though fighting with their usual savage intensity, were defeated in the end and Hawkwood and his lieutenants taken prisoner.

It had been twelve months of impatience, of anger, of self-recrimination. A caged tiger could not have paced nor raged as much against its loss of freedom as Hawkwood. But the year had also given him time to think, a look into his innermost self, an activity he had always shunned. Time to ponder his own mortality. Strangely enough, considering the risks, the daily danger of his life, he had never given much thought to death. Now he did, looking at it, facing the inevitable for the first time. Die he must, but like a good many men, he wanted something of himself to live on after him. It was then he remembered his sons by Roscilla. They were his key to perpetuity, his lasting, living monument, his line. When and if his present employer, Bernabò of Milan, ransomed him, he vowed to return to England to fetch the twins, bring them back to Italy and rear them as his rightful heirs.

In his castle prison he had thought of Joanna, too. He had

not forgotten her; he never would. The sweet curve of breast and hip, the honeyed mouth, the smooth silky skin that shivered and trembled under his touch had haunted the edge of his dreams during those long, lonely nights. No woman he had bedded could compare to the passion she roused in him. No other woman had made him feel so vulnerable, so tender, so loving. But male vanity, the warrior's code he lived by, forbade confessing it, even to himself.

Joanna. In the shadows he smiled to himself again. She had tried to fob off Edmund as his son—natural enough, but futile, since the boy in no way resembled him. But he had decided to forgive her, to forget Sir Thomas had been her lover. Hawkwood needed her. He would bring Joanna back to Italy along with the boys. His sons he would leave under the care of a *tutore* in his villa near Pavia, and Joanna would live with him.

It never occurred to him that she would refuse to go.

But he erred as he had done at Arezzo. Overconfident, he had miscalculated Joanna and her pride.

"Joanna!" he called, smiling broadly, holding out his arms.

Her first impulse had been to turn and run. But she realized that such a course might be fatal. He would only follow and confront her at the Smithbornes', something she had to prevent at all costs. So she crossed the courtyard to where he stood, her mind a whirlwind of conflicting emotions; love, hate, bitterness, fleeting nostalgia and galling resentment.

His arms dropped. "Are you not glad to see me, love?" White teeth flashed in a face paled from his imprisonment. The lines at the corners of his eyes had deepened, and there was a permanent furrow between his brows. His tawny, sun-bleached hair, streaked with gray now, was worn short above his ears, shaped to the nape of the neck. He was clean-shaven, the assertive, arrogant jaw exposed. Older but still ruggedly handsome.

"Why—why are you here?" Joanna asked, the familiar question echoing down the years in her head.

"To see you, sweet."

The same voice, the same false words.

"Well, now that you have seen me, good day!" She turned to go, and he moved swiftly, grasping her arm.

"Do not play games, Joanna. I haven't time. I went to a good bit of trouble to find you. Thorsby, Nareham, Kenham Abbey, why can't you stay put? Nay—don't try to get away.

I want you to listen. I have traveled many miles to see you, the least you can do is hear me out."

"Say what you have to say and be quick!" Damn him! Why did he have to turn up again, just when—at last—her prospects for a better life had brightened? And—she glanced hurriedly from left to right—if anyone friendly to the Smithbornes should notice them together, Elizabeth Wheelwright, for instance, there would be the devil to pay. She had already seen Elizabeth head to head with Tom Smithborne, giving him an earful, the topic, Joanna felt sure, her "adopted daughter's" perfidy. And now if she had this...

"I cannot stand here all day, Sir John, I am wanted elsewhere."

Had Hawkwood sensed Joanna's anxiety, her fear of being seen, he might have eased the situation by drawing her back into the shadows. But John thought her nervousness was due to a natural agitation at his unexpected appearance.

"I will make it brief. I am here to tell you that of all women, you are the only one who pleases me. I am asking you to go back with me to Italy."

"Are you mad?"

She struggled to free her arm, but he had a firm grip on it and would not let go.

"I was never more sane. I want you, Joanna. I want you to return to Italy with me."

"Return as your mistress, that's it, isn't it? *Isn't it?*"

"You never objected to being my mistress before. In fact, I can remember when you begged me to go along."

"You—you scurvy dog! Well, you have wasted your time, your breath."

"Come now, darling, you know you do not mean it. I saw your face a minute ago, and you were happy to see me, *happy.*"

"I'll be happy to see you in hell. God's bones, you must think me a mewling female to come flying into your arms whenever you show your face."

"I think you a wondrous female," he said. "I remember, as you must, our last time together in bed, the way we folded into one another, the way you sighed and moaned under my hands."

"You are sure your memory serves you right? There must have been a dozen or more women since me who have sighed and moaned under your hands."

"None. I swear there have been none."

"Ha—liar! But it makes no matter. I would not come with

you had you offered me a queen's crown. You see, my sweet John Hawkwood, *Sir* John, I am to be married in three weeks, *married*, and to a knight."

He let go of her. "I do not believe you. You little minx, you are lying." He smiled. "You are trying to make me jealous, poor darling."

"I am trying to do nothing but tell you I am to be married. The banns have already been read. You have only to ask the priest at the chapel to find out whether I am lying or not. I am betrothed and am to marry Sir Richard Smithborne on April the eighth in this year of our Lord."

He searched her face, and she met his gaze with cold contempt.

"So ..." He let out his breath. "You have managed to snare yourself a prize. Did you tell him you were pregnant, as you did once to me?"

"You have a low, vile mind. But then you have always thought the worst of me and acted accordingly, contrary to Richard, who has behaved from the start with the utmost propriety. He *respects* me."

"Does he?" He narrowed his eyes.

A little thrill of fear ran through Joanna. "You are not going to make trouble?"

"I shall do as I choose."

"John..." She had made a terrible mistake by telling him. There was something cruel and vindictive about John she had only dimly suspected in the past, but now she could see it plainly in the impassive face, the set of his mouth, the narrowed eyes. "John..."

"So it's to be a marriage," he interrupted, brushing her protest aside. "A lawful wife to some petty knight, but a man who *respects* you. Does he know about your bastards?"

She drew herself up, a spot of high color on each cheek. "Aye," she lied, "he does."

"And still wants you? Then he won't mind if I tell him one is mine."

"Yours? You have never acknowledged Edmund."

"Not to you. But your Sir Richard need not know that."

"You—you wouldn't!"

His brows went up and his thin mouth twisted into a derisive smile.

She wanted to claw at him, to wipe that snide look from his face. "I shall kill you if you say one word. I swear I shall kill you!"

He threw back his head and laughed. "Foolish girl. Beautiful, foolish girl. Come away with me. To hell with the marriage, with respect, the so-called honorable life. Come away and I will teach you what it means to be happy."

"Nay," Joanna said, clenching her teeth on the word. "Nay. Never. Go take yourself, your boasts and your threats back to Italy." And turning, she hurried off almost at a run, rounding a corner, pausing, peering out to see if he would follow.

But he did not, and when she reached the loft, rather breathless and pale, Ellen said, "Bad news?"

"'Twas only a message from an old friend. There's been a death in the de Ander family, my husband's old master."

"Did he leave a bequest?"

"None that I am heir to."

Her answer seemed to satisfy Ellen, for she asked nothing further.

A week before Easter, Richard came home unexpectedly.

Joanna had been at the window to get the last good light as she mended a shift. Hearing the sound of horses' hooves, she looked down and saw him in his light-yellow jupon trotting across the yard. His squire, Henry, carrying shield and lance, rode by his side. They drew up at the forge, and Joanna watched as Tom Smithborne ran out to greet his son. She heard the questioning voices, the note of surprise in Tom's voice, and her heart froze. Richard did not look ill, and only that or a similar catastrophe could have torn him away from the tournament, which had another ten days to run. What had happened to bring him home?

"Richard's here!" Joanna exclaimed to Ellen, hoping the nervous tremor in her voice would be interpreted as joy.

"Richard?" Ellen echoed in disbelief.

Joanna nodded, pressing icy hands to her hot cheeks.

When he came into the room, the drooping mouth and the sadly accusing blue eyes gave him away. He knows, Joanna thought, tasting bitter gall. Hawkwood has carried out his threat and told him. Damn him! May his tongue rot, may he die a slow lingering death. The low, deceitful churl! And now she was finished, the marriage snatched away from her. It had been all for nothing, the subterfuge, the coy blushes, the fluttering eyelashes. Nothing. Again just when she had been on the brink of pulling herself up in the world, she had been pushed back. She was going to be poor, shamed, scorned for the rest of her life. Damn John Hawkwood!

"Why are you here?" the uncle and aunt asked Richard in unison. "What has happened?"

He said, "Joanna and I must speak alone."

She could feel their hostile eyes shafted at her.

"Come outside," Richard said.

She followed him down the ladder on legs of straw. He took her by the arm and led her around to the back of the forge, a not altogether private spot, but at least out of earshot and view from the Smithbornes.

"Joanna," he began, his tone not angry, but hurt, "you know that I love you, that I want nothing in this world but happiness for you, but why...?" He broke off. "Why did you not tell me?"

Joanna chewed her lips, her gaze fixed beyond him, as the tears slowly filled her eyes.

"A man, Hawkwood, Sir John Hawkwood, a mercenary captain, came to me at Windsor," Richard went on. "He said— he said you had two bastards, one his. Is it true?"

For a fraction, an infinitesimal fraction of time, she thought of denying it. But her innate good sense told her that one lie would only compound another, making her situation far worse. Better to admit the truth, invent a plausible excuse, and throw herself on his mercy.

"I was afraid to tell you," she murmured in so small a voice he had to bend his head to hear.

"But, Joanna..."

"Oh, Richard," she cried, flinging her arms about his neck. "I love you so, I could not bear to lose you. I couldn't, even if it meant holding back the truth."

"Joanna..."

She pressed her hand to his lips. "If I had confessed, if I had told you how two dastardly men forced me—aye, forced. I know John Hawkwood boasts of conquest, but he did not seduce me. It is a terrible lie. He raped me—he took me when I was hardly more than a child. I was walking in my lady's garden at Nareham..." And here she burst into a torrent of sobs.

He gathered her into his arms, he patted her shoulders, muttered little words. "'Tis all right, don't cry, don't cry. You poor, brave little girl..."

She clung to him, her breasts hard against his chest, her body fitting tightly into his. "I could not, I could not..." she sobbed over and over.

"And the other?" he asked into her hair, his voice edged with the faintest doubt.

"Aye. God in heaven, how could it happen to me? Twice. Alys de Ander's son was another—I had no recourse but to submit. The lord's son—how could I not? Oh, Richard..." She pushed herself away, grasping him by the shoulders. "If you would disown me, repudiate our betrothal, I would understand. For there is more. I was never married." She might as well confess it all; nothing now could make her situation worse. "I am not a widow. I only posed as one to keep the lechers away, to try to lead a decent life. But I should have known better. It is too late, too late. I release you, my love. I do not want my misfortune to cast dishonor on your name."

"Joanna..."

She uptilted her tear-stained face, her eyes large and poignant. "Oh, Richard, I do love you, that is the one thing I never lied about. I will always remember you, always. My honorable, good knight. I will pray for you. I will carry you in my heart to the end of my days."

"Joanna..."

"Nay, 'tis best—'tis best I go." Once more she leaned against him and wept.

Tenderly, he took her face between his hands, and bending, kissing her salty sweet lips, he forgave her.

"God has given me a test," he said, his voice catching a little, his blue eyes moist with feeling. "'Twould be a poor love that failed at the first trial."

They were duly married a week after Easter and moved from the Smithborne quarters to a house Richard had rented on Lime Street near Corn Hill from a wine merchant, a wealthy burgher of scattered properties. A small house, it had a long narrow hall (or parlor as they were beginning to be called) on the ground floor, a dim room with an open fireplace and a small window which looked out on a patch of neglected garden and the street. To the left of the parlor beyond a wooden screen was the kitchen and to the right a shallow flight of steps which led to the bedchamber. Furniture had come with the house; chairs, a table, some coffers, a bed hung with dusty brocade on which rested a lumpy, musty-smelling mattress. Not an elegant house, but contrasting it with what Joanna had lived in for most of her life, it seemed fine indeed. Here she felt mistress more than she ever had at Thorsby. It was *hers*, really hers, not Dame Joanna's pretend home, but Lady Smithborne's. Lady, *lady!* Sometimes she could hardly believe it, even when looking at the small beryl ring Richard had placed on her finger. More, her husband was to have his own blazon, anvil and flames displayed on a field of vert, the heraldic device to be registered in the Roll of Arms, a privilege not many of the come-lately knights shared.

What plans she made, what dreams she had of their future life together. She would bring Aleyn (it would not seem right to leave him with Alys) and Edmund, her heart's love, to London. They would share Richard's name too, for he had offered to adopt them. No one need ever know that they were illegitimate. She would make the house on Lime Street beautiful. She would add to the furnishings with tapestry-covered chairs, little tables, carved chests, new beds, fanciful mugs and silver-handled knives. What fun it would be to choose and pick, to be able to buy her own things.

Alas, Joanna soon, all too soon, found that she had married a man of limited means. Having missed most of the tourney at Windsor, he had gone into debt renting the house, borrowing to pay the required six months in advance. The servants he procured, a cook and two menials, had been promised their wages as soon as he returned from his next tourney at Grove's Court. What little cash he had left must be reserved for the daily necessities. Joanna's tapestry-covered chairs, her beds and silver-handled knives, her journey to fetch her children would have to wait.

But Richard was good to her, apologizing for his inability to provide better. He would give her the moon if he could, and she knew it. A pity his lovemaking was so pedestrian. There were times when lying naked beneath him while he went at her she had to fight the urge to change positions, to straddle him, legs apart, to grasp his manhood in her hands and show him what it was all about. But she had shocked him enough. He must never guess that she was in any way knowledgeable about lovemaking, must never suspect she had been anything other than the innocent victim of a man's unbridled lust.

When Richard departed for the tourney in June, he left with her a small purse, and Joanna had to put off the grumbling servants with more promises, menials who, at best, were lazy and inept. She learned quickly that if she sent the cook to the marketplace it cost her dear. The woman, a feckless idiot, could not count her own fingers and toes and overpaid for everything, whether it was a sack of flour or a scrawny hen. Joanna therefore had no choice but to do her own buying. Fortunately she had learned how to dicker years ago at Thexted Fair and had not forgotten any of the old tricks. She knew how to haggle, knew how to pretend indifference, to choose obliquely, to shrug her shoulders, knew the right moment when the seller would or would not yield another farthing. It demeaned her—that is, it demeaned the Lady Joanna, but the peasant in her enjoyed the process, the give and take, the uncertainty, the challenge and the eventual victory, for she was a hard, shrewd bargainer.

In the meanwhile she had a scribe write to Alys at Nareham apprising her former mistress of her changed situation, married, a lady, and asking to have Aleyn back.

The reply arrived in a shockingly short time. "Nay—he is yours no longer. Sir Thomas is marrying Joan Hadley and wishes me to continue raising the boy."

Joan Hadley? And what had become of Lady Rosamonde? But no matter. Joanna, thinking of her own affairs and hearing the message, experienced a surge of relief followed by a stab of guilt. She should put up more of a fight to keep Aleyn even though his father had prior rights. She ought to insist, any decent mother would. But if she did, would the child be happy to come to London? Most likely not. She assuaged her guilt then by assuring herself that Aleyn had long since forgotten her, was well cared for and content at Nareham.

But Edmund...

She did not write to the abbot. She did not want to give him the opportunity of refusing. As soon as Richard could scrape up the money to provide her with a horse and escort, she would go to Kenham Abbey, present herself and say simply, "I have come to fetch Edmund." No *asking*, only the announcement, and if need be, the demand.

It was two years, however, before Richard could manage to clear himself of debt and have the money to spare. When he returned from a spring tourney at Bury St. Edmunds he brought with him fifty pounds, a carnelian ring and a silken scarf for Joanna. He had done well, very well, much better than expected. At home he paid the servants, who went from grumbling to fawning the moment they heard the clink of coins. He paid the landlord, the candlemaker, the saddler and baker. To his wife, he said, "Tomorrow, early, I shall see to buying you a palfrey for your journey."

She knew the purchase of a decent palfrey would eat into

Richard's winnings and for a moment thought of demurring, but she did not want to arrive at the abbey on muleback, looking like a pauper, so she said nothing. Richard's squire, Henry, the snub-nosed yeoman's son from Kent, would accompany her, and for greater safety they planned to wait for and join a band of pilgrims on their way to Walsingham.

The little troupe got on well together and were pleasant company for Joanna. They made good time without incident until passing through Epping Forest they were waylaid by a quartet of ugly-looking ruffians, brigands on stolen mounts wielding dagger and sword and making wild, incoherent cries as they rushed from the surrounding trees. The pilgrims were unarmed except for a bowlegged little friar who carried a well-honed bread knife and Henry, the squire, who wore a light sword and a dagger in his belt. But they were two, if you counted the friar, against four.

"All ye riding, dismount!" bawled the leader, a scoundrel with a mouthful of black rotting teeth. He wore a tarnished surcoat of cloth of gold and felt shoes, the highly exaggerated points of which were tied to his ankles by laces.

Startled, the band stood in the road, mouths agape, those on muleback, those afoot, unable to move or utter a word. Henry, who had been riding nose to tail with Joanna, shuffled his horse back a step closer to her.

"Dismount!" the man in the surcoat shrieked.

His companions stationed themselves on the flanks of the frightened, huddled little group; a beefy, black-bearded rogue to the left, a pock-faced knave with a squint on the right and the third, a brute wearing a greasy black pancake-shaped hat, behind.

"Sheep! I'll show ye!" the leader shouted, whirling his sword over his head. He rode forward and slashed at a hempen-cloaked old man astride a mule. The pilgrim gave a cry and fell forward; a woman screamed in terror, another began to sob.

The squire leaned over and whispered to Joanna, "Do as they say," at the same time drawing both sword and dagger. Plunging forward, he took the beefy brigand on the left by surprise, knocking him from the saddle, then whirled to meet the hatted rogue, who came at him with his own weapon, a lethal, heavy, two-edged battle sword. The pilgrims whimpering and milling about tried to get out of the way, some rolling themselves in the ditch by the side of the road. But

Joanna, furious at the thought of losing her costly mount, her saddle, her purse of coins and perhaps her life to these crude outlaws, stood her ground, loosening her heavy saddlebags to use as a bludgeon. Seeing that the man Henry had felled was about to rise, she rode him down, throwing him back to the ground, and just to make sure he would not attempt to rise again, she galloped over him, grinding his body into the dust. It gave her a curious, almost overpowering sense of triumph, and although she still could not recall Sarah's death at the hands of just such outlaws years ago, she had the feeling that she was repaying a long-overdue debt.

Meanwhile the bowlegged friar on foot was busily attacking the leader with his breadknife, stabbing at his legs, running in and out under the man's flashing sword. The squint-eyed outlaw coming to his comrade's rescue was making straight for the stabbing friar when his horse stumbled over the body of the slain pilgrim, throwing him headlong over the horse's head. As he fell his head hit the edge of a rock, and he lay still, very still. Joanna pranced over him, saddlebags at the ready and aimed a blow at the hatted man, who, having shattered Henry's sword, had raised his own to finish the squire off. Joanna's blow caught him rising in his stirrups, unbalancing him and sending him toppling. Henry quickly slid from the saddle and without pausing for breath plunged his dagger into the brigand's chest.

Now the man in the surcoat, who had been on his way to decapitate Henry, suddenly turned his mount, jumped the ditch and disappeared into the trees.

They buried the dead old man in his coarse, hooded cloak, tenderly placing his script covered with cockle shells, the symbol of the pilgrim, on his chest. The slain outlaws they dragged to the side of the road where the crows could pick their ugly bones clean.

"My lady," Henry said to Joanna, "you did well. You have a brave heart. Sir Richard would be proud of you."

And the pilgrims murmured their approval too. "My lady, God bless you." "Such courage, my lady."

My lady! How it delighted her to be called that, even now.

The abbot received her with a friendly smile. Glad to hear of her good fortune, he congratulated her on her marriage. Privately he felt that a woman of her sort should not be so rewarded for a life of sin. This thought passing through his mind lasted only a few moments, however, for the abbot was not a narrow, vindictive man.

"Edmund is learning his letters with such speed it astounds me," the abbot told her. "And Latin too. Already he knows more than many a parish priest."

"You are not thinking of making him one?" she asked, looking directly at him, her violet-blue eyes suddenly anxious.

"His birth precludes it, lady." He had made inquiries. The Bishop of Lincoln owed him a favor—it could be done, the illegitimacy swept aside, given the right word in the right ear.

"You remember in our last conversation you promised..."

"...to consult Edmund and you. Of course, and it shall be done."

The abbot's aim for a long time had been to achieve one good, a single honest, incorruptible priest for the church, but recently it had become a vow. Through the years at Kenham he had acquired a taste for business, a taste for sharp bargaining, for accumulating wealth—all done for the abbey's good. And he believed this myth for years until one night he dreamed of St. Francis of Assisi, dressed in rags, a crow perched on his shoulder, the saint's eyes black pits in a death's-head skull, pointing a bony finger at him, accusing him of grinding the faces of the poor.

It was after this terrifying yet revealing dream that he decided to start a school and from it each year to take the likeliest of his young students and shape them for the priesthood, knowledgeable, pure of soul, devout lads, his, the abbot's, gift to the church.

The vow was made shortly after Edmund arrived, the school was started and Joanna's son installed. In a short while it was clear to Mark that he had been right about the boy; Edmund had a calling, he was bright, intelligent, honest, painfully so, and he loved the monastic life, the beauty of long meditative silences, the prayer, the books, the easy mellifluous flow of Latin. What a find! What a gem!

And now his mother was here to take him away.

"May I see him?" she asked.

"Of course." He nodded to the cellarer, and the monk rang a little bell. Presently another monk with a harried look on his face came into the parlor.

"Pray, fetch Edmund Coke."

When he had shut the door behind him, Joanna turned

her sweetest, most engaging smile on the abbot. "Your grace, may I ask a boon? I should like to see my son privately. Pray do not be offended. 'Tis...'tis..." She managed to blush. "I am loath to give way to emotion in your presence."

"By all means, Lady Smithborne." He nodded to the cellarer. Clever woman. He wondered what she would promise Edmund to come away.

The world, if she could. When she saw her son, how he had grown in the past few years, how his handsomeness shone despite the thin, knobby wrists gangling from the plain jerkin which was several sizes too small, her eyes filled with tears of pride.

"Edmund...!" She clasped him, kissing him again and again, letting him go, holding him at arm's length. "Edmund—almost as tall as your mother!"

He laughed. Ivo's laugh, Ivo's face and hair, but Hawkwood's eyes.

"The most wonderful thing has happened, my darling. I am married!" She proceeded to tell him of her good fortune, of the marvelous change in her life. She painted the house on Lime Street with glowing colors, Sir Richard as the noblest, the most warm-hearted and gentlest of men. "He wants to be your father. He loves you already just from what I have told him about you and can hardly wait until I bring you home." Of Edmund's real father she had never spoken; the boy did not even know his name. He remembered a knight coming to Thorsby once, a broad-shouldered, heavily muscled man with a nose that had an arch to it, a man who had denied having fathered him. But he did not need a father; he had the abbot, Father Mark.

"Mama, I should like to stay," he said when she paused for breath.

"Stay...! Why, you foolish child. You are only nine, too young to know your own mind. Don't you *want* to go with me? Don't you love your mother?"

"Oh, Mama, I do. I shall always love you. But I like it here. I like the books—and the monks are so kind. We have a school now—there are other boys, and I am never lonely. I do not even miss Aleyn any more."

"You are saying that simply because you have become accustomed to the abbey. So much nicer than Thorsby. But when you see the house on Lime Street you will feel differently. You will have an alcove all to yourself, and as for friends—why, I shall send you to a school in London, a proper school. Mary St. Le Bow…"

"Thank you, Mama, you are very generous and good. But I should prefer to stay here."

For the first time in her life Joanna had the urge to box his ears. The jackanapes! But she could not really blame the child. It was Father Mark who had turned the boy's head.

"My dear Edmund, your place is with your mother. You are not an orphan, you have a loving mother and a loving man at home who wants to be your father. I know what is best for you. Trust me."

She told Father Mark to have the boy's bundle packed, that they would leave on the morrow. "He is reluctant to part with his friends here—'tis only natural for a boy of his age. But I know once he reaches London, he will have forgotten the abbey. Children are like that."

She never knew what Father Mark said to Edmund, what promises he made, but Edmund came without fuss, never once voicing a word of complaint or regret. He rode pillion with her in silence. At night he did as she asked—"Aye, Mama," "Nay, Mama,"—curling up beside her on the straw pallets of the various inns where they sought shelter. He was good, an exemplary child, too good, like a pietist who had been ordered by his conscience, or his confessor, to accept. Again and again she cursed the abbot for making her son into this spiritless boy of straw. When I get home, she promised herself, all will change. Richard will take him in hand, teach him the manly arts, riding, swordplay, archery.

But her plans had to be postponed, for when she returned to London she found that the city had been struck by another outbreak of the dread plague. Sir Richard, about to depart for a tourney in the north of England, was loath to leave Joanna at such a dangerous time. "I've had the sickness," she told him, urging him to go. They needed the money. The pounds Richard had won at Bury St. Edmunds had dwindled to an alarming few. Aside from paying for Joanna's journey and other household expenses, Richard had loaned his father ten marks, had bought his old aunt a new gown and his nephew a pair of shoes. Generous to a fault. But Joanna, remembering her vow not to scold, could only gnash her teeth in silence. He was too much like Ivo, too soft-hearted, too open with money once he had it in his hand. If they were to avoid lean times she could not allow him to stay home because he felt his presence would protect her and the boy. Whether he was there or not, she pointed out, would make little difference; if they were marked for the plague, they would get it.

When Richard left, Joanna provisioned the house as though it were faced with imminent siege. She gave the servants the opportunity to leave if they so wished, but they chose to stay. Where could they go to be safe? they asked, eyeing the casks of ale, the hams, the smoked herring, the cheeses. Joanna boarded up the windows and ran heavy wooden bars across both doors. Preparing to wait the sickness out, relieved that their dwelling did not sit in the midst of the more crowded quarters of London, she was congratulating herself on the wiseness of her move when the serving boy became ill. She recognized the symptoms—it was the plague. She knew how contagious the disease was, how once it started in a household it spread to every member. Her concern was for Edmund, a fierce, blind maternal protectiveness that blocked other feelings out. She had the serving boy carried to the lean-to at the back of the garden. She refused to go near it and forbade the cook to do more than leave him bread and water. He had been ill four or five days (no one knew for sure how long) when he died, but by then Joanna had another more terrible concern. Edmund himself became ill.

It was a nightmare. She relived those agonizing days of her own childhood when she herself tossed and turned upon a sweat-soaked pallet, the fever burning her face, pain knotting her limbs, her head pumped up like a pig's bladder. Tight-lipped, out of her mind with worry, she sat by Edmund's bedside putting cool cloths to his brow, coaxing him to take a sip of broth, a little wine. In his delirium he spoke of nothing but the abbey, the abbot, the cloisters, the dim, cool, cool corridors where he had been so happy. He sobbed, he whispered, he implored God to take him back. And Joanna, watching him, slipping to her knees, promised the same implacable deity that if He should bring her child through his ordeal, He should indeed have Edmund as His servant.

"Only make him live," she begged. To lose Edmund, to have him die . . . no, she could not think of it. "I promise," she prayed passionately. "I will give him up without a murmur. I promise. Holy Virgin, Mother of God, Mother to mother, if he dies, I die too."

Edmund passed the crisis, the buboes burst, the fever died, and very slowly he began to recover. She fed him rich soups, sops in wine, honeyed custard, cajoling him to eat, gently teasing him to take another bite. Outside the house the rampant plague gradually died; the mournful bells of London's 146 churches, which had tolled almost incessantly for two months, rang intermittently now. With Edmund up and about, safely past danger, Joanna would have pushed her earlier frantic vow to the back of her mind (somehow, in some way, she would make it up to God), but the child, though recovered in body, remained low and sick in spirit. Joanna tried in every way to cheer him, amusing him with stories, with songs and ditties, but nothing she said or did sparked a light in his pale solemn face. He would sit for hours by the window, looking out with blank eyes, numb, a hollow shell.

She could not bring herself to ask it, but she knew she must. "Would you want to go back to the abbey, Edmund?"

His face broke into a smile, a radiant smile that cut her to the heart.

Chapter XIX

On Easter Sunday, seven months after Edmund's return to the abbey, a daughter was born to Richard and Joanna. They named her Cristina. The baby commenced life not in the house on Lime Street, but in a much shabbier, smaller one in the shadow of St. Giles near Cripple Gate, the move having been forced upon them by a lack of funds. Because the plague had decimated the ranks of both knightly contenders and spectators, tourneys became fewer and farther between, and Richard's earnings diminished accordingly.

The dwelling, only a few notches above a village cot in comfort, had a main room, a kitchen, a sleeping loft and furniture of the crudest sort. Drafty in winter, stifling in summer, in need of whitewashing and the carpenter's hammer, it made a poor home for a knight and his lady, and Richard was always promising that his next purse, his next ransom money, would be used to obtain quarters more appropriate to his station. What money he did bring, what gold or silver cups resold for shillings and pence, however, went toward food and drink, for rent and for the one servant they could now afford. In short, they had only enough to meet the expenses of daily life and none to lay by for improving it.

Joanna, mindful of her prenuptial vow, hid her bitterness as best she could, and Richard, unaware of his wife's secret discontent, remained cheerful, optimistic, a kind, loving, attentive husband who never failed to bring some little gift from his travels, even if it was only a flower or a ribbon, gallantly kissing Joanna's hand and cheek at each farewell and return. He adored Cristina with her blond hair and blue eyes and small pointed nose, never for a moment regretting she had not been born a boy.

Joanna herself felt cool toward the child, not as distant as she had toward Aleyn, but cool nevertheless. The rush of maternal warmth, the desire to protect and champion, had all gone to Edmund, and she could not summon these feelings for another. Besides, the baby, though not ugly, was decidedly plain. A girl should be pretty, especially a poor girl without prospects of a decent dowry. But she had a pointed nose and close-set eyes, admissible on a male but damning to a female.

There were other things which fed Joanna's feeling of blighted hope. Being Lady Smithborne seemed to have made very little difference in her life. The acceptance from those who were now her equals had not been forthcoming. When she was still living on Lime Street she had organized a small gala supper, had ordered the wine, the meats, the savories, intending to cook the meal herself. She had sent a neatly dressed boy around to the various intended guests Richard had suggested, knights who had fought with him in tourneys and were now in London to contend in King Edward's famous Spring Tournament at Smithfield. Five knights and their ladies had been invited. Only one pair had come, a Sir Gilbert Cartwright, a former yeoman, like Richard knighted in the field, and his lady, clearly of peasant stock. The others, all nobly born, had not even bothered to say yea or nay. It was a humiliating affront she found difficult to excuse or forget.

Nor were she and Richard asked to sit at nobilities' board. There had been one exception, however; they had dined at the Savoy.

John of Gaunt, the Duke of Lancaster, the Savoy's illustrious chatelain, was gathering another English army for the purpose of recovering Aquitaine, the larger portion of which had been lost piecemeal to the French. Throughout Britain the earls and barons were calling up their knights, men-at-arms and archers for the military muster to be held at Calais across the channel. From there, with Sir Hugh Calveley in the vanguard, they planned to march on Paris in the initial stage of their campaign.

Richard Smithborne was one of the first to offer his services, and he and Joanna, along with a hundred or so other knights, had been invited to a farewell banquet at the great palace. The feast had been a long-drawn-out and not wholly satisfying affair.

In the first place, they were put at a trestle below the salt, a seating arrangement all too familiar to Joanna. She and Richard were wedged between two very young knights, quite drunk, who got into an argument across them, wielding their cutting knives and swearing loudly until Richard threatened them both with a head cracking. In the second place, they drank an inferior wine and were served the tougher cuts of meat. There were few women guests of equivalent rank, and she had no opportunity to speak to anyone, nor even to see much of the entertainment, minstrels, dancers and tumblers, since their seat was at the side of the hall with a crowd of tables between them and the cleared space in the center. She did not feel like Lady Smithborne, not even like the Joanna of old who had at least dined with the steward close to the dais.

Her life was a daily reminder of past poverty. She had gained little by her marriage except a worthless title and a legitimate child. Save for the beryl and carnelian rings she had no jewels of value and no clothes but two gowns, one for marketing and cooking, the other to be worn at church. She would walk by the mercers' stalls and eye the bolts of silks and wools longingly. Though they had enough to eat, the food was of mediocre quality. At Nareham or even at Thorsby (when they were not starving) they dined on fresh meat, fresh vegetables, fresh bread. Here everything tasted stale, old, tainted.

The narrow lane on which they lived had a ditch running down the center. Here offal, bones, fish heads, dead dogs and cats were thrown into the dirty water, the entire refuse-choked stream exuding a noisome odor, relieved only by a heavy rainstorm or the occasional employment of rakers (cleaners). The house had a small garden, a neglected, half-dead apple tree and a tangle of thorny weeds. Joanna spent much time trying to clear a small space in which to plant kitchen herbs, a few cabbages. She wore gloves to protect her hands, clumsy things, though she wondered, what was the use? Richard spoke of booty he would gain by this new war, but she remembered John Hawkwood telling her six years earlier (was it that long, was she twenty-five now?) that France had been picked clean by brigands even then. But she said nothing. Richard was the perennial optimist. Tomorrow he would win the big prize, tomorrow his luck would turn, in this war he would become rich, and she had not the heart to tell him that miracles happened only to saints, long dead, their claims beyond refute.

Before Richard left he moved her and Cristina back into his father's house, a move Joanna protested. But Richard pointed out that he could not go off and leave his wife and child protected only by a dim-witted servant (though such an argument had not been made when he rode to distant tourneys) for God alone knew how long. Furthermore, and this was the reasoning which convinced Joanna, it would cost so much less. The purse he gave her, all he had, even if used sparingly could not sustain her beyond four months, far too soon to look for her husband's return.

The Smithbornes took her in, a little more graciously than they had before. She was now part and parcel of the family, no matter what their personal feelings, and she had given birth to another Smithborne. Though a girl, it was manifestly their own, a child with a remarkable resemblance to Richard.

Lady Smithborne, living above a blacksmith's shop, wore a gray shapeless gown and a matronly wimple now, as befitted a married woman, a nunlike headdress which hid her glorious hair. She had grown thinner, paler, her mouth set in anxious lines. She seldom spoke and rarely smiled. Sometimes catching a glimpse of herself in the well, she felt as though what she saw was not the Joanna she knew but the mirrored image of a stranger.

One afternoon a week after Cristina's third birthday, she was hurrying across the courtyard to fetch the Smithborne loaves from the communal oven when a man-at-arms wearing an unfamiliar badge stopped her.

"Many pardons, mistress, but can you direct me to Joanna of Thorsby?"

"*I* am Joanna," she said, surprised and curious. "What is it you want?"

He peered closely at her before he replied. "But—you do not answer the description."

"Whose description?" she asked tartly. "I assure you I *am* Joanna, Lady Smithborne now."

For a moment she wondered if this man was an old creditor, one that Richard had forgotten to pay. But then he said, "I have word of your son, Edmund."

"Edmund?" Her hands flew to her breast. "Mother of God!" Only bad news could come by word of mouth from the abbey; if it were good Edmund would write himself. "Is he ill? Has something happened? What is it? Tell me!"

"I know nothing except that a monk from Kenham Abbey has sent me to fetch you."

"Where is he? Here? Where?"

"He has put up at an inn down the strand a little way. The Bell."

"Aye, I know where 'tis."

The man-at-arms hovered by, as if waiting for a coin for his trouble, but Joanna was busy thinking. Should she get the loaves first or go at once? The Smithbornes knew about Edmund but only that he was a nephew, her dead brother's son, a relationship subject to much suspicious conjecture on their part.

"I'll go!" she exclaimed. Hang the loaves.

At the Bell she inquired if a monk from Kenham Abbey was staying there. The innkeeper raised questioning brows. "He was looking for a Joanna of Thorsby," she added.

"Ah!" He pointed with his thumb to a ladder which led to the loft.

It was dim in the room, but the moment she set foot in it she saw that she had been knavishly tricked. No monk awaited her, no messenger from Kenham Abbey. Only John Hawkwood, grinning at her as he stood by the window.

She turned at once to go, but he strode across the room and grabbed her arm.

"Let me be, you dirty rat. You brigand! To deceive me so vilely! Liar!" Angry tears choked her voice.

"Forgive me, but 'twas the only way I could see you alone. Would you have me come to your door and ask for an interview?"

"I would have you go to hell. After what you did to me the last time—I never want to see you again."

"Joanna..."

"Lady Smithborne, pray."

"So he married you." Older, dressed in a blue silk surcoat, he smiled down at her.

"Surprised? Aye, he married me. A loving, honorable man. And I have his child, one whom he acknowledges. Legitimate."

"And you love him, the man who married you?"

"Dearly."

He threw his tawny head back and laughed.

She wrenched her arm away, but he grasped it again, his fingers bruising her flesh. "You lie, my beauty, you lie. You don't love him. Look at you!" His eyes raked the drab gown, the wimpled face and hidden hair. "He has made an old woman of you. Or is trying. No one in love could look like you."

"Whoreson!" she spat, trying to struggle free.

He released her. "I still want you, sweeting," he said, his voice suddenly low, and intense. "But I won't force you, that is not my way. Remember, Joanna, my name is carved on your flesh, on your very bones. I was the first, Joanna. The two of us, you and me, have what few men and women share. We belong. We are made for one another."

"Are you saying you love me?" she asked, irony underlying her tone.

He gave her an odd look, an elusive one she could not define. But the next moment his lips curved in a mocking smile.

"If that be love—ah, Joanna, can't you see? I have not forgotten. I must care if I carry you in my mind—aye, very well, in my heart." He made a mock gesture, placing his hand on his breast. "I am not good at flowery language, pretty words. I have told you so before."

"You were clever enough with them once." But it had not been his words, she thought bitterly. He did not need words. Even now, knowing him as she did, hating him, she could feel his vitality, the strong, bold masculinity that seemed to charge the very air in the room with excitement.

"'Tis you I want, Joanna."

What if he meant it? What if he really loved her, but in a perverse masculine way could not come out and say the words, words which fell so easily from Richard? Ah—but how could she compare the two? One was decent, honest, the other a rogue.

"Come away with me," John urged. "Come away, my sweet Joanna. What is there here for you? What is there here that I cannot give and more, much more? Tell me truthfully, has there been a man in your bed, aye, in your heart, who has contented you half as much as I? The truth."

She lifted her chin and looked at him defiantly. "Nay. But that is not all of life. There are other things besides a tumble in bed that can make a woman happy."

"What? Clothes, gowns, jewels? I can give them to you; satins, silks, the sheerest of linens. Pearls, rubies. I have a villa, a townhouse in Florence, a farm in Fiesole—houses with servants. My stables are stocked with blooded horses, my cellars with the best wine. You will never want, Joanna."

"So, you will give me everything except the one thing Richard provides so generously—love. Richard..."

"You fool!" he broke in, his eyes blazing. With a suddenness that startled her he pulled her into his arms, crushing her to his chest, the jeweled emblem on his tunic biting into her flesh.

"John...let me..."

But his mouth was on hers, the warm, mobile mouth of a hundred erotic memories, claiming hers with a hungry, bruising intensity. And Richard, the Savoy, the world outside faded to nothingness as she gave herself up to abandonment, to the wild surge of blood, the heady intoxication, that only he could evoke.

When he finally released her she felt a pang of disappointment, a pang she quickly squelched. Clawing her hands into fists to keep her legs from trembling, she stepped back and drew in her breath.

"Well, Joanna?" He grinned.

She swallowed. "You kissed me. Aye, you kiss well enough. But what happens if you tire of me, Sir John? Then what?"

"Have I forgotten you these past ten years? Have I? Nay, I have come back across a continent and a sea, have found you at great cost to myself..."

"You have not made the journey solely on my account. You have had business here, I am sure."

"True. My brother died at Hedingham, and there was his estate to claim, but I could have easily sent another to settle my affairs. As you see, I did not. I wanted to find you, Joanna. I want to take you back with me. I have thought of nothing else this past year."

She half believed him. Half. He seemed so earnest, so sincere. And if he wanted her now, now when she appeared her least attractive, wimpled, shapeless, with the sourness of disappointment beginning to purse her lips, then he must love her, must mean what he said.

"And what of my husband? My children?"

"Leave them. Your husband will find another wife soon enough. As for your children, you were able to part with them before."

"Not my daughter. She is still too young."

"She has loving grandparents, no doubt. Aunts? Uncles? A father."

"I couldn't. Adultery. I would be committing adultery. I couldn't add that to the sin of deserting the child."

"Mark me, Joanna. Of what good are you to her now? You are not happy. I can see it in your face, your eyes. It is Thorsby all over again. If you went with me you could send your child money. You could help *all* of them in a way you could not possibly do in a thousand years with that feckless young knight you married. He will never have the wherewithal to make you even comfortable. One look at him and I could tell. A man, honest, upright, but one who will always be poor."

"You do Sir Richard a wrong."

But did he? If she had money, she had often thought in the past, she could send gifts to Aleyn, reminding him that he had a mother, she could help Edmund procure a good living, a decent if not rich and comfortable parish, and she could dower Cristina properly. Money to spend, to give, to lavish. What was there one could not do with it? Money that Richard would never have. As for her leaving—well, he would get over it. Or would he? Richard.

"I cannot," she said.

"Think it over. I shall give you a day and a night. I am sure you will decide in my favor. Come tomorrow evening. Meet me at the riverbank just beyond the Savoy mews. I shall have a small boat waiting. It is not necessary to take anything but your cloak. I shall buy you whatever you may need."

"You are assuming much."

"I am assuming you love me." He lifted her hand and kissed it. "Lady Smithborne." He smiled into her eyes, his own dancing, the lines crinkling at the edges. "Tomorrow night."

She had no intention of going. Once out of his presence she wondered why (never mind his kisses) she had contemplated such a scheme even fleetingly. Leave husband, child, country, the little security she had for a man who had once deserted her so cruelly in her time of need? Why, she would be daft. Crazy. Oh, she was still in love with him, she knew it, she knew that Richard could never take his place, she knew that living with Hawkwood, no matter how precariously, would give her a wild excitement she could never hope to have with her husband—or any other man. And thinking of the excitement, remembering the way John's hard mouth could weaken her bones, melt her flesh, she had a momentary stab of poignant regret. It passed, however, shoved aside quickly by a surge of righteous guilt.

She slept little that night, her mind full of Hawkwood, but the next day she busied herself with a thousand and one tasks and so managed to purge him from her thoughts. The second night was like the first—worse, for this was the night when he would be awaiting her. But she must not think of it, she must pretend she had never seen John Hawkwood, never spoken to him. Forget it. Think of something else. Nevertheless, as she lay on her pallet next to Cristina, staring wide-eyed into the darkness, she asked herself, had *he* appeared at the rendezvous? Was he waiting now by the mews, peering into the darkness, listening for her footsteps? She could picture it, Hawkwood standing legs apart, impatient, muttering, fuming, while behind him the river lapped, the boat bobbed.

Let him wait, she thought with a twist to her lips, let him wait until Judgment Day.

Supposing, however, her mind conjectured, as she turned from one side to the other, he had been playing with her, that he had never meant a single word of that impassioned plea, that he had had no intention of meeting her, of taking her away, that he had baited her? Revenge? Mayhap. He had been angry at her marriage and now he was paying her back. But could she be sure?

An hour later she was still tossing and turning, her mind still seesawing, still debating. The room had grown oppressively hot. Bess Smithborne, the old aunt, believed that open shutters at night brought diseased humors, and consequently the loft, sun-baked during the day, was like an oven at night, a malodorous oven rebounding with the snores, snorts, murmurs and rustlings of eight, sometimes more, sleepers. She was sweating now, her face flaming as if fevered. Finally, feeling that in another moment she would suffocate, she rose, threw a cloak over her naked body and climbed softly down the ladder.

She had no intention of going near the mews. She only wanted a breath of fresh air, a little walk to the well and back so that she could clear her mind, cool her blood. But curiosity drew her. She wanted to see if Hawkwood had really made an appearance or if he had indeed played a trick. A quick peek, nothing more. She would not show herself; he need never know she had been there at all.

Keeping to the shadows, she crept silently across the court through an archway, down a shallow flight of moss-covered stone steps. She saw the outline of the long, low building where the duke's falcons were housed, valuable birds, as prized as his fine-bred horses. A guard, crouching on his haunches, his head resting on his chest, leaned against the wicker gate. Asleep, she surmised.

She slid from shadow to shadow until she reached the edge of the mews and the river came into view. A crescent moon threw a thin silver streak across its wide expanse. Tied to the stone jetty were three or four cockle boats. Nothing else. The jetty itself, the walk on either side, was deserted. I might have known, she thought wryly, I might have guessed. The pig-headed jackanapes! The...

Suddenly a hand whipped across her mouth, an arm like steel gripped her waist. She had a moment of heart-bursting panic as she thrashed legs and arms, and then a coarse sack

294

was thrown over her head and the scream rising in her throat echoed in the muffled blackness.

Water lapping, water, and movement and suffocating darkness. She tried to shout, "Help! God in heaven, help!" but nothing came from her mouth but a meaningless, moaning mumble.

The sack was lifted from her head, and she found herself looking into the harsh blinding light of a lamp. She shut her eyes quickly.

"If you promise not to bellow, I shan't gag you." The voice—Hawkwood's. "Promise?"

She nodded, the light still bright against her closed lids. A dream, a nightmare? She creased her brow and remembered the mews. Had she fainted? Had he hit her?

"Why...?" she whispered, her throat as dry as paper. "Why have you abducted me?"

"For your own good, silly girl."

"You must—have you any water?" The light moved away and she opened her eyes.

"Only a little wine in a flask."

The moon had gone in. The small lamp placed on the bottom of the boat cast an eerie upward glow illuminating a pair of oars and Hawkwood's bulk. Beyond that the darkness lapped and gurgled.

Hawkwood lifted her head and put a flask to her lips. The wine was sweet and cool. It revived her. She levered herself up on her elbows. Nothing hurt, not her jaw, nor her head.

"Have more."

She took another long drink. Then, looking up at him, she said, "That was a terrible thing to do. You who claimed you would not take me by force."

"I haven't raped you, my sweet. Merely carried you off as any romantic lover would." He gave her a feline grin.

"You must take me back. Nay—you must! Before they miss me. God in heaven...!"

"I cannot, 'tis too late. I'd be rowing against the tide."

"Where are we going?" She sat up, trying to peer through the gloom. "Where are you taking me?"

"You will see."

"This is madness. You will be punished, you will pay. Richard's family—his father and brother will cut your throat and throw you to the fishes."

He laughed. "You forget that I am a soldier, a knight. I have faced far worse than a pair of doddering smiths."

"John—please..."

But he had turned his back on her and taken up the oars.

Strangely she did not feel frightened, nor very angry. The wine had been potent, but not strong enough to make her tipsy or even light-headed, but it had relaxed her, made her predicament seem less dire.

It was cool on the river and calm, a peaceful silence broken only by the sound of the dipping oars. From some hidden garden along the way came the scent of late-summer roses mingled with the rotting odor of the water, for the Thames, like the street gutters and the Fleet, acted as the city's sewer. Still, it was a broad stream rising and falling with the sea's tide and could cleanse itself more readily than the smaller rills. Joanna had never been on the river before; she had watched the boats on occasion with little curiosity, but now she realized how pleasant a river ride could be. The fine ladies at the Savoy sailed in curtained barges, lolling on cushions of silk, she had heard, passing the time as minstrels sang and played to them.

Passing time! she thought with a start, rousing herself from lassitude. In a few hours, perhaps less, it would be dawn; Cristina would wake, would see the empty space on the pallet and begin to cry. Gone. The others would wonder. She had to get back.

"John...! You must turn about this instant. At once!"

"Hush!"

A shock went through the little boat and the lamp went out as they hit a stone jetty. Above her Joanna could see the dim outline of a two-story dwelling. Light filtered through the chinks of a shutter on the ground floor, light and the sound of roistering, loud tipsy laughter, men's drunken voices.

"Where are we?"

Hawkwood jumped out of the boat, tied it expertly to a spike, then, reaching down with his outstretched hands, said, "Come."

"I shan't budge. You must return me to the Savoy."

He leaned forward and grabbed her arms, dragging her out of the boat, heels kicking, knees scraping against the stone.

"Be quiet!" he warned, and lifted her into his arms. "If you scream no one will pay the slightest attention."

They were climbing an outside wooden staircase which creaked and swayed at every step. Overhead, clouds scudded across the moon, a feeble crescent that cast no light on the blackness around. And now suddenly she began to be afraid. She opened her mouth and screamed, and the echo rebounded in the night. "Damn you!" Hawkwood cursed softly. Down below (a tavern? an inn?) the noise went on, the laughter, the voices. Someone was singing in a full-bodied, belching baritone. "Hey ninny, hey non. Drink now at her pleasure..."

A door creaked and they went over a threshold into a dark room. Hawkwood put Joanna on her feet, and as she started to speak he slapped her soundly across the face. "That is for breaking your promise," he said in a smooth, tight voice. "Do not do it again."

Stunned, her hand went to her hot cheek. She heard him moving in the darkness, saw the red eye of an ember on a hearth, and then a candle bloomed. He held it high and surveyed her silently. It was warm in the room but she found herself shivering.

"The accommodations are crude, my sweet," he said mockingly. "But we must make do for now. I promise you will be sleeping in a silk-sheeted bed, once we have reached Milan."

"I have no intention—none—of going to Milan," she said, clenching her jaws to keep her teeth from clicking. "Not of my free will. You will have to knock me insensible, as you have already done on this night. You will take with you only reluctant flesh."

The candlelight slitted his eyes, made the smile on his lips animal-like and cruel. "I doubt that."

With a quick motion—and she always wondered how a man of his breadth and size could move so rapidly—he set the candle on a table behind him and, turning back, pulled her roughly into his arms.

She arched her back and, gathering wrath in her mouth, spat at him. With a growl his mouth came down on hers, bruising, hurting, angry. She went limp, pretending, and when she felt his muscles relax, she brought her hand up hard against the side of his head. He fell away, but only for a moment. Then he was back at her, holding her against his chest, looking down at her in the candlelight. "You do yourself a disservice. Your blows only whet my appetite."

"Dog!"

His lips brushed her cheek, and bending his head he kissed the hollow in her throat. It was one of her sensitive places, sometimes as sensitive as her breasts, and though she steeled herself against the shivering thrill, it came nevertheless, raising bumps along her arms. His tongue licked her neck and she trembled again, the last of her anger draining away.

"John, if..."

He kissed the hollow once more, his arms tightening around her. She felt the hard muscles of his thighs, the clasp of his tunic pressing into her flesh. A wave of fiery blood rushed to her face. It had been so long, so very long since she had felt lost in a kiss, since she had had rough arms force her to stay, make her receive a passionate kiss, part her lips, receive the hungry, probing tongue. She felt splintered, sundered, helpless, the voice within her crying, "Nay—do not," growing weak, weaker, finally stilled.

"Your cloak," he murmured, and not bothering with the laces he wrenched it open. She felt it sliding from her shoulders, past her hips, slithering to the floor. His hands were warm on her naked skin, moving sensuously up from her hips, cupping the full mounded breasts, firm and shining with a white luminescence in the wavering light, the tips puckered, growing, blossoming, pink, coral, as he caressed them with his thumbs.

"Three children," he said, "and still lovely, still beautiful."

Pride of body shot through with sudden desire impelled her to fling her arms about his neck. She wanted to take him into herself, to be one with him, to join, to meld her body with his. He picked her up and carried her to a low bed deep in the shadows. She heard the rustle of his garments, saw his black shape looming, and then the candle went out. She ached for him, felt cold, hot, cold again, before he lowered himself and embraced her. She held him tightly as a miser clutches his purse. The skin across his buttocks was satin-smooth under her hands, the narrow hips bony-hard. He began to kiss her again, quick, stinging little kisses, hungry kisses, the eyes, the cheeks, the lips lingering at her throat, across her shoulders, moving his mouth to her breasts, taking a nipple, biting it, so that her hips arched, and wild with unbearable desire, she cried out.

He entered her, jamming, thrusting, going at her savagely, his breath coming faster and faster, and she, exultant, catching his frenzied rhythm, rose and fell with him, her nails digging into his back, her legs wrapped about his waist. She felt him shudder, heard him groan. "Not yet," she muttered between clenched teeth, and still hard, he kept at her until she reached the exploding, blinding pinnacle too.

No words were spoken; there was no need. He held her, tucking her head under his chin, and she fell asleep in his arms.

When she awoke in the morning he was gone. She sat up staring at the empty place beside her, a hollow feeling under her heart. He had slipped away in the night while she slept without a word, a kiss of farewell. She retrieved her cloak from the foot of the bed and thrust it about her naked shoulders. Tears welled up in her eyes, and she bit them back angrily. Duped, swindled, made the fool—again. Again! How many times did it have to happen before she would learn? He had brought her here so that he could have her in comparative comfort and privacy, had used her, had humped and left her as he would any common whore. If he had booted her down the stairs and tossed three pence after her she could not have felt more shamed. And more empty, more desolate.

She got up, her body stiff and sore, the little bites on her breast, her belly, smarting, bringing back the night and her wild response. Fool! Fool! She called herself all the names she had cursed herself with twice before; *fool, trollop, bawd, harlot, imbecile!* As for *him,* he was nothing more than a lecher, a cockmonger, a lying rogue. But how well he had summed her up, how easily he had led her on.

And he was gone—he wanted her above all others, but just for a night, once every few years.

Now she would have to find her own way back to the Savoy, without money, her hair in disarray, barefoot and naked beneath the torn cloak. She dared not cadge a ride, for she was sure she looked every bit the soliciting whore. She had no idea how far she had been brought from home, how many miles she must walk to reach it or in what direction it lay. Upriver, perhaps, she thought, since John had made some mention of not being able to row against the current. Upriver. And she was hungry, thirsty.

Oh, *damn* him! Damn him to everlasting purgatory!

The door suddenly opened and the object of her vilification walked in. Smiling. "Good morning, sweet." Self-castigation, the curses, the bitter hate died a sudden swift death. His eyes glowing, his face happy, John bent to kiss her, and unwanted tears, tears of gratitude, of relief, of love, crowded her lashes. He had come back. He had never gone away. He had not deserted her, not played her the fool.

"What's this?" he asked, tipping her head back with a finger thrust under her chin. "Crying?"

"I—I thought..."

"You thought I had left you? Here? In this place?" He kissed her and she clung to him.

"You have a low estimation of my character," he chided. "I have been up early to see about passage to Calais. And more." He turned and called, "In here, boy!"

The "boy," an ancient with a limp and a white, bushy beard, entered, carrying a parcel wrapped in gray linsey.

"For your trouble," Hawkwood said, dropping a coin in his hand.

The old man wheezed a thanks and, bobbing his head, backed out through the door.

"Open it," John commanded.

She unwrapped the cloth with trembling hands, and there folded neatly was a blue-and-silver-striped gown. Tenderly she lifted it, shook it out, the silver braid glinting and gleaming.

"Oh...!"

"Put it on, sweet. Go on, put it on."

The silk felt like a caress next to her skin. "I shall have to get a shift," she said happily. "'Tis shameful without one."

"Not to me," he said, drawing her into his arms.

"Careful," she laughed. "You'll tear my new gown."

They were to sail in three days on the *Trinity*, an English cog bound for Genoa by way of Calais, Bordeaux, Cádiz and Marseilles. In the meanwhile John gave Joanna a purse. "'Tis *all* for you. Buy yourself some pretty shifts, another cloak, a gown, shoes—whatever your heart desires. There's more when you've finished with that."

Never, *never* had she so many gold pieces to spend on herself alone. It opened new doors, new vistas—"whatever your heart desires"—and she who had desired so much for so long had almost forgotten what it was she wanted. For years, for nearly the whole of her life, the struggle to survive had absorbed her will, her strength. Crimped with the necessity to make do, to stretch a loaf, to scrape yet another meal from boiled chicken bones or a stringy mutton leg, to mend and refurbish and mend again the same shabby gown, she had been confined by an austerity which had blanched her dreams to vague, half-remembered fantasies. Now, with John's purse in hand, she felt like a prisoner suddenly set free.

Since the inn was situated on the riverfront, a teeming

neighborhood of dark, narrow, noisome lanes swarming with drunks, beached sailors and city thugs, Hawkwood would not let Joanna go out alone, but assigned one of his men-at-arms to accompany her. A dour soldier (the same who had accosted her at the Savoy), unhappy at having to play duenna to a woman when his job was *fighting* (by God!), he preceded her at a great pace, pushing the crowd aside with his pike, shouting, "Make way! Make way or I'll bust your head!"

Ramshackle wooden buildings lined the streets; taverns, inns, wine shops, sleeping dens, whorehouses (though the latter were supposedly confined by law to Cock Lane and Bankside), all crowded together with hardly a hand's breadth of space between. Decent folk in search of accommodations avoided these rat- and lice-infested hostels if possible, but their landlords had no lack of custom, providing food, shelter and divertissement to a transient population of sailors who came and went with the ebb and flow of the tide.

The faces Joanna passed, swarthy, fair, sunburned and scarred, were from Dover, Sandwich, Hythe, Dartmouth and from across the sea, the Rhine, St-Malo, Venice. The ships tied up at the quay were as varied as the faces; galleys from Bordeaux and Gascony laden with casks of wine, scuts of Flanders unloading bales of cloth, great lumbering vessels from Norway, cogs from Pisa, galliots from Venice, whelk boats, kettes, barges and lighters. The ships that could find no space at the quay were anchored in the Pool below London Bridge, a sea of patched, gaudily colored sails with the emblems of their nationality sewn on them, a rainbow of blue, green, scarlet and yellow cloth wings ballooning and billowing with every puff of wind.

As they threaded their way through the traffic past a small chapel, Joanna could hear a chorus of voices raised in the sailor's "Hymn of Praise to the Virgin," a paean sung whenever a voyage was safely concluded. "Our Lady we thank Ye, God give Ye grace..."

Joanna hurried to keep up with the man-at-arms, who had been stopped at the corner by a procession. A crowd of men and women were dragging a man on a hurdle through the streets. He must have been a baker who had short-weighted a customer, for the faulty loaf was tied about his neck, dangling under his dewlapped chin as he kept his head lowered. Behind the hurdle a troop of youngsters followed, pelting him with stones, offal, rotten vegetables, whistling, catcalling and shouting obscenities. Watching the scene, Joanna shuddered.

In Thexted the citizens ran their whores through the streets as a matter of course twice a year. Whores and adulteresses.

The sight sank her into gloomy apprehension. Had she made a terrible mistake? Suppose someone from the Savoy should see her now or later on Bow Lane at the tailor's, the mercer's. Suppose she were apprehended, hauled before the constable, judged, the punishment meted out, a similar hurdle ride on the fencelike contraption. Could she face the shame of having her skirts hoisted and tied, could she bear the mockery, the derision?

Presently, however, as she walked on, the purse at her girdle swinging and jingling with coins, her spirits lifted. Here she was just a face among many. No one would notice her in the crowd, no one pay the slightest attention. And, oh, she wanted new gowns, she wanted a fancy cloak ("... with fur, mind you," she pictured herself instructing the tailor) banded in miniver or coney. After all, she was a lady, and the law allowed ladies—unlike upstart burgesses' wives—to wear fur.

It was on the way back, her arms laden with parcels, instructions having been left at the tailor's to have cape and gown ready in two days' time, that she and her escort came up behind a man on horseback, a bareheaded knight wearing light armor. Joanna could not see his face, but the thick blond hair, the straight spine, the set of narrow shoulders, were Richard's. Richard! Her heart shrank, cold sweat broke out at the nape of her neck, on her brow. Richard! God in heaven, help me. She wanted to run, but hemmed in on the narrow street by passersby and a lumbering cart, she could not.

The knight turned, bending to adjust a stirrup, revealing a snub-nosed profile and a bearded chin. Not Richard. Nothing like Richard, who must be somewhere in Aquitaine by now. The relief was so great she felt giddy. When the relief and giddiness wore off a few minutes later, however, the old guilt crept back into her veins like a mortal infusion. She had betrayed her husband, a good man who had forgiven her, who had been willing to accept her bastards, who had *married* her despite her lies, her attempts to deceive him. She remembered the vows on her wedding day murmured in gratitude, a gratitude she swore never to forget. And how quickly she had done just that, all because of a man's kisses, a gown, a pair of new slippers. She had sinned often enough in the past, but now she added a new one, adultery. If Ivo—God rest his soul—had known he would have disowned her once more.

302

It wasn't too late. She could go back to the Savoy, she could pretend she had sleepwalked or had awakened with a delirious fever and gone out, wandered off, anything to placate her husband's kin. Go back. Confess, do penance, forget John Hawkwood, forget that this day and night have ever happened, she told herself, don't close the door on redemption, on salvation.

But she was already at the inn and he was standing there at the bottom of the stairs, waiting for her, smiling with the same impish glint in his eye that had charmed her as a child, bending over the bundles in her arms, kissing her, John Hawkwood, her lover, smelling of wine and cloves and faraway places where the eternal sun beckoned and a wind fragrant with roses and lime blossoms blew, where she would be free to love the only man capable of giving her happiness.

Chapter XX

Sir Richard Smithborne returned to England in June of 1374 with the remnants of the Duke of Lancaster's army.

The campaign had been a disaster. Though they had never once met the French in pitched battle, the English straggled back to their home shores as dispirited, as thinned in ranks as any defeated host. Hunger, disease, the long exhausting march through large stretches of barren countryside, the harrying attacks of the Frenchman du Guesclin, had been as decisive in their rout as any clash of arms. At Paris, the French refused to sally forth and fight, and the duke lingered there too long. Time lost, supplies running low, he continued his march via the Auvergne, crossing uninhabited mountains where starvation and wolves stalked them, where horses died and the knights on foot in clanking armor struggled up steep inclines, stumbling, falling, many taking their last unshriven breath in some rocky ravine watched by the rapacious crows wheeling high overhead.

Richard, tough from a childhood spent at the forge, survived. Though he had lost both squire and horse and had been forced to abandon his costly armor, he had by sheer doggedness arrived with the decimated army in Bordeaux. There the duke, taking stock, realized that he could not possibly hope to recover the lost territories of Aquitaine, the apparent aim of this expedition. Nor was he able to invade Spain (as was his ambitious hope), recapture Nájera and set himself up on the Castilian throne. The duke tarried for a few months in Bordeaux, then, running out of money to pay his troops, set sail for England. He, along with his father, King Edward, and the Black Prince, considered this futile and costly exercise only a temporary setback, not a defeat, and thus England was fated to continue her war with the French for another seventy years.

Richard, being of an optimistic nature, also felt that the English would return and successfully recover the lands that rightfully belonged to English kings. He would be ready to go when the time came. He was not disillusioned, only tired, bone-weary. And he had been reduced to penury. A knight without a horse, armor or squire was little better than a beggar. But he was alive, that was the important thing, alive, and he was coming home to Joanna. The thought of her had sustained him through thirst, hunger and fever. The picture of her as he kissed her goodbye, the black-fringed, violet eyes, the curve of her lips as she smiled, the dark hair braided into glossy ropes, had made one more climb surmountable, one more faltering step possible when all he wanted to do was to lie down and never have to get up again. It was her image which had prodded him over mountain passes, kept him from falling, from failing, her image which had solaced his grief at the death of his faithful friend, Henry, and her face which had softened the loss of his most prized possessions, horse and armor.

The voyage across the sea had taken a lifetime. He could think of nothing, no one, but Joanna, imagining in a thousand different ways how she would run to him when he appeared in the courtyard of the Savoy, how she would kiss him, weep and clasp him to her breast. Once the ship tied up, he was over the side, hurrying at a trot toward home. Home meant Joanna.

And she was not there.

"She went off," his father said.

If she had died in his absence he could not have been more stunned.

"She went off," Tom Smithborne repeated sourly. "I allus knew she would. She had the look, didn't she, Ellen?"

Ellen nodded in agreement. "The look of a trollop. I knew, right from the start, the woman would make a bad wife."

"When?" Richard heard himself ask hoarsely.

"April," his father answered. "Late April. We woke one morning and she was gone."

"Where—where did she go?"

"Where?" He shrugged. "Adam, the tanner's son, saw her climbing aboard the *Trinity* on the riverfront down by Queenhithe. She was with a man dressed as a knight, he said."

Richard sat down and passed his hands over his eyes. "I don't believe it," he murmured. They were lying to him. Joanna had died, she had been ill of a fever and had perished, and they were trying to spare him, trying to explain her absence with this falsehood.

"You can ask Adam. He will tell you."

"Adam was drunk. He did not see her. 'Twas someone else. Not Joanna. It *cannot* be true."

"'Tis true, all right. And good riddance, I say, eh, Ellen?" Tom Smithborne asked of his daughter-in-law.

"Aye. There's no reason to lie about it."

Richard stared at their faces, stared at the wall, the settle, at the shuttered windows, at the bed where he and Joanna had slept, the hearth, the kettles, and saw nothing. Whatever had happened, the truth of the matter was plain—she was gone. Gone. Gone since last April. Christ my Lord, is it so?

"You wait a bit, Richard," Ellen counseled. "When you've had a few good meals and a proper rest you'll feel better."

Feel better. As if he were suffering from the gripes, instead of a deeply gashed, bleeding wound. She was gone. It *was* so.

"Afore long you'll find another wife," Ellen was saying, "a modest girl, not a stuck-up goose like that one, and you'll forget you ever had another."

Forget Joanna? God, how could he? How? He should have died on the Auvergne, finished it there, rather than come back to this, this emptiness and desolation. To think of the times he had forced himself to go on, to shuffle forward another inch, a foot, a mile, to take one more breath, to wake one more morning, because she was waiting for him at the end of that long, torturous road. But she wasn't there, she had gone off. In April. Oh God, what was the use of it all?

"Papa?" He felt a slight tug at his knee. "Papa?"

He glanced down and saw the small white face, the cornflower-blue eyes, the little pointed nose. Cristina.

"Papa...?" Her look was anxious, a little frightened. "Are you ill, Papa?"

He stared at her for a moment more, then suddenly scooped her up on his lap, clasping her as a drowning man clasps a floating spar, holding her so tightly she squealed.

When he released her, she put her arms about his neck and laid her face against his chest. "Papa—I did so miss you."

How could he break apart now when this motherless mite needed him? How could he be so selfish as to think only of himself? The child was his, deserted by one parent; could he make an orphan of her? Cristina loved him; she looked to him for a father's protection. He must do whatever he could to care for her, to make up for her loss.

So Richard, forced to stagger up again after this last and most terrible blow, went on with his life, though he had little heart for it.

He came to accept Joanna's defection, though the wound had gone too deep ever to heal completely. Adam, questioned, described Joanna, what she wore, "a silk gown shot with silver," and the man, "broad-shouldered in a velvet surcoat."

Every word spoken brought another throb of pain, and yet he must hear it all, again and again, like a tongue probing an aching tooth.

"Who was he?" Richard asked Adam.

"Someone said John Hawkwood."

Hawkwood, the father of her oldest child, Edmund. Had Joanna loved him? Had she given herself to Hawkwood and not been raped as she claimed? What other lies had she told him? "I love you, Richard." Was that one the most killing lie of all? Oh, Joanna, Joanna!

There followed a short period during which he thought she might return. He dreamed of her coming back, bedraggled, sick, pale and weeping, falling to her knees, begging his forgiveness, saying she had been carried off against her will, she had been forced to go; she regretted every moment spent with the rogue, she missed Richard; she loved only him. But common sense told him that once having left England Joanna would not return.

He then began to dream of avenging his honor, of pursuing the two lovers, of meeting Hawkwood and challenging him to combat. In his fantasy he pictured himself on horseback thundering across a field, the clash of swords, Hawkwood falling from the saddle and Joanna crying, "My darling, Richard—'tis you I love." Again common sense dispelled the dream. Even if he had the wherewithal to leave England and search for Hawkwood, he had no idea where to look.

In the meanwhile, practical matters had to be considered. Grieving still, he managed to pull himself together and ask for an audience with one of the duke's army captains. He wished to be reinstated, he said, explaining how he had lost all in the abortive Aquitaine campaign. There was some delay, money being short and no immediate need for a penniless knight who could not equip himself, but in the end his reputation for valor and for skill in the tilting yard won him a place in the Savoy guard.

He was grateful his duties did not require him to travel. Fitted with armor, provided with a horse and a squire, some, if not a great deal, of his manhood was restored. As soon as he began to draw pay, he moved himself and his daughter from the Smithborne hearth. Though he could have found separate quarters in the Savoy compound, he preferred to rent the upper story of a house near Temple Bar, putting as much distance as he could between himself and the carping of his father and sister-in-law, who reminded him daily of

Joanna's perfidy. He hired a servant, a country woman of middle age, widowed, decent, without kin, Lydia. She proved competent and loyal though a little lacking in warmth and a bit of a martinet toward Cristina. But he would rather have a chilly nurse who took her charge seriously than one who oozed affection while tippling at ale and neglecting her duties.

Cristina soon became the center of his life. He never thought he could love a child so, could be intrigued by everything his little daughter said or did. She was his mirror, his other self, balm for his thwarted love. He spoke to her of places he had been, battles he had fought, foes he had quelled, finding words, weaving stories with a skill he'd never dreamed he possessed. And she listened, this child of his, with half-open mouth, her blue, blue eyes filled with wonder. He worried about her too, what would happen when she grew older, how he must provide a dowry for her, so that she could marry well, though truth was he hated to think of her marrying at all.

Cristina in turn adored her father. To her Richard was a saint. Early on she had been taken to watch him joust—for he still entered tourneys at Westminster and Smithfield—and seeing him armored astride his great horse, the blue steel of his hauberk sending off sparks of light in the afternoon sun, filled her with awe. It was hard to believe that this fearsome creature thundering down the turf to meet and best a bristling opponent was her own father, the same gentle man who took her on his knees and made her laugh. But it was true, true, for there he was, wearing her crimson ribbon tied about his arm and the flower she had given him stuck in his crested helm. *Her* father.

She remembered little of her mother; a vague recollection of sweet scent, of swishing skirts, black, black hair and a white brow that frowned. "Not now" and "Go away" were the two phrases she associated with Joanna. And she sensed too, with the unerring insight of young children, that her mother somehow had wronged her father. Not that Richard ever said a word against Joanna, or even mentioned her name, but Aunt Ellen often spoke of her, her voice dripping with venom.

As Cristina grew older she began to get the meaning of her aunt's diatribes, for Mistress Smithborne never tired of repeating the story, and Richard, though he tried, could not keep her from visiting her own grandniece.

"She deserted your father—went off with another man," she would tell the child. "Sinful whore. She'll roast in hell, sure as there is one." Mistress Smithborne with her nodding head and turned-down mouth frightened Cristina, and the picture she painted of Joanna remained. Her mother was evil, she had left husband and child, willfully causing them pain, because she hated them. But then Cristina began to wonder; perhaps she herself had done something terribly wrong, forcing her mother to leave. The thought preyed on her mind until one day she asked her father if it was so. He became angry, the first time she had ever seen him show temper.

"You must never think that. Whoever gave you such an idea? Of course not. Let us not speak of such things again."

Cristina never did. But she puzzled over her mother's fate, wondering what pitchforks, what fiery torments, awaited this whore, this adulteress, in hell.

She knew all about hell. Lydia had given her a graphic and vivid description. More, the good woman took Cristina to Mass each morning and at the Sunday service the priest, a conscientious, God-fearing, superstitious old man, sermonized, going on and on about pitfalls, about sin, about the horrors of purgatory. The devil figured prominently in these talks, a horned and tailed devil with cloven hoofs who hung sinners by their tongues from trees of fire and fed murderers and adulterers into the flames of a red-hot oven. He painted these unfortunates in such vivid colors they haunted Cristina's nightmares, peopling her dark, sleeping hours with contorted bodies and suffering faces. The grim inscription over the entrance to the chapel, *Salvandorum paucitas, damnandorum multitudo*—few saved, many damned—did not help either, for it was translated often, a reminder that she, along with many others, was doomed. Only when she became older and was able to look about her with a clearer, less impressionable eye did she realize that good people often worried about hell more than the bad. Not that she doubted the existence of the devil, not that sin ever tempted her; she *knew* there was a hell, but its imminence seemed more remote, its punishments pushed to some far distant future.

A year after Richard's return from France, a lawyer by the name of Walter Fynche came to the Smithborne freehold near Temple Bar. He explained to Richard that a relative of Ivo Coke's had died, a merchant of Thexted, and had willed the issue of Joanna Coke, "if there be any," an income of twenty pounds a year. Richard had never heard of this generous merchant, but then Joanna (he remembered bitterly) had revealed very little about her past. Still, it was a nice sum. Richard could have accepted and received it in Cristina's name, spending the money on himself—his armor needed refurbishing, his horse, growing old, must soon be replaced, and lastly there was always the nagging urge to find Hawkwood and demand satisfaction. But he would not touch a farthing. It belonged to his daughter. Scrupulously honest, he had Fynche set the yearly sums aside for her dowry, happy that she would be provided for.

If he had known the real source of the gold Fynche received twice a year with such regularity, he would have scorned and repudiated this "legacy" even in Cristina's name. The relative in Thexted was nonexistent; the money came from Joanna. It was blood money, guilty florins changed to guilty pounds, but the giving of it (each of the children had received the same mysterious bequest) helped ease her conscience.

She was living in Rimini now, where Hawkwood had installed her in a villa overlooking the sandy beaches of the blue Adriatic. Her lover had been rehired by the pope under instructions to invade Tuscany and spent most of his days consulting with engineers about a new type of weaponry called "bombards." These were massive iron siege guns which, when aided by gunpowder, could hurl huge stone cannon balls at an enemy's walls with devastating effect. Though John could appreciate the worth of these clever contrivances—the threat of using them alone could bring a city to its knees—he worried over their transport. Clumsy, awkward, weighty, they would slow an army down, particularly one like the White Company, which depended on its speed of movement for surprise and quick victory. Still, he was eager to try them.

Joanna might have shared his eagerness or at least understood what kept him from her bed until the small hours of the morning if she had known about the bombards. But she did not. John never discussed matters of war with women, on principle—it was a man's job, although he sometimes could not help boasting of his victories.

Women's vocation, he maintained, was love and pretties. And Joanna could not complain for lack of either. When John did join her he made up for his absence by such a passionate assault as to leave her weak and trembling, his body assuring her again and again that he was hers and that she belonged to him. He showered her with silks, costly gowns of gold brocade thickly sewn with semiprecious gems, with perfumes from Araby, and on her saint's day gave her a rare white falcon, the bird of kings, though she knew nothing of falconry.

She soon learned. Introduced at a small banquet to Pandolfo Malatesta's mistress, Bianca, a pretty, honey-haired, slim-waisted young woman of her own age, she found a friend who offered to teach her. The ladies of Rimini were not allowed the freedom enjoyed by English women of rank. They went nowhere, even to the shops, without a heavy escort and the presence of elderly duennas. And they did not hunt with the men. Still, again under guard, they would ride out to the sandy marshes beyond the gates of the city to throw their falcons at larks and sparrows. Joanna envied the grace of these women, their languid movements, the bright chatter, the careless tinkle of their laughter. Bianca, though living in sin, was one of them, accepted without demur by the best families. An illegitimate daughter of a count, she had noble blood in her veins, and her lover's family, the Malatestas, owned Rimini. Bianca was proud of her position as Pandolfo's mistress. In Italy such things were looked upon with more grace than at home. Noble blood or not, these women all had something in common—wealthy origins. They had never known hunger or deprivation, never worked with their hands, cooked a meal or scoured a pot. They sat their horses with ease as they galloped over the plains, an ease which Joanna tried hard to imitate.

By now Joanna had lost the last vestiges of regret. In the beginning she had often wakened in the predawn darkness with a vague feeling of unease. Lying in her silken bed in her lover's warm arms, she would crease her brows trying to remember the dream which had disturbed her. Then suddenly with a needlelike stab of guilt she would recall everything. Sometimes she dreamed of Richard, sometimes of Cristina or Edmund, on several occasions—that was the worst—of Ivo, his voice ringing out, "You are no daughter of mine." She wept when she thought of Ivo.

"Sweet, you are crying," John, awakened, would say as he gathered her closer to his chest. "What is it?"

"Nothing—nothing at all." She did not want to tell him her dream, that she wept for her father. He would not understand. From what he had told her, he had never shed a single tear for his.

"Nothing?" Hawkwood would query. "A fine answer. One does not weep for naught." Then after a pause, "You are not sorry you came with me?"

"Oh, nay. Never." Then she would begin to kiss him to keep him from saying more.

Her kisses would always rouse him, and he would throw her on her back, mounting her, his mouth finding her breast, the hollow in her throat, his knee sweeping her legs apart. Bound mouth to mouth, swept up in his urgency, she would forget her dreams, her guilt, and live only for the moment.

He was a lover of infinite variety. He knew all the forbidden paths of love and took her down every one, knew a hundred little ways to make her gasp and moan with pleasure. She who had always thought physical delight was limited to two lovers lying full length, face to face, on a pallet or a bed, preferably at night, soon learned otherwise. She remembered well the shock of her first encounter with Hawkwood's impulsiveness. It was one early morning; she had thrown a bedgown over her bare skin and gone out to pluck a few roses in the garden. As she stooped over a bush of dew-glistening blooms, John's arms suddenly snaked about her waist.

"John...!"

He was stark naked, his hard-muscled legs pressing urgently against her buttocks.

"I thought you were asleep."

"Not now, love."

Holding her in a viselike grip, without turning her, he opened her robe and began to stroke the inside of her thighs, his exploring fingers slowly, deliberately, silkily, inching upward and at last touching and gently caressing the secret moist place between her legs. She started, gasped, a wild tremor running through her body.

"Not here—the servants, nay—oh, God...!"

He went on, his breath in her ear, his heart beating heavily, his manhood growing, pressed to her, hard and pulsating.

"John! Not here...!" He was bringing her to the brink of madness, and out in the open for all to see.

"John...!" She tried to wrench herself away. He muttered, "Hush!" and suddenly stooping, lifted her, hoisting her over his shoulder, her unbound hair hanging down in a dark silken fall over his naked back. He carried her under the grape arbor and lowered her to a marble table. Before she could protest again, he straddled and entered her, his mouth devouring hers, savoring her lips, her tongue, his hands cupping her breasts.

And now he was moving, and the protest became a moan low in her throat. She did not feel the cold hardness of the marble table, only the terrible urgency of his savage movements. Her arms twined and clung, her nails digging into his shoulders, her senses dimly conscious of the aroma of crushed rose petals mingling with the scent of his male ardor. Deep, deep in the back of her mind came the words—*forbidden, forbidden*—but it made their passionate lovemaking, the frenzied rhythm of their nude bodies, all the more sensuous, the blinding throes of their final union like the bursting of a thousand fiery stars.

Hawkwood made love to her without shame, with laughter, with tenderness, with feline stealth or feral violence, whatever his mood; in the bath, on the Saracen carpets, in their bedchamber, in a hammock, in the loggia by the light of the moon. What she loved best was when he fitted her back into his chest and bent knees like a spoon and came at her from behind. His movements would send shock after shock of shivering pleasure through her, raising her very scalp, until she rose to climactic ecstasy with a cry of hoarse triumph.

She loved him completely; he made her feel whole, sheltered, safe. And he would not leave her, not again, never again. He would go off to battle, true, but he would always return. They were linked to one another, a link that would last. And as time went on, her bad dreams became fewer and fewer and finally vanished altogether. She had never been so happy, never imagined she could be. Hawkwood allowed her to buy whatever she wished, gave her money to send to her children, housed and clothed her like a duchess. Strangely enough, though he always drove a hard bargain with his employers, his own tastes were simple and he never became absorbed as some in accumulating wealth for wealth's sake.

Money flowed through his hands, the bulk of his income going for the upkeep of his small army, which must and did have the best of everything in the way of armor and accouterments. The men of the White Company were among the highest-paid on the peninsula. He would sell a villa or a piece of country property or a coffer of jewels to meet the wages of knights and soldiers rather than make them wait until he collected from a tardy pope or a reluctant lord who had hired him. He had his black moods, his tempers, his cruelties, but in those first years Joanna only saw the pleasanter side of him, her impassioned love blinding her to everything else.

Then one day Joanna had an unexpected visitor, a caller who shattered her idyl and brutally brought the past back to her.

Richard had found her.

She and her lover were living in a palazzo outside of Romagna now, and John, hired out to the pope, had gone off to do battle with the Florentines on his holiness's behalf, so Joanna was alone when Richard arrived.

"God's greetings, Joanna."

"Good morrow."

The two years since their last meeting had aged him. The bright blond sheen of his hair had dimmed, and there were lines in his forehead, an unwonted grimness in his blue eyes.

He accepted her proffered cup of wine with a hand that trembled slightly.

She did not know what to say. A thousand questions crowded her tongue. Cristina? Edmund? How did you find me? Should she say, "I am sorry," when she was not? Seeing him seared her with guilt. He had been generous, had given her his heart and his good name, and she had deserted him for another man, gone off without a word.

"You look well, Joanna. Sin agrees with you."

She blushed. "I had not expected..." she began.

"...to see me here?" he finished wryly. "Your lover's fame has traveled wide. I heard that he was in the pope's employ, that he headquartered in Romagna now. And when I was fortunate to win a large prize at the Dover tourney, I decided to come."

"I am glad you are doing well," she said, embarrassed, nervous. Had she slept with this man, borne his child? God, that he should appear this way, suddenly, like an apparition from the dead.

"I am not here to castigate, nor to be congratulated," he said coldly. "I have made a journey of no little distance and no mean expense to avenge my honor. You have wronged me, Joanna, and God will deal with you as He sees fit. But Hawkwood..." He swallowed; the wine cup shook in his hand. "Hawkwood has done more. He has given me a cuckold's horns, made me the object of fun. He has shamed me."

"Richard..."

"You cannot deny it." His fingers tightened about the cup in a white-knuckled grip. "Chivalry demands I challenge Sir John Hawkwood to combat."

"Combat!" She took a deep breath, forcing her voice to calmness. "Be reasonable, Richard. Hawkwood is no longer a young man, but he has spent a lifetime on horseback with battle sword. And he has survived."

"Are you telling me he is a better knight than I?"

Aye! She wanted to shout. You fool! You prideful fool!

"I am in no way faulting your skill, Richard. You are one of the best knight-errants in England. But Sir Hawkwood does not joust in tourneys, does not abide by rules, he..."

"Whereas I do. I see. He is not only a lecher, but he fights unfairly."

She made a helpless gesture with her hands. "Pray, I pray you, forget this need to revenge yourself."

"You do not understand," he said impatiently. "You are a woman."

"Maybe that is why I *do* understand. Can't you see how such combat would be folly? In any case," she added thankfully, "Sir John is not here. It may be months before he returns."

"I shall wait. There is a village nearby. I will find shelter there." He rose and made for the door.

"Richard..."

He turned.

"How is Cristina?"

"Well, very well."

"You have told her?"

"She knows," which did not quite answer her question.

To Joanna's dismay Hawkwood returned much sooner than expected. She was hoping he would stay away long enough—weeks, months, even—so that Richard would grow tired of waiting and return to England. But the Florentines had offered Hawkwood a substantial sum not to attack them for a period of five years, and the moment the agreement was signed and sealed, he had hurried back to Rimini.

Joanna ran out to meet him in the courtyard, and as they climbed the stairs arm in arm to the chamber above, she told him about Richard.

"So the wronged husband has come to seek satisfaction," Hawkwood said, flinging his cape aside.

"Oh, John, you must go away at once. I do not want him to find you here."

"Have you lost your senses? Would you have me run like a rabbit?" He lifted her in his arms and kissed her soundly.

"Oh, put me down! Heed me! You will kill him."

"He wants to kill *me*. My love, I cannot deny him that chance. I stole his wife. I *must* give him the opportunity to fight. Not to would be unfair. Let the little cock have his day."

"You *want* him to die."

"Ahhhh..." He let out his breath, his eyes suddenly narrowing. "So that is the way it is. You still love him, you still think of him as your husband."

"Nay! I do not. I do not."

"And have you slept with him while I was gone? A little bed sport for old times' sake?" He grasped her arms, his steely fingers biting into her flesh. "Well—did you?"

"You know better than that."

"Do I?" He searched her face. And though his hands hurt her cruelly, she met his gaze without flinching.

"Never mind," he said, throwing her arms from him. "I shall settle with him, soon enough."

"One would think *you* were the wronged husband," she said.

"I am your husband in the eyes of God. I am the man who took you first, remember that. *He* is the interloper."

But *you* never wanted to marry me and *he* did, she wanted to fling at him. But before she could utter a word his arm was around her waist and he closed her mouth with a kiss.

They met on a flat piece of ground at the edge of a wood, Richard riding a mount lent to him by Hawkwood, Hawkwood himself astride a brown stallion, each man with a lance resting in the crook of his arm, each with his sword at his belt. Up until the last minute Joanna had pleaded with them, first John, then Richard, pointing out the folly of the duel, urging them to give it up. Neither had heeded her.

She had not wanted to watch them, had not even wanted to be present, but there she was, sitting on a rock under an ash tree at the edge of the field, hands clasped tightly in her lap. The chaplain from a nearby village, much against the encounter also, but beholden to Hawkwood, gave the men his blessing, his voice ringing out in the misted morning air. "God go with the righteous!"

The contenders faced each other across a wide stretch of dew-drenched turf, the wronged husband's face grim under his visor, the lover's smiling. A few spectators, mainly soldiers of the White Company, had lined the field, chatting among themselves as they placed their bets. Presently a herald came forward and blew a trumpet, a weak, trembling sound shivering the mist, and when the last note died, the chaplain raised his hand. Joanna abruptly turned her head away. She could not bear to look after all. Over the heavy beat of her heart she heard the thundering hooves, heard the harsh impact of lance on shield, the onlookers shouting. She took a quick glance—both still in the saddle, turning now. She closed her eyes. A moment later the sound of the galloping charge reverberated across the field, then the mighty crash which told her the two had met again. This time a cry of triumph rose from Hawkwood's men, and Joanna knew that Richard had been unseated.

She opened her eyes.

John had dismounted and, sword unsheathed, was standing over Richard, who, obviously hurt, was struggling to draw his own weapon with his left hand. The right arm hung limp.

Joanna sprang to her feet. "Don't! Don't!" she shrieked. "He is wounded, can you not see?"

"Do you yield?" John asked Richard.

"Yield, for God's sake yield!" Joanna cried as Richard went on trying to draw his sword.

"You have fought honorably," Hawkwood said. "I cannot do battle with an injured man."

He turned and walked away.

Joanna rushed up to Richard, who was being helped to his feet by the chaplain. "Are you hurt badly?"

His face under the raised visor was blanched, his blue eyes pools of pain. "Nay—do not trouble yourself."

"Richard..." And seeing him thus, a courageous man, one who had come so many leagues on a long, hazardous journey to right his wrong, she was filled with pity and remorse. She remembered only too well how Hawkwood had once tried to poison Richard's mind against her, how Richard had forgiven her, had vowed his love over again, despite her two bastards. And he had married her, lifting her from infamy and shame. Why could she not love him? He was as handsome as John, when it came to it, and certainly more gentle and tender. Why could she not love him as passionately as she did John?

"My husband," she said, looking up at him, her eyes filling with tears. "My husband, for what I have done to you, I ask your pardon. I will go home with you."

He removed his helm with his left hand, and she had the impulse to sweep the sweat-matted hair from his brow, had started to in fact by reaching out, when he pushed her hand away.

"Nay. I want you not. Not now." There was no anger in his voice, only a despairing weariness. "If I had won you fairly in battle, 'twould be different. But I have not. Stay." A grimace of pain crossed his face and when he spoke again his voice was edged in bitterness. "Stay then with your paramour."

"Richard..."

But he had turned from her and, leaning on the shoulder of the chaplain, limped from the field.

"He did not want me," Joanna said incredulously. She and Hawkwood were sitting at the noon meal. John paused with a speared gobbet of beef on the edge of his knife.

"You offered to go back with him?"

"Out of pity."

"Pity?" A hard look crept into his eyes. "Did you think"—he leaned forward—"that I would ever let you go? Did you?"

"I did not think of anything except that he was my husband and suffering. I have never felt rancor against Richard."

"And me? What do you feel for me?" His free hand shot out and grabbed her wrist. "Lust, love, pity, hate?"

"It has nothing to do with you."

"I will never let you go. Do you hear? Never! Even if I should tire of you, my beauty—and remember I might, I just might—*I will never let you go.* I shall kill you first."

Joanna, looking into his flint-hard eyes, suddenly understood how this man's very name struck terror in the hearts of his enemies. She understood how he had earned the reputation for being ruthless, formidable, single-minded. He never made idle threats. Aye, he would kill her. Even now he was perfectly capable of plunging his eating knife into her breast. And this was the brigand, the *condottiere,* she had given herself over to, a murderer who never once had told her he loved her.

Suddenly a bubble of hate formed in her throat.

"I shall leave whenever I choose," she blazed at him. "And if need be, *I* will kill *you!*"

"Ha!"

She picked up her wine cup and flung it at him, catching him at the side of the temple, the wine spattering and dribbling down his face. He reached over and pulled her across the table, upsetting wine, platters, cups, dragging her into his lap. "God's blood, but you are beautiful." Before she could bring up her balled fists to strike him again, he kissed her, a savage kiss that hurt and bruised.

"Joanna," he growled after a long moment, still holding her tightly, his forehead pressed to her hot, rebellious cheek, "why do you say things you do not mean?"

How could she answer? He buried his head in her breasts, kissing each softly. The hatred, the anger seeped from her veins. She did not struggle again, she could not. The man, whatever she might think of him, however blame him, had become more than an obsession, he had become a part of herself, her life.

Chapter XXI

With his fall on the field outside Romagna, Richard's career as a member of the duke's Savoy guard and as a knight-errant came to an end. Aside from the broken arm, which had healed crookedly, he had sustained another injury just below the ribs, one that made breathing sometimes difficult. This hurt he hoped would fade in time, but the arm he knew would always be useless.

Useless.

The word kept echoing like a death knell in his brain. The questions what to do, where to go, how to live, faced him each morning as he rose from a sleepless bed, plagued him all through the day and stayed with him after he laid his head down at night once more. The situation was worse than it had been when he returned from Aquitaine, to find Joanna gone. Then he had come back in rags like a beggar, without horse or armor, but at least he had still possessed his health and the use of his limbs. He could and had started over again.

But now fighting and jousting were out of the question. Nor could a one-armed man be of much good in a smithy should he want to go back to his father's forge. Even the boy who worked the bellows had two stout arms, to say nothing of Richard's brother, who wielded hammer and anvil. He could do menial jobs in the shop, if he chose, sweep out, shovel horse dung, fetch and carry. His pride would suffer, but he could bear that if he must. What he could not bear was his father's incessant caviling.

Tom Smithborne, of course, blamed Joanna for this latest calamity. Her fault, the bitch, hers alone. If she had been a decent Christian, remained faithful to her husband and not run off like a harlot, nothing of this sort would have happened. Married to a virtuous spouse, Richard would not have felt it necessary to redeem his honor by doing battle with a murderous brigand like Hawkwood. He always knew Joanna would bring him bad luck, and God would surely punish her in His own good time, but in the meanwhile his son had been made to suffer for her sins. Nor were the other members of the Smithborne family remiss in damning Joanna.

Richard, suffering the scourge of their constant I-told-you-sos in addition to his own bitterness, teetered on the edge of despair. It was not like him to give in to brooding dejection so easily. But the loss of his wife, whom he had loved with all the passion his simple nature could engender, the blow to his manhood, the termination of his knightly vocation, combined to defeat him. He had no money—Cristina's he would not touch—and no means of support, and to throw himself on his family's charity was the last thing he wanted. For a brief while he toyed with the idea of taking to the highways as a peddler or a begging pilgrim, disguised in rags so that no one would know him. At one point suicide flashed through his mind, but the idea was too horrifying to contemplate. Everyone knew that God rejected those who died by their own hand, sending them directly to hell, where Satan's demons flayed them, then tossed the screaming sinners into vats of perpetually boiling oil. The few who risked such a fate were either mad or beyond redemption in any case. No, he must find another way out of his difficulties.

Suffering in silence, he tried to rally, tried to make some plan to go on with his life, not so much for himself as for Cristina. Humbled, he went to speak to his captain, a man like himself who had risen from the ranks. Sir Peter listened with sympathy and afterward gave Richard the position of assistance to the ward of the Savoy's outer gate. Richard's job of keeping an eye out for suspicious characters who might enter the palace grounds was one usually relegated to older, rather decrepit men and so carried very little prestige. Still, it was gainful employment, and though it paid little, it was enough to buy food and ale and put a separate roof over his and Cristina's head. He, the child and the old nurse, Lydia, moved back to Temple Bar, and gradually, despite the pain of his internal injury, which stubbornly refused to go away, his resiliency and his natural optimism began to return.

The outer world went its way around them, making small historic landmarks. The famous Long Parliament convened, the Lollards began to preach in the streets against the abuses of a bloated and corrupt clergy, the Duke of Lancaster, never as popular as his brother, the Black Prince, standing up in defense of the heretic John Wycliffe, became the butt of criticism, and at one point a mob threatening to kill him advanced on the Savoy itself. Bishop Courtenay dispersed the angry crowd, but the mutterings went on, and Richard was required to stay at his post day and night for the better part of a month.

Except for her father's absence, these events hardly touched Cristina. It was the everyday occurrences which mattered; a saint's day, the changing colors of leaves in the fall, the excitement of Christmas, the street pageants at Easter, a pair of new slippers, a treasured trinket lost, a straying pet found. Richard, anxious to have his daughter educated (for he hoped she would someday be a knight's lady), hired an elderly widow with vague noble connections, a Dame Brandone, who instructed Cristina in stitchery, spinning, lute playing, dancing and deportment. Cristina also expressed a desire to learn to read, a whim Richard indulged her, much to the good dame's disapproval, by making an arrangement with a friar at St. Giles to take Cristina on as a pupil, each lesson at home to cost ten pence.

Cristina spent a lonely childhood without playmates, closely watched by her female mentors, Lydia and the dame, as well as by Richard himself. They rarely saw the Smithbornes. The girl did not learn she had two half-brothers until she was ten. Her father's relatives had never met Edmund during his brief, plague-ridden stay in London, and having thought of him as an unfortunate nephew who did not take to city life promptly forgot him. Richard himself did not mention Joanna's eldest son. So it was somewhat of a shock when one late afternoon Edmund came to the door in search of his mother.

Edmund had had no word from Joanna since her scribe-written letter had arrived at the abbey announcing Cristina's birth some ten years earlier. Edmund's subsequent message of congratulation and a later missive had remained unanswered. A call at the Lime Street house had drawn a blank, and it was only through lawyer Walter Fynche that he had located Richard's present abode. Edmund, having used the money he had received from what he believed was Grandfather Ivo's Thexted relative to help pave the way toward his goal, had recently been ordained a priest. In addition he had been able to procure his choice of a living, the one at Nareham, his birthplace, where Sir Theobold, now old and feeble, had asked for a younger man to take over the bulk of his duties. Before setting out for Nareham, Edmund had decided to visit his mother.

At twenty, young for a priest, but making up for it with an air of poise and dignity far beyond his years, Edmund had attained full growth. Of middle height, somewhat thick-set, though without an inch of fat, he was—in figure at least, for his face remained Ivo's—much like the father who had refused to acknowledge him.

"Cristina—at last!" Edmund exclaimed, pleased to have finally met his half sister. "You have mother's smile, too. Exactly."

Cristina did not know whether to take his remark as flattery or to be dismayed, since Joanna had been painted in such scurrilous colors. Besides, the priest introduced as a brother took getting used to. Had her mother been married before? Not married? Was Edmund a bastard? She lowered her lashes as Dame Brandone had taught her to do when receiving a compliment and murmured, "Thank you, brother." Or should she call him "Father"? Perhaps "sir"?

Edmund was just as delighted at meeting Richard again. He had only the dimmest recollection of his stepfather, having seen him only briefly before Richard had gone off on tourney those long years ago on Lime Street. Now Edmund's assessment, though quick, was more observant. Richard, he noted gladly and with not a little surprise, was unlike what he had heard of Hawkwood or had remembered of Thomas de Ander, a straightforward man with an air of simplicity dignified by a hint of suffering in his candid blue eyes. A decent soul, a knight too, but from his accent less lordly than most. He wondered if his arm had been lamed in war, but out of a sense of delicacy refrained from asking.

"And where is our lady mother?" Edmund asked, smiling, looking around.

The embarrassed silence which followed forewarned him—falsely—for during that pregnant pause he was suddenly certain Joanna had died. A possibility he had never contemplated. His mother dead? Oh, God! Guilt, regret, grief hit him like hammer blows. Holy Mother, all-merciful God, forgive me, he thought. Why had he not come sooner? Dead. Joanna had loved him, she had given him up to the church because *he* wanted it, a sacrifice which had distressed and pained her. Why had he not tried harder to communicate with her? Why had he not asked the abbot for a leave to come to London years ago?

"She saw best to leave us," Richard said, speaking at last.

Compassionate soul, Edmund thought, this was his tactful way of saying Joanna was in God's care now.

"I did not know," Edmund murmured, stricken. "I . . ."

Another pause, then Cristina, still child enough to be honest, if not blunt, burst out, "She ran off with John Hawkwood."

Richard frowned. It pained him to have Joanna's mortal sin and his own shame exposed. He himself would have said nothing more unless questioned directly.

Edmund, shocked but disbelieving, said, "Sister, you must not say things like that."

"But 'tis true," she insisted.

Edmund looked at Richard. He nodded in the affirmative.

"Ran off? God!" How could she? Better that she had died, his beloved, loving, sinful mother, than to have behaved in such an abominable fashion. When she had come to the abbey and told him she had married he had been happy for her, and happy again when she had written she had borne her husband a daughter. The abbot, who once had pointed out the error of Joanna's ways, now felt she had given up concubinage forever. "By being an exemplary wife and fond mother," he told Edmund, "I believe she can redeem herself." Edmund himself had always felt his mother possessed a pure heart. But this latest—this latest iniquity was an act far worse than the others; she had left her lawful husband, left her young child, and had bolted with a brigand, a man who had misused her in the past and would again. She had truly become the scarlet woman of Babylon, an adulteress.

"Where—where did they go?" Edmund asked, suddenly remembering how the abbot was fond of saying, "While a sinner still breathes there is hope of redemption."

"I am given to understand they are somewhere in Italy," Richard replied. He did not want to say anything about his own meeting with the pair. It was too painful; in fact, this entire conversation pained him. "I have heard that—that Hawkwood is in the service of the pope now."

"The pope at Avignon?"

The present schism of the church had created two popes, the true one, according to the abbot, at Rome, and the false one in Avignon.

"Rome," Richard said.

Somehow the pope's name seemed to mitigate his mother's heinous crime, made her salvation more possible. But Italy! It might as well have been the ends of the earth. Yet—yet with the abbot's help he might, he just might, be able to undertake a pilgrimage and from his holiness learn of Joanna's whereabouts.

"How long has it been since she left?" Edmund asked.

"Over six years," Richard answered, more shortly than he intended.

"And you have not seen her since?"

The question Richard dreaded. He wished he could tell a lie, a falsehood, make up a story. "Aye—I have." The words seemed to catch in his throat.

Edmund realized at once what he had failed to see earlier, that the subject was a torture to Richard. Of course. He had been thinking only of his own disappointment, his own distress, not of this honest, dignified man who had been so shamefully cuckolded. A fine priest he would make if he were to be so blind to another's anguish.

"Sir Richard, you must forgive me." The man suddenly looked ill, too, white, almost trembling. "Forgive me for putting you through an inquisition. I wish there were something I could do. Some words of real consolation I could offer. Is there no way I can be of help?"

Richard shook his head. "I can think of nothing."

"Prayer eases pain. I know 'tis banal advice, but it *does* soothe. God listens, He hears. Lean on Him and it will comfort you."

"I have prayed. Mayhap in time..." His voice trailed off. "But you should not concern yourself too deeply. I do have Cristina. God has been kind to me in that way."

They fell silent. Then Edmund said, "Sir Richard, you say it has been over six years since you were left. You could marry soon again, you know. The church allows that if a man or woman is seven years without a spouse, he or she is considered widowed."

Richard looked at Cristina and gave her a wan, loving smile. "I do not think I wish to take another wife. I am really quite content as I am. Pray do not trouble yourself over me."

Invited to supper, Edmund needed little persuasion. He had taken a liking to Richard, as indeed Richard had to him. Richard was pleased, in an odd, perverse way, to find that Joanna had such a fine son, bastard or not. Though the two had little in common, divided by age and inclination, one a servant of God, the other a servant of war, they found much to talk about.

"This John Wycliffe—what do you make of him?" Richard asked, interested because of the duke.

"A heretic, no doubt of it. But he has some good arguments in his favor. There *are* abuses in the church, there *are* bishops and priests who have grown rich and forgotten their Christian mission."

"Tell me more of what he says."

As the evening wore on, they went from religion to the recent death of the Black Prince, to the state of the streets in London, to the wool trade, to Sir Richard's choice of soldiering over smithing and Edmund's choice of the priesthood. Listening to them, fighting heavy eyelids, Cristina learned that she had yet another brother, Aleyn, also a bastard, at Nareham Castle, reared by his natural father's family and about to be knighted. It gave her a warm feeling to know she had kin other than the sour Smithbornes, two brothers, Aleyn and Edmund; Aleyn, she hoped, just as likable and warm-hearted as Edmund.

"Will Aleyn come to see us?" she asked sleepily.

"Mayhap," her father said.

Though Sir Richard had enjoyed his talk with Edmund it had tired him. During the last hour the pain under his ribs, never absent for long, had returned with knifelike force, making it difficult for him to breathe. He had tried his best to hide any sign of discomfort, but when he finally closed the door on Edmund (with the priest's promise to return in the morning) he sighed with relief. Not wanting to ask for a poultice and have Lydia fuss over him, Richard went to bed, lying flat on his back to ease the pain, wishing he had saved some of the precious wine he had offered his guest to help him into sleep.

After a restless night he awoke in the early dawn feeling nauseous. The pain had fanned out in his chest. He elbowed himself up and in the halflight saw that his pillow was covered with blood. Fear set his heart to thumping. God knew he had seen blood often enough in the wars, his blood, too, for his shoulder had once been pierced by a lance and had gushed like a geyser. But this silent message which had come in the night was different. He shuddered. He did not want to think of dying. All must, he knew that, but not now; some time in the future, next month, next year, five years hence. Not now. Life, however hard, however sad, was better than lying in the cold grave. He shook his head as if to dispel the blasphemous thought. Edmund would scold him for that. What of life everlasting that Our Lord promised? Had he been free of sin, so free as to go straight to heaven? Ah, nay, only a saint could do that, not Richard Smithborne, the blacksmith's son.

He coughed, and bloody froth rose to his lips. If he were bled, given a physic, his painful disability would go away. He could not give up, say all was lost, because of an ache and a little blood on his pillow.

"Lydia...!"

After a leech, a friar from St. Botolph's, had bled him and given him a potion containing a few drops of poppy infusion, Richard felt better. The good friar's treatment, he believed, had done the trick. It was only a question of lying still for a day—two at the most—and he would be right as new. He had Lydia send a message to the sergeant-at-arms at the outer gate, explaining his absence—an indisposition—and that he would be at his duties day after tomorrow at the latest.

He slept until noon, waking again to the knife edge of pain. His breath now came in labored gasps. A dribble of blood had dried on his cracked lower lip. Beyond the bed curtains he heard voices, Edmund's and Lydia's.

"He's sick, sorely sick," Lydia was saying. "Mayhap you'd best return tomorrow."

Richard, through a fog of pain, gathered his strength and called, "Father Edmund!"

He was there in a moment, bending over him, a compassionate face, the brown eyes filled with concern.

"You are ill, Sir Richard," Edmund said, brushing the invalid's sweat-soaked hair from his forehead. "You said nothing last night. I thought—so pale. What is it? What ails you?"

"'Tis an old wound. Nothing." He closed his eyes, wanting to grit his teeth, trying not to groan, to scream at the wrenching sharpness in his chest. "I—Edmund..." A bubble of blood rose to his lips. The pain expanded, grew, throttling his throat, rushing up into his head, bringing with it a swirling red darkness. He sought to fight it, to push it back, but could not. The struggle was too much for his weakened body.

"I am dying, Father," he whispered through bloodied lips. "Pray—absolve me."

Edmund did not argue. He could see death stamped on the knight's blanched features. He sent Cristina and Lydia away from the bedside and, closing the curtains, knelt by Richard's side. Unprepared, without the accouterments of the last rites, he must nevertheless perform them. No host for absolution. "Lydia!" he called. "A morsel of bread."

Confession came brokenly from a hoarse throat in unintelligible words. A string of petty offenses—pride, envy, falsehood, mixed with the names of battles and men—issued from

Richard's cracked, swollen lips. Pity flowed through Edmund as he recited the Latin liturgy which would speed this good knight on his way to paradise. That a man who had spent such a blameless life should die in so much agony grieved him.

"Pax vobiscum," he whispered. "Peace be with you."

The child was brought. Cristina, kneeling by her father's side, gazed at him with wide frightened eyes, baffled, not comprehending. The final rites were for others, an old neighbor, Aunt Ellen's infant grandchild, the miller's wife, not for her father, not in this house. "Papa!" she implored. "Papa, speak to me!"

Still lost in fevered memory of the past, he did not recognize her, did not know who she was. He talked of Joanna now, his love, the black-haired beauty, Joanna, his happiness, his despair, the sum of his life. On and on the words jerked out brokenly, spaced with short, labored breaths. "...a ribbon, a red ribbon, a carnelian ring—I brought—Joanna. The witch of Thorsby—ah, love, love..."

"Papa!" Cristina begged. "Why are you ill? How did it happen? Who hurt you?"

And Richard, hearing her question through a maze of revolving images, honest to the end, replied, "Hawkwood."

He died before cockcrow, never having recovered consciousness, unaware of Edmund, who prayed at the foot of the bed, nor of Cristina, who wept forlornly in heart-wrenching sobs at his side.

Chapter XXII

They were residing in Milan now.

John Hawkwood had quit the pope and gone back to his former employer, Bernabò Visconti, the Lord of Milan, one of the most ruthless of tyrants in a land where ill-natured despots and their cruelties were fairly common. Avaricious, sly, possessed of a savage temper, Bernabò tortured citizens, servants and hapless prisoners alike for the slightest infractions, sometimes simply on whim. He and his brother, Galeazzo of Pavia, had between them devised the notorious *quaresima*, a punishment which lasted forty days, the digits of its victims amputated one by one, each amputation interspersed by a day of rest, until at the end, the poor wretch, if not already dead, was beheaded.

Bernabò lived in extravagant splendor. He dined on gold plates, wore silks, ermine and precious jewels and maintained a retinue of hundreds, all appropriately clad at his expense. A passionate hunter, he owned five thousand dogs, aleuts and greyhounds, hundreds of falcons and horses, and often spent days in the saddle chasing his favorite quarry, the boar. Hunting was not the lord's only obsession. Women he loved and bedded by the score. A man of boundless sexual appetites, he was said to have acknowledged fathering some thirty-seven children, seventeen of whom were legitimate. One visiting prince of the church likened his household to a sultan's seraglio.

Joanna, by now somewhat conversant with the Italian language, had garnered enough tidbits of gossip to piece together this unflattering picture of her husband's overlord. She had never before probed into Hawkwood's activities and rarely questioned him. But she felt obliged to ask of Bernabò, "Does not this man's manner of living offend you?" Certainly she and John were not saints, but it seemed the devil himself could take instruction from the Lord of Milan.

John, however, felt the visconti's private affairs were his own business. "I am a soldier and in his pay. I object only when Bernabò attempts to instruct me on how to wage war, a fault he has, and over which we dispute. But other than that, what he does and with whom I care not." He frowned. "And if you are really looking for a monster, my dove, you need go no further than the papal legate, Robert of Geneva. If God sees fit to keep me in purgatory 'twill be because I took part in his butchery at Cesena."

She had no reply for that. She knew, as did everyone, how Cesena had been put to the sword on the legate's orders, defenseless men, women and children slain in a horrible bloodbath, a massacre which had revolted even a hardened soldier like Hawkwood. So that when Bernabò had asked him to come back to Milan, he had grasped at the opportunity to be free of both the pope and his savage cardinal.

Joanna was presented as Lady Joanna of Thorsby to the Lord of Milan at a banquet given in honor of one of Bernabò's sons. Her position as Hawkwood's mistress, hardly a secret, was here acknowledged openly. Other guests had also appeared with their ladies of love, Bernabò himself sitting next to his favorite mistress, Porina. No one seemed to think much of it. Joanna, observing their ill-famed host, saw a tall man with red hair, short beard, wide nose, and cold, narrow, very keen eyes. She noted how little he spoke, how the guests seated next to him fawned, how the servants, quick and sure, nevertheless cringed in his presence.

The hall in which they dined would have put the Savoy to shame. Marble-columned, paved in terrazzo, its cornices gilded and fluted, the vast chamber soared to dizzy, white-arched heights. Thousands of candles in sculptured bronze sticks vied with torches and chased flambeaux to give light, sparking the jewels worn by the guests, gems at ear, throat, wrist and hair catching flame. Never had Joanna seen such tableware, golden platters, crystal goblets and mazers set with precious stones. Nor had she ever eaten such food. Dozens of courses borne in by liveried varlets were set before them; suckling pigs, trout, quail, ducks and capons, sturgeon, eel pies, meat galantines, roast kid, shivering junkets, fresh fruit and a host of tasty cheeses. Bread light as air, wine sweet and acid, and brandy wine from the Low Countries.

For the occasion John had ordered a seamstress to make her a gown "fit to be seen in," as if the others were simply make-do. The new costume set off her figure to shapely advantage, a sky-blue surcoat trimmed in ermine over a dark-blue velvet gown embroidered at the low neck with pearls. Her waist was girded with cloth of gold, the hips of the skirt, according to the latest fashion, slashed narrowly to show her *robe-linge,* the fine gossamer linen shift underneath. From her ears dangled long aquamarine earrings, and around her throat hung a necklace of the same jewels. Her hands sparkled with gems, one a ring which John had lately given her, a blue sapphire of such purity and size it covered a third of her forefinger. Her hair was fixed again according to the latest fashion—a pity, for its black glossy beauty was hidden under jeweled cauls surmounted by a flat cloth-of-gold cap hung from behind with a transparent veil which fell to the shoulders.

Looking about her, scarcely able to eat for excitement, Joanna never bothered to wonder whence all this wealth came. If she had asked, John he might have told her—taxes. Everyone—all from peasant to and including the highest of the church's clergy—was taxed; a *gabella* on salt, a *citimo* on income and property, duties on wine, flour, flax and cattle. The merchants who did well in this period of Milanese history could afford to pay, but the assessments fell hard on the poor. Forced to pay and pay more, the peasant and the urban artisan as well were slowly bleeding to death. The *condottieri* avoided the tax if and when they could, growing rich on the spoils of war, booty won in victory, the sack of town and village, or bribery from some overlord for "protection." John's captains and their women, if dressed a little less splendidly than the nobility, still wore velvets, jewels and furs of the finest quality.

Joanna rarely thought of the past now. Nareham and Thorsby, even London, seemed like places dim and far away as though someone else had been there, not she. She loved Milan more than any other of the Italian cities they had lived in. It was larger, busier, different, exciting. Its sights never failed to thrill her; the sixteen columns of white marble in the midst of the Corso di Porta Ticinese, remnants of the once great Roman baths, the beautiful Basilica of St. Ambrogio with its vast atrium and roofed cloisters, and the Cathedral of St. Lorenzo with its graceful dome. There were walled gardens and lovely villas and a thousand splashing fountains, shops that displayed merchandise from distant places, wide gold bracelets from Nubia, silks from Cathay, exotically feathered birds from tropical islands, glass cups, silver knives and jewels of every description, black opals, pink pearls, beryls, carnelians, rubies, emeralds, and figures carved in onyx and jasper.

One morning emerging from Mass at St. Lorenzo's Cathedral, Joanna noted a pilgrim of middle height near the bottom step. Leaning on his staff, his round black hat shielding his head and brow from the sun, he scanned the faces of the passersby as if searching for someone. Pilgrims dressed in sackcloth cloaks, carrying staffs, and cockle-shelled scripts, were a common sight, and Joanna would have hardly given this one a passing thought had he not looked vaguely familiar. As she descended the steps the feeling of familiarity grew stronger, and when the man suddenly lifted his face and looked at her, she felt her heart stop. For an infinitesimal moment she thought that it was Ivo come back from the dead in the guise of a phantom pilgrim to confront and denounce her anew. But it isn't Ivo, she thought, closing her eyes. He is not tall enough, he has brown eyes, not blue, and Ivo is resting peacefully in his grave as a good Christian should.

"Lady Mother..."

The deep voice came so suddenly her body jumped.

"Mother..."

Her eyes flew open, shock, disbelief, wonder passing swiftly across her face. "Edmund! Is it you? Mother of God...!"

She rushed into his open arms, sobbing, laughing, hugging and kissing him over and over. "Edmund—I never thought...oh, let me look at you!" She wiped a tear from the edge of a shining eye. "Edmund, Edmund. You have come on pilgrimage..."

"Partly. I am a priest now."

"Your birth..."

"Overlooked." He smiled. "Some relative of Grandfather's died in Thexted, and with the money I was able to give a new screen to the bishop's church."

"I am so happy for you. It is what you have always wanted, but tell me—oh, I am so excited!" And she gave him another hug. "Where are you staying, how long have you been here? Did you travel on foot? Are you bound—?"

"Wait, Mother, wait. Not so quickly. I cannot answer all at once. I am staying at a nearby hostel."

"You must come home with me. I won't have you sleeping there—and they give such poor fare. I live but a stone's throw."

"With *him,*" he said.

"Aye—with your father."

"My father. *He* does not think so, and you, you are living with him in a state of adultery." He had not meant to plunge

332

into the heart of his mission so abruptly, but the reference to Hawkwood had goaded him into it.

"I love him, Edmund. I always have. Surely God will forgive me."

"Only if you renounce him."

"I—I cannot...Edmund..." She glanced up. A small knot of curious loiterers, pilgrims and beggars mostly, had gathered around them to watch.

"We cannot talk here," she said quickly. "Let us go from the steps at least."

She hurried down and, rounding a corner, paused in the shadow of the church wall. "Edmund," she pleaded, "I love John Hawkwood. I have loved him since childhood. Believe me, 'tis not a passing fancy. Oh, my dear son, how can I make you see?"

"I see nothing but that you have left your child and lawful husband, a man who was crippled—"

"What?" she asked sharply. "What did you say? Crippled? What means this?"

"His right arm..."

"It did not heal?"

"My lady mother, he has gone to the Healer of all. He is dead."

"God in heaven!"

She had thought of him only once or twice in the last few years, but now the news of his death shocked her, and for a moment she seemed to see his face again, the bitterness in the set of his mouth as he stood before her on the field at Romagna.

"He spoke of you to the very last," Edmund said, reaching out, taking her arm to steady her, for she had gone deathly pale.

"Did he curse me? Did he? Ah—you won't answer."

"He said he still loved you." A half-truth. Nay, he must tell her all. "He called you witch, too, his beautiful witch."

"And rightly. Holy Mother, forgive me. His arm—he was unseated—I did not think 'twas a serious wound. And I offered, Edmund, I swear it upon the cross, I offered to go back with him."

"The Smithbornes told me he had been wounded in combat, but they said nothing of your offer."

"And *he* did not speak of it? 'Twas a shameful business. I tried to persuade Richard not to fight, and I tried—I did—the same with John. Neither would listen. And when Richard fell, I said I would go back with him. But he would not have me."

"He did not want your pity, Mother. He wanted your love."

She made a helpless gesture. "I—I could not—I could not love him. My heart is John's."

"Why? Why and how can you love such a rogue? Because he has given you jewels and gowns?" His eyes swept her disdainfully. "I can well guess that you have much in the way of luxuries. You live like a princess, no doubt. Are you happy?"

"Oh, Edmund, God forgive me, aye. Happy."

"Are you? Are you, Mother? Even when you think whence came these riches? Your paramour is a brigand, a mercenary. He kills not the infidel, the unbeliever, but Christians. Think on it."

"He is a man of the sword. An honest man. Even the pope has hired him."

"Does that make it right? Catherine of Sienna herself has admonished the holy father to wage his crusade not against brothers but against the Saracen."

"I know nothing of that."

"Do you not? Do you not hear the cries of the murdered, of the robbed and mutilated? Is your conscience not burdened by the despair, the hopelessness of the peasants who must watch their fields and huts put to the torch? Who must see their children trampled to death under the hooves of paid mercenaries' horses? *They* are the victims of battle, not the lords who sit safely behind their walls. *They* are the ones who pay dearly. The baubles you wear about your neck and in your ears come from blood-tainted gold."

"John is a soldier by trade. If he were not the captain of the *condottieri* then another would be in his place. Giving it up would not rid the world of war."

"But he, and more importantly *you*, would have no part in it."

"I do not honestly see that it matters much in the scheme of things. I have little enough. What? A few jewels, some gowns. You begrudge me those? You begrudge me happiness? My son, sweet, sweet son, I have earned what little I have. Aye. You speak of peasants. No one knows more than I their travail. Hunger? Pestilence? Hard work? Humiliation? I have suffered it all. Aye. I know what it is to grub in the earth for mere existence. I know what it is to be spat upon, to be reviled, to be alone and despised. And now that I have a little of something that raises me above the meanness of life you would throw it in my face. Do you think—honestly, my son, the priest—that if one of those peasants you speak so pityingly of had the chance to change places with me he would not grab at it?"

"That argument does not excuse you."

"My son, where did you think the money with which you bought the bishop such a grand gift came from?"

"A relative..." he began and stopped short at the expression on her face.

Wrong. No relative. He might have known, might have at least guessed. The deceased merchant in Thexted, one that Joanna had never spoken of, leaving his money to her children. A fictitious benefactor. "It was you, *you*. But how?"

"Through Sir John's agents. I did not want to tell you for fear the money would be refused. Now that you are a priest it does not matter, since you have what you always wanted. But you must never tell Cristina. Promise me."

"Aleyn too..."

"Cristina is the one who must be kept in the dark. Do I have your promise?"

He did not know what to answer. He was not thinking of Cristina but of the "tainted gold." What would the abbot say, he wondered, if he knew? What would he have said had he known beforehand? The abbot was such a mixture of the worldly and the pious it was hard to tell. Perhaps he would have reminded Edmund that more than one rich, cheating burgher or cruel, battle-scarred overlord facing death and subsequent purgatory had willed a part of his ill-gotten gains to erect a chapel or nunnery in his name, a memorial accepted gladly by the church.

"Edmund?"

"I shan't tell her," he said.

"You condemn the money—and me—because you have no love for John Hawkwood."

His eyes widened, an expression so like Ivo's it caught at her heart. "Why should I love him? Aye, I know 'tis Christian to love all—but 'tis hard, very hard in this case. And how *you* can love him is beyond me. He has two sons—"

"Two sons?" she interrupted. "What sort of nonsense is this?"

"Mother, did you not know? He has not told you, I see. Quite by chance I found out from a vicar who came to the abbey—he was from Hedington. It seems that Hawkwood was

335

married quite young and his wife died shortly after she gave birth to twins."

"Nay," she said, shaking her head, a smile on her lips. "You are mistaken. Impossible."

"He has brought them to Italy."

"'Tis a fable, sweet. Gossip. I do not believe it. He would have told me long since."

"Does he tell you everything?"

"Of course," she lied.

"Ask him then."

"I shall. And I want you to be there when I do. I want you to hear the denial from his own lips."

Hawkwood was not happy about Edmund's visit. "So he has made this pilgrimage simply to see you and throw your sins in your face."

"I am his mother—it has been over ten years since I took him back to the abbey. He loves me still. And"—she gave him an oblique look—"you are his father."

"I am *not* his father."

She lifted her chin. "Stubborn." But she smiled when she said it.

"There is something else," she went on. "But I shan't say a word of it until we break bread with Edmund."

They had eaten and drunk, Joanna taking more wine than her wont, for despite her chatter, her efforts to lessen the discomfort between father and son with talk of trivial matters, the weather, the Milanese sights, the pope's latest foray, she felt a hard knot of fear, a sense of impending disaster, in the pit of her stomach.

The savories had been brought to the table, their gilded mazers fluted with pagan figures of Dionysus and Leda refilled.

"Sir John," Joanna said, a little thickly, lifting her cup, meaning to jest with him, "Sir John, I drink to your sons, the twins."

She saw the flicker in his eyes, saw him swallow, and could hardly believe it when he said, "How did you know?"

She would have thrown the wine in his face had Edmund not restrained her, holding her wrist, the wine spilling from the cup, splattering her wrist and her gown. "You—you varlet! 'Tis true then, *true!* You never told me you had two sons whom you acknowledge. You never *told* me! You coxscomb!"

"I did not want a fuss made," he said calmly, "such as I see you making now."

"And why should I not? God knows what else you have been hiding from me, another mistress, mayhap even a wife." She wanted to plunge her knife into his breast; to wipe that cool what-of-it look from his face.

"No wife, no mistress but you, dove."

"And no other offspring—no sons, no daughters."

"None but the two."

"Three," Joanna corrected. She knew she was far from sober, knew she ought to curb her anger until they were alone, but she could not help herself. "You have three sons. Three! Damn you!"

"Two," Hawkwood said, implacable, unruffled.

She sprang to her feet, knife in hand. "A murrain on you! You churl, you meaching, lying dog!" she shouted, brandishing the knife.

"Bitch!" Hawkwood reached up and twisted her wrist just as Edmund rose in his seat, catching the knife as it dropped from his mother's hand. For a moment nothing could be heard at the table but Joanna's heavy breathing and the tinkling of a distant fountain.

Edmund said, "I will not be a party to this." He had gone very white, a small pulse ticked in his cheek. "A pox on both of you! Your quarreling sickens me."

He placed Joanna's knife carefully on the table, trying to compose himself, dismayed at his quivering hands. "I need no brigand as a father," he went on. "The Almighty is my Father, as He is to all who love Him. Do you think I *care* whether this man recognizes me or not? Do you, Mother? Do you feel that I should go on my knees to him, begging a—a cutthroat, an outlaw?"

"Take heed, shavetail," Hawkwood warned. "Men greater than you have been reduced to mash for saying less."

"Reduce me then," Edmund said. His voice was steady, but the tick pulsed. "Reduce me. I am not afraid of you—or your varlets." The two men's eyes met, Edmund's hard and blazing, Hawkwood's steady, unfathomable.

"I cannot eat under this roof. I cannot stay, Mother."

"Edmund," Joanna pleaded, her tipsy rage suddenly gone, "please do not leave. If you will stay…"

"I cannot. If you wish to speak to me I shall be at St. Maria's hostel."

"Edmund…"

337

John put his hand on her arm. "Let the black cowl go."

She turned on him. "Because of you! All because of you, *you!* You have driven him away."

"What would you expect? I know why he has come to Milan. He wishes to persuade you to return to England, to that mealy-mouthed husband."

"Richard is dead," she said flatly. "Edmund is concerned only with my sins."

"So..." John let out his breath. "So the blacksmith's knight has left you a widow. And now your priestly son is trying to save you from the flames of hell."

"Jest. But you believe in hell as we all do, and you shall roast there along with me. You are a fornicator and adulterer no less than I."

"True. But when the time comes, and not before I am an old bent graybeard, you may be sure, I will make my confession and be shriven."

"And how can you be sure you will die in your bed? Suppose you are mortally wounded on the field?"

"I always take a pastor with me on campaign. So you see, I have no fear of being unabsolved."

"How smug you are."

"No more than the next man. Listen, sweet, you have only to tell yourself that you can do the same. Be absolved when the time comes. Give money to have Masses said for your soul."

"How easy you make it sound." There was no winning an argument with John. She had tried it too many times.

She rapped her mazer on the table, and the page behind her chair refilled it. She drank slowly, watching Hawkwood, who was carving a chunk of cheese from a wheel with his knife.

"John," she said, breaking a silence, "I know the best way to shrive ourselves. I am a widow now. We can marry."

His brows flew up. "Marry? And spoil what we have, my pretty?"

"We could have it all. Our love and be man and wife."

He turned his gaze away and looked out through an arched window which was open to the late winter garden. "It would certainly make Edmund very happy," he said dryly.

"What in God's name have you against Edmund?" she flared.

"You keep pushing him at me."

"Oh—Jesus save us!—but you are impossible." She rose.

"I cannot talk to you. Impossible!" And she left him, hurrying away before her anger should set them to quarreling again.

She could not allow Edmund to leave Milan without seeing him again. As he refused to come near the palazzo Joanna shared with Hawkwood, she sent word that she would meet him in the garden of a ruined villa not far from his hostel. The villa had once belonged to a silk merchant, a descendent of the illustrious del Torro family, a man who had had the audacity to criticize Bernabò publicly. In retribution the Lord of Milan had ordered his personal guard to fire the house in the middle of the night while the family was sleeping. No one had escaped the flames, which had consumed all but the outer stone walls and the pillars of the loggia. Though the fire had taken place some ten years earlier, the ruins still seemed to exude a charred odor, and Joanna, who arrived before Edmund, had some minutes of uneasy waiting.

The garden, the vegetation and trees surrounding the villa had gone to wild. Black, unpruned cypress spread dense-needled arms across the weed-choked, graveled pathway, blocking out sun and sky and casting dark, unsettling shadows beneath. Here a crooked almond bloomed, white and ghostly in the gloom, there two leafless beeches leaned upon one another while a twisted ash and a giant magnolia struggled together for the light. Overgrown hedges tangled with vines and pale-flowered bushes which grew raggedly rank and moistly green. In the center of four mossy paths a leaf-choked fountain stood, its little stone faun lying on its side, the pipe in its hand shattered. Joanna waited there, drawing a shawl tightly about her shoulders. The April air so soft and sweet beyond the ruined walls blew chill and damp here. The garden depressed her, gave her a feeling of impending doom. She was beginning to regret her choice of a meeting place when Edmund came hurrying under the trees toward her, his pilgrim's cloak sweeping the grasses and dead leaves.

"Ah, Mother!" he exclaimed happily. He might disapprove, even condemn, but he was too fond of Joanna to let anything, even anger, come between them. "I would not leave Milan without saying goodbye. You see," he said, taking her hands, "I still hope to convince you to come back to England with me."

"Edmund—Edmund. You are as stubborn as your father."

His brow darkened. "Let us not speak of *him*. Let us speak

339

of you. Have you no care for your immortal soul? Is hell so far away you would dismiss it until some future date?"

Joanna thought she could. Hawkwood's argument had been very persuasive. Why worry about sins when one could have them all absolved at the last moment?

"You think you can be absolved without doing penance," Edmund said, guessing her thoughts, "but you are wrong. For every act of sinful fornication you will be called to task. Every one. And the more you delay, the harder it will be to achieve God's grace." He paused, and suddenly his amber-brown eyes filled with tears. "Oh, Mother, come home with me. Devote yourself to your daughter, who needs you."

Edmund's plea moved her in a way it had not done before. Though the son she had borne and loved, planned for, hoped would be her comfort, had left her and chosen another life, he still loved her. And she saw him coming to Milan, not as a pilgrim to visit a shrine, a priest to save a soul, but as a son to redeem a beloved mother.

She touched his cheek with her fingers. "Do not weep, Edmund. All will be well."

"How? I do not mean for my tears to persuade you. That would be womanish. I mean for *you* to decide, for *you* to leave this man of your own will."

"Edmund, I cannot—I ..."

The clatter of hooves and cracking of branches interrupted her. Looking down the tangled avenue of cypress, Joanna saw Hawkwood approaching on horseback. The mount, nervous and high-bred, kept shying and rearing, apparently disquieted by the dark, brooding trees.

"Joanna!" Hawkwood called.

Suddenly the horse stumbled over a hidden, sprawling root and Hawkwood was thrown. Joanna heard an ominous thud as his head hit a tree trunk. She screamed and ran to him. He lay crumpled, on his side, his eyes closed, his face gray as ash.

"John! Oh, John—speak to me!"

Her hands trembled so she could not find his pulse. "Edmund ..." she appealed.

He came to her and, lifting Hawkwood's arm, pressed his fingers to his wrist. "He lives."

"His flask—he always carries one in his saddlebag. Get it—hurry!"

The horse, quiet now, stood a few feet from them, head lowered, snuffling at the green undergrowth. Edmund found the flagon, unstoppered it and gave it to his mother. Joanna gently eased John over on his back. She lifted his head and put the flask to his mouth. When it remained closed, she dribbled the wine on her hand and wet his forehead, his cheeks, his lips. After what seemed a long time John opened dazed eyes.

"Where does it hurt, love?" Joanna asked.

He looked at her without recognition, and her heart shrank. Again she pressed the flask to his mouth. He drank, blinking his eyes.

"Why is it so dark?" he asked.

Joanna shot an appealing look at Edmund, who stood beside her, his face expressionless.

"Joanna...?"

"I am here, sweet," she said, hope rushing back on joyful wings. He knew her, the blow had not injured his memory. "What is it? Where do you hurt?"

"All—over." His body was wrapped in pain. He saw Joanna's face through a haze against the backdrop of a darkening sky crisscrossed with the cypress's dense, shadowed branches. He heard the wind whisper, and a shudder of impending doom shook him. He had been wounded in battle, had lain ill of fever, had faced death a thousand times, but never, never had he had this feeling of an implacable fate closing in. Was he dying? He was not afraid, only cowards feared death, but it was what came afterward, after the flesh became quiescent and the soul went from the body, that frightened him. For despite his scoffing and his lighthearted jesting he was as fearful of dying unshriven as any.

"Joanna, I—I must see a priest."

"Oh, love, nay. You have just had a fall. You will be all right. I'll send for someone to carry you home."

"There isn't time. Is—is that Edmund? Is he still here?"

"Edmund—aye."

John closed his eyes. It hurt to talk, to breathe. Hearing a crow caw, his eyes flew open in terror. High above he saw the huge bird wheeling, a glint of sun catching one black wing. The bird of death. And he unabsolved.

"Edmund," he whispered. "Shrive me. I have sinned and I wish to repent." The sins in his life, he could not remember them all. Crécy, Avignon, Pisa, Cesena—ah, Cesena. He must not omit Cesena. "Edmund...?"

Edmund said nothing but stood looking down at the prone man, his eyes and face passive.

341

"Edmund!" Joanna cried. "For God's pity. Do as he says. He is dying."

But Edmund could not speak. Something hard and cold had risen in his breast, a feeling the Christian in him tried futilely to deny. *Humble thyself before thine enemy, forgive.* Christ on the cross told the thief next to him, *I will see thee in paradise.* A thief. But like a palpable second heart the rancor of years lay beating so loudly under his ribs he was certain his mother and her injured paramour could hear it. Absolve this man who had denied him, who had made a whore of his mother? And what of the thousands of clamoring souls this brigand had sent to perdition, the villages he had laid waste, the poor and innocent he had murdered? How could any priest absolve such a man?

"I cannot," he said through stiff lips.

"You must!" Joanna said. "How can you call yourself a man of God?"

How? If this creature were a stranger, the worst blackguard, the most infamous scoundrel in the world, asking for pardon, would he not go down on his knees? It was John Hawkwood he hated, God forgive him, not the sinner.

And Hawkwood, looking up, his head grown to an enormous size and pounding with pain, saw himself, not Edmund, standing there in the dark pathway, in the shadow of the cypress, the broad shoulders, the sturdy body, the clenched fists, the stubborn, arrogant tilt of the head. Himself, twenty, thirty, forty years ago? Time had become blurred, but not his vision. Not any more. How could he have missed it? His blood. Himself. There in Edmund, his flesh. How could he have been so blind, so deaf? Joanna had been a virgin; she had loved him and he had branded her trollop, denied the boy. Even now he did not fully know why.

The world was growing darker; large black crows were perched now on every mournful branch, their beady eyes watching him, watching. "Edmund—my son." His voice came out like a croak. "My son—I beg of you . . ." He closed his eyes. "My son."

Joanna, rigid, shocked, her hands pressed to her breast, thought—he has acknowledged him, the stubborn old fool! God! She did not know whether to laugh or cry. Not laugh—never laugh. "Edmund, he calls to you. Your father calls."

"He is afraid. Dying men will say anything."

"Thumbscrews would not make him say such a thing unless he meant it."

Still Edmund stood, unmoving, unmoved.

"Oh—! You two are so alike!" she cried in exasperation. "You will be as much a sinner as he if you deny a baptized Christian."

The truth, she spoke the truth. What would the abbot say of him now if he knew? Father Mark may have been practical, a little too businesslike in running the abbey and its various properties, but his piety had never been questioned. And he had never carried a grudge. He had been kind, even to the Shurbridge villagers who had tried to burn his mother as a witch.

Edmund removed the wooden cross which hung about his waist and knelt in the dust. "Mother, leave us."

As she stood with her back to them, staring down at the debris of the broken fountain, she heard faintly the words, *"In nomine Patris et Filii..."*

John Hawkwood did not die. He was too tough for a mere spill from a horse to finish him off. He had suffered a bad knock on the head and a multitude of bruises, but nothing else. Looking back, he was amazed at himself for thinking he was done for. It must have been the blow, which had jolted his reasoning and set him to fancying he was breathing his last. He was glad to be alive, of course, but ashamed of his weakness in demanding absolution, though he did not deny a word of what he had uttered. Perhaps the whole embarrassing episode was meant to be. Always skeptical of what the clergy called "God's workings," he was not so uncertain now. His experience had been a revelation in that it had shown him plainly, beyond doubt, that Edmund was indeed his son.

While still recovering from his fall, he summoned Edmund to his bedside. "My son, I want to make amends for the years I have neglected you."

Hawkwood was not accustomed to apology, but he could do it when the occasion demanded, and skillfully too. He had learned diplomacy, the art of tactful speech, while negotiating contracts and dealing with his former enemies. Not that he lied or even dissembled, he simply withheld words that would not serve his purpose. But this situation was somewhat different. The set of Edmund's jaw (again so like his—not the shape of it, that was still Ivo's, but the *way* he held it) put him off. "You have little respect for me, that is plain. Am I right?"

Edmund said simply, without rancor, "Aye."

Edmund had given him absolution after a string of horrendous confessed sins, and he had tried in his heart to forgive him. But he would never, never like this man, father or not.

"I cannot blame you, my son. I should feel the same were I in your place. But I am sincere. Ah..." A small smile curled his lip. "I see you have second thoughts. Ask anyone in the whole length and breadth of this land what the word of Sir John Hawkwood means. They will tell you that I never go back on a promise once it has been given."

Edmund found it hard to look his father directly in the eye, and it bothered him. Never in his entire life had he failed to meet another's gaze. Perhaps his experience had been too narrow, perhaps the cloistered walls of Kenham Abbey had kept him too removed. How could God's servant have reluctance, even hate, in his heart? But he did. This man had sired him, and he, Edmund, carried Hawkwood's blood in his veins whether he liked it or not. But he could not bring himself to call him Father. Was he unnatural, then? *God help me, give me strength*, he prayed silently, shrive me of emnity, make my heart accepting, loving.

"Mayhap in time you will come to see I am not the devil you take me for," John went on. "But this is neither here nor there. I said I wanted to make amends. And I do. There is an old ruined abbey in Lombardy on land I won some years back. I give it to you. More, I will have the abbey restored, a Cistercian abbey, and you will be its abbot. Does that please you?"

Edmund drew in his breath. An abbot at twenty! It was something he had never dreamed of. He wavered. To be like Father Mark, to be the apex, the fountainhead. To hold the strings of other lives in his hand. The bastard, Edmund. He must not disdain the gift, nor the giver. He saw that Hawkwood was sincere, and the part of his mind that looked coolly on possibilities, on opportunities (the abbot's influence, or was it inherited from Hawkwood?), was sorely tempted. But he would have to live here, in Lombardy, far from home, for the rest of his life. He would never see England again. Could he do that? And he knew, even as the question turned over in his mind, that he could not. He wanted to go back to Nareham, to the English countryside. He wanted to see the hedgerows in spring, to feel the cold crisp autumn days, drink new ale, smell the smoking fragrant logs, hear his native tongue spoken. He could not put into words why these things mattered. Italy was beautiful too. But it was alien. Not home.

"I thank you, Sir John, but I have already given my promise to Nareham."

"You won't reconsider? You would not want to stay on?"

"I think not."

"Still, I wish to do something." He gave Edmund one of his rare smiles. "Surely Nareham could use a new church? If I remember correctly the old one was falling into disrepair. A sorry place for worship."

Again an argument took place in Edmund's mind. Should he accept this man's "tainted" gold? This time, however, the debate was brief. Who was he to deny God a decent church, no matter where the money came from? Should not God's house have a stout roof and walls, His parishioners an appropriate place to worship? Of course. He had given up trying to appeal to his mother. Neither she nor Hawkwood would ever reform their ways; they enjoyed sinning too much. His only hope was that they might marry and in a small way redeem themselves. But the new church he would take.

"You are very kind," he said.

"Not kind. Never *kind*. But wanting to help my own flesh and blood."

Edmund winced.

He stayed on for another two weeks, waiting for a party of pilgrims that were setting out for Compestella, a shrine he dearly wished to visit before returning to England. He continued to lodge at the hostel, preferring it to Hawkwood's palazzo. Though he made up his quarrel with his mother's lover, he knew he would feel uncomfortable under his roof, even if the bed was softer and the fare more palatable than the monks' hard bread and sour wine.

To Joanna he expressed the hope that the two would marry, and she in turn thought that John, if not pushed, would come around in time. But one day, quite by accident, Edmund heard disturbing news which put an end to any expectations in that direction.

One of the monks, Brother Bramante, acted as barber for hostel guests, charging a penny or two to trim hair or shave a beard, and Edmund availed himself of the man's services. He liked to listen to Bramante's gossip, spoken in an amusingly garbled English.

"Have you heard the latest concerning Bernabò Visconti?" he asked Edmund as he soaped his face in preparation for a shave. "He is giving his *bastarda*—how you say—bastard daughter, Donnina, in marriage. *Sì*, the daughter by his favorite mistress, Porina. A ripe girl, mmmm." He smacked his lips. "Like a plum. And who is the fortunate one, you might ask? *Comandante* Sir John Hawkwood, a man three times her age, but—"

"She is to wed Hawkwood? Sir John Hawkwood? Are you sure?"

"Certamente! The Visconti's *legittima* daughter, Elizabeth, will take Count Lucius Landau as *marito* on the same day. Bernabò likes for his wellborn *figli* to marry into the old nobility, though you see the bastards do well too. Only last year..."

But Edmund did not hear the rest. Shocked, angry, he could only surmise how this latest turn of events would affect Joanna. And she was certain to hear of it if she had not already done so. Why hadn't John Hawkwood told her of his plan long before this? This decision to marry was certainly not made on the spur of the moment. The lowliest peasant made arrangements, had banns read weeks, sometimes months before the wedding. So Hawkwood must have known about Donnina even as he tried to prevent Joanna from leaving him. The sly fox. He had concealed the existence of his two sons and his former marriage from Joanna, and now this. It seemed incredible that such a man could go on deceiving her and suffer no consequences.

The moment Bramante had done with him, Edmund hurried to the Palazzo de Fontana. Joanna was sitting at a window of her bedchamber feeding a pet cockatoo which had perched on her shoulder. When she saw Edmund hurrying along the path toward the loggia doors, she called out to him, "Up here, Edmund, come up and join me."

Joanna, watching his figure disappear under the loggia, wished that he had accepted Hawkwood's offer and stayed in Lombardy. It would be so wonderful to have him close, to know he was there, to visit him every so often.

"Edmund!" she said, going toward him, smiling as he came into the room. "How glum you look—come and sit down. Have some wine. 'Twill cheer you."

"I want no wine. And I think *you* had better sit down."

"Something has happened?" She searched his face. "You have bad news." She sank into a chair, one hand pressed to her throat. "What is it? John...?"

346

"Aye, Sir John. But not what you think, Mother. He has not hurt himself, but I fear he has hurt you."

"How? How? Speak out, tell me!"

"Did you know he is to be married in three weeks' time?" Joanna gazed at her son without understanding.

"Bernabò Visconti, in order to ensure Sir John's loyalty, is giving him Donnina as a bride."

"Nay—nay. You are wrong. You have been listening to gossip in the streets. They will say anything. It cannot be true." Then, suddenly suspicious of Edmund's motives, she asked, "You are not telling me this to persuade me to leave Milan, are you?"

"Have I ever lied to you, Mother? Have I? As God is my witness, 'tis true. I went to the church where the ceremony is to take place and spoke to one of the priests. The banns have been read. Hawkwood is to marry this bastard."

She stared at him, her throat working. "He cannot," she said finally in a weak, dazed voice. "How? She is young enough to be his granddaughter. A snip of a girl. I met her just a month ago." She paused, remembering. Donnina had sat on Porina's right, hair the color of burnished copper, slanting sky-blue eyes, slender arms encased in green velvet, a bodice so low it exposed all but the nipples of small white breasts, a beautiful child, virginal, yet seductive. Seductive.

"But—it cannot be!" She scanned his face, and the compassion in his eyes told her that it was indeed so.

"Nay—nay—nay! Mother of God!" Her hands flew to her head. "How can he? How can he? *How can he?*" She began to rock to and fro on the chair, pulling at her hair like a madwoman.

"Mother, pray—pray, do not take on so."

"The bastard! Churl! Villain! Turd!" She rose and, scooping up the wine flagon, hurled it across the room. Two mazers followed, one after another, with a crashing and tinkling of broken glass. "Pig!" She shouted every foul word she could think of, language she had not heard since she was a child running barefoot through Nareham village.

Edmund did not try to speak or calm her, but waited patiently until the worst of her anger should pass. However, just as she was beginning to grow less furious and more coherent, Hawkwood himself came into the room.

"I heard you shouting, Joanna. Are you and Edmund quarreling? Love…"

"Love!" she shrieked at him. She looked wildly around for

347

something to throw and finding nothing but a lap dog, which was cowering under a chair, she lifted it and hurled it at Hawkwood. He dodged it easily, and the dog, yelping and howling, thumped to the floor. Joanna ran to a chest, swept up a heavy, gilded candelabrum and pitched that also.

"What's this—what have I done?" Hawkwood ducked his head. He invariably found Joanna's passionate outbursts entertaining if they did not go on for too long.

She whirled and ran to the wall, wrenched a jeweled dagger from its pegged holder and turned a wild, white face to him.

"Enough!" Hawkwood commanded.

Edmund now wished he had broken the news more gently, perhaps spoken to Hawkwood first. He had never seen his mother in such a violent rage. She seemed to have lost her senses completely.

She started to come at Hawkwood with the knife; he grabbed her arms and pinioned them behind her back. "At least tell me why you are going for my blood like a she-cat."

"You—you!" Fury choked her. "You have been lying to me, *lying!* Donnina—Donnina...!" She could not finish. "Oh, you outlaw, you filthy lying brigand. May that black heart of yours be torn from your breast!" She struggled to free herself, but Hawkwood held fast. Half dragging, half carrying, he brought her to a chair and forced her down. She hung her head, panting like an exhausted animal.

Hawkwood, still holding her shoulders, turned his head to Edmund. "What have you been telling your mother?"

"That you are to marry Donnina, the whore Porina's daughter."

"Meddler! Could you have not held your tongue?"

"She would have found out in any case."

Joanna's head came up, her cheeks streaked with tears. "This—this is the last—I have reached the end. The end, do you hear? I curse the day I ever laid eyes on you. Damn you! I am not staying, not a minute longer than it takes me to throw a bundle together. I am going, Edmund! I shall go with you, if I have to walk every mile of the way. I am going. Let me up, churl!"

"Hush! Be quiet!" Hawkwood ordered. "Will you listen? Stop your jabbering and pay heed to what I say."

"I do not want to listen."

"You will if I have to strangle you. I am marrying Bernabò's daughter because he wishes it. A marriage of convenience that binds a contract, nothing more."

"Nothing more? If she were old and ugly I daresay you would think twice. You have never, *never* done anything in your life you really did not want to do. You want to marry her! *You want to marry her!* I was not good enough, a steward's daughter, a peasant. So you take the girl bastard instead—do her tits come stuffed in gold?"

Edmund, as unobtrusively as he could, started for the door.

"Don't go, son!" Joanna called. "Edmund, for God's sake, don't go! Do not leave without me."

Hawkwood said, "What's this nonsense, leaving? Over a marriage."

"A marriage, aye. And you will go to bed with her, no doubt you are panting for it. Fifteen years old. Someone young to warm your old bones."

Though John was well into middle age, he was anything but old. He still carried himself with that same arrogant air, the straight spine, the purposeful stride; his muscles were still hard, not an inch of fat on his well-proportioned body. He still fought in battle and made love with fierce vigor, with a virile vitality that a man much younger would envy. And he *was* looking forward to bedding the Donnina plum; a man would have to be a eunuch not to.

"You are jealous," John accused. "That is the trouble. Jealous. And you have no need to be."

"Nay," Joanna said, sinking back, her fists uncurling. "I am jealous no longer. I want to go home. I want to keep a little of my dignity. I cannot stay on with you—and your wife. I am not like Regina." (Regina was Bernabò's wife. She tolerated all his mistresses, his parade of bastards, with a calm benevolence.)

"You are speaking twaddle," John said. "In a few days you will look at things differently."

"Nay, I have made up my mind."

Hawkwood stepped back and surveyed her coolly. "I do believe you mean it. But, sweet, you cannot leave me, you know that. I shan't allow it. I told you more than once I will never let you go. I have not changed."

"You do not love me." Joanna's voice rose again. "God knows if you ever truly have. You certainly have been chary of telling me so. You do not love me. You want me here beside you because you are greedy, aye, greedy and superstitious. Oh, I know you, how well I know you. You feel I possess some gift, some charm against your dying. As long as I stay you live, once I go you die. That's what it is!"

"You blather like a fishwife. I have no mind to listen." He turned from her.

Joanna shot him a look of intense hatred. Then swiftly she sprang for the knife which had fallen to the floor earlier and went after Hawkwood. He wheeled quick as a cat, as Joanna's fist with the knife clutched in it shot over his shoulder.

What happened next happened so quickly Edmund, who saw it all, had difficulty later in piecing together the swift sequence of events. He saw John struggle for possession of the knife, saw Joanna raise her arm again, bring it down, and then heard her cry out. She had inadvertently plunged the knife into her own breast. A look of utter astonishment widened her eyes before they closed.

"Holy Jesus!" John caught her as she fell. He wrenched the knife from her breast and, lifting her slumped body, carried her to the bed. With strong hands he tore a bed curtain from its mooring and wadded a swath of it into the wound.

"Edmund—wine!"

Edmund had never seen so much blood. Sick with fear and remorse, he ran out, calling for a servant. *"Vino! Vino!"* he shouted. If anything happened to her it would be his fault. He should never have come, never tried to redeem her soul; never gone to her with the tale of Hawkwood's marriage. *"Vino!"*

He ran back into the room. Hawkwood was kneeling at her side. "You did yourself a hurt, sweet, when there was no need."

Hawkwood's uncharacteristic tenderness, his gentle speech, only served to increase Edmund's fear.

"Is she wounded badly?" he asked, forcing himself to approach the bed.

Joanna lay with closed eyes and blue lips, her face the color of paste. Despite the wadded curtain the whole front of her gown had turned a deep crimson.

"Shall I get a physician?" Edmund asked. He did not feel like a grown man, a priest, he felt like a child again, and incongruously a scene at Thorsby rushed back to him, the time when the howling villagers tried to storm the castle, and his mother had stood straight and tall while he clutched at her skirts.

"He can do no more than we. But I shall send for one nevertheless," John replied.

A manservant entered with the wine. "Here—here..." John took it from him. "What kept you so long? Go run for Lodovico Giogio."

He lifted Joanna's head, and her eyes flickered open. Already they seemed sunk into her face, the deep black pupils staring out at them.

"Does it hurt?" Hawkwood asked, pressing the goblet to her bloodless lips.

"Aye," she whispered.

"Drink. You will feel better. Ah—no more than a sip?"

"I cannot."

Hawkwood lowered her head to the pillow, and Joanna closed her eyes again.

Edmund asked, "Has the blood been staunched?"

"I think so." He tore another piece from the curtain, removed the blood-soaked cloth from her wound and replaced it with the new. "I have had much experience with wounds, and..." He looked up at Edmund. The terrible truth was written on Hawkwood's face, in those brown eyes, always so cool, so impassive, and now eloquent with a fatalistic despair. "And though it bleeds much 'tis not a mortal one."

It was a lie; both Edmund and Hawkwood knew it.

The cloth at Joanna's chest grew bright crimson again. She opened her eyes, and a ghost of a smile played over her lips. "Did you think I could leave you, my heart? Did you think another would take my place?"

"Joanna..." Hawkwood paused, swallowing painfully. "There has never been another woman for me. I told you so long ago. I mean it. I—I love—only you."

"Do...?" Her trembling hand reached out and touched his sleeve. "Oh—John. Say it—I—I want to hear it again."

"I love you, sweet. I love you. I know now that I always have."

"Ahhhhh..." It was a flutter in her throat, that one sound, but filled with a floating happiness.

He leaned over and kissed her tenderly on the mouth.

"John," she whispered. "I shall not see tomorrow. I want to be buried at Nareham."

"You are mad. Of course you shall see tomorrow. Are you trying to frighten me?"

"Nay. Where is Edmund?"

"Here," Edmund answered, tears burning his eyes. "Mother..."

"Give me your blessing, my son, my eldest, my best-beloved child."

"Mother..."

Hawkwood grabbed his arm. "Heed me, Edmund. I want you to marry us."

"But the banns, the..."

"Now—now! To hell with the banns. I say marry us." He turned back to Joanna. "Sweet dove, I have asked for you in marriage. Do you find that to your liking?"

A painful smile drew her lips up. "Aye. I shall be proud to be your wife, Sir John Hawkwood."

"And you will be my lady, just as it should have been all along. Edmund...?"

Edmund could not remember the words for the marriage rite. His mind drew a blank. "There should be a Mass," he said. "I have not the—"

"Marry us, you fool. The best way you can. I have a ring. Say whatever comes into your head. You must know a few Latin words."

He looked at his mother and saw that her face had become miraculously young again. She had never seemed more beautiful, the eyes luminous, her features lighted from within.

"As God is our witness," he intoned, "do you, John Hawkwood, take this woman, Joanna Coke Smithborne, as your lawful..."

Edmund choked back the tears.

John had slipped a ring on Joanna's finger. She looked up at Edmund, then at her new husband, her eyes, those beautiful violet eyes, swimming.

They watched as the light faded from her face, became sunken, ashy. An hour later while the physician stood by helplessly and John and Edmund knelt in prayer, she took her last breath, dying just as the bells of St. Girionia were tolling Vespers.

PART III

CRISTINA

"And so began there a quarrel
Between love and her own heart."

John Gower

Chapter XXIII

Honoring his mother's last request, Edmund brought her body back to England in a sealed lead coffin. It had not been easy. Though Hawkwood had given him money to oil the way (money whose purity he no longer questioned), there had been many who would not carry a corpse no matter what the bribe. He had to wait in Genoa an entire month before he could find a sea captain, an irritable old sailor with a red face, who would take him on board. The vessel, a battered merchant galley manned by a crew of ugly rogues, leaked and listed dangerously with every chance gust of wind, every slap of a wave. Edmund was convinced that his prayers alone were responsible for bringing the ship across the buffeting sea into safe harbor.

When he finally stepped ashore on shaking legs he found that England had a new king, Richard II. Edward II had died in June, and his grandson, a boy of eleven, had been crowned in extravagant pomp. But Edmund gave himself little time to reflect on the change of monarchs. Once he had had the coffin removed to a shed for safekeeping he hurried to the Savoy in search of Cristina. To his surprise, he learned that she no longer lived with the Smithbornes, where she had moved after her father's death, but was now situated in the palace proper, a member of the ducal household. It seemed that she had found employment as an apprentice maid through the offices of Dame Brandone.

It took Edmund some time, wandering through a labyrinth of corridors and rooms, questioning a dozen minions before he came upon Cristina. She was in an alcove of the stillroom—a chamber given over to the mixing of elixirs, perfumes and cosmetics—standing on a stool at a table pounding a chalky substance with a pestle, powder for a lady-in-waiting's fading complexion.

"Cristina!"

Her eyes lit up. "Oh, Edmund." She got down from the stool and gave him her cheek to kiss. "What a surprise! I am so happy to see you."

"And I you. How long have you been here?"

"Nine, mayhap ten months."

"You are too young to be working in the Duke of Lancaster's court." Licentious, he had heard. The duke himself, though married to Costanza of Spain, had a mistress, Lady Katherine Swynford, a mistress he openly flaunted. Even the duke's father, the late King Edward, the doddering old fool, made no secret of his leman, Alice Perrers. And the court nobles, following suit, bedded and copulated with abandon.

"I am eleven," Cristina said proudly, lifting her chin, a movement that reminded Edmund poignantly of Joanna. "Grandfather Smithborne and Aunt Ellen were always after me about—well, never mind. I am much happier here."

"But you are a knight's daughter, and in any case need not work like a slavey. You have an income."

"Aye, and the Smithbornes would have liked nothing better than to get their hands on it. This was the only way I could honorably leave them. Brother, there's no need to worry on my account. My tasks are simple, I am well fed and have a comfortable bed. In time I hope to work my way up to a position of importance in the duchess's retinue."

"You are very ambitious."

"Mayhap. Are you staying in London for long?"

"Passing through. I have just come from Milan, where I saw our lady mother."

She said nothing. Her expression hardened as she resumed her position on the stool and began pounding the pestle.

"Cristina—she is dead." He had planned not to tell her the circumstances and if pressed only to say it had happened through an accident. But it seemed she was not going to ask how her mother died. She was not going to ask anything.

"I know you have had harsh thoughts about our mother," Edmund went on, "but I am hoping you can forgive her now."

Again he waited for her to say something, a word, a murmur of regret, of apology, of forgiveness. But she remained silent.

"I have brought her body back. She wished to be buried at Nareham. I—I was hoping you would come with me to the funeral."

She wet her lips. "I cannot."

"It could be arranged. I have the money for the journey, and I will speak to the chamberlain. He would let you go."

"I do not *want* to go," she said, turning a white, angry face to Edmund. "Whoever you have in that coffin is a stranger to me."

"She is your mother."

"I have no mother."

"But you do. She bore you, suffered to bring you into this world."

"A cat suffers too, and a bitch dog. And furthermore, Edmund, they have more feeling for their babies than the woman you call our mother ever did."

Edmund shook his head. "You have a hard heart, child."

"If I have a hard heart, it is because she gave it to me. She—she killed my father." Tears swam in her eyes, and her lower lip began to tremble. "She killed him just as surely as if she had used a lance and struck him through the heart."

"You have been listening to the Smithbornes. Mother tried to dissuade your father, and Hawkwood, from dueling. She begged them both not to go on with it."

"Aye—and why did my father have to fight in the first place? Because *she* ran off with a—with a thieving scullion."

"The thieving scullion married your mother when—when he knew she was free."

"Long life to him," she said derisively.

"You will not change your mind? Will not reconsider?"

"Never."

"Sister, I am sorry. To forgive is Christian." The banal words rang with an uncomfortable familiarity. Had he, Edmund, a priest rather than a child, rushed to forgive his father?

"I am sorry too, Edmund, but I cannot."

He sighed. He was tired; the unburied lead coffin weighed on his heart. He still had to hire a drover and cart to carry it to Nareham, and the village seemed more distant now than it had in Genoa. When he thought of the long journey behind and the one yet to come, his will faltered. He had a great longing to be back at the abbey, walking the shadowed cloisters, sitting beneath the green-fronded trees in the courtyard, listening to the bells marking the hours with their patient tolling, each day, each hour ordered with a never-varying serenity. How peaceful it had been there, safe, comforting, free of turmoil and care, free of impossible decisions demanding to be made.

"I shall pray for you, my little sister. Will you visit me at Nareham?"

"Oh, Edmund," she answered, her expression softening, "I should like to. I have nothing against you, believe me. It is just..."

"I understand."

"Mayhap you can come to London again and bring my brother Aleyn with you."

"At least you have not disowned us." He gave her an affectionate smile. "I shall do my best to persuade him."

But Cristina was fourteen before she saw Aleyn.

By that time she had become one of Costanza's ladies-in-waiting, a meteoric rise from her former humble position. It had come about purely by chance. Costanza had been criticized for having a retinue composed entirely of her own Castilian women, a situation which had done little to increase the duke's popularity, recently sunk to a particularly low ebb. Costanza, with her arrogant airs, her cold religious zeal, her unconcealed distaste for everything English, was not liked. She knew it; she did not care. She resented any sort of interference in her own personal affairs, resented the beefy-faced, ungainly nobles that peopled her husband's court. Nevertheless, urged to act by her closest friend and adviser, her confessor, she decided to obtain a "young English lady of obscurity, discretion and modesty" rather than some well-known noble's daughter who might find an excuse to refuse the honor. If Costanza must have a native lady-in-waiting, let it be a nonentity.

One gusty March morning as Costanza, accompanied by two of her women, was leaving the Savoy's outer chapel, nearly empty at this hour, her eye fell on Cristina, who gave her a deep curtsy as the duchess swept up the nave. Somehow the girl made an impression on her. So few at the Savoy attended daily Mass, and when Costanza saw her a second and a third time kneeling in prayer she wanted to know her identity. Told that Cristina was an orphan, fourteen years of age and a knight's daughter, the duchess summoned her for an interview. Persuaded by the young demoiselle's unassuming demeanor, Costanza after a brief interrogation carried on through an interpreter chose Cristina to become part of her retinue. If she had inquired further she would have been shocked to learn that her new lady-in-waiting's father had been a blacksmith's son and that her mother had been a peasant. In all probability, she would have sent Cristina back to pounding powders and mixing elixirs. But no one thought to tell the duchess, and Cristina was never asked.

On the whole, Cristina had been happier in the stillroom. There her fellow apprentices conversed in her own language, although she never had what one would call a "friend." Aloof, guarded, she had been too much on her own as a child to

358

share her thoughts and feelings with another. Still, working among powders, lip unguents and fragrances had been pleasant, much pleasanter than being at the beck and call of a cold-hearted woman who spoke only in a strange Spanish gibberish.

Ordinarily, Cristina rarely took note of the affairs of the outer world, but in June of 1381 an event occurred which affected the whole of England, including the duke's household. The peasants, whose dissatisfaction had been smoldering for a long time, revolted. Many of them were virtual slaves without the right to plead their grievances against a harsh overlord or to voice their complaints against the rich abbeys and monasteries which held them in thrall. They were tired of poverty, of eating black bread when their lords feasted on white, tired of being scorned and vilified when it was they who made the luxuries of the nobility possible. The last straw had been a particularly stringent poll tax, one that had been imposed on the populace to raise another army for the Duke of Lancaster, who still had aspirations toward the throne of Castile. Led by Wat Tyler, a disgruntled tiler from Maidstone, and John Ball, a wandering priest who had railed against the aristocracy, preaching equality for years, the peasants, armed with billy hooks, rusted swords, kitchen knives, clubs and axes, marched upon London. Burning castles, beheading those they felt were "lawyers and servants of officialdom," they demanded an end to servitude. And in their rebellious zeal they set about London with torch and sword, murdering the hapless Flemings, foreign weavers, who for some arcane reason they despised, beheaded the Archbishop Sudbury and the king's treasurer, Sir Robert Hales. Descending upon the Savoy, they broke every stick of furniture, every window, every gold chalice, glass cup and gilded plate, slashed the hangings, bed curtains and tapestries, throwing every movable object into one great heap in the main courtyard. Then, dragging out stored barrels of gunpowder, they set fire to the lot, sending the entire palace up in an explosive burst of flame.

Fortunately neither the duke nor the duchess was in residence. Lancaster was away in Scotland, and Costanza, traveling north, had sought refuge with her retinue at Knaresborough. Cristina herself had viewed a company of the marching peasants as she sat in one of the duchess's concealed wagons on a hillside, looking down through a screen of trees on the Great North Road. She saw them brandishing their scythes, spades and clubs and heard them chanting Wat Tyler's song. She had no way of knowing the devastation they would bring to the Savoy, nor that the entire Smithborne family would perish in the smoking rubble, until much later when she returned with the duchess to London.

In the end the rebellion, starting with such high hopes, came to little. King Richard, then only a boy of fourteen, accompanied by a small band of knights and exhibiting great courage, met the rebels at Smithfield. There he promised the leaders all they asked, only to rescind his pledges at a subsequent meeting when Wat Tyler was killed by a royal aide and his head stuck on a pike.

Returning to London, the duchess and her household, unable to occupy the destroyed Savoy, set up residence at Kennington. Cristina managed to get away a day after their arrival, and taking a man-at-arms as an escort, she rode to the palace which had once been her home. A group of idlers were gazing at the ruined walls, the blocks of stone piled in the gateways, the windowless, gutted buildings which had remained standing. Cristina, drawing rein among them, caught the stench of burned flesh and acrid smoke and shuddered. Nevertheless, she had the man-at-arms help her dismount.

"You are not going in, damosel?" he asked gruffly.

"I shan't be long."

Picking her way over the gritty stone, past the gatehouse, through the courtyard littered with charred beams and fallen masonry, she came to the place that had once held the Smithborne forge and the loft above. Built of wood, it had been entirely consumed by flames, and in its place only the anvil stood on a block of stone. All gone, burned, destroyed, dead. It did not seem possible. If she closed her eyes she could picture the hearth fire, hear the hammer ringing on steel, the hissing of a shoe thrust into the leather bucket of water. A tightness formed in her chest. She had never thought she could feel anything for the Smithbornes, never imagined she could mourn their passing. They had been harping, gross, critical, and she had been glad enough to get away from them. But now she recalled a dozen and one little kindnesses they had shown her; sweet cakes the old aunt had baked for her birthday, a brooch mended by Master Tom, who had added a twisted bar of gold, given to her gruffly, but given, she was sure now, out of the heart; Aunt Ellen scolding her for getting her feet wet lest she take cold; her young cousin throwing his arms about her neck, kissing her; all small acts of caring which she had chosen to ignore.

She could not weep for them. She had not wept since her father died, and she no longer knew how. But she felt bereft. Her father dead, her grandparents, uncle, cousin and aunts gone, kin, family she had been bonded to. Only Edmund was left, a half brother whom she scarcely knew, and Aleyn, whom she did not know at all, both living in a place called Nareham, far, far away. She wondered if they ever gave her a thought. Her singular aloneless struck her with an odd, empty feeling, and for a few moments she felt herself on the edge of panic. But then the man-at-arms called to her—it was getting late— and turning her back to the scene of desolation she walked quickly away.

Two days later one of the duchess's ladies informed Cristina that the duke and Costanza were leaving for Bordeaux, and since the duchess saw no necessity for taking an Englishwoman to France, Cristina was herewith dismissed. No provision had been made for her, no thought given to where else she might be employed or where she could go.

However, Cristina was not dismayed. She would make other plans, exactly what she did not know, but at least, she reminded herself, she was not without means. Her twenty-pound income left to accumulate with the lawyer Fynche through the years must now have added up to a tidy sum. In addition she still possessed the fifteen pounds she had realized from the sale of her father's effects. Not rich, mayhap, but comfortable.

She mulled over the possibilities open to her, a girl of good name without a protector, alone in a large city. She could enter a nunnery as a lay sister, if she chose; lay or novice, the prioress would welcome her if she brought a dowry. Or she could set up a shop on London Bridge, an unpretentious establishment where she could sell simple nostrums, unguents, paints and ribbons. Or she could buy a small house and live quietly, modestly, with a companion. The nunnery had little appeal—too cloistered, too confined, too dreary. The shop would expose her to snide customers, to discourtesy, to unpleasant haggling which she felt was beneath Sir Richard's daughter. The house, however, appealed to her. She would ask Dame Brandone, old and doddering now, but still in possession of her wits, to live with her. And she knew just the house she wanted, a freestone, one-story dwelling on Watling

Street standing in the shadow of a walled manor. It had once been an abbot's private residence jutting out from a monastery, the monastery so long gone no one could remember its name. Nonetheless she had passed the house again only yesterday on her way to the Savoy and saw that it was without an occupant. Perhaps the owner would sell it to her. But first she must ascertain from Fynche how much money she could count on.

She went to see him the next morning, alone, on foot, dressed in a plain russet cloak with a brown hood. It was the first time she had gone out on the streets unaccompanied, a necessity now since men-at-arms were no longer at her disposal. But, she reasoned, if she walked quickly with purpose, using a main thoroughfare, her hood drawn tightly to hide face and hair, she would attract little notice.

Fynche, she remembered from an earlier childhood visit with her father, lived on Candlewick Street, both street and house not difficult to find. The lawyer's dwelling stood out among the others, a rich man's abode, half-timbered, enclosed by a tall hedge, with a painted sign picturing his calling—a blind goddess of justice holding a pair of balanced scales—dangling from a front gable.

Ushered into a small alcove on the ground floor by a varlet who turned a sour eye on her inelegant cloak, she was told in a hissing whisper to wait until the master spoke first. The lawyer sat at a table a few feet from Cristina, a frown between his eyes, busily scratching on a parchment with a quilled pen. It was warm in the cubbyhole, airless, the one glazed window nailed shut. Cristina, her face flushed, threw back her hood and opened her cloak, wondering if she might ask for a sip of water. It had been a long walk from Kennington and a dusty one.

When Fynche finally looked up he seemed surprised to see her. "And who be you?" he wanted to know, raising hairy brows.

She had forgotten how ugly he was, a sallow-faced man with a high-arched nose that curved to meet colorless lips. And he was older than when Cristina had last seen him, much older. His age should have been reassuring but was not. His yellowed eyes kept traveling from her neck to her breasts, neck to breasts, a distasteful, intimate assessment.

"I am Cristina Smithborne. Sir Richard's daughter."

"Sir—? Ahhhh—aye—Sir Richard! I remember now. Damosel Cristina, I did not recognize you. My, how you have

362

grown. Sit you, pray." He leaned over and pulled a chair close to his own.

Cristina sat down, surreptitiously pushing her chair, a backless stool, a few inches away in an attempt to put distance between them.

"Pretty, pretty," he observed, blowing fetid breath in her face. "How pleased I am to have you here."

"I came on business," she said primly.

"Good—good. But I would be a poor host if I did not offer you refreshment. Aubri!" he shouted, and the varlet appeared. "Wine. Bring the silver mazers—we have an honored guest."

Cristina protested, "Master Fynche, water would do."

"Nonsense."

A flagon was brought, the wine poured. "Aubri," Fynche said, "I want you to fetch some parchments from Master Aldyne on Berrybinder Lane. At once, pray. Well, don't stand about and gawk! Off with you!"

The servant bowed his way out.

"Now, my little bird," Fynche said, raising his cup, "here is to our reacquaintance. Drink—drink, 'tis not meet for you to refuse a toast."

She sipped at the wine, feeling more and more uncomfortable. Fourteen, still chaste, she nevertheless knew a lecher when she saw one. There had been a few at the Savoy, at Pontefract, at Hereford and at Bolingbroke. Wherever the duchess's retinue moved, male birds of prey congregated, the debauchés, the amorists, the seducers, eyeing the women speculatively. Cristina herself, now blooming from plain girl child into lovely womanhood with tawny gold hair and large limpid blue eyes, had been the object of several advances, one or two rather bold ones, but she had always successfully managed to fend them off. She thought she could do the same with Master Fynche. However, in the meantime, she felt obligated to show him some courtesy, a situation which embarrassed and angered her.

"Finish your wine. Go on, finish," he urged, patting her hand with his own liver-spotted one.

Her insides shrank from his touch. She had a great distaste for pawers, male or female, who patted, squeezed, pinched or stroked while they spoke. The Smithbornes had not been a demonstrative family, and she and her father had shared this trait. She found it impossible to squeal with delight, embrace and kiss as the other ladies-in-waiting at the Savoy frequently did even when they had met only an hour earlier. She thought their show of gushing affection hypocritical, since they gossiped incessantly and jeeringly about each other. And because she stood apart from this false show of affection she was called cold and lacking in feeling.

Moving her hand away, she plunged into the object of her visit. "Master Fynche, I wish to withdraw some of my money."

"I am sure that can be arranged. Are you hankering to buy yourself a trinket? A ribbon for your pretty hair?" He leaned over and rumpled the fringe on her forehead.

"'Tis not for a trinket," she said coldly. "I would like a goodly sum. You see, I wish to buy a house."

"What—*you?* A house? My sweet child, whatever for?"

She explained about the duchess's leaving England and how she could not stay on at Kennington.

"And you want to purchase a *house?*" he repeated incredulously. "You are japing. I never have heard of such folly, a young girl like you living alone."

"Not alone. I will have Dame Brandone."

"An old crone. She was old when your father was alive. What protection can she offer you? Nay, the idea is entirely without merit. Witless."

Cristina flushed. "I am well prepared to take care of myself."

"Pshaw! Sweet thing, you should marry. Marry! You ought to have a husband, someone to bed and cosset you."

"I shall never marry." It was a statement uttered with conviction. She had seen enough in the duke's household to know the hollow, meaningless flummery of marriage. Though she understood nobility arranged matches for expediency, wellborn wealth wedded to wellborn wealth, their open flaunting of sacred vows repelled her. Adultery at the Savoy had been rampant. The duke's own mistress had often been there under the same roof with his lawful wife, and this same concubine already had two (or was it three?) bastards by him. Mistresses and bastards seemed just as plentiful as legitimate wives and children. She had only to look at her own mother to see what one licentious spouse could do to the other. Marriage was a misery, and she wanted no part of it.

"Of course you shall wed. And if I were a widower," and Fynche lowered his voice and rolled his yellowed eyes toward the ceiling, "which I may shortly be, since Mistress Fynche ails, I would ask you myself."

"Thank you, but I have made up my mind on the matter. I much prefer having a house."

"You could have a house, dove, and more." He leaned over and whispered, "Six months, a year at the outside, and she'll have hopped the twig. Then you and me..."

"Master Fynche!" She drew away. "Such talk is not seemly."

"And why not? Don't hold your cloak so tight, I'll not harm you. And," peering into her cup, "drink the rest of your wine."

"I don't want it," she said, trying not to sound petulant. "I have come to claim the money you have been saving for me." And then a terrible thought struck her. "You do have it?"

He drew himself up. "What do you take me for? Of course I have it. But I have my wits about me, even if you do not. What would your father have said if I handed over a large sum to you, a mere snip?"

"My father is not here to say anything. The money is mine. And if you..."

"Never mind. Let us not quarrel, pigeon. Let us not quarrel." He stroked her hand again. "Let us be good friends, eh? I see where I have not gone about this business in the right way. Tender words are what a girl likes to hear when she is being courted, eh? I am not a bad catch. Sweet dove, darling."

"Master Fynche, pray, I have no wish to be courted. But I *would* like to have my money."

"I have known you since you were no higher than a grasshopper's knee," he went on, refilling his cup. "I knew and loved you. And when I looked up and saw you today 'twas like the sun shining. Such golden hair." His hand snaked up and stroked it.

"If you will, Master Fynche, pray." She shrugged away.

"Why don't you think on it?" He drank, smacked his lips, then wiped them and the tip of his curved nose with his sleeve. "My proposition is a sound one. I own this large house. Solar, kitchen, hall, bedchambers—two bedchambers." He held up two ink-stained fingers. "I have servants and far more money than your little savings. And in addition I know how to please women." He winked lewdly. "Aye, once I came to your bed you'd be eager for me."

If she had not been so revolted she would have thought the situation comical. But Fynche, old enough to be her grandfather and then some, proposing marriage while his poor wife lay sick abed somewhere in the house did not seem very funny to her.

"I do not need time to think on it. I do not *want* to get married."

He wagged his head, giving her a toothy smile. "I hope 'tis only coyness makes you reluctant. Do y'know who I could have if I wanted? Half a dozen wenches, all with large dowries. Aye. There's a horsemonger's daughter, ripe breasts, big hips, only fifteen, she comes with a thousand pounds. One thousand. Rich, rich, rich, and the tits thrown in with it. But I have taken a great fancy to you, sweet, though you are dowerless by comparison. A great fancy."

Suddenly he lunged at her, grabbing her around the waist, bringing his hot moist lips to her mouth. She wrenched herself away, stumbling to her feet as he grabbed her cloak.

"Master Fynche!" She tried to free herself, but the old satyr had tenacity and more strength than she imagined. When she heard the cloth rip, she slipped her arms free and, leaving the cloak behind in his hands, dashed from the alcove. She took a wrong turn in her panic and found herself running down a short, dark passage before she realized her mistake. Her heart pounding wildly, she doubled back and came out into the central hall through which she had passed earlier—it seemed ages ago—only to find the grinning Master Fynche barring the door.

"Now, my pretty, let us not play too boisterously, eh? We might disturb Mistress Fynche, and what would she think?"

"She would think that you are trying to force me, which is the truth. In fact I shall scream if you do not let me pass."

"Scream, wench, and I shall give her another story. I shall say you came on a pretext, that you made lewd talk and fondled my tool. And then we shall see."

"She will never believe you. Who would want anything to do with your foul body?"

"Why—you bitch!—you tempting bitch. We shall see." He took a step forward to grasp her arm, but she sidled away. "Do your little dance, sweetheart, but I will have you in the end. As for my good wife, she will take my word to yours. A girl unescorted, alone, coming to see a man—what would she think?"

A cold lump formed in her throat. She saw her mistake. She should never have come alone. She should have brought Dame Brandone, a servant, one of the maids at Kennington, anyone. But how could she have known? The few times she had seen Fynche in the past she had been with her father and the lawyer had hardly noticed her. Or was it that she had not noticed him? She rubbed her damp palms along the sides of her skirt, and making an effort to keep her voice steady she said, "Let me pass, Master Fynche. I promise I shan't breathe a word of what has happened here—if—if you let me leave."

He made a sound in the back of his throat like the rasp of dried husks. "You do not really want to."

"I do."

He considered her for a long moment. "Very well." And he stepped aside.

She had her hand on the door latch when he grabbed her shoulders and spun her around. Again she was astounded at his strength. Caught unaware, she lost her balance, and he began to drag her toward the cushioned settle opposite the hearth. She fought, clutching at his wispy hair, pinching and slapping his face.

"Grrrrump—grrrrump," he mouthed, shaking his head free. She brought her hand across his cheek with a resounding blow, and he let her go. But now the settle was in her way. Before she could get around it he had her by the waist again. She turned in his arms and went limp. Later she could not remember how she had had the presence of mind to do so, for she was as terrified of him, as revolted, as she had ever been of anyone in her entire life. But she forced herself to yield.

"That's better," he grumbled. When he lowered his face, his lips screwed up for a kiss, she shoved him violently away. Surprised, he staggered back, tripping over a stool and falling, his head hitting a pair of fire tongs on the hearth with a loud crack.

Crumpled, he lay at her feet.

For a few moments the only sound in the room was Cristina's heavy breathing.

Then from somewhere above a faint, querulous voice appealed, "Walter...? Walter...?"

Horrified, Cristina stood frozen, unable to move. Every muscle, every nerve screamed, *Run! Run!* But her legs refused to budge. Holding her breath, she gazed wide-eyed down at Fynche. The color had fled from his face, even the nose had turned white. She knew without touching him that he was dead. Dead. Guilt coupled with a new fear crept through her veins like an infusion of icy water. In a flash she saw herself discovered, brought to justice, a murderess. She would be hanged, if lucky; if not, tortured, burned at the stake or left to rot in some dank dungeon. God! God! What had she done?

"Walter...?"

Cristina heard dragging footsteps overhead. Terror broke her trance. She ran to the door, fumbling in desperation with the handle, an eternity passing before she finally managed to lift it. Flinging open the door, she dashed out into the street, running, fleeing blindly into the sun-shafted afternoon light.

Chapter XXIV

Her flight through the London streets back to Kennington was a nightmare. Twice she lost her way, blundering once into Puppekirt Lane, where a huge mongrel suddenly came at her with bared yellow fangs, grabbing the hem of her skirt and tearing a portion of it off before a sympathetic woman beat the hound off with a stick. Her braids had come loose; frayed and half undone, they hung down her back, a temptation to male idlers who pulled at them as she hurried by. Ruffians smacked their lips, whistled, flung lewd invitations. When a man in a peaked hat, ragged drawers and stained jerkin tried to forcibly detain her she managed to dodge him and escape into St. Katherine Cree. She knew she presented an uncouth, disreputable sight without a cloak, her gown torn, her hair in wild disarray, and so was grateful to find the church nearly empty. Halfway down the nave, she slid to her knees, her heart clamoring in her breast, resting her chin on upraised, folded hands. There were only four others besides herself present, all women in the same kneeling position as she, listening to a priest at the altar chanting a Mass. No one seemed to have noticed her entrance.

The drone of Latin came to her through the erratic thrumming in her ears. She could think of nothing, see nothing, but Fynche's ugly face, the bloodless pursed mouth, the staring eyes, the gray mottled skin. It had been an accident, she had meant only to push him away, not for him to die. A sudden anger rose in her throat. Why? Why did it have to happen? Why did the old lecher have to hit his head and make everything so final? No one would believe she had meant him no harm. They would say she had killed him, that she had picked up those fire tongs and given him the lethal blow, then had fled. Does an innocent person flee? she could hear the coroner ask. Guilty—guilty! Guilty! And the cloak left behind...why had she not had the sense to take it with her? No time to think, too frightened. The cloak would damn her. Had Mistress Fynche heard them speaking, arguing? Oh, but the servant had seen her, the scornful varlet. He would come home from his errand and finding his master dead would raise the hue and cry. Already it seemed to Cristina she could hear voice and horn, the running feet of the wardsmen, see their cressets and red lances, feel a hand on her shoulder. "'Tis she!"

She swallowed, crossed herself, and began to pray in an earnest undertone, "Hail Mary full of grace..."

Gradually a measure of calmness eased the painful beating of her heart, and she raised her head. Two of the women had left, one was rising to go. The priest had disappeared. The smell of incense and burning wax permeated the air, drifting on little trails of smoke from the tall tapers lit at either transept. Above Cristina painted angels, wooden figures with outspread wings, looked down from gilded beams. And on the walls were scenes of the nativity, the Virgin Mary holding the Babe, the Three Wise Men kneeling, the Lord blessing the fishes and the loaves. Blue and crimson shafts of light came in through the painted windows, dust-moted and golden where they touched the statue of St. Katherine herself. Cristina took comfort from her serene face, the eyes lowered, the white stillness of her brow. Perhaps Fynche's death would be deemed natural, an accident; perhaps it was time for him to die. Perhaps they were not looking for her, not looking for anyone.

When Cristina reached Kennington at last she went directly to the dorter she shared with six of Costanza's other ladies-in-waiting. Her disheveled appearance aroused curiosity, and questions were asked. But she was saved from answering by Lady Isabela, who said, "Someone looks for you."

"Who? *Qui?*"

"*Un hombre.* A man. I know nothing else."

Cristina shrugged. She knew no man, no one who would seek her out at Kennington. Isabela had misunderstood.

Cristina was combing her hair when a page appeared in the room. "Damosel Cristina Smithborne?" he inquired.

"I am she."

"A Sir Aleyn of Nareham wishes to see you. He waits in the antechamber next to the hall."

Aleyn, the half brother she had never seen. Astonished that he should trouble to find her after all these years, not knowing whether to be happy or dismayed, she hesitated a moment before she said, "Tell him I shall be there in a few minutes."

She finished braiding her hair, twining an indigo silk scarf in each of the golden ropes. Then she changed, putting on a gown of blue perse embroidered in pink rosebuds and girded with a white sash, though she felt more like donning sack-

370

cloth and ashes. But she did not want her brother to be ashamed of her. The terrible thing that had happened earlier she could hide deep inside, but her face and dress must reflect tranquillity, a serenity she did not feel.

She came down the staircase slowly, heart beating fast, wondering if she should kiss Aleyn on the cheek as she would have done with her father or Edmund. What would she say? What if he should mention Fynche? What if the antechamber held a crowd of people and she addressed the wrong man as brother?

She went through the arch and entered the room, relieved to find it occupied by only two young men, one elegantly dressed. It was he who came forward. "Damosel Cristina?"

"You are Aleyn?" He did not look at all like Edmund. He had curly brown hair and was very handsome, but vain. She could tell by his jaunty self-assured air and by the peacock plume stuck rakishly in his narrow-brimmed hat.

"That is I, sister." He embraced and kissed her soundly on the brow, then held her away, looking at her with a pleased smile.

Tears suddenly stung her eyes. (Why? Why tears, now?) She fought them, she did not want to make a spectacle of herself, but it was a losing battle. As long as she had imagined herself alone in the world, she had been able to stiffen her will. Fear she had felt, not the need to weep. But now her brother's affectionate gaze melted the stone in her heart, and she felt the terrible urge to lean her head against his chest and sob all her misery out.

"Cristina! You must laugh, be happy, not sad at such a moment."

"Aye," she agreed tremulously, blinking through a misted blur, conscious of the tall figure hovering over Aleyn's shoulder.

"And here—here is my cousin, Phillip, come with me all the way to London, and a merry time we had. Cristina, you— you must not..."

The tears slid down her cheeks, faster and faster. Her face screwed up, and Aleyn, who could not abide weeping women, shrank back, but Phillip stepped forward, and it was into his arms Cristina blindly went. She sobbed, mumbling a string of sentences between catching breaths, but all the two men could make of it was that Fynche was dead.

Finally when her storm of weeping subsided and she lifted

371

her face, she was astounded to find herself looking not into Aleyn's brown eyes but into Phillip's sympathetic gray ones.

"Feeling better?"

"I—I did not know. I am sorry to lose hold of myself."

"Pray, demoiselle, think nothing of it, I have young half sisters myself. Come sit." He motioned to a bench.

She sat down, wiping her eyes as delicately as she could on the edge of her fringed girdle. "I am so ashamed—so ashamed."

Now that she was no longer weeping, Aleyn became once again the affectionate brother. "You need not be ashamed, Cristina. Is something troubling you? I am sure those tears were not caused solely by my unexpected appearance."

Her lips lifted in a faint smile. "I don't know how—how to explain." She looked from Aleyn to Phillip.

"You can speak in front of our cousin," Aleyn said. "He is one of the family."

Phillip de Ander was the son of Andrew, the youngest of the de Ander brothers, who had died of a gangrenous infection before Phillip had been born. A half cousin, he was related to Aleyn—but not Cristina—through his uncle, Thomas.

"I—I don't know," Cristina stumbled, giving the tall Phillip an oblique look.

Phillip bowed courteously. "Damosel, you may rest assured that I will not betray your confidence."

She was able to observe him better now, a young man with a pleasant, clean-shaven face and dark, waving hair.

"And if any wrong has been done to you," Phillip added, "I shall be the first to avenge your honor."

"Thank you," she murmured weakly. She could not, she *could not* tell them what had happened. She could not explain Fynche's lewd advances to these two, even if Aleyn was her half brother and Phillip "one of the family."

But Aleyn, his curiosity now aroused, pressed her. "What is it? Something to do with Fynche?"

She bit her lip. "'Twas nothing."

"But you must tell us. Such weeping does not come from naught. What has Fynche done? I myself am meaning to see him. My allowance has stopped this past year, and I wish to know why. Has the same happened to you?"

She looked at him, not knowing how to answer.

He, taking her silence for agreement, said, "Then I shall take him to task for both of us."

"Oh . . . !" She caught at his arm. "Oh, Aleyn, he is dead. And I . . ." Again tears brimmed her eyes. "I killed him."

"You?"

"Aye."

"Cristina, sister—how?"

Head lowered, her eyes fixed on the tile floor, speaking in a low, barely audible voice, she recounted her visit, its purpose, Fynche's dismissal of his servant, the wine, the advances, his proposal, the struggle and the manner in which he fell.

"He—he must have died the very moment he—he hit the tongs," Cristina stumbled in conclusion. "I could think of nothing but to run."

Phillip drew in his breath. "If he had not died, I would kill the dog myself."

Aleyn said, "The lecher did not deserve such an easy death."

"But the law will not feel the same," Cristina said ruefully. "The servant saw me—and I left my cloak."

"Never mind the law, the servant or the cloak," Phillip said. "You had every right to defend yourself."

Aleyn agreed. "Leave it to us, sister."

"Aye," Phillip said. "We shall make inquiries and see what has happened. Meanwhile, speak of this to no one."

Three days passed before she saw Aleyn and Phillip again.

"You have nothing to fear," Aleyn said. "The varlet Aubri has confessed and he has been charged with murder."

"The servant?" she exclaimed, aghast. "Confessed to a crime *I* committed?"

"Damosel," Phillip said, "you committed no crime. I pray you remember that. *You committed no crime.*"

"I wish I could believe that. I wish I could. But to have an innocent man pay for my own misdeed, to . . ."

"Aubri was far from innocent," Phillip interrupted. "He killed Mistress Fynche. Aye, the cook discovered his mistress's body upon coming home from market. It was half in and half out of the bed, her throat cut from ear to ear. Cook surmised that the culprit must have bludgeoned the lawyer first and then, surprised in the act by his mistress, cut her throat, then dragged her upstairs before he ransacked the coffers. Since the chest had not been broken into but opened by keys, the cook reasoned that one of the servants was to blame. That evening when Aubri did not appear, he knew the varlet—whom everyone heartily detested—was the rogue."

"He will hang?"

"If he is lucky; else he will be broken on the wheel."

She shuddered.

Aleyn said, "Cristina, you are not to think on it any longer."

"I will try. If I could confess to a chaplain..."

"Mayhap it would be best to wait," Phillip advised.

There was a short silence. Cristina, glancing at Phillip, met his eyes, gray with short bristly lashes, eyes that were looking at her with admiration and tenderness. It sent a shock through her, a sudden spurt of strange excitement, before she lowered her gaze, embarrassed, vastly annoyed with herself. She had no desire for male approval, not that kind. Phillip had tried to help her, and she was grateful, but she preferred him at arm's length.

Aleyn said, "Did you know that Fynche has been using monies put into his trust, including yours, Cristina, for his own benefit over the years?"

"Mine?"

"Aye. His records were such a muddle I had another lawyer look into it. Apparently his figures were all a sham. I had nothing but the income, but you say you had savings? Well, I'm afraid there's nothing left now."

She had already reconciled herself to the loss—Fynche dead and she fleeing in terror and guilt. She never expected to ask for, much less to receive, her money.

"A blow for me, a year's income, I can tell you, sister," Aleyn went on. "I have expenses, and my erstwhile father has become very mean with his purse of late."

"Come now, Aleyn," Phillip admonished. "You know that your father has had quite a few blows himself these past few years. One trouble following upon another."

It was true. Thomas de Ander seemed to have suffered nothing but misfortune ever since he had evicted Joanna from Thorsby. First he discovered that Lady Rosamonde, to whom he had been betrothed, was illegitimate and her mother a serf, and so had no claim to the vast properties of her father, Simon of Tribourne. Breaking off this alliance, he married Joan Hadley, a wealthy London mercer's daughter, a young woman with a rich dowry. In 1369 as a result of a plague outbreak Thomas lost both father and mother, thus making him master of Nareham and sundry de Ander estates, an inheritance he was astonished to discover much reduced by debt and bad management in the last years of his father's life. His wife's money helped. But she, though healthy, had difficulty conceiving, and when she finally managed to become pregnant and carry the baby full term, giving birth to a son, he thought the bad times were over. Then the child, sickly from the moment it drew first breath, died at the age of three, and Joan could not seem to quicken again.

Adversity continued to dodge his heels. During the peasant revolt his wife's holdings, the wealthy dowry she had brought to their marriage, was virtually annihilated, three houses on the Strand, two seagoing ships and a half-dozen shops burned along with the looting and firing of the Savoy.

It was enough to make any man sour, if not miserly, and Thomas, who had always indulged his bastard son, now felt he could no longer do so. Nareham itself was producing less and less; they had little surplus to sell, not like the old days when they could send cartload after cartload of hay, corn, barley and foodstuffs to market each week.

"Still," Aleyn said, gazing disconsolately at his yellow doe-skin shoes, "he could have spared a few pounds to pay my gambling debts. I hated to sell my good horse. I am ashamed to be seen on the one I have now—a cart nag, little better than a mendicant's mule. A few pounds. And now Fynche stealing what was mine."

"I am sorry," Cristina said.

"Why should you be sorry? No fault of yours."

Phillip added, "Certainly not." Then, after a moment, "What will you do now, damosel?"

"I know not." She repressed a sigh. "I suppose there is some nobleman's wife with whom I can find employment as a tiring woman." Gone was her dream of a house, of living a quiet, tranquil life. Again she would be at someone else's beck and call, having to arrange her time at another's pleasure.

"Have you no guardian?" Phillip asked.

"Nay, my portion was not deemed large enough to have one chosen for me."

"Mayhap your brother could see to your future. Aleyn?"

"What?" Aleyn, who had been listening with half an ear, sat up.

"Arrangements should be made for your sister," Phillip said, his voice edged with annoyance. "You and Edmund are the damosel's closest living male relatives, the only ones, if

I am correct, and since you, Aleyn, are here and not Edmund, I should think you would try and..."

"Pray," Cristina interrupted, "it is not necessary to find me a husband, if that is what you are thinking. I do not want one."

"Nonsense," Aleyn said. "Every girl does."

"I am not *every* girl," she retorted.

The admiring flame sprang up in Phillip's eyes, and again Cristina's heart leapt. But when she spoke her voice was cool and controlled. "I have no mind to put myself in bondage—for that is what a wife must do."

"Fair damosel," Phillip said, "that is not always true."

"As far as I have been able to see it is," she replied.

She knew she was acting discourteously, that Phillip ill deserved it, but his fervent glances disturbed her, not in the same way Fynche's had done—those had been sickening—but disturbed her nevertheless.

"You could come to Nareham," Aleyn suggested. "I am sure Joan could find a place for another tiring woman."

Cristina repressed with difficulty the retort that rose to her lips. She told herself that Aleyn in an obtuse way was only trying to be helpful. But how could he be so insensitive? How could he fail to see how demeaning it would be for her to act as waiting woman to the wife of her mother's former lover?

"Aleyn, thank you, your offer is kind, but I cannot go to Nareham."

He shrugged. "Do as you see fit, then."

Phillip, who understood Cristina's situation (though not her cold attitude toward himself), had another suggestion. "My mother has been looking for a damosel of rank to join her household."

It was a half-truth. His mother had been remarried to Sir Michael de Leys, a wealthy noble, the past sixteen years, and while not actively seeking a tiring woman could always use one more.

"My mother, Cecilia de Leys, stays mostly at Connington Castle, a comfortable place three leagues to the south of Nareham. You will find her comfortable too, easy to serve, generous and kind."

Would she seem churlish if she declined? She did not want to hurt him any more than she had to, but if she lived under his mother's roof then she would be bound to see him, to show him courtesy. And the thought disturbed her. Yet what else could she do, where go? She had never before felt so helpless and confused. Her father's death had left her grief-stricken but not fearful. She had moved from the Smithbornes' into the Savoy and thence into the cold, alien Costanza's orbit without too much ado. Why this churning agitation now?

"Think on it," Phillip urged. "I do not want to press you for an answer if you are not ready."

How kind he was; only an ingrate would refuse. Impelled by shame and a desire to end her own uncertainty, she said on impulse, "I should be honored to serve your mother."

Again the eyes leaping flame. She looked down at the hands folded in her lap, the fingers, the single garnet ring, her ears burning. I cannot, she thought, I cannot let him want me.

Aleyn, bored with the conversation, had since wandered off. They were alone in their corner of the antechamber.

"You will not regret your decision," Phillip said, giving her a reassuring smile.

He knows, she thought, he knows I am frightened. And I do not like him any the better for it. God help me, I should, but I do not. I do not want him in love with me because I cannot love him back. Nor any man.

"I should like to escort you myself," Phillip said, "but unfortunately I have business here in London which promises to detain me for some time. However, I will see that you make the journey in safety."

She could only murmur, "Thank you," with lowered eyes.

Castle Connington was fairly new, having been built in 1365. Since de Leys had the means, he had spared nothing, making what he termed his "private abode" a thing of beauty and comfort. Crenellated and fortified, it had the prerequisite moat, the portcullis, the watchtowers. But the manor house— not a keep—had been constructed according to ideas copied from the townhouses of the wealthy along London's Strand. Though Connington did not begin to compare to the opulent Savoy, it offered amenities rarely found in many castles—a garderobe, or latrine, with cushioned seats, rooms partitioned with walls instead of the simple arras, chimneyed hearths and a number of glazed windows.

Cristina, bearing Phillip's letter, presented it to the Lady de Leys, who had it read for her by a clerk. Pregnant with her sixteenth child, though not yet showing it, she smiled sweetly at Cristina when she heard that the girl was an orphan.

A small person, plump going to flabbiness, with dark lively eyes, she never questioned her role in life. A woman bore children, thanking God for her fruitfulness, served her husband, tried to see that the household ran smoothly, helped the less fortunate, had pity for orphans and widows. A model of good wifehood, she nevertheless had two weaknesses. One, rather obvious, was Phillip. He had been fathered by Andrew de Ander, a boy who had seduced her and was then forced to marry her, and she preferred Phillip above the other children, though she swore she loved them all equally. Her other flaw was a strong streak of possessiveness, a jealous tenacity she thought unbecoming and therefore kept well hidden beneath a placid exterior. But her fondness for Phillip she could demonstrate openly. Unfortunately the boy had only his good looks to commend him. Landless, he owned nothing but his golden spurs, his horse and his illustrious de Ander name. He had to—*must*—make a good marriage. And thinking of that now, Cecilia, squinting down at Cristina with her near-sighted eyes, wondered if Phillip had sent the girl out of charity or because he had developed a liking for her.

"And so you were with the duchess. How unfortunate—about the Savoy." It must be charity, Cecilia thought. Though the girl was pretty, she was too retiring, too prim, not the sort to catch a man's eye. Nay, nothing to fear here; charity.

Cristina, rising from her curtsy, kissing the lady's hand, did not resent the close scrutiny, the narrowed assessing eyes. She had been subject to much worse when she had first been introduced to Costanza. Close inspection by a chatelaine, a castle's mistress, showed good sense. Cristina would have done the same.

"My dear child," Cecilia said, "I shall be happy to have you with me at Connington."

"I thank you, lady, you are very kind. I promise to do my best to please you."

"We shall get on well together, I can see that," Cecilia said, rewarding Cristina with another smile, certain now that the girl would be useful, unobtrusive and soft-spoken, never causing her a moment's uneasiness.

But she was wrong. It was not Phillip, however, she had cause to worry about. It was her husband.

Sir Michael, approaching his forty-fourth year, felt as young and as strong as he had in his twenty-fourth, certainly far from past his prime as some would have it. He had fought with the Duke of Lancaster at Nájera, had distinguished himself in the Scottish border wars and most recently had campaigned alongside the Earl of Buckingham in Burgundy. He still had a good eye, a strong arm and a capacity to endure. He could travel the day from dawn to dusk in the saddle, reach his destination that night and banquet with his host until morning without showing signs of fatigue. Tall, broad-shouldered, his narrow waist only just beginning to thicken, he possessed a handsome ruddiness despite the creases in his forehead and the furrow between his eyes brought on by years of squinting into the sun. The women still cast admiring glances at him, causing Cecilia a secret pang now and then, but she never had any real reason to doubt him, for he was not a lecherous man by nature. Of course, when he was away he sometimes took a camp whore, and once, nay twice, he had had a brief affair with a noblewoman, but for the most part he was remarkably faithful to his wife, an unusual attribute among his peers.

He could not explain why Cristina attracted him so violently almost from the moment he saw her—young, still a child really, a pretty child, but very different from the mature, full-breasted, beautiful women who might conceivably tempt him. Very different. What did Cristina have that could possibly make his heart beat in a way it had not beat in years?

She had been sitting at an embroidery frame with Alette, one of his wife's tiring ladies, when he had come into the solar, a room he rarely entered, for it was the women's domain and he felt awkward intruding upon them. But on this occasion, having decided to join Thomas de Ander at Nareham for a boar hunt, he went up to the solar himself to inform his wife of his intended absence, a matter of a week or more, instead of sending a servant. It was his policy to ignore the other ladies—he thought it shameful the manner in which some of his friends carried on with the female members of their households—and did not notice Cristina until he stumbled over a lap dog on the floor.

Cristina cried, "Oh—! I am sorry, Sir Michael." It was her duty to tend to Cecilia's pets—a half-dozen or so—and the girl, jumping forward to snatch the offending animal away, collided with Sir Michael. He caught her arms to keep her from falling and suddenly found himself looking down into a white upturned face and two startled, lash-fringed, very blue eyes. For a long moment he gazed at her, completely lost in those eyes, the dog's yelping and his wife's voice reaching him from a far-distant place.

"Come here, Pooh-Pooh, come here, now, now, you're not hurt..."

Cristina, her face hot, feeling the way Sir Michael's arms trembled as he held her, said, "Sir..."

He let go, a dusky flush staining his cheeks.

"Michael?" Cecilia said sharply. "Have you something to tell me?"

"I—I'm off to Nareham to hunt with Thomas," he answered unsteadily, still shaken as he approached her. "Don't look for me until a week from Tuesday or Wednesday."

Cristina, seated now, her head bent, was painfully aware of Sir Michael's interest. The way his eyes had turned dark with surprise and the tenseness of his hands as he held her had conveyed his feelings eloquently enough. If he had shouted, "I want you!" his desire could not have been plainer. Later, however, she had tried to convince herself that it had been her imagination, that the intense look he had given her was his natural manner. But when Alette remarked rather maliciously that evening, "I see you have taken Sir Michael's fancy—we could be made of wood for all the notice he ever takes of *us*," Cristina felt a sick knot form in her stomach. She was afraid of Sir Michael, afraid of him in the same way as she had been of Phillip. But whereas Phillip had managed to be gallant, cautious and respectful, she sensed that Michael would make no such effort. To her he seemed overpowering, a man who exuded an animal warmth, a vitality, a musky, sweaty male odor that both drew and repelled her. She prayed that Cecilia had not seen, would never know how her pulses thrummed and the hot blood had rushed to her face. She would die if Lady de Leys even suspected.

But later, she thought, Can I be condemned for a look? Aye, she could; for had not the chaplain of Connington preached even this past Sunday that 'twas a sin to lust in the heart?

She confessed; she said one hundred *Aves* on her knees. And later she told herself that she had not lusted, that it—her feelings—had only been a brief, very brief aberration. And gradually as the days passed she began to feel safe. Sir Michael had gone off; his absence, she hoped, would give her a sufficient interval in which to recover.

Two weeks later he returned, heralded by the sound of a trumpeteer and the gateward's shout of welcome. It was a warm autumn afternoon and the ladies were sitting in Cecilia's pleasaunce, a garden laid out in clipped hedges, beds of flowers, stone benches and small burbling fountains. A minstrel sat crosslegged at Cecilia's feet strumming on his lute, singing of thwarted love. The lady had become heavy now, and when she heard the blare of the gateward's trumpet which signaled her husband's return she sent Cristina to tell him welcome, that if he wished she would receive him in the garden.

Cristina, hating the chore, could not think of a way to refuse without arousing suspicion. "Hurry!" Cecilia called after her.

Cristina found him dismounting at the stable door. She curtsied and, looking at the hem of her gown, said, "My lady awaits you in the pleasaunce."

"Thank you." Then, abruptly, "They call you Cristina?"

"Aye, Sir Michael."

"Look at me, Cristina."

She lifted her face, consciously stiffening the muscles, wanting to show him only blank indifference. But she could not hide the fear and an almost imperceptible quiver of anticipation.

He lowered his voice. "I wish to speak to you alone. Nay, do not shrink away. I shan't harm you, but I must speak to you. Come to the stable in an hour's time."

"Forgive me, but I cannot. My lady..."

"You must," he insisted, frowning. "I command you. Her ladyship has nothing to do with it. In an hour."

She nodded and murmured, "Aye, sir."

She was late. She hurried along, hoping not to be seen, certain that every eye in the yard and manor was watching, the servants and household noting her movements, speculating, whispering, "Where is she going?" A crimson sun gilded the gray-tiled roofs of the outbuildings as it sank slowly in a streaked western sky. The chapel bells began to ring, filling the courtyard with their jangling unmusical cacophony, and Cristina quickened her step. She had excused herself from Vespers, pleading a stomach upset, the only pretext she could think of which would be accepted without question. She hated subterfuge, hated having to lie. But how could she defy Sir Michael's command? He might make trouble if she did not appear as promised, she reasoned, and would have hotly denied that her breathlessness may have been due to excitement rather than fear and a need for haste.

The barn door was open. A red-combed rooster pecking on the threshold gave a startled squawk as Cristina brushed
381

past. She paused for a moment in the dimness, her heart beating painfully in her ears, the smell of manure and new hay washing over her. She heard the shuffle of hooves, the whickering of a horse, the clank and jingle of harness, men's voices. A single shaft of the dying sun illuminated only one stall, the rump of a mare; the rest lay in shadow. Where was he? Mayhap he had changed his mind, had reconsidered and had decided against the meeting.

Gradually her eyes became accustomed to the gloom. The voices came from somewhere in the back of the stable, but she could see no one and was too nervous to move from where she stood. Presently she heard footsteps, a rustling sound, and gooseflesh rose along her arms. Frightened, she turned to leave.

"Cristina!"

It was Sir Michael, standing in the shadows beside an empty stall. "You are late. I was beginning to think you had disobeyed me."

"Nay, sir," she answered in a small tremulous voice.

"Come closer."

She stood before him, not daring to meet his eyes.

"Look at me," he ordered.

Reluctantly she raised her chin.

"Do you think me an old man, child?" he asked, his voice low but harsh.

"Nay—oh, nay." His eyes seemed black in the gathering dusk, his cheeks, chin and beard planes of darkness. She smelled him, that feral odor so strangely persuasive, saw a muscle at the edge of his mouth twitch.

"Do you think you could love me, Cristina?" He did not touch her, but his eyes moved to the neck of her dress, to her breasts, then back to her face. Nothing like Fynche's lewd assessment, different from Phillip's, a man's appraisal, a mature, compelling man accustomed to getting what he wanted.

"Sir Michael—I cannot," she said in a low, uncertain voice. "My lady—I would be doing her a disservice—she would be angry. I ..."

"She need never know." His eyes softened, caressed her face, then grew hard again, narrowed, as they fastened on her breasts. She felt the nipples grow taut, felt them pressing against the linen cloth.

"I—I cannot. 'Twould be—a sin."

382

"God forgives sin. And if you love me—if you want me—He will overlook our transgression."

They were stock phrases; Cristina had heard them before, but now they seemed strangely persuasive.

"You are so beautiful. So lovely. I will not force you, sweet beautiful girl." He brought his face closer, his fingers lightly touching her upper arm. "Give yourself to me—pray, I beg of you."

"I—I cannot." Her voice strangled in her throat.

His arm looped about her waist, and he brought his mouth down on hers in a kiss that was surprisingly gentle. But then suddenly with a sound in the back of his throat he grasped her tightly, crushing her body against his chest. His kiss became savage, bruising. He cupped her head with one hand; the other slid down and grasped her small buttocks, pressing them to his rising manhood.

She had meant to fight, whatever his strength, whatever his power. She had determined beforehand to struggle; but the moment his arm circled her waist and she felt his hot breath on her face, her will deserted her. Limp, sinking, drowning, going down and down into a bottomless, rapturous abyss, she clung to him. His hand, moving up to her breasts, cradling them, his thumb brushing her nipples, sent a sharp twist of desire through her loins, and she opened her mouth wider to receive his probing tongue. *Sin, sin, sin,* a voice deep inside hissed, but she pushed it aside. Never, never had she dreamed that a man's hard-muscled arms crushing her so painfully, his mouth biting, sipping, kissing, could make her blood sing so. Never, never would she have believed she was capable of such feelings, such giddiness, such madness. She wanted him, she wanted him, her mind and her body fused in that one overwhelming yearning—she wanted him. He was drawing her into the shadows, his hands tearing at the neck strings of her gown. He meant to undress her; she would be naked, she did not care. She wanted her skin to burn under his hands, his lips.

"Sir Michael!"

He let her go so suddenly she had to grasp at the wooden post of the stall to keep from falling.

"What have we here?" a woman's voice questioned, a voice that Cristina was all too familiar with. "Cristina, my virginal tiring woman?"

Cristina turned, her face flaming.

Cecilia stood just inside the doorway, her fingers laced across her ballooning stomach. "You disgust me! Seducing another woman's husband. What have you got to say for yourself?"

Cristina could not answer. She wanted to disappear, to sink into the floor, to die.

Sir Michael spoke. "My dear, you are mistaken. We have done nothing wrong."

Lady de Leys's rage carried her over the barrier of ingrained habit. To contradict her husband had been unthinkable until this moment, but now, finding him pawing one of her tiring women, a girl young enough to be his daughter, and the vixen complying, not fighting him off, not even protesting, made her blood boil.

"I saw you with my own eyes," she accused Cristina. Cecilia might have contradicted her husband, but never, never would she acknowledge him as the guilty party. The woman was always to blame. "I saw you—you whore! Baggage! Doxy! Trollop!"

Cristina, aghast, stunned, reeling, clutched the post tighter as if it could protect her from the woman's lashing tongue.

"Get out of my sight, you slut!"

Cristina, holding the neck of her gown together, brushed past Cecilia and fled. Running across the sunset-flooded courtyard she made for the stairs, climbing them, panting, sobbing, her eyes blinded with tears. *Whore! Baggage! Doxy!* She was her mother's daughter; she carried Joanna's tainted blood. Why else would she have met Sir Michael in the stable, why? A girl of honor would have died first. But she...oh, God, God!

The dorter, thankfully, was empty, the women still at their prayers. She opened her coffer and withdrew a square linen cloth, stretching it out on the floor. Then she hastily piled into it shifts, a gown, her vial of gillyflower essence and a pair of slippers, quickly tying the four corners of the cloth together. From the bottom of the coffer she took a purse. Three, no, four, nobles. She tucked them into her bosom. Then, lifting the cloth and slinging it over her arm, she hurried out, ignoring the stare of a varlet who passed her in the corridor. Outside the sky had darkened to a cobalt blue pricked by a few glimmering stars. She heard voices from the chapel; they were coming out. God! Like a trapped animal she looked wildly about, then began to run in the opposite direction toward the postern gate. She had no idea where she was going, she did not even think of it. Her only wish was to escape, to leave her shame behind.

Chapter XXV

Stumbling through the gate, she found herself on the brink of a glacis and grasped at the stone wall behind to keep herself from sliding into the moat. It was dark now and she could not see the water, but she could smell the fetid stench rising from it. A deep ditch whose primary purpose was defense (though no one as yet had attacked Connington and would not for another sixty-three years until the War of the Roses) it was also used as an outlet for latrines and all manner of refuse. In the heat of summer and early fall, before the heavy rains of winter arrived, one could smell the effluvium for miles around. It was an odor that castle folk were accustomed to, and Cristina, who had spent most of her life living over a London gutter, felt not aversion but anxiety about its murky depths, for she could not swim.

After a slight hesitation she began to inch along the scarp and had gone some distance when suddenly her foot stepped into space. She experienced a moment of horrified, hair-raising disbelief before she stumbled, fell, and began sliding down the steep slope. She scrabbled desperately, clutching at tufts of coarse grass to stop herself, but the grass came away in her hands. Dislodged stones clattered past her, and her feet sought frantically for purchase, but nothing held her and she continued slipping, slipping. Through her fear, far, far below she heard a faint plop! Her bundle. Lost in the fall, all her worldly possessions gone forever in the waters of the moat toward which she herself was fast falling. Already it seemed she could feel the stinking pool closing over her, choking the breath from her lungs. Her death, God's claim, His retribution.

Frantic at the thought, she flailed out, her hands suddenly grasping the branches of a prickly bush. She held on, and though the thorns tore at her fingers, the bush stopped her downward slide. She lay for a long time, face down, tasting the sour, rubbled earth, listening to her heart knocking against her ribs and the whistling of her frightened breath.

Presently she began to haul herself up toward the castle wall, using elbows, fingers and toes, carefully reaching out with probing, torn and bleeding hands before she inched from one spot to a higher one. She reached a small stunted tree with a twisted trunk and rubbery leaves and gratefully pulled herself up, leaning against the branches, her knees shaking so badly she could hardly stand. The milky night sky luminous with starshine cast a faint light on the castle wall above her. Below, the moat glimmered. She had only a few yards to go, no more, and she would reach the gate tower. Studying the terrain, she now saw why she had fallen. She had stepped off into a rain-washed gully. But the rest of the way seemed safe enough. If she went more slowly, carefully feeling her way, she would reach the bridge without mishap. Only a short distance.

Still, she was loath to leave the firm support of the tree, and so she lingered. A slight breeze stirred the branches, shook the leaves above her, ruffled the hem of her gown. She began to think again of Sir Michael, painful, shameful thoughts. She was not in love with him, never had been, never could be, and yet she had enjoyed his kisses. Admit it! Admit it! *Bitch, whore!* Oh, why had she been such a fool? Why?

She heard a sudden clap and rustle of wings overhead, and it startled her. A bird of prey? She couldn't stay there all night; she must move.

On her knees once again, slipping and sliding, she crawled to the top of the slope and taking hold of the wall pulled herself up. Using the rough stone for support, she resumed her step-by-step progress toward the bridge. After what seemed a long, heart-thumping age, she finally reached the tower and paused in its shadow to catch her breath. The drawbridge stretched before her, its wooden planks deserted now, gleaming dully in the starlight. She could still change her mind, turn back, knock on the gate, ask for readmittance. Once across the moat, she would be on her own. Where she would go, how to get there on foot, she had no idea. The unfamiliar and the unnamed lay ahead, a void; while behind—no mystery there—lay humiliation and dismissal.

She chose the void and, stepping on the drawbridge, started across. She had gone only a short distance when a voice from the tower roared out in the stillness, "Ho! Ho! Who is it? Give your name! Stop, there! Stop!"

The gateward! Picking up her skirts, Cristina began to run, her leather-shod feet pounding on the slats as she fled.

When she reached the other side she kept running, though the gateward had ceased to call. Feeling like an outlaw, she sped across a field, stumbling over stones and rabbit warrens, her breath coming in short-winded gasps. Down a winding road she went toward the whitewashed church which marked the beginning of the village, Barnum. There she paused in the shadow of the steeple, nursing the painful stitch in her side. To her right behind a broken hedge lay the cemetery, headstones of different sizes and shapes, some tall, some squat, some gray, some bald and gleaming white, others lichen-covered, grave markers crowded together like hunched, whispering old men. They seemed to be muttering among themselves, grumbling about damnation, hell and purgatory, about eternal pits of fire.

Cristina shivered and crossed herself. She could not stay. At midnight the skeletons danced. They emerged from the buried shrouds into the upper world and to the piping of the wind, two by two, danced a stately pavane. Lydia had described the whole scene to her once long ago, remarking that all graveyards were the same. She crossed herself again. She must go on. Where? Should she knock on a peasant's door and ask to be taken in? What would she say, how explain? Would they think her a thief running from justice?

An owl began to hoot from the branches of a large oak tree. Hooooot—hoooooo—hooo! She listened, head bent, eyes straining, the hairs along her arms going stiff. Hoooot—hoooo—hooo. No, no, not an owl, but the voice of a tormented soul. She kept staring at the tree, and presently from one of the stones beneath it a thin scarf of vapor arose. Gradually it grew larger and began to take shape as it floated out from under the shadow of the branches. Hoooot—hoooo—hooo; almost mocking, like laughter. The vapor, a tall column now, was forming itself into a human figure, first the feet, then the edge of a gown, a man's old-fashioned mantle such as was worn a hundred years earlier, a buckled belt, fingers clutching it, hands, arms, a neck...God in heaven, help me! Hooot—hooo...

She turned and ran down the darkened village street. The thatched cots, silent, dark and shuttered, seemed to shrink away from her. Their occupants slept; each varlet, each villein and peasant lying safe abed behind a closed door, secure among his fellows. And she alone, on the outside, cold and friendless. It didn't seem right. She had stopped before a cot with the intent of knocking when a pair of dogs began to growl, then to bark in sharp staccato notes. A man's voice inside shouted a curse, and a shutter was thrown open.

"I—I come in peace—I..." Cristina began, only to have a stone flung at her, striking the side of her head.

The dogs growled and whined to be set loose. Another stone. She should have known. No one in his right mind would open a door to a stranger at night. Another stone. She picked up her skirts and took to her heels. Fleeing down the village street, she came out on to the common; one side was a wood, on the other the fields. The road led over a slight rise. She had no choice but to continue. Dry-mouthed, breathing hard, looking neither to the left nor right, she hurried forward. A twig snapped underfoot, and she flinched. She had the notion that if she moved silently, without a sound, the malevolent ghosts who haunted the night would leave her undisturbed. But her feet *would* make noise, rattling loose stones, crunching dead leaves. If she could float like the phantoms she had seen—but no, she must not think of that. She must not think of anything except the way ahead. And hurry! Hurry!

The backs of her legs began to ache, and a hole must have worn in the sole of one shoe, for she could feel the rutted ground beneath. Twice she stumbled into potholes, once twisting her ankle cruelly. Her walk had now slowed to a painful limp. But she could not stop—to stop would be death or worse, for she knew that spirits sometimes entered unwary sleepers' bodies and snatched their souls away. She must walk until daylight. Then she could sit down and rest. But oh—if only she had a drink of water, a small sip to wet her parched lips and ease her dry throat. On and on the road went, on and on, now over a stone bridge, now past a clump of forbidding trees. The wind whispered and skulked in the tall sere grasses, a frog belched, a cricket sang in a muddy ditch. Soon a sickle moon rose, a sliver of yellow against the backdrop of the starred night. It grew colder, and Cristina felt her face and arms going numb. A windmill reared itself out of the darkness, and she could hear the splash of water as its paddles hit the stream. She crossed over to it and knelt at the bank, cupping her hands in the cool water. The drink revived her, though not enough to restore her strength. She wanted to stay there, sink, lie down in the sweet-smelling grasses and sleep. But she dared not; it was still dark. So picking herself up she limped back to the road and turned her face toward the horizon. Was ever a night so long?

After a while, an eternity it seemed, she came upon a cairn of stones topped by a large wooden cross. Beneath it, under a plank and enclosed on three sides by granite slabs, stood a small plaster saint, the red of its painted cheeks washed away by the imprint of beseeching and prayerful lips. Which saint it was Cristina could not even guess, some local one perhaps, but a wayside shrine was a holy place, sanctified even as the great Canterbury and Walsingham. Here she knew she would be safe. Grateful, exhausted, she sank down on her knees and rested her head on the stones.

Just before her eyes closed she suddenly remembered Nareham, not the castle where Aleyn resided but the village Nareham, and Edmund, who was priest there now. Why had she not thought of him earlier? Edmund would help her. Edmund would understand her predicament, he would not condemn her, he would offer shelter, a plan for the future. And Nareham was not far from Connington. Tomorrow she was bound to find a traveler on the road from whom she could obtain directions. Nestling closer under the overhang of the shrine, she fell instantly asleep.

At Nareham Castle, though it was well past midnight, Thomas de Ander, his bastard son, Aleyn, and his nephew, Phillip, still diced with their guest, Sir Richard Scrope. An illustrious visitor, the Duke of Lancaster's own chamberlain, Scrope (the same Scrope so distrusted and disliked by the rebellious peasants) was making the rounds of the various fiefs to raise money and men for the duke's latest plan to regain Castile. Bandy-legged, with a hooked nose and poppyseed eyes which rarely betrayed the keen and perceptive intellect behind them, he had judged almost at once that Nareham would yield him nothing. The manor seemed to be going to decay, the fields looked sickly, the castle smelled of damp rot. Thomas de Ander himself, though far from his dotage, looked little better. He had put on weight, lardy, unbecoming fat; his jowls hung to his collar and his waist had been lost to a paunch. The yellow bags under his eyes spoke of sleepless nights, his reddened nose of excessive drink. He wheezed when he climbed the stairs; not a man likely to go forth and do battle for any cause. Nevertheless Scrope, though his mission here had proved fruitless, decided to make the most of things. At the least he could rest and enjoy himself for a few days.

He liked gambling as well as the next man. Besides, he was winning. They had been throwing dice for the best part of the evening, and now they went on to the game called quek, played on a board checkered in black and white where pebbles were moved at the toss of the dice. Before long Thomas de Ander, weary, and Phillip, bored, dropped out, leaving Aleyn playing against Sir Richard. The chamberlain's luck began to change. No matter how he rolled the dice upon the board, he lost. Aleyn gleefully raked in his winnings, chuckling, muttering to himself. Finally after the sixth or seventh throw, Scrope said, "Wait!" He drew the board toward him and ran his fingers over the squares. A slow dusky flush crept up from his neck, suffusing his face.

"Pardon, sir knight—but I believe this board is defective."

"How so?" Aleyn asked, surprised, rather affronted.

"See for yourself," Sir Scrope said. "All the black squares are lower than the white."

Aleyn took the board and ran his hand over it. "I see nothing amiss."

"Then you have lost your touch." Scrope turned to Thomas de Ander. "Far be it for me to question my host or his family, but examine this board and tell me what you think."

Thomas said, "Sir Richard, you realize what you are implying is an accusation?"

"Aye, and one I would not make without just cause. See for yourself."

Thomas, gripping his wine cup, stared at the board but did not touch it. Finally he turned to Aleyn. "Will you swear on pain of eternal damnation that this board has not been tampered with?"

Aleyn swallowed. It was a terrifying oath his father wanted him to take, and over a board! Rather ridiculous. Yet there he and Sir Richard sat, both watching him. Aleyn did not relish eternal damnation—who would?—yet the truth would be devastating. Could he lie, somehow smooth it over with a falsehood, a half-truth? He must, he had to.

"I bought the board from a peddler in good faith," Aleyn said with a forced easiness, looking his father in the eye. "If 'tis ill made then the scoundrel cheated me."

"Swear," his father commanded.

"I—I swear by God in Heaven." Was he sweating? Did it show? Would God strike him dead? "I am truly sorry, Sir Richard. Of course I am returning your money," he insisted, shoving the coins across the table. "Aye—aye, you must take them, they are yours, not mine."

There were apologies all around, one final goodnight cup. Thomas said, "Phillip, show our guest to his bed."

As Aleyn rose to leave also, his father put a detaining hand on his arm. "A word," he said in a low voice, "after the others have gone."

Aleyn felt sweat gathering in his armpits once more. He sank down on the bench and, lifting the flagon, refilled his wine cup with a hand that was none too steady. Why? Why should his hand shake? Why should he feel so apprehensive? True, his father's tone had not suggested a friendly chat, but he had gone through many a paternal tongue-lashing before without any harm being done. Of late his father had grown a little more cantankerous—the matter of gambling debts—but that was to be expected, given his father's age, no heir and a wife growing hard and brittle. Aleyn knew his father's affection for him had not diminished. Thomas was still proud of his handsome son, bastard or no.

Thomas turned from the doorway, where Scrope and Phillip had disappeared, and came back to his seat. "Pour me some wine," he ordered in a chilly voice. The look on his face did not augur well.

Aleyn tipped the flask, forcing his hand to steadiness as he filled the silver-chased goblet.

Thomas took a long draft. "That board," he said, indicating it with his chin. "I want to speak to you about that board. No peddler cheated you."

"I swore."

"Your swearing means nothing. You could swear on the Holy Sepulcher itself and lie. You are a heathen, just as your mother was, a heathen. But you will get your due in the hereafter, I have no doubt. All liars do."

"Father, I am innocent, believe me."

Aleyn had bought the board thinking it a cunning device by which to recoup his losses. He should never have tried it on an experienced man like Scrope.

"You are far from innocent," his father said, eyeing him with distaste. "You have been a liar and a deceitful churl from the day you were born."

"Father, I..."

"Hold your tongue!" Thomas shouted in a sudden explosion of anger. "Son of a whore! Prevaricator! Knave!" Breathing hard, he mopped his brow with his sleeve. "You will be the death of me yet. How could you shame me so? And before one of the most respected knights of the realm? How could you play your dirty tavern tricks here in my house?"

"Father—pray, believe me—I knew nothing of the board's

defects." He should have thrown it in the fire. Gotten rid of it.

"Liar!" Thomas pulled the flagon closer and spilled more wine into the mazer. "A prince could not have treated his own true-born son the way I have treated you." Thomas gulped at his wine, swallowed and opened his collar. "Your knighting alone cost me a pretty penny. And what do I receive in payment? What gratitude do you show? Whoreson!"

"Father—pray, 'tis over—nothing. I assure you Sir Richard has already forgotten."

"Him? Forgotten? Never! He will take the tale back to London, to the king's court. I will be a laughingstock. God, that I ever acknowledged you! I should have let you go with the bitch, your mother, though now that I recall she did not put up much of a fuss to keep you. I can see why. Ingrate!"

The insults were not new; Aleyn had heard them all before. His father was angry, a little drunk now, but in the morning he would have only a vague recollection of their quarrel; he would act toward Aleyn as if nothing had happened at all.

But Thomas was not as inebriated at Aleyn believed. "My wife," he said after a long sour pause, "is expecting again."

"God praise her!" Aleyn exclaimed, managing to put a hearty cheerfulness he did not feel into his voice.

He had hopes of inheriting Nareham himself, hopes that had been fostered years earlier when his father had adopted him legally, giving him the de Ander name, and in addition had told him that he had made out a will in which he specified that should he die without issue, Aleyn would receive the bulk of his property. It was unusual but not unheard of for a bastard to inherit, and as time passed and Joan de Ander remained barren, he began to imagine himself in his father's chair. After all, his uncle, Robert, had died childless too. But now...

"A boy, God willing," Thomas said. "And if 'tis a girl I shall see that she marries well, that my son-in-law will be a worthy master of Nareham after I am gone."

Aleyn groped for some little remark to politely echo his father's sentiment, but could think of nothing. Still, he did not despair. Far from it. Joan had been pregnant before, many times, and it had come to naught.

"If," his father began, reaching for the flagon, pouring out the last of the wine, "if God does not see fit to bless us now or ever—ah, but I don't like to think of that." He stared glumly into his wine, then, as if suddenly remembering Aleyn, raised his head and fixed him with a bleary eye. "I am changing my will. Tonight was the last straw. Should—God forbid—I leave no heir, then Phillip gets Nareham."

"Phillip?" Aleyn could not conceal his indignation. "And pass me over?"

"Pass *you* over? And who are you to inherit the de Ander manor? You do not even rightfully have our name. There's peasant blood in your veins, while Phillip—now, there is a lad—Phillip comes of noble issue on both sides."

The "peasant blood" hurt. Aleyn was well aware of the Coke family, his mother's half brothers who lived in the village. Charles Coke, in particular, a blond, surly knave, a disgruntled, troublemaking farmer who had sympathized with the rebel peasants in '81, was a thorn in his side. And to be put on the same level with him...it wasn't fair.

"But I am your son," Aleyn insisted.

"You are a bastard." His father belched.

"You did not mind before," Aleyn said bitterly. "And now all because of a quek board, you find me wanting."

"I have found you wanting for a long time, believe me. You are a liar and a cheat—nay, worse, you are soft. You can gamble, you can be a spendthrift, fond of clothes and women—those are the prerogatives of a knight—but to flinch from combat—aye, don't turn away, I heard how you hired someone to take your place at the king's tourney last Easter. The shame of it!"

"You put spies upon me," Aleyn said sullenly. "And they got it all twisted. I was ill, I could not fight and do honor to myself."

"Ill? Ha! You heard that you were to battle with Sir Errenguard, a knight who has a reputation for being skilled as well as savage, and you did your best to get out of meeting him. You should have been a baldpate like your brother Edmund. You are weak and a coward."

Aleyn rose to his feet, fists clenched. "'Tis untrue! Untrue! Such an accusation. You..." He bit the curse back. A knight did not curse his overlord, especially if he was his own father. But he had called him coward. Coward! And yet wasn't there a germ of truth to it? Nay, nay!

"I shall fight Sir Errenguard now or at any time. I am no coward."

Thomas turned his head wearily away. His stomach rumbled, and he belched again. "It grows late. This talk is beginning to tire me."

"I shall go with Sir Richard," Aleyn went on with heat. "I shall offer my services to the duke. And if I die in Spain..."

"Do as you like," his father said, heaving himself up from the bench. "But tomorrow I will name Phillip in place of you."

Aleyn, watching him leave the room, thought, There's always a slip betwixt cup and lip. Joan would lose this one as she had the others, his father would change his mind, or mayhap—mayhap Phillip would die.

Phillip was not told of Thomas's sudden decision to change his will, and if he had been he would have thanked his uncle and thought no more on it. These days his mind was full of only one thing—Cristina. Ever since he had met her in London and she had agreed to go to Connington he had been thinking of her. He tried to imagine how his mother had accepted her, what they said, how Cristina had taken to the other tiring women. A lovely, delicate flower among nettles. He speculated daily as to how soon he could safely visit Connington Castle. He did not want it to seem as if he had placed her there for his own convenience and benefit. Very young, she was a maid who must not be hurried, she had turned away from him, but that was only out of modesty. He must approach her with tact, with kindness, with restraint. He loved everything about her. He loved her hair, the way she smiled, the little cleft in her chin, her sweet, low voice. Never before had he known a girl he could love, a girl he would want to marry. And it was not from lack of encountering eligible damosels, since Cecilia, eager for him to marry well, had introduced him to quite a few.

His mother's standards included noble lineage, comeliness if possible, good health and a substantial dowry. The dowry was most important of all, since Phillip had no land or wealth of his own. Cecilia had found several would-be brides who more or less came up to her expectations, but Phillip would have none of them. She had reminded him time and again that *his* choice had nothing to do with it, that he must obey his mother and that love came afterward. He was glad now he had put her off. Cristina—no other—would be his wife.

Phillip waited another week, feeling as though he were tethered on a short leash, vaguely aware that his Uncle Thomas and cousin Aleyn were not speaking to one another and that Joan, his aunt, lay abed all day. He passed the endless time tilting with the quintain in the courtyard, currying and exercising his horse and playing chess with his squire.

Finally he thought enough time had elapsed. At any rate he had already waited beyond his endurance. He had his squire pack his gear and then he went to bid his uncle farewell.

"I go to Connington, to see my mother."

"I shall miss you. Will you be back soon?" Thomas asked.

The question caught Phillip by surprise. He knew his uncle, though fond of him, did not find his company very diverting, preferring instead to spend his time with more roisterous drinking companions.

"I cannot truthfully say, Uncle, but I shall try." Phillip did not want to mention Cristina. That her mother, Joanna of Thorsby, had been Thomas's mistress was a fact he shut from his mind. What did such an innocent as his love have to do with a parent's sins? He did not believe children came into the world with a stigma as the priests averred, in Cristina's case especially.

"My lady wife is with child," Thomas said, his finger scratching a sign of the cross on the table.

"God give His blessings." Phillip meant it. He himself wanted five sons—with Cristina, of course—and he had always secretly pitied his uncle. Nothing was more of a blow to a man's vanity, to his virility, than an empty nest. "I wish the lady a safe delivery."

"Pray for a boy," Thomas muttered, making the sign again.

"With all my heart."

Phillip set out the following morning. At the last moment Aleyn, disgruntled and in the doldrums, decided to accompany him.

As the two men trotted down through the village to the high road, Phillip, noticing Aleyn's long face, asked, "Why so morose, cousin? Are you still fretting over the quek board?"

"Quek board? I wish to God it were only that. My father has disowned me."

"Oh, come now, it has hardly come to that."

"Just as bad. He is writing a new will and naming you to my place. Oh, yes, he went on and on about it, says he has dizzy bouts, complains of numbness in his left arm, swears he has not long to live and wants to make sure someone with 'a strong shoulder and level head like Phillip' steps into his shoes when he is gone."

Phillip smiled. "Uncle has many, many years yet, I am

sure. Besides, his lady is expecting a child. 'Twill be a son, and after, many more. So who is named in the will makes little difference."

"That is easy for you to say." Aleyn spurred his horse and rode on.

Phillip shrugged. He was accustomed to his cousin's bad temper. Overindulged, Phillip thought, as if his uncle by pandering to his bastard son was paying some sort of penance. And now the indulgent father was losing patience with the prodigal; Aleyn's scrapes were becoming too much for him. Less coddling of the child would have served the parent better. Phillip's own childhood had been far from easy; a half orphan living on charity in his grandfather's house, the lowest seat at high table, a stint as page at Racote, where he slept on straw and was beaten once a week as a matter of course. The beatings, however, were shared by all and inflicted without malice. No harm done. When his mother had remarried, his stepfather, Sir Michael, had taken a great liking to him, had paid for his knighting and had treated him like a son. Through de Leys's connections at King Richard's court, Phillip had recently obtained a position as butler of the pantry, and going up to London to accept it, he had met Cristina. Ah—Cristina! He smiled, his mood softened. Cristina. He had much to be grateful for, despite his landless condition. And now he was riding to pay court to *her,* a lovely girl whose hand he felt sure he would win.

Phillip and Aleyn arrived at Connington late in the day. As always, Cecilia kissed and embraced her son as though he had been away for years fighting a foreign war instead of having spent a few weeks in London and Nareham.

"Well—and have you seen the king?" Cecilia beamed.

"Briefly."

"When do you take office?"

"In the spring. April." He gave the tiring women a quick glance. "By the by, Mother, how did you find the damosel I recommended, Cristina Smithborne?"

She bristled. "Not at all to my liking, not at all. My dear Phillip, she must have fooled you. I am sure you sent her in good faith, but—it pains me to tell you—she was little better than a whore."

Phillip's face turned a fiery red. Had he heard right? Was she speaking of the same girl? He turned again and looked at the women, this time more closely. Not one was familiar, not one the face he had come to see.

"Surely, Mother, you are mistaken. I meant the Damosel Cristina."

"I am not deaf, son, not yet, you need not shout. Cristina Smithborne—aye—'twas she." She lowered her voice. "She took a sinful desire for your stepfather and enticed him to her bed."

Has his mother's wits strayed? Had frequent childbearing, this latest perhaps, muddled her brain? *His* Cristina, a whore? *His* Cristina, enticing his stepfather to her bed?

"Faddle! Why, she's as innocent a maid as ever I have met."

"So! She has bewitched you too. Innocent, indeed! I caught them. I saw them with my own eyes." Her small eyes blazed. "Do you doubt me?"

Certainly. He doubted her eyesight, and her reason, and felt sure she had confused Cristina with someone else.

"Let me speak to her," Phillip said. "I wish to question her myself."

"You are too late. She has gone—like the guilty bitch she is."

"Gone? Where?"

Cecilia shrugged. "No one knows. She took her belongings and sneaked off when we were all at our prayers, crept away like a common criminal. Now, tell me, would an innocent woman behave like that? The baggage! She—"

"When did this happen? How long ago?"

"Son, she is not worth..."

"When?"

"A week—ten days, mayhap. You are making a fuss over nothing."

"Have you any idea where she might be?"

"None." Cecilia did not appreciate this interrogation. She liked her life to run smoothly, without fuss. Curse the girl for causing so much trouble. First with Michael—now with her son. If she had had any inkling that Phillip cared the least bit for the wench she would have refused to accept her. But Cecilia's instincts had betrayed her, first as to Phillip's feelings, then as to Cristina herself. But how could she tell? How could she possibly have known? The girl had seemed so demure, so modest.

"She went alone?" Phillip found this unexpected, calamitous situation difficult to understand. Sir Michael was not one to seduce young girls; never had there been a whisper of scandal connecting him with his mother's ladies. Yet supposing . . . ? Had Cristina . . . ? Could his mother be right? But how? His Cristina, a girl who gazed at the world through artless, childlike eyes, a maid who blushed at the slightest hint of intimacy, could such an angel lure a man to her bed? Unthinkable. More than likely it was the other way around. Michael *must* have seduced, mayhap even forced Cristina to his will. And his mother blamed the girl.

"Where is Sir Michael?" he asked.

"Phillip . . ."

"Never mind, I shall find him myself."

Phillip came upon his stepfather in the courtyard giving instructions to his groom concerning the care of a newly purchased horse, a sleek, leggy stallion.

"Phillip! God's greetings, son. How good to see you." He clapped Phillip on the back. "Is this to be a short visit, or are you planning to stay longer than usual?"

"I haven't decided."

He had always liked his stepfather, but now, observing him, the ruddy face, the gray eyes, the stocky figure, he saw him differently, saw him naked, obscenely straddling his lovely Cristina. And he wanted to hit him, to smash his fist into the bearded jaw, hear the bone crunch, send him reeling, kill him.

"Why are you eyeing me in such a wild manner?" Sir Michael asked, bewildered. "Have I done something?"

Phillip's fist unclenched, then clenched again. "I have something to ask you, stepfather," he finally said in a strangled voice.

"Ask—if there is aught I can do for you, I will. What is it?"

"It concerns the Damosel Cristina."

Michael's smile vanished. Avoiding Phillip's eyes, he stroked the stallion's dark muzzle.

"Is it true . . . ?" Phillip began and faltered. He was afraid of what the answer might be. He did not want to hear that Cristina had thrown herself at his stepfather, nor did he want to hear that Michael had succeeded in debauching her. His virginal love. Christ! Why had he ever sent her to Connington? And yet he had thought it would be the safest place. His dream of marrying her now was shattered. If she had been forced by a stranger, mayhap he would feel differently, but every time he looked at his mother's husband . . .

"Phillip, you are distressed. Did this girl mean much to you?"

"I..." Phillip swallowed, trying to dislodge the painful lump in his throat. "I—I loved her."

"Aheee!" Michael sighed. "What a coil!"

"Why do you say that? What happened?" He grasped Michael by the arm. "Tell me what happened. Did you...?"

"I am ashamed of myself. I do not know what possessed me. I must have been mad."

Not Cristina's fault. Michael's. Should he challenge him? He must; he would never be able to rest easy unless he did. His honor demanded it.

"'Twas as if I were struck with a sudden illness," Michael was saying. "And she so young, so..."

His glove. He could strike his stepfather with his glove, but he did not have one with him. In his earlier anxious confusion he had left the pair somewhere with his squire, in the hall, mayhap. He could spit. But his mouth was too dry. Hit him then, just as he had had the urge to do a minute ago, hit. His stepfather? Aye. Hit. Smash his jaw. Remember Cristina. Hit him!

"...no harm done. A kiss, that was all. Cecilia found us, and I can tell you there was hell to pay, but no harm done, son."

"W—what are you saying?" Michael's words had reached him through a red mist.

"I said no harm was done. I kissed her, not an innocent kiss I will be the first to grant, but thank God it went no further."

Phillip felt as though the air had been squeezed from his lungs. He couldn't breathe, he was stifling, his face afire.

"Stepfather—you did not...?"

"Nay, not I. I told you 'twas a kiss, no more. I did not take her maidenhead. I swear it. I swear by the tears of the Holy Mother Mary. Son, I cannot tell you how that one kiss has troubled me. The poor child—not her fault. And that very evening she disappeared."

"Where? How? Did no one see her go?"

"I myself did not realize she was gone until the following morning. I wanted to apologize—or have someone do it for me, coward that I am. But she had already left. My wife— well, one can understand. Women have their little jealousies, and she did not tell me at once. You can imagine my consternation. Because of me, this unfortunate child had run off. Well, I sent my squire to search for her, discreetly, of course.

He returned in three days, saying that he could find no one who had seen a girl of that description."

"She could have drowned in the moat," Phillip said, his voice choked with anguish.

"Aye, but if so her body would have floated to the surface by now. Phillip, believe me, I deserve to be whipped. Had I known...Can you forgive me?"

Phillip, looking at his earnest face tried. Tried. But could not.

"I am going to find her," he said.

Chapter XXVI

Cristina, awakening at the feet of the enshrined wayside saint, found herself looking into a pair of green-flecked, inquisitive eyes.

Startled, she sat up abruptly. "Who—who are you?"

The eyes instantly became lively. "I may well ask the same of ye," a hoarse feminine voice averred.

Cristina pulled her cloak together. It was morning, a bone-chilling morning with a dismal leaden sky. "I am known as the Damosel Cristina Smithborne."

"A damosel," the woman said. "I guessed as much. And how is it ye are here? Has some accident befallen ye?"

The woman, outlandishly dressed, wore a ragged short cloak trimmed in moth-eaten rabbit fur over men's baggy hose. Her muddied felt slippers had their points cut off, revealing naked, twisted, knobby toes. Of an indeterminate age, anywhere from thirty to fifty, she had the leathery, toughened skin of a person exposed for long periods to every caprice of weather.

"I—I must have fallen asleep," Cristina replied cautiously. The woman was not the kind to inspire confidence. "I was traveling to Nareham."

"Alone?"

No female, even the lowliest whore, traveled alone. "N—nay." The lie came with difficulty, and Cristina would have left it at that, but the woman kept looking at her, as if expecting an explanation. "I—we—that is, my companions and I got caught by the dark before we could reach an inn—and I was separated from them."

The woman made a sound of sympathy in the back of her throat. "A pity. And they—the others—no doubt are looking for ye now?"

Cristina mumbled, "Aye." She could tell the woman found her story dubious. How separated? A damosel on foot? Where is the cart, mule, horse? And so on. But her spur-of-the-moment tale was the best she could do.

"Mayhap I and my family can help you find your friends."

It was then that Cristina, looking past the woman, saw three men dressed in the colorfully patched and belled costumes of jugglers and tumblers. They were standing off to one side, gazing at her with covetous curiosity. Beside them were two mules with large packs strapped to their backs and sides.

"We are a traveling company of entertainers," the woman explained. "I am called Idonia Merrymouth. This"—pointing to a youngish man with a short clipped beard and a squint—"is my husband, Tom, and there"—indicating the other two, one flaxen-haired with boiled gooseberry eyes, the other a lad of about fourteen, fair-haired also—"my two brothers-in-law, Waldus and Hamo."

All three blinked their eyes and went on staring.

"Now," Idonia said briskly, reaching out to help Cristina to her feet, "let's get on our way. I'd offer ye the back of one of the mules, but as ye can see there ain't no room."

"That is quite all right," Cristina assured her. Her body felt numb and bruised, and she was hungry. A chunk of bread would have been welcome. But she was too proud to ask.

"We're aiming in the same direction as ye," Idonia said as the men and mules fell in behind them.

"I am most grateful for your company," Cristina murmured, torn between shame at having been reduced to accepting aid from such a motley crew—entertainers!—and actual gratitude at not having to make the journey alone.

"Thexted is where we go now. Harvest fair. We earn our bread by doing tricks and turns for the crowd." She paused and gave a deep, soulful sigh. "'Tis not an easy life. Ye cannot believe how mean and tight-pursed folk can be. They expect to be amused as their rightful due. But," and she sighed heavily again, "there's always a kind few who'll throw us a penny." She cast a sidelong look at Cristina. "We did poorly at our last place. Not even the kindly few were there. Nothing but idlers and gawking peasants who wouldn't part with a ha'penny if their lives depended on't. This past week we ain't had naught but hard crusts to eat and river water to drink."

The woman and the trio of men plodding behind looked too well fed to give the story credence. Cristina had enough experience with a variety of people at the marketplaces in London not to recognize the familiar prelude—crusts and water—to a more elaborate hard-luck story, a tale calculated to leave one in such a state of pity as to persuade the listener to either buy at a higher price or to drop a few pennies into the wretch's outstretched palm.

"And if that were not all," Idonia went on, "someone stole

our packs from the mules as we slept. And them packs had most of what we owned. No more inns for us. We must sleep in the open, and the nights—have ye noticed how cold the nights are getting? Ah—but how could ye when ye wear such a lovely warm cloak?" She stretched out her hand and fingered Cristina's cloak. "Pretty, and so warm."

Cristina said nothing. She had begun to limp again. In addition to the twisted ankle, she had acquired a blister on her heel, which now burned like fire at every step.

"But a damosel like you would not know of such things, eh? Ye've never been hungry, I trow."

Had she? Had she ever been hungry? She could not remember. Already her past life seemed to have been lived long ago, far away, in another world. Had it been only yesterday, nay, the day before that she had felt secure, content, *decent?*

They plodded on. Every once in a while Idonia would look nervously over her shoulder, not at the men but beyond them as if she were expecting someone to follow. Perhaps Cristina's friends.

Presently Idonia broke the silence. "There's an alestake up ahead where they serve a passable stew. But—alas—we have no money." And when Cristina still said nothing, she added, "If ye, kind damosel, could see yer way to helping us? We would guide ye all the way to Nareham in payment."

Cristina knew the woman and her cohorts were well able to buy themselves a meal, but she was too hungry to argue.

"I have only one noble," she lied. "But I shall be glad to pay."

"Well said, well said!" The woman clapped her on the shoulder. "Husband, brothers!" she called behind. "This fair damosel has offered to treat us to our dinner."

Outside the Swan and Bell the stake and swinging sign were garlanded with ribbons and autumn foliage. Cristina stood blinking in the doorway. A thin square of pale light came in through one unshuttered window, disclosing a narrow, long room, a smoking hearth and two trestle tables. A stout woman bustled forward.

"Madam," she said, addressing Cristina, recognizing her as the superior one, and hence the mistress of the party, although she was hard put to understand why her servants wore jugglers' garments. "God give you good health and good luck!"

"God wish you the same," Cristina replied.

"Ye be welcome. Is it lodgings ye wish?"

"Nay, a meal, for me—and my—my companions."

Companions? The goodwife's eyebrows went up, but Idonia stepped forward and said in an authoritative tone, "What have ye to serve?"

"I have salted cod and herring, pottage, and for special guests, a little dearer but well worth it, a rabbit stew."

Idonia looked at Cristina. "Damosel, I would humbly suggest the rabbit stew."

It was served in a large wooden bowl rimmed with a thick crust of grease, under which floated leeks, garlic, beans, thin strands of thyme plus a few lumps of gray cooked flesh. It had a sour taste, and Cristina, her first pangs of hunger satisfied, lost her appetite when she espied a large dead cockroach clinging to a translucent wedge of onion. The others, however, ate everything, mopping up the oily remains with oaten bread.

A leathern bucket of thin, watery ale had been placed beside the stew bowl, and Idonia and the men dipped their horn cups in frequently. Cristina, without a cup, thirsty, licked her lips, but none offered to let her drink. Finally she asked the alewife if she could spare the use of a ladle.

Finished at last, Idonia's husband, Tom, said, "The mules could do with a bit of feed. Landlady, d'you have hay and oats?"

"Aye, I do. That will cost ye six pence extra."

Tom looked questioningly at Cristina. She did not think she should be expected to pay for the mules also, but not wishing to quibble over six pence, she said, "Include that in my accounting," to the goodwife. At any rate, she thought, we shall be in Nareham by nightfall.

The men went out to attend to the mules. "I could do with another hanape of ale," Idonia said.

The request irritated Cristina, and she ignored it.

Idonia sighed. "Thirsty—the stew was too salty, do ye not think?"

"Nay," Cristina said shortly.

Another heavy sigh. Idonia put her head down on the table and a moment later began to snore softly.

Cristina got up and went to the door. She saw the mules nibbling at hay under the roof of a lean-to shed, but the three men were nowhere in sight. The sun had gone in and a stiff wind had come up, blowing dust and debris and a swirl of brown leaves across the yard. The alestake's sign above the door creaked and groaned. High overhead, gray clouds were

404

rapidly building up into craggy mountains and frowning battlements. Rain, Cristina thought with dismay. And even as she stood there she felt the first drop on her forehead.

She went back inside and sat down at the table, leaning her head against the soot-streaked wall. Idonia slept on. There were no other patrons. The landlady poked at the fire, releasing a puff of smoke. She sneezed and cursed under her breath. A rickety dog wandered in and began to nose amid the floor-strewn rushes for discarded scraps. The landlady, rising from her knees, kicked the dog, and he let out a yelp, slinking under the table. Rain began to patter on the doorsill. The three men sauntered one by one into the room, sitting down on the bench across from Cristina, eyeing her with silent hunger. She glared back at them until they averted their gaze. The air became smokier, darker; Cristina closed her eyes and, listening to the rain, falling heavily now, fell asleep.

Her dreams were a feverish jumble of faces, her father's, Sir Michael's, the lawyer Fynche's, Aleyn's, the Smithbornes', Costanza's, a nightmarish hodgepodge that made no sense. Fynche's face loomed suddenly large, and he thrust his hand down her bosom. She shouted, catching at his wrist, and at the same time her eyes flew open. Idonia was bending over her, and Cristina had hold of her hand.

"My dear," Idonia said, "I was brushing a fly from yer cheek. I meant no harm."

Cristina's mouth tasted of sour stew. "I was having a bad dream," she mumbled.

"We shall have to spend the night here," Idonia said. "The rain has stopped, but 'tis drawing on to evening. The lady of the house has sleeping quarters above. She says she can put us up—three pence for each."

"I had wished to be in Nareham by now," Cristina said.

"We wished the same. Can't be helped. And I did not think ye wanted to spend the night out of doors."

"Nay." She would have to pay for the beds along with everything else. She was being fleeced, but she did not know what to do about it.

The chamber above was reached by way of a ladder, a stuffy windowless room under the eaves furnished with filthy straw pallets. The air stank of urine, stale sweat and rotten straw. A furry gray mold grew on the walls, cracked in places to show the rubbled filling between the wattles.

Idonia and Cristina shared a pallet, the three men another.

The landlady, having lit the way with a stinking tallow candle, disappeared down the stairs leaving them in total darkness. Cristina did not trust the men; the way they had been looking at her boded ill, and she was not too sure she had dreamed the hand reaching down her bosom.

However, Idonia must have divined her thoughts. She said, "Ye needn't fear my boys. They like to look, but they know their places. They won't lay a finger on ye—not on pain of having an arm lopped off."

Nevertheless it took a long while before Cristina was able to fall asleep. Her own tenseness, the little rustlings in the thatch overhead, and the fleas which attacked her with sly, stealthy jabs kept her awake long after the others were snoring. But finally her eyes closed and her mind floated off to dream of Cecilia scolding her for making crooked stitches on an altar cloth. "This way, whore," the lady instructed. "You cannot make a cross straight because you are a sinner. This way, trollop, not that."

She awoke some hours later with a start. The unfamiliar surroundings frightened her for a few moments, until memory and realization returned. She sat up. A few chinks of gray light came in through the breaches in the walls, showing empty pallets and a littered wooden floor. She could hear the clamor of magpies in the roof's thatch. Morning. Had they gone? Deserted her? But no, she heard Idonia's hoarse voice speaking down below. She rubbed her bitten ankles, half listening to the rumble of the men's voices, not paying close attention until Idonia said, "Hush—do ye want to waken her?"

Cristina went rigid.

"We are not taking a chance, I tell ye," Idonia said, so low Cristina had to strain to hear. "If someone were looking for her they would have come this way by now. I tell ye, she has committed some crime, who knows what? Murder, mayhap, and she's running away."

"But she's nobility," protested a voice which Cristina recognized as Tom's.

"Pshaw!" Idonia replied. "Even they have their outcasts."

"I should like to get between the legs of that outcast," Waldus guffawed. "My, my, a virgin—I can smell 'em a league away."

"Ye shan't do anything of the sort," Idonia scolded. "She's worth more to us as a virgin than not."

"How d'ye mean?" Tom asked.

"Why, we shall sell her, a damosel, young, still in possession of her maidenhead. Some rich merchant will pay dear for it."

Cristina felt the blood drain from her face. Instinct had warned her against this quartet of rogues, but she had never dreamed they could be so base, so foul. And she had fallen into their clutches so easily, without a murmur. She was surprised they had not already stripped her of her money and clothes. Perhaps that would come later.

She clenched her fists, pressing them against her breast. Well, she would not play the sacrificial lamb. Sell her like a potion, a sack of grain? Not if she had a breath of life in her. Somehow she would manage to elude them—not at the moment, for there was only one exit from the loft, the ladder. And *they* stood at the bottom of it. But later she would give them the slip, or failing that she would throw herself on the mercy of the most likely traveler at the first opportunity. On the road there were always pilgrims or friars, holy men journeying to some shrine or other. They had passed two the day before. In the meanwhile she would pretend she knew nothing, lulling them into thinking they had a compliant pigeon in their grasp.

Drawing on her cloak, she rose and, squaring her slim shoulders, went down to meet them.

"Damosel!" Idonia exclaimed cheerfully. "You are awake. Did you have a good sleep?"

"A very good sleep." She gave them all, each upturned, inquisitive face with raised brows, a smile, though her knees were shaking.

"With your permission, fair mistress," Idonia said, "we thought to break our fast with a cup of ale."

Cristina did not know whether to agree with enthusiasm or with reluctance, but decided on the latter as the most natural. "I have not much money left, but if you think..."

"'Twill sustain us, dear lady, until we get to Nareham."

So, she had been elevated to lady, and they were still perpetuating the fiction of Nareham.

"Very well, then."

The ale finished, they set out once again, Idonia in the best of spirits, the men behind singing a merry tune: "Tom the tinker and two of his knaves..." The mules, their packs swaying, plodded along.

Presently they overtook a peddler, his wife and two children in a mule-drawn cart clanking with blackened kettles and rusty trivets. Cristina looked at the man's wind-bitten, hard visage and the wife's thin gauntness that spoke of hardship and want. She could not ask them for help, weighed down, as it seemed, with troubles she could only guess at. What concern would they have for her when they scarce had the strength to care for themselves?

On they walked, the men still singing cheerfully, passing a peasant now and again, a shepherd with his flock, a boy leading a cow, but no one who could be of any use to Cristina. At noon Idonia called a halt before the Blind Goose.

"We'll tarry and have a bite here," she announced.

Once inside, Cristina quickly looked over the assemblage, a plowman, a pardoner and a harlot, her upper lip cut away (the punishment for whores who loitered too near a royal residence). In a corner sat a gray-robed priest and his two servants. Cristina watched the priest covertly as she and her companions seated themselves at a trestle and were served a loaf and bucket of the landlady's brew. The cleric, wearing a large wooden cross suspended by a chain around his neck, was an older man, one who seemed to have an intelligent, kindly face. Cristina waited, rehearsing her little speech, and when the priest happened to glance in her direction she rose. Idonia tried to grasp her skirt, but Cristina pulled it away and hurried over to the priest.

"Sir, Father—I beseech you..."

Startled, the cleric looked up.

"I am in dire need of aid." The words came tumbling out. "I am captive to those people yonder. They—they wish to sell me into bondage. If you could hear my story. My name is Cristina Smithborne—damosel—I am the daughter of a good knight now dead—God keep his soul—and having lost my way—they—those thieves offered to escort me to Nareham, where my brother, the vicar of Nareham, Father Edmund..."

Conscious suddenly that the priest was not listening but looking past her, over her shoulder, Cristina turned to find Idonia there, winking knowingly and twisting one pointed finger at her forehead.

"Sir," Idonia said, giving the priest a quick curtsy, "please forgive the intrusion. This girl is my poor demented sister. Ah—she denies it, as always—such is her madness. She imagines herself to be a fair lady, one of the nobility, taken in bondage. You have met several such, I am sure. She is so clever in her madness as to imitate their speech, their manner. But believe me, sir, she means no harm. She is quite docile. Have pity and forgive her."

"'Tis untrue!" Cristina cried. "All untrue!"

"Tsk, tsk." Idonia winked again. "She *will* deny it."

The priest, clearly uncomfortable, removed a small piece of linen cloth from his sleeve, dabbed at his mouth and then mopped his forehead.

"Heed her not, sir," Cristina implored. "For the love of God, do not listen."

The priest crossed himself and moved his lips silently. The mad were often possessed of the devil, and to fool the unwary they appeared sane. As this one did. Sane and dressed in the clothes of a noblewoman.

"My dear child," he said, speaking thickly, "you would do best to mind your sister."

"She is *not* my sister!" Cristina cried, fear, anger, frustration making her voice shrill. "She is a fraud, she has used up my money, promising to take me to—"

"Ask her," Idonia interrupted, "ask her, my good Father, where she came from and why, *why* she left that place."

The priest, grasping his crucifix with both hands, lifted his brows. "Can you answer, my poor afflicted child?"

Cristina could not tell him. She was too ashamed; the words, the explanation spoken aloud, would sound weak if not suspect. Tell him about Sir Michael? She couldn't.

"Aha!" Idonia trumpeted. "There you see, good Father. Come along, sister, 'tis all right. I shan't put you away. Harmless," she assured the priest again. "She does get a little wrought, but harmless."

Tears formed in Cristina's eyes, and she fell to her knees in one last desperate attempt, clutching at the priest's gray robe. But his servant lunged forward and lifted her by the collar, ripping her cloak. "You are not to touch him, he is a holy man."

Cristina wanted to throw herself upon the floor, to beat at the rush-strewn planks with angry fists, shout that she was sane! Sane! But a shred of good sense still clinging to the whirling red anger in her brain warned her that shouting would only confirm her madness even more. The priest had already shrunk from her in horror, his lips moving in a hurried wordless prayer. The landlord and his wife glared at her from the hearth; the plowman, his cup of ale held in midair, stared at her, his mouth agape.

"Take the dummy from here," the alewife commanded. "Take her away at once! Do ye wish to spoil my custom?"

Tom threw four pence upon the table. Idonia grasped a subdued and miserable Cristina's arm and led her outside.

"Ye made a fine exhibition of yerself," Idonia muttered under her breath, pinching Cristina's arm cruelly.

"Let me go, slut!" Cristina ordered.

"Let you go," Idonia mocked. "Aye, and then what? How far would ye get alone—and the way ye look—half mad as 'tis. Look at ye!"

Cristina looked down the length of her cloak, streaked with dust, stuck with odd bits of straw and the hem mud-caked. Her hair had come loose and hung down her back. She had not been able to brush or rebraid it, since both brush and comb had gone into the moat with the rest of her belongings.

"And ye might as well give over the rest of yer money," Idonia advised unpleasantly.

"I shall do nothing of the sort." They were walking again, with the men and mules behind. The road had been worn into ridges and ruts by the passage of heavy wheeled carts, and Cristina, in her indignation, not looking ahead, stumbled and nearly fell. One of the men snickered. Idonia said, "Clumsy!"

Cristina thought: Let them laugh. They haven't got the better of me. Not yet.

"If ye do not give me the money," Idonia went on, "then I'll have Tom—or better still, Waldus—take it from ye. And I warn ye, if he does, it shan't be pleasant. He'd enjoy sticking his hand down for a feel o' yer tits. Believe me—if not more. 'Tis Cristina that keeps the men in line."

Cristina's face flamed. If she had had a knife in her hand she would have killed the woman. She reached inside her bodice and took out her small leather pouch, and threw it as far as she could into the ditch. Idonia ran after it, screaming, "The money!" and the men followed her.

Cristina turned and, picking up her skirts, ran, leaping the ditch, crashing through a stand of oaks, racing under them across a carpet of dried, crackling leaves. There was no path, but the underbush grew sparsely beneath the tall, intertwined trees, and she ran unimpeded, her milling mind urging her to go fast, faster, *faster*, to put as much distance as she could between herself and the others. She heard them shouting behind her, and she spurted forward, dodging a low branch, her breath soon coming in ragged gasps, the blood whistling in her ears. A startled bird flew up, squawking harshly as she sped on, a squirrel scampered up a tree trunk.

She streaked past a clearing where thorny vines and great scarlet flowers like saucers of blood grew, past a rotting stump, a patch of waving ferns. She heard the snap of trod-upon twigs behind her, the shout, "Stop!" and she ran faster, sobbing, stumbling over a root, her feet squishing through a damp boggy place, on and on until a rough hand grabbed her shoulder and whirled her around.

Her knees buckled and she went down. It was Waldus, he of the boiled gooseberry eyes. He was upon her before she could lift herself, pinning her arms to the ground above her head with one hand and with the other tearing at her skirts. She kicked, she twisted, and he let go, giving her a cuff that jarred every tooth in her head. Then he was pulling at her gown again, splaying her thighs apart with a knee. She screamed and a moment later felt Waldus's weight lifted from her.

"Ye fool!" Idonia shrilled. "Ye idiot! Ruin her and ye do us all out o' a good price."

"Don't see why I can't have a bit o' fun." He pouted.

"Ye can't see beyond yer nose." She reached down and dragged Cristina to her feet. "See what a bloody mess you've made o' her face. Pretty—and now look! Dummy!"

Cristina touched her throbbing jaw, already swollen to the size of a goose egg.

"And ye, ye skinny wench," Idonia said. "If ye try that again I'll let him have ye. 'Tain't worth the trouble chasing after ye. More, I don't want ye speaking to anyone—*anyone,* d'ye hear? First time ye get close to a parson or whatever I'll have ye bound hand and foot, put in a sack and strapped to one of the mules. Now, come along, like a good girl, d'ye hear?"

Cristina said nothing. She was trying desperately not to cry.

Tom and Hamo were standing on the road holding to the mules, which were grazing on the verge. Tom said, "Give her a good wallop for me—bitch!" And he spat.

"Let's not stay here and gabble," Idonia said. "Come along, then."

They had been walking for perhaps half an hour when a carriage pulled by four horses, one harnessed behind the other and mounted by a single postilion wielding a short-handled whip of split thongs, forced them from the road. Only the very rich could afford such large conveyances, clumsy four-wheeled wagons whose wooden beams rested directly on axles, the springless bed jouncing its occupants unmercifully. But the discomfort was made up by extravagant embellishments of the wagon itself; gilt beams, carved wheel spokes, a gaily painted top bearing the noble blazon of its owner. A glimpse inside past looped silken curtains showed a lady reclining on yellow and indigo velvet pillows. On either side and behind the wagon a guard rode on a crimson-caparisoned horse. Cristina, watching the small cavalcade rattle past, felt a stab of envy. She imagined the woman riding within had not a care in the world, nothing to think of but her destination, some castle mayhap up ahead where she would be received with ceremonial grace, offered a bath, fresh clothes and a seat at the high table, where she would dine on tasty delicacies. While she, Cristina, limped along the dusty road, captive to cutthroats.

Still, it could be worse. They might have bound, gagged and trussed her in a sack, as Idonia had threatened to do earlier, or robbed and killed her at the outset. As it was now she had her limbs free and could walk and breathe, and while she had that she had hope. There would be a way to escape, and God willing it would come soon.

Presently the road became more crowded. Apparently they were approaching a town, which one Cristina did not know, but she felt sure it was not Thexted nor any place close to Nareham. They would not risk bringing her to a district where she might be recognized or known. A bishop riding in a horse litter, a corpulent churchman, his crest embroidered in gold thread on purple curtains, rode past them. Idonia grasped Cristina's arm again. "Keep yer lip tight," she advised in an undertone.

A train of pack ponies clip-clopping slowly caught up with them, their backs loaded with huge bales of wool. A man walked at the head of the train whistling between his teeth, hugging a whip under one arm. He gave them all a hearty good day, his eyes sliding along to rest on Cristina. She stopped, tried to speak, but Idonia shoved her forward, muttering a curse.

By late afternoon they reached the walls of the town. Meading, a crudely painted sign said; not Thexted but a strange place, just as Cristina had earlier surmised. A bailiff stood at the gate, collecting a penny per cart and a farthing for every horse or mule. Idonia paid grudgingly as they filed through. The Poultry Fair was to be held on the morrow, and

Idonia led them to the fair site, a large grassy square in the center of town.

"We'll stay here the night and be early," Idonia explained to the men, who grumbled about not going to an inn. Since Idonia now had Cristina's purse she had returned to her tight-fisted habits. "Ye're getting soft. A snooze on the ground won't kill ye. And mayhap in this way we can dodge the fee."

But no sooner had they unloaded the mules than a little bandy-legged man with a large belly and a pockmarked face came to collect his four pence, a sum charged to all stall holders and entertainers. Idonia parted with the coins as if they had been the fingers of her right hand.

For supper they shared a loaf, two, three days old, hard, beginning to grow mold, spread with dabs of rancid lard and washed down with a weak watery ale. Idonia and Cristina slept on a thin blanket with no covering but their cloaks, and Cristina was kept awake long into the night by the bitter cold. In the morning she awoke to find her hair rimed with frost.

Before the sun rose over the town wall, the farmers from the surrounding countryside began to arrive; carts piled high with produce, barrows trundling pigs, mules carrying faggots and cut rushes, young girls driving geese, oldsters clutching the legs of squawking hens, goodwives laden with baskets of eels and herrings. They poured into the square with a clatter of wheels and the gabble of fowl, their voices ringing out in the morning air. The four-legged beasts tethered and fed, the various sellers threw up their tents and stalls and began to set out their wares. Yellow onions, green leeks, bunches of purple garlic and tender parsley, pale cabbages, early rosy-cheeked apples and late blushing pears piled in pyramids for all to admire and buy. Hens, cocks, geese, ducks clamored and fluttered amid a snowy shower of feathers. Ells of cloth, hersey, burel, worsted motley, scarlet; gloves, hose, caps, pins and needles, boots, cradlebows, purses, paper, beads of ala-baster, statues of saints and spices—ah, the spices watched and guarded like gold—were displayed and hawked by their vendors. Soon the savory smell of meat pies and sausages and hot gingerbread mingled with the homely farm odors of ma-nure and hay.

Tom Merrymouth and his brothers squared off their al-lotted space with a rope, spreading the ground with blankets, erecting a platform at one end. Idonia supervised, giving instructions in her loud, raucous voice, meanwhile keeping an eye on Cristina.

A trumpet blast signaled the opening of the fair. The mayor of Meading, a heavy-jowled bald man wearing a velvet robe looped with gold chains, was helped onto a mounting block, where he stood for a few minutes with a raised hand waiting for silence.

"Welcome to Meading's Poultry Fair! I beg of you all to remember you are guests of our beautiful city and behave as such. Honor the peace, keep holy the Sabbath and abide by the rules."

He went on to enumerate them, calling for honest representation, just bargaining and true weights. He warned against counterfeit coins, foysters (pickpockets), shavers (filchers of cloaks, swords, spoons, mugs and such) and horse thieves. The piepowder court would be set up to the side of the spice booth, he said, where complaints could be heard and judgment rendered on the same day.

The crowd began to get restive. They had heard it all before, since "law merchant" was customary law carried from fair to fair. They wanted to get on with their business and the fun, which was as much a part of the Poultry Fair as trading. "God bless this day!" the mayor exclaimed in conclusion against a rising babble of voices.

While the mayor spoke, Cristina for one flaring moment thought she might make another run for it, disappearing into the crowd. But Idonia, fooled once, was sticking close to her elbow, and there was not one face among those she saw that looked sympathetic enough to come to her aid.

The Poultry Fair was not much different from the market at Chepe except here there seemed to be a plethora of sideshow attractions, shambling bears on chains, bulls and dogs for bull baiting, strong men with their greased pigs tucked under their arms, gypsy women with rackety tambourines, pardoners with false relics, mummers with grotesque masks, not to speak of the quacks and drug sellers, the minstrels, tumblers, preaching friars and beggars.

"Come one, come all!" Idonia shouted. Wearing a colorful hat, its horned peaks stiffened with straw and tinkling with bells, she stood on the platform of their roped-off section. "See the men twist themselves into shapes ye never thought possible for the human body. See them tumble and twirl! Here—here—here!"

Tom stood by juggling three wooden platters and a crimson

ball. A pair of children stopped and gawked, an old man with a thorn stick paused, a woman carrying a babe on her hip stepped across from another booth.

"Here—here—here!" Idonia called, thumping now on a small tabor.

Tom's platters spun faster and faster. Waldus and Hamo began to tumble and leap, cavorting and jumping through hoops. A peasant in scruffed boots and a leather jerkin joined the other onlookers, and presently, slowly, the crowd began to grow. Waldus jumped onto Hamo's shoulders, then Tom, still juggling, stepped carefully onto Hamo's upturned palms, and from there Waldus hoisted him on his own shoulders, Tom never missing, never dropping a plate. The crowd laughed, applauded, and a few pennies were tossed into the large round red cloth laid out for that purpose.

"Come closer! Good folk, closer!" Idonia begged. "There, there, a little closer. Hark—I have something here will astound ye. A powder given to me by a lady who has made four"—she held up her fingers—"four pilgrimages to Compestella, who has drunk of the waters at Walsingham and Canterbury. The lady, good people, wishes the poor and rich alike to benefit from her infusion. The powder must be steeped in cow's milk, then taken with a sip of ale. If ye do this for seven days straight, I promise you all your maladies will disappear. *All*, no matter what. Ye have worms? Over there, am I right? Worms the powder will kill. Have ye tight bowels, loose ones, stomachache, headache, spots before the eyes? The powder will cure you. Never, good people, will ye be able to buy for so little—three pence for a packet—a better nostrum. Ah—this goodwife wants to know if 'twill cure barrenness. My dear—of course, of course! I had a woman in Devises, married to a strong, virile man for fifteen years, no children, not ever had she come in pod. One dose of my powder and she conceived the very next moon. Aye, she is the proud mother of five, five *boys*. Now give ear..."

The three Merrymouth men had long ceased their tumbling and juggling. Cristina saw them in the crowd, as if jostling and elbowing for position. Their actions puzzled her, for surely they must have heard and seen Idonia go through her paces many times before. Watching Tom, she caught a tiny glimmer of steel in his hand, then observed him stuff something inside his jerkin. It happened so fast she thought at first she had imagined the glimmer until Tom moved on and the same little flashing glint caught her eyes. She drew in her breath. Aye—aye, he was cutting purses! And the two others? She craned her neck. There were Waldus and Hamo, and though she could not see them too clearly, she had no doubt they were doing the same thing. Cristina realized that she now might have a way of freeing herself from the Merrymouths. But she must do it cleverly. Mayhap she could inform the mayor's deputy, the market overseer or the constable, but she saw no one who looked like an official. Still...She got to her feet, ready to shout a warning, when the same peasant who had been among the first to stop and watch the tumblers suddenly yelled, "Thief! I got yer! Hand in my pocket, eh?"

And he sent Tom reeling with a cracking blow to the jaw. The hue and cry went up, other men discovered their pockets picked or their purses gone. Waldus and Hamo, trying to slink away, were tripped up and held. Strong hands grabbed Idonia and tumbled her, fighting like one possessed, from her perch. The constable came running.

"What's this? What's happened here?"

A jumble of voices all tried to explain at once as the thieves were hustled forward. The old man with the thorn stick grasped Cristina by the collar. "Here's another—she's one of 'em too."

"Nay!" Cristina protested, trying to wriggle free. "They—those cutpurses have abducted me. I have nothing to do with them. Nothing!"

But her objections were lost in a surge of angry voices. The crowd, swindled and robbed, was in no mood to listen.

"I swear it! I am innocent!" Cristina cried.

A fat woman shook her fist. "Thass what they all say!"

No piepowder court for these, the constable assured the mob. Gaol for all of them. Gaol, where they would await sentence, a quick justice. Thieves in most places were punished by hanging.

Chapter XXVII

At Connington, Sir Michael had begged Phillip to have a meal, a sip of wine at the least, before he started out, offering his own men-at-arms to aid in the search. But Phillip, unable to bear a delay or to receive any aid from Sir Michael, declined. He ordered his horse saddled and together with his squire, Adam, galloped out under the portcullis, through the same gateway he had entered only an hour earlier.

A mile from the castle he came to a fork in the road and drew rein. Which way to go? Left? Right? Could Cristina have returned to London, taken that long road on foot? She had no friends in the city except Dame Brandone, so old and senile now she would have offered a poor refuge. Nareham to him seemed more logical. Cristina had spoken once or twice of Edmund, the vicar half brother, in fond terms, and it seemed to Phillip that the girl in her distress might have turned to him. Or Aleyn. The thing that troubled him about Nareham, however, was that he had just come from the castle and had not seen nor heard of a young girl's arrival. Still, if she had gone to the village, he might have missed her.

That she could have fallen prey to brigands, highwaymen or some unscrupulous band of vagabonds he would not allow himself to think.

He arrived at Nareham in good time before dusk to the dolorous resonance of the chapel bell. His heart congealed as he cantered into the manor-house courtyard; the mournful, slow clang-clang-clang meant a death had occurred, and his mind, which had dealt solely on Cristina during his hasty ride, immediately jumped to the conclusion that it was she for whom the bell tolled. Dismounting, giving his reins to a solemn-faced groom, he was afraid to ask, "Who?" In his perturbed state he had forgotten that Cristina was all but unknown at Nareham, and he fancied that if he did not ask, the dreaded answer which would make everything so irrevocably final would be forestalled.

In the hall, Thomas de Ander, sitting at the high table alone, his head bowed over a cup of wine, did not notice Phillip's arrival. Drunk, Phillip thought with a spurt of resentful anger.

"Uncle!"

Thomas lifted his head, and Phillip saw that his eyes had tears in them.

"Ah—nephew, she is dead."

Phillip said, "She...?"

"Joan, Joan and the unborn babe."

A shameful surge of relief washed over Phillip, but he managed to keep it from his voice. "The lady—but how?" It had been foolish of him to think, even remotely, that it had been Cristina.

"A miscarriage, and the midwife could not stop the bleeding."

"May God absolve her soul," Phillip said, crossing himself. "She seemed all right when I left. When did it happen?"

"Barely three hours ago."

"So quick. I shall miss her, Uncle. A good woman, she is surely with God now."

"Aye, she is in paradise, no doubt of that. But what of me? Without a wife, no child, no heir." His voice and face, so full of self-pity, reminded Phillip of Aleyn. How alike the two were, father and son.

"In time..." Phillip began.

"Ach—I don't want to hear of it."

Phillip watched as Thomas drained his cup. After a long silence, he said, "Uncle, I am truly sorry about your loss, and I don't wish to intrude on your grief with my own troubles, but I am looking for a damosel who has disappeared from Connington. Cristina Smithborne." He hesitated. "She is Aleyn's half sister."

"Half...?"

"Cristina Smithborne," he repeated. "Joanna Coke's daughter."

"Cristina...aye, aye. I have heard of her from Aleyn. Joanna's spawn. Joanna the witch they called her in Shurbridge village. It was she who put this curse on me, everything turning to ashes. Witch! Damn her!"

"Uncle, I am inquiring about Cristina. Have you seen her?"

"Here, at Nareham? Nay, I thought she was at your mother's castle."

"She was, but no longer. There—there was some disagreement, and she ran away. A foolish thing to do, but she is so young."

"How young?" Thomas asked with sudden red-eyed interest.

Phillip's stomach knotted sickly. The old roué, the lecher, and his wife not even in the grave. "Fifteen, I believe. Thomas, you are not thinking of another wife so soon?"

"Nay, nay. 'Twould be unseemly." He shook his head sadly. "Marriage will have to wait. But in the meanwhile...I do not like a cold bed, nephew. I am not used to it. Now, if this girl—this Cristina—Smithborne, was it?"

Phillip clenched his fists and said through his teeth, "Cristina may be half peasant and dowerless, but she is a pure girl who would kill herself before she became any man's leman."

"Oh ho ho!" He wagged his finger drunkenly. "So that is the way the wind blows. Cristina, Cristina, Cristina. You want her for yourself."

"I want to marry her," Phillip said, drawing himself up.

"Has she a portion? Never mind—never mind her inferior lineage, but if she—she brings nothing..." He paused to belch. "If she brings nothing to the marriage your mother will never approve."

"We shall see. But first I must find her."

"And leave before your aunt has been properly buried? I think not." He lifted his cup and, fixing Phillip with a dismal eye, added, "I have sent for Aleyn."

"Aleyn? I thought that you were no longer speaking to him."

"What has that to do with it? He should be present at my wife's funeral. That in no wise means that I have changed toward him. You, Phillip, are my heir now." A large tear slowly rolled down his cheek.

"Come now, Uncle, you are not old yet. You will marry after you have properly mourned. There are many heiresses who would be glad to have you."

"You think so?"

"I am sure of it. When is my lady aunt's funeral?"

"Tomorrow morning. They are laying her out now."

"Then I shall have time to go into the village. I want to consult with the priest, Father Edmund."

"Another one of her bastards," Thomas said with a wry twist of his lips. "I should have married one like that—witch though she was, at least she bred sons."

Edmund was reading by the light of a flickering wick set in a dish of grease. Books were rare, and this one, Richard Rolle's English translation of the Psalter, had been lent to him by the abbot, who still remained his dearest friend. The

419

book's beautifully illuminated text absorbed him so completely that when he heard the knock on his door, he jumped.

He answered it himself. "Sir Phillip! This is a pleasant surprise." They had met several times at castle festivals and had spoken, though briefly.

"May I come in?"

"Of course, enter, enter."

"You are alone?" he asked, looking around.

"Except for old Betsy, who's tucked herself in."

Sir Theobold had finally gone to his reward the previous spring, and Edmund now lived alone with his ancient housekeeper, who by her own reckoning was past eighty. Still nimble and spry, she was a thin old woman above reproach, in contrast to the various youngish, buxom females who had shared the parson's house in the past.

"I thought the Damosel Cristina might be here," Phillip said.

"Cristina?" Edmund asked in surprise. "Here? I have heard she was with your mother at Connington Castle. I have not seen Cristina since—well, since our mother died years ago."

"And you have heard naught—lately, I mean—a message, word?"

"Nay. Sit you, Sir Phillip, you look distraught. What is it? Tell me."

"I am in love with her, Father. You see..." And he began to tell Edmund the entire story, how he had met Cristina, how careful he had been not to press his suit, how he had found a position for her among his mother's ladies and what had happened at Connington.

"She ran away," he concluded in despair. "And I had thought she might have come to you. But it seems she has not. As soon as Joan de Ander has been buried I shall set out at once for London."

"Why the haste? Cristina, if I remember, is a sensible girl. She would not have left Connington without some plan. She is probably resting now with a friend or a relative of her father's. Calm yourself. Be patient. Wait. You might hear from her yet."

"I shan't hear from her. I cannot wait. I cannot stay here. I don't want to lose her, I must do something, *something*. You do not understand, Father—how could you? A priest who has never been in love."

Edmund's face went stiff. *Never in love.* God, if that were only true! Had it been only a month ago that he had struggled with his weak flesh, had fasted, prayed, had begged God to forgive his lapse, even if it had only been in thought? But then he had felt more than a physical desire for the girl, more than a wish to bed her. He had loved her; he wanted to protect, to cherish, to make her happy.

"If you could only know what Cristina means to me," Phillip was saying. "She has become my whole life, everything else..."

My whole life...everything else... Each syllable rang with his own anguish. He remembered the first time he had become aware of the girl—Gena Melker—one of the innumerable Melker tribe, a cousin of sorts on his father's side. When he had first arrived in Nareham he had visited every cot in the village, and while tactfully putting in a good word for the ailing and still popular Sir Theobold, he had also taken pains to make his own person known. He told the parishioners that he was there not only to perform the duties of a priest but to help them in any way he could. He was Nareham born, one of them, and though he had left the village when still a child, he felt as if he had come home. All the same, the peasants regarded him as a stranger, an outsider, and far too young for a priest. Nevertheless, it was not long before they took a grudging liking to him. His cheerful manner, his willingness to listen, his quick response to a call from the ill, his ability to comfort the bereaved, his celibate life, his devotion to prayer, all earned him their respect and affection. Gena's had been one face in many until she came to him one early weekday morning, begging him to hear her confession. She had a low whispery voice, and he had to strain to hear her words, the usual little sins of pride, of vanity, of disobedience. He had heard them all before and was wondering how he could cut her short so that he might prepare for morning Mass when he suddenly became aware that she was weeping.

"What is it, my child?"

"I—I don't want to marry him."

"Who? Who must you marry?"

"Charles Coke. My father says I must—and my mother agrees. He has asked for me, but—oh, Father Edmund, can you not think of some excuse to prevent this marriage? Mayhap if you consulted your kin book you would find us related."

Everyone in the village was related in some tenuous way or another. Charles Coke was Edmund's half uncle, Ivo's eldest son by Katrine. The kinship rules had to be applied loosely, Edmund realized, for people in Nareham did not like to marry outside the village and were particularly loath to see their daughters go elsewhere with their dowries, no matter how meager a portion they had. However, Gena's concern was clearly not her kinship with Charles Coke.

"What have you against the young man in question? I have seen him here in church and he appears to be a decent fellow, clean, not bad-looking."

"He has a temper, an ill temper, and..." She lowered her voice to a whisper. "He says terrible things against Thomas de Ander and those at the castle."

"What terrible things?"

"He says that everyone has the right to call himself a freeman, that every Englishman should be allowed to sell his labor in the open market and to work where he likes. Oh—and to share in the timber and game of the wood, which, as you know, have always been the lord's."

Exactly, Edmund thought, what Wat Tyler had preached at the insurrection which had been so bloodily put down.

Edmund came out from behind the leather curtain. "My child, I must prepare for Mass now, but if you can come to me later we shall talk more about this." He certainly would have to speak to Charles, warn him that such ideas bandied about would get him into serious trouble.

"Can I hope then?" she asked, lifting a tear-stained face to him.

The face, not beautiful but delicately formed, was framed by hair of such lightness as to seem like a halo. She had full lips (nothing saintly about that mouth), thin nostrils and gray eyes. But she had something more, much more, something he could not define, something he was drawn to, something he wanted to touch, to embrace. And it shook him. He had thought himself luckier than his fellow seminarians, they who had to fast, wear hairshirts, practice flagellation to free themselves from the desires of the flesh. Not he. But now...For one long moment his eyes held hers, a naked mutual coming together, as if he and she had been lovers who had known one another intimately, a man and woman who had shared a vital, enduring passion in a different time, another place.

Edmund tore his gaze away. "Later," he muttered and hurried to the altar behind the screen.

He went through the rite in a numb trance, waking at odd moments to castigate himself for sinking into such a state of indifference to the ceremony that had always given him a feeling of renewal. Women are snares of the devil, his mind mocked. Beware! *Jesus labentes respice.* No, no, that was a hymn—oh, God forgive me...

Somehow he managed to stumble through the final amen. Then quickly, before anyone could detain him, he left, walking through the passageway to the little two-room house which made up his dwelling place, closing the door, thinking, I cannot see her. I cannot. I shall send someone else. But who? He had no assistant, not even a deacon—and besides, he had promised to consult the kin book and meet with her again.

Phillip was still talking, and Edmund forced himself to listen, but soon his mind slipped away, remembering.

It was the next morning, he recollected, when a knock on the door sent his heart racing like a schoolboy's. "See who it is," he called to Betsy, who was busy in the kitchen kneading bread for the day.

Grumbling, she went to the door. "'Tis Gena Melker, Father," she said, returning a moment later. "She says you asked her to come."

What could he do? He got the large, iron-hasped kin book down from its shelf and was turning the yellow, cracked parchment pages when she came in, shyly, hopefully, giving him a gaze of such faith and trust as to make his heart shrivel.

Coke, Coke, Coke—his finger went down the page. Melker, Melker, Melker. Fourth cousins. He could, of course, ban the marriage; there was the ancient rule of marriages forbidden to the fifth degree. But it had long fallen out of custom.

"Surely a bad temper is hardly a reason for not wanting to marry this man," Edmund said, trying to make his voice stern. "And his bold ideas and thoughts on his place in the world need have nothing to do with you, his wife. What have you against Charles Coke?"

"I do not love him," she said simply.

"Love, my child—we can love only God." The familiar words, so often uttered with heartfelt sincerity, now sounded sterile and empty.

"I do love God," she assured him. "But 'tis not the same."

Not the same. Of course, *that* was carnal love, love of the flesh. *He* could have spent his life just looking at her, hearing her sweet voice, he could—but why fool himself, he wanted her too. And in a matter of moments a lifetime of ecclesiastic discipline, of study, of dedication, stood tottering on the brink. Where God had been, Gena now existed, filling every crevice of his soul with her presence, a longing, a need, a love. Should he let her go? To take her as a mistress was unthinkable— a disgrace. But there was a way. He could renounce his vows, disappear, go to Ireland, the Netherlands, and there make her his wife. Should he forbid her marriage to Charles Coke? It was in his power.

"Let me think on it," he said.

The next day he spoke to Charles, a conversation that was difficult, not because Charles was his half uncle and four years his senior, but because of the disturbed state of his mind. They touched on many topics, the weather, the crops, livestock, Charles's ideas as to peasant rights (a warning here from Edmund, and Charles's fair sunburned brows came together), and finally, almost delicately, Edmund got around to Gena.

"All maidens are reluctant to be bedded," Charles assured the priest. "She is modest, a virtue I respect, but once she is broken she will tame down nicely."

And into Edmund's turbulent thoughts there came a picture of the naked Gena and this loutish fellow, his desire swollen, mounting her, tearing at her like a beast in rut. He seemed to hear the sound of Charles's panting, Gena's sobs, her weeping, and for a moment he was filled with such blind rage he wanted to kill the man.

"You are cousins," Edmund said in a tightly controlled voice.

Charles looked surprised. "Are we? Much removed, I would say." He paused. "Surely you are not going to forbid this marriage?"

Edmund thought: I could, I can forbid it. I can abjure the priesthood and take this lovely, pure girl to wife. I can live with her in love for all of my days.

And for the first time he had a true glimpse of the world he had renounced so gladly; a wife, children, a hearth blessed by little ones, the warm conviviality which only comes with tears and laughter closely shared. He understood now, also for the first time, his mother's long concubinage, her clinging to John Hawkwood despite the threat of damnation and hellfire. He understood. She had loved the brigand. Earthly love.

He looked away from Charles, then down at the cross he wore around his neck. It had been given to him by the abbot, a black cross with a beautifully carved silver Christ nailed to it, the sorrowful face, the crown of thorns, the pierced hands, each tiny detail exquisitely wrought. The abbot had been so proud of him! So proud; the servant of God he had fashioned himself. Could he, Edmund, turn his back on the man who had been dearer than a father to him? Could he cause him pain, he who had given him nothing but gentle kindness? And if he broke his vows, could he live with his betrayal? What of Gena and the children that would come— would they not feel the weight of his own sinful burden? But more, he would forswear his joy in the mystical rites which brought him so close to God. Never to celebrate the Eucharist, Communion, to feel himself transformed as he dispensed the Host to his parishioners? He could not imagine it.

He married Charles and Gena, telling himself that it was a ceremony like any other, repeating the nuptial mass, trying to ignore the pain under his ribs. He could scarcely look at Gena; her face so pale under a crown of flowers, her eyes puzzled—*betrayer! Judas!* Afterward he had done something he had always felt was beneath a priest—he got soddenly drunk on sacramental wine.

And now Phillip was repeating, "You don't understand."

Edmund would never tell him, of course; only God and someday the abbot would know, but no one else.

"Sit down, calm yourself," Edmund advised. "'Twill do no good to pace to and fro like a penned beast. Come, have a chair. We shall put our heads together. Have you had anything to eat today? I thought not. Betsy's made an excellent blood pudding. I shall have her warm it."

Phillip protested he wasn't hungry, but nevertheless when the pudding was set before him he devoured it to the last crumb, washing it all down with a large horn cup of ale.

"'Tis possible Cristina did not set out for London," Edmund said. "How was she dressed?"

"No one saw her go, that is the worst of it. Not even the servants. A pox on them all!" He drove his fist into the palm of his hand. "Selfish churls! They think only of themselves."

"She went alone?"

"As far as I can tell."

Now for the first time Edmund began to feel alarmed. Surely even in her anger and shame Cristina would have had enough presence of mind to take someone with her, even if it was only a servant boy. But apparently she had not.

"Suppose," Edmund said, keeping his voice calm, "supposing she set out on the road to Nareham, stopping along the way somewhere, at an inn. Suppose..." He paused, suddenly remembering an incident. It might have had nothing to do with Cristina, but then again, how could he be sure? "I had a visitor yesterday, a priest traveling from Meading to Glastonbury with his two servants. He told me a strange story. He had stopped at an inn, the Blind Goose, I believe he said, and there a fair-haired, mad girl in the company of a troupe of jugglers and tumblers begged him to save her."

"A mad girl—surely you do not think...why, I see no connection."

"Cristina traveled alone. How easy 'twould be for some unscrupulous folk to promise her safe passage, rob her and take her along for God knows what nefarious scheme."

"But it could be a beggar—a lackwit, some poor creature."

"He did say the curious thing about her was that she was dressed as a noblewoman."

"What?" Phillip sprang up.

"Disheveled, her cloak tattered, but not the sort of garment a peasant or a juggler would wear. He wondered at that. The woman who claimed to be her sister said that the girl in her madness insisted on dressing that way."

"Do you think...?"

"'Tis worth a try, Phillip. We have no other clue."

Phillip rose early, before dawn, and went to the chapel, where his Aunt Joan lay in a silk-lined coffin atop a velvet-covered bier. Tall white tapers bent and flickered over the pale marblelike face, the hands folded about a silver crucifix. Two priests were in attendance, chanting the prayers for the dead. Phillip knelt beside them, lowered his head and prayed in his own way for his aunt's soul, begging God to make her time in purgatory short, quickly raising her to paradise. Phillip felt he could do no more than that. Getting to his feet, he left the chapel, gave orders to have his horse saddled and instructed a page to tell his uncle he could not stay for the funeral; urgent business called him away. Thomas would be displeased, but he could not help that. The funeral would take all day, and he could not wait even if God Himself had asked.

He found the Blind Goose without difficulty. The landlady certainly did remember the "mad girl," how could she forget?

"Such a scene, sir, falling on her knees, foaming at the mouth, her eyes staring from her head. And then when the good priest said he could not help her, she rolled all over the floor. Broke a chair and two mugs, and the churls who were with her refused to pay. Good sir, is she related? A servant? The chair was a sound one, cost me two shillings."

"What did the girl look like? Can you describe her?"

"Pretty—blue eyes, fair, blondish hair, cleft chin, slender..."

It was her, Cristina. "I am given to understand she was with a troupe of jugglers. Did they say where they were going?"

"Nay."

"A fair, mayhap?"

"The only fair I know of was the Poultry Fair at Meading."

He was out the door before she could finish. She followed him. "Two shillings for the chair, sir..."

He mounted his horse and flung her several coins.

Arriving in Meading, he learned that the fair had taken place a few days earlier. He began to question the shopkeepers; the mercer, the postelier, the wax chandler, the shoemaker and a smith; did they remember a troupe of jugglers, three men and a woman, and a girl, a "mad" girl?

A nobleman asking questions meant trouble, especially a nobleman they did not know. He could be the king's man, slyly inspecting their premises with this innocent interrogation in order to assess them a new tax. So one and all—though they remembered very well the troupe in question—professed ignorance.

Phillip's squire, Adam, who had more experience with folk of this sort, advised his master to seek out the mayor. But the mayor, a member of the artisan class himself, shared the townspeople's suspicion. Who was this Sir Phillip of Nareham? Why should he want to know about a troupe of jugglers and a mad girl?

"Sir, are you here on the king's business?" he asked bluntly.

The young knight felt the mayor had stepped beyond his authority to question him thus. He said as much. The mayor resented the rebuke, and a shutter came down behind his eyes.

He said, "Sir, so many jugglers and tumblers pass through on fair days, I would be hard put to recollect any of them. They may have been here, they may not have been here. I cannot honestly say. However, there's a big fair at Finchester. A stock fair. You might try that."

Phillip paused only long enough to water the horses and

let each feed on a helm full of oats, while he and his squire refreshed themselves with a tankard of ale. Then they rode out through the city's gates.

The mayor, watching from his window, was glad to see them go. He, the constable and the village council had been debating for two days what to do with their prisoners. Felons were hanged, as a rule. Sometimes if they were cutpurses, as these were, their hands were severed, but all agreed this punishment might be too lenient for such rogues, strangers who had come to fleece the good citizens of Meading. Hanging, then. But what of the women?

"They could be boiled in oil," one elder suggested. "Or kept in prison on bread and water, a little less each day until they died of starvation."

"I hear the French have taken to hanging women," the mayor said. For some inexplicable reason which led back to shadowy antiquity, Meading had been reluctant to hang female criminals. But the mayor had got his information a little twisted. Women had been hanged in Paris and later in London at the time of Henry III, more than a century earlier.

"Ahhhh." The contemplative sigh went around the room.

"'Twould be simpler," the mercer said. "Hang the lot and let their corpses swing from the gibbet until their bones are picked clean. 'Twill be a warning for the next nipper who tries his tricks in Meading."

The mayor looked around at the small assembly, the twelve good men who formed the "leet" court. "Is there any among you will gainsay hanging? What think you all?"

A murmur of assent and a nodding of heads.

"Agreed," the mayor said. "Tomorrow at dawn. You, John, have the town crier spread the word. We shouldn't want to deprive our folk of enjoying the sight of justice done."

Cristina squatted on her heels, supporting her back against the slimy wooden wall. The stench which arose from the filthy matted straw under her feet churned in her stomach and brought the taste of vomit to her lips. She was certain that in one of the murky corners a former prisoner had died and his corpse had been left to disintegrate and decay. There were no windows. A thin ray of light seeping in through a slit in the raftered ceiling revealed four walls, the straw, a slop jar and a few rusting chains. The prison had two stories, the upper chamber, given over to women, where she and

Idonia were the only occupants, and the lower, housing the jailer, the kitchen and the male criminals.

No nightmare, no stretch of Cristina's imagination could equal the horror of the pit she found herself in now. It was hell, a cold, dank hell without satanic flames or the smell of brimstone, but hell nevertheless, and what hope she had managed to sustain all through these past days since her ordeal had begun was gone now, in fact had vanished the moment the nail-studded jail door had slammed behind her.

She hated Idonia, but instinctively knew that if she had been thrust into this blackness alone, she would have gone mad. Another human being, no matter how vile, was better than none.

"They won't hang us, that you can count on," Idonia said cheerfully. She had reviled her jailers in colorful language, using every dirty epithet, every variety of "son of a bitch" and "son of a whore" she could think of, all the way to the jail. She had sworn by her mother's grave that she did not know the men, that she was innocent, that she had no idea they were stealing, that Cristina alone was to blame for forcing the tumblers to cut purses. "They never hang women in Meading."

Cristina was too steeped in misery, too ill, to pay much attention. Hanging, she thought, trying not to breathe the fouled air, would be a blessing.

"Of course, they might drown us," Idonia went on. "That's been done." She got up and began to thump on the walls. "I once was thrown into the dungeon of an abbey—now, that's a frightful place to be—and managed to get out through a stone passageway. It had been blocked by a fall of the roof and no one knew it was there." Her teeth gleamed in a grin. "Never can tell, can ye?" She gave another thump. "Ah, I could do with a drink of ale."

Cristina's dry throat worked. She tried not to think of thirst. Hunger she did not feel, but if she could only have a sip of water, just one sip, to ease her parched mouth. She ought to pray. This might be her last night on earth. But the familiar words of the *Ave* and the *Credo* were jumbled in her mind. She wondered if her jailers would let her see a priest before they put her to death—in whichever way they chose— please God that it would not be too painful. She was not prepared to suffer. Nor, for that matter, despite her misery, was she really prepared to die.

And as she sat there trying to assimilate the appalling fate

which had engulfed her, her thoughts swinging from one
dreadful possibility to another, she suddenly recalled a dark
childhood figure of the London streets—the death crier. He
was an official appointed by the mayor whose duty it was to
make the rounds of the city and publicly announce the death
of prominent citizens. One night, awakened by his ringing
bell, she had crept to the window and peered out. He was
standing in the street shaking the bell with one hand while
the other held a lantern. His dress was enough to frighten
a child even in daylight, a stark black tunic sewn with ma-
cabre white skulls, but at night in the flickering lamplight
with his dark shadow looming ominously and the bleached
death's heads grinning and winking at her, she became terrified, certain he had come to take her away. In a panic she
had fled from the window and wakened her father. He calmed
her, told her not to be afraid, that the crier's function was
merely to call out names. But she had never fully believed
that, and now he was here, in this place, the death crier. She
could not see him, but if she listened hard enough she could
hear the little bell—

"Cristina!"

Idonia's harsh voice jolted her.

"Cristina, are ye attending to what I have to say? Somewhere I recollect hearing townfolk are soft-hearted when it
comes to women in pod. Now, if I were t'say I'm yer mother
and ye be my daughter and expecting—are ye listening, damosel?"

Cristina forced herself to attention.

"All is not lost, I tell ye. There's a way out. Believe me,
I been in worse spots. If ye'll not sit there like a dummy, but
heed me..."

Gradually as Idonia spoke, Cristina's fears dropped away.
Idonia's voice, the positive way she outlined her plan, kindled
a new ray of hope. Perhaps the woman was right. She had
had much experience—a thief's experience—battling with
the law, and she had survived. Was it not logical to think
that she might do so again?

"...ye must sound convincing when ye swear on the cross
that I be yer mother," Idonia was saying. "Never mind the
sin of a lie—ye can repent later, God will forgive ye. Ye are
my daughter, a widow, and ye are three months gone with
child. Ye have no one in the world to support ye or the babe
but me. Can ye remember that?"

"Aye—but do you think..."

"I *know*. Listen, these townfolk are fools. Flatter the mayor, call him 'sir,' a wise man, and the council too. Show meekness and modesty, and weep. Above all, weep as if yer heart were breaking. I'll do the same."

"And what of the others?"

"Let them look out for themselves," she answered shortly.

Idonia kept up her chatter, her instructions to Cristina, for most of the night, and in the morning as first light seeped in from under the door, she woke the girl, rehearsing her once more on how to act, what to say.

They waited through another long day, Idonia's tongue still clattering, her voice growing hoarser and hoarser. She exhorted Cristina to have hope, not to give up, to do exactly as she advised.

"Remember to weep, real tears, 'twon't be hard, I daresay."

Toward dusk the bolt screeched as it was withdrawn and the constable appeared, outlined in the doorway against a pale milky sky, and announced in solemn tones without preamble, "Cristina Smithborne, Idonia Merrymouth—you have been found guilty."

Idonia fell to her knees.

"Kind sir, would ye put a mother to death? Aye—my daughter here is a widow and with child. I am her only kin."

"Hush, you shrew, I have heard that tale before. You are no more kin to this thieving slut than I am. By order of the town council you both have been condemned to die. You will be allowed to confess, then you will be hanged until there is no breath left in you."

"Sir..." Cristina began. "Sir..."

Before Cristina could finish the constable stepped back and slammed the door so hard it shivered the walls.

And Cristina, sinking down beside Idonia, her heart hammering with an unspeakable dread thought: So this is where it all ends. On a gibbet. In a place called Meading.

Chapter XXVIII

Three miles out of Meading, Phillip's horse cast a shoe. Angry, frustrated at the loss of time, he turned back to the town, reaching it just before the gates jolted shut for the night. The blacksmiths were putting up their shutters as Phillip and his squire rode through the darkening streets, and they refused to attend him, since they were forbidden by law to work at night. But Phillip finally found a farrier in a back alley who agreed to replace the shoe for an outrageous fee.

"Hurry is as hurry does," the farrier advised, prodding his apprentice into working the bellows. "Ye'll have to stay the night in any case."

"Aye," Phillip agreed sourly, "but I shall be gone by cock-crow."

"What, and miss the fun? There's to be a hanging at dawn. Five of them. Hey there, blow, you churl! Blow! How d'ye expect me to work without a good fire? Five of them, sir, 'twill be something to see."

"I have more urgent business than to stand idle and watch some poor wretch dangle."

He and his squire put up at an inn. There too the common room was abuzz with talk of the hanging, but Phillip, sitting in his corner, brooding over a mug of inferior wine and a two-penny pie, heard nothing. His mind was busy galloping down the highways and byways. He would visit every town, every village and hamlet, knock on every door, question every inhabitant throughout the length and breadth of England. He had to find her. And God help her captors once he did—he would throttle them with his bare hands.

He slept little that night and rose well before first light to a loft black as pitch and resounding with snores. Hurriedly donning cape and boots, he shook his squire awake, and they both clambered down the ladder, stepping over more sleeping bodies to get to the door. The goodwife dozing at the hearth cocked an eye open.

"Shame!" she called. "Are ye leaving without settling yer bill? And ye of gentle birth. For shame."

Phillip in his haste had forgotten. "What do I owe?"

"Five shillings, two pence."

Phillip's squire said, "Isn't that rather dear?"

"Not at all," the woman replied, holding out her hand. "Ye got the best bed in the house."

The sky had paled to a deep gray by the time Phillip's squire had saddled both horses. The town was already stirring as the two men clattered through the streets; dogs barked, roosters crowed, shutters banged, voices called, and smoke began to rise in the morning mist from the chimneys and windows. They reached the gates just as the sergeant-at-arms descended from his tower chamber yawning in the rosy light. Beyond the walls a babble of voices rose, urging the sergeant to open up—why did he keep them waiting so long?

"A murrain on you," he cursed. "'Tis not a market day."

But they had not come to market, these peasant folk from the hinterland; they too had heard of the hanging and were eager to witness it, arriving at Meading's gates as if to a fête. Phillip, listening to their cries of impatience, felt repugnance. It was one thing to kill in battle, one thing to slaughter one's enemies, but to stand as an onlooker, to see, to enjoy watching men die a painful death, filled him with distaste. God knew he was not a coward, not one of those soft-hearted creatures that shuddered to squash a fly, but he had never been entertained by the suffering of others, even should they justly deserve it, as these thieves or murderers, or whatever, most likely did.

The gates swung inward, and before Phillip and his squire could ride out the crowd surged forward, a press of men, women and children on foot, on muleback, some riding in carts, a mass of shoving people stampeding through, rushing down the narrow street toward the marketplace. Phillip, cursing, used his whip, but to no avail. On they came, not one would be deterred, not one ready to stand aside, even if they had been able to.

Phillip's horse shied, rearing and curvetting, and Phillip, in trying to control him, lost his reins for a moment. The horse, turning with the onrushing mob, began to gallop with the tide toward the town. It had gone some distance before Phillip was able to bring it, frothing and wild-eyed, under control.

"Make way! Make way!" the town crier's voice echoed in the canyon of houses on either side of him. Phillip pulled his horse aside to let the tumbrel bearing the accused thieves to the gallows pass.

* * *

433

The priest who was sent to hear the prisoners' confession was a small, gnarled man in a greasy robe. Plainly he did not relish this duty, but was there only because the bishop felt that such an occasion should be attended with some Christian dignity. Even the most foul of sinners should be allowed to recant at the last moment, should be allowed the grace of God's forgiveness. The priest did not see it so. He thought these wretches deserved hanging, or worse; they had not earned the right to absolution. He himself was of peasant stock. He had seen his family, mother, father, sisters and brothers, robbed daily as a matter of course and had always harbored a burning rancor in his heart for those human wolves who preyed on the weak and the trusting.

The moment the priest appeared, Cristina fell on her knees and once more proclaimed her innocence. But when she looked into the stony face above her and saw no sympathy there, she realized it was useless to beg. He, like the constable, had turned a deaf ear to her plea. Still unprepared to die, she ticked off her sins, little breaches, the largest of which was her brief infatuation with Sir Michael de Leys. She knew the priest was not listening, hardly heard, that his absolution would be automatic, empty, and she tried to speak directly to God. "Forgive me," she whispered. "Oh, God Almighty, forgive me." But the words were meaningless. She had no idea of *what* God should forgive her. Why must she die, and so cruelly? Surely her sins had not merited it? The priest mumbled, *"Benedicite omnia opera Domini Domino,"* making the sign of the cross.

Idonia confessed a few paltry sins, then began affirming her blamelessness of the particular crime for which she had been accused, saying there had been a mistake which she momentarily expected to be rectified. The priest refused to give her absolution—it stuck in his throat, he said, to see a culprit unwilling to show remorse. Idonia, in a rage, spat at him, called him a venal shavepate and the devil's whoremaster. A guard, hearing her screech, entered the room and gave her a clout across the mouth, while the priest beat a hasty retreat.

The four members of the troupe and Cristina were placed on a two-wheeled tumbrel, their hands tied in front of them. Idonia still cursed loudly through a broken, bleeding lip; Waldus, sunk into some kind of stupor, gazed into space with blank eyes; Hamo blubbered and sobbed, the tears streaming down his grimy face. Tom jostled and wriggled, now trying to free himself from his bonds, now trying to throw himself from the cart.

Cristina made an effort to separate herself from the others as they rumbled along, but the five of them crowded the small cart, and she was forced to stand squeezed between the shrieking Idonia and the stupefied Waldus. Head lifted, her eyes fixed on the passing wedge of gray sky above the black silhouetted house gables, she watched as the heavens gradually began to blush pink and gold. Shutters were flung open and epithets, insults and rubbish were hurled down upon their heads. An egg dropped, broke and spattered on Cristina's shoulder. A vessel of slops followed, splashing over Tom. A rotten onion hit Cristina's temple, and her eyes suddenly blazed, a spurt of anger shaking her from her trance.

"Damn you all!" she shouted, raising her fist threateningly. She had no way of knowing that these were the exact words and the precise gesture by which her grandmother, Mariotta, had cursed her enemies years earlier. To her under the circumstances, so unfair, so *wrong,* it seemed the last straw to be so reviled, and anger, the like of which she had never experienced before, a blinding red fury, engulfed her like a sheet of flame.

But rage died quickly as the tumbrel, creaking and jouncing on its springless wheels, lurched into the market square, already filled with onlookers, who cheered at the sight of the hand-bound criminals. So dense was the press the sergeant-at-arms had to force the people back with staves and lances to let the cart through. A crude gibbet had been hastily constructed, and from its arms dangled five nooses. The priest (the same greasy-smocked one), his crucifix raised, the executioner, the mayor, the constable, and the council stood at the foot of the scaffold ladder facing the crowd.

The first rays of the sun gilded the heads and faces of the townfolk and the country peasants dressed in their Sunday best, some holding children aloft on their shoulders to get a better view. There may have been a sprinkling of sober faces or eyes reflecting compassion, but they were few and far between. For the most part the throng exuded an expectant holiday air. They had not seen a hanging for at least two years.

The trumpeteer blew a high shrill note. The tumbrel, brought to a halt, was tipped forward and the prisoners prodded out. Tom and Idonia put up a fight and were struck with clubs for their trouble—not too hard, however, as the ceremony would be marred if the prisoners had to be carried instead of mounting the scaffold on their own.

"Go to your death like a man," the sergeant urged Tom.

"And ye can go to hell!" Tom spat and was given another blow.

The executioner, having received God's forgiveness from the priest, was the first up the ladder. A tall man wearing a black jerkin, he seemed to loom like a giant against the blood-tinted sky. The crowd looking up at him turned from jeering the prisoners to jeering the hangman, flinging lewd, bawdy insults at him while he squared his shoulders and pretended not to hear.

The priest addressed Tom. "My son, do you fully forgive judges and hangman?" It was a question asked of all facing execution.

"A pox on ye!"

Still objecting, he was pushed up the rungs of the ladder, the sergeant threatening to run him through and hack off his legs if he did not hurry. Tom, his mouth full of bloody teeth, managed to crawl up to totter beside the hangman. Next came Hamo, sobbing and pleading.

"Be of good heart!" a peasant shouted. "Ye'll be with the angels soon, lad."

Waldus, ignoring the priest, mounted after Hamo, moving like a sleepwalker, his face devoid of expression. Some in the crowd, seeing his blank eyes, crossed themselves, sure that he had fallen under the spell of the evil eye. When it came to Idonia's turn, she, like Tom, fought savagely, fending off the blows raised on her with some success, until one crashing across her head stunned her into insensibility. She would have fallen, but the sergeant held her up.

"You fool, look what you've done!" the sergeant exclaimed to the man who had been overzealous. "Get some water, ale, anything. We must revive her."

A bucket of wash water was passed through the crowd and dumped on Idonia's head. She came to sputtering, cursing, and before she could fully regain her wits was hurried up the ladder.

Now it was Cristina's turn. She did not want to make that climb any more than the others. But she found it impossible to put up an ignominious fight as Idonia and Tom had done, to shriek and struggle like a chicken dragged to the chopping block. She was a knight's daughter.

So holding her chin high, her hands clasped behind her,

still wearing her torn and dirty cloak, her hair matted with straw and sweat, she slowly began her ascent. She tried to empty her mind, tried not to notice, tried to pretend the sun-flooded sky, the outline of church tower beyond the square, the tile-roofed houses, the trees on the rim of the marketplace shedding the last of their leaves in the morning breeze were all part of a dream. In a moment she would wake and would find her father bending over her, his blue eyes smiling, his cheerful voice bidding her good morrow, his...

She stumbled, and a cheer went up, bringing her harshly to the present.

The platform swayed under the weight of six, the five condemned and the hangman. Cristina looked out on a sea of faces and wondered if a single one felt her agony, her fear. That was the worst of it, the fear. Would she die quickly or would she hang for hours, as she heard some did, choking slowly, agonizingly, to death? The hangman went from one to the other, placing the nooses around their necks. Tom, who had no spittle left, spat nevertheless. The executioner gave Tom's noose an extra twist, jerking the rope so tightly as to make his eyes goggle. "I'll hang ye before ye get yer feet off the ground, you churl," he growled.

Cristina, feeling the rasp of the rough hempen rope on her skin, closed her eyes and began to pray. "Our Father, who art in heaven, hallowed..."

"Cristina!"

Someone calling her name? Someone in the crowd taunting her?

"Cristina!"

She looked down and saw nothing but a throng of upturned faces.

"Executioner!" The voice rang out. "Executioner—stay! In God's name, stay your hand!"

And now she saw him, a horseman plowing through the crowd, a mounted knight waving his sword. "Stay—on pain of the king's displeasure!"

The hangman stood mouth agape; the mayor and the no-tables craned their necks to see. A murmur of voices went up from the watchers. "Who's he, what's he want?"

"Make way!" the horseman cried at the red-faced sergeant who tried to catch hold of his bridle. When he would not let go, Phillip's sword, whistling through the air, neatly took the man's leather helm from his head, and he shrank back.

"What's this?" the mayor asked, regaining his composure.

Vhat would you have, sir knight?" The same troublesome knight who had harried him yesterday. "We are not in liege to the king, we are a free town."

"You have my wife—wrongfully—up there on the scaffold! And I want her down—this very moment!"

The world whirled red and green and black faster and faster before Cristina's eyes, and her head sagged against the rope.

"She is in a faint. I say!" Phillip cried beside himself. "Cut the rope before she does harm to herself!"

Without waiting for the mayor's orders, Phillip sprang from his saddle and, bounding up the ladder, cut the noose from Cristina's neck. Her face was so white he thought her already dead, but when he bent his head he saw a tiny pulse beating in her throat.

Tenderly he lifted her and carried her down.

"This woman," he said, "was abducted by the scoundrels above. She is my wife, Lady de Ander—had she not told you so?"

The mayor, a little stunned by this turn of events, nevertheless was determined to show his constituents that he was not in awe of the nobility. Puffing out his chest, he said, "Sir, she called herself Cristina Smithborne, and the others said she forced them to steal. If she is your wife indeed—"

"Do you doubt the word of a knight in the king's service?" Phillip asked, drawing his brows together. "You may think yourself mayor of a chartered town, but you have not the right to hang my wife. Further, I shall see that suit is brought against you in this matter."

"Now sir..." the mayor protested.

"Let us see to my wife. Some wine, Adam, if you will."

The squire brought out a leather flask and tipped it to Cristina's lips. She stirred and fluttered her eyelids, but they remained closed.

Thinking quickly, the mayor said, "You may use my house to bring the lady around," in a low conciliatory voice, wishing to hurry them off before the others might be mysteriously and precipitately freed also. "'Tis on the next street, a brown house with carved sickles on the gables."

Phillip, assisted by Adam, mounted his horse and with the unconscious Cristina in his arms rode off to the blaring of a trumpet. A moment later four bodies dangled from the gibbet—the Merrymouths' last public performance.

* * *

Mistress Mathilda, the mayor's wife, hearing the interchange between her husband and the knight, had hurried home as fast as her short, plump legs would allow. Trundling the youngest, a girl of five months, on her hip, a servant following her, she panted audibly as she came upon Phillip's squire banging on the front gate. Of course, no one was at home; everyone down to the potboy and kitchen maid had been given leave to attend the hanging. What a coil, she thought, to have come close to putting an innocent noblewoman to death.

Phillip brought Cristina into the house, the goodwife bustling behind, showing him up to the parlor. There pillows were plumped up, the lady's face bathed with vinegar, her wrists rubbed, her collar loosened. Phillip, looking down at Cristina, the white brow, the pinched cheeks, the lank hair, felt his heart twist with love and pity.

"The mayor was duped," Mistress Mathilda claimed. "You can hardly blame him, good sir. The others caught red-handed cutting purses, and she was among them, the lady, she..."

Phillip gave her a withering look. "I would like to be alone with my wife."

"Aye, forgive me, if there is anything..."

"Nothing."

She drew the curtain, and Phillip sat beside Cristina, stroking her wrists. After a while she opened her eyes and stared at him, fear and incomprehension in her eyes.

"Cristina, be not afraid. You are safe."

"Phillip," she said. "Oh, Phillip, it—it seems like a dream. Am I truly saved?"

"Aye. You must not think on it."

"But how?"

"I thought it best to tell a lie. I said you were my wife, which"—his anxious eyes scanned her face—"I truly hope you will someday be."

She closed her eyes to ward off his gaze. She was not prepared for it. She felt sick, weak, so filled with loathing for the whole human race that not even Phillip, her rescuer, appealed to her. She had only one emotion, a wish to hide, to retreat from life into some kind of dark, hidden limbo.

Phillip, intuitively aware of her distress, said, "Sweet, forgive me. You must have time to recover from your ordeal. Nay, you need not explain. I know why you left Connington, and believe me, Sir Michael regrets—is penitent—but let us not dwell on it. You are young, you have a life ahead of you—

a wonderful life. And for the present you must regain your strength. I will take you to Nareham."

"Nareham?"

"Just for now. I know you have been reluctant to go to the castle in the past. However, 'tis the only place I can think of where you will be cared for."

In a few days, Cristina, wearing a clean gown and a scrap of linen on her fair hair, was strong enough to make the journey. Phillip had purchased a palfrey for her use, an extravagance he could ill afford, but he realized that to ride pillion with him would have made her uncomfortable. She had been through a terrible nightmare, he reasoned, and her present malaise would disappear as soon as she was among people whom she could trust, people who could make her feel harbored and safe.

At Nareham, Thomas de Ander did not find it in him to give Phillip a warm welcome. Disgruntled because his nephew had gone off before Joan's funeral—an affront from a kinsman—his temper was further acerbated by the sight of Cristina, to him a pale excuse for so fervent a love on Phillip's part. He saw no resemblance between this girl and his former mistress, Joanna, whom he remembered as a vibrant woman; this was a bloodless creature as different from her mother as day from night. How Cristina could have ensnared Phillip as well as Sir Michael (he had heard all about the girl's disgrace) remained a mystery to him.

"The damosel is not well," Phillip confided, thinking it best not to mention her Meading ordeal unless Cristina herself wished to speak of it. "And she has nowhere to go. She is in need of good nursing, and of kindness also."

"She shall receive all she requires. At Nareham we do not stint," Thomas said haughtily, yet feeling put upon.

The funeral had been costly, more than he had anticipated, and his coffers were nigh empty. Two more mouths to feed hardly mattered, but how to meet the Christmas Day dues on his mortgage? After he paid his soldiers—and he could not do without a small contingent—there would be very little money left. He could ask for an extension on his credit, but he had already done that twice. And in addition to everything else there were the expenses for Aleyn's upcoming wedding, for while Phillip had been gallivanting about looking for his lady love, Aleyn had gotten himself betrothed.

* * *

Aleyn had met the girl's father, Sir Henry de Mayre, at his stepmother's wake feast. De Mayre, on his way to London and traveling a few days ahead of his family, had stopped at Nareham to break the journey, a break that coincided with the funerary banquet. A long-jawed, grizzled knight who had lost an arm at Nájera, Sir Henry had known Thomas de Ander's father, though not Thomas himself, and was sorry, he said, to have met the son under such sad circumstances.

The funeral, because death had been sudden and unexpected, was sparsely attended. Besides Sir Michael de Leys and the pregnant Cecilia (the sight of whose burgeoning stomach and numerous offspring made Thomas flinch) and Sir Henry, there was only the bereaved widower and Aleyn. Thomas told one and all he would never forgive his nephew, Phillip, for his absence, but he also informed a hopeful Aleyn that he was in no way reinstating him. Aleyn would have to look elsewhere for his patrimony.

Hearing that Sir Henry had a marriageable daughter, Lenore by name, with a substantial dowry, Aleyn played up to the old man, flattering him, but subtly, since Cecilia (the source of his information) had warned him Henry was no fool.

Sir Henry, far from a fool and divining Aleyn's intent, sized him up and decided bastard or no he would do. He waited a few days for form's sake, then consulted with the boy's father, Thomas. After some polite fencing he came to the nub of the matter, a match between Aleyn and Lenore, making the terms of the marriage agreement weigh somewhat heavily in his daughter's favor—such and such to be retained in her name, such and such property to go to her male issue, that income and that to her female issue. But Thomas, delighted at having relieved himself of further embarrassment through Aleyn's escapades, pleased with the alliance in general, found no fault with the contract. The betrothal was announced and the wedding set for Christmas.

Aleyn had been assured that Lenore was "not unattractive," that she played both lute and gittern admirably and that her cross stitch was the envy of damosels from Dover to Bannockburn. Was she dark, fair, tall, short? No one could say for certain. Her exact age remained vague, also; "young" was the closest he could get to it. Nevertheless he preened like a peacock as if he had singlehandedly brought off a great coup. He managed to borrow money from a knight in Sir Michael's entourage and hastened into Thexted to buy his intended a ring, something large and expensive that would establish his worth as a generous knight in the girl's and her father's eyes. The marriage terms had dismayed him only a little, for he felt that once the knot was tied, he could in some way get around the restrictions and lay his hands on some much-needed ready cash.

Lenore with her mother and attendants arrived a few days after the contract had been signed. Aleyn with the others, who were still wearing the black bands of mourning, stood in the courtyard waiting to greet the prospective bride. He himself helped her dismount, a thin girl wearing a braided cloak, a flat hat and a veil.

"God's blessings on you," Aleyn said, bowing. Should he lift the veil and kiss her on the cheeks as was customary?

"God's greetings," the muffled voice replied. He tried to see beyond the folds of the cloth, but the mother, a portly woman in magenta, hurried her off, saying they needed rest and refreshment.

He did not see her until that evening when she entered the great hall, an hour after the meal had begun. She was wearing a horned headdress, the latest in fashion from King Richard's court, the hair hidden beneath a coif. The headdress, unflattering even to the comely, was grotesque on Lenore, emphasizing her beaked nose, her angular cheeks. Thin, almost gaunt, she had a sallow complexion, the daub of red paint on her lips only emphasizing the yellowness of her skin. And she was not young, not to Aleyn. He thought her old, old, old. In point of fact, Lenore was thirty-five. Her father, despairing of getting her married, had accepted Aleyn because he knew without consulting his daughter that she would be delighted to get a young, handsome husband.

She was.

Aleyn, however, did not share this delight. Sitting next to her through the meal, he was hard put to imagine bedding such a stick. Flat-chested, she had no breasts that he could see; her neck and arms were thin as reeds, and her collarbones stuck out like two shiny knobs under the olive skin. He should have known, have considered, that what God gave with one hand He took away with another. What rotten luck! Why couldn't she at least have had tits? Damn her father for perpetrating such a fraud. The betrothal had not been solemnized, and he could still wiggle out of it. He could suddenly become violently ill, develop a marked limp, say he already had a wife, one he had forgotten about in London, or simply vanish. His mind raced past and around and through these possibilities.

"Do you have good hunting at Nareham?" Lenore asked in a sweet submissive voice. Her eyes, usually lackluster, held an excited, almost feverish glow. Ever since her mother had informed her that the handsome young man who had helped her dismount in the courtyard was to be her husband, she had been in a state of twittering excitement. It had taken her all afternoon to dress, choosing one gown, discarding it for another, debating about the headdress, the jewels she should wear. She loved him instantly and looked up to him as if he were God.

"Very good, damosel," Aleyn replied, warming toward her somewhat. No man could help but be flattered by such open admiration. Suppose, Aleyn thought, I do not marry her, then what? I have no money, no prospects, and if I should force Father to break the marriage contract, then things will be black indeed. He might even forbid me Nareham, throw me out to fend for myself. On the other hand, if I marry her I will be lord of my own manor, Waddington, which came with Lenore's dowry, not a large estate, but far better than being lord of nothing. And who knows, she might die of a miscarriage like Joan, and I will be the richer for it, able to choose my next wife with care.

"Christmas seems such a long time from now," he said, gallantly kissing her hand.

The betrothal had been formalized a fortnight before Cristina's arrival. Shortly afterward the de Mayres had continued their journey to London and Aleyn had gone off somewhere on his own. Cristina, given a choice of accommodations—sharing a dorter with several female de Ander kin or a small chamber above the great hall—chose the chamber. Still in a state of despondency, she preferred being alone as much as possible.

Her mood did not lighten. Her experience had left a deep mark, and she found it hard to like, to trust, or sometimes even to speak to anyone. Phillip she tolerated because he had saved her and she knew he was basically good and kindhearted. But not the others. From high to low, men and women were warped, selfish creatures who cared for nothing but satisfying themselves. Sir Michael de Leys had done her a great injustice; an older man, he should have realized the consequences of a seduction, and Lady de Leys should have had a more understanding, a gentler heart. The band of rogues who had abducted her, the priest who had refused to help her, the townspeople of Meading, the mayor, all had shown a cruel indifference to her plight. Looking back over her short life, she saw that the only ones who had cared, the only persons who had shown her true affection, were her father, Dame Brandone, Edmund and lately Phillip, but he, unhappily, was laying siege to her, a siege which dismayed and sometimes frightened her.

She felt uncomfortable at Nareham Castle. Thomas de Ander, her mother's former lover, had come as a shock. What had Joanna seen in him? A jowled man with bags under his eyes, hair thinning on top and a petulant air (so much like Aleyn's), he hardly presented the picture of a dashing lover. Aside from his short, blunt words of greeting he had ignored her, making her feel like a poor unwanted relation whose visit he secretly hoped would be short.

When Edmund came to see her she told him she wished to leave Nareham. "Thomas does not want me. Everyone knows what happened at Connington, and the women whisper behind my back."

"What women?"

"Lady de Ander's tiring women and cousins. I know what they are saying, and it angers me. I have done nothing wrong, and they—I doubt if there is one among them who has remained chaste or who has not betrayed a husband."

"True. But in time they will forget and talk of something else."

"They? They have nothing else to do but talk. Oh, Edmund, if I could stay with you, for a little while, until I can arrange to enter a convent."

"A convent? My dear child, without a dowry I fear they will not accept you."

"I have heard there are small, poor houses that will take in orphans such as me. I am young, strong; I will work hard."

"The poor houses do not take laypersons."

"Surely there must be *one,* Edmund?"

He smiled. "I daresay every young girl at one time or another wishes to become a nun. But remember, nuns for all their religious bent are women too; they have their foibles, their petty squabbles, their jealousies and gossip. If you could not get along with the castle women, how do you expect to get along elsewhere?"

"Are you saying I am spoiled, vain?" she asked, hurt to the quick.

"Somewhat—and stubborn."

"How can you think me stubborn? Why?"

"Because you will not listen to Phillip. He loves you. He wants to marry you. Do you realize how fortunate you are?"

"I don't want to talk about it. You are against me, like all the others."

In the end Edmund advised Phillip to send Cristina to one of his married aunts. "Aelenor," he suggested, "who is wed to Sir Edgar du Trolaine. They live in a remote part of Northumberland near the Scottish border, I understand. Cragwell Castle? Aye. Good. Let Cristina cool her heels there for a spell."

Cristina did not like to be disposed of in such an arbitrary fashion. She much preferred the convent. Why send her to strangers?

"And I suppose the convent is not peopled by strangers? How many nuns do you know?" Edmund asked.

"Still, it seems you are shunting me off to Cragwell for punishment. I won't change my mind about Phillip," she added. "I will *never* marry."

Chapter XXIX

The gray lichened towers and crenellated walls of Cragwell rose out of the late-afternoon mist, floating like a mirage on the chill white air. Below it lay the valley, the winding River Coquet and a tiny hamlet now obscured by the fog so that the castle seemed isolated, a lone, ghostly habitation anchored in a vast colorless sea. As the little cavalcade drew closer, its shape took more substantial form. Squarely built, ugly, Cragwell had been raised as a fortification on an old Roman site and since its inception had acted as a bulwark against the marauding Scots who would sweep down from the hills from time to time. The castle had an air of grim desolation even when the fitful sun shone upon it, its walled ramparts frowning over a barren, stony landscape where winter came early and stayed late.

Cristina shuddered and pulled her mist-dampened cloak closer. They had been riding for almost a fortnight now, taking the journey in easy stages. They were a small company; Cristina, Phillip's squire, one man-at-arms (grudgingly lent by Thomas) and a maidservant for Cristina, not the wellborn one Phillip would have preferred, but a rawboned peasant girl, Janet, who made up in willingness what she lacked in experience. Phillip, riding at Cristina's side, solicitous of her comfort, had tried to put up at the castles of friends along the way rather than at the shoddy, flea-ridden inns. When forced to remain the night in a public house, however, he had ordered the best accommodations, the best wine, the choicest food. Cristina did not have a hard heart, and she made an attempt to show her gratitude for Phillip's concern—a smile, a thank you—but the leap of light in his eyes whenever she did was so disquieting as to make her wish she had said nothing or that she could receive such looks with indifference. Why did Phillip disturb her? Because he was a man? Or because he was Phillip? In her heart she knew the answer, but her mind shied away from it.

At Cragwell they had some difficulty gaining entrance. Even though Phillip's squire had gone ahead to announce their arrival, the gateward, made suspicious by past enemy ruses, was reluctant to lower the drawbridge until Phillip himself appeared and hailed him. Once inside, however, the

446

castle became alive with welcome. Sir Edgar hurried out into the courtyard followed by his lady and her youngest son, Roger, their faces wreathed in smiles. Edgar clapped Phillip on the back, Aelenor kissed him on both cheeks. She wept a little. Visitors were rare here in this remote corner, especially those from Nareham. And she could not have been happier to see a kinsman. Cristina, introduced as a cousin, was greeted with the same warmth. It was difficult to set one's heart against Aelenor. The lady had such a cheerful air about her. When she smiled her face lighted up, changing it, smoothing out the furrowed brow and the grooved mouth lines, so that one hardly noticed her high-bridged hawkish nose and the close-set eyes.

But Cristina refused to be charmed; polite, courteous, aye, but not charmed. She had liked Cecilia too.

"You poor child," Aelenor said, taking Cristina's chilled hands and rubbing them, "you look half frozen. There's a fire in the hall—warm yourself while I have servants bring water for a bath."

Aelenor herself supervised the bath, improvised from an empty wine vat, and afterward wrapped a linen towel around Cristina, clucking at her marblelike paleness. "We shall have to put roses in your cheeks, I can see," she said. Phillip had managed to take Aelenor aside earlier and had quickly given her an outline of Cristina's trials, glossing over the episode at Connington as a "misunderstanding."

Aelenor, a maternal soul, had eleven children, five of whom had lived. All, except Roger, were gone from home now, married or in service, and she welcomed the opportunity to mother the orphan girl.

She took the brush and comb from the maid and began to comb out the tangles from Cristina's newly washed hair, all the time talking in a low sympathetic voice. Under Aelenor's soft hands Cristina's tenseness vanished and she found her eyes closing, her head growing heavy. She imagined herself a little girl again, sitting in her father's lap while he crooned under his breath as he stroked her head. A tear formed in her eye and slid slowly down her cheek. "Child, you have nothing to fear," Aelenor said, bending to kiss her. "We shall protect you."

At supper Cristina heard rumors of war. The Scotch-English treaty negotiated by the Duke of Lancaster two years earlier had run out, and Sir Edgar expected trouble.

"The treaty barely held those devils in check," Sir Edgar said. "The lairds have been champing at the bit for months now."

"I had no idea your situation was so grave," Phillip said in a low voice, trying not to alarm the women. "If I had guessed, I might have thought twice before I exposed the damosel to peril. God knows she has seen enough these last months."

"There is no need for uneasiness," Edgar assured him. "If they attack 'twill be further east. Besides, we are well able to repel any force, no matter how large, should they change their minds and strike at us here. The Scots have never breached a Cragwell wall yet."

"I hope you are right," Phillip said gloomily.

"Of course I am!" Edgar cried, lifting his cup. "Let us drink to the English and damn the Scots!"

A month after she had arrived at Cragwell, on a late afternoon toward dusk, Cristina lay soaking in a perfumed bath, the wooden vat placed for warmth before a roaring fire. However, the water, hot only a short while earlier, had begun to cool rapidly, and she was debating whether to climb out, an awkward procedure without assistance, or to wait for her maid, who had been sent to procure fresh towels, when there was a knock on the door.

"Oh, do come in," she said impatiently, for Janet had been gone some while.

She heard the rustle of the woolen arras which shielded the door from drafts, and rising, with her back to it, she said, "I had nearly given you up."

"Had you?"

She whirled about.

Phillip was standing near the arras, gazing at her, his eyes slowly traveling her nakedness with a look of masculine appreciation mingled with awe and wonder. Cristina unclothed was ravishing. She knew it, because even the ladies of Costanza's retinue had often commented, not without envy, on her slender waist, her full, firm breasts, the delicate curve of her hips so well hidden by the gowns she wore. And Cristina, standing there, her dewy skin rosy in the firelight, her piled-up golden hair held by a black Spanish comb, seeing the admiration in Phillip's eyes, was torn between an odd vanity and a need to speak sharply, to object to his staring at her in such a bold, sexual manner. But she could not find the words, words which would have come quickly enough were it someone else. Was she pleased with Phillip's look of frank appraisal? God forbid, she thought in annoyance.

"I believed you to be my maid," she said with dignity, breaking the silence. "Would you—pray, my chamber robe...?"

She pointed to a stool where it lay, a sky-blue velvet garment lined with rabbit fur.

He scooped it up and brought it to her as she stood in the water, now gone quite chill. "If you will give me your arm..." she began.

Instead he reached over and, slipping one arm around her waist and the other under her knees, lifted her out. She had a momentary sensation of surprise at the muscular hardness of his chest, at the same time aware that his mouth was buried in her tangled hair.

"Cristina, you smell so sweet."

"Put me down—please, please..."

Setting her on her feet, he wrapped the robe about her. "Cristina..." His hands lingered on her shoulders, and she hesitated a moment before she eased herself away, moving closer to the fire, fastening the clasp at her neck.

A small strained silence ensued, punctuated with the crackle of the fire.

Cristina was the first to speak. "You came upon me at a most inopportune time," she said, not looking at him, wishing he would leave, more aware of him as a man than she had ever been.

"I came to say goodbye."

She turned then. "You are going?"

"Aye. I would gladly stay at Cragwell the winter, but Edmund advised against it." He gave her a wry smile. "He claims absence makes the heart grow fonder."

"Phillip, 'twould be best—"

"Don't," he broke in abruptly. "I don't want to hear you say you won't ever marry, you won't ever love me. I do not want to hear it."

She turned back to the fire. "You are angry now."

He did not answer at once, and she was aware of his smoldering eyes, could almost feel them on the back of her neck. Outside the wind keened, rattling a shutter, tapping at it, sighing. A log sputtered and settled in a fiery shower of sparks. Their shadows danced upon the wall, his large and looming, hers small and slender.

When Phillip spoke at last it was in a subdued voice. "Let

us part friends, Cristina. We need not quarrel. God knows when we shall see each other again. You cannot be so hard..."

"Nay," she said, facing him. "I do not mean to be hard, believe me, Phillip. I am most grateful for all you have done. And I would like to—to part friends."

"Then you will let me kiss you goodbye—as friends do."

She gave him her cheek, and as his lips touched it in a brushing kiss, a little tremor worked itself down her spine. He must have felt it too, for he put his hand on her arm, and when she looked up into his eyes she saw that they were dark and eloquent with yearning and something else—pain. A sudden compassion flooded her heart, and leaning up, she kissed him lightly.

She felt him tremble, and before she could draw back his arms went around her, crushing her tightly to his hard, lean body.

"Phillip...!"

But his mouth silenced her, his lips commanding hers in a kiss that grew with hungry intensity. She did not think, she could not. Through a whirling darkness she was aware of the primal female in her, the woman she tried to deny, clinging to him, kissing him back, her mouth opening under his.

She felt his hand undoing the clasp at her throat, felt the robe slip from her bare shoulders, felt his mouth trailing fiery kisses along her neck, across her white shoulders, her breasts, pausing at the dark fragrant cleft between.

"Phillip..."

He was kissing her lips again, stilling her voice, lifting her against his chest, carrying her, moving through firelit shadow, while the winter wind howled outside the window ledge, closing them in, she and Phillip together in this halflit, flickering chamber, she and Phillip alone, the everyday world of thought, of reason, of doubt, dropping away into dark, sweet forgetfulness.

He lowered her on the bed, and she sank down into the deep feather mattress with a sigh that was half moan, turning her hands against his chest, feeling his strong heavy heartbeat through the cloth of his tunic. His head bent to her breasts and she arched her hips as he took a nipple in his mouth, the surge of pleasure suddenly striking an echoing chord in her memory, taking her back in time. It seemed to her she could smell hay and horses, the sweaty feral aroma of a man aroused, and into her swaying mind there came a picture of Sir Michael, the dust-moted barn, the agony of her

450

shameful desire, and she could hear again Cecilia's shrill voice, "Whore! Slut!"

With a cry, Cristina tore herself away and flung herself from the bed. "I cannot! I cannot!" She sank to her knees, pressing her head against the bedpost. "Oh, dear God, I cannot."

Phillip lay where she had left him, and for a few moments nothing could be heard but the sound of his measured breathing. Gradually it lessened, and when he spoke he did so in a low, controlled voice. "I love you, Cristina. I want you, as any flesh-and-blood man who loves a woman does. And I believe you want me too."

"Nay—nay, 'twas but a moment's weakness—you—I cannot."

"I will not force you, Cristina. I want you to come to me of your own free will."

"I cannot. Pray, pray, go—leave me."

"You tempt a man, arouse him, and then ask him to go."

"I did not mean to tempt you. If I did, forgive me. But I cannot."

"Cristina..." He moved toward her, and she shrank away.

"Have you forgotten your promise, the one you made to me at Meading, Phillip?"

He drew back sharply and rose from the bed. "I have not forgotten," he said in a voice edged in bitterness. "I am not to speak of love, of marriage. So be it, then. I shan't bother you. Goodbye, Damosel Cristina. May God watch over you."

"Phillip..."

But he had already turned and, striding toward the arras, swept it aside. A moment later she heard the door slam shut.

"I cannot," she whispered to the still-swinging curtain, an ache constricting her throat, her eyes brimming with tears.

The days drew in and the wind skittered and shrieked outside the castle in ever stronger gusts. Though tapestries and woolen rugs covered the walls of the great hall and the upper chambers, chill drafts and damp eddies swirled through the rooms. One could keep warm only by staying close to the smoking peat fires. Cristina often wore her cloak to meals, rubbing her aching chilblained hands, curling and uncurling her toes to keep them from going numb. The heated bricks put under the blankets to warm her bed at night turned to cold stone long before morning, when she rose to find ice in the water bucket.

Still, it had been a long while since she had been so much

at peace, though wariness always lurked beneath her content. Would it last? Would something happen to make Aelenor turn on her? In the meanwhile, however, under the lady's loving care the pucker between her brows disappeared and her cheeks turned pink with health. Every now and then, caught off guard, she even found herself laughing, when she had never thought to laugh again. Life was pleasant at Cragwell despite the cold and the austere surroundings, despite a diet heavy in bread, sour cheese, rabbit and fowl and the lack of visitors. She liked Sir Edgar (but took care not to show it), a cheerful man with a short, iron-gray beard and curly brown hair peppered with white. He was courteous to Cristina and made her feel like an honored guest, a knack he had with all who received his generous hospitality. What surprised and intrigued Cristina was his fondness for his wife, and his wife's for him, a fondness which seemed to have lasted after so many years of marriage. Not a breath of scandal had ever linked either of them with a different partner. Sir Edgar, from what she could learn, had never taken a mistress, nor had Aelenor given herself to a lover.

If the pair had their differences they gave no sign. Cristina never heard a discourteous word pass between them. She noticed how Sir Edgar greeted his wife even if he had been away for a few hours, a resounding kiss on the cheek and on the lips, kisses which brought a glow to Aelenor's eyes. They conversed together, sitting at the table or by the fire, talking sometimes for hours, each interested in what the other had to say. Edgar discussed everything with his wife, hid nothing, unlike most lords, who thought talk of arms, horses and hunting suitable only for male ears. This friendship between man and wife was something new for Cristina, something to puzzle and wonder over.

December arrived with a flurry of snow. Aelenor's married sons, Hubert and Simon, together with their families, were to spend the Twelve Days of Christmas at Cragwell, but a week before the holiday commenced two messengers arrived almost simultaneously, one bringing word that Hubert's youngest had fallen ill with smallpox and the other that Simon, facing a lawsuit concerning water rights, must ride up to London to consult a lawyer. Neither family would come.

Aelenor put a good face on her disappointment. "We shall have to wait now until Easter to see them. I do hope Hubert's wife does not forget to hang red cloth in the chamber against the others catching the pox. Ah, well, we shall make merry without them."

Nareham celebrated *its* Christmas with a wedding.

Aleyn had awaited the nuptials with as much impatience as his bride, not because of any eagerness to bed her, but because of a desperate need for money. A noble to whom he owed a large gambling debt had threatened him with Ludgate Prison unless he paid by the first of the year, and Aleyn had no way of laying his hands upon such a sum except through access to Lenore's dowry.

The bride's mother, however, did not share Aleyn's eagerness. She had never liked the match. She had heard vague rumblings about Aleyn—a gambler, a coward, a womanizer—nothing for sure, but enough to make her look at him with a sour eye. Nevertheless the day had long since passed to hope for a better offer. Aleyn, the bastard de Ander, it had to be. But why, she wanted to know, should the marriage take place at Christmas, so shockingly soon? A virgin, betrothed decently, did not rush into marriage until a suitable time had elapsed, a year at least from the day the contract was signed. God knew how the gossips counted on their fingers if the bride gave birth less than nine months after the wedding night, especially when said bride married in haste. Lenore's mother was all for delaying the ceremony, but Lenore would not hear of it. She did not care what others thought, she wanted to get married *now*, today if she could. Her trousseau had long been ready, her wedding gown too. "Mother, he will forget me, change his mind. He might even die—God forbid—and then where would I be?" she asked tearfully.

So two days before Christmas, amid the roisterous clang of bells, the couple were joined at St. Katherine's of the Angels in Thexted. They—the wedding party—set out immediately for Nareham, the bride, her face aglow with excitement and cold, riding a pure-white palfrey. Earlier, Thomas de Ander in a burst of tipsy generosity had insisted the marriage feast be celebrated at Nareham, an impulsive gesture which he later regretted.

However, once committed he had to go forward. He hated being considered a pinchpenny, and though extravagance was not expected in the case of a bastard son, he had his reputation as an open-handed lord to protect. Raising the money for such a banquet, to say nothing of housing a multitude of guests, some of whom would stay for weeks and months, had been difficult. Afraid to touch Joan's jewels (her father was asking for them back—the skinflint!), he had found it necessary to levy an additional tax on his peasants. The amount so garnered had not been bounteous but sufficient to make a notable display.

Nareham's great hall, decked out in holly and ivy with a huge Yule log blazing on the hearth and an ox turning on the spit, presented a welcome sight to the chilled and hungry guests. The wedding couple ceremoniously escorted to the high table were seated at the place of honor. Speeches were made, toasts drunk. The minstrels who had been hired for the celebration made up for their lack of talent by a great musical din: tabor, harp, gittern and the loud, cracked voice of a baritone. Aleyn drank copiously and dutifully pinched his bride's thighs under the table, his gaze meanwhile scanning Lenore's bridesmaids with a practiced eye. One among them, a flaxen-haired beauty, had caught his attention at the church. She had pouting pink lips and high breasts outlined by a low-necked clinging gown of white, and as he drank, he thought more and more of those breasts, and less and less of the new wife beside him who had none at all.

Finally the moment arrived when they were both led to an upstairs chamber for the bedding ceremony. The girls undressing Lenore fluttered, giggled, hiccoughed, exclaimed and chattered like a flock of magpies.

Aleyn, divested of his garments by the groomsmen, stealing a glance at the flaxen-haired girl, happened to meet her eye. He winked broadly, and she blushed. Aha, he thought, life is not over for me. Wait—wait, my beauty.

Fortified with wine and determined to get his first-night duties over with quickly, Aleyn attacked his new wife as if she were a haunch of beef. Poor Lenore, having prepared herself for bliss, tried her best not to cry out at the unexpected assault. Baffled and in pain at the thing thrusting back and forth inside her, she bit her lip, while her eyes swam with tears. Not even a kiss? Except for the chaste meeting of lips at the altar and her husband's cruel pinching under the table, he had not shown the least sign of affection. But perhaps, she thought, this is what happens on the first night. Men, her mother had warned her, are all the same beneath their finery—beasts.

But later as her husband lay asleep on her breast, she felt happier. I am a wife now, she mused, a wife. I shall be like other women, have a husband in my bed, bear his children, be a mother. Lady de Ander. People will look up to me, will show me courtesy, will address me differently than they did when I was the plain spinster, the Damosel Lenore de Mayre. I am someone to envy. And thinking of it, smiling to herself, she fell asleep.

Some hours later she was awakened by a low, drawn-out moan. For a moment she lay dazed, a little frightened, listening, her ears and eyes straining in the blackness. A thumping sound came from a corner of the darkened chamber, as if someone were beating upon the floor. She sat up. Aleyn was gone and she was alone. Fearful, apprehensive, she slid out of bed soundlessly and approached the corner on bare feet. Passing the hearth on the way, where the dying fire glowed redly, she stooped to light a brand, and as it flared into flame she thrust it on high.

There in startled pantomime, frozen for an interminable instant, was her naked husband mounted on one of her bridesmaids, the Damosel Marianna. In that moment Lenore went from grateful, submissive bride to furious, betrayed woman. No gradual change, no painful deliberation, no hemming and hawing, but a shockingly swift transformation. Meek to implacable.

She did not cry out, in fact, did not utter a word. She had been too well schooled in restraint. Reared from childhood by her mother to keep her feelings well hidden and never to give way to emotion, her face betrayed nothing, not a glimmer of her abysmal disillusionment. Up until then Aleyn had seemed to her the epitome of a girl's dreams, a spinster's impossible vision and fantasy realized. Fakery, all fakery. She had always known that God's rule against fornication and adultery applied more strictly to females than males, that the wife must accept a husband's whoring or the taking of a mistress as a matter of course. But to copulate with another on her sacred wedding night—and in the very room where she slept—too much, far more than any woman should be asked to bear. She should have been crushed. Wanting to die, she should have bowed her head, forgiven, tried to forget. But no. Something, a feeling she had never known before, surged through her veins. Anger, anger mingled with hurt and an acid pride. Pride. A new sensation for Lenore. Yet it must have been there all along, uncultivated, unnoticed, submerged under the endless tide of her mother's scoldings. Pride. Her father's daughter too. She came of a long line of stiff-legged nobles, and their blood was hers. Pride. A de Mayre did not accept an affront gladly.

"Lenore!" Aleyn cried, adding fatuously, "You are awake."

Lenore stood, still speechless, her face white and rigid under the flickering torch. Even had she chosen to, she could not, did not know how to express her anger.

"Love, my sweet." Aleyn jumped up. "I—I did not know." Then to the girl, whose face gazed up at them both in horror, "I think you had better go."

She drew a bedrobe about her nakedness and scrambled to her feet. Lenore wanted to shout, "Slut! Whore!" but again she found speech impossible. The girl threw one shamed look at her, then fled.

"Lenore," Aleyn began in a soothing voice, "love, I want to explain, nay, I owe you an explanation. I—I was not entirely sober, and she came to me while I was sleeping. I thought—I thought in my wine-befuddled mind 'twas you—'twas dark—you can see how I made such an error, can you not?"

Error? Did he take her for an utter fool? Her mother had warned her that Aleyn de Ander had a wild reputation, but she would not listen. He looked and acted so devoted, and she had begged and wept to be his wife. Now it was too late. She could not complain, must never let anyone know, least of all her mother.

"May I be forgiven, sweet lady?" Aleyn put his arm about her shoulders.

She forced herself not to shrug him off. Strange how a man's touch which only hours earlier had set her aflutter could now turn her cold as ice. "Aye," she answered, the word sticking in her throat.

"Let's to bed, then, sweet. And we'll think no more on it."

It was daylight before Lenore fell asleep again. She had lain the long hours staring up into darkness, seeing over and over again the two naked bodies entwined. What made her humiliation worse was the realization that Aleyn would not have dared to behave in such a gross manner had he married a younger and prettier bride. But because she, Lenore, was older and plain, he had thought she would accept anything, thought she would be grateful for crumbs thrown her way. God! God! How she hated him! She wanted revenge. She wanted to grind his face in the dirt, to hack off his eyes, nose, to castrate him. She wanted him to suffer. If she were a man she would challenge him to battle, meet him on the field, impale him on a lance, slice him in two with a sword. But she was not a man, only a helpless woman. She could withold nothing that rightfully belonged to him, neither her body nor that part of her dowry signed to him in the marriage contract.

"I shall kill him," she promised herself. "I shall murder him slowly so that I can watch his agony with pleasure."

It was a notion conceived in anger, and she recognized it as such once she arose the following morning. But as subsequent days and weeks wore on and Aleyn openly flaunted his affair with the girl, taking her with him to London, where he planned to spend some of his newly acquired gold pieces, the idea began to solidify in Lenore's mind and heart.

There was another person at Nareham, Nareham village more correctly, who nurtured a murderous anger. It was Charles Coke, Ivo Coke's eldest son by Katrine, now a young man of twenty-four. Though for the time being his resentment had been pushed aside, temporarily banished in anticipation of his coming marriage, his animosity still smoldered, an animosity he had felt toward the de Anders from the day Harold de Ander had cheated his widowed mother of Ivo's legacy. Through death dues and a series of fines (one having to do with the purchase of a horse for the lord years ago) and a false charge for tardy rent, Katrine and her children had been left penniless. Forced to leave the keep, they had moved in with Katrine's family at the mill, where eight people were already crowded together in two rooms and a low-ceilinged loft above.

It was a hard life; hunger stalked them, for though the elder Flemyng did better than most he had difficulty feeding so many mouths. As a consequence, Charles was sent out to work at six, laboring from dawn to dusk at a series of odd jobs, giving over every grubby coin he earned to Grandfather Flemyng. Not until he reached the age of sixteen and demanded a portion of his pay as his right was he allowed to keep some of it.

Charles had been twenty when for the first and only time he heard John Ball preach his sermon about equality of all men, claiming that none should be held in servitude to another. The priest's words had struck a responsive chord in Charles, still simmering against the injustice done to his family and to his father's memory. He had wanted to join the peasants in their march on London in 1381, but his grandfather flatly forbade it, and his mother on her deathbed made him promise he would not go.

So he had to give up the Great Revolt and regretted it

even though it had ended in defeat. The cruel reprisals afterward, the broken promises, the hangings, the beatings and brandings, only served to make Charles angrier. He felt sure that someday the peasants would rise again, a rebellion that this time would succeed.

In the meanwhile he continued to work, hiring himself out as a laborer to surrounding manors, going sometimes leagues away to aid in the harvest, or thrashing, wherever he could get the highest pay, despite the statute enacted by the late King Edward setting a limit on wages. Soon he had put enough aside to buy back a portion of his father's land from Thomas de Ander and began bit by bit to cultivate it.

He had no intention of marrying. Charles could see where a wife did nothing for a man but load him down with a cot full of brats. He would remain single, work hard, save his money, keep his eyes open and when the hour was ripe take up where John Ball had been forced to leave off.

No, he had not reckoned on marriage, not until one late afternoon he rescued Gena Melker from a charging bull and fell astonishingly, suddenly and irrevocably in love.

He began to court her in the circumscribed way that peasants courted young girls, first speaking to her parents and with their consent "walking out." She was reluctant and came only because she had been prodded by her mother. He understood that; her shyness, her modesty, only increased his desire to wed and have her.

The first reading of the banns took place in late November. Charles, with the aid of his family and neighbors, erected a house in the meantime, a cot very much like the ones he had helped others raise. And by the time the wedding took place it was finished, the shutters in place and the roof neatly thatched. After a modest feast put on by the bride's parents, amid ribald jests and cheering, Charles and his bride retired to their new home.

He knew that she was frightened, and because he cared, because he wanted more than anything for her to feel toward him as he did toward her, he went slowly, carefully, tenderly, a little surprised, a little amazed at his own restraint, for his desire had burgeoned the moment he had slipped into bed beside her and felt the warmth of her naked skin.

She, for her part, froze when he touched her. She had not wanted this marriage; she loved—God forgive her—Father Edmund, the priest. To love a priest was a sin; but, she told herself, she loved him purely, a love without embrace, without as much as a chaste kiss. She would have been content to adore him from afar. She had not dared confess this, even to him—and he, *he* had advised her to marry. She must marry a man known for his wicked temper, for his simmering rancor, and couple with him like a beast.

And now he was kissing her softly on the cheek, tenderly, not at all like a man with a "wicked" temper. He was saying, "I will not force you, Gena. I swear by all that is holy I shall never force you. If you wish me to sleep on the floor, so I will do."

The only light in the cot was from the dying fire, so that she saw his face only as a shadow, but the trembling of his voice reassured her.

"'Tis my wifely duty..." she began.

"Aye, but I am not a rapist. I care for you, my sweet Gena."

She raised herself on an elbow and tried to peer into his eyes. "And you would not take me if I say nay?"

"'Twould sadden me, but if you are not ready, I can wait."

This was something she had not expected. From what her mother, her sisters, her friends had told her, the first night was one of brutality and pain, a night to be endured with gritted teeth and clenched fists.

He touched her cheek with a callused finger, "Words come hard with me. I cannot woo you—I do not know how."

Suddenly softened, she leaned over and kissed him lightly on the lips. He took them gently at first, meaning not to press her, but he was only flesh and blood, and after the first moment his mouth possessed hers, engulfing it, swallowing, demanding, hungry. Gena, flooded with a new, frightening, yet not unpleasant sensation, tried to draw away, but Charles's hands, cupping her skull, held her prisoner. And presently she found that she liked his kisses, liked the feel of his hard-muscled arms crushing her to his bare chest, liked the warm male smell of his body, the way his mouth devoured hers, ravaging it with a wildness that sent every nerve end humming. But when his hands began to play, stroking her shoulders, descending to her breasts, fondling each a little clumsily, she gasped with pain and, pulling from him, edged away, trying to put some distance between them on the narrow bed.

"Gena, I don't want to hurt you," he said earnestly. "I—I wish I could please us both." But he did not know how to do it any more than he knew the sweet words of love. His only sexual experience had been a now and again rough bout in the hay with a promiscuous goose girl, a quick in-and-out,

459

over in a wink, a performance that had always been furtive and unsatisfactory. "If you could help, tell me..."

But how could she? She knew even less than he. "I—I liked the—the kisses," she said hesitantly, blushing hotly in the dark.

He moved closer, cradling her head in one arm and lifting himself slightly, and bent over and kissed her again, again and again, his passion rising as she clung to him. Now, now he could wait no longer. He turned, straddled her, pinning her to the mattress, pushing her legs apart, and thrust his hand between.

"Nay, nay," Gena mumbled in panic, trying to struggle free.

But he had found the place and entered her, his manhood plunging deep, bringing a sharp cry to her lips. She tore at his hair, pummeled his back, but he did not seem to feel her blows; his wild pumping to and fro became more and more frantic, until a series of shudders ran through his body and he collapsed.

After a long silent moment he raised himself and looked down on Gena. She lay very still, without speaking, her head turned away.

"Are you angry with me, sweet?"

"Nay. Why should I be angry? You have had your will, as a husband should."

"I did not mean to..." He leaned over and kissed her cheek. "I love you," he added simply. "If I have ill used you..."

"Nay, you have used me as gently as you could. 'Tis I who have failed."

"Oh, nay, nay, never say that, sweet." He touched her mouth lightly with a finger tip. "To have you as wife has made me happy beyond—well, I did not know a man could be *so* happy."

She smiled faintly up at him in the dark.

He sank back and, drawing her head upon his shoulder, sighed contentedly. In time, he thought, in time she will feel as I do about her. And I will take care that she does not become a drab like other men's wives. I shall see that she does not work too hard, that she always has plenty to eat, decent clothes, shod feet and a husband who can treat her with kindness and respect, as my father treated my mother. She shall never want, never regret her life with me.

So dreaming of future love and good fortune, he fell asleep.

Chapter XXX

At Cragwell, Cristina, the wound of Phillip's bitter parting slowly healing, went her round of days, outwardly calm and content, but inwardly tiptoeing, wary of pitfalls. She was afraid to be happy. She had made that mistake too many times before, allowing herself to be deluded into a sense of well-being, even of joy. And what had happened? God had punished her, and those she trusted had either left, died or cast her out. She wanted to be fond of Aelenor—so much like the mother she had pictured and longed for in her childhood, warm, maternal, understanding—but she held back. The lady had guessed Phillip's feelings for Cristina—it would have been hard not to miss the substance of his ardent, yearning gaze—and urged the girl to accept his suit.

"You may never have such an opportunity again," Aelenor pointed out. "He is not rich, but he comes of noble lineage. And he is a kind, tender man who loves you deeply and cares not a whit for your dowerless state."

"But—I—I do not love him," Cristina said, embarrassed, for it pained her to discuss Phillip. "He *is* a good man. 'Tis simply that I do not think it is in my nature to love any man as a wife should."

"You will learn. It may take time, but you will learn."

Cristina shook her head. "I think not. You, my lady, are more fortunate than most women. For I think you have always loved your husband, as he has you."

"You are wrong. 'Twas not always thus."

"But you must have had some feeling for him as a bride."

"None at all," Aelenor replied. "I thought him a hairy beast."

They both laughed. That was what Cristina admired about Aelenor—she knew how to laugh, and she did not make Cristina feel guilty because she had refused Phillip.

Dead winter brought more snow and freezing cold. The wolves, finding prey scarce in the highlands, became bolder, moving down to the valley in packs and attacking anything that moved. They could be heard during the clear frosty nights, howling beyond the castle walls, their wails sending shivers down Cristina's spine as she drew closer to the fire. When the villagers complained of the beasts' depredations, Sir Edgar organized a hunt, and Aelenor asked if she and Cristina might ride out to watch.

"At a distance, of course," she assured her husband. "We have been confined so long, and a little canter in the open might do us good."

They set out one dark, slate-colored dawn, wrapped in furs, their faces muffled in their collars to keep out the bitter cold. As they rode through the gates the sun made a feeble attempt to break through, reaching out with tentative pale golden fingers, striking a dazzling spark or two on the frozen river, then withdrawing, leaving the world gray again. Snow covered the ground, softening the bony ridges and brutish jagged rocks, lacing the bracken with ice, powdering the black twisted skeletal trees that grew in sparse clumps. They rode through the village, past thatched, snow-shrouded cots, coming to life now with the crowing of cocks and the lowing of cows.

Cristina, riding in the rear with Aelenor, could hear the echoing cries of the huntsmen and the crack of their whips on the still frozen air as they kept their dogs in line. The peasants, armed with scythes, hoes and sticks, their faces rosy with cold, their breaths smoking, fell in behind the horsemen. Cristina had never been on a hunt, never had learned to cast a falcon, to shoot an arrow or take her mount over a hedge as many of the country ladies did. But today she was not required to do any of these things, she had only to enjoy the outing. And she found it to be a pleasant experience. The contagious excitement of the hunters, the air of nervous anticipation, the muffled clip-clop of the horses' hooves on the crusted ground, the jingle of harness and the creak of leather took her out of herself into a strange and interesting world. Above them hawks wheeled, zigzagging over the crests of barren, snow-ridged hills, a lonely country, desolate, remote, a landscape made even more godforsaken by winter's hushed silence. Cristina, safe and secure in the fur-lined cape and gloves, riding by Aelenor's side, looked about her with curiosity, her cheeks tingling with the cold.

"Ware! Ware! Ha, ha, ware!" the huntsmen called.

They crossed the river at the ford, the horses cracking the ice and sending spray flying in cold droplets. Aelenor pointed out a "bastle," one of the many defensive homes built by country families, little self-contained fortresses which dotted the Northumberland border. As they passed, a woman wearing a black shawl over her head flung open the shutters of an upper window, and Cristina waved. The woman called to the men-at-arms, "'Tis the wolves ye be after?"

"Nay, the Scottish lassies," someone replied, and there was a burst of loud laughter from the peasants of their party.

The country grew rockier. "The Cheviots," Aelenor said, pointing to the grooved, white-rimmed hills.

The wind sweeping down from the north blew in gusts, now skirling the powdered snow, lifting the hem of Cristina's cloak. She pulled her hood tighter, rubbing her icy nose with a gloved hand. Her feet in the stirrups had become numb with cold.

"Is it true," Aelenor asked, "that our King Richard's Anne has brought a different way of riding for ladies from her native France?"

"So I have heard," Cristina answered. "'Tis called side-saddle. They consider it more elegant for a lady than riding astride."

"Indeed. And how is one to keep from sliding off?"

"The saddle, they tell me, is specially constructed."

"I don't see how," Aelenor said after a moment. "I predict the fashion will never take hold."

They rode on, climbing a little now, along a narrow path. Below them a frozen stream wound its way between snowy banks; above loomed a rise topped with immense boulders. Suddenly something made Cristina look up. Was it a shadow she saw? Her imagination? Or a man's figure outlined against the sky? Paralyzed for a moment with nameless dread, she stared at it. It *was* a figure, for now she perceived the raised bow. She screamed, and at the same time several of the mounted men ahead shouted.

Arrows hissed through the air. A boulder began to tumble down, gathering speed, sending pebbles, sticks, snow and black earth flying. The horses, whinnying and rearing, stampeded, and the peasants began to scramble out of arrow-shot down the bank to the stream.

"Back! Turn back!" Aelenor cried, wheeling her horse.

Terror-stricken, Cristina followed, kicking the horse's flanks, urging her on. Down and around and down they flew until they reached a small copse of firs. Here Aelenor paused. In the distance they could hear shouts, shrieks, and the shrill nickering of horses.

"God damn them!" Aelenor swore under her breath.

"Scots?" Cristina whispered, her heart knocking in her breast.

"Aye. They must have stumbled upon us by chance. A hunting party like ourselves, mayhap. God pray they are not many. Did you see?"

"Only the one man. I did not have time..."

"We can do nothing but wait."

It was not long before the shouts of battle died down. Aelenor bit her lip impatiently, wondering if she should ride up to see how it went. She was about to send spurs to her horse when a man, one of her husband's squires, came cantering round the bend.

"Thank God, 'tis you," Aelenor breathed. "Did you beat them off?"

"Aye, lady. We killed four. Made short shrift of the devils. Halard and John are in pursuit and will bring down the few who got away, never fear."

"And Sir Edgar?"

"Sir Edgar, lady, has been wounded."

"Where? How?" she cried and without waiting for an answer pulled her horse aside and galloped off.

Cristina followed, apprehensive, feeling again that awful dread she had experienced when she saw the dark shadow raise itself against the horizon.

Sir Edgar lay on the churned, blood-spattered snow, an arrow protruding from his chest. Aelenor was kneeling beside him, trying to staunch the flow of blood with the hem of her cloak. The horses, held by the grooms, stood with hanging heads, their flanks still quivering nervously, while the scattered hounds could be heard barking in the distance. Stretched out on the ground were two huntsmen, dead, their bows still in their hands. The little knot of men made way for Cristina, and a squire helped her dismount. Aelenor was whispering the Lord's Prayer, and even before Cristina knelt beside her she knew that Edgar was dead.

Aelenor, beside herself with grief, declining food or drink, spent three days and nights on the cold chapel floor at the foot of her husband's bier, refusing to leave until she was carried to her bed in a faint. When Henry Percy, Earl of Northumberland, himself, hearing of the attack, came to Cragwell, Aelenor could not muster the strength or will to see him. "Tell him I am ill." Strangely she was not interested in revenge or the earl's promise to pursue and punish the Scottish clan whence the attackers had come.

"What does it matter who pays the price? Will it bring Edgar back? Will it restore my beloved husband to me?" she asked Cristina. "If I thought for a moment that it would I myself would give the order to butcher every Scot in the land."

The arrival of Aelenor's two sons and their families for the funeral seemed to restore her. Weak though she was, she got up out of bed to organize the household for its influx of mourners. No one but she could manage, so she had no choice. There were beds to find for everyone, and the preparation of the wake feast to supervise. She was the only person who could decide how many kegs of wine should be brought up from the cellar, how many oxen should be slaughtered, how many loaves baked. Cristina, watching Aelenor bustle about, could hardly believe it was the same woman who had refused to eat a week earlier. She appeared almost cheerful. Had she forgotten her husband so soon? Cristina wondered.

But no, far from it. On the evening after Sir Edgar had been laid to rest in the chapel vault, Cristina offered to help a weary Aelenor to bed. As she was brushing the lady's hair, Aelenor said, "He will always be alive to me. That is what I have finally come to understand. He is still in my heart; he will never die. Oh, I shall miss him, but God gave me good years, happy years, enough of them to tide me over for the rest of my life. And I am grateful."

Cristina thought it a strange way to look upon the death of a loved one. She had been anything but grateful when her father had died, and she could not help saying so.

"My dear child," Aelenor replied, "was not your father the best a daughter could have? Certainly. You told me so yourself. I am not saying you should feel indifferent at losing a cherished one or swallow without question the homily that what God takes we cannot dispute. There is a time for grief and anger. But after a decent interval it must be put aside. What I mean to tell you is that we should remember the happy part of the past, treasure the fond memories and be thankful we have them."

Aelenor's words gave Cristina food for thought. Had she herself brooded overlong on the dark side of her life? Had she been a little self-pitying or even a little harsh? Had she been wrong to turn Phillip away? And for a moment his face came back to her, his ardent gray eyes looking down at her in the firelit room, the sound of the wind, the feel of his arms. But no, no, she had been right to refuse him. She had been right.

In March, Cristina expressed a wish to return to Nareham. Aelenor had begged her to stay on, but Cristina and the new heirs to Cragwell, Hubert and his wife, Maude, did not get on. Hubert drank, and Maude reminded her too much of Cecilia, suspicious and hotly jealous. So Cristina wrote to Edmund asking again if he would give her temporary shelter, and Edmund passed her letter on to Phillip.

Young Phillip, about to assume his new post in King Richard's court, gave his excuses and set out immediately for the North Country to fetch Cristina. He found her silent and withdrawn.

Moved at the sight of her, forgetting their former unhappy parting and his promise at Meading, he again asked her to marry him. "There is no need to tell you how much I love you, sweet. If only you would say yes."

They were standing in a corner of the great hall, and as he spoke, her blue eyes slowly filled with tears.

"Phillip, I cannot..." she began in a choked voice.

A knot formed in his stomach and he had to fight the sharp retort which rose to his tongue.

"Phillip, I..."

"'Tis all right," he managed to say, swallowing his incipient anger. "I shan't press you."

He was a patient man, but there were times when he truly wondered why he should love her, why he should not find himself a woman whose eyes would light up when he looked at her, who would welcome his courtship, encourage and meet him at least a little of the way. But those thoughts were always fleeting. He loved Cristina and felt an overwhelming tenderness, a compassion for her plight. Poor child, she seemed so lost, so hounded with ill fortune.

And Cristina was thinking of love too; that to marry a man no matter how the marriage turned out meant unhappiness and suffering in the end. Even Aelenor for all her cheerful talk had been left to grieve and mourn.

At Nareham, Edmund's ancient housekeeper, Betsy, made room for Cristina in her own small bedchamber. Phillip had attempted to persuade the girl that she would find accommodations more agreeable in the castle, but Cristina had courteously declined the invitation, saying she preferred the village. She tried to be useful, mending and sewing, even carding and spinning some wool donated to the priest by a grateful parishioner whose child Edmund had christened. Nevertheless, as Edmund had previously pointed out to her, her situation under his roof did not escape unpleasant comment. There were some who looked askance and sneered behind her back—"Half sister, indeed!"—and Cristina knew that she would have to make other, more permanent arrangements. Again she spoke of a convent.

"My dear," Edmund said, "you have no vocation. 'Twill seem like a refuge for a while, but then you will bitterly regret your decision."

It was the same old argument, and they went around and around with it.

"You do not have a true Christian's forgiving heart, for one," Edmund said. "If you remember, you never forgave our mother."

"How could I? After what she did to my father, not to speak of abandoning me—you—Aleyn."

"Aleyn and I did not hold it against her. But you did, you do. Dear Cristina, she spoke of you, you were in her thoughts."

"That I find hard to believe."

"Do you? I will tell you something—God forgive me for breaking a promise to that dead woman, but I cannot help it. Who do you think sent you money all those years when your father had difficulty in keeping you both in bread? Who?"

"'Twas a merchant of Thexted, a relative."

"So she had you think, but 'twas your mother."

"My mother?" She gave him a look of incredulous disbelief.

"Aye, your mother. She made me swear that you would never know. She wanted you to have a dowry, wanted you to find a good husband and be happy. 'Twas a gift from the heart."

Cristina looked away, then down at her hands, her brows drawn together in a frown. After a few moments she took a deep breath and said, "'Twas guilt money."

"She would not have felt guilty if she did not love you." Edmund's voice became stern. "Cristina, you are not a child any longer. I urge you to put away your childish feelings and act the grown woman. Try to understand. Be humble. Forgive."

Cristina felt a lump gather at the back of her throat. "I never knew her," was all she could say.

"I think if you could have, you would have felt differently. She was a brave woman; she suffered from hunger and cold and poverty, aye, and scorn, but she would never bend, never break. She had courage, the kind of courage the bravest knight would envy. Her one weakness was love, love for a man who treated her rather shabbily. Would you condemn her for that?"

"She did not love my father," Cristina murmured, a little ashamed, because she could hear herself, hear how unbecoming, how uncharitable, she sounded. "'Tis hard, hard to forgive."

"Hard because you have a heart of ice, my child. Aye, do not look distressed. 'Tis true. A heart of ice. I wish I could thaw it before it is too late, before this good man, Phillip, gives up and sees that he has wasted his honest love on a selfish child."

"Edmund..."

"Listen to me. I loved a girl once—but..." He hesitated; the confession did not come easily, more so since it was only a half-truth. He *still* loved her. Gena seemed happy in her marriage and he was glad, but there were times when, seeing her with her husband, he felt a stab of jealousy. "But I had to give her up because of my vows. The sacrifice was necessary, do you understand? Necessary. But you—how can you give up happiness simply out of mule-headed stubbornness?"

"Mayhap," she said in a bitter voice, "I have no heart at all."

He smiled. "But you do, you do, sister dear. A little cold, a little icy, but the heart is there."

Cristina, gazing at him with moist eyes, said "I wish..." but not knowing exactly what she wished was unable to go on.

Aleyn for the first time since early childhood was ailing; a stomach complaint, vomiting, loose bowels and a weakness that he could not seem to overcome. Bleeding did not help; it only made him feebler. Lenore nursed him with hot poultices of wild mustard and a concoction of herbs she herself had brewed, a beverage heavily laced with deadly purple foxglove.

He lay in one of the bedchambers at Nareham, having come home with his wife to celebrate his father's saint's day. Thomas had invited the couple, together with Lenore's father, Sir Henry, to a grand feast, hoping to borrow money from this illustrious and rich relative by marriage. Thomas's debt at Nareham had come due, and the moneylender had refused to extend his credit. Sir Henry, when asked for help, stroked his beard, became thoughtful, finally saying his own funds were tied up, that he himself must make a payment on a mortgage, but that he would be glad to plead for a continuance with the moneylender, with whom he was on good terms.

This did not help Thomas very much. Sooner or later the day of reckoning would come, sooner, it seemed, for the moneylender grudgingly agreed to wait another three months if Thomas could pay the interest at once. So Thomas turned to the tried-and-true method to raise the necessary marks. He put a hearth tax on the villagers.

The tax came at the worst of times, at the end of a long, hard winter when supplies were low or exhausted, when many of the peasants who had not been able to hoard seed for the spring planting must now buy it with their last worn coin. Thomas's levy, five pence on every hearth, was bitterly resented by those who could afford to pay and impossible for those who could not. To Charles Coke this seemed the last straw.

"If we all banded together and refused," he told his fellows one night at the alewife's, "Sir Thomas can do nothing to force us."

"Can he not?" John Crykes asked sourly. "He can stop the mill or refuse to bake our bread, or he can shove us into the stocks."

And Buford Bagley added, "'Tis all well and good for freemen like ye, Charles, to feel ye can thwart the lord, but what of us serfs in bondage? He can throw us out of our cots and wait until we starve."

Charles mulled the situation over. Now that he was happily married his blood had simmered down somewhat, and he began to think he could reason with Thomas. So one morning, cap in hand, he went to speak to him.

The master of Nareham received him in the great hall, lolling on a high-backed chair under the blazoned shields of the de Anders, a jeweled wine cup in his hand. He listened to Charles with a sneer on his lips.

"Why, you baseborn villein!" he interrupted before Charles had finished. "God's bones, but you make too much of yourself by advising me. You—all of you are the same, insolent, greedy, sullen, tricky. A dirty lot who stink to high heaven.

469

You befoul the air here. Phew!" He pinched his nose. "Go back and tell the peasants they are lucky to get off so lightly."

"Sire, I am neither baseborn nor villein. I—"

"Get out!" Thomas shouted. "Here—you two," he called to a pair of husky house carls, "throw this churl out!"

An enraged Charles sent one minion reeling and gave the other a bloody nose before a half-dozen servants came running. Subduing him with cudgels and painful kicks, they dragged him from the hall and tossed him into the courtyard, mocking and jeering at him, then slamming the door so violently it shivered on its hinges.

Charles picked himself up out of the dust, his heart black with hate. He was done with talk. He nursed his grievances that night, planning and plotting with the Crykeses, Flemyngs and Melkers on how best to show Sir Thomas that he had something more to deal with than "stinking churls."

Aleyn's health did not improve. Too ill to return to Waddington, he stayed on at Nareham while his wife continued to minister patiently to his needs. He was a peevish invalid, hot one moment, cold the next, wanting more blankets, wanting fewer or none. He complained of thirst, that his heart beat too slowly and painfully, that no one came to see him, except Phillip, who remained at Nareham, reluctant to leave for London, putting off his departure from day to day. He would look in on his ailing cousin occasionally and listen sympathetically to his grumbling. Aleyn had moments when in a half-drugged, thick-voiced anger he blamed Lenore for his illness, calling her an ugly bitch whose face made him sick, clamoring for his mistress or the other women he had known, strumpets, he vowed, who were far better than his wife. Through it all Lenore tended him with forbearance and kindness, secretly enjoying his torment.

Cristina, hearing of Aleyn's complaint, paid him a visit. At first he did not recognize her, but when she spoke to him and his glazed eyes focused, he whispered, "Cristina!" and seemed pathetically glad to see her.

She took his hand, so dry and feverish. "I am here, brother."

"Do not leave me," he begged. His eyes rolled to where his wife was sitting, hands busy at embroidery. *"She..."* He lowered his voice to a hoarse whisper. "She is poisoning me."

"What an idea!" Cristina chided, adjusting the pillow behind his damp, tousled head.

"Phillip did not believe me, but *you* must. You are the only friend I have."

"What of Edmund? He tells me you refuse to see him."

"A priest? I am not dying, sister. It is a bad omen to see a priest, even if he is my own brother." His eyes suddenly widened and he groaned as a spasm of pain cramped his stomach. "Promise, Cristina, promise you won't leave me, sister. Promise—nay, swear it!"

"I swear." She wiped the sweat from his forehead with a cloth.

He fell into a doze, and waking a half hour later gazed up at Cristina, a smile lighting his reddened eyes.

"Mother," he whispered.

"Nay, Aleyn, 'tis Cristina."

"Mother," he repeated, "so you have come. You have not failed me. I always knew you loved me, even when you scolded. Remember how you stroked my brow when I had a fever?"

"Aleyn," Cristina insisted, upset, "'tis me, Cristina." But he did not hear, did not see; his mind had wandered back in fantasy to the past, a different time.

"...and you told me not to be afraid. Do you recall? When they came to burn you as a witch, you did not take fright, but stood there, so straight and tall. 'Dame Joanna!' they shouted, and I clung to your skirts, how I clung, because I knew no one could harm me as long as you were there. Mother—for Christ's pity!—help me! Mother, mother, I don't want to die!"

Something inside Cristina seemed to turn over, and for the second time that week she found herself contemplating Joanna through another's eyes. Could this mother, a woman who had betrayed her father, have the qualities—courage, maternal feelings, strength—her sons had given her? As the shadows deepened in the room Cristina seemed to feel the presence of Joanna in the gathering dusk, a straight-spined, dark-haired woman with a proud head and unflinching eyes, Joanna of Thorsby, her mother, a woman who, according to Aleyn, had faced almost certain death just as she, Cristina had done. Joanna...

"Mother—I thirst."

Cristina rose from the side of the bed, but Lenore had heard her husband's request and was already filling a cup with cooled wine. She stirred it with her finger, then lifted it and took a sip.

"You had best give it to him," she told Cristina. "He accuses me of poison. You can see that I have drunk of it too."

"Aleyn speaks in the confusion of illness," Cristina answered. "You are the best nurse a husband could ever have."

Lenore smiled faintly, a smile that stirred a momentary uneasiness in Cristina, a disquieting thought quickly put away as the sick man called again.

Aleyn drank eagerly, then fell back on his pillow and turning his head soon began to doze, his mouth open, his breath coming in labored gasps. Lenore lighted an oil lamp and resumed her seat, picking up her embroidery again. Cristina sat on, tired, her head drooping, her chin finally coming to rest on her breast.

She opened her eyes some hours later to the smell of smoke and the sounds of shouts. Lenore had gone. Except for the feeble flickering circle of light thrown off by the oil lamp, all was darkness. Numb, stiff with fatigue, half awake, Cristina arose to fetch the lamp. She brought it over to the bed and, lifting it, she saw that Aleyn lay exactly as he had fallen asleep, drawn up on his side, mouth agape, except that his breath had stilled.

He was dead.

Guilt washed over her. Had he called out for her while she slept? Why had she not sent for Edmund or the castle chaplain? Perhaps, she thought, that is where Lenore has gone, to fetch the chaplain.

Suddenly Cristina became aware that the smell of smoke had grown more acrid, more pronounced. She turned her head, frowning. There from under the door, like a drift of dirty wool, smoke was seeping in. She ran to the door, flinging it wide, only to shrink back as a gray choking billow poured through. Beyond the threshold far down the passage an orange tongue licked along the paneled wall.

Coughing, she ran to the window, unfastened the shutters and opened them. The night was alive with fire, the outbuildings, barn, stable, smithy, all in flame, the thatched roofs burning like tinder. By craning her neck and looking down she could see a portion of the bottom story of the manor house aglow with fire. People ran about in panic, milling and shouting, some making for the gates, some with buckets drawn from the well ineffectually trying to put out the blaze.

Cristina, her heart beating frantically, rushed back to the

door. The tongue of flame had become two, three, four, a dozen, crackling now, eating away at the walls, coming closer.

"Cristina! Cristina!"

It was Phillip.

"Cristina...!"

"Here, Phillip—oh, Phillip..." And as he came running toward her a ceiling beam fell, crashing and sparking, hitting the back of his head. He went down at her feet like a stone. The strength of terror, of panic, a strength Cristina had no idea she possessed, enabled her to push aside the beam and to drag Phillip across the threshold and slam the door on the holocaust in the passage.

He lay very still, his face ashen in the flickering lamplight. Cristina, her hands pressed to her mouth, thought he was dead, and a sudden, shocking feeling of desolation swept over her. She was moved in a strange and terrible way, as if she had known this young knight all her life and had just killed him herself. How boyish he looked, how vulnerable. She thought of all his kindnesses, his patience, his concern for her welfare, and how she had given him nothing in return. She thought of the night he had kissed her so passionately, and her own wild response, and how in the end she had cheated him by fleeing from his embrace. And now it was too late, too late...

He stirred and she whispered, "Phillip...?" Quickly she got the wine jug and, kneeling beside him, lifted his head and pressed the rim to his lips. He opened his eyes.

"Thank God," she breathed. Her throat ached. She wanted to say more, to say, "I am sorry, I am sorry," but he was already staggering to his feet.

"Aleyn?" he asked, looking toward the bed.

"He is dead, Phillip. He died a short while ago."

He crossed himself. "Poor devil. God absolve his soul." He clutched Cristina's shoulder. "The fire—my God!"

Little pennons of flame were working themselves up the stout door.

"We cannot help Aleyn now, but..." Phillip strode to the wall and tore down two wool hangings. He threw one around Cristina, winding her in it from head to toe. The muffled, woolly darkness terrified her.

"I can't see."

"Best that you cannot." He wrapped the other hanging around himself, leaving only a peephole for his eyes and a slit for one arm. Then he flung open the door. The swoosh of air acted like the updraft of a chimney, and the door went up in a fountain of flame. Phillip pushed Cristina through and followed, propelling her down the timber-strewn corridor, where the fire had nearly burned itself out. The smoldering roof beams, those that were left, sent showers of hot ashes down upon them, the charred floor searing through their shoes.

Cristina worked her head free. "Oh, Phillip—look!"

The wooden staircase, the pride of Nareham manor, had burned away, and they could see down into the great hall, where the fire still raged. Phillip turned and pulled Cristina under an archway past an arras hanging in tattered, black strips and through a heavy oaken door into a bedchamber that had thus far miraculously escaped the flames.

"Help me," Phillip ordered as he tore covers and linen sheets from the bed, cutting and ripping them with his knife into long lengths. Cristina threw the singed tapestry from her shoulders and began to braid the strips together. Soon they had a rope. Phillip went to the double window, unbarred it and tossed their makeshift rope over the side.

"I'll hold it," he said. "You go."

"Phillip, I cannot leave you to..."

"Go!" he ordered angrily, grabbing her by the shoulders, pushing her toward the window. "Out! There, hold tight. The garden is below you—not far."

She grasped the cloth rope with slippery hands and found herself swinging out into the flame-shadowed night. Lifting her head, she had a glaring view of Phillip's face, the sculptured brow, the assertive chin, a strong face and suddenly a dear one.

"Cross your legs and slide—slide!" he called.

"Will you come too?" she shouted, but his answer was lost in the din of voices below.

She slipped down and down, down past a flaming window, quickly turning her eyes upward to the livid sky. She did not think of what a drop it was to the garden beneath or if the rope would hold but of Phillip above surrounded by the burning manor. Down and down, with the roar and crackle of the fire in her ears, she slid and swung. Then suddenly a strong pair of hands grasped her and she was standing on firm ground. The hands, she saw, belonged to Charles Coke, a peasant farmer, once pointed out to her by Edmund as "our cousin, the village rebel." She did not wonder why he should

474

be there at night in the manor garden, her only thought was of Phillip.

"You must help him—Sir Phillip—he is up there—hurry, for God's sake!"

But Phillip was already working himself down, hand over hand, swinging far out to escape the same burning window. Charles had disappeared for a few moments, and now he returned, wheeling a cart of hay. He placed it under the spot where the edge of the rope dangled.

Cristina, gazing up, saw Phillip pause. "'Tis all right!" she called. "Why do you stop? Oh, darling, sweet—don't stop."

And then in a burst of flame from the nearby stable she saw that the rope had torn, was tearing. Suddenly Phillip plummeted down. The hay broke his fall, but he lay stunned, unable to rise.

"Help him!" She turned to Charles. But he had vanished into the night.

As Cristina started to climb into the cart, Phillip sat up, rubbing his scalp. "Twice in one night. 'Tis a wonder I still have a head. But did I hear you right, love, when you called me darling?"

"Aye, but, oh—we cannot stay here, Phillip." The grass and bushes around them were beginning to catch fire.

Phillip jumped down from the cart and grabbed Cristina's hand. They ran from the garden through the burning gate, just as a portion of the manor roof caved in, sending up a geyser of sparks and a shooting tower of flame.

"God in heaven!" Phillip exclaimed. "Thomas—Lenore..."

"Mayhap they escaped as we did, Phillip."

They made their way across the drawbridge, jostled by the fleeing mob, house carls and servants, stableboys, grooms, soldiers, squires and herdsmen driving cattle before them, refugees like themselves with their charred, ragged clothes and sooty faces.

Halfway over, Cristina turned her head. "Mother Mary! The manor—the castle!"

"Don't look back," Phillip said, putting an arm about her shoulders. "Don't look back."

Chapter XXXI

Three months had passed since the fire. Nareham Castle stood, an empty charred shell, its manor house gutted, the stone keep rising above the heaped ashes and rubbled stone like an accusing finger. The stench of burned bodies still hung over the ruins, though workmen had slowly begun to clear the debris away. Thomas de Ander and his two squires had perished in the fire, along with a great number of servants, no one knew for sure how many. Lenore had escaped. She had gone to the garderobe, she said, and looking out through the slit window had seen the first flames leaping at the main doorway of the house. Panicked, she had run down the stairs and out through the kitchen door.

Phillip was now master of Nareham, lord of a devastated estate bogged down with debts. Grubbing about in the charred desolation he had managed to find enough booty, several silver chalices, a coffer of coins, two suits of armor, five swords, three cups and two jeweled buckles, the sale of which had netted him enough to have what he believed to be Thomas's and Aleyn's remains decently buried and to pay off some of his creditors.

His position at King Richard's court had gone by default and another man had been appointed to fill it. He had not asked Cristina to marry him again—how could he now that he was overburdened with financial obligations?—though she longed for him to do so. Her heart had thawed, just as Edmund had hoped it would. Not suddenly, not overnight, but melting daily in patches. The night of the fire she had felt fear, not so much for herself as for Phillip. That had startled, surprised her. She had never really felt fear *for* anyone except her father. How odd it felt. She had called Phillip "darling, sweet," too, the words coming to her unbidden.

It set her to thinking. She remembered Aelenor, her face shining with memories of happiness and love. Should she, Cristina, try, take the step, give herself over to Phillip? But he was no longer pressing her, no longer begging her to be his wife. Too poor, he said, he loved her too much. What better proof could she have of his love? She watched him covertly, the straight-nosed profile, the little furrow between his

476

brows, the dark wavy hair, the cleft chin. And the more she looked, the more she liked that face, and the more she liked it the more her heart melted. She wanted to be his wife, to live with him, to bear his children. So she asked him to marry her.

"But I have nothing—there is no way I can procure another position at court, no way I can support you," he protested. "You would have to live like a peasant."

"You forget," she said with a smile that lighted up her eyes and face in a way he had never seen before, "I have peasant blood and I have never lived grandly. So 'twill be no great hardship."

But Phillip was not easy to convince. How could he take a wife, a woman he loved so dearly, and give her naught but his name?

"Sweet, I do not love you for what you can give me." Was she saying it? The word "love"? She could hardly believe her own voice. It seemed as if she were inside someone else's skin, talking with a stranger's tongue. She felt so different, elated, sure of herself, almost giddy.

Finally, with the help of Edmund and her own argument, sprinkled generously with kisses, kisses Phillip found impossible to fend off, she managed to convince him. They were to be married on Maundy Thursday, and now she sat in Edmund's small house sewing on her wedding dress. The material was not brocade or silk, but a blue-dyed linen of coarsest weave. She did not mind. As she had told Phillip, poverty was not new to her, she had never been arrayed in cloth of gold. She would be as happy a bride as any, though she would not be decked with jewels or carried to the church in a painted litter.

They would live in one of the stone buildings left standing in the outer courtyard, Phillip told her, a granary made habitable by installing a hearth for cooking and partitioning the one huge chamber into several with brick walls. Phillip planned to continue farming at Nareham. But he would be his own bailiff and steward and most likely, if they were shorthanded, reeve, hayward and laborer too. The serfs still in bondage were set free.

"Men put more heart into a task when they work for a wage," Phillip declared. He abolished the hearth and plow taxes, lowered the milling fees, made the rents more equitable and permitted householders to build their own bake ovens if they so chose.

What he could not do was allow the peasants responsible for firing Nareham to go without punishment. The alewife in whose house the men had met, hoping for a reward, had turned the guilty ones in. Charles Coke, she said, was the ringleader. But because he had been of assistance to Cristina and Phillip in their escape from the burning manor and because of his kinship to Cristina, Phillip decided to give the culprit a light sentence. However, the rebel and his wife had fled, apparently the same night as the fire, and no one could say—or was willing to say—where they had gone. (Years later Cristina learned that Charles by dint of hard labor had managed to obtain a sheep farm in Yorkshire, but he never returned to Nareham.) For the others, Crykeses, Flemyngs and Melkers, Phillip ordered banishment, although he would have been well within his rights to instruct a manor court to have the arsonists hanged. But he did not want corpses dangling on a gibbet to mar his wedding, nor to set a somber tone upon his new lordship.

Ironically, at this time Edmund finally received Sir John Hawkwood's promised gift of gold florins with which to re-build his church. The coins, stamped with the city of Florence's emblem, came with no message, only the sender's name. It was a generous amount, far more than Edmund needed, since he thought it inappropriate to build a large, lavishly endowed church for his simple parishioners, so he put a sum by for charitable purposes and offered another sum to Phillip. Sir Phillip would only accept it as a loan to be repaid with interest, a loan that would be instrumental in making a spring planting possible, the start of Nareham's climb back to solvency.

In the meanwhile, Edmund married them in the old and still-shabby village church in a simple ceremony, first on the porch, as was the custom, then at the altar rail. All of Nareham had been invited as a matter of course, but of the nobility only a few attended, close friends of Phillip's, knights and their wives, and Phillip's squire. His stepfather and mother had also been asked, but Cecilia had refused and Sir Michael, bowing to her wishes, had remained away. Cecilia sent word that she would never forgive Phillip for such an ill-made match, nor accept Cristina as her daughter-in-law. Phillip tried not to let his mother's bitterness sour his happy day. In time, with the birth of his first son, he felt sure she would come around.

The nuptial feast, held in the refurbished stone granary,

was by aristocratic standards a poor one—only a single ox and a lone hart turned on the spit—but what the meal lacked in fine victuals was made up in laughter and merriment and the handsome couple's glowing faces.

Bedded at last, Cristina grew suddenly shy. Phillip overcame it by teasing her and soon had her laughing. He cradled her in his arms, the laughter dying as he gazed down at her. Then silently he bent his head and kissed her, a long, lingering kiss. It was a kiss far more sensuous than the one he had given her at Connington, because for one, they were naked, and the touch of bare warm skin to bare warm skin had aroused her quickly, sending a rush of heat to her head. Secondly, her lover, young and ardent, was her husband now, *her husband*, and she reveled in the thought. She belonged to him; she loved him. Thirdly, she put no bar upon herself. Her passionate nature willed to her by Mariotta and Joanna, her legacy so long buried, was there, out in the open now, acknowledged, welcomed, and she let it carry her along on its rising tide.

Trembling under Phillip's caresses, not with timidity but with excitement, with thrilling little shivers of pure animal pleasure, she clung to him as he kissed and stroked, taking a pink nipple in his mouth, touching her where no man had touched her before.

When he eased himself over her, lying full-length against her, nuzzling her ear, and whispered, "Cristina, I shall try not to hurt you," she flung her arms about his neck, holding him tightly.

"I don't care, sweet. I don't care!"

She hardly felt the loss of her maidenhead, an irritation, a pinprick of pain, no more, and afterward she sighed, nestling her head in the crook of his neck. "I am truly Lady de Ander now, am I not?"

"Truly."

Later she awoke to Phillip's kisses, different now, urgent, feverish, wild, as if he were acting out an erotic dream. It took only a moment or two before her desire rose to meet his. She returned kiss for kiss, her mouth opening, her tongue twining with his, her hands gripping the corded muscles of his shoulders. His lips moved, trailing fiery kisses from cheek to throat to shoulders to breasts, closing on a nipple, sucking at it until it flowered, going to the next, making it bloom pinkly too.

"Phillip—if . . ."

But he was kissing her mouth again, and she felt his hand between her thighs. And then he was touching her *there,* in *that* place again, his finger slipping inside, moving slowly, deliciously. She wanted to cry out, to scream, to fight for her very sanity, which seemed to be swiftly ebbing away. Gasping, she clutched his hair and clung to him.

"Phillip!"

When he entered her she arched her hips without being aware of it, intent only on his hard urgency, moving with him now, a pulse throbbing in her throat, rushing up and up and up with her lover into winged darkness until the final blinding light. And in that exploding moment she suddenly understood.

She understood, she understood!

She understood and forgave, for she, like Joanna, knew passionate love and the sweet intoxication of forbidden wine.